CHILD HEALTH AND NUTRITION IN INDIA

CHILD HEALTH AND NUTRITION IN INDIA

Editors

Sanjay Prasad

H.G. Sadhu

Suman Vaishnav

PRABHAT PRAKASHAN

Mahatma Gandhi Labour Institute
(An Autonomous Institute of the Government of Gujarat)

Tel : (079) 40013700, 40013703, 40013704 • Fax : (079) 27912617
E-mail: info@mgliahd.org • Website: www.mgliahd.org

Published by
PRABHAT PRAKASHAN PVT. LTD.
4/19 Asaf Ali Road,
New Delhi-110 002 (INDIA)
Tele : +91-11-23289777
e-mail: prabhatbooks@gmail.com

ISBN 978-93-90366-62-0
CHILD HEALTH AND NUTRITION IN INDIA
Edited by Sanjay Prasad • H.G. Sadhu • Suman Vaishnav

Edition
2025

Price
₹ 900.00 (Rupees Nine Hundred only)

Printed at
R-Tech Offset Printers, Delhi

Brief about Contributors

Aneesh Kumar P. is an Assistant Professor of Psychology at the Department of Psychology, Christ University, Bengaluru. He has worked as project officer for Indian Council for Social Sciences Research (ICSSR) in Pondicherry University and was Head of the Department of Psychology, Wadi Huda Institute of Research and Advanced Studies affiliated to Kannur University, Kerala. He did his doctoral research on the topic "burden of child abuse and neglect in Kerala: risk factors and impact". He has published and presented papers at various National and the International forums in the area of public health, child and adolescent psychology. His research interests include child mental health and school counselling programs. He teaches papers in Child and adolescent counselling, counselling special population, development psychology and qualitative research methods. The author can be reached at aneeshksree@gmail.com

Aparajita Chattopadhyay is currently an Assistant Professor in the Department of Development Studies in the International Institute for Population Sciences (IIPS), Mumbai. Dr. Chattopadhyay is specialised in the field of nutrition, ageing, gender and environmental issues. She is having extensive experience in teaching and research for the last 16 years. Her papers are published in high ranked National and International journal, and she has been coordinating many research projects related to population ageing, environmental issues and child nutrition etc. The author can be contacted at apachat@rediffmail.com

Apoorva Patel is currently working in Gujarat National Law University, Gandhinagar as an Assistant Professor of Social Work. She acquired research experiences while working with the Public Health Foundation of India (IIPH-G) Ahmedabad, and Azim Premji Foundation, Uttarkashi, Uttarakhand. She has pursued her Masters in Social Work from Tata Institute of Social Sciences, Mumbai with 'Health & Development' as a field of practice. Her areas of research interests include early childhood care and education, child health and nutrition, child-centred disaster risk reduction; with focus on marginalised and vulnerable populations. The author can be contacted at apoorva.tiss@gmail.com

Aparna Mukherjee

B.B. Patel is the former professor of Labour Economics at the Mahatma Gandhi Labour Institute, Ahmedabad and is at present, Professor Emeritus. He has worked extensively on employment and unemployment, wages, social protection for workers in the organised and unorganised sectors. He also worked in human development issues in Gujarat. He was one of the key National Level resource person on issues of social safety net and retraining of displaced workers in India under the National Renewal Fund (NRF) India.

D.C. Baxi is the Deputy Commissioner of Labour, Ahmedabad under Labour and Employment Department, Government of Gujarat. He holds M.Sc., L.L.B. (Special), D.L.P., from Gujarat University, Ahmedabad and Ph.D. from Saurashtra University, Rajkot (Labour Laws). He has teaching experience of over 18 years and is an eminent Professor, taught Labour Laws at Gujarat State Judicial Academy, Gujarat High Court, Gujarat State, Sardar Patel Institute of Public Administration (SPIPA), B.K. School of Management, Gujarat University, Ahmedabad and remained panellist at IIM, Ahmedabad. He has various publications in the journal of National and the International repute. He has also remained a member of the expert committee, constituted for framing rules under the Building and Other Construction Workers Act, 1996. He further acted as Government Nominee for interviews conducted by Gujarat Public Service Commission during 15th September, 2014 to 17th September, 2014. The author can be reached at baxidharmang@yahoo.co.in

D. Sriram is the head of the Department of Public Policy and Administration, School of Liberal Studies, Pandit Deendayal Petroleum University. He is teaching Public Administration at PG and UG level. He has completed his Masters and Ph.D. from Osmania University, Hyderabad. Currently, He had worked with DST Sponsored Research Project in E-Governance. He was selected as Doctoral and Post-Doctoral fellow by Indian Council for Social Science Research, New Delhi. He is also associated with IPAA and NEPASI in India. He was selected as an observer for the United Nations Committee on Experts of Public Administration (UNCEPA) for its 14th and 15th sessions. His areas of interests are Public Health, Public-Private Partnerships and Service Delivery. At present, he is guiding five Ph.D. Scholars. Dr. Sriram recently completed Panchayati Raj Devolution Index Project for Gujarat and Dadra and Nagar Haveli. He can be reached at sriram_divi@yahoo.co.in

Dipti Govil is working as an Assistant Professor with International Institute of Population Sciences, Mumbai. She has a Ph.D. in Population Studies from IIPS, Mumbai. Since the past 15 years, she is working in the health sector and has completed many research projects and evaluation studies. She has worked as a researcher with Indian Institute of Management, Ahmedabad and a faculty with Indian Institute of Health Management Research, Jaipur. Her specific research interest lies in health policy analysis, program evaluation, menopause and hysterectomy, public health, vector-borne diseases, ethics, mental health, qualitative research, maternal and child health, quality of care, health financing, migration and health. She has skills in using both qualitative and quantitative methodology. Currently, she is associated with the Longitudinal Aging Study in India. She could be reached at diptigovil@gmail.com.

H.G. Sadhu has worked for more than 27 years in the field of Occupational Health as Research Officer, Sr. Research Officer, Asst. Director, Dy. Director and Scientist F at ICMR-NIOH, Gandhinagar Gujarat. He had been associated with various studies carried out by the ICMR-National Institute of Occupational Health on the occupational health hazards related to salt production, dusts (silica, asbestos, cotton, etc.), heavy metals (lead, mercury, thallium, etc.), pesticides, dioxin, health hazards among the community due to air and water pollution caused by the industries, and non-occupational dust-related diseases. Presently he is serving as visiting faculty and examiner at various PG and diploma courses in the field of occupational health and industrial hygiene conducted by different university/organisations in the country. He attended and presented papers at various national/international conferences and published about 40 research papers and technical reports. He assisted Hon'ble high courts of different states, Hon'ble Supreme Court of India, Hon'ble NHRC, Hon'ble SHRCs and Hon'ble NGT in various matters related to workers' and community/environmental health.

Keshab Das is a Professor at the Gujarat Institute of Development Research, Ahmedabad, India. He holds M.Phil. (Applied Economics) and Ph.D. (Economics) degrees from the Jawaharlal Nehru University, New Delhi (through the Centre for Development Studies, Trivandrum). He also holds a Bachelor's degree in Journalism and Mass Communications. He is a recipient of the VKRV Rao Prize in Social Sciences (Economics) and had been empanelled as an Indian Council of Cultural Relations Chair Professor in Economics. He has been a visiting research fellow/faculty at the following: Tshwane University of Technology, Pretoria, South Africa; University of Insubria, Varese, Italy; International Institute of Social Studies, The Hague, Netherlands; University of Manchester, Manchester, UK; Institute of Developing Economies, Chiba, Japan; CNRS-REGARDS, Bordeaux, France; Maison des Sciences del Homme (MSH), Paris, France; and University of Sussex, Brighton, UK. With eight books, his research focuses on local and regional development; industrialisation strategies; micro, small and medium enterprises (MSMEs), clusters and globalisation; informality; innovation; labour, basic infrastructure and politics of development. The author can be reached at keshabdas@gmail.com

Kranti Vora is an Additional Professor with Indian Institute of Public Health Gandhinagar, Gujarat. Dr. Vora has completed her MD (ObGyn) from Gujarat University, MPH from Johns Hopkins School of Public Health, USA and Ph.D. from University of Maryland, USA. Her experience extends from private practice specializing in infertility to working in UNFPA led Government of Gujarat (GOI) project. She started her public health career as a consultant in SEWA, Ahmedabad and worked on "Averting Maternal Death and Disability" project at Indian Institute of Management, Ahmedabad. Before starting her doctoral program at the University of Maryland, she worked on a SIDA project to improve midwifery practise in India and authored case studies on the maternal health situation in India and Gujarat. After completing her Ph.D., she conducted a qualitative study for evidence-based policymaking with RAND, Europe in India. At IIPHG, she has been involved in evaluation projects and other related projects to improve the evidence base for advancing reproductive health in India. The author can be reached at kvora@iiphg.org.

Laxmi Kant Dwivedi is an Assistant Professor, Department of Mathematical Demography & Statistics with International Institute for Population Sciences, Govandi Station Road, Deonar, Mumbai. He earned Ph.D. degree in Population Studies from the same Institute. His specific area of interest lies in the field of Mathematical Modelling; Multivariate Analysis; Fertility and Family Planning; Public Health; Impact Evaluation; Large-scale Survey Research Methods. The author can be reached at laxmikdwivedi@gmail.com.

Madhu Jain is a Professor at the Department of Obstetrics and Gynaecology, Institute of Medical Sciences (IMS), Banaras Hindu University (BHU), Varanasi, UP India. She has done her MBBS from K.G. Medical College, Lucknow and MD from IMS, BHU. She has a teaching experience of over 39 years and research experience of over 33 years. Her area of specialisation is in Obstetrics and Gynaecology as well as diverse issues related to women and child health. She achieved various prestigious awards, distinctions and honours throughout her academic career such as Silver Medal in Anatomy Dissection, National Scholarship under GOI, and Award in Scientific Symposium on Menopause, She is a Fellow in The International College of Surgeons, Member of National Academy of Medical Sciences. She is a member in various eminent organisations like Founder Life Member of Indian National Society for Lymphology, Member National Academy of Medical Sciences, New Delhi, National Thalassemia Welfare Society, New Delhi, National Haemophilia Welfare Society,

New Delhi, Life Member, Menopausal Society of India and the like. She is Executive member of Genetic & Foetal Medicine FOGSI, Executive member of UP chapter of Obstetrics & Gynaecology, Hon. Secretary, VOGS, 2011; Vice-President: 2012, 2013, Regional Coordinator of PGDMCH—IGNOU since 2014. She has published over 67 research papers in various journals of the National and the International repute. The author can be reached at drmadhujainbhu@gmail.com

Manisha Chandra is an IAS Officer of Gujarat Cadre and is currently serving as Director (ICDS). She is a visionary and is deeply interested in planning and implementing programmes with rigour so that the health, educational and nutrition status of children and adolescent girls improve. She considers that policies and programmes which influence the lives of such important group should be framed in a simple manner which is easily understood and accepted by the grassroots functionaries. She firmly believes that creative ways of programming for reaching people, proper training, IEC and research are the pillars which have the potential to influence public health programming. In this article, she recognises the sincere efforts put by Ms. Ankur Vaidya, Sabla Consultant, who took the initiative to implement the programme with zeal and enthusiasm and assisted in structuring this article. Above all, she earnestly acknowledges the contributions by ICDS functionaries at all levels, most importantly, the Anganwadi workers who took time out to attend the sessions of SATCOM and implemented the entire programme with utmost dedication. This article is just the beginning of the focused work which ICDS has started to improve the health and nutrition outcomes of adolescent girls in the State.

Manoj K. Sahoo has ten years of teaching and research experience. Currently, he is working as an Assistant Professor with Faculty of Economics, School of Liberal Studies, Pandit Deendayal Petroleum University, Gandhinagar, Gujarat. He holds M.Phil. and M.A. degree in Economics with UGC-NET from Centre for Economic Studies and Planning, Jawaharlal Nehru University, New Delhi and FDP from IIM, Indore. Previously he worked as faculty with School of Management, KIIT University, Bhubaneswar and was an Economic Consultant with Twelfth Finance Commission, Govt. of India, New Delhi where he worked on centre-state tax devolution issues and fixing norms for mineral royalty. Mr. Sahoo also worked as Co-Principal Investigator on the Global Development Network Project under United Nations Conference on Trade and Development (UNCTAD) on estimating Outward FDI of Indian MNCs. As a Research Associate with Indian Institute of Public Administration, New Delhi he worked on the viability of State Road Transport Undertakings in India states. Mr. Sahoo has to his credit about ten national and international research papers, UNCTAD Report etc. and he works extensively on socio-economic issues related to grassroots underdevelopment, financial inclusion, and problems of the informal sector and WTO issues related to intellectual property rights. Mr. Sahoo is a Life Member of Indian Economic Association and Indian Society for Technical Education, New Delhi. The author can be reached at sahoomanoj1@rediffmail.com

Mukesh Ranjan is currently pursuing his Ph.D. from the International Institute for Population Sciences, Govandi Station Road, Deonar, Mumbai. He obtained his M.Phil. degree in Population Studies from the Institute. Since the past five years, he is actively involved in demographic research activities. His specific area of research work is related to infant and child mortality and associated issues. The author can be reached at mukeshranjan311984@gmail.com

Mukesh Ravi Raushan is a Senior Project Officer in Longitudinal Ageing Study in India (LASI) at IIPS, Mumbai. He has submitted his thesis for the award of Ph.D. in Population Studies at IIPS, Mumbai. His research interest includes sexual, reproductive & child health; food security and nutrition, inequality, gender and human capital. He has presented 21 research papers at various seminars /conferences/workshops of national and international repute. He is having 15 research paper publications in peer review journals, edited books and working papers in his name. The author can be reached at mrr.iips@gmail.com

Marita Saldanha has submitted her Ph.D. thesis to the University of Mysore. She is currently working as faculty in Post Graduate Department of Corporate Psychology, St. Aloysius College, Mangalore. Her interests include Montessori education, Learning, Memory, and Psychological Assessments & Remediation of Dyslexia, Dysgraphia, Dyscalculia and mental health of school children. The author can be contacted at marisal1784@gmail.com

Neetu Purohit is currently working as an Associate Professor at IIHMR University, Jaipur (www.iihmr.org). She has earned her Ph.D. in Psychology from Rajasthan University, Jaipur. She has upgraded her skills by attending a summer program on Health Behaviour and Society at Johns Hopkins University, Baltimore, USA. She worked with the University of Manchester as a consultant in elementary education and as a counsellor in family courts. Since the past 15 years, she is working in the health sector and has completed multiple research projects and evaluation studies for state and central government and multilateral funding agencies. While her keen interest lies in Behaviour, notably Behaviour Change Communication and community mobilisation via various forms of communication and organisational behaviour, she is equally engaged in child health, malnutrition and reproductive health and is proficient in using both quantitative and qualitative methodology. She could be reached at neetupurohit3@gmail.com, neetu@iihmr.edu.in

Niharika Rao is a Ph.D. scholar in the field of Population studies in the International Institute of Population Sciences (IIPS), Mumbai, with particular interests in the field of Ageing, Migration, Nutrition and Child Health. Having completed graduation in Economics from the University of Mumbai, she has persuaded her Masters and M.Phil. in Population Studies at IIPS Mumbai and has worked as a research assistant in developing a Manual for Health Statistics for Ministry of Health, Government of India and TISS, Mumbai. The author can be contacted at niksun20@gmail.com

Prakash Padakannaya is a Professor and the Chairman at the Department of Psychology, University of Mysore, Mysore, India. He is a Fellow of National Academy of Psychology, India and Fellow, Association of Psychological Science (APS), USA. He is an accomplished academician, and his research interests are majorly cognitive dynamics of reading, dyslexia, and psycholinguistics. He works in the said areas by using multiple techniques that include behavioural (including eye-tracking), neural (includes brain imaging such as MRI), and genetic basis of reading deficits of dyslexia. The author can be contacted at prakashp99@gmail.com

Pooja Sahu is a Research Scholar in the Department of Psychology, Banaras Hindu University, Varanasi, India. She has earned a Ph.D. in Psychology from the Banaras Hindu University, Varanasi. Since the past six years, she is engaged in research on pregnant working women. Her specific interest lies to give focus on servitude and improving the community around us, especially women in remote and backward regions. She is also interested in the area of working women engaged in the workforce. She could be reached at the poojabhu2012@gmail.com

Pradeep K. Mehta is currently the Director of Research, Monitoring and Evaluation (RME) at S.M. Sehgal Foundation, Gurgaon, Haryana. He holds a Ph.D. degree in Economics from Mysore University through Institute for Social and Economic Change (ISEC), Bangalore; an M.Phil. degree in Planning and Development from Indian Institute of Technology (IIT), Bombay; and M.A. and B.A. degrees in Economics (honours) from Punjab University, Chandigarh. As a development specialist, he has over ten years of experience in teaching and research in the National and International organisations of India. His areas of expertise are rural development, agriculture, climate change, gender, water, and impact evaluation. The author can be reached at p.mehta@smsfoundation.org

Praveen Kumar Pathak is currently an Assistant Professor of Geography at the Delhi School of Economics, the University of Delhi since March 2014. Earlier, he worked as an Assistant Professor in the Department of Geography at the University of Pune (2013-2014), Shivaji University, Kolhapur (2010-2013), and Ravenshaw University, Cuttack (2010). He has obtained his Master's degree in Geography from the Banaras

Hindu University (BHU), Varanasi, and earned Master of Philosophy (M.Phil.) and Doctor of Philosophy (Ph.D.) in Population Studies from the International Institute for Population (IIPS), Mumbai, India under the UGC-Junior/Senior Research Fellowship Program. His research focuses on the social determinants of population health and nutrition from the spatial perspectives; social networks and demographic behaviour; assessment of population health inequalities. He was a Policy Communication Fellow (2013) at the Population Reference Bureau (PRB), Washington, D.C., USA, and a Young Scientist (2013) in the World Population Program at the International Institute for Applied Systems Analysis (IIASA), Vienna, Austria. He was also a Guest Researcher at the Vienna Institute of Demography (VID), Austrian Academy of Sciences, Vienna, Austria (2014). The author can be reached at pkpathak@geography.du.ac.in

Priscilla U. is a counselling psychologist who is working with Kendriya Vidyalaya ASC Centre, as a school counsellor, Bengaluru. She has graduated in Commerce from Kristu Jayanti College and worked for a year in TESCO–Tesco Bank as a Payroll officer. She has also interned with several NGO's such as CWC, Chennai, Respect for Life, India and International Justice Mission. She has done her research on postpartum experience on First-time mothers for her postgraduate degree program. Her research interests include mothering experiences and child and adolescent psychology. The author can be reached at priscy.priscilla8@gmail.com

Priyanka Kacker is working at the Institute of Behavioural Science of Gujarat Forensic Sciences University, Gandhinagar since 2013 as an Assistant Professor of Psychology, teaching and researching Neuropsychology and Forensic Psychology. She is trained in cognitive electrophysiology, cognitive neuropsychology and hypnotherapy; engaged in computerised EEG and ERP analyses, especially in the use of Brain Electrical Oscillations Signature (BEOS) profiling for forensic and clinical-sleep studies. She advocates police officers of the National and the International stature in the area of Forensic Psychology and Investigations. Also, she is a member of the Core Committee of Juvenile Justice Rules of Gujarat Government, which is currently engaged in a developing preliminary assessment module for Gujarat State. She has 56 research and other presentations in the National and the International conferences, and 28 research publications in the above areas. She is a Member of the Editorial Board of the 'International Journal of Indian Psychology', 'International Journal for Transformation of Consciousness', Executive Committee and Editorial Board of the 'Cognitive Neuroscience Society of India (CNSI)'. The author can be contacted at drpriyankakacker@gmail.com

Rahul Mishra is currently pursuing his Ph.D. from International Institute for Population Sciences, Govandi Station Road, Deonar, Mumbai. He obtained his M.Phil.

degree in Population Studies from the Institute. His specific area of research work is related to maternal and child health. The author can be reached at iips.rahul@gmail.com

Rajesh Raushan is an Assistant Professor at Indian Institute of Dalit Studies (IIDS), New Delhi. He obtained a Ph.D. in Development Studies with specialisation in Population Studies from ISEC, Bangalore. His research interest includes inequality, health and demographic techniques, vulnerability, gender, human development and multi-level modelling. He has worked with Institute of Economic Growth (IEG), Jawaharlal Nehru University (JNU), New Delhi and Institute for Social and Economic Change (ISEC), Bangalore. He has presented papers at various Seminars /Conferences/ Workshops of National and the International repute. He is having 25 publications in peer review journals, edited books, working papers and discussion papers in his name. His upcoming book on "Child Health in India: Caste and Neighbourhood Effect" is in a publication with Routledge, New York & London. The author can be reached at rajesh.rajiips@gmail.com

Ritu Sharma is currently working as an Assistant Professor and Heading the Department of Psychology of Pandit Deendayal Petroleum University (PDPU) Gandhinagar, Gujarat. Dr. Sharma is a gold medallist and holds a Ph.D. degree in Psychology. She has over 13 years of work experience. She is involved in the complete gamut of academic activities such as teaching, research and institutional development. The author can be reached at dr.sharmaritu@gmail.com

Sanjay Prasad was an officer at the Indian Administrative Service (IAS) of 1986 batch. He did Graduation in History from St. Stephen's College, University of Delhi and Post Graduation in History from Jawaharlal Nehru University (JNU). Previously, he also served as the Principal Secretary, Social Justice & Empowerment Department, and as Principal Secretary, Labour and Employment Department, Government of Gujarat. He retired as Additional Chief Secretary, Gujarat. Presently he is the State Election Commissioner, Gujarat.

S. Parasuraman has over 25 years of experience as a teacher, trainer, activist, administrator and development worker. He is a Professor and the Director (Vice-Chancellor) of Tata Institute of Social Sciences (TISS), Mumbai. He held various prestigious positions of the national and the international repute such as Senior Advisor to the United Nations Human Rights Commission, UNESCAP, Bangkok, Thailand (responsible for auditing all specialised UN organisations and have been programming development work in rights framework in countries in Asia region). He also has held Asia Regional Policy Director, Action Aid International, Asia Regional Office, Bangkok, Thailand (January 2001-June 2004), Team Leader of the Secretariat and Senior Advisor to the Commission, World Commission on Dams (Employee of World Bank and IUCN: September 1998-December 2000), Programme Director, Oxfam GB, India Programme, New Delhi (October 1995-December 1997), Professor and Head of Unit for Rural Studies, TISS (1993-1998), TISS, Reader in Social Sciences, TISS, (198-1992), Visiting Senior Fellow, Institute of Social Studies (ISS, The Hague) Lecturer, Unit for Child & Youth Research, TISS (198-1986). Prof. Parasuraman has over 50 publications in the form of articles in the International and the National journals, books and research reports. He was awarded the Bharat Shreshta Acharya Award in 2012 by MIT, Pune

S.V. Subramanian is a Professor of Population Health and Geography at the Department of Social and Behavioural Sciences, Harvard Chan School of Public Health, and a senior core faculty at the Harvard Centre of Population and Development Studies, Harvard University, Boston, USA. He is also the founding director for an interdisciplinary Ph.D. program in Population Health Sciences that is currently being developed at Harvard. He received him under- and post-graduate training at the University of Delhi, and completed his Ph.D. in Geography from the University Of Portsmouth, the UK in 2000. Prof. Subramanian has published over 425 articles, book chapters, and books in the field of social and contextual determinants of health, health inequalities in India with a special emphasis on nutritional inequalities among children and adults, and applied multilevel statistical models. The author can be reached at svsubram@hsph.harvard.edu

Shachi Barot is currently pursuing her Ph.D.. from School of Liberal Studies, Pandit Deendayal Petroleum University, Gandhinagar, Gujarat. She has completed her Masters in Psychology and Criminology. Her areas of interest are Criminal Psychology, Forensics, Social psychology and Criminology. The author can be reached at shachi8@gmail.com

Shahin Saiyed is working with the Indian Institute of Public Health Gandhinagar (IIPHG) as a Research Assistant since 2013. Ms. Saiyed has done her post-graduation in Business Administration in Healthcare Management from Sikkim Manipal University and graduated in Science with Mathematics from St. Xavier's College, Ahmedabad. She has been working in public health for the past ten years. She started her public health career as a researcher at Foundation for Research in Health Systems (FRHS) and worked for different research projects funded by WHO, UNICEF, Oxfam, Government of India and Government of Gujarat. During her career, she coordinated and monitored 24 NGOs on "Capacity building of Village Health and Sanitation Committees in Gujarat State" and was a part of Health Monitor 2004. At IIPHG, she has been a part of prevalence study for Cervical Cancer and capacity building of field workers. The author can be reached at ssaiyed@iiphg.org

Tanya Khanna is presently working as a Project Coordinator with Centre for Health Research and Development, Society for Applied Studies, New Delhi. She obtained her Master's degree in Public Health and Nutrition from the Maharaja Sayajirao University of Baroda, Vadodara, Gujarat and has also been a gold medallist during her post-graduation. Her Master's thesis work was on assessing the relationship between infant and young child feeding practices, nutritional status and developmental progress among 0-3 years old children in rural Vadodara. She has gained exposure in the field of public health by working in rural as well as tribal communities in India since the past two years. She has done extensive work in rural communities related to nutrition, health, water, hygiene and sanitation, food security and child development. The author can be reached at tkhanna2393@gmail.com

Uma Joshi is the Director at Amity University, Jaipur (Rajasthan), and a senior core faculty and dean of Faculty of Family and Community Sciences at the Maharaja Sayajirao University of Baroda Vadodara. She served as a director in various prestigious institutions such as Institute of Fashion Technology and Institute of Hotel Management and Catering Technology. She also served as Interim Vice-Chancellor, M.S. University of Baroda since 12th June-6th July, 2011. She was Member of Planning Commission working group on Nutrition Mission for 12th Five Year Plan, Member of Core Committee, National Open School Programme, of MHRD—UNFPA, Member of Advisory Committee for Life Skills Programme for Adolescents, MHRD—GOI, Academic Staff Review Committee Member MHRD—GOI, Member of National Assessment and Accreditation Council (NAAC). She received her under- and post-graduate training in food and nutrition and home Science education and extension, and completed her Ph.D. in home science and education extension. Prof. Joshi has published more than 200 articles, book chapters, and books in the field of social and contextual determinants of health and inequalities in India with a special emphasis on nutritional inequalities of maternal and child health. She could be reached at the following email address: ijanjoshis@gmail.com

Urmila Rani Srivastava is presently working as an Associate Professor in the Department of Psychology, Faculty of Social Sciences, Banaras Hindu University (BHU), Varanasi, UP India. She has done M.Sc. (Psychology) Moreover, Ph.D. from (BHU). For the last 20 years, she has been actively engaged in teaching and research in the area of Organisational Behaviour, Occupational Health, work-Family interface and Reproductive Health of Women. Her specific interest lies in studying the work-family conflict, challenges of managerial and professional women and reproductive health with special reference to working women. She has participated and Presented 37 research papers in various National and the International Conferences and published

24 research papers in various National and the International Journals of repute (such as American Journal of Industrial and Business Management, International Journal of Management Excellence, Journal of Health Management, Management and Labour Studies and Psychological studies etc.). She has been the active member of Gender Sensitisation Committee Faculty of Social Sciences BHU since, 2016. She has edited a Book entitled Health and well-being: Emerging trends (Edited by S. Ojha, U.R. Srivastava and S. Joshi, 2010) Global vision publishing House, New Delhi. ISBN: 978-81-8220-284-9. She has been the recipient of various awards and prizes such as 'BHARAT JYOTI AWARD' with 'CERTIFICATE OF EXCELLENCE' by India International Friendship Society New Delhi, 2014, GOLD MEDAL for standing first in Masters of Psychology (FINAL) Examination, 1990. The author can be contacted at urbhu_24@ yahoo.co.in

Vanisha S. Nambiar is a Professor at the Department of Foods and Nutrition, Faculty of Family and Community Sciences, The Maharaja Sayajirao University of Baroda, Vadodara. She has a Ph.D. in Nutrition and is engaged in teaching as well as research since the past 25 years in the same university. Her research has focused on transforming Food Science and Public Health Nutrition knowledge into action through policymakers and program administrators. Her area of research focuses on maternal and child health and nutrition (urban, rural, tribal), micro-nutrient malnutrition (VAD, IDD, IDA), healthy school initiatives for reduction in Non-Communicable Diseases, behaviour change communication and advocacy for improving developmental programs and policies related to nutrition, Food and Nutrition Security, Antioxidants from Underutilised plant species in improving food and nutrition security (FNS) in health and inflammatory disorders. She has completed 26 major/minor research projects funded by Harvest Plus/IFPRI/CIAT, Washington, USA, International Diabetes Federation, Diabetes Foundation of India, Mid Day Meal Section, Department of Education, Government of Gujarat, Gandhinagar, CSR cell of Transpek Silox Industry Pvt. Ltd. and Surat Municipal Corporation, Surat, Gujarat. She has published four books, 8 chapters in books, 45 research papers in peer-reviewed journals, is an invited eminent speaker in various international and national forums and has received 5 international and 7 national awards including the Junior and Senior Young Scientist Awards, Sight and Life Awards and Tata-Cornell Initiative Award. The author can be reached at vanishanambiar@gmail.com

Introduction

Concerns about the well-being of children, adolescents and mothers have grown as the Nation has embarked on a significant restructuring of welfare, income support, and health and social services policies over the recent years. The attention of those who pursue the welfare reform proposals have been focused mainly on the objective of the health and well-being of the children. The outcomes also warrant assessment as the effects of the welfare reforms require acceleration and optimisation. A growing number of interdisciplinary teams are engaged in empirical evaluation work focused on children living in poverty and families receiving welfare assistance. Research also needs to be addressed to issues that relate to the holistic understanding of health and nutrition, and the complex inter-linkages of various socio-cultural determinants influencing the health of children in India.

According to the World Health Organisation, nutrition is central to the achievement of the 2030 Sustainable Development Goals (SDGs) Agenda. At least 12 of the 17 SDGs contain nutrition-related indicators. In this regard, the 2012 World Health Assembly recognised six nutrition targets for mothers, infants and young children as well as several non-communicable disease targets to be achieved by 2025. These global objectives aim at setting the direction for national nutritional policies and programmatic measures to solve the problem of malnutrition and to provide a better path for inclusive human and economic development for all.

National Health Family Survey-4 reports show that 38 percent of children under the age of five are stunted for their age in India. Twenty-one percent of children under the age of five are wasted, which is a sign of acute undernutrition, while 36 percent of children under the age of five are underweight. Two percent of kids are also overweight. The prevalence of stunted children is highest in Bihar 48%. Overall, 59% of children had some level of anaemia (haemoglobin levels below 11.0 g/dl), 28% of children had mild anaemia, 29% had moderate anaemia, and 2% had severe anaemia.[1]

1. http://rchiips.org/Nfhs/NFHS-4Reports/India.pdf

The Government of India in 1995 launched the National Programme of Nutritional Support to Primary Education, popularly known as the Mid Day Meal Scheme to enhance enrolment, retention and attendance in schools while simultaneously improving nutritional levels among children, however, the scheme had been introduced earlier by one of the state Government. Gujarat was one of the pioneer states in the country to have started the Mid Day Meal scheme in 1984. The Scheme aims at increasing the enrollment rate by reducing the dropout rate, improving child nutrition and reducing the burden of poverty on poor parents as well as caste discrimination in society. It involves the provision of serving a hot cooked meal to the students of primary and upper primary classes. MDM includes Government Schools, Government Aided Schools, and students of Special Training Centres.

The present volume is an effort to encourage discussion of diverse issues related to Child Health and Nutrition in India. An effort has been made to identify the gaps stemming out of the various dimensions of health and nutrition of the children and also to provide a way forward for the increased efficacy of welfare policies.

Children's state of wellness has an obvious effect on their development and ability to perform as a human resource. The understanding of factors that shape and influence a child's well-being, including nutrition, environmental conditions and emotional and social health; needs to be improved with ongoing research on these topics. The research inputs can lead to noteworthy changes in views about health, approaches to health care, help in resolving issues and improve outcomes of child health and nutrition schemes.

Children represent the hope and future of the world. Nutrition to a child means not only health but also growth and development. It is generally recognised that the development of child healthcare is inseparable from political, economic, and cultural development. Every child's health is of paramount concern for the mother and her country because the future of the country depends on their children's achievements. A healthy child has to have a healthy mother and environment free of harmful practices and violence, providing adequate shelter, nutrition, clean water, primary education, and therapy. However, the reality is that the world is fundamentally complex and heterogeneous, with extreme disparities. The social inequalities and uneven access to the welfare mechanism of the state lead to a variety of outcomes that could impact the health of the child.

The relationship between nutrition and health is undeniably strong: nutrition is one of the three significant factors that impact a child's development while genes and environment are the other two factors. Research studies show that nutrition in a child's early years is linked to his/her health and academic performance in later years. Giving a child solid nutritional start can contribute to his/her physical, mental and social development. Malnutrition weakens the immune system, making a child susceptible to disease, increasing the severity of illness and impending recovery. A sick child, in turn, can quickly become malnourished. This vicious cycle can be broken with age-specific breastfeeding and complementary foods and proper health care. Before conception, the food future of a child begins with the nutritional status of the mother before pregnancy. A chronically malnourished mother give birth to an underweight baby who may also get stunned as a child. A well-nourished woman over 18 years old has a far higher likelihood of survival as well as good possibilities for her child's healthy growth. [2]

Maternal and Child Health has been the epicentre of attention in health, and a large number of welfare schemes of the government are attempting to improve child and maternal health. This topic represents the convergence and synergy between various disciplines of public health and public policy to achieve the health objectives of the health-related to children and their mothers.

This volume on Child Health and Nutrition in India attempts to, provide a comprehensive approach and well-documented understanding of children's health and nutritional needs. These can enable and provide a pathway to better understand and improve the health and nutrition of mothers, newborn babies and children with particular attention to poor and marginalised communities. This book is an attempt to present, in a consolidated form of research articles that can provide a common platform for communication and discussion healthcare and service providers, functionaries, scholars and social workers involved with child health and nutrition. The scope of this book to present an overview of child health, maternal health and community issues in India and also attempt to highlight some of the important issues in this field.

2. https://www.unicef.org/nutrition/index_role.html

An Overview of Child Health and Nutrition

B.B. Patel, in his paper on **National Perspective on Malnutrition,** provides an overview of the status, progress, challenges and further action related suggestions to accelerate the achievements on the elimination of malnutrition among women and children. It also focuses on strengthening nutritional intervention and health care services.

It highlights the considerable progress on most of the indicators of prevalence of malnutrition among women and children, between 2005 and 2015-16 all across the states. However, the levels of these indicators of malnutrition, as observed in 2015-16, are high. The prevalence rate of anaemia among children are higher than those among women. The author expresses his concern towards lack of awareness or lack of access to the right type of food and feeding practices among women. He indicates gaps in access to food, ignorance about feeding practices, lack of timely medical attention and care.

However, it was also found that health care services like antenatal care, postnatal visit, immunisation etc. have made significant progress and have their impact on maternal and child health, institutional delivery etc.

The National Nutrition Strategy, 2017 prepared by NITI Aayog, Government of India aims at a very comprehensive approach from the stage of pregnancy of woman to the childbirth and beyond that, till the child becomes 18 years of age. This author concludes with emphasising the importance of local-level institutions and the grass-root level functionaries for effective implementation. It places a sharp focus on the role of Anganwadi workers, ASHA and ANMs at the village level and *Panchayats* and other local bodies so that they own the programme and work for desired outcomes in a time-bound manner.

S. Parasuraman and Aparana in their paper: The Situation of Child Health and Nutrition in India: Approach challenges and way forward to meet SDGs the authors present the background of child Health and Nutrition in India explaining the concept & dimension of Nutrition in India. They explained child Health and its determinants in the contest NFHS_4. They also throw light on the current trends and patterns of this child Mortality and Child Health in India. It also includes challenges and intervention for sustaining nutrition in India while explaining in detail the reasons for the prevalence of malnutrition among children in India. They have focused on policy and legal aspects of malnutrition and emphasis the future thrust area in the field of child health. They concluded his article with suggestions.

B.B. Patel, in his paper, **Malnutrition: Incidence and Challenges in India, focusing on Gujarat,** brings out that the incidence of malnutrition among women and children in India is a big challenge. Both in terms of the hunger index and the nutritional status of the population, India is faced with a big challenge. Some of the states have an alarming situation in terms of indicators like underweight children, wasting, low birth weight children and mortality of children under the age of 5. The paper analyses the status and the change in some of the key social indicators such as infant and child mortality rates, nutritional status of children, anaemia among children, maternal and child health services and delivery care. The paper includes the reference period of 2004-05 to 2015-16 across selected states—Gujarat, Maharashtra, Tamil Nadu, Bihar, Odisha and Madhya Pradesh by using secondary data from NFHS-3 and NFHS-4 of the Ministry of Health and Family Welfare, Government of India. The paper argues that all selected states have made notable progress in achieving positive changes in the indicators. Maternal and child health services play a decisive role in advancing outreach across the states. However, the total desired outcomes of health interventions are still to be achieved. Poverty level reduction has had a positive impact on health outcomes; however, this is only medium to long-term measure. It is on preventive health care and additional social welfare and nutritional intervention which can help break the vicious cycle of malnutrition and morbidity.

H.G. Sadhu, in his paper **Occupational Health of Children and Adolescents in India,** provides the scenario of occupational health of children and adolescent in India with the national legislation and ILO convention. He also includes causes for child labour focusing on the unorganised sector of industry and its occupational hazards in the context of child and adolescent in India. He throws the light on the magnitude of the problems related to the occupational health of children and adolescent in India. He suggests to spread awareness on occupational health of children and adolescent and to include need-based research for the elimination of child labour as a longer-term objective.

D.C. Baxi in his paper **Legal Aspect of Child-Specific Health Care Policies** sets out the adequate constitutional provisions, constitutional and legislative framework for child health and nutrition policies and implementing departments of the states as well as constitutional monitoring bodies like National Human Right Commission and National Commission on Protection Child Rights are already in existence. However, the issue of infant mortality, malnutrition and health-related issues of the child continue to persist. The author points out that the children below the 0-14 years numbers over 35 crores and account 27.71% of the total population of the country. Children being the biggest strength and future human resource of the nation, the author draws the attention towards the need for quality and effective implementation of constitutional provisions, Acts and Schemes of the government which should be supported by effective monitoring and social audit.

Child Nutrition in India

Uma Joshi, in her paper, **Nutrition Education-Key to Sustaining Child Health,** provides an interdependent synthesis between children and sustainable development. The author believes that providing child rights and health can contribute to sustainable development. However, nutritional status in India, both at undernutrition and over-nutritional-levels need to be tackled in the first place. Data from development agencies have repeatedly highlighted the high prevalence of stunting, wasting and underweight among children as well as the poor condition of nutrition among women, high maternal mortality rates and high incidences of non-communicable diseases in the country. Development initiatives that involve academicians, policymakers and activists should increasingly focus on the policy agenda related to children's survival. Promoting adequate nutrition and clean environment for all children shall make them potential contributors to a sustainable society. The author through her study calls for initiatives that have a significant impact on the children's health. These can be created through health promotion from the early years of life by educating and sensitising them about healthy eating, sanitation practices and regular physical activity. This is the core of the Anganwadi school-based nutrition education programmes. Efforts should be made to increase health awareness, communication and consciousness through effective educational strategies and skill development. The paper discusses the content of nutrition education and how it should be imparted in order to make it useful.

Priyanka Kacker, in her paper **Protein: An Important Nutrient for Cognition and Brain Development of Children** emphasises the cognitive development among children through protein intake. The research study points out that nutrition plays a significant role in the growth of the nervous system. Research has shown that malnutrition causes a variety of cognitive and behavioural deficits over a lifetime. The severity, timing and duration of malnutrition are crucial determinants of its possible effect on the neurological development of the child. Proper nutrition with adequate amounts of necessary micronutrients, and calories, given at the appropriate time, may ensure healthy brain development. Therefore, for ensuring an intelligent child a high protein diet is the key ingredient, and this should be a significant part of mid-day meals in schools for optimum results in improving child health.

Apoorva Patel though her paper **Malnutrition Among Tribal Children** explores the magnitude of malnutrition among the children of tribal villages in Rewa district of Madhya Pradesh. She attempts to find out the role of various factors and the effectiveness of nutrition interventions and welfare programmes in addressing malnutrition. These villages comprising of Kol, Gond and Khairwaar Tribes are regarded as the most malnourishment affected areas with associated morbidity. Anthropometric measurements are used to assess the nutritional status of the children in the study area. The findings show that 76% of children were malnourished as per 'MUAC measurement criteria for 6-60 months of children' and 54% were malnourished according to WHO weight-for-age standard growth criteria. It seems that socioeconomic factors and health factors, along with traditional practices, contributed to the poor nutritional status of children. Cultural beliefs related to healthy habits practised in the community have also a confounding influence on health which is further accentuated due to the poverty cycle of debt and mortgage of the tribal families.

Niharika Rao and **Aparajita Chattopadhyay** explore the nutritional status of young school-going children aged 6-9 years in an eastern part of Mumbai through their paper **Nutritional Status of Primary School going Children in Mumbai, India: A Case study.** Socio-economic characteristics, food intake practices, daily routine and morbidity pattern were used as the critical determinants for measuring the nutritional status among the study children. Data were collected 557 students of schools in the eastern suburb of Mumbai to assess the nutritional status of the primary school children. Anthropometric measurements like height and weight of children were measured using electronic machines. Nineteen percent of children were found to be stunted, about a quarter had low BMI, and 27% were underweight. The study brings out the factors that have a significant negative impact on nourishment like intake of baby canned baby milk powder, avoidance of breakfast, use of certain types of cooking oil, drinking of inadequate water and chronic childhood diseases. Food habits rather than socio-economic factors have a positive impact on undernourishment. The authors suggest measures such as the provision of nutritious school breakfast, frequent intake of safe drinking water; and a school-based deworming programme that can help to curb undernutrition among young children in India.

Praveen Kumar Pathak and **S.V. Subramanian** in **Parental Child Marriages and Childhood Under-nutrition in India: A Cross-Spousal Analysis** present an analysis on the influence of parental child marriages (marriage below legal ages) on childhood nutritional status using a nationally representative data. The study population consists of nationally representative cross-section sample of singleton children (n=16756) aged between 0 to 59 months from the 2005-2006 Indian National Family Health Survey. Modified logistic regression models that account for multistage survey design and sampling weights were applied to estimate the association between parental child marriages and childhood under-nutrition. The outcome measures were child underweight and stunting; parental child marriages 18 years among mothers and below 21 years among fathers was the primary exposure variable. In the mutually adjusted regression models, the authors do not find any significant association between parental childhood marriage and underweight children. However, in the case of child stunting, they found that children born to early married mothers were significantly more likely to be stunted. The findings between the association of parental child marriage and childhood underweight indicate that early age of marriage of parents may not explain childhood malnutrition in India.

Mukesh Ravi Raushan and **Rajesh Raushan** state that along with food shortage, feeding practices are essential factors for child malnutrition along with nutritional knowledge and awareness among mothers. In their study **Nutritional Awareness, Feeding Practices and Nutritional Status among U5-Children in India.** They investigate nutritional awareness and dietary diversity among children in India. Data for this study were primarily collected from National Family Health Survey: 2005-06 (NFHS-3) considering the youngest child living with the mother. Dietary diversity was assessed by constructing the composite score of dietary diversity, named as Complementary Food Diversity Score (CFDs) based on the World Health Organisation-Infant and Young Child Feeding model. The findings reveal that only 40 percent mothers were aware of nutritional details of the food provided to their children during the infancy, ranging from a highest of around 82 percent among mothers in Tamil Nadu to the lowest of only 14 percent in Bihar. The study further demonstrated that the children who consumed milk products were less likely to be malnourished than their counterparts who did not consume milk products. Overall, both the CFD and the frequency of the food given to the child were found negatively associated with the child malnutrition in India. The study concludes that increasing nutritional awareness of complementary dietary diversity may be one of the significant ways to reduce the poor nutritional status and adverse health outcomes during infancy and young age among children in India.

Manoj K. Sahoo and **D. Sriram** in their paper **Nutrition and Health Status of Construction Workers' Children in Gujarat: An Empirical Study of Gandhinagar** examine the implementation process of the Unorganised Workers Social Security

Act 2008. The policy intends to provide social security benefits to the workers by providing the Smart Card or identity cards. These cards enable the workers to avail the benefits of schemes such as special Balwadi/Anganwadis for children to provide nutritious food at the construction sites, maternity benefits and free treatment at the government hospitals. The Gujarat Building and Construction Welfare Board has implemented schemes like hostel facility, temporary housing facilities at the worksites, *Shramik Sahay Suvidha*—a helpline facility for any problem including health problems of the construction workers, medical aid for major disease under *Mukhyamantri Amrutam Yojana* and *Mukhyamantri Amrutam Vatsalya Yojana* for mother and child. Through this study, the authors address the issues of on-ground access and availability of all the above facilities to the construction workers' children. The study covered fifty children from ten construction sites in and around the capital city of Gandhinagar in Gujarat. The findings show that the construction workers' children in the study area avail vaccine facilities and medicine and treatment facilities for routine health problems like fever, cough and cold, diarrhoea etc. However, there is potential for further improvements in the delivery of mechanism for nutritional and health services to the construction workers and their families.

Neetu Purohit and **Dipti Govil** in their paper **Reasons to Review, Reflect and Restructure ICDS: A Case from Rajasthan** evaluate the implementation of ICDS programme with a focus on supplementary nutrition and growth monitoring. For this, an observational study was conducted in the state of Rajasthan. A total of 488 Aangan Waadi Centres (AWC) from all blocks of 33 districts of the state were observed, and 482 Aangan Waadi (AAW) Workers were interviewed over six months. Also, a total of 2442beneficiaries, including mothers of 6 months to 6 years old children, pregnant and lactating women, were interviewed from the catchment area of AWCs covered by the team. The findings suggest there is a need to establish mechanisms that will facilitate the availability of supplies and equipment, enhancement of the knowledge and competency of the worker and accountability towards beneficiaries. Providing the right services in the right manner can help address the problem of malnutrition more effectively.

Shachi Barot and **Ritu Sharma** through their paper **Challenges and Scope of Mid day Meal Intervention: A Systematic Literature Review** evaluate the mid-day meal implementation to discuss the challenges and scope of the scheme in the Indian context. Social audits of MDM revealed that it had reduced the burden of providing a one-time meal to their children and was considered great support to the beneficiary families. Teachers opined that mid-day meal aided in active learning of children, which indirectly improved their academic performance. The scheme has played a significant role in bringing social equality among all the sections of society. However, the authors call improvement in the infrastructure of the MDM scheme to enhance its optimum utilisation among the targeted beneficiaries.

Vanisha S. Nambiar and Tanya Khanna in their paper Developmental **Programmes, Under-nutrition and Developmental Progress of Young Children** detail the functioning and progress of Integrated Child Development Scheme (ICDS) and attempt to identify the bottlenecks in the implementation of the programme. ICDS, the centrally sponsored scheme implemented by the state governments which aims to provide supplementary nutrition, preschool education and primary health care to preschool age. The scheme intends to fight malnutrition and improve overall development among children. Early intervention services are offered by community-based organisations and paraprofessionals in most cases under the supervision of trained professionals. The government needs to increase resource allocation for public health, especially schemes aimed at the poor and weaker section of the society. There is a need to intensify efforts to increase public as well as private investment and spending on key social services, particularly education, social welfare and nutrition, water supply, sanitation, housing, and often suits schemes which have direct and indirect impact on children's health.

Maternal and Child Health

Pregnancy-related stress and its impact on neonatal well-being and caregiving are well documented in the paper **Conceptualizing the Components of Pregnancy-Specific Stress through Qualitative Investigation among Pregnant Working and Non-Working Women** by **Urmila Rani Srivastava and her colleagues**. Nine major themes, along with their subthemes, had emerged from the analysis and these themes were highly stressful for both the working and non-working pregnant women. The findings of the study reveal that to get a positive solution for pregnant women, we should be aware of the psychosocial relationship between maternal health and well-being. This study is an essential addition to the existing literature on pregnancy-specific stress and has the potential to provide useful information for clinicians and practitioners.

In the article **Improving Health Outcomes Across Life Cycle Continuum By Focusing On Adolescent Girls**, the author **Manisha Chandra** identifies and discusses the lessons learnt in the implementation of programme together on adolescent girl, which may contribute to positive health and nutrition outcomes through nutrition and health education. Apart from improving reproductive health, this is also essential to improve the health of adolescent girls for their well-being as *'Individuals'*. As adolescence is a transition period between childhood and adulthood, it provides an opportunity to educate and inform the girl to prevent nutrition-related problems.

The author calls it an appropriate time to provide health promotion programmes so that they understand the importance of healthy eating and make correct food choices. Therefore, an attempt was made under the Integrated Child Development Scheme (ICDS), Gujarat to revitalise the existing programmatic framework of *Sabla*. This has now changed to Scheme for Adolescent Girls, a Central scheme and PURNA, a state scheme and Kishori Shakti Scheme and impart nutrition, health and life skill education to girls. This actively engaged them in creative and simple activities where they could learn through the approach of learning by doing helped by the active support of the Anganwadi worker.

Pradeep K. Mehta, in his paper **Improving Child Health And Development In Mewat: Role and Limitations of Community-Based Mechanisms** analyses the impact of the health system on maternal and child health. He begins by discussing the main elements of a health care system versus health system, examining the key difference between the two. In this context, he highlights Mewat, one of the districts in Haryana, which has very high Infant Mortality Rate (IMR) (117) and Maternal Mortality Rate (447) indicating an alarming health situation. In this context, this paper examines the role of participation mechanisms by rural people in improving service delivery under the ICDS. A case study is presented of a community-based organisation in Mewat that attempts to increase awareness about the rights and entitlements and Redressal mechanisms in the implementation mechanism of ICDS. The results highlight that is increasing access to information about rights and entitlements that provides the community with tools to demand accountability from service providers. This has an important role in improving implementation of ICDS resulting in better and improved access to child health and development facilities. However, the process of transformation through awareness is slow and needs to be accelerated. Further, there is a need for providing regular training to Anganwadi *workers* on budget utilisation and provision of services p under ICDS which can improve t responsiveness to the demands raised by the local community.

Kranti Vora and **Shahin Saiyed** in their paper **Maternal Health Scenario in Gujarat** make a systematic review of literature of existing government reports and analysed trends in maternal health indicators, health infrastructure and, programmatic successes and failures. It also evaluates new initiatives and different strategies implemented by the government of Gujarat for improving maternal health indicators of the state. Human resources related issues, however, need to be resolved for the efficient implementation of schemes.

In recognition of the importance of perinatal care-giving in the field of maternal and child health **Priscilla U. and Aneesh Kumar P.** in their paper **Mothering and Child Development: Impact of Mothers' Well-being and Beliefs on Early Child**

Development provide an overview on maternal health and child-rearing practices. Thus aim to understand maternal well-being and beliefs among mothers in India about child development and child-rearing practices, and how this affects early child development. The paper brings out the importance of understanding mothers' postpartum experiences, the beliefs they hold regarding childrearing practices like breastfeeding, illness and the use of corporal punishments and their impact on physical and mental health of children. The existing health care policies and programs in India are also discussed in the paper, highlighting the need for evidence-based interventions and programs. The findings of the study call for the need for training, support and knowledge at family and community levels.

Community Health Issues

Saldanha, M.P.J. and **Padakannaya, P.** portrays the dimension of mental well-being in their paper **Remediation of Alphabetic-Alphasyllabary Bi-Literate Dyslexia: A Bridge from Despair To Hope**. The authors claim that children having a high rate of dyslexia should be diagnosed in the early stage as an essential preventable measure. This can avoid the vicious circle of academic failure and other socio-economic consequences. Different writing systems deploy varying cognitive demands on the reader and shows varying degrees of challenges faced in mastering efficient reading and spelling. The focus of remediation needs to be customised so that the problem can be alleviated and the children integrated into the mainstream of socio-psychological development. The authors, through their findings of the stud, confirm the view that phonological awareness training is a vital element in any dyslexia remediation protocol.

Mukesh Ranjan and **his colleagues** in their paper **Death Clustering Among The Tribes Of Central And Eastern Indian States** attempt to understand the intra-family clustering of deaths of children due to the occurrence of deaths of previous siblings in families. It also includes unobserved factors such as the contribution of maternal level behavioural factors in child-rearing, genetic factors, etc. in the concentration of deaths of children within the families of the Tribes of Central And Eastern Indian States namely Jharkhand, Madhya Pradesh, Orissa and Chhattisgarh. The analysis of the data brings out a number of traits which can account for the clustering of mentality among children of these tribal families. The conclusion has important policy implications for improving the health and survival prospects of children, especially among underprivileged communities.

Through **Children's Right to Safe Sanitation in Urban Gujarat: Evidence from the Margins, Kesab Das** presents an overview of the safe drinking water and sanitation issues, bringing out that their absence increases children's vulnerability to various infectious diseases. He engages with the issues of children's access to sanitation and a hygienic living environment both in the private and public spheres. The findings underscore the need for sustained efforts towards educating and informing slum dwellers regarding benefits of sanitation and hygienic living. Increased investment towards building drainage and sewerage facilities, provision of water and regular management of collection and disposal of solid and liquid waste is an essential prerequisite for promoting a safe sanitation environment for children and adults. The study further considers that the widespread provision of sanitation infrastructure along with awareness regarding hygienic practices would contribute immensely towards ensuring children's right to safe sanitation and healthy living.

—Editors

Acknowledgment

We would like to acknowledge the contribution of all the authors of these articles for devoting their time and effort. We would also like to express our gratitude towards Government officials, Mahatma Gandhi Labour Institute (MGLI), Labour and Employment Department (Government of Gujarat) and UNICEF. Last but not least, we would like to convey special thanks to everyone, who were; directly or indirectly, involved in the preparation of this volume.

We would also acknowledge children of Blind Peoples' Association—an NGO based in Ahmedabad for creating the delightful drawings that enabled us to create the cover page.

Contents

1

Malnutrition in India: A big Challenge

—B.B. Patel

Introduction

The text book of Preventive and Social Medicine defines malnutrition as "A pathological state resulting from a relative or absolute deficiency (or access) of one or more essential nutrients". Undernutrition is the condition, which results when insufficient food is eaten over an extended period of time. In extreme situation it may become starvation.

Prevalence of malnutrition among children and adult women and men damages the foundation on which a society can build a super structure of human capital and attain the goals of human development.

Malnutrition-morbidity-mortality-poverty form a vicious circle and hence, even if the nation has young population it may not be in the position to get demographic dividend rather, it might result in a demographic disaster. About 2/3rd population in India is below 35 years in age. Unless this young population is healthy on key parameters, it poses a big challenge for formation of human capital and economic prosperity.

The Comprehensive National Nutritional Survey (CNNS) released by the Union Health Ministry finds some shocking results regarding the status of nutrition of children in India. Only 6.4% of Indian children aged less than 2 years get a 'Minimum Acceptable Diet' there are wide variation across the states from 1.3% in Andhra Pradesh to 35.9% in Sikkim. In Andhra Pradesh, Maharashtra, Gujarat, Telangana and Karnataka (all 3.6%) and Tamil Nadu (4.2%) on the other hand the percentage of children who receives minimum acceptable diet above the national average is in the relatively poor states like Odisha, Chhattisgarh, Jharkhand and Assam.

The survey CNNS finds that 35% of children under the age of 5 are stunted (low height for age) in this age group 17% are wasted (low weight for height) and 33% underweight (low weight for age).

It was further found that in the age 5-9 years 22% were stunted, 10% were underweight. This findings point to the almost alarming situation although during the preceding decade situation has improved.

The paper is focusing on the nutritional status of children and women and changes over time in India and in some selected states in India. Along with that, it also highlights the nature and extent of outreach of maternal and child health services and key interventions which are designed to improve the nutritional status and overall health of children and women in particular. The main source of the data is the National Family Health Survey (NFHS-4), 2015-16.

The National Family Health Survey (NFHS-4) is the fourth in the series. The Ministry of health and family welfare Government of India has designated the International Institute of Population sciences, Mumbai as the nodal agency for these surveys.

The survey was carried out from January 2015 to 4th December, 2016 and covered 601509 households, 699686 women and 103525 men for eliciting information.

The problem of malnutrition, morbidity and diseases in India cannot be seen in isolation from the status of some indicators of preventive health care. Also, many of the health and nutrition related variables are influenced by the characteristics of the population in the sample. Hence, it is useful to have understanding of the profile of the population covered in the survey. The profile data, concepts and definition used bellow are as per their definitions adopted in the NFHS-4.

Children (female) who Ever Attended School

The female population age 6 years and above who ever attended school was 68.8% in the total. Also 63% of the rural female children in the sample and 80.6% children in the urban population had ever attended a school. Thus, illiterates (never gone to schools) accounted for about 31% in the total number of HHs in the Survey. Moreover, mere attending school gives no idea about the years of retention in school and hence, many among these school attending children may be hardly literate.

Child Birth Registration

The percentage of children below the age of 5 years (born in the last 5 years) and have their birth registered was 79.7% in the total, 76.1% were in the rural and 88.8% in the urban areas. Thus, about 20% of the children born in the last 5 years did not have their birth even registered.

Households with Electricity

It was found that 88.2% of the households in the sample had electricity at a home. Even in rural areas the coverage with electricity at home was 83.2%, which is quite significant.

Improved Drinking water source

As regards the access to improved drinking water source, It was found that 89.9% of all HHs in the sample had access to improved drinking water source. Even in rural areas it covered 89.3% of the sample households. In other words access to improved water supply was significant for the HHs in the sample.

Improved Sanitation Facility

The households who used improved sanitation facility were only 48.4% of the total. The percentage was only 36.7% for rural households and 70.3% for urban households. However, due to Mission mode implementation of sanitation and hygiene program and *Swachchhta Abhiyan*, the coverage of HHs by improved sanitation facility is likely to have become more wide spread in the last five years.

Use of Clean Fuel for Cooking

Only 43.8% of all households were using clean fuel for cooking. In rural areas, the percentage was very low i.e. only 24%. This has the implication for cooking two hot meals a day in the family. Before we analyse nutritional status, an overview of the status of hunger across the states will provide an appropriate context.

Hunger Index

In the discussion on malnutrition or under nutrition, the calorie malnutrition refers to the daily intake of food which gives certain level of calorie to an individual. In the estimation of poverty in India by Prof. Dandekar and Rath (1971) 2250 calorie was taken as a cut off point to determine the poverty line. In other words if the daily consumption of food by a person does not give 2250 calorie per day that person will be classified as below poverty line. This mainly referred to the adults. Later on in 1979, the planning commission of India took 2400 calorie as the cut off point for an adult in rural areas and 2100 calorie as the cut off point for urban areas etc.

The India hunger index 2008 which was based on the data from National Family Health Survey-3 (NFHS-3) and 61st round of the National Sample Survey (2007) took the calorie cut off point of 1632 per person per day and thereby calculated National Calorie Under Nutrition rate of 20% in 2008. Thus, even with the use of conservative methodology calorie undernutrition was 20%. However, the hunger index calculation takes two other variables also. The proportion of underweight children under five years of age which indicates the proportion of children suffering from weight loss or reduced growth or both. This is a second variable used in hunger index calculation.

The third variable in the hunger index is the mortality rate of the children under the age of five years which to some extent indicates an interplay between dietary intake and unhealthy environment–lack of access to clean drinking water, lack of sanitation and hygiene.

The hunger index for India 2008 had the score of 23.30. The lowest score was 13.63 in Punjab and the highest score was 30.87 in Madhya Pradesh. The range of hunger index varies from less than 5 to 30 and above. If the hunger index value is less than 4.9, it is classified as 'low'; if it is less than 5.0-5.9 as 'moderate'; 10.0-19.9 as 'serious'; 20.0-20.9 as 'alarming' and, 30.0 and more as 'extremely alarming'.

According to this India hunger index of 2008, there was not a single state with less than 10 score of hunger index. 12 out of 17 states in India were classified in the category of alarming status while the state of Madhya Pradesh with the index score of 30.9 was classified as extremely alarming status. Assuming that in the decade after 2008 significant achievements have been made, the overall situation is likely to have remained grim. The recently calculated Global Hunger Index (based on data 2014-18) shows that the position of India has worsened. In 2019 India ranked at 102 position (as against 97 in 2016).

The GHI ranks countries on a 100–point scale, with 0 being the best score (no hunger) and 100 being the worst. Values less than 10 reflect low hunger, values from 20 to 34.9 indicate serious hunger; values from 35 to 49.9 are alarming; and values of 50 or more are extremely alarming. **India's score was 30.3 putting it in the serious hunger category.**

We may note that, in a country like India, food intake is also affected by a variety of factors such as cultural and religious practices, food habits, occupational compulsions forcing them to have only one proper meal in the case of casual labourers and low income self employed persons who account for more than 85% of the working population.

The Manifestations of inadequate food intake, unbalanced diet, lack of facility to cook twice in a day etc., are the poor maternal and child health, malnutrition, morbidity and mortality. The NFHS-4 (2015-16) and the previous one NFHS-3 (2005-06), provide insights not only into the present status but also the changes which have taken place in some of these key variables in health, nutrition, mortality as well as the role played by a range of health and medical services.

Nutritional Status of Children Under 5 Years of Age

The nutrition status of children under five years of age in terms of underweight, stunted and wasted children in India is given in Table-1.

Table-1: Nutritional Status of Children below five years of age in India (%):

Nutritional Status	NFHS-4 (2015-16) (in %)			NFHS-3 (2005-06, total)(%)
	Urban	Rural	Total	
Underweight (weight-for-age)	29.1	38.3	35.7	42.5
Stunted (height-for-age)	31	41.2	38.4	48
Wasted (weight-for-height)	20	21.5	21	19.8
Anaemia among children below five years of age (%)	55.9	59.4	58.4	69.4

Source: National Family Health Survey-4, 2015-16, India Fact sheet, International Institute for population sciences, Mumbai.

Under Weight Children

Among the three measures of malnutrition among the children below the age of five, the percentage of underweight children (weight-for-age) was 35.7% in 2015-16. In rural areas however, 38.3% of the children were under weight as against 29.1% in urban areas. Also the percentage of underweight children in India decreased by 6 percentage points from 42.5% in 2005-06, to 35.7% in 2015-16.

Stunted Children

The second measure of malnutrition among children is height-for-age or stunted. It can be seen from the table that 38.4% of the children below the age of five years were stunted. In rural areas the percentage of stunted children was 41.2% as against 31% in urban areas. The proportion of stunted children however was reduced significantly from 48% in 2005-06 to 38.4% in 2015-16. It can be seen that the percentage of stunted children–who have failed to attain adequate height for their age, is even higher than the percentage with underweight.

Wasted Children

The third measure of malnutrition is weight-for height or wasted. The percentage of wasted children was lower to 21% and, there were not any significant differences either in rural or urban areas or between 2005-06 to 2015-16 .

Interstate Variation in Nutritional Status of Children

Table-2: Interstate variations in prevalence of malnutrition (children less than 5 years of age) in 2015-16 and change between 2005-06 and 2015-16.

States	Years	Stunted (height-for-age), %.	Wasted (weight-for-height), %.	Underweight (weight-for-age), %.
Tami Nadu	2015-16	27.1	19.7	23.8
	2005-06	30.9	22.2	29.8
Maharashtra	2015-16	34.4	25.6	36
	2005-06	46.3	16.5	37
Gujarat	2015-16	38.5	26.4	39.3
	2005-06	51.7	18.7	44.6
Bihar	2015-16	48.3	20.8	43.9
	2005-06	55.6	27.1	55.9
Odisha	2015-16	34.1	20.4	34.4
	2005-06	45	19.6	40.7
Madhya Pradesh	2015-16	42	25.8	42.8
	2005-06	50	35	60
All India	2015-16	38.4	21	35.7
	2005-06	48	19.8	42.5

Source: National Family Health Survey-4, 2015-16, India Fact sheet, International Institute for population sciences, Mumbai.

While 35.7% of the children below 5 years of age were underweight in India in 2015-16, these percentages were much higher in Bihar, Odisha, Gujarat and Madhya Pradesh. The proportion of underweight children was the lowest in Tamil Nadu while, it was highest in Madhya Pradesh.

Similarly, while 38.4% of the children were stunted in India in 2015-16, the percentages were much higher in Bihar and Madhya Pradesh.

Nutritional status of adult men and women (15-49 years of age)

The nutritional status of children can be looked at on the basis of the nutritional status of adult man and women.

The nutritional status of adults is measured in terms of the Body Mass Index (BMI) with the standard value of 18.5 Kg/m^2. If the value is less than the standard, it shows chronic energy deficiency and affects the growth and development of the newly born child.

Table-3: Nutritional Status of Adults men and women (age 15-49 years) in selected states, 2015-16 and 2005-06.

		NFHS-4 (2015-16)(%)			NFHS-3 (2005-06) (%)
	States	**Urban**	**Rural**	**Total**	**Total**
Man<than 18.5Kg/m2,%)	Tami Nadu	10.7	14.3	12.4	27.1
	Maharashtra	14.5	23.7	19.1	33.5
	Gujarat	19	29.6	24.7	36.1
	Bihar	18.9	26.9	25.4	35.3
	Odisha	12.6	21.4	19.5	35.7
	Madhya Pradesh	22.5	31.1	28.4	41.6
	All India	15.3	23	20.2	34.2
Women<than18.5Kg/m2,%	Tami Nadu	10.9	18.5	14.6	28.4
	Maharashtra	16.8	30	23.5	36.2
	Gujarat	18.1	34.3	27.2	36.3
	Bihar	22.2	31.8	30.4	45
	Odisha	15.8	28.7	26.4	41.4
	Madhya Pradesh	20.6	31.8	28.3	41.7
	All India	15.5	26.7	22.9	35.5

Source: National Family Health Survey-4, 2015-16, India Fact sheet, International Institute for population sciences, Mumbai.

It can be seen from Table-3 above that, by an large, the percentage of women with below normal BMI is higher than that for men in India and across the selected states (except in urban areas).

One can observe that, there is striking reduction in under nutrition among adult men and women across the states between 2005-06 to 2015-16.

Tamil Nadu has the lowest percentage of men and women who have BMI less than normal.

Madhya Pradesh, Bihar and Gujarat have higher percentage of men with below normal BMI than in India.

Similarly, Bihar, Madhya Pradesh, Gujarat and Odisha have significantly higher proportion of women with below normal BMI than in India.

There are also significant differences in the percentages of adult men and women with below normal BMI as between rural and urban areas all across the states. The percentage of women with below normal BMI were higher in rural areas than in urban areas.

It will be noted that the under nutritional status for men as well as women (BMI) was significantly lower than the proportion of children below the age of five who were either under weight or stunted. **This means that although parent's health has some link with the child health the deterioration of child health is more affected by lack of proper food and care of the child after birth.**

Anaemia Among Children

Apart from the measures relating to age-weight and height, it is equally important to study the haemoglobin (Hb) level in blood of a child. If the Hb level is less than 11.0 g/dl, it will be classified as anaemic child . An anaemic child or a man or woman become susceptible to all types of infections and diseases. Moreover, if a child is anaemic it is most likely that it will be also under weight and stunted. Probably the mother of a child will be also anaemic.

The prevalence of anaemia among children under five years of age and among women in the reproductive age was wide spread across the states.

Table-4: Children age 6-59 months who are anaemic, selected states and change over time.

States	NFHS-4 (2015-16)			NFHS-3 (2005-06)
	Urban	Rural	Total	Total
Tami Nadu	48.6	52.5	50.7	64.2
Maharashtra	53.6	54	53.8	63.4
Gujarat	59.5	64.6	62.6	69.7
Bihar	58.8	64	63.5	78
Odisha	38.1	45.7	44.6	65
Madhya Pradesh	66.3	69.9	68.9	74
All India	55.9	59.4	58.4	69.4

Source: National Family Health Survey-4, 2015-16, India Fact sheet, International Institute for population sciences, Mumbai.

It is a matter of serious concern that 58.4% of the children below five years of age in India were found to be anaemic in 2015-16. The differences in the proportion of anaemic children in rural and urban areas was not very significant although the overall proportion of anaemic children decreased significantly from 69.4% in 2005-06 to 58.4% in 2015-16.

Anaemia Among Adult Women

The problem of health and nutrition among children are directly linked with health status of women in particular. This aspect is examined in terms of the prevalence of anaemia among women.

The table below brings sharp focus on the prevalence of anaemia among the women in India.

Table-5: Anaemia among women in the age group 15-49 years in selected states in India, 2015-16 and 2005-06.

States	NFHS-4 (2015-16)(in %)			NFHS-3 (2005-06, total) (%)
	Urban	Rural	Total	
Tamil Nadu	53.4	56.8	55.1	53.2
Maharashtra	48.2	47.8	48	48.4
Gujarat	51.6	57.5	54.9	55.3
Bihar	58.7	60.5	60.3	67.4
Odisha	47.6	51.8	51	61.1
Madhya Pradesh	49.7	53.8	52.5	55.9
All India	50.8	54.2	53	55.3

Source: National Family Health Survey-4, 2015-16, India Fact sheet, International Institute for population sciences, Mumbai.

53% of the adult women (age 15-49 which is the reproductive age) were found to be anaemic in India (50.3% pregnant women and 53.1% non pregnant women were anaemic in year 2015-16).

The percentage of adult women who were anaemic was much higher than the national average in Bihar, Tamil Nadu and Gujarat. However, almost half or more percentage of adult women across the states were found to be anaemic. The rural, urban differences in the percentage of anaemic women are not significant except in Gujarat.

Use of Family Planning Methods

Apart from food habits, calorie intake and prevalence of morbidity, adoption of family planning is a major factor affecting the health of women. Only 53.5% of the currently married women in the age 15-49 years use any method of family planning in 2015-16 (NFSH-4). Among the states, only Maharashtra and Odisha had 64.2% and 57.3% of the women who used any family planning method in 2015-16. While only 24.1% of the women in Bihar, reported the use of any method of family planning in 2015-16. **Moreover, it is striking to note that the percentage of women using any method of family planning had decreased all across the states between 2005-06 and 2015-16.**

Unwanted pregnancies, more children in the hope of getting a male child and male domination in matters relating to man and women relation are also the factors which affect the health of the young women.

It is also found that 58% of the mothers who delivered low birth weight babies were less than 20 years in age and 76% of them weighed less than 50Kg. This is bound to have serious negative effect on the newly born child.

It is however, interesting to note that, the prevalence of anaemia among the pregnant women was somewhat lower (50.3%) as against 53.1% among the non pregnant women. This is Probably because of the improved outreach of a range of antenatal services targeting the pregnant women.

The pregnant women in urban areas probably have better access to health care which is evident in the lower percentage (45.7%) of anaemic women as against 52.1% in rural areas.

If we relate this prevalence of anaemia among adult women to the percentage of anaemic children below five years of age, it is quite clear that to a large extent, anaemia among the adult women is directly linked with the anaemia among the children. In fact, the percentage of anaemic children is somewhat higher (58.4%) as compared to among adult women.(53%). **Which shows that in addition to the spill over effect of mother's anaemia the child does not seem to have proper food intake which would hamper the mental and physical development and expose them to the higher risk of mortality.**

Breast Feeding Practices

For infants and children below 23 months, breast feeding practices have a critical role in their survival and growth of an infant.

Exclusive breast feeding (infants in age 0-6 months)

Table-6: Children under age 6 month exclusively breast fed (%) in selected states in 2015-16 and 2005-06.

	NFHS-4 (2015-16)(%)			NFHS-3 (2005-06)(%)
States	**Urban**	**Rural**	**Total**	**Total**
Tami Nadu	47.8	48.7	48.3	34.1
Maharashtra	51.3	60.6	56.6	53
Gujarat	48.7	60.2	55.8	47.8
Bihar	46.8	54.2	53.5	28
Odisha	64.3	65.8	65.6	50.8
Madhya Pradesh	54.2	59.6	58.2	21.6
All India	52.1	56	54.9	46.4

Source: National Family Health Survey-4, 2015-16, India Fact sheet, International Institute for population sciences, Mumbai.

54.9% of the infants in India were on exclusively breast feeding in 2015-16. The proportion of breast fed children was above average in Odisha, Madhya Pradesh, Maharashtra and also in Gujarat. However, in Tamil Nadu the proportion of breast fed children was only 48.3%. There is noteworthy progress in exclusive breast feeding to infants particularly in Madhya Pradesh, Bihar and Tamil Nadu. (Table-5), it can be also noted that exclusive breast feeding is more in rural areas than in urban areas.

Feeding Practices Among Children age 6-8 Months

It can be seen from the Table-7 that the children in age 6-8 months receiving solid and semi solid food along with breast milk accounted 42.7% in India in 2015-16. Even in urban areas only 50.1% of such children were receiving the food along with breast feeding.

Table-7: Children age 6 to 8 month receiving solid or semi solid food and breast milk, in selected states in 2015-16 and 2005-06.

	NFHS-4 (2015-16)(%)			NFHS-3 (2005-06)(%)
States	Urban	Rural	Total	Total
Tami Nadu	76.4	59.8	67.5	81.2
Maharashtra	48.8	38.8	43.3	45.5

Gujarat	55.4	44.4	49.4	54.1
Bihar	41.2	29.5	30.7	54.5
Odisha	57.5	54.4	54.9	65.5
Madhya Pradesh	45.3	35.7	38.1	46
All India	50.1	39.9	42.7	52.6

Source: National Family Health Survey-4, 2015-16, India Fact sheet, International Institute for population sciences, Mumbai.

The percentage of the children in age 6-8 months receiving solid or semi solid food and breast milk were above average in Tamil Nadu, Odisha, Gujarat and Maharashtra. However, in Bihar and Madhya Pradesh only 30.7% and 38.1% of the children age 6-8 months received solid or semi solid food along with breast milk which were the lowest,(Table-7).

Breast Feeding Children in Age 6-23 Months Receiving Adequate Diet

The percentage of the breast fed children in age 6-23 months who received adequate diet was very low in India as well as across the selected states. Only 8.7% of these children received the adequate diet. It is striking that the percentage of these children was quite high at 21.4% In Tamil Nadu In rest of the states except Odisha, these children in the age 6-23 months who got adequate diet along with breast feeding was almost negligible, (Table;-8).

Table-8: Breast Feeding Children age 6-23 months receiving an adequate diet in selected states in 2015-16 and 2005-06.

	NFHS-4 (2015-16)(%)			NFHS-3 (2005-06)(%)
States	**Urban**	**Rural**	**Total**	**Total**
Tami Nadu	20.9	21.8	21.4	0
Maharashtra	6.9	4.1	5.3	0
Gujarat	6.1	5.6	5.8	0
Bihar	8.4	7.1	7.3	0
Odisha	9.4	8.8	8.9	0
Madhya Pradesh	8.9	6.2	6.9	0
All India	10.1	8.2	8.7	0

Source: National Family Health Survey-4, 2015-16, India Fact sheet, International Institute for population sciences, Musmbai.

This requires an effective communication with mothers on feeding practices along with making them aware about locally available food items, food preparation etc. by the local functionaries. It is also necessary that the local functionaries are well qualified and trained so that, they do their job professionally.

Poverty and Malnutrition

Generally the problem of malnutrition in the population, is identified with the issue of poverty or population below the poverty line. However, when we examine the percentage of population below poverty line across the major states in India, it is found that the incidence of anaemia is much higher than the percentage of population below the poverty line. Table-9, below shows the percentage of population below poverty line as per the estimates of the Reserve Bank of India for the year 2012.

Table-9: Percentage population below poverty line in India.

States	% of persons (rural) below poverty line.	% of persons (urban) below poverty line.	% of persons (combined) below poverty line.
Tami Nadu	15.83	6.54	11.28
Maharashtra	24.22	9.12	17.35
Gujarat	21.5	10.14	16.63
Bihar	34.06	31.23	33.74
Odisha	35.69	17.29	32.59
Madhya Pradesh	35.74	21	31.65
All India	25.7	13.7	21.92

Source: Reserve Bank of India, Annual Report, 2012.

According to the estimates of the population below the poverty line by the Reserve Bank of India and published in their annual report 2012, the overall percentage of population below poverty line in India in 2012 was 21.92%, 25.70% in rural and 13.70% in urban areas. In contrast the proportion of women in the age 15-49 years and who were anaemic was 53% in the total, 54.2% in rural areas and 50.8% in urban areas in 2015-16.

In Bihar for example 33.74% of the population was below the poverty line, 34.06% were in rural areas where 31.23% in urban areas. In contrast all women in the age group 15-49 years and who were anaemic accounted for 60.3% in the total, 60.5% in rural areas and 58.7% in urban areas in the total.

In Odisha, the population below the poverty line was 32.59% in the total, 35.69% in rural areas and 17.29% in urban areas in 2012. In contrast all women in the age of

15-49 years who were anaemic accounted for 51% in the total, 51.8% in rural areas and 47.6% in urban areas.

In Madhya Pradesh, the population below the poverty line was 31.65% in the total, 35.74% in rural areas and 21% in urban areas. In contrast all women in the age 15-49 years who were anaemic were 52.5% in the total, 53.8% in rural areas and 49.7% in urban areas, in 2015-16.

In Tamil Nadu, the population below the poverty line was 11.28% in the total, 15.83% in rural areas and 6.54% in urban areas. In contrast, all women in the age 15-49 years who were anaemic 55.1% among them were found to be anaemic in the total, 56.8% in rural areas and 53.4% in urban areas in 2015-16.

In Maharashtra 17.35% of population was below the poverty line in the total, 24.22% were in rural areas and 9.12% were in urban areas in 2012. In contrast among all women in age of 15-49 years who were anaemic were 48% in the total, 47.8% in rural areas and 48.2% in urban areas in 2015-16.

In Gujarat, 16.63% of the population was below the poverty line, 21.50% were in rural areas and 10.14% in urban areas. In contrast among all women in the age 15-49 years who were anaemic 54.9% in the total, 57.5% were in rural areas and 51.6% were in urban areas in 2015-16.

It may be mentioned that the Rangrajan Committee was set up to review the poverty estimates and methodology adopted by the Tendulkar committee, it submitted his report in 2014, and the estimate of poverty related to 2011-12. The Rangrajan committee fixed Rs. 972 per capita per month or Rs. 32 per day for rural areas and Rs. 1407 per capita per month or Rs. 47 per day in urban areas. According to this methodology the population below the poverty line in 2009-10 was 38.2% and 29.5% in 2011-12. Which also shows that the problem of anaemia among women and children has many other dimensions such as unwanted pregnancies and their termination, frequent pregnancies in the hope of a male child and lack of use of family planning method, customs and traditions and male domination in the family particularly among the socio economically backward classes do not seem to allow any effective say as to how many children the family would like to have. Irrespective of the gender of the child. This also focuses on the issue of lack of adequate diet apart from the balanced diet. The Global Hunger Index (GHI), 2018 shows that India still has a major challenge to provide adequate food to the majority of the people.

Multi Dimensional Poverty Index (MPI) which is Called a Semi-economic Measure of Poverty

United Nation's Multidimensional Poverty Index (MPI) is a comprehensive measure unlike the income or nutritional intake based poverty line. The MPI takes in to account deprivation in respect of a number of indicators such as nutrition, child mortality, years of schooling, school attendance, cooking fuel, sanitation, drinking water, electricity, housing and assets. The indicators are grouped in to three category of health, education and standard of living, each category with equal weight of 33.3.

According to MPI the percentage of population which was below poverty was 55.1% in 2005-06 but, reduced drastically to 27.9% in 2015-16. In absolute numbers 2071 million people were lifted out of poverty in 10 years in India.

Significant progress has been achieved on specific indicators in all the three categories. The table bellow shows the extent of progress made on each of the indicators between 2005-06 to 2015-16.

Table-10: Progress under key indicators of multi dimensional poverty index in India between 2005-06 to 2015-16.

Dimension of Poverty	Indicator	Deprived if Living in a household were:	2005-06, % HHs	2015-16, % HHs
Health	Nutrition	Any person under 70 years is under nourished.	43.3	21.2
	Child Mortality	There was death of an under–18 child in five years leading up to survey.	4.5	2.2
Education	Years of schooling	No member 10 years or older has studied beyond primary school.	24	11.7
	School attendance	Any child eligible up to middle school is not attending school.	19.8	5.5
Standard of living	Cooking fuel	Cooking is done with dung, wood, charcoal or coal fuel.	52.9	26.2
	Sanitation	Sanitation facility is not improved or is shared with others.	50.4	24.6
	Drinking water	There is no drinking water within at least a 30 minute walk from home, round trip.	16.6	6.2
	Electricity	There is no electricity.	29.1	8.6
	Housing	At least one of roof, walls and floor is not *pucca*.	44.9	23.6
	Assets	More than one of these is lacking: Radio, T.V, Phone, Computer, Animal cart, Bicycle, Motor bike or Refrigerator and does not own a car or truck.	37.6	9.5

Source: United Nation's Report (2019), Global Multi Dimensional Poverty Index.

The UN report highlights significant progress which India has achieved in reducing multi dimensional poverty and argues that India is on Track to ensure that there is no child without primary education in next 10 years. 99% of the school going children are expected to complete the primary school by 2030. While only 37% of the children completed upper secondary education in 2000, 84% are expected to complete it by 2030.

In terms of gender parity in school, only 53% of Indian girls were completing lower secondary education as compared to 66% of the boys in 2006. In 2015-16 however, the proportions were similar at 79%-82%.

Maternal and Child Healthcare Services

As revealed in the NFHS-4, there is significant progress in providing maternity services in India. For example, the percentage of mothers whose last birth was protected against neonatal tetanus were 89% in India in 2015-16 while it was 76.3% in 2005-06.

However, the coverage of the pregnant women for ante natal check up in the first trimester was only 58.6% and those who had at least 4 antenatal care visits were only 51.2% in 2015-16.

There is noteworthy progress in terms of institutional deliveries in India. It was only 38.7% in 2005-06 but increased sharply to 78.9% in 2015-16.

Similarly, the children in the age 12-23 months who were fully immunised were only 43.5% in 2005-06 but increased to 62% in 2015-16. This shows that much more needs to be done. It can be seen that although, incremental improvement has taken place in most of the variables across the states between 2005-06 and 2015-16, a much larger effort is required not only to ensure full coverage but also to achieve desired outcomes.

Interstate Variations in Access to Services

62.4% of the mothers in India have received post natal care from a qualified medical personnel within two days of the delivery in 2015-16 as against 34.6% in 2005-06.

However, only 24.3% of the infants in India had received a health check up within two days of the birth in 2015-16.

Gujarat was ahead with 73.9% regarding anti natal check up, Gujarat was also slightly better (63.4%) than all India average regarding the post natal care of the mother. However, only 15.8% of the infants received health check up within two days of delivery in Gujarat in 2015-16 which is lower than the all India average.

However, the state of Bihar and Madhya Pradesh were below the National averages in terms of these indicators of maternal and child health. In contrast Odisha was above the national averages on these indicators.

Healthy States, Progressive India

Niti Ayog, Government of India, has just released Health Index Report titled 'Healthy States, Progressive India'. The report ranks states and union territories on their year–on–year incremental changes as well as overall performance with respect to each of the 23 health indicators between 2015 and 2016 and 2017-18.

The report takes a comprehensive look at health in terms of health outcomes in several health indicators, governance and impact of policy decisions. Among the larger states, Kerala is the best (index score 74.01) and is followed by Andhra Pradesh (index score 65.13) and Maharashtra (index score 63.99). Punjab which had third rank in 2015-2016 is pushed down to the 5th rank and Tamil Nadu is now pushed down to the 9th place.

In the bottom end is Uttar Pradesh with the rank of 21. Bihar had 19th rank in 2015-2016 but is pushed down to 20th rank in 2017-18. Odisha ranked 19th in 2017-2018 from the earlier rank of 18th in 2015-16.

The overall health index score for Gujarat was as good as for Maharashtra state (63.52) in 2017-18 (reference year) as compared to 61.99 in 2015-16 (base year). Gujarat was ranked 4th among the larger states in 2017-18 but in terms of incremental improvement it was ranked 10th among the larger states.

Kerala, Tamil Nadu, Maharashtra and Punjab have already achieve the Sustainable Development Goals (SDG) targets relating to under-five mortality rate and have almost achieved the goals on neonatal mortality (12 neonatal deaths per 1000 live births).

However, achieving SDG targets remains as a big challenge for most of the other larger states in India.

Gujarat shows poor performance in terms of improvement in sex ratio, reduction in T.B. cases and percentage of children born with low birth weight.

The state government is constituting grass root level committees for effective communication strategy, awareness creation and for providing timely health and medical care along with nutrition to children, pregnant women and lactating mothers by effective implementation of many relevant schemes.

Policies and Programs to Reduce and Prevent Malnutrition in India

The analysis of the data in the preceding pages clearly establish that there is some definite improvement in most of the nutrition, health and maternal and child care indicators across the selected states between 2005-06 (NFHS-3) and 2015-16 (NFHS-4).

However, it is also quite clear that the levels of most of these indicators of problems in 2015-16 are quite high and hence, continue to pose a big challenge to reduce and eliminate the persistent malnutrition among children and women across the states in India.

Second, the problem of wide spread malnutrition among children and women was well recognised and accorded high priority ever since the launching of the Integrated Child Development Scheme (ICDS) across the states in India.

Integrated Child Development Scheme (ICDS) the ICDS is a Major flag ship program and is a centrally sponsored scheme. It targets preschool age children, pregnant women and lactating mothers. The ICDS is run through Anganwadi centres through out the country and are managed by Anganwadi workers and helpers. It has the objective to break the vicious cycle of malnutrition–morbidity and mortality among children and women.

Third, the policies and programs to reduce and eliminate malnutrition have also evolved over a period of time in terms of the coverage of different target groups, direct as well as indirect programs, allocation of funds and institutional mechanism. In what follows, we have looked at some of the key aspects of policies, programs emerging comments and suggestions for the improvement as highlighted in different reports, report of the Working Group on Nutrition for the 12th five year plan which also gives Mid-term appraisal of nutrition policy and program in the 11th five year plan.

- The working group report of the 11th five year plan nutrition programs found that the total financial outlay on ICDS increased from Rs. 12147 crores in the 10th plan to Rs. 44400 crores in 11th plan, (2012-17), which is spectacular increase.
- There was significant increase in the number of beneficiaries of supplementary nutrition program.
- There was also a government directive to provide hot cooked meals to children although, the report did not favour over burdening of Anganwadi workers with the responsibility of cooking.
- **The MTA also observed that the Angan Wadi workers (AWWs) who were expected to be trained or qualified for multitasking, most often were ill equipped both in terms of skills and equipments.**
- The AWWs were found to be overburdened, ill paid and had neither supervision nor guidance.
- The report recommended a second AWW for the centre so that there is clear cut division of work and responsibility for the target group 0-3 years of age and the target group in 3-6 years of age.

- The introduction of Rajiv Gandhi scheme of empowering adolescent girls was considered as additional burden on AWWs.
- It also noted the need for **greater integration but with specific role and responsibility among AWWs, ASHAs and ANMS.** It emphasised the need for imparting skills in the village level functionaries so that they have the capacity to bring about behavioural change in the target group families.
- Village level Report Card: with the evolution of the policies and programs there is now specific focus on village level institutions and manpower. It is suggested that there should be check on the regularity of functioning of the Anganwadi centres to see whether all eligible beneficiaries are in fact covered continuously and review the nutritional status–growth charts for children in the gae 0-1, 1-3, 3-6 years. Availability of WHO charts, equipments should also be checked.
- Award may be given to one village in one block for achieving targets of normally growing children. The government can introduce colour cards– green card showing good progress, yellow card showing mediocre and red card showing poor progress. Such an approach, has the potential to become a community or village movement for achieving nutrition goals.
- It is known that in order to achieve sustainable results on nutrition, direct measures/interventions alone will not be sufficient or sustainable. Hence, there is also emphasis on long term programs which create enabling conditions for the people to succeed. These are for example, Mahatma Gandhi National Rural Employment Guarantee Scheme, National Rural Health Mission, Total Sanitation Campaign, Public Distribution System, Drinking Water Mission etc.
- However, in order to bring focus on nutrition in different sectoral policies and programs, a village level institutional mechanism is established for convergence and is anchored on *Panchayati raj* institutions.
- The village health and sanitation committee under National Rural Health Mission is expanded to include nutrition and ICDS and the committee is recognised as sub committee of *panchayat.*
- It is also observed that almost all across the states, the child feeding practices remain highly unsatisfactory. Exclusive breast feeding for infants (0-6 months) and breast feeding along with semi solid and solid food for children in the age 6-23 months is the most crucial period of intervention. The progress on this aspect has been very dismal. This requires up to date information on ANC registration, institutional delivery and the follow up visits by health persons.

Unless these persons are fully trained in counselling on breast feeding, nutrition and the mother and child health they are unlikely to succeed. It is suggested to develop Management Information System (MIS) to monitor the processes as well as the progress on targets.

- Moreover, immediately after the child birth the mother must have rich and nutritious food at least for 10-15 days. This, apart from restoring the health of the mother, is essential to aid breast feeding.
- **Traditionally, on the birth of a child, the parents of the mother use to send rich food like *gunderpak*, *sukhdi*, *ghee* to prepare *seera*. SEWA Ahmedabad, had introduced the distribution of 1 Kg of *ghee* tin to such mothers in one of their projects. It is suggested that the cash benefit under the maternity benefit scheme be substituted this type of rich food packet including 1 Kg *ghee* tin.**
- **Integrated management of neonatal and childhood illness:** Under this program a range of health and medical services are provided to mothers and children in public health institution.
- **Janani Surksha Yojana:** The yojana is centrally sponsored and provides cash assistants, nutritional support, medical care after child birth, it also encourages institutional delivery.

Vision 2022—"Kuposhan Mukt Bharat—free form malnutrition across the life cycle".

The National Nutrition Strategy, 2017 is committed to ensuring that every child, adolescent girl and women attains optimal nutritional status, is specially those from the most vulnerable communities. The focus is on preventing and reducing under nutrition across the life cycle particularly in the first three years of life. This commitment also builds on the recognition that the first few years of life are for ever the foundation for ensuring optimum physical growth, development, cognition and cumulative life long learning. The national strategy will contribute to more inclusive growth by reduction of maternal, infant and young child mortality by focusing on following outcomes.

- To prevent and reduce under nutrition (underweight prevalence) in children (0-3 years) by three percentage points per annum from NFSH-4 levels by 2022.
- To reduce the prevalence of anaemia among young children, adolescent girls and women in the reproductive age group (15-49 years) by 1/3rd of NFHS-4 levels by 2022.

The implementation of the national strategy will adopt a life cycle approach with the focus on critical periods of nutritional vulnerability, will emphasis early prevention of under nutrition in the life, will have inclusive and gender sensitive approach will work for community empowerment and ownership and make the best possible use of local level key functionaries like Anganwadi workers, helpers and ASHAs workers. It is suggested to involve women members of the self help group if any, elected women members of *panchayat* or municipality. These program's ownership will be of *panchayati raj* institutions and local bodies etc. In the strategy there are several other initiatives which aim at directly focusing on reducing the under nutrition and anaemia among women and children.

Sustainable Approach to Prevention and Reduction of Under nutrition and Anaemia among Children and Women

The direct measures to prevent and reduce under nutrition and anaemia can be only short term and transitory. If the scale of the program goes on expanding and is continued for a long period of time it will raise question about effectiveness of interventions and the availability of resources. Hence, along with the above mentioned initiatives it is suggested to focus on the following.

- Effective and highly targeted Public Distribution System (PDS) with the following characteristics—cleaned and packed food grains (wheat and rice), 1 Kg of edible oil, 1 Kg of *gur*/sugar delivered at home as a package with biomatric identification of the family.
- Ensure cooking gas connection to all these more vulnerable families so that we are able to cook two meals a day even under the compulsion of being out of home for the whole day either as a casual labourer or a low income self employed person.
- Ensure that each ration card family has a toilet at home and safe and potable drinking water.

Key Intervention

The evolving policies and programs to prevent and reduce malnutrition including the latest nutrition strategy 2017, and *Niti Ayog* new initiative of health index recognize that in the end, it is the lowest administrative unit i.e. *Panchayat*/municipality which must own these programs and the role of the local health functionaries like ASHAs, Anganwadi workers and ANMs is critical to achieve desired out comes on nutrition and health issues of children, women and mothers.

These local functionaries will require intensive and high quality training to comprehend the nutrition and health issues and the action required from them. They must freed from the administrative hierarchy so that they have freedom and time to devote to these critical task for which they should be accountable.

These local functionaries must be well trained to conduct focus group discussions (FGDs) on identified subjects at *Moholla* (street) level with the target groups of adult women and adolescent girls.

The FGDs must be based on well structured questions on the identified theme/ sub-theme and it should be conducted in a participative and interactive mode.

The suggestions, comments and problems raised by the participants on each question matter should be recorded or documented and sent to the highest level of the authority without any editing. This may turnout to be the best feedback.

References

1. Ministry of health and family welfare, Government of India: National Family Health survey, 2015-16: Fact sheets of states and India.
2. Text book of Preventive and Social Medicine, K. Park, Jabalpur, India, 2015.
3. Ministry of Women and Child Development, Government of India: Report of the Working Group on Nutrition for the 12th five year Plan, 2012-2017.
4. NITI Aayog, Ministry of Health and Family Welfare : Healthy States, Progressive India, Report on the Ranking of States and Union Territories–Health Index, 2019.
5. NITI Aayog, National Nutrition Strategy, 2017, Government of India.
6. International Food Policy Research Institute (IFPRI), Welthungerhilfe (NGO), and Department of Economics, University of California, 2008: India State Hunger Index, 2008.
7. The Times of India, Ahmedabad, Saturday, 13th July, 2019: United Nations, 2019, The Global Multidimensional Poverty Index (MPI).
8. Comprehensive National Nutrition Survey (CNNS), 2019, Ministry of Health and Family welfare, Government of India, the times of India, 8th October, 2019.
9. Global Hunger Index, 2019 (Times of India) 16th October, 2019.

□

2

The situation of Child Health and Nutrition in India: Approach, Challenges and Way forward to meet SDGs

—*S. Parasuraman*[3] *and Aparna Mukherjee*[4]

"We are guilty of many errors and many faults, but our worst crime is abandoning the children, neglecting the foundation of life. Many of the things we need can wait. The child cannot. Right now is the time his bones are being formed, his blood is being made, and his senses are being developed. To him, we cannot answer 'Tomorrow'. His name is 'Today'."

—*Gabriela Mistral, 1948*

Background

One of the important agendas of Sustainable Development Goals is to ensure zero hunger and functional health and well-being of all, particularly women, children and adolescents".These goals not only target to improve the health of children and women only but it, in turn, has ripple effect towards achieving other sustainable goals like ending poverty, achieving gender equality and education, controlling climate change and others. Malnutrition, for instance, can induce and Perpetuate poverty, which can also cause a cycle that hinders economic and social development and tends to unsustainable use of resources and environmental degradation. Along with the SDG is the United Nations General Assembly in 2016 adopted a resolution proclaiming the UN Decade of Action on Nutrition from 2016 to 2025.[5] It aims to catalyse policy commitments that result in measurable action to address all types of malnutrition. The aim is to ensure that all people have access to healthier and more sustainable

---

3. Former Director at Tata Institute for social Sciences, Mumbai
4. Assistant Professor at Tata Institute for social Sciences, Mumbai
5. Who | What Is Malnutrition? (n.d.). Retrieved from https://www.who.int/features/qa/malnutrition/en/

diets to eradicate all forms of malnutrition worldwide, with a particular focus on children and adolescents.

It is now globally acknowledged that investment in human resource development is a pre-requisite for any nation and a country like India, it is of paramount importance as it is potential to the demographic dividend will depend on that. It is the Fundamental duty of the state and inalienable right of children that they are provided with an environment where they can grow and develop up to their most. They need to be provided with nutritious food, quality education, necessary medical facilities and a safe family and social environment. Early childhood up to the first six years is the most crucial period in life when the foundations for cognitive, social and emotional language, physical/engineering development and lifelong learning are laid. The young child under three years is most vulnerable to the vicious cycles of malnutrition, disease/ infection and resultant disability, all of which influence the present condition of a child at a micro level and the future human resource development of any nation at the macro level. Thus it is of the utmost importance that findings on the nutritional and health status of the children should be well investigated and based on the evidence policies and programmes should be framed.

Child health and nutrition remains a significant matter of concern, particularly among the less developed and developing countries, and India is no exception to it. The 2016 UNICEF State of the World Children Report indicates that India is the 48th highest in child mortality among 193 nations. In comparison with other developing markets and even with neighbours such as Sri Lanka, Nepal and Bangladesh, India also has poor prices for under-5 stunting, waste and underweight indices. Precisely, an estimated 159 million children are stunted, and 50 million are wasted, while 41 million children under the age of 5 years are overweight or obese. The 2017 Global Nutrition Report, which looked at 140 countries, including India, found three major forms of malnutrition using ' significant burdens ' as indicators of measurement trends. These include stunting in children, anaemia in women of reproductive age, and adult women with overweight. It found that 38 percent of children under five are affected by stunting, and about 21 percent of children under five are defined as 'wasted' or 'severely wasted' due to lack of nutrients, suffering irreversible damage to cognitive development. In India, most people are not able to fulfil the minimum calorie intake which is 2100 per day in the urban areas and 2400 calories in rural areas, but children become the worst victims of poor nutrition (Deaton and Dreze, 2009).

Previous studies have found that it is the combination of complex factors like poverty, low educational status, lack of health care facility, malnutrition and health education, poor maternal health are responsible for the poor health status of children's in India. It is important to have proper measures and implementation of new programmes to improve child health and nutrition in India. Consequently, malnutrition is both a health outcome and a risk factor for disease and exacerbated malnutrition, and can increase the risk of morbidity as well as mortality. Despite the continuous improvement in the indicators related to child health and nutrition, India, India remains far from eliminating cases of malnutrition among children. Also, certain pockets of India have a higher concentration of children with malnutrition with significant inequalities across states and socio-economic groups–like female children, rural areas, the poorest and scheduled tribes and backward castes are the worst affected and such inequalities appear to be increasing (NHHS-4).

It is important to look at the scenario of child health and nutrition, but before that, we need to understand various concepts and dimensions of nutrition.

Concepts and Dimensions of nutrition

According to the World Health Organisation, "Nutrition is the intake of food, considered about the body's dietary needs. Good nutrition–an adequate, well-balanced diet combined with regular physical activity–is a cornerstone of good health. Poor nutrition can lead to reduced immunity, increased susceptibility to disease, impaired physical and mental development, and reduced productivity." [6]Improper intake of food leads to the existence of malnutrition. Fighting hunger and reducing the occurrence of malnutrition are common goals to various national plans, which has also grab the attention on the international level.

Malnutrition is usually associated with several diseases, each with a specific cause related to one or more nutrients, such as protein, iodine, vitamin A, or iron. Malnutrition is synonymous in the current situation with protein-energy malnutrition, which means an imbalance between the supply of protein and energy and the body's demand to guarantee ideal development and operate. This imbalance includes both inadequate and excessive energy intake; the form resulting in waste, stunting and underweight malnutrition, and the latter resulting in overweight and obesity.

Malnutrition in children is the consequence of a range of factors, that are often related to poor food quality, insufficient food intake, and severe and repeated infectious diseases, or frequently some combinations of the three. These conditions, in turn, are closely linked to the overall standard of living and whether a population can meet its basic needs, such as access to food, housing and health care. Growth assessment thus not only serves as a means for evaluating the health and nutritional status of children but also provides an indirect measurement of the quality of life of an entire population.

---

6. Who | Nutrition. (n.d.). Retrieved from https://www.who.int/topics/nutrition/en/

"Malnutrition refers to deficiencies, excesses or imbalances in a person's intake of energy and nutrients. The term malnutrition covers two broad groups of conditions. One is 'undernutrition which includes stunting (low height for age), wasting (low weight for height), underweight (low weight for age) and micronutrient deficiencies or insufficiencies (a lack of important vitamins and minerals). The other is overweight, obesity and diet-related non-communicable diseases (such as heart disease, stroke, diabetes and cancer)"(World Health Organisation, 2005). Globally, more than one-third of under-five deaths are attributable to under-nutrition.15 About 20 percent of children under age five in India are wasted, 43 percent underweight and 48 percent stunted. (UNICEF, 2011)

Chronic Hunger: Inability to obtain enough food to satisfy the minimum requirements of a nutritionally adequate diet. The process could be temporary-seasonal, sudden or persistent, permanent and prolonged over a long period covering the entire life span. The extent and intensity could vary accordingly. Broader external events, as well as internal processes, can entrench hunger. Various factors and processes can not only precipitate endemic hunger into acute crisis and starvation but also push comparatively secure households into hunger. 'Listening to poverty-Parasuraman'.

One of the crucial way to ensure child health and survival is breastfeeding. According to WHO breastfeeding was scaled up to near universal levels, about 8,20,000 child lives would be saved every year. Globally, only 40% of infants under six months of age are exclusively breastfed. Exclusive breastfeeding up to 6 months can protect infants from childhood diseases, particularly diarrhoea and pneumonia, which are the two primary cause of child mortality worldwide. More important breast milk is readily available and affordable, which help to ensure that the infant gets proper nutrients. Specifically, the mother's first milk, colostrum is the most beneficial to boost the immunity of the new-born. However, unfortunately, there are many misconceptions around breastfeeding practices in India, depriving children of vital nutrients that they may otherwise get only from mother's milk.

The transition period from exclusive breastfeeding to family food, known as complementary feeding, covers a 6-23-month-old child and is a vulnerable period. It is the moment when malnutrition begins in many infants, which contributes to the elevated incidence of malnutrition in kids under the era of two. Optimal first-year breastfeeding and complementary feeding practices include adequate diet, and together, according to the United Nations Children's Fund, can prevent nearly one-fifth of deaths in children under five years of age. An 'adequate diet' is defined as the introduction of nutritionally adequate and safe complementary (solid) foods at six months together with continued breastfeeding up to two years of age or beyond.

Catch-up growth or nutrition for 1000 days is a notion that involves the restricted potential for catch-up growth among stunted kids after two years of age, especially when such kids stay in bad environments. Recently, however, few studies have shown that some catch-ups between the ages of two and eight and a half years are possible for kids who have not been born with low birth weight or have been severely stunned in childhood. However, children who were stunted at the age of two years, whether or not they reached catch-up growth later, were discovered to suffer considerably from subsequent cognitive deficits, a finding that further emphasises the need to avoid early stunting.

Especially in the age, up to 6 years are a very crucial age because most vital and intense care must be given at this age only. This period determines most of the future of the child. It is a crucial period of development in a child's life. Improper caring and lack of basic needs for development can lead to further problems in the future. An adequate amount of calcium and vitamins must be given to the child at this age. Many of the children got through hunger these days. This hunger may not be the hunger of food but through 'hidden hunger'. Hidden hunger exists where the child is not getting the required amount of nutrition in his daily food consumption. Inappropriate consumption of nutrition is termed as hidden hunger. There might be a supply of food but not of nutrition. (Breckenridge, 1942)

Other Determinants of Child Health

India is a significant contributor to child deaths in the world, that is, more than 20 percent . The mortality rate of children under the age of 5 years was 66 per thousand live births in 2011 (UNICEF 2011). According to the National Family Health Survey 4 (2015-16), the under-five mortality rate in India stands at 50 per 1000 live births, which were earlier 74 in the 2005-06 and. It ranges from 78 in Uttar Pradesh to 7 in Kerala, one of the best states in the country when it comes to effective health systems. Previously, the Millennium Development Goals placed special emphasis on reducing the child mortality rates, which made countries conscious and mindful about preventing diseases among children to serve a larger purpose (DLHS-3 2008). Child health does not solely depend on nutrition but other factors like immunisation, safe water and sanitation along with other socio-economic characteristics. To improve the socio-economic environment for children at large, it may take time but ensure that all children are fully immunised and provided with clean water and sanitation facility can be possible in the short run.

Immunisation refers to the process of getting vaccines that make a person immune to certain diseases as a result of those vaccines. Immunisation begins as soon as a child is born to protect the child from diseases. It is seen as the most economical way of ensuring and maintaining public health. To prevent the communication of vaccine-preventable diseases, children must be immunised on time. Six diseases can be prevented by vaccination: tuberculosis, diphtheria, whooping cough, tetanus, polio and measles. The government has taken many initiatives to administer vaccines against these diseases to reduce mortality and disability and improve and maintain the health of children, and the population at large, in India. (DLHS-3, 2008)

India is one of the countries with the lowest immunisation rates in the world and has the largest annual birth cohort of approximately 26 million newborn children (UNICEF 2011). These poor vaccination rates have been the main cause of high child mortality rates in India. (Shrivastwa 2015). The Government of India adopted the World Health Organisation's Expanded Programme of Immunisation or EPI in 1978 which was later renamed the Universal Immunisation Programme or UIP in 1985. This effort was aimed at attacking those above six vaccine-preventable diseases in order to prevent mortality and disability and produce a healthy population. (DLHS-3 2007-08) As part of this, an immunisation schedule was prepared, which mentioned the vaccine to be given, at what age and how many times. Vaccination cards are prepared for every child, which maintain the record for every vaccination. As per guidelines, all six primary vaccinations must be administered to children by the age of 12 months. Full vaccination includes one dose of BCG, three doses against DPT, three doses for polio, and one vaccine against measles. There are many children who are under-vaccinated, that is, do not receive all these vaccination, while there are still many children who do not receive even one vaccination. (DLHS-3 2007-08) Despite the Indian government's efforts to of providing vaccinations to children and having in place a national programme focused on immunisation, disparities exist.

Trends and Patterns

Table-1 given below shows the scenario of child mortality and child health in India as per the latest NFHS data. (2015-16). Infant mortality rate and the under-five mortality rate has come down in the last decade, but the still the numbers are yet too high. Mainly, the rural-urban difference is very wide. For example, IMR is estimated at 29 per 1000 live births in urban areas as compared to 46 per 1000 live births in rural areas, which is almost double than that of rural areas. Almost half of the children surveyed reported suffering from diarrhea in the last two weeks preceding the survey. Only 41 percent of the children were breastfed within one hour of birth, whereas 52 percent were received exclusive breastfeeding. It is clear from the recent data that a significant proportion of children in India are suffering from malnutrition. Thirty-eight percent of children are stunted, and 21 percent are wasted of which 7.5 percent were severely wasted.39 percent of children are reported underweight in rural areas as compared to 29 percent in urban areas. It is important to note that around 60 percent of the children are anaemic. Clearly, data shows that children in rural areas are more vulnerable and susceptible to poor health. Therefore, we need to look at the prevalence of malnutrition in the context of rural India. It is clear from the map below that the percentage of underweight children are concentrated more in the Empowered Action Group (EAG) states. Similarly, NFHS-4 data shows that the worst performing state was Rajasthan was only 3.4 percent of children in the 6-23 months' age-group reportedly got adequate diet, followed by Gujarat (5.2 percent) and Uttar Pradesh (5.3 percent). The best performing state/Union Territory was Puducherry (31 percent), followed by Tamil Nadu (30.7 percent) and Meghalaya (23.6 percent).

Table-1: Indicators on Child Health and Nutrition, National Family Health Survey 3 & 4

	NFHS-4			NFHS-3
Indicators	**Urban**	**Rural**	**Total**	**Total**
IMR	29	46	41	57
U5MR	34	56	50	74
Children age 12-23 months fully immunised (BCG, measles, and 3 doses each of polio and DPT) (%)	63.9	61.3	62	43.5
Prevalence of diarrhoea (reported) in the last two weeks preceding the survey (%)	8.2	9.6	9.2	9
Children with diarrhoea in the last two weeks who received oral rehydration salts (ORS) (%)	58.5	47.9	50.6	26
Children under age three years breastfed within one hour of birth(%)	42.8	41.1	41.6	23.4
Children under age 6 months exclusively breastfed(%)	52.1	56	54.9	46.4
Total children age 6-23 months receiving an adequate diet (%)	11.6	8.8	9.6	N.A.
Children under 5 years who are stunted (height-for-age)(%)	31	41.2	38.4	48
Children under 5 years who are wasted (weight-for-height)(%)	20	21.5	21	19.8
Children under 5 years who are severely wasted (weight-for-height (%)	7.5	7.4	7.5	6.4
Children under 5 years who are underweight (weight-for-age)(%)	29.1	38.3	35.7	42.5
Children age 6-59 months who are anaemic (<11.0 g/dl) (%)	55.9	59.4	58.4	69.4

State wise distribution of children under five years who are severely wasted in rural India, NFHS-4 (2015-16)

- 19.17 - 27.00
- 27.01 - 31.40
- 31.41 - 37.60
- 37.61 - 48.30
- Missing Value

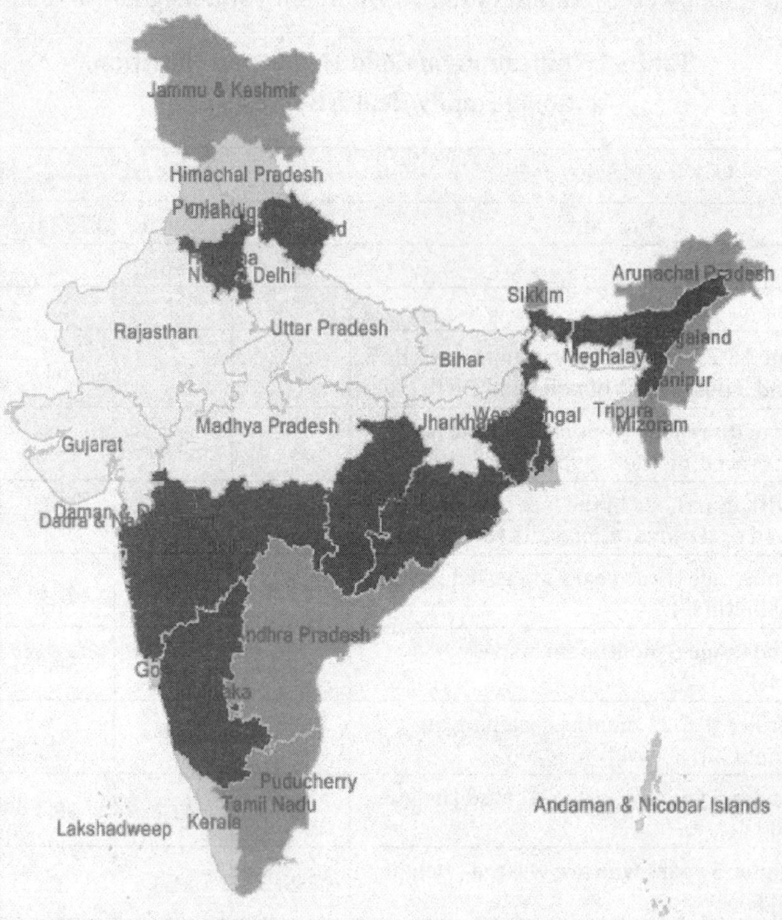

There is also a significant inter-state variation in underweight patterns and trends. In six states, Maharashtra, Orissa, Bihar, Madhya Pradesh, Uttar Pradesh, and Rajasthan are underweight in at least one in two children. More than 43 percent of all underweight children in India is represented by the four latter nations. In addition, in the high prevalence states, the incidence in underweight is falling more slowly. Lastly, state-level demographic and socio-economic trends do not necessarily reflect those at domestic level (e.g., in some states, underweight inequalities are narrowing and not widening, and in some countries, children are more likely to be underweight than women) and nutrition policy should be aware of these differences.

Deficiencies of micronutrients are also common in India. More than 75 percent of pre-school children suffer from iron deficiency anaemia (IDA), and 57 percent of preschool children have sub-clinical Vitamin A deficiency (VAD). Iodine deficiency is endemic in 85 percent of districts. Progress in reducing the prevalence of micronutrient deficiencies in India has been slow-IDA has not declined much, in part due to the high prevalence of hookworm, and reductions in sub-clinical VAD slowed in the second half of the 1990s, despite earlier gains. As with underweight, the prevalence of different micronutrient deficiencies varies widely across states. (World Bank, 2005)

In India, in 2007-08 as per DLHS-3, the number of children aged 12-23 months that were surveyed were 64,702, out which just a little over half the population (54%) of children aged 12-23 months were fully immunised. This had shown improvement from DLHS-2 (2002-04) when the full immunisation coverage was only 46 percent . However, these figures are not encouraging at all. In our country, almost half the children are under-vaccinated or not vaccinated at all. If we compare DLHS-3 and DLHS-4, some states have shown an improvement in the full immunisation levels while in some states the immunisation levels have dropped from 2007-08 to 2012-13. This is shown in the graph below.

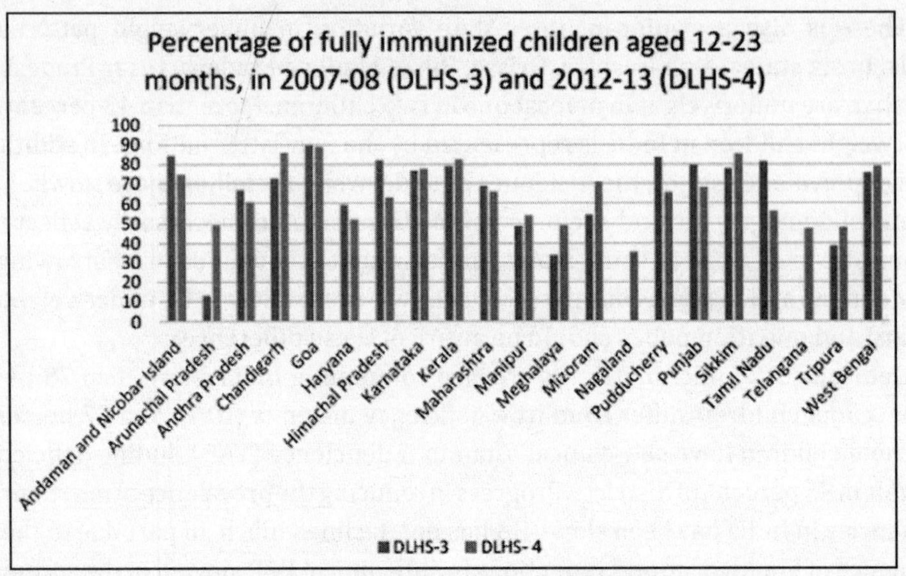

Nutrition-specific Interventions	
Indicators	**In percentage**
Pregnant women who availed supplementary food under ICDS	40.7
Mothers (of children under-36 months) who received 3+ antenatal check-ups	63.4
Children (12-23 months) who are fully immunised	65.3
Anganwadi Centers (AWCs) without functional adult weight scales	48.4

Source: Rapid Survey on Children (RSoC), 2014

The NFHS–4 data also shows a decline in stunting among children under five from 43% to 32%. Similarly, there is a decline in the prevalence of underweight children under five from 39% to 29%. However, there are stark regional differences. The poorer states continued to have low levels of health and nutrition. Poor nutrition is less common than reported in the last round of the National Family Health Survey. In nine states and union territories, fewer than one-third of children are found short for their age. In Bihar, Madhya Pradesh and Meghalaya, more than 40% of children are still stunted.

In all the states (except Goa), more than 50% of children and women are anaemic. To be more precise, 50 percent of the children under five are anaemic in 10 states.

According to the National Family Health Survey, 2015-16, at least six out of 10 children received full immunisation in 12 of the 15 states and union territories. In

Goa, West Bengal, Sikkim, and Puducherry, more than four-fifths of the children have been fully immunised.

Due to the launch of the programmes like the National Rural Health Mission after NFHS-3, the improvements in public health systems have shown some results. While there is an improvement in immunisation coverage in many states, few states have shown a slight decline. There is an urgency to include new vaccines in the national programme.

ICDS and Nutritional outcomes			Stunting Rank
States	ICDS performance Rank	Under-weight Rank	
Karnataka	1	11	7
Maharashtra	2	10	9
Andhra Pradesh	3	7	10
West Bengal	4	12	8
Jharkhand	5	20	18
Tamil Nadu	6	9	2
Orissa	7	16	13
Kerala	8	3	1
Madhya Pradesh	9	18	15
Haryana	10	8	11
Gujarat	11	14	16
Himachal Pradesh	12	4	5
Chhattisgarh	13	15	17
Jammu and Kashmir	14	1	4
Punjab	15	2	3
Uttarakhand	16	5	6
Rajasthan	17	13	12
Uttar Pradesh	18	17	20
Assam	19	6	14
Bihar	20	19	19

States	% Underweight children	% Stunted children	% of Households practising open defecation	%Low birth weight babies
Kerala	18.5	19.5	1.9	13
Goa	16.2	21.3	13.9	16.7
Tamil Nadu	23.3	23.3	43.4	16.5
Mizoram	14.8	26.9	3.8	2.3
Sikkim	15.8	28	4.6	10
Arunachal Pradesh	24.6	28.4	31.7	11.2
Nagaland	19.5	29.1	14	19
Delhi	19.4	29.2	2.5	21.9
Punjab	16.1	30.5	9.7	20.6
Tripura	30.5	31	3.5	18.8
Jammu & Kashmir	15.6	31.9	33.2	16
Manipur	14.1	33.2	12.6	7.3
Himachal Pradesh	19.5	34.2	21.8	17.7
Uttarakhand	20.5	34.2	21.6	14.3
Karnataka	29	34.7	33	17.2
West Bengal	30	34.7	28.3	16.9
Maharashtra	25.2	35.4	36.5	20.3
Andhra Pradesh	22.3	35.5	39.2	18.5
Haryana	22.7	36.5	25.6	21
Rajasthan	31.5	36.5	59.1	23.2
Odisha	34.4	38.2	77.7	19.2
Assam	22.2	40.6	37.5	13.3
Madhya Pradesh	36.1	41.6	63.4	23.2
Gujarat	33.5	41.8	38.1	19.4
Meghalaya	30.9	42.9	30.6	10.3
Chhattisgarh	33.9	43	69.6	16.8
Jharkhand	42.1	47.3	75.6	14.6
Bihar	37.1	49.4	74.8	14.9
Uttar Pradesh	34.5	50.6	57.7	22.3

Challenges and Interventions for Sustaining Nutrition

The fact that improvement in water, sanitation and hygiene (WASH) can reduce stunting among children and has been shown to have resulted in height increase among children much more than other nutritional interventions. Household risk factors affecting child health, especially malnutrition, are mainly basic amenities such as drinking water, toilet facilities, housing, and cooking fuel. In studying the nutritional status of children of indigenous people living in remote and inaccessible regions, the importance of local contextual factors is especially important. The contextual factor, the collective impact of basic amenities measured by a specially constructed index operates at both macro and micro-level, i.e. state and household level. Contextual factors as potential factors of child malnutrition in northeastern India, home to the country's largest the number of tribes.

Solid fuel use has been suggested as a risk factor for stunting as it causes indoor air pollution—a factor highly conducive to childhood diseases. Household allocation of scarce family resources to affects child health. Children born with low birth weight are more likely to be exposed to the risk of developing malnutrition and are also likely to be at high risk of mortality. Malnutrition can even trigger cerebral palsy and mental retardation. The association between live attenuated measles vaccine and malnutrition is found to be positive due to adverse nutritional effects of measles experienced by all children. Regardless of the context of the residence, the probability of stunting rises with era, but there is no proof of underweight and waste.

About 53 percent of India's population defecates in the open, exposing children to faecally-transmitted infections. The 'Asian enigma', the phenomenon of the shorter height of Indian children, is attributed to the lack of access to toilets, and the stunting of children to open defecation. Maternal weight or body mass index (BMI), and excessive vomiting during pregnancy are significant risk factors of child malnutrition. Poor nutritional status of the mother, leading to the child having a low birth weight, further increases the child's susceptibility to infections and aggravates the situation. Christian and Sikh children have relatively better nutritional status than Hindu and Muslim children, but there is no statistically significant difference. Undernutrition is a significant health problem among tribal children and is associated with the literacy status of mothers, household wealth index, and morbidities. There are mixed findings of the association between the sex of a child and malnutrition—no association, higher malnutrition among girls as they were fed less than boys and girls having the edge over boys in the case of NE India. Literature available on child malnutrition in India has considered a few of the risk above factors. However, these studies have not considered the household environmental health risks as a potential determinant of child malnutrition.

DLHS-3 surveyed the reasons given by mothers for non-vaccination of children. The major reason was given by almost half the mothers (45.4%) as they were unaware of the need for immunisation. This implies that despite the government's efforts to ensure health care reached all and despite its efforts to raise awareness on child immunisation, lack of awareness persists among people and is the major cause for non-immunisation. Another major reason was the sex of the child. It was found that 18 percent of the mothers did not vaccinate their child because she was a girl. This shows how son preference becomes a hurdle for health. Almost seventeen percent of women stated that they had to travel a great distance to get their children immunised as the reason for non-immunisation. Then, about fourteen percent women said that the time and place of immunisation was unknown. Fourteen percent of women also said that they feared the side effects of the vaccinations and hence, did not get their child or children vaccinated. Other reasons were no faith in immunisation (10%), ANM absence (10%), the mother too busy (approximately 10%), etc.

Policy and Legal Aspects of Child Nutrition

Despite the continuous efforts of the government to tackle the problem of child nutrition, India is home to over 40 million stunted and 17 million wasted children. Although there are so many programmes for the children, children with under-nutrition and anaemia in India is highest in the world Protein Energy Malnutrition (PEM), and growth retardation is seen as a result of such problems. Various health policies have been established from the government to contour these issues and to prevent these issues. Various schemes like Integrated Child Development Service (ICDS), Mid Day Meal Schemes and others have been started by the government for promoting nutrition among the children. These schemes are promoted in the grass root level for reaching it out to a maximum number of people possible.

India's main early child development intervention, the Integrated Child Development Services program, has been sustained for about 30 years and has been successful in many ways. Integrated Child Development Service (ICDS) is a government scheme which is established to mitigate the problem of hunger and malnutrition. ICDS was established in 1975 and started to work as a pilot project. This also led to the further establishment of many ICDS centres in various blocks and districts of the country. ICDS represents the world's largest programme for childhood care and development. The main focus of ICDS is for the proper care of children below six years of age as well as including the pregnant and lactating mothers. Along with the children, the health of the mothers is also taken care of. The Centre also provides regular food and pre-school education services. Mother's care and checkups are done regularly. Even the pregnant and lactating mothers are provided with daily food free of cost. The six packages of the ICDS is another area which provided them with a stronger base. These are:

- Supplementary nutrition
- Immunisation

- Pre-school and formal education
- Nutrition and health education
- Health checkups
- Referral services

These above mentioned are the different areas where the ICDS functions and the services are rendered to the people in these areas. The reason the ICDS is considered one of the largest program is because of its services being delivered in different areas. Also, the program targeted to function at the grassroots level within the community level. This further lead to the establishment of millions of ICDS centres where people can get easy access to. Most of the rural settings of India are poor; having the facilities of free food for the children generated an attraction for the people to get accessed with.

However, a significant dent in child malnutrition has not yet been achieved. This is mostly due to the priority the program has placed on food supplementation rather than nutritional and health education interventions, and because the program targets children after three years of age when malnutrition has already occurred. Interventions to address good caring behaviours, which have been proven cost-effective in many places, including India, require substantial development of grassroots workers ' skills and an efficient system of management. Although progress has been made towards offering training and growth of skills, much emphasis has been placed on universalizing the program rather than reinforcing the quality of its execution and tracking in a manner that improves its effect. Transforming ICDS into an intervention that effectively combats undernutrition will yield enormous benefits for India, both in terms of human development and economic returns, but will require substantial changes in the program's design and implementation. In particular, public investments in ICDS should be redirected towards the younger children (0-3 years) and the most vulnerable population segments in those states and districts where the prevalence of undernutrition is high. The focus should be on those ICDS components that directly address the most important causes of undernutrition in India, specifically improving mothers' feeding and caring behaviour, improving household water and sanitation, strengthening the referral to the health system and providing micronutrients.

Among the larger states, only Tamil Nadu met its millennium development goal (MDG) target with a reduction of 67 percent in infant mortality rate to 19 deaths per 1,000 live births in 2015. Despite having an Integrated Child Development Services (ICDS) scheme, a flagship programme of the Central government since 1975 and one of the world's largest for child-care and development, and increasing the budget for child health by more than three times over a decade to 2014-15, India missed its MDG targets. Many ICDS deficiencies have been recorded, ranging from not covering all eligible kids to having infrastructural gaps. For under-nutrition, especially, major efforts are needed to close the inequality gap. In the latest research by LANSA, a global research partnership comprising multi-national research organisations and voluntary organisations has outlined the huge siphoning of government finances in the supply of take-home rations and cooked meals in Uttar Pradesh, with no local authority supervision, little community involvement, and unresponsive ICDS machinery. This contrasts with the scenario in neighbouring Chhattisgarh, where decentralisation of authority to societies and *panchayats* has ensured far better delivery to mothers and children of ICDS services.

India has many nutrition programs, some of which have had success in several states in addressing the needs of poor households and reducing the instances of malnutrition. These programs include:

- Integrated Child Development Services (ICDS);
- the Mid Day Meals Program;
- the Public Distribution System (PDS);
- community public works programs; and
- Annapurna Program.

All of these programs have potential, but they do not form a comprehensive nutrition strategy, and they have not addressed the nutrition problem effectively so far. For example, several evaluations of ICDS have shown it to have low coverage, poor targeting, and little impact on reducing child malnutrition. Moreover, two factors that do seem to affect under-nutrition are open defecation and the status of women. States with low rates of open defecation seem to have better nutritional outcomes, while states with high rates of open defecation seem to have worse nutritional outcomes, as the chart below shows. In the absence of sanitation facilities, children face a hostile environment and frequently fall prey to common infectious diseases which reduce their ability to absorb nutrients and grow.

Need for Research

Prevalence of under-nutrition among under-five children is relatively high and varied widely depending on the assessment methodology adopted, and there are limited studies on assessment of over-nutrition. The distribution of risk factors and its influence on malnutrition among children in a given set up should be analysed in planning diverse control measures. Strengthening public health interventions for mild malnutrition cases among the vulnerable groups with a focus on socioeconomic development and research on overweight, obesity and its aetiological factors in the country are the prerequisites required to tackle malnutrition among under-five children in India. These disparities are a cause of alarm. In a country like India, which has a large young population, public health cannot be neglected. Some steps can be taken to address this issue of low immunisation and disparities in immunisation. The need of the hour is to raise more awareness on the need for immunisation as that was the main reason for non-vaccination. Proper and sufficient information must be disseminated on the various vaccinations, the time of these vaccinations and where to go for these vaccinations. The rural infrastructure must be worked on so that access to health care services does not become a problem. More efforts must be made to educate people, especially women. Gender sensitisation and programmes focused on the girl child must be continued and intensified.

Underweight, unhealthy mothers deliver babies with low birth weight, perpetuating the cycle of malnutrition between generations. Therefore, India's children rise with a disability that is exacerbated by financial and cultural variables as well as a absence of concentrated focus from the enormous paraphernalia of the employees of Public Health and Integrated Child Development Services (ICDS).

In policy formulation and implementation there is a paucity of real-time data. Although the ICDS scheme requires a monthly weight record of each child under the age of 5, this demand is noted more in its violation. Nearly no state positions information in the public domain on aggregate ICDS project-wise monthly baby weights.

Maharashtra, the only state that does this on a regular basis, has uploaded aggregate child weight data on the internet–but only until December 2016. It is not feasible to define the particular areas of child malnutrition where targeted measures are needed without real-time information on infant weights. More critically, this information shortage absolves the performance accountability equipment of the ICDS.

Nutrition and health administrators in Delhi are strangely reluctant to adopt the WHO-recommended height measurement criterion for under-5 children as of 2008. Stunting in under 5 children, representing chronic malnutrition, can not be assessed without height assessment. Stunting contributes to disabled growth in children, both physically and cognitively, with implications for their potential safety and productivity. In the absence of height statistics, wasting in under-5 children, one of the contributors to infant and child mortality, can not be readily evaluated.

Because maternal and child undernutrition is a common cause of infant and infant mortality, the policy must break the connection between undernutrition, disease, and child death. Most significantly, in the integrated health and growth strategy of the government, nutrition must be provided greater consideration. The mild pace of advancement over the past two centuries has resulted to a long-overdue reorientation from discussing post-birth undernutrition to measures targeting preventive, premature intervention–prenatally, in the neonatal era, in premature childhood, and in the first two years of adulthood.

Way Forward

Establish a nodal body for multi-programme coordination on nutrition

- Strengthen and restructure the Integrated Child Development Services (ICDS) programme, and leverage the Public Distribution System (PDS)
- Extend coverage of food fortification of staples
- Target multiple contributing factors, for example, water, sanitation, and hygiene (WASH)
- Align agricultural policy with national nutritional objectives
- Boost private sector engagement in nutrition-interventions through PPP

For a country that aspires to be an economic powerhouse and is already one of the largest markets in the world, investing in the health and productivity of its future generation is an imperative which can no longer be ignored.

References

1. The Incidence Of Malnutrition In Children (age 0-5 Years). (n.d.). Retrieved from http://jalsnet.com/journals/Vol_1_No_2_December_2014/10.pdf
2. Breckenridge, M. (1942), the Pre-School Child Nutrition, the American Journal of Nursing, Vol. 42, no. 5, pp 533-537./ retrieved 22nd September, 2017.
3. Deaton, A., and Dreze J., (2009), food and Nutrition in India: Fact and Interpretation, economic and political weekly Vol. 44 no. 7, pp 42-65./ retrieved 22nd September, 2017.
4. Arnold, F., Parasuraman, S., Ariokiasamy, P., and Kothari, M., 2009. Nutrition in India. National Family Health Survey (NFHS-3) India 2005-06. Mumbai, In
5. International Institute for Population Sciences, 2016. National Family Health Survey (NFHS-4) State Fact Sheets 2014-15. Available from: <http://rchiips.org/nfhs/factsheet_NFHS-4.shtml> [Accessed 12th October, 2016].
6. Water Aid, 2016. Caught short: how a lack of toilets and clean water contributes to Malnutrition. Available from: <http://www.wateraid.org/what-we-do/ourapproach/research-and-publications/viewpublication?id=3622F9E333B24DA399F5227D10E38D5B> [Accessed 12th October, 2016].
7. Ministry of Women and Child Development (MWCD), Government of India, 2014. Rapid Survey on Children (RSoC) 2013-2014 National Report. Available from: <http://wcd.nic.in/sites/default/files/RSOC%20National%20Report%202013-14%20Final.pdf> [Accessed 12th October, 2016].
   Read more at http://www.millenniumpost.in/opinion/opinion-241222
8. Rapid Survey on Children 2013-2014. India Fact sheet. Provisional. Ministry of Women and Child Development. Government of India. Available from: http://wcd.nic.in/issnip/National_Fact%20sheet_RSOC%20_02-07-2015.pdf. Accessed 29th August, 2015

9. International Food Policy Research Institute. 2014. Global Nutrition Report 2014: Actions and Accountability to Accelerate the World's Progress on Nutrition. Washington, DC.
10. Source: NFHS, RSOC, The Economist, 'Revival of Rural Public Distribution System' by Andaleeb Rahman [EPW May 2014]
11. India's Children Need A Better Deal | The Indian Express. (n.d.). Retrieved from https://indianexpress.com/article/opinion/indias-children-need-a-better-deal-nfh
12. Malnutrition Is Still A Serious Problem For India: Report ... (n.d.). Retrieved from https://www.thehindubusinessline.com/economy/malnutrition-is-still-a-serious-pro
13. Children Not Getting Adequate Diet Between 6-23 Months Can ... (n.d.). Retrieved from https://www.therahnuma.com/children-not-getting-adequate-diet-between-6-23-month
14. Executive Summary-World Bank. (n.d.). Retrieved from http://siteresources.worldbank.org/SOUTHASIAEXT/Resources/223546-1147272668285/u

□

3

Malnutrition: Incidence and Challenges in India focusing on Gujarat

—*B.B. Patel*

Abstract

About 65% of India's population is below 35 years in age. However, without education, skill and health, this demographic advantage cannot be converted into a resource. The incidence of malnutrition among women and children in India is a big challenge. Even hunger continues to be a challenge in a majority of states in India. With hunger and unbalanced diet malnutrition–morbidity–disease–mortality form a vicious circle. Both in terms of hunger index or nutritional status of the population, India is faced with a big challenge, and some of the states have even alarming situation in terms of some indicators. The paper is analysing the status and the change in some of the key indicators of these issues during 2005-06 to 2015-16 across selected states–Gujarat, Maharashtra, Tamil Nadu on the one hand and Bihar, Odisha and Madhya Pradesh on the other. The paper is based on the data from NFHS-3 and NFSH-4 of the Ministry of Health and Family Welfare, Government of India. The paper argues that during the period under consideration, all selected states have made notable progress in achieving positive changes in the indicators. The poor states, however, had unfavourable status in 2005-06 but have progressed relatively faster than the relatively developed states. Hence, there is some convergence in these indicators over time. The analysis of indicators of nutritional status and anaemia indicates that although the progress is significant, it is yet a long way to achieve a satisfactory level. Maternal and child health services have now significant outreach across the states and yet, the total desired outcomes of health interventions are at the most halfway. Poverty level and reduction over time have a positive impact on health outcomes. However, this is only medium to long term measure. In the meanwhile, focus on preventive health care can help to break the vicious cycle of malnutrition–morbidity etc.

Introduction

Nearly 65% of the population in India is below the age of 35 years. Thus, India happens to be the only country in the world with this tremendous advantage of demography. In this sense, the population is a resource rather than a problem for all-round development in India.

However, this advantage of demographic dividend depends on the ability to equip young people with skill, education and healthy life. A healthy population is a foundation for human resource development, which is the key resource for the nation.

It is in this context that the issues of malnutrition among children and women assume great significance. It is of concern that even hunger is still a challenge in India. Lack of balanced diet together with hunger set into motion a vicious cycle of morbidity-malnutrition–disease–malnutrition–mortality. It is a fact that hunger is at the root of multiple issues in malnutrition, maternal and child health and mortality. The hunger index of India takes three indicators, namely the percentage of the undernourished population, the percentage of underweight children and mortality rate of children under the age of five. The hunger index of India was 23.30 in 2010. The hunger index score between 5.0-9.9 is considered moderate. This means that we still face a very big challenge to eradicate extreme poverty and hunger, which is a Millennium Development Goal (MDG).

However, between 2005-06 to 2015-16, the key social indicators for India as revealed in National Family Health Surveys (NFHS–3 and 4) indicate remarkable progress in reducing mortality, malnutrition and in making maternal and child health services effective (Table-1).

Table-1: Key Social Indicators and Changes as per NFHS-3 and NFHS-4 in India.

	Social Indicators	**NFHS-3 (2005-06)**	**NFHS-4 (2015-16)**
Infant and child mortality rates (per 1000 live births)	Infant mortality rate(IMR)	57	41
	Under five mortality rate (U5MR)	74	50
Nutritional status of children (Under five age) %	Children U5 who are stunted	48	38.4
	Children U5 who are wasted	19.8	21
	Children U5 who are underweight	42.5	35.7
Nutritional status of adults (age 15-49 years) %	Women whose BMI is below normal (BMI < 18.5 kg/m^2)	35.5	22.9
	Men whose BMI is below normal (BMI < 18.5 kg/m^2)	34.2	20.2

Anaemia among children and adults %	Children age 6-59 months who are anaemic (< than 11.0 g/dl)(%)	69.4	58.4
	Non pregnant women age 15-49 years who are anaemic (< than 12.0 g/dl) (%)	55.2	53.1
	Pregnant women age 15-49 years who are anaemic (< than 11.0 g/dl) (%)	57.9	50.3
	Men age 15-49 years who are anaemic (< than 13.0 g/dl) (%)	24.2	22.7
Maternal and Child health services %	Mothers who had an antenatal check-up in the first trimester (%)	43.9	58.6
	Mothers whose last birth was protected against neonatal tetanus (%)	76.3	89
Delivery care %	Institutional births (%)	38.7	78.9
	Institutional births in public facilities (%)	18	52.1

Source: India Fact Sheet, National Family Health Survey, NFHS-4, 2015-16, Government of India.

It can be seen from Table-1 that, both IMR and U5MR have decreased significantly in 10 years–28.07% in IMR and 32.43% in U5MR. As a result, IMR in 2015-16 was 41 and U5MR was 50 in India. At this rate of progress, it is likely that as the major government interventions gather momentum, India will reach the Millennium Development Goals (MDG) shortly.

Nutritional Status of Children age 6-59 Months: Stunted and Underweight

A stunted child is short in height for that given age while an underweight child is less than of required weight for that given height.

More than 1/3rd of under five years age children in India were stunted (38.4%) and also underweight (35.7%) in 2015-16. The percentage of stunted and underweight children, however, was reduced by 9.6% points (stunted) and by 6.8% points (underweight). While this progress is commendable, it can be realised that we have yet to go a long way to make it a significant reduction.

Nutritional Status of Adults

Nutritional status of adults–men and women are measured by Body Mass Index (BMI). If the BMI is less than 18.5kg/m^2, it is an indication of malnourishment.

35.5% of women in India had Body Mass Index (BMI) of < than 18.5kg/m^2 in 2005-06. This, however, decreased to 22.8% or reduced by 12.6% points over the decade.

Among the men, 34.2% had BMI < than normal in 2005-06. The reduction during the same period was higher–14% points (from 34.2% in 2005-06 to 20.2% in 2015-16).

Anaemia among Children, 6-59 Months: The anaemic children and women fall easy prey to morbidity, disease and malnutrition; which in turn, leads to the anaemic health condition of children. Apart from children, anaemia is rampant among women in the reproductive age group and low socioeconomic strata of the population. It reduces the capacity to learn and work. Anaemia in pregnant women leads to adverse pregnancy outcomes such as high maternal and neonatal mortality, low birth weight, increased morbidity etc.

In the year 2015-16, 58.4% of the children in India were suffering from anaemia. On the whole, however, the incidence of anaemia among children decreased from 69.4% in 2005-06 to 58.4% in 2015-16. It is a matter of concern that more than half of U5 age children in India were suffering from anaemia in 2015-16.

Anaemia among Non-pregnant Women: More than half (53.12%) of the non-pregnant adult women (15-49 years of age) were suffering from anaemia. There was little progress in reducing the incidence in the span of 10 years.

Anaemia among pregnant women: What is noteworthy, however, is the substantial reduction in the incidence of anaemia among pregnant women. It was 57.9% in 2005-06 but reduced to 50.3% in 2015-16. Probably this is the outcome of increasing coverage of target groups and increasing effectiveness of mother and child care services. The challenge, however, is that 50% of pregnant women were anaemic in 2015-16.

Anaemia among men: So far as the incidence of anaemia among adult men is concerned, it can be noted that it is only half of that among women. However, there is very little reduction over time in the incidence of anaemia among men and non-pregnant women.

Maternal and Child Health Care Services: There is a remarkable increase in the percentage of mothers who had an antenatal checkup in the first trimester–from 43.9% to 58.6% or by 14.7% points between 2005-06 and 2015-16.

The achievement is even higher in terms of the percentage of mothers whose last birth was protected against neonatal tetanus. It was 76.3% in 2005-06, which itself was notable, but increased to 89% in 2015-16.

Institutional Deliveries

One of the most desirable objectives in maternal and child care is to ensure that the deliveries take place in medical/health institutions. This not only ensures the safety of the mother but also protects the child on birth and in the subsequent weeks.

The progress achieved is remarkable. Only 38.7% of the deliveries were institutional in 2005-06 but increased to 78.9% in 2015-16.

What is also noteworthy is the significant use of public health care institutions for deliveries. Only 18% of the deliveries were in public medical facility in 2005-06, but it increased to 52.1% in 2015-16.

Study of Inter Sate Variations

The above analysis provides a bird's eye view of status and changes in key social indicators in India. However, there are sizeable variations in many of the social indicators across the states. Moreover, many of these variations are not necessarily related to the level of economic development or the incidence of poverty. In order to explore these dimensions, the paper focuses on these issues of malnutrition among women and children as reflected in the National Family Health Surveys (NFHS), 2005-06 and 2015-16 in Six States. Three among these, i.e. Gujarat, Maharashtra and Tamil Nadu are relatively economically developed states with a low percentage of the population of below poverty line while, the other three states, i.e. Bihar, Madhya Pradesh and Odisha are comparatively poor states with a high percentage of population below the poverty line (Table-2).

Table-2: Percentage of population below poverty line (Poverty Ratio) in selected states, 2011-12

States	Rural	Urban
	%age of persons	%age of persons
Gujarat	31.4	22.2
Maharashtra	22.5	17
Tamil Nadu	24.3	20.3
Bihar	40.1	50.8
Madhya Pradesh	45.2	42.1
Odisha	47.8	36.3

Source: Rangrajan Committee report on poverty estimation, 2012, Planning Commission, Government of India.

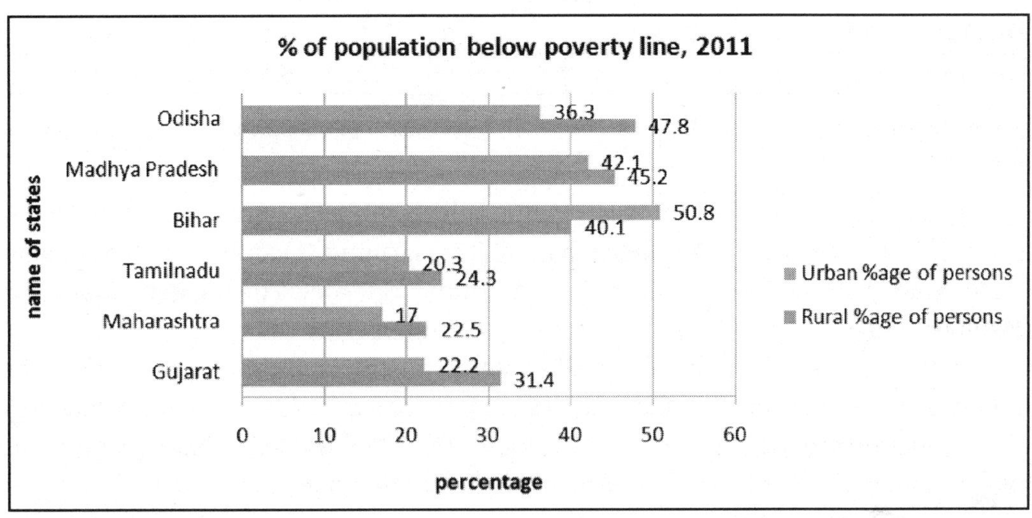

Source: Table-2

Poverty Levels

On the whole, the percentage of population below the poverty line either in rural areas or urban areas is higher in Bihar, Madhya Pradesh and Odisha than in Gujarat, Maharashtra and Tamil Nadu. Also, except in Bihar, the incidence of poverty is higher in rural areas than in urban areas.

Hunger Index in the Selected States

Hunger is at the root of many of the issues of morbidity, malnutrition and mortality. As noted earlier, the hunger index is measured by three variables, i.e. calorie undernourishment, underweight children below five years of age and under-five mortality rate.

Status of hunger among the selected states is shown in Table-3:

Table-3: Hunger Index of Selected States in India, 2008.

States	Prevalence of Calorie under Nourishment (%)	Proportion of Underweight Children less than 5 years of age (%)	Under five mortality Rate (per 100)	Hunger Index (HI)
Gujarat	23.3	44.7	6.1	24.7
Maharashtra	27	36.7	4.7	22.8
Tamil Nadu	29.1	30	3.5	20.87
Bihar	17.3	56.1	8.5	27.3

Madhya Pradesh	23.4	59.8	9.4	30.87
Odisha	21.4	40.9	9.1	23.8

Source: Hunger Index of selected Indian states, 2008, India Human Development Report, 2011. (Quoted from Menon et al. (2009)

The hunger index score if it is < 4.9 it is low, 5.0-9.9 is moderate, 10.0-19.9 is serious, 20.0-29.9 is alarming, more than 30 it is alarming. It can be seen that hunger status among all the selected states is in 'Alarming' category. The hunger situation in Madhya Pradesh is categorised as extremely alarming.

It can also be seen that calorie undernourishment, is more of a problem in the relatively developed states rather than in the poor states. Calorie deficiency affecting the population is least in Bihar but is the highest in Tamil Nadu and Maharashtra. The overall food habits of the people probably also matter, and hence, poverty alone is only a partial explanation.

However, the percentage of underweight children was high in Madhya Pradesh, Bihar and even in Gujarat. Under-five mortality rates are lowest in Tamil Nadu followed by in Maharashtra. The under-five mortality rate in Gujarat comes under the middle position between the developed and the poor states. The hunger index is the lowest in Tamil Nadu followed by in Maharashtra and in Odisha. The hunger index of Gujarat ranks in the middle; thus, the hunger index of Gujarat is adversely affected by a relatively higher proportion of underweight children and calorie undernourishment.

The result of poverty and malnutrition is reflected in mortality rates. IMR and U5MR in the selected states are shown in Table-4.

Table-4: IMR and U5 Mortality Rate Across Selected States, NFHS-3 (2004-05) and NFHS-4 (2015-16).

Name of States	IMR		U5MR		Percentage points differential -IMR	Percentage point differential in U5MR
	2005-06	2015-16	2005-06	2015-16		
Gujarat	50	34	61	43	16	18
Maharashtra	37	24	46	29	13	17
Tamil Nadu	30	21	35	27	9	8
Bihar	61	48	84	58	13	26
Madhya Pradesh	69	51	93	65	18	28
Odisha	65	40	91	49	25	42

Source: State Fact Sheets of selected states, National Family Health Survey–4, 2015-16.

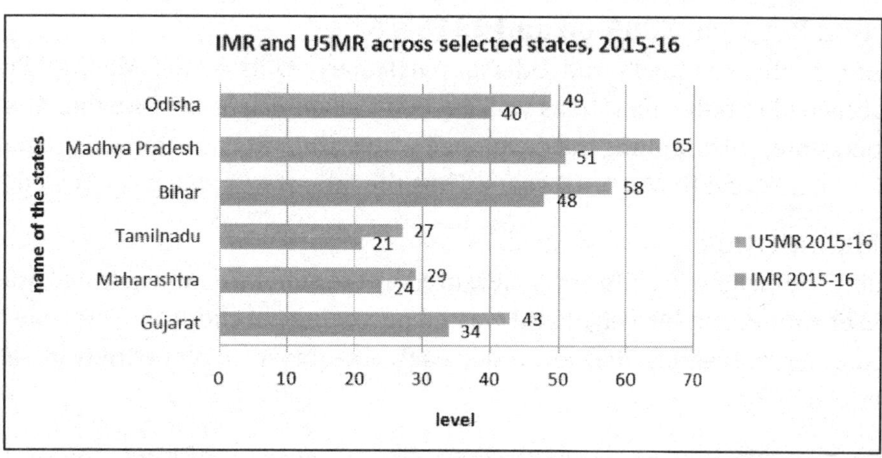

Source: Table-4.

It can be seen that both IMR and U5MR are distinctly lower in Tamil Nadu followed by in Maharashtra in 2015-16. The mortality rates are very high in Madhya Pradesh, Bihar and Odisha. These mortality rates in Gujarat are in the middle, i.e. IMR of 34 and U5MR of 43, although Gujarat is one of the Industrialised states. The graph below shows the changes in IMR and U5MR between 2005-06 and 2015-16 across the selected states.

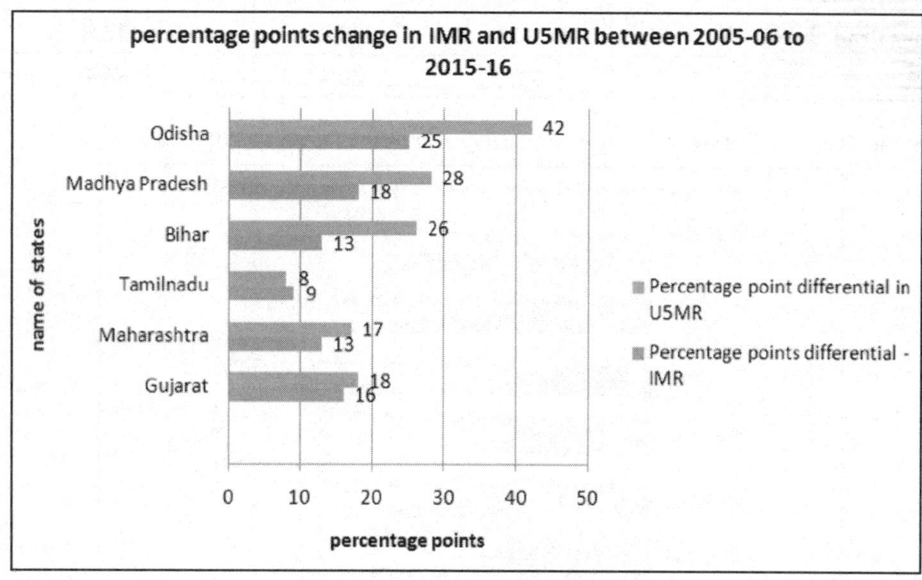

Source: Table-4.

Reduction Between 2005-06 and 2015-16

Bihar, Madhya Pradesh and Odisha, particularly Odisha and Madhya Pradesh have succeeded in reducing IMR as well as U5MR at a much faster rate than the more developed states. Also, among the developed states, Gujarat has achieved a significant reduction in IMR and U5MR in 10 years. Thus the interstate gap has narrowed.

Child Malnutrition

Malnutrition among children is measured by the standard international practices in terms of stunted, underweight and wasted percentage of children. The table below shows the percentage of children under each category of malnutrition in selected states in 2015-16.

Table-5: Nutritional Status of Children below the age of five (% of Children) in selected states, 2015-16.

States	Stunted	Wasted	Underweight
Gujarat	38.5	26.4	39.3
Maharashtra	34.4	25.6	36
Tamil Nadu	27.1	19.7	23.8
Bihar	48.3	20.8	43.9
Madhya Pradesh	42	25.8	42.8
Odisha	34.1	20.4	34.4

Source: State Fact Sheets of selected states, National Family Health Survey–4, 2015-16.

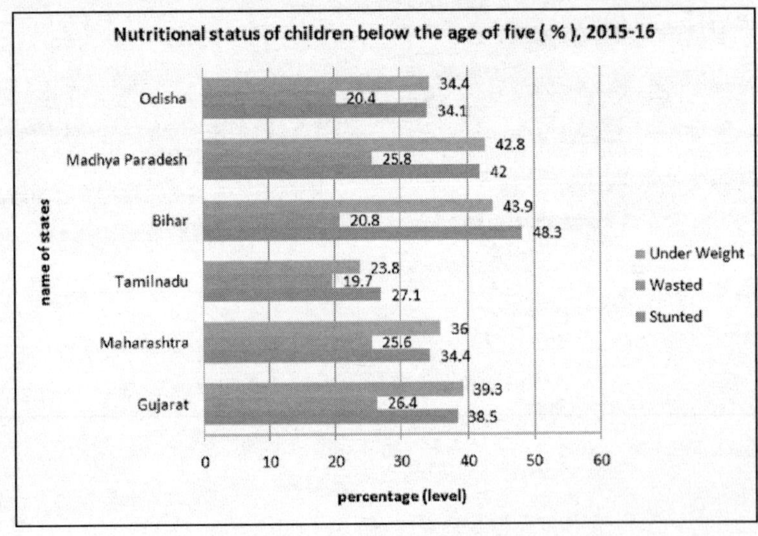

Source: Table-5

Stunted Children (height-for-age)

The stunted children are those who fail to gain the required height for that given age. Tamil Nadu has the lowest (among the six states) percentage of stunted children in 2015-16 (27.1%). It is followed by Odisha (34.1%) and Maharashtra (34.1%). The percentage of stunted children in Gujarat (38.5%) is quite high and is lower than only in Bihar and Madhya Pradesh.

Underweight Children (weight-for-age):

The underweight children are those who do not have the weight that is required to be healthy at that given age.

It can be seen that the problem of underweight children is more widespread across the selected states–rich or poor. In Gujarat and Maharashtra in particular, the percentage of underweight children is almost at the level found in Bihar and Madhya Pradesh. While in Odisha the percentage of underweight children is the second lowest after in Tamil Nadu. Hence poverty alone cannot explain this type of malnutrition among children.

Percentage of wasted children (weight-for-height):

If a child does not have standard weight for a given height, it is categorised as 'wasted'.

Gujarat has the highest percentage of U5 wasted children in 2015-16 (26.4%) followed by in Madhya Pradesh (25.8%) and in Maharashtra (25.6%). It was the lowest in Tamil Nadu (19.7%) and Odisha (20.4%) and Bihar (20.8%).

Change in the incidence of malnutrition among children, between 2005-06 and 2015-16

Table-6: Percentage point change of children below the age of five between 2005-06 and 2015-16.

States	Stunted	Wasted	Underweight
Gujarat	13.2	-7.7	5.3
Maharashtra	11.9	-9.1	1
Tamil Nadu	3.8	2.5	6
Bihar	7.3	6.3	12
Madhya Pradesh	8	9.2	17.2
Odisha	10.9	-0.8	6.3

Source: State Fact Sheets of selected states, National Family Health Survey-3, 2005-06 and 4, 2015-16.

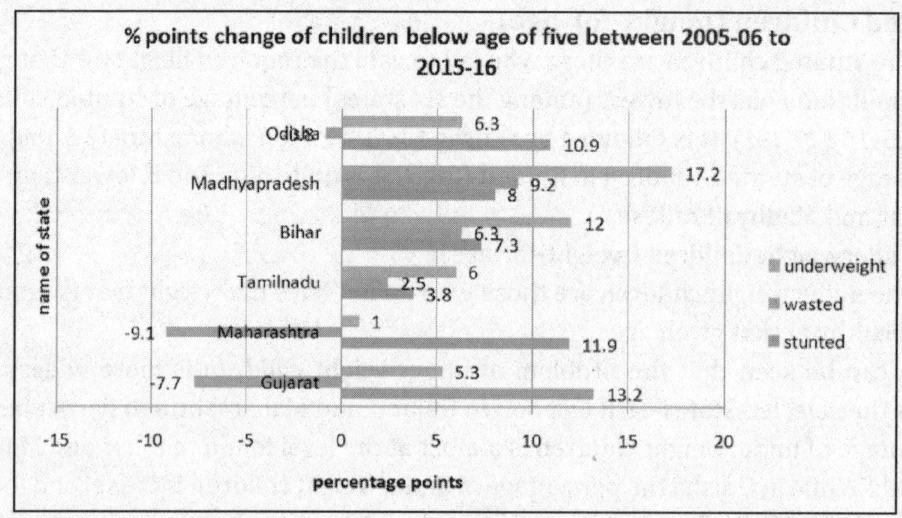

Source: Table-6.

However, if we look at the change in the proportion of stunted children between 2005-06 to 2015-16, the maximum progress has been achieved by Gujarat (13.2%). The percentage of stunted children was reduced by 13% points in Gujarat while the reduction was 11% points in Odisha. In this respect, Tamil Nadu and Maharashtra have lagged behind the other states. Gujarat is fast catching up with the developed states in reducing the problem of stunting among children.

There is no significant reduction in the percentage of underweight children in the developed states, while the reduction is significant in the poor states. Thus Gujarat and Maharashtra face a bigger challenge to reduce the incidence of 'underweight' children than in other states.

As far as the percentage of wasted children under the age of five is concerned the real problem is found with the developed states as in fact the proportion of stunted children has increased in Gujarat and Maharashtra and there is a negligible reduction in Tamil Nadu between 2005-06 and 2015-16. On the other hand, there is a significant reduction in the proportion of wasted children in poor states.

Nutritional Status of Adult Women (BMI):

Nutritional status of adults–men and women are measured by Body Mass Index (BMI) if the BMI is less than 18.5 Kg/m², it is an indication of malnourishment. We have shown the percentage of adult women who are having BMI < than 18.5 Kg/m² in 2015-16.

Table-7: Percentage of Adult women with Body Mass Index (BMI) of less than 18.5 Kg/m2 in 2005-06 and 2015-16 across and percentage point change. Selected states.

States	BMI less than 18.5 Kg/m² in 2005-06	BMI less than 18.5 Kg/m² in 2015-16	Percentage point difference
Gujarat	36.3	27.2	9.1
Maharashtra	36.2	23.5	12.7
Tamil Nadu	28.4	14.6	13.8
Bihar	45	30.4	14.6
Madhya Pradesh	41.7	28.3	13.4
Odisha	41.4	26.4	15

Source: State Fact Sheets of selected states, National Family Health Survey-3, 2005-06 and 4, 2015-16.

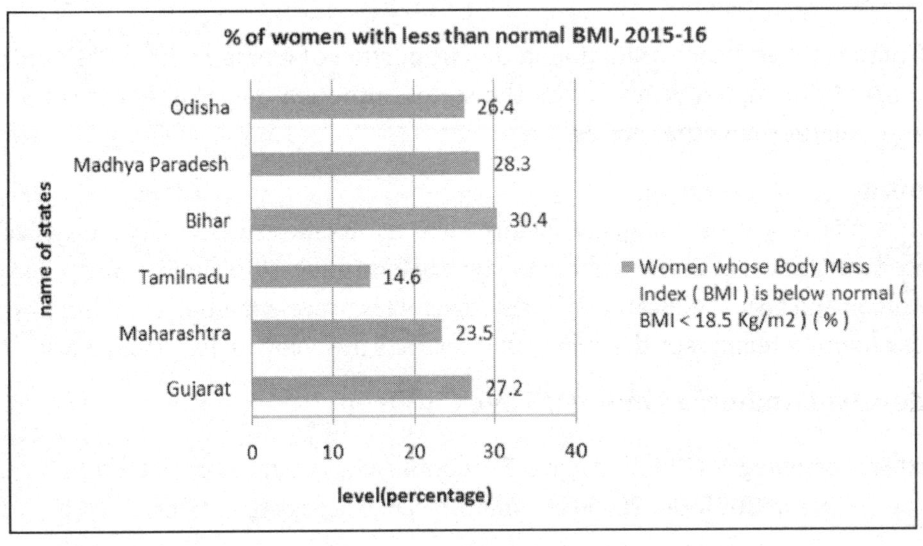

Source: Table-7

Only 14.6% of adult women in Tamil Nadu were with a BMI of less than 18.5 Kg/m2 in 2015-16, and 23.5% were in Maharashtra. Gujarat with 27.2% of women with less than normal BMI was closer to Madhya Pradesh, Odisha and Bihar.

Percentage points change between 2005-06 – 2015-16

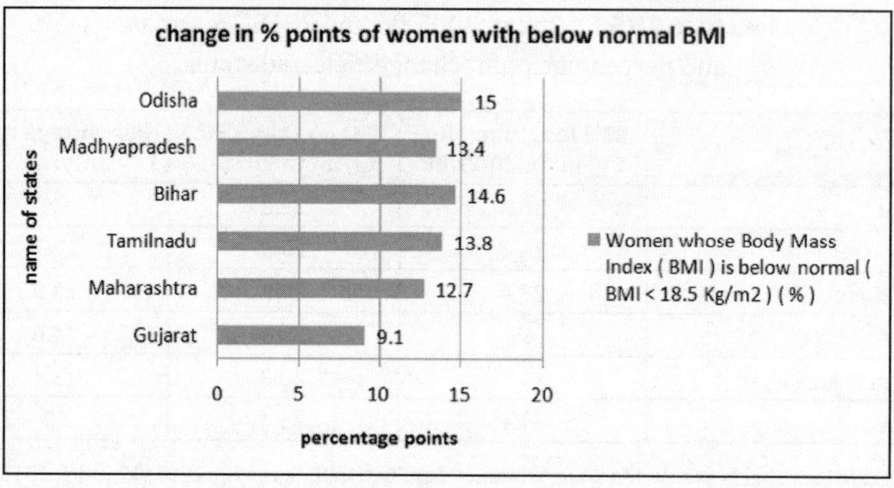

Source: Table-7

There is a significant reduction in the proportion of women with a BMI of < than 18.5 Kg/m2 during ten years across the states, although the progress is somewhat lower in Gujarat than other states.

Anaemia

Anaemia is a result of many factors such as assetlessness and poverty, lack of balanced diet, lack of awareness about the type of food intake, discrimination against girls and women and lack of education of girls. Anaemia is prevalent among children, women and also men. Anaemia saps the energy and restricts the ability to learn and work.

Incidence of Anaemia among U5 age Children

Table-8: Percentage of Children age 6-59 months who are anaemic (< than 11.0 g/dl) in 2005-06, 2015-16 and difference across the states.

States	% anaemic children 2005-06	% anaemic children, 2015-16	percentage point difference
Gujarat	69.7	62.6	7.1
Maharashtra	63.4	53.8	9.6
Tamil Nadu	64.2	50.7	13.5
Bihar	78	63.5	14.5
Madhya Pradesh	74	68.9	5.1
Odisha	65	44.6	20.4

Source: State Fact Sheets of selected states, National Family Health Survey-3, 2005-06 and 4, 2015-16.

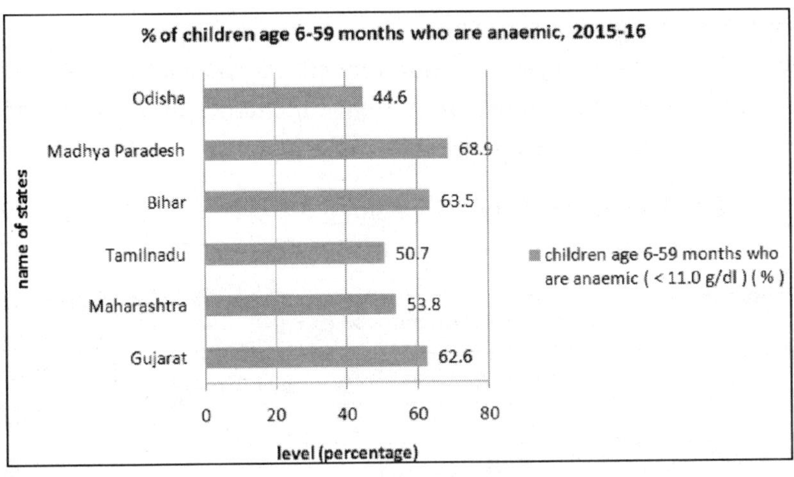

Source: Table-8

It can be seen from the Table-8 that the incidence of anaemia among children U5 age is significant across the states in India ranging from 68.9% in Madhya Pradesh, 63.5% in Bihar to 44.6% in Odisha. 62.6% of U5 age children in Gujarat were anaemic as compared to 50.7% in Tamil Nadu and 53.8% in Maharashtra in 2015-16.

The highest reduction in the incidence of anaemia between 2005-06 to 2015-16 was in Odisha, Bihar and Tamil Nadu. Gujarat and Maharashtra relatively lagged in reducing the incidence of anaemia.

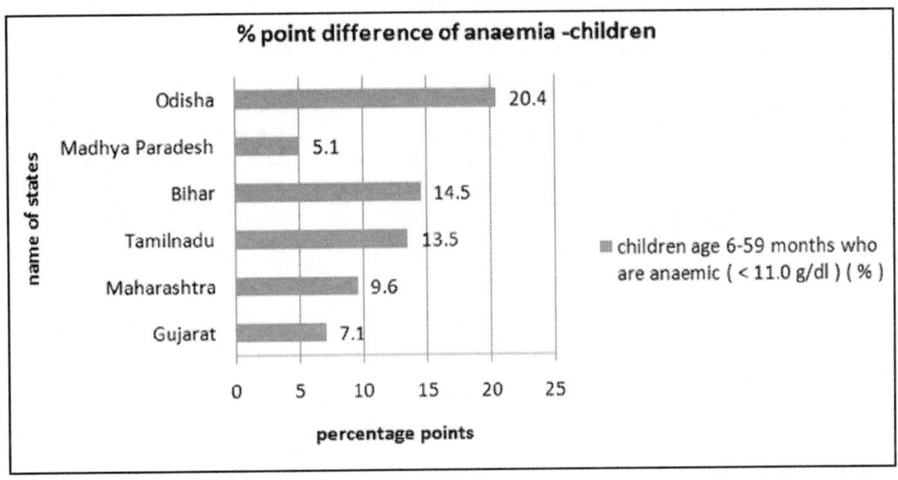

Source: Table-8

Anaemia among Pregnant women

Anaemia among pregnant women not only affects the health of women but also affects the health of the newly born child. Hence incidence and changes in anaemia among the pregnant women are analysed in Table-9.

Table-9: Incidence of anaemia among the pregnant in selected states and changes during 2005-06 to 2015-16.

States	% pregnant women with anaemia, 2005-06	% pregnant women with anaemia, 2015-16	Percentage point difference
Gujarat	60.8	51.3	9.5
Maharashtra	57.8	49.3	8.5
Tamil Nadu	54.7	44.4	10.3
Bihar	60.2	58.3	1.9
Madhya Pradesh	57.9	54.6	3.3
Odisha	68.1	47.6	20.5

Source: State Fact Sheets of selected states, National Family Health Survey-3, 2005-06 and 4, 2015-16.

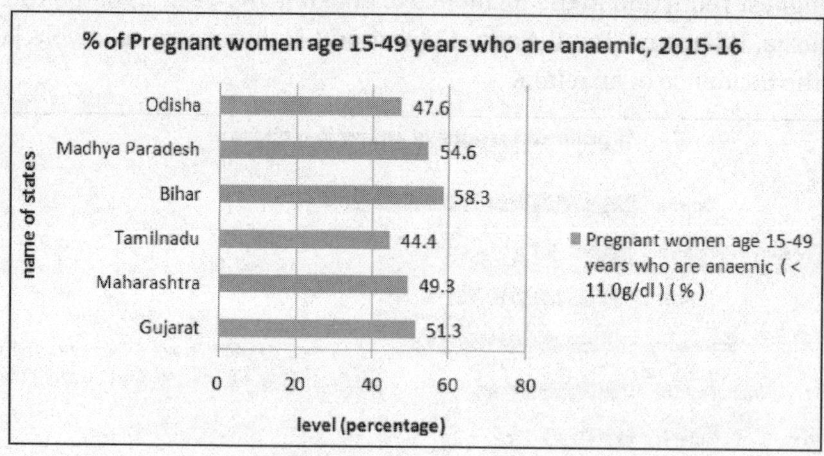

Source: Table-9

It can be seen that the incidence of anaemia among the pregnant women was comparatively low in Tamil Nadu and Odisha states; while, it was 50% and above in other states, highest being in Bihar (58.3%). Even among the developed states, the incidence of anaemia is almost 50% in Gujarat and Maharashtra.

Percentage points difference in the incidence of anaemia-pregnant women

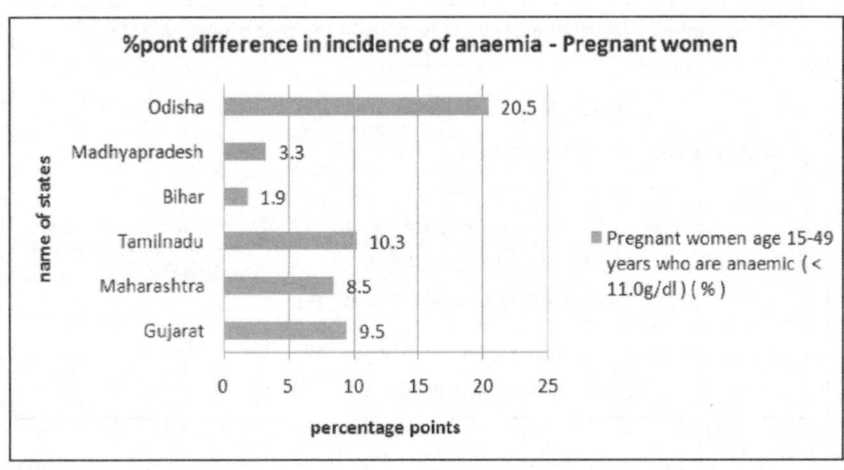

Source: Table-9

The striking reduction in the incidence of anaemia among the pregnant women was in Odisha (20.5% points) compared to nil or negligible reduction in all other states.

Maternal and Child Health

Table-10: Percentage of mothers who had an antenatal checkup in the first trimester, 2005-06 to 2015-16 and the changes

States	% of women are receiving an antenatal checkup in the first trimester, 2005-06.	% of women are receiving an antenatal checkup in the first trimester, 2015-16.	Percentage points difference. (2015-16-2005-06)
Gujarat	55	73.9	18.9
Maharashtra	62.1	67.6	5.5
Tamil Nadu	75.3	64	-11.3
Bihar	18.7	34.6	15.9
Madhya Pradesh	39.3	53.1	13.8
Odisha	48.3	64.1	15.8

Source: State Fact Sheets of selected states, National Family Health Survey-3, 2005-06 and 4, 2015-16.

It is observed that Gujarat has the highest percentage (73.9%) of mothers who had an antenatal check-up in the first trimester. It was also 64% in Tamil Nadu and

67.6% in Maharashtra. However, it was the lowest at 34.6% in Bihar and 53.1% in Madhya Pradesh.

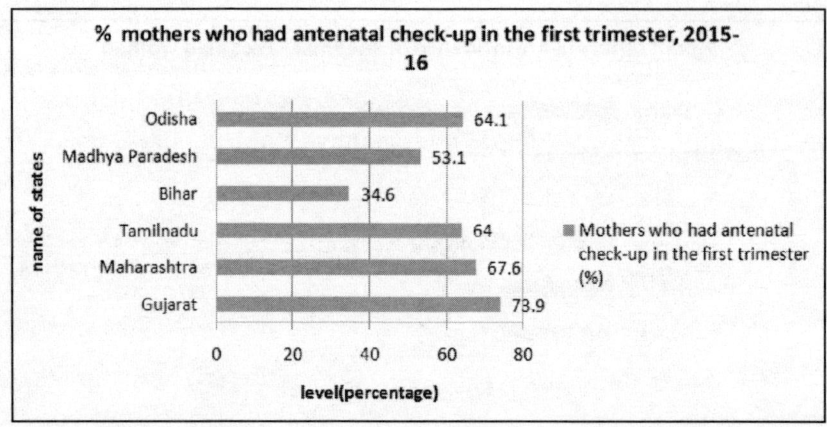

Source: Table-10

Percentage Points Change

The percentage points change of mothers who had an antenatal checkup in the first trimester was the highest in Gujarat (18.9% points) while in Tamil Nadu and Maharashtra the changes are negative. The poorer states, on the other hand, have made noteworthy progress. Thus ANC program targeting pregnant women in Gujarat has become much more effective than in other states.

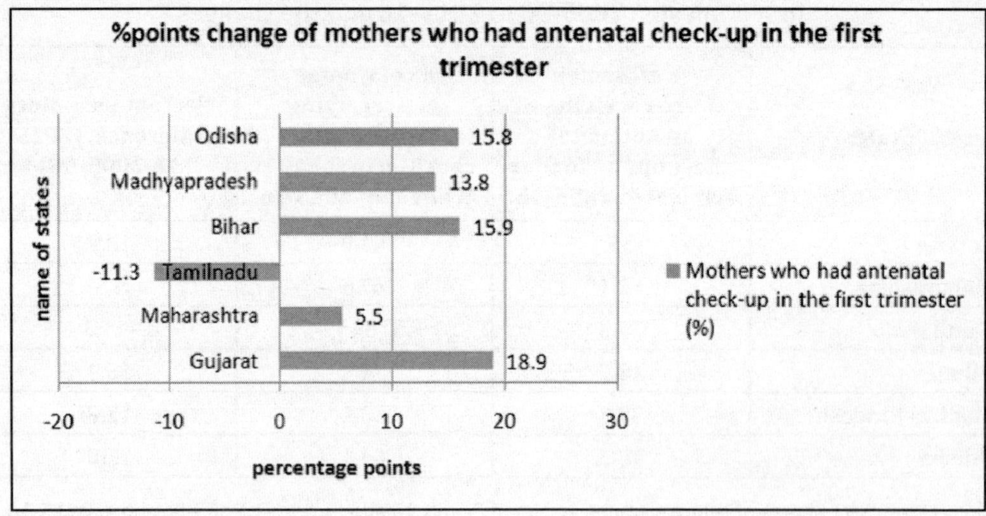

Source: Table-10

Delivery Care

Institutional Delivery: Except in the state of Bihar, in all other states, 80 or more percent of childbirths were found in medical institutions in 2015-16. However, in Gujarat, Maharashtra and Tamil Nadu, the percentage of institutional delivery was 90% and above. It is also noteworthy that most of the institutional births are in a public health facility in Tamil Nadu, Bihar, Madhya Pradesh and Odisha. In Gujarat, however, only 32.6% of the deliveries were in public health care facility.

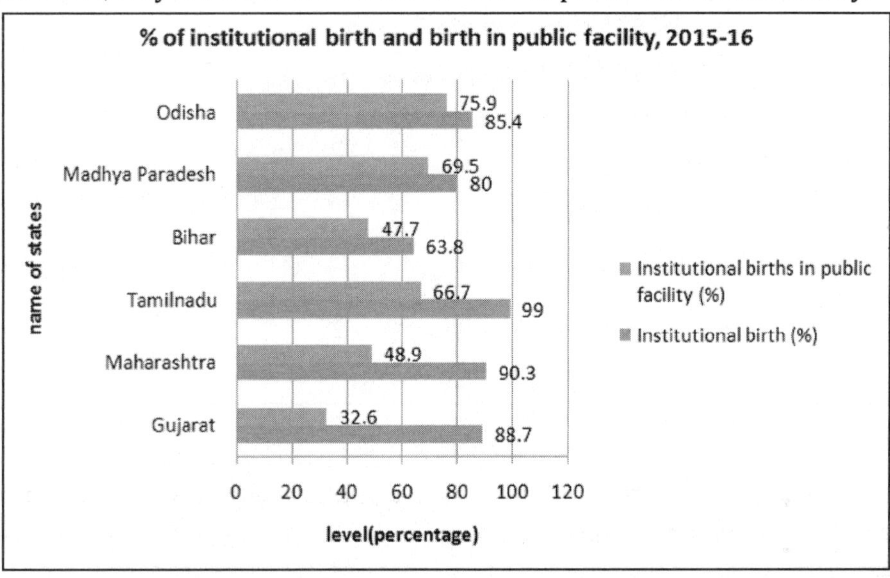

Source: Table-11 and 12, State Fact Sheets of selected states, National Family Health Survey-4, 2015-16.

Percentage Points Change in Institutional Births

Table-11: Percentage of Institutional delivery and percentage points change between 2005-06 and 2015-15.

States	% institutional delivery 2005-06	% institutional delivery 2015-16	Percentage point difference
Gujarat	52.7	88.7	36
Maharashtra	64.6	90.3	25.7
Tamil Nadu	87.8	99	11.2
Bihar	19.9	63.8	43.9
Madhya Pradesh	26.2	80	53.8
Odisha	35.6	85.4	49.8

Source: State Fact Sheets of selected states, National Family Health Survey-3, 2005-06 and 4, 2015-16.

The poor states like Odisha, Madhya Pradesh and Bihar have achieved very rapid progress in terms of ensuring institutional births between 2005-06 and 2015-16 as compared to the developed states, which have already very high coverage in 2015-16.

It is noteworthy that, the increase in the institutional births in the public health care facility was maximum in the poor states than in the rich states.

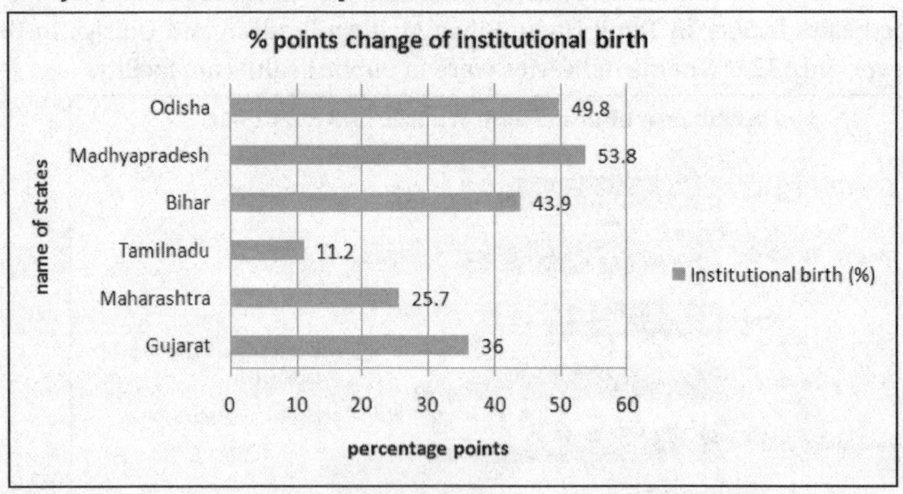

Source: Table-11

Table-12: Percentage of Institutional delivery in a public health care facility and percentage points change between 2005-06 and 2015-16.

States	% institutional delivery in a public health care facility 2005-06	% institutional delivery in a public health care facility 2015-16	Percentage point difference
Gujarat	13.9	32.6	18.7
Maharashtra	26.5	48.9	22.4
Tamil Nadu	48.1	66.7	18.6
Bihar	3.5	47.7	44.2
Madhya Pradesh	18.4	69.5	51.1
Odisha	28.8	75.9	47.1

Source: State Fact Sheets of selected states, National Family Health Survey-3, 2005-06 and 4, 2015-16.

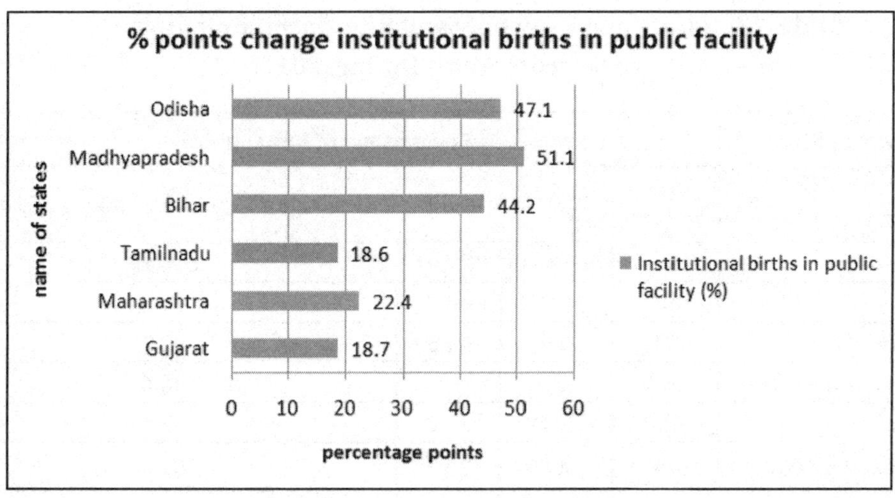

Source: Table-12

The cases of home delivery attended by a skill health person are found in mainly in Bihar. Most of the progress in ensuring institutional delivery is achieved by the states between 2005-06 and 2015-16 except in Tamil Nadu were the percentage was very high even in 2005-06.

Per Capita per Day Net Availability of cereals, pulses (grams) and the availability of the food grains in Public Distribution System:

The net availability of cereals in India in 2014 was 444.1 grams as compared to 334.2 in 1951. However, the availability of cereals has fluctuated from year to year. On the whole, it has remained at around 400 grams in the last two decades.

On the other hand, the per capita availability of pulses has decreased over time. Between 1951and 1971, the net availability of pulses was between 50-69 grams as against 42-47 grams during 2012-2014. Thus, the per capita per day availability of pulses has decreased. This has a negative impact on a balanced diet.

However, the procurement for public distribution has gone up significantly from 8.9 million tons in 1971 to 42.6 million tons in 2001 to 60.7 million tons in 2015. The subsided sale of food grains through public distribution, which was only 7.8 million tons in 1971 increased to 13.2 million tons in 2001 and which was 43.5 million tons in 2014.

Access to Basic Amenities as a Measure of Preventive Health

Preventive health care is as important as curative healthcare to ensure a healthy population. The drinking water facility and access to toilet facility are two indicators the status of which is shown across the selected states. (Table-5).

Table-13: Nature and Extent of Sanitation Facilities in Households in Selected States During, 2012.

Name of States	Percentage of households			
	Without latrine facility		Having access to an improved source of latrine	
	Rural	Urban	Rural	Urban
Gujarat	58.7	6.2	40.7	93.6
Maharashtra	54	6.9	44.3	92.7
Tamil Nadu	66.4	12.2	33	86.6
Bihar	72.8	20.8	25.8	78.4
Madhya Pradesh	79	14	20.7	84.9
Odisha	81.3	18.2	17.3	80.5
All India	59.4	8.8	38.8	89.6

Source: Swachchhta Status Report, 2016. NSSO, GOI.

Sanitation Facility

59.4% of the households in rural areas and 8.8% in urban areas did not have a latrine facility in India in 2012.

Among the developed selected states, Gujarat and Maharashtra as compared to India have a lower percentage of households without latrine facility in rural as well as urban areas.

On the other hand a very high proportion of the households in rural areas in Madhya Pradesh, Bihar and Odisha were without latrine facility. Even in urban areas between 14 to 21% of the households did not have a latrine facility.

As regards having access to improve the source of latrine in rural areas between 41 to 44% of the households in Gujarat and Maharashtra had access to an improved source of latrine as compared to 33% in Tamil Nadu. In these developed states, more than 90% of the households in urban areas had access to an improved source of the latrine.

In the poor states, however, less than 1/4th of the households in rural areas had access to an improved source of latrine although between 78 to 85% of the households in urban areas in these poor states had access to an improved source of the latrine. Thus in rural areas yet, a very high percentage of households are without latrine facility and even among those who have access to latrine facility only a small percentage of having access to an improved source of the latrine. In urban areas, however, the access to latrine is generally access to an improved source of latrine

Drinking Water Facility

Table-14: Households with access to drinking water facility in selected states, 2011

States	Drinking water facility, Tap water	Drinking water facilities, within the premises
Gujarat	69	64
Maharashtra	67.9	59.4
Tamil Nadu	79.8	34.9
Bihar	4.4	50.1
Madhya Pradesh	23.4	23.9
Odisha	13.8	22.4

Source: Census of India, 2011.

As far as the drinking water facility is concerned, the census of India 2011 data shows that 43.51% of the households had tap water facility which was mostly within the premises. In the relatively developed states, 68-80% of the households had tap water, although within the premises facility was highest in Gujarat. 34.9% of the households in Tamil Nadu have access within the premises. 64% of the households in Gujarat had access to drinking water within the premises, followed by 59.4% of the households in Maharashtra.

Among the poorer states, Bihar has the highest percentage (50.1%) households with access to drinking water within the premises whereas in Madhya Pradesh and Odisha only 22-24% had access within the premises.

Thus the low level of preventive health measures as mentioned above in the poor states seems to compound the problem in achieving better results. Although the status of health and nutrition is influenced by more complex factors which is evident in the fact that in the state of Odisha despite the low level of preventive health measures as mentioned above, it has achieved much better results.

Major Programs to address the Problem of Hunger and Malnutrition:

Food and Nutrition Security and Right to Food:

Under the act (2010), every identified BPL family will be entitled to receive 25 Kg of food grains every month at highly subsided prices.

The overall calorie deficiency and hunger status indicate the challenge before the public distribution system.

Nutrition Interventions

It may be mentioned that nutrition interventions are through a variety of programs, most of which are either partially or fully funded by the central government. States are implementing a plethora of schemes and programs with suitable modification as per the local requirements.

Kuposhan Mukt Maha Abhiyan

Under the program, all children below the age of five, are screened by the health workers, and complicated cases are referred to the nearby malnutrition treatment centres or nutrition rehabilitation centres for follow up.

Mamta Divas

To reduce malnutrition among children, Malnutrition Assessment and Monitoring To Act (MAMTA) is organised in each village on Wednesday once in a month.

On the MAMTA day, activities such as ANC registration, growth monitoring mother and child, immunisation etc. are carried out.

Kasturba Poshan Sahay Yojana (KPSY)

The target group is pregnant women, and the objective is to reduce malnutrition linked, morbidity and mortality. All BPL mothers become eligible to receive conditional cash transfer so that they can avail services, nutritious food and other supplements during pregnancy. The scheme provides for a total of Rs. 6000 cash support to each pregnant women and the cash is disbursed by three instalments to ensure full compliance with the requirements under the scheme.

Malnutrition among Women and Children

In order to address the challenges of malnutrition among women and children, the government of India and state government are implementing a major all India program (funded by GOI) of Integrated Child Development Services (ICDS). The target groups are all children in the age of 6 months to 6 years, pregnant and lactating mothers. Anganwadi Centres (AWCs) are equipped with necessary manpower, physical infrastructure, and equipment. Thus an Anganwadi centre is the key entry-level institution to fight the incidence of malnutrition among women and children.

Supplementary Nutrition

Under the scheme, all families in the community are surveyed and identified for supplemental nutrition intervention. Supplementary feeding support is provided for 300 days in a year through AWCs. This is an attempt to bridge the protein energy gap between the recommended dietary allowance and average dietary intake by children and mothers.

Fortified Blended Food

In order to upgrade the nutrition status of children below the age of three years, ready to eat energy dense fortified blended food in the form of ready packets are provided to be taken home for feeding the children.

Sheera, Sukhadi, Upma

A mix to prepare the above items at home is given to ensure 600 calories and 18-20 grams of protein for pregnant women, lactating mothers and adolescent girls.

Hot Cooked Breakfast:

Children in age 3-6 years in Anganwadi centres are provided with hot cooked breakfast for six days in a week. ***Sukhadi* (take home ration):**

Under the scheme, ration to prepare *sukhadi* is given to the target families. Sakhi Medals/Mahila Mandals etc. are implementing the scheme.

Dudh Sanjeevani Yojana

All tribal taluka in the state and Anganwadi in developing taluka are covered. 100 ml pasteurised flavoured fortified milk is given to the children for five days in a week. Moreover, 200 ml of milk is given two days in a week to pregnant women and lactating mothers.

There are also schemes to provide fruits twice in a week to children, and there is also a provision to provide third Meal to children who have been identified as severely malnourished. It will thus we saw that there is a large number of schemes, yet the outcomes in terms of reducing malnutrition are not commensurate with the money spent and efforts made.

Conclusion and Observations

While there are large numbers of schemes and programs to fight malnutrition, they need to be sustainable and hence, these interventions cannot substitute what the women or a child eat at home.

It is therefore suggested to focus on two major programs which can be further strengthened and innovative methods can be used.

Public Distribution System (PDS):

Although several initiatives have been taken for proper targeting and effective outreach to the beneficiaries, there are problems relating to the quality of food grains and availing of the benefits.

It is therefore suggested to go for cleaned, packed and certified grain for distribution. Further, it is suggested to add an entitlement of two litres of edible oil at the subsided price and adopt home delivery mechanism through a mobile van system once in a month.

Integrated Child Development Service (ICDS)

ICDS is the key all India program focusing on children, pregnant women etc. It is suggested to revamp the workforce to manage Anganwadi centres. The minimum qualification suggested is 12th Pass plus rigorous six months training in nutrition and food, child care, child psychology, sanitation and hygiene etc. Moreover, it is suggested to adopt at least the competitive district process for the recruitment of the personnel.

Regarding the salary, it is suggested to fix a basic salary plus incentive paid or bonus based on the evaluation of performance indicators every quarter.

Third, it is suggested to experiment with some pilot projects for running centralised kitchens for a cluster of villages at the Taluka level.

According to the district level Household Survey (2002-04), the incidence of malnutrition among the tribal population is much higher than in the 'others' population across the states.

Moreover, the habitation pattern in the villages in tribal areas is on undulated and uneven topography. Even within the villages, settlements are scattered in fali as and homesteads. As a result, any service if it is to reach every household, it is a big challenge for health personnel. A high percentage of Schedule Tribe population in states of Odisha, Chhattisgarh, Jharkhand, Madhya Pradesh and Gujarat pose a special challenge to reach out to such families.

Due to high illiteracy, there is not much awareness, and motivation to seek health services proactively.

Even when there is awareness among some, the further challenge emerges from the nature of their occupation likes agriculture labour, construction labour, farming etc.

In a way, such population groups are away from their home from morning till evening for work.

What is more, is that in a large number of the villages in tribal areas in Gujarat and Madhya Pradesh etc. the tribal households out-migrate seasonally for 6-8 months either as agriculture labour, annual farm servants, share croppers, contract labour, salt workers etc.

Once they are out with their families, there is hardly any follow up to mainstream the children into the local schools, local Anganwadies or even facilitated access to public distribution system and health care services.

Thus, such groups of families remain deprived of all those benefits due to seasonal migration. Adhaar card can be used to ensure universal access to avail the benefits by such migratory households.

Further, due to scattered habitation in villages, the location of even Anganwadi centre cannot be an ideal one. It does involve covering about 1 Km distance in many areas. In monsoon, the problems compound further and therefore, frequent absenteeism is also observed.

It is not that the government is not aware of some of these challenges for upgrading the nutritional status of women and children. However, it is a question of adjusting the timing and delivery system of many of these programs to suit with the compulsions of earning livelihoods. Anganwadies need to be converted into Day Care Centres in tribal areas.

The governments have introduced special programs to specifically focus on tribal population, which is an attempt to overcome some challenges.

It is because of such special programs and overall strengthening of the programs for improving nutrition status and health care delivery that, in10 years between 2005-06 to 2015-16 significant progress has been achieved in a majority of these indicators in the selected states.

Probably it will accelerate the progress if some of the below-mentioned measures are also contemplated:

While supplemental programs are helpful to upgrade the nutritional status of women and children, it cannot be a sustainable substitute for what the family has to manage at their level. The sustainable arrangement requires that they have means and awareness to have balanced food items particularly of milk and milk products, eggs, meat and green vegetables and pulses and therefore goat and sheep, poultry and vegetable growing the economy of many of these vulnerable social groups need to be promoted as a priority. The dairy activity has almost bypassed this specified livelihood support and nutritious food supply activities of the weaker sections.

Proactive seeking health care services

In order to make people proactive to seek health care services for children and women, in particular, a strategy to motivate the people through their own/community girls who are either studying or are educated within the village is suggested.

Setting up some common facilities

In the district like Kutch, the population density is extremely low. Thus, apart from the challenges in tribal areas, the long distances and small villages in Kutch district too represent special challenges to reach out to the people with health and education services and veterinary services.

The doctors and other health personnel, as well as teachers etc. who are posted either in tribal areas or semi-desert areas of Kutch, also have certain problems of living, education of children etc. Therefore, motivation and dedication are not of the required level in many cases. It is suggested to consider the setting up of a common residential facility comprising of studio type 1.5 room facility as one unit and provide basic facilities of bathrooms, toilets etc. If 25 to 30 functionaries stay to gather at Taluka level in such accommodation and facility, it will give tremendous synergy and provide a high level of motivation for performance.

References

1. National Family Health Survey (NFHS-4), 2015-16. Ministry of Health and Family Welfare, Government of India.
2. Swachchhta Status Report, 2016, National Sample Survey Organisation, Ministry of Statistics and Program Implementation, Government of India.
3. Census of India, 2011.
4. Rangrajan Committee Report on Poverty Estimation, 2012. Planning Commission, Government of India.
5. India: Human Development Report, 2011, Oxford.
6. Economic Survey, 2016-17, Ministry of Finance, Government of India.

□

4

Occupational Health of Children and Adolescents in India

—Dr. H.G. Sadhu

Occupational Health is the promotion and maintenance of the highest degree of physical, mental and social well-being of workers in all **occupations** by preventing departures from **health**, controlling risks and the adaptation of work to people, and people to their jobs. (ILO/WHO 1950).

Child labour, an extensive and complex problem, has been an important global human right issue since many decades. Elimination of child labour is a formidable challenge faced by today's world. It is associated with inadequate educational opportunities, poverty and gender inequality.[1] In addition to causing damage to a child's physical and mental health, child labour is also responsible for the deprivation of basic rights to education, development, and freedom of a child.

The International Labour Organisation (ILO) describes child labour as 'work that deprives children of their childhood, their potential and dignity, and that is harmful to physical and mental development'.[2] This definition includes types of work that are mentally, physically, socially or morally harmful to children; and interferes with their schooling. Forced labour, including begging, child trafficking, sexual exploitation, the use of children in illicit activities or crime (e.g. drugs) and hazardous work are the worst forms of child labour on the streets.

A total of 152 million children–64 million girls and 88 million boys–are in child labour globally, accounting for almost one in ten of all children worldwide. Nearly half of all those in child labour–73 million children in absolute terms–are in hazardous work that directly endangers their health, safety, and moral development. Children in employment, a broader measure comprising both child labour and permitted forms of employment involving children of legal working age, number 218 million.[3] Child labour declined during the period from 2012 to 2016, continuing a trend seen since the publication of the ILO's first global estimates of child labour in 2000. The 16-year period starting in 2000 saw a net reduction of 94 million in children in child labour. The number of children in hazardous work fell by more than half over the same period. There were almost 134 million fewer children in employment in 2016 than in 2000. Real advances have been made in the fight against child labour, providing an important foundation for efforts moving forward.[4]

As per Census 2011, the total child population in India in the age group (5-14) years is 259.6 million. Of these, 10.1 million (3.9% of total child population) are working, either as 'main worker' or as 'marginal worker'. Together, Uttar Pradesh (21.5%), Bihar (10.7%), Rajasthan (8.4%), Maharashtra (7.2%) and Madhya Pradesh (6.9%) constitute nearly 55% of total working children in India. Also, more than 42.7 million children in India are out of school. However, the incidence of child labour has decreased in India by 2.6 million between 2001 and 2011. Though the decline was more visible in rural areas, the number of child workers has increased in urban areas, indicating the growing demand for child workers in menial jobs. Child labour has different ramifications in both rural and urban India.[5]

National Legislations and ILO Conventions

Child labour is a brake on sustainable development and anathema to just societies, and its eradication must be pursued with utmost determination. The enactment of the Child Labour Amendment (Prohibition and Regulation) Act, 2016 and The Right to Education Act, 2009 have paved the way for ratification of ILO's two core conventions:[6]

1. Convention No 138 stipulates that the minimum age at which children can start work should not be below the age of compulsory schooling and in any case not less than 15 years; with a possible exception for developing countries.
2. Convention No. 182 prohibits hazardous work which is likely to jeopardize children's physical, mental or moral health. It aims at immediate elimination of the worst forms of child labour for children below 18 years.

These Conventions emphasize that freedom from child labour is a human right and that the elimination of child labour is a universal and fundamental value.[7]

The constitution of India, under the fundamental rights Article 24, prohibits child labour. The Child Labour (Prohibition and Regulation) Act was implemented in India in 1986 that prohibits child labour in certain occupations and processes.[8] The ***'Child'*** *is defined as a person who has not completed his 14 year of age* and the ***'Adolescent'*** *as a person who has completed his 14 year of age but has not completed his 18 year of age* as per the act (Section 23). The main objectives of the act are to prohibit the engagement of children in certain employments (as specified in the Section 3,

Schedule-Part A and Part B) and to regulate the conditions of work of children in certain other employments (Section 6).

In 1992, India became the first country to join the "International Programme on the Elimination of Child Labour", a global programme launched by the ILO in 1991.[9] Under the National Child Labour Project (NCLP), 7328 special schools opened for the children withdrawn from work and providing them education, nutrition, vocational training, stipend and health care, etc.[10]

Causes for the Child Labour

The various government studies and policy statements and also as per different social and economic scholars the following are some of the major reasons for the problem of child labour in India.[11]

1. Poverty
2. Lack of education
3. Economic uncertainties
4. Indebtedness
5. Employment (or lack of employment)
6. Landlessness at rural areas for majority of the population
7. Weak policy of legal framework
8. Weak social awareness

Children from lower socio-economic class are more commonly known to be inducted as child labour. Family poverty plays a significant role for child labour.[12] The assumption that more working hands will enhance the income of the family with subsequent alleviation of poverty is a driving force for parents to encourage child labour activities. Further, due to the parents' wish to keep alive the family tradition, the children are compelled to learn and grow in the same occupation against their own desire to attend school like their peers. Whatever the reason for getting engaged in child labour, such child inadvertently misses out the opportunity to gain an education. This very fact finally leads to further perpetuating household poverty across generations, slowing the economic growth and social development.

Unorganised Sector of Industry

The informal economy or the unorganised sector of industry harbours most child labour. The 'informal sector' is the part of the economy that includes the income-generating activities carried out by the majority of the urban poor. Further as it is not recognised or protected under the legal and regulatory frameworks, informal workers have a high degree of vulnerability.[13] The informal economy is spread across all economic sectors and may be closely linked to formal sector production, for example, in situations where formal sectors outsource work to the informal economy.[14] On the other hand, illegal industrial activities such as mining also employ a sizable work force including child labour.

Occupational health hazards

All types of work carried out by children are not necessarily considered as child labour. For example, engagement of children or adolescents in work that does not influence their health and schooling such as working on farms and making handicrafts is usually regarded positive.

Children and adolescents form a very special group of humans, as they are passing through an important phase of both physical and mental growth of variable stages depending on their age. The health as well as growth and development of working children is liable to be affected due to exposure to various forms of mechanical, physical, chemical, biological, physiological/ergonomic and psychosocial hazards prevailing in the workplace environment. Working children are more prone to misjudge, ignore or take a risk that they cannot manage. Due to the smaller physical dimensions, they may be exposed to vapours and gases heavier than air, particularly in cases of leakage and accidents and also do not fit in personal protective equipment (gas masks, earplugs, gloves, goggles and others) designed for adults.[15] Since the bodies and minds of children are under the stage of growth and development, exposure to workplace hazards and risks can be more devastating and long-lasting for them.[16]

A vast majority of working children is employed in agricultural sector. According to the ILO, an estimated 70% of the world's child labourers (more than 150 million girls and boys under 18) are agricultural workers.[17] The child and adolescent workers are also employed in hazardous activities like stone polishing[18], in other activities in markets[19] and different cottage industries.[20] The construction industry is also one of the most important sectors where hazardous working environments prevail, especially for children. Operating or working near the dangerous machinery may lead to non-fatal or fatal injuries among the children. Strenuous labour, in addition to fatigue, can affect the musculo-skeletal development of the children. Long work hours, are responsible for often denying the child labourers a basic school education, normal social interaction, personal development and emotional support from their family. Continuous work in sitting postures at ill-lighted and ill-ventilated room affects the physical growth. The verbal and physical child abuse has its undoubted impact on social and mental growth of the child.

Magnitude of the problem

The child labour has still remained a major concern, despite the reported decline from 1995 to 2000. In 2016, it was estimated that ~150 million children under the age of 14 are engaged in labour worldwide, with most of them working under circumstances that denies them a playful childhood and jeopardize their health.[21] Most working children are 11-14 years, but around 60 million are 5-11 years old.[22] Though the exact numbers of the distribution of child labour are not available globally, the available statistics show that 96% of child workers are in Africa, Asia and Latin America.[23]

Research into the impacts of child labour suggests several associations between child labour and adverse health outcomes. Child labour is associated with certain exposures like silica in industries, and HIV infection in prostitution.[24] Additionally, as child labour is associated with maternal illiteracy and poverty, working children are more susceptible to malnutrition,[25] which predisposes them to various diseases.

A meta-analysis on the topic was published in 2007.[26] However, authors reported only an association of child labour with higher mortality and morbidity than in the general population, without reporting individual outcome specific effects.[27] Another meta-analysis investigated the effects of adverse childhood experiences (ACEs), including child labour, on health. They reported that ACEs are risk factors for many adverse health outcomes.[28]

Studies on occupational health of children and adolescents in India

The magnitude of child labour in India has witnessed a decline over more than two decades, both in terms of magnitude and workforce participation rates. As per the National Sample Survey data, India's child workforce was estimated at 2.155 crore in 1983.[1] As per the Census 2011 data, out of the total child population of 25.96 crore in the age group (5-14) years, 1.01 crore (3.9%) were working, either as 'main worker' or as 'marginal worker'. In addition, more than 4.27 crore children were out of school.[2]

The Census data of children in the age group of 5-14 working in the non-agricultural sector has been classified according to occupations. Though the occupations in the Census data do not match with the occupations listed as hazardous under the Child Labour (Prohibition and Regulation) Act, a tentative segregation of data into hazardous and non-hazardous occupations gives a broad estimation of children working in different occupations. As per this data, 36.43 lakh children in the age group of 5-14 years are working in non-agricultural sector in the country, out of which 12.19 lakh children are working in hazardous occupations. The distribution of child workers in some major hazardous occupations is presented in Table-1.[3]

Table-1: Number of child workers (5-14 years) engaged in Hazardous Occupations as per 2001 Census

Occupation	No. of child workers
Pan, *Bidi* and Cigarettes	252574
Construction	208833
Domestic workers	185505
Spinning/weaving	128984
Brick-kilns, tiles	84972
Dhabas/Restaurants/Hotels/Motels	70934
Auto-workshop, vehicle repairs	49893
Gem-cutting, Jewellery	37489
Carpet-making	32647
Ceramic	18894
Agarbatti, *Dhoop* and Detergent making	13583
Others	135162
Total	1219470

In spite of a large child labour force in the country, a relatively small number of epidemiological studies covering the occupational health perspective of the child labour is available. Non-cooperation from the employers, parents and even the child labourers themselves is the major factor responsible for the paucity of such studies. Awareness about the illegality of the child labour and fear of losing cheap labour are the chief reasons for non-cooperation on the part of the employers/occupiers. Loss of income due to child losing the job subsequent to the participation in such study as a threat from the employer is the primary concern for the parents for such non-cooperation. Detection of the adverse health effects due to hazardous workplace exposure with resultant loss of job perceived by the child worker himself and forbidding pressures by the parents are major factors for non-cooperation.

Epidemiologic evidence suggests that a greater impact of some occupational exposures on the health of children as compared with adults.[4] A study among young and child workers revealed that 85.7% were unaware of the materials they were using. Sixty-nine percent of children were working in improper light, 71% of workers experienced high levels of noise, 83% were working in high temperatures and 55.3% were working with improper ventilation. Health problems experienced by children included joint pains, backache, vertigo, numbness of fingers and fatigue.[5] Another study found that the most common reason for taking up child work was to earn money needed by parents. Current health problems reported were skin infection, diarrhea, fever, upper respiratory tract infection, visual problems and musculoskeletal disorders. Thirty-six percent of these children were underweight. Fifty-three percent of the children had at least one health problem during the survey period. Twenty-eight percent of the children reported that they had inju-ries.[6]

Some of the studies on occupational health of children and adolescents employed in industries in different parts of India are discussed below:

Gem Polishing Industries, Jaipur, India[29,30]

This cross sectional study was conducted in different working units of the gem polishing industries of Jaipur. The raw stones are subjected to different work processes before they attain the semiprecious stone characteristics as a finished product. The raw stones are cut with the help of a rotating saw to remove those parts that contain some impurities. After sorting the raw stones on the basis of their colours, the stones are preshaped into the desired shape and size with the help of a rotating wheel. This is followed by multiple faceting to impart a shine to the stone. Finally, these stones are polished with chromic oxide powder and quartz powder to increase the shine and lustre. Some of these finished materials are used for preparing neck jewelleries and are converted into beads with a drill. The cutting, faceting and drilling processes pose the hazards like cuts, abrasions and piercing type of injuries, respectively making the children prone to such injuries during work.

The study included randomly selected 588 child labourers (not yet 18-year-old), out of which 270 (46.1%) were boys and 316 (53.9%) girls. The high proportion of female subjects probably reflect the fact that females constitute a source of cheap labour. This may further worsen the female literacy rates in the country. The mean age of these child labourers was 11.3 (±5.3) years with mean duration of work for 20.2 (±0.9) months and the mean hours of work of 6.3 ±1.9) per day. Though most of the children have taken the job only recently, many of them work for almost six hours or more per day under unsafe working conditions of ill-ventilation, poor illumination, awkward posture, unhygienic conditions, and dust exposures. These unsafe working conditions along with working beyond bodily capacity by these children set in an early fatigue. All these factors are also known to affect the human health in adverse ways independently. In most instances, parents compelled the child to take up the job. Although the job was supposed to increase the family income substantially, more than half of the working children earned less than five rupees (US$ 0.08) per day.

The most frequent complaints reported were injuries to finger (37.5%), eye strain (29.5%), headache (28.8%), and respiratory symptoms (27%). Other complaints included gastrointestinal symptoms (e.g., abdominal pain, nausea, vomiting, and diarrhea) in 10.1%, musculoskeletal symptoms (e.g., back pain, pain in limbs, neck pain, and joint pains) in 4.9% and skin disease (e.g., scabies, and dermatitis) in 1.5%.

Almost a quarter of the working children had one or other morbidities. The most common morbidity was repeated finger injuries. This is important as such injuries combined with poor personal hygiene may result in wound contamination and more complications. The reported eyestrain and headache may partly be attributed to the high degree of visual concentration, which is required for the processes like sorting and calibration of semi-precious stones. Moreover, the poor personal hygiene may also be associated with poor ocular hygiene that would cause more problems as contamination of eyes with certain chemicals such as chromium oxide, quartz powder, etc. causes irritation and lacrimation.

The gender-wise differences in the prevalence of injuries showed no significant difference suggesting that the work processes are equally injury prone irrespective of the gender. The observation that the children working for more than 6 hours sustained more injuries than those working for a shorter time each day can be attributed to both mental as well as physical fatigue, thereby increasing the chance of injury as the precise nature of the work demands more concentration. The shorter duration of employment was found to be a statistically significant risk factor for the occurrence of injuries as children working for more than 2 years reported fewer injuries than those working less than 2 years. This may be attributed to the lack of proper awareness of the injury prone nature of machine parts and processes and lack of required skill development during a shorter work duration.

A sub sample of 67 children was subjected to the questionnaire based assessment of injury care practices. The majority children reported frequent injury inflictions. The causes identified were rapidly revolving sharp cutting wheels for injuries to fingers and small pieces of cut stone flying out at high speed for eye injuries. The majority of the subjects mentioned that the fingers were common sites for incisive types of injury. This is attributed to the unsafe manufacturing process because there is no enclosure of the sharp moving parts. A small proportion of children did not care about washing hands after getting the injury. This is very important as wound contamination can hamper normal healing processes and breach in the integrity of skin may lead to enhanced absorption of harmful chemicals such as chromium oxide, quartz powder, etc. used in the polishing process. Further, about half of the subjects reported applying medications known to heal the wound, while nearly 30% of the subjects didn't care for the wound and yet another 11% either applied harmful substances such as mustard oil or kerosene oil. Such poor injury care practices by the children are also reported by other studies.[29, 30] Such practices should be stopped and awareness on proper wound care should be generated. Under the assumption that latex material will help prevent the cut injuries the children practiced wearing ruptured balloons as protective devices. However, their efficacy was not evidenced by the fact that they still suffered from injuries in spite of majority of them wore it necessitating the use of more efficient protective measures such as hard finger caps.

Stone quarries

This cross-sectional study was undertaken in the stone quarries operating in the central part of India. The industry falls under the unorganised sector and usually employs contract workers for different quarrying and supportive activities. The stone quarrying units operate on the surface at low heights and involve manual work activities. Relatively large, stout tools (mostly used by adult workers) are used for initial breaking of stones. Small hand tools like hammers are used in breaking the stones into smaller ones. After this, the stones are loaded onto trucks (usually smaller vehicles) and dispatched. The overall work environment is open under the sun with full exposure to light and heat. Hardly any personal protective equipment is used by the workers.

Young (child and adolescent) workers are also working in such units. In the absence of information on the exact number of such workers, an estimated number of 2,000 obtained from local authorities were used for calculation of sample size. With the prevalence of injury predicted as 10%, the minimum sample size for a 5% level of significance was calculated as 130. From 12 units randomly selected from the list of 36 operating units in the area, 147 child and adolescent workers participated in the study. With the help of an interviewer-administered questionnaire, detailed information of their demographic as well as personal, occupational and work-related morbidity (including occupational injuries) was collected.

The results showed that 126 (85.7%) workers were children (age <14 years) and the rest (14.3%) were adolescents (age ≥14 years and <18 years) with the mean age as 11.34 (± 1.9) years and mean body mass index (BMI) of 14.9 (± 1.8). The majority (65%) children were illiterate, whereas the rest attained only up to primary level education. Their mean job duration was 26.3 (± 14.6) months, the mean work hours were 4.56 (± 1.7) per day and the mean income was 27 (± 26) Indian rupees per day. The majority of the workers (90.5%) were engaged in the act of stone breaking, while 9.5% were engaged in the loading activity. The morbidity pattern revealed that the workers were suffering from repeated injuries (28.6%), recurrent backache (8.8%) and joint pain (15.6%), cough (6.8%) and breathlessness (2%). Musculoskeletal morbidity (backache, joint pain or both) was reported by 21.8% subjects. The univariate analysis of the data showed that the musculoskeletal morbidity was the only characteristic of the workers that showed a significant effect on injury causation.

However, it was observed on the multivariate analysis that age, nature of work, work hours per day, musculoskeletal complaint and education had a significant effect on workplace injuries.

The hands and legs are the most predominant sites of injuries in these workers. The young workers are mostly engaged in breaking bigger stones into smaller pieces as well as loading the stones onto a vehicle. They do their job manually using small tools, which are usually designed for adults and hence may be uncomfortable for young workers leading to the common occurrence of hand and leg injuries. They work on barefoot and without any protective covers for the hands. In addition, this kind of job also considerably predisposes to other injuries, especially those of the eyes.

There is epidemiologic evidence suggesting that such occupational exposures may have a greater impact of on the health of children as compared with adults.[31] So far as workplace injuries are concerned, there are reports showing that young workers confront occupational injuries very frequently.[32] A workplace injury poses additional risk on the growing systems of a young or child worker apart from the injurious effect of adverse occupational hazards. Hence, prevention of such injuries is of utmost importance, and recognizing the determinants of such injuries is the key to protection. Although studies conducted with child and young workers have already highlighted that work-related injury is a major problem area, very few studies have explored the determinants comprehensively. The present study has made an effort to identify the probable factors responsible for such work injuries so that this knowledge can ultimately help in their prevention.

The finding of younger age, stone breaking and longer working hours being contributing factors for workplace injuries necessitates that specific intervention measures be aimed at alleviating these components. Mechanisation of jobs, redesign of the workplace, stopping employment of children (up to 14 years of age) in such work, a proper work rest schedule and shorter working hours per day may be effective interventions to lessen such injuries.

The job contents and procedures may also be suitably modified. Mechanisation of such jobs should be seriously considered. Tools used for work may also be redesigned to suit the young workers, and the working area (workplace) for such work may be suitably rearranged (e.g., instead of breaking stones on site, the stones may be mechanically shifted to a nearby shade for further breaking/processing). Taking special precautions, especially during stone breaking, and arranging for suitable personal protective equipment to safeguard hands and legs during work may reduce the occurrence of work-related injuries in a significant manner. Training of young workers with regard to safe work practices (especially material handling), provision for education, musculoskeletal morbidity alleviation measures, suitable restriction of work hours per day and awareness generation among parents regarding the imminent danger of such labour in their children will ensure a positive impact in protecting young and child workers from occupational injuries. Special emphasis should be given to hand and leg injuries, and provision of safety shoes and proper hand gloves may minimize such injuries when combined with other steps of job and workplace modification.

Footwear industry[33,34]

The Indian footwear industry, a significant segment of the leather industry, ranks second in the world next to China. The industry is labour intensive and is concentrated in the small and cottage industry sectors. The major production centers India are Chennai, Ranipet, Ambur in Tamil Nadu, Mumbai in Maharashtra, Kanpur and Agra in Uttar Pradesh, Jalandhar in Punjab and Delhi. Children are employed in the manufacture of shoes, particularly in the Agra. It is estimated that as many as 25,000 children may be involved in shoe making, both for the domestic and international markets. The processes in the footwear making include *chappals* last making, pattern cutting, clicking, sewing, assembling and finishing. Each of these processes is associated with certain type of hazard and workers, especially child-workers are more prone to such hazards.

Children between 10 and 15 years old are mainly employed in assembling shoes. Some 80 percent of the children work for contractors at home. Children work on soling (fixing upper portions of shoes to leather or rubber soles with glue). Children in cramped poorly lit rooms suffer from continuous skin contact with industrial adhesives and breathe vapours from glues. These child workers are exposed to leather dust, physical factors like poor illumination, noise and poor ventilation, and fumes emanating from adhesive solutions. These adhesives contain a mixture of organic solvents such as hexane, benzene, propane, dimethyl heptane, cyclohexane, xylene, cyclopentane. Most children suffer from respiratory problems, lung diseases and skin infections through constant exposure to glue and fumes. Poor illumination and possibly organic solvents fumes can lead to eyestrain (asthenopia), a symptom complex that involves sensations of irritation to the eye itself, changes in vision (such as blurred or double vision), and associated symptoms such as headache.

The present study aimed to assess the prevalence of eyestrain among 139 child labourers (not completed 18 years) working in the footwear making unit at Agra as exposed group and 160 age and socio-economically matched children from government run NCLP schools from the neighbouring areas as comparison group. Eyestrain was assessed through evaluation of self-reported common symptoms including itching, burning, lacrimating or irritated eyes; tired or heavy eyes and difficulty seeing clearly (including blurred or double vision). Univariate and multivariate analysis of eyestrain was carried out according to the risk factors which included age ≥12 years, female sex, daily working duration ≥4 hours, and experience in the job >2years. The age, daily working hours and duration of employment were arbitrarily dichotomised.

The mean age of the child labourers was 10.8 ± 1.5 years while the same for the comparison group was 11.0 ± 1.5 years. The difference was statistically non-significant. The mean duration of work exposure for the child labourers was 20.5 ± 16.2 months while the mean daily hours of work were 3.9 ± 1.9 hours.

The prevalence of eyestrain in child labourers was 25.9%, which was significantly higher than the 12.4% prevalence in comparison group subjects (*P*=0.01). Working children of footwear making units were at 2.4 times higher risk of developing eyestrain as compared to comparison group children (OR=2.44; 95% CI: 0.81-2.69), though statistically non-significant. The gender wise comparison showed that boys had more asthenopia than girls, which can be attributed to high proportion of boys working in the process of soling where organic solvents are used. The organic solvent fumes irritate the eyes resulting in lacrimation and itching.[33] The poor illumination at workplace further adds to the eyestrain. The high prevalence in > 12-year-old can partly be attributed to the cumulative exposure to the poor illumination and solvent fumes causing strain on eyes. The proportion of those complaining eyestrain was more in those working for more than 4 hours daily. This can be partly attributed to the development of fatigue. A study among visual display users working for more than 4 hours a day was found to be a significant risk factor.[34] A non-significantly higher prevalence of eyestrain in those working for more than 2 years as compared to those who have worked for lesser duration was also observed.

Conclusions and the Way Forward

The paucity of scientific/epidemiological work in the country on the front of occupational health of working children and adolescents, is highly disappointing. Lack of awareness about the occupational health among the medical professionals, employers, parents and child workers, those concerned with the implementation of the existing legislation and other stake holders are the major factors for the deficit of required knowledge on the subject. Non-cooperation (for participation in occupational health studies), apathy and ignorance of the employers, parents and child workers, migration of the workers, etc. also play a very important and negative role for the management of the issue.

The cross-sectional studies conducted in three different industries viz. gem polishing, stone quarries and footwear manufacturing discussed in this paper have reported various occupational health morbidities/symptoms such as injuries, musculoskeletal (backache, pain in limbs, neck pain and joint pains, etc.), eyestrain (asthenopia), headache and respiratory symptoms like cough and breathlessness. Other complaints included gastrointestinal symptoms (abdominal pain, nausea, vomiting, and diarrhoea) and skin disease (scabies, and dermatitis). It is also observed that these symptoms/morbidities occur on repetitive/recurrent manner. The lack of understanding and necessary training for the work processes, unhygienic work practices, non-use of personal protective devices and working with the equipments that are meant for adults are identified as the prime factors for occurrence of these health effects.

It should be noted that the cross-sectional design of the above studies has certain limitations. The studies suffer from the restriction of lack of temporality (have no dimension of time), so they cannot support conclusions on the risk of disease, nor on cause-effect relationship. Furthermore, as these studies are conducted only in one set up, the generalizability of the findings to all those engaged in similar work or to all those working children is limited. Nevertheless, this type of study is used to generate descriptive statistics regarding the disease/outcome burden in a population, or to determine background exposure rates. Cross-sectional studies may also exhibit recall bias, because disease or assessment of disease may influence subjects' responses to questionnaires. To overcome these limitations, further studies using analytical epidemiology should be planned.[7]

The elimination of child labour is a long-term objective. It is well appreciated that much more research needs to be conducted in the field. However, one important aspect of the management of the occupational health appears to be totally neglected. It is a well-known fact that in spite of no curative treatment available, the occupational morbidities can be easily prevented, as is evident from these and the studies conducted world over. The causal agents for the occupational health effects–machinery, ventilation, illumination, chemicals, etc. being present in the workplace itself, are easily identifiable and almost always measurable and therefore, controllable. There is sufficient knowledge and means to prevent the harm by controlling these agents. Implementing appropriate control measures aided with regular training and awareness programmes as an urgent short-term action can go a long way by avoiding injury and harm to working children with the preservation of their health.

Prevention is always considered better than the cure for the management of health. The healthy working population with decreased sickness absenteeism/ premature death and expenditure on medical treatment can efficiently and effectively

7. Cross Sectional Study-An Overview|Sciencedirect Topics. (n.d.). Retrieved from https://www.sciencedirect.com/topics/biochemistry-genetics-and-molecular-biology

work for a longer tenure with increased production, as is one of the important concerns from the industry's point of view. If the costs of a long lived, healthy and productive working population in general and the working children in particular, leading to a useful and meaningful life for the nation can be calculated and included to the cost benefit analysis, the **prevention may not just remain better but invariably, cheaper than the cure.**

References

1. Parker D.L. Child labour. The impact of economic exploitation on the health and welfare of children. *Minn. Med.* 1997; 80:10-2.
2. Hilowitz J. *Child Labour: A Textbook for University Students.* International Labour Office, 2004.
3. Global estimates of child labour: Results and trends, 2012-2016. ILO, Geneva, 2017: 11.
4. Child labour in India. ilo.org/india; www.ilo.org/sacl.
5. Child Labour (Prohibition and Regulation) Act, 1986. https://labour.gov.in/sites/default/files/ act_3.pdf.
6. IPEC. Ministry of Labour & Employment. https://labour.gov.in/childlabour/ipec.
7. Jyoti Rao. Assessing Child Domestic Labour in India. UNICEF. unicef.in/Story/1139/Assessing-Child-Domestic-Labour-in-India
8. Sudeep Limaye, Milind S. Pandey. A study of Child labour in India—Magnitude and challenges. Available from: https://www.researchgate.net/publication/261709693_ A_study_of_Child_labour_in_India_-_Magnitude_and_challenges [accessed Jun 11 2019].
9. Lieten G.K. The Causes for Child Labour in India: the Poverty Analysis. Available from www.childlabour. net/documents/kristoffel%20publicaties/PovertyAnalysis.pdf (Accessed 6th February, 2012).
10. ILO (2002) International Labour Organisation. Decent work and Informal Economy. 2008, Available from www.ilo.org/public/english/employment/infeco/download/report6.pdf (Accessed 6th February, 2014).
11. Occupational Risks and Children's Health. Children's Health and the Environment. Global Occupational Health Programme. WHO Training Package for the Health Sector. World Health Organisation. www.who.int/ceh.
12. Hurst P. Health and child labour in agriculture. Food Nutr Bull 2007; 28: 364-71.
13. International Labour Organisation. The end of child labour: Within reach. Global report under the follow-up to the ILO Declaration on Fundamental Principles and Rights at Work. Geneva: International Labour Organisation, 2006.
14. Chiavegatto C.V., Carneiro A.P., Dias E.C., Nascimento M.S. Diagnosis of severe silicosis in young adults working in stone polishing and mining in Minas Gerais, Brazil. Int. J. Occup. Environ Health 2010; 16: 147-50.
15. Omokhodion F.O., Omokhodion S.L. Health problems and other characteristics of child workers in a market in Ibadan. Afr. J. Med. Med. Sci. 2001; 30: 81-5.

16. Baig L.A., Rasheed S., Zameer M. Health and safety measures available for young labourers in the cottage industries of Karachi. J. Coll. Physicians Surg. Pak. 2005; 15: 7-10.
17. UNICEF. The state of the world's children 2016: a fair chance for every child. Technical Report, United Nations Children's Fund (UNICEF) 2016.
18. Roggero P., Mangiaterra V., Bustreo F. et. al. The health impact of child labour in developing countries: evidence from cross-country data. *Am J Public Health* 2007;97(2):271-5.
19. Hughes K., Bellis M.A., Hardcastle K.A. et al. The effect of multiple adverse childhood experiences on health: a systematic review and meta-analysis. *Lancet Public Health* 2017;2(8): e356-66.
20. Fassa A.G., Facchini L.A., Dall'agnol M.M., Christiani D.C. Child labour and health: problems and perspectives. Int. J. Occup. Environ Health 2000; 6: 55-62.
21. R.R. Tiwari, A. Saha. Morbidity Profile of Child Labour at Gem Polishing Units of Jaipur, India. www.theijoem.com Vol. 5, Num. 3; July 2014.
22. Rajnarayan R. Tiwari, Asim Saha, Jagdish R. Parikh, Habibullah N. Saiyed. Injuries and injury care among child labourers in gem polishing industries in Jaipur, India. J Occup Health 2004; 46: 216-219.
23. R.R. Tiwari and S.P. Zodpey: Knowledge and practices of urban and rural high school children regarding minor injuries. Indian J Community Health 5, 6-11 (1999).
24. R.R. Tiwari, P.N. Kulkarni and G.B. Ganveer: Wound care in animal bites. The Antiseptic 96, 236-237 (1999).
25. Asim Saha and H.G. Sadhu. Occupational Injury Proneness in Young Workers: A Survey in Stone Quarries. J. Occup Health 2013; 55: 333-339.
26. Tiwari, R.R. Child labour in footwear industry: Possible occupational health hazards. Indian J. Occup. Environ. Med. 2005. 9:1; 7-9.
27. Rajnarayan, R. Tiwari. Eyestrain in Working Children of Footwear Making Units of Agra, India. Indian Pediatrics. April 2013. 50: 411-413.
28. Piccoli, B.A. critical appraisal of current knowledge and future directions of ergophthalmology: consensus document of the ICOH Committee on 'Work and Vision'. Ergonomics. 2003;46:384-406.
29. Sánchez-Román FR, Pérez-Lucio C., Juárez-Ruíz C., Vélez-Zamora N.M., Jiménez-Villarruel M. Risk factors for asthenopia among computer terminal operators. Salud Publica Mex. 1996;38:189-96.

□

5

Legal Perspective for Child Specific Health Care Policies

—D.C. Baxi

Abstract

In spite of the Constitutional provisions, perspective, an adequate framework of Legislation, implementing Departments of the States, Constitutional monitoring bodies like National Human Rights Commission and National Commission on Protection Child Rights, the issue of infant mortality rate or malnutrition or health-related issues of a Child has marginally increased and hence require more attention. This can be considered as a serious issue to deal with, as the children below the 0-14 years' accounts for about 27.71 % (about 35.10 Crores) of the total population of the country. Being the most significant strength and future human resource of the nation, the author brings the attention towards the need for quality and effective implementation of Acts and Schemes, supported by effective monitoring.

Background

As per the data of India Demographic Profile, 2017, the children below the 0-14 years accounts for about 27.71 % (about 35.10 Crores) of the total population of the Country which will be the biggest strength of our Country in the World in decades to follow, if we can manage their total development, i.e. Mental, Physical, Social, Educational and Cultural Development. Inclusive development of a child before and after birth has always remained challenging, despite Constitutional perspectives, Legislative framework, Administrative monitoring and policies and programmes. The infant mortality rate shows that about 41 child dies per 1000 childbirth (India Demographic Profile, 2017).

There may be various reasons for Infant Mortality Rate and Child's lack of inclusive development, and one of the reasons that people lack awareness about Child's rights. The very purpose of this paper is to raise awareness among people about constitutional, legal, administrative aspects, policies and programs implemented by the Gujarat government on child health care.

UN Convention on the Rights of the Child

In 1959 the UN General Assembly adopted the Declaration of the Rights of the Child, which defines children's rights to protection, education, health care, shelter and proper nutrition. The UN Convention on the rights of Child with respect to health is listed as under;

Article 6 (Survival and Development): Children have the right to live. Governments should ensure healthy survival and development of children.

Article 23 (Children with disabilities): Children who have any disability have the right to special care and support, as well as all the rights in the Convention so that they can live full and independent lives.

Article 24 (Health and health services): Children have the right to good quality health care–the best health care possible–to safe drinking water, nutritious food, a clean and safe environment, and information to help them stay healthy. Rich countries should help poorer countries achieve this.

Children and the Sustainable Development Goals

For 15 years, the Millennium Development Goals (MDGs) were a guiding force on many issues affecting the lives of children, young people and their families. Over this time, tremendous progress was made in reducing preventable child deaths, getting more children into schools, reducing extreme poverty and in ensuring more people have access to safe water and nutritious food.

However, progress has been uneven and many of the most pressing issues for the world—including addressing inequalities, promoting inclusive economic growth, protecting children from violence and combating climate change-were not adequately covered in the Millennium Development Goals.

With the adoption of the new Sustainable Development Goals (SDGs) in September of 2015, world leaders have committed to ending poverty by 2030; however, unless accelerated efforts are made, by 2030.

Constitutional provisions and perspective on Rights related to health and overall development of Child

The Constitution of India under Article 15 (3)—Provides for the guarantee of a right to equality without any discrimination, empowers State to make special provisions relating to Child

The Constitution of India under the Article 39(e)—State to direct its policy towards securing the health and strength of tender age of children and are not abused are not forced by economic necessity to enter avocations unsuited to their age or strength.

The Constitution of India under the Article 39 (f)—State to direct its policy towards securing that children are given opportunities and facilities to develop in a healthy manner and conditions of freedom and dignity; and childhood and youth are protected against exploitation and moral and material abandonment

The Constitution of India under Article 42—Provides for just and humane conditions of work and maternity relief. The said article foresees child care by women employees during pregnancy, and it commands the employer to provide certain benefits to such female employees.

The Constitution of India under Article 45—State shall endeavour to provide early childhood care and education for all children until they complete the age of fourteen years.

The subject Health is under the State list of the Constitution of India. The Item No:6 of the State list provides for Public health and sanitation; hospitals and dispensaries and Item No. 9 of the State list provides for Relief for the disabled and unemployable.

Thus, fundamentally the Constitution of India fully empowers the State Governments to formulate relevant Laws, policies and programmes for the protection of child rights, including health, nutrition etc.

Constitutional Bodies to Look After the Rights of the Child

(1) The National Commission on Protection of Child Rights: The National Commission for Protection of Child Rights (NCPCR) was set up in March 2007 under the Commissions for Protection of Child Rights (CPCR) Act, 2005, an Act of Parliament (December 2005). NCPCR is a statutory body under the CPCR Act, 2005 under the administrative control of the Ministry of Women & Child Development, Government of India. The Commission's Mandate is to ensure that all Laws, Policies, Programmes, and Administrative Mechanisms are in consonance with the Child Rights perspective as enshrined in the Constitution of India and also the UN Convention on the Rights of the Child. The Child is defined as a person in the 0 to 18 years age group.[8],[9]

The Commission visualises a rights-based view that flows into national policies and programs, along with nuanced state, district, and block-level answers, taking care of each region's specifics and strengths. It seeks a deeper penetration into communities and households in order to touch each Child and expects all authorities at a higher level to take into account the ground experiences gathered on the field. Thus the Commission considers the State's indispensable role, sound institution-

8. (18th March, 2018). National Commission for Protection of Child Rights (NCPCR)–Steel .... Retrieved 14th June, 2019, from http://steelframeofindia.org/national-commission-for-protection-of-child-rights-ncpcr/

9. (n.d.). List of allocated IP addresses in 139.59.0.0 ...-Quick Ip Look Up. Retrieved 14th June, 2019, from http://quick-ip-lookup.info/139.59.1/index.jsp

building processes, respect for decentralisation at local and community level, and greater societal concern for kids and their well-being.[10]

The National Commission on Protection of Child Rights monitors the implementation of THE COMMISSIONS FOR PROTECTION OF CHILDRIGH RIGHTS ACT, 2005. The said Act is implemented by the Women and Child Development Department at National level and Social Justice and Empowerment Department in Gujarat State.

The said Act provides for the constitution of a National Commission and State Commissions for Protection of Child Rights and Children's Courts for providing speedy trial of offences against children or of violation of child rights and for matters connected therewith or incidental thereto.

CHAPTER II of the NCPCR Act, 2005 provides for the NATIONAL COMMISSION FOR PROTECTION OF CHILD RIGHTS and accordingly Government of India has constituted the National Commission under the Section 3 of the NCPCR Act, 2005.

CHAPTER III of the NCPCR Act, 2005 provides for the . FUNCTIONS AND POWERS OF THE COMMISSION

Section 13.

(1) The Commission shall perform all or any of the following functions, namely: Examine and review the safeguards provided by or under any law for the time being in force for the protection of child rights and recommend measures for their effective implementation;

Present to the Central Government, annually and at such other intervals, as the Commission may deem fit, reports upon the working of those safeguards;

Inquire into violation of child rights and recommend initiation of proceedings in such cases;

Examine all factors that inhibit the enjoyment of rights of children affected by terrorism, communal violence, riots, natural disaster, domestic violence, HIV /AIDS, trafficking: maltreatment, torture and exploitation, pornography and prostitution and recommend appropriate remedial measures;

Look into the matters relating to children in need of special care and protection including children in distress, marginalised and disadvantaged children, children in, conflict with law, juveniles, children without family and children of prisoners and recommend appropriate remedial measures;

Study treaties and other international instruments and undertake periodical review of existing policies, programmes and other activities on child rights and make

10. "Recruitment-National Commission for Protection of Child Rights ...." http://ncpcr.gov.in/index1.php?lang=1&level=0&linkid=33&lid=906. Accessed 17 Jun. 2019.

recommendations for their effective implementation in the best interest of children;

Undertake and promote research in the field of child rights;

Spread child rights literacy among various sections of the society and promote .awareness of the safeguards available for protection of these rights through publications, the media, seminars and other available means;

Inspect or cause to be inspected any juvenile custodial home, or any other place of residence or institution meant for children, under the control of the Central Government or any State Government or any other authority, including any institution run by a social organisation; where children are detained or lodged for the purpose of treatment, reformation or protection and take up with these authorities for remedial action, if found necessary;

Inquire in to complaints and take suo-motu notice of matters relating to, deprivation and violation of child rights non-implementation of laws providing for protection and development of children;

Non-compliance of policy decisions, guidelines or instructions aimed at, mitigating hardships to and ensuring welfare of the children and to provide relief to such children; or take up the issues arising out of such matters with appropriate authorities; and,

1. Such other functions as it may consider necessary for the promotion of child rights and any other matter incidental to the above functions.[11]
2. The Commission shall not inquire into any matter which is pending before a State Commission or any other Commission duly constituted under any law for the time being in force.

CHAPTER IV of the NCPCR Act, 2005 provides for the constitution of the STATE COMMISSIONS FOR PROTECTION OF CHILD Rights

Section 17

1. A State Government may constitute a body to be known as the, (name of the State) Commission for Protection of Child Rights to exercise the powers conferred upon, and to perform the functions assigned to, a State Commission under this Chapter.
2. The State Commission shall consist of the following Members, namely:
   (a) a Chairperson who is a person of eminence and has done outstanding work for promoting the welfare of children; and,
   (b) six Members, out of which at, least two shall be women, from the following fields, to be appointed by the State Government from amongst persons of eminence, ability, integrity, standing and experience in:

11. Functions and Powers-National Commission for Protection of children http://ncpcr.gov.in/index1.php?lang=1&level=1&&sublinkid=5&lid=600

(i) education;
(ii) child health, care, welfare or child development; .
(iii) juvenile justice or care of neglected or marginalised children or children with disabilities;
(iv) elimination of child labour or children in distress;
(v) child psychology or sociology; and
(vi) laws relating to children

(2) The National Human Rights Commission: The International Movement for Human Rights was reinforced by the adoption of the Universal Declaration of Human Rights (UDHR) by the United Nations General Assembly on 10th December, 1948. For the first time in human history, the Declaration, drafted as' a common standard of achievement for all peoples and nations,' outlined basic civil, political, economic, social and cultural rights that should be enjoyed by all people.[12]

The Convention on the Rights of the Child Adopted and opened for signature, ratification and accession by General Assembly resolution 44/25 of 20th November, 1989 and came into force on 2nd September, 1990, in accordance with article 49.

Article 24

1. States Parties recognize the right of the child to the enjoyment of the highest attainable standard of health and to facilities for the treatment of illness and rehabilitation of health. States Parties shall strive to ensure that no child is deprived of his or her right of access to such health care services.
2. States Parties shall pursue full implementation of this right and, in particular, shall take appropriate measures:
   (a) To diminish infant and child mortality;
   (b) To ensure the provision of necessary medical assistance and health care to all children with emphasis on the development of primary health care;
   (c) To combat disease and malnutrition, including within the framework of primary health care, through, inter alia, the application of readily available technology and through the provision of adequate nutritious foods and clean drinking-water, taking into consideration the dangers and risks of environmental pollution;
   (d) To ensure appropriate pre-natal and post-natal health care for mothers;
   (e) To ensure that all segments of society, in particular parents and children, are informed, have access to education and are supported in the use of basic knowledge of child health and nutrition, the advantages of

12. 'International Law-OHCHR.' https://www.ohchr.org/en/professionalinterest/pages/internationallaw.aspx. Accessed 17 Jun. 2019.

breastfeeding, hygiene and environmental sanitation and the prevention of accidents;

(f) To develop preventive health care, guidance for parents and family planning education and services.

3. States Parties shall take all effective and appropriate measures with a view to abolishing traditional practices prejudicial to the health of children.
4. States Parties undertake to promote and encourage international co-operation with a view to achieving progressively the full realisation of the right recognised in the present article. In this regard, particular account shall be taken of the needs of developing countries. [13]

Article 25

States Parties recognize the right of a child who has been placed by the competent authorities for the purposes of care, protection or treatment of his or her physical or mental health, to a periodic review of the treatment provided to the child and all other circumstances relevant to his or her placement.

Article 26

1. States Parties shall recognize for every child the right to benefit from social security, including social insurance, and shall take the necessary measures to achieve the full realisation of this right in accordance with their national law.
2. The benefits should, where appropriate, be granted, taking into account the resources and the circumstances of the child and persons having responsibility for the maintenance of the child, as well as any other consideration relevant to an application for benefits made by or on behalf of the child.

Article 27

1. States Parties recognize the right of every child to a standard of living adequate for the child's physical, mental, spiritual, moral and social development.
2. The parent(s) or others responsible for the child have the primary responsibility to secure, within their abilities and financial capacities, the conditions of living necessary for the child's development.
3. States Parties, in accordance with national conditions and within their means, shall take appropriate measures to assist parents and others responsible for the child to implement this right and shall in case of need provide material assistance and support programmes, particularly with regard to nutrition, clothing and housing.

13. "Convention on the Rights of the Child-OHCHR." https://www.ohchr.org/en/professionalinterest/pages/crc.aspx. Accessed 17 Jun. 2019.

4. States Parties shall take all appropriate measures to secure the recovery of maintenance for the child from the parents or other persons having financial responsibility for the child, both within the State Party and from abroad. In particular, where the person having financial responsibility for the child lives in a State different from that of the child, States Parties shall promote the accession to international agreements or the conclusion of such agreements, as well as the making of other appropriate arrangements.

Our Country has ratified the Convention on the Rights of the Child (CRC), 1989 on 11th December, 1992

India's National Human Rights Commission (NHRC) was created in 1993, as a response to increasing international awareness of human rights, after India entered the global economic arena. The United Nations Human Rights Commission adopted the 'Paris Principles', a guiding light for resolving international human rights issues.

The National Human Rights Commission in India derives its power from The Protection of Human Rights Act (TPHRA). Its composition enjoys a robust legal fortitude, with a panel that features former judges of the Supreme Court, High Court, and people experienced in human rights policy and execution. It is presided by a retired Chief Justice of India, and Chairpersons of national commissions of key human rights concerns-Minorities, India's Scheduled Classes and Tribes, and Women.

The Functions of the National Human Rights Commission

NHRC today enjoys a very wide mandate, receiving over 70,000 complaints every year. Through recommendations and requests for inquiries, the Commission seeks to resolve human rights violations across India.

Child Rights in India: A Vital Function of the NHRC

Child rights are often considered the most critical of all human rights reforms as they define the future for both current and upcoming Indian generations. 'Children's rights' have radically changed; from the middle ages, which refused to recognize the concept of a childhood and saw children work side by side with adults to today's understanding of nurturing a child's unique identity while providing him access to necessities.

Children's rights apply to the special protection and care that minors under the age of 18 are provided. Based on international legislations, these include right to association with both parents, physical protection, food, free education, healthcare, and legal protection from violence or discrimination.

THE PROTECTION OF HUMAN RIGHTS ACT, 1993—An Act to provide for the constitution of a National Human Rights Commission, State Human Rights Commission in States and Human Rights Courts for better protection of human rights and for matters connected therewith or incidental thereto.

Section 3. Constitution of a National Human Rights Commission

1. The Central Government shall constitute a body to be known as the National Human Rights Commission to exercise the powers conferred upon, and to perform the functions assigned to it, under this Act.
2. The Commission shall consist of:
   (a) A Chairperson who has been a Chief Justice of the Supreme Court;
   (b) One Member who is or has been, a Judge of the Supreme Court;
   (c) One Member who is, or has been, the Chief Justice of a High Court;
   (d) Two Members to be appointed from amongst persons having knowledge of, or practical experience in, matters relating to human rights.
3. The Chairperson of the National Commission for Minorities, 1 [the National Commission for the Scheduled Castes, the National Commission for the Scheduled Tribes] and the National Commission for Women shall be deemed to be Members of the Commission for the discharge of functions specified in clauses (b) to (j) of section 12.
4. There shall be a Secretary-General who shall be the Chief Executive Officer of the Commission and shall exercise such powers and discharge such functions of the Commission [except judicial functions and the power to make regulations under section 40 B], as may be delegated to him by the Commission or the Chairperson as the case may be. 1 Subs. by Act 43 of 2006 for "The National Commission for the Scheduled Castes and Scheduled Tribes." 2 Subs. by Act 43 of 2006 for "as it may delegate to him." 2 3 43 of 2006 43 of 2006 20 of 1990 45 of 1860 (5) The headquarters of the Commission shall be at Delhi and the Commission may, with the previous approval of the Central Government, establish offices at other places in India.[14]

Functions and Powers of the Commission

Section 12. Functions of the Commission

The Commission shall perform all or any of the following functions, namely:

(a) inquire, suo motu or on a petition presented to it by a victim or any person on his behalf [or on a direction or order of any court]1, into complaint of
   (i) violation of human rights or abatement thereof; or
   (ii) negligence in the prevention of such violation, by a public servant;

(b) intervene in any proceeding involving any allegation of violation of human rights pending before a court with the approval of such court;

14. "The Protection of Human Rights Act, 1993-MHA." 8 Jan. 1994, https://mha.gov.in/sites/default/files/Humman_Right_Act_1993_15052017.pdf. Accessed 17 Jun. 2019.

(c) visit, notwithstanding anything contained in any other law for the time being in force, any jail or other institution under the control of the State Government, where persons are detained or lodged for purposes of treatment, reformation or protection, for the study of the living conditions of the inmates thereof and make recommendations thereon to the Government;
(d) review the safeguards provided by or under the Constitution or any law for the time being in force for the protection of human rights and recommend measures for their effective implementation;
(e) review the factors, including acts of terrorism that inhibit the enjoyment of human rights and recommend appropriate remedial measures;
(f) study treaties and other international instruments on human rights and make recommendations for their effective implementation;
(g) undertake and promote research in the field of human rights;
(h) spread human rights literacy among various sections of society and promote awareness of the safeguards available for the protection of these rights through publications, the media, seminars and other available means;
(i) encourage the efforts of non-governmental organisations and institutions working in the field of human rights;
(j) such other functions as it may consider necessary for the protection of human rights.[15]

The Section 21 of THE PROTECTION OF HUMAN RIGHTS ACT, 1993 provides for STATE HUMAN RIGHTS COMMISSIONS Constitution of State Human Rights Commission, that is every State should constitute such Commission.

The Juvenile Justice (Care and Protection of Children) Act, 2015

The Juvenile Justice (Care and Protection) Act, 2015 is an Act to consolidate and amend the law relating to children alleged and found to be in conflict with law and children in need of care and protection by catering to their basic needs through proper care, protection, development, treatment, social re-integration, by adopting a child-friendly approach in the adjudication and disposal of matters in the best interest of children and for their rehabilitation through processes provided, and institutions and bodies established, herein under and for matters connected therewith or incidental thereto.[16]

Section 2(14) (iv) defines child in need of care and protection with reference to health as who is mentally ill or mentally or physically challenged or suffering

15. "Role of the National Human Rights Commission (NHRC) in the ...." https://www.srdlawnotes.com/2018/01/role-of-national-human-rights.html. Accessed 17 Jun. 2019.

16. "Juvenile Justice (Care and Protection of Children) Act, 2015 ...." https://advocatetanmoy.com/juvenile-justice-care-and-protection-of-children-act-2015/. Accessed 17 Jun. 2019.

from terminal or incurable disease, having no one to support or look after or having parents or guardians unfit to take care, if found so by the Board or the Committee; or (v) who has a parent or guardian and such parent or guardian is found to be unfit or incapacitated, by the Committee or the Board, to care for and protect the safety and well-being of the child.[17]

Other Legislative Provisions for Child Care Under Labour Laws for Women Employees

Women Labour: Women are an integral part of the workforce of India. According to the 2011 census, there are 149.8 million female employees in India and 121.8 and 28.0 million female employees in rural and urban regions respectively. A total of 149.8 million female employees, 35.9 million female farmers and 61.5 million female farm employees. 8.5 million of the remaining female employees are in the household industry and 43.7 million are categorised as other employees.[18]

According to the 2011 census, women's labour participation rate is 25.51% compared to 25.63% in 2001. Women's Work Participation Rate dropped marginally in 2011, but there was an improvement from 22.27% in 1991 and 19.67% in 1981. In rural regions, women's involvement in job is 30.02 percent compared to 15.44 percent in urban fields. With regard to the thorough industry, women employees represented 20.5 percent of the country's total unorganised industry of jobs.[19]

The Article 42-Provides for just and humane conditions of work and maternity relief. The said article foresee the child care by women employees during pregnancy and it mandates the employer to provide certain benefits and welfare to such female employees before and after the child birth under the Maternity Benefits Act, 1961, and the Factories Act, 1948.

The Maternity Benefits Act, 1961

The Maternity Benefits Act, 1961 provides for regulation of the employment of women in certain establishments for certain periods before and after child birth and to provide for maternity benefit and certain other benefits. This Act applies to all the establishments registered under the Factories Act, 1948 and to shops and establishment employing 10 or more employees. The Act provides that every eligible women employee shall be paid maternity benefit at the rate of average daily wage for maximum period of twenty six weeks and medical bonus.

17. "THE JAMMU AND KASHMIR JUVENILE JUSTICE (CARE ...-JK ICPS." http://www.jkicps.org/wp-content/uploads/2018/10/Draft.pdf. Accessed 17 Jun. 2019.
18. "A Study on Women Education, Employment and Income in Nagaland." http://fac.ac.in/facj/04-FACJ-6-2016.pdf. Accessed 17 Jun. 2019.
19. "About Women Labour | Ministry of Labour & Employment." 18 Nov. 2015, https://labour.gov.in/womenlabour/about-women-labour. Accessed 17 Jun. 2019.

Further, every establishment having fifty or more employees shall have the facility of crèches within such distance as may be prescribed, either separately or along with common facilities. The employer shall allow four visits a day to the crèches by the such woman employee, which shall also include the interval for rest allowed to her. Thus the fundamental object of the Act is to provide legal cover to such women employees during and after pregnancy, so that she can look after the child health and nutrition etc.

The Factories Act, 1948

The Factories Act, 1948 provides for Creches in every factory wherein more than fifty women workers are ordinarily employed. The Act further provides for that employer should maintain a suitable room or rooms for the use of children under the age of six years of such women employees. Such rooms shall provide adequate accommodation, shall be adequately lighted and ventilated, shall be maintained in a clean and sanitary condition and shall be under the charge of women trained in the care of children and infants.

The Act also provides that the State Government may make rules—(a) prescribing the location and the standards in respect of construction, accommodation, furniture and other equipment of rooms to be provided under this section; (b) requiring the provision in factories to which this section applies of additional facilities for the care of children belonging to women workers, including suitable provision of facilities for washing and changing their clothing; (c) requiring the provision in any factory of free milk or refreshment or both for such children; (d) requiring that facilities shall be given in any factory for the mothers of such children to feed them at the necessary intervals.[20]

Similar provisions for Creches also have been made for women employees under following Labour Laws

Section 44 of the Inter State Migrant Workmen (RECS) Act, 1979.

Section 12 of the Plantations Labour Act, 1951.

Section 14 of the *Beedi* and Cigar Workers (Conditions of Employment) Act, 1966.

Section 35 of the Building and other Constructions (Regulation of Employment and Conditions of Service) Act, 1996.

Conclusion

Thus, our Country is quite progressive since our Constitution was constitutes in social sector especially in inclusive development of child, supported by UN convention on child rights. The Constitutional bodies namely National Commission on Protection

20. "Factories Act, 1948 | Bare Acts | Law Library | Advocate Khoj." https://www.advocatekhoj.com/library/bareacts/factories/index.php?Title=Factories%20Act,%201948. Accessed 17 Jun. 2019.

of Child Rights and National Human Right Commission has always remained vigilant on the issues of violation of child rights. The apex Court of the Country is also monitoring the compliance of Juvenile rights. The Government of India and State Governments also implements various schemes related to inclusive development of child. Probably what is missing is the awareness among the people at large about legal aspects related to the health and nutrition of child. We hope that this compendium will help to everyone for awareness on the subject.

Recommendations

There are Constitutional provisions, perspectives, adequate frame work of Legislation, implementing Departments of the States, Constitutional monitoring bodies like National Human Rights Commission and National Commission on Protection of Child Rights are already existing in the country since long . However, it is evident that be it the issue of infant mortality rate or malnutrition or health related issues of children, they have remained either standstill or even marginally increased. It is alarming as, the children up to 14 years account for about 27.71 % (35.10 Crores) of the total population of the Country, which is the biggest strength of our Country in the World in decades to follow and therefore, it is the need of the day for quality implementation of Acts and Schemes, supported by effective monitoring.

References

1. Retrieved from http://www.shrc.tn.gov.in/files/humanrightsact.html 5. Health. (n.d.). Retrieved from http://www.childrensrightseducation.com/5-health.html
2. Advocatekhoj.com. (n.d.). Factories Act, 1948 | Bare Acts | Law Library. Retrieved from https://www.advocatekhoj.com/library/bareacts/factories/48.php?Title=Factories Act, 1948
3. Child health. (31st January, 2019). Retrieved from https://www.who.int/maternal_child_adolescent/child/en/
4. Cutler, L. (2007, 12). Human Rights Guarantees, Constitutional Law, and The Military Commissions Act of 2006. Peace & Change, 33(1), 31-59. doi:10.1111/j.1468-0130.2007.00475.x
5. Dhar, K. (2012). Human Right Commission in India-The Protection of Human Right Act, 1993. SSRN Electronic Journal. doi:10.2139/ssrn.2007961
6. International Law. (n.d.). Retrieved from https://www.ohchr.org/en/professionalinterest/pages/internationallaw.aspx
7. Juvenile Justice (Care and Protection of Children) Act, 2015. (6th June, 2018). Retrieved from https://advocatetanmoy.com/juvenile-justice-care-and-protection-of-children-act-2015/
8. National Commission for Protection of Child Rights. (n.d.). Functions and Powers. Retrieved from http://ncpcr.gov.in/index1.php?lang=1&level=1&&sublinkid=5&lid=600

9. National Commission of Protection of Child Rights. (n.d.). National Commission for Protection of Child Rights, Government of India. Retrieved from http://www.ncpcr.gov.in/
10. Role of the National Human Rights Commission (NHRC) in the implementation and enforcement of human rights in India | Human Rights and International Law. (n.d.). Retrieved from https://www.srdlawnotes.com/2018/01/role-of-national-human-rights.html
11. The Welfare and Safety provisions of Factories Act, 1948 | Labor Law. (n.d.). Retrieved from https://www.srdlawnotes.com/2017/11/the-welfare-and-safety-provisions-of.html
12. Http://ljournal.ru/wp-content/uploads/2017/03/a-2017-023.pdf. (2017). doi:10.18411/a-2017-023
13. श्रम एवं रोजगार मंत्रालय (n.d.). Retrieved from https://labour.gov.in/womenlabour/about-women-labour

□

6

Nutrition Education: Key to Sustaining Child Health

—*Uma Joshi*

Abstract

There is a symbiotic relationship between children and sustainable development. Provisions for child rights and their health can contribute to lasting and equitable development. Childhood conditions of children have persistent and profound impacts on their later life. Healthy and educated children make a healthy society. Adequate maternal and child health, nutrition and clean environment for all children make them potential contributors to the sustainable society. Major impact on the sustained children's health can be created through health promotion from the early years of life by educating and sensitising them about healthy eating practices and regular physical activity. This is the core of all school meals and school-based nutrition education programmes. Efforts should be made to increase health awareness, communication and consciousness through effective educational strategies and skill development. The paper discusses what nutrition education is and how it should be imparted to make it effective.

Introduction

Sustainable development is the pathway to future social, economic, emotional, physical development of people. It is increasingly realised that promoting sustainable development; we need a shift in our value systems, our education and understanding, our practices to change our mindsets towards unsustainable practices. This requires mobilising children and young people by educating them and preparing them to be the catalytic agents for sustainable development. There is a symbiotic relationship between children and sustainable development. Provisions for child rights and their health can contribute to lasting and equitable development.

As per UNICEF figures, 20% of children under five years of age suffer from wasting due to acute undernutrition in India. The rate of underweight children in India is among the highest in the world and is nearly double that of Sub-Saharan Africa, according to the

World Bank . With slight regional variations, the overall scenario in the country requires a serious concern and calls for urgent and immediate action. In childhood, the conditions of children have persistent and profound impacts on their later life. Healthy and educated children make a healthy society. Adequate maternal and child health, nutrition and clean environment for all children make them potential contributors to the sustainable society. Major impact on the sustained children's health can be created through health promotion from the early years of life by educating and sensitizing them about healthy eating practices and regular physical activity. This is the core of all school meals and school-based nutrition education programs. Efforts should be made to increase health awareness, communication and consciousness through effective educational strategies and skill development.

Nutrition Education

'Nutrition education' does not apply the same to all nutrition professionals. A fundamental distinction is between education teaching about nutrition (traditional information-based study) and education in nutrition for action, which aims at practices: it has been defined as "learning (WHY NUTRITION EDUCATION MATTERs) Nutrition and consumer protection division experiences designed to facilitate the voluntary adoption of eating and other nutrition-related behaviours conducive to health and well-being". This approach centres on people, their lifestyles, motivation and social context, and has an action-based methodology. It has developed under various names, for example, social marketing, behaviour change communication, community nutrition and health promotion.

Nutrition Education is one such systematically planned set of activities as an essential component to improve the nutritional status of a population and is crucial for the well-being of people in general. It aims at information dissemination approach, which facilitates behaviours conducive to health and focuses on environmental change for sustainable development. Nutrition education can help children understand that diet is related to their health and can provide information on what food to eat for good health. It promotes access to a variety of nutritious food. It develops personal skills and motivation among children to adopt healthy eating practices. Scientists and health experts worldwide agree that children who are well-nourished are much more easily able to develop the cognitive and behavioural skills they need to reach their full learning potential. It also provides the basis for public health policies and to develop nutrition advisory services and nutrition education of the public thereby increasing participation in coordinated community nutrition programme to improve the nutritional status/ level in the community.

According to FAO (2016), "Nutrition education is also coming into the limelight. It is now acknowledged as an essential catalyst for nutrition impact in food security, community nutrition and health interventions. It is also demonstrably capable of improving dietary behaviour and nutrition status on its own. Moreover, it has long-term effects on the independent actions of parents and through them on the health of their children. At the same time, it is low-cost, practical and sustainable.

It requires experience and expertise to plan, conduct and assess and nutrition programme at global, national, community and household levels. It involves work on food composition, nutrient requirements and nutrition assessment, food and nutrition security policy and nutrition education.

By the nature of its mandate, Food and Agriculture Organisation (FAO), 2016 emphasises approaches which focus on food as the main way to improve diets and fight malnutrition. These approaches look at all links in the food chain from production and purchase to consumption; promote home gardens for better diets; understand the social significance of food, and recognize people's need to act for themselves to improve their diets and lifestyles. They promote "a wide variety of good quality safe and culturally appropriate foods in-sufficient amounts to meet nutritional requirements within a hygienic environment and coupled with a healthy lifestyle"—in simple terms, an all-around good diet, all the year round. It also has a very wide scope. It contributes to all the pillars of food and nutrition security but is mainly concerned with whatever influence food consumption and dietary practices: food habits and food purchasing, food preparation, food safety and environmental conditions. Many causes of poor nutrition are attitudes and practices which can be influenced by education: food taboos, long-established dietary and snacking habits, agricultural production decisions, food distribution in the family, and ideas about child feeding, misleading food advertising, ignorance of food hygiene, or negative attitudes to vegetables. Education is becoming critically necessary in countries affected by globalisation and urbanisation, which are experiencing a dangerous dietary transition to cheap processed foods rich in sugar, fat and salt."[21]

Nutrition is the key to a healthy body and mind. The study of various nutrients, their functions, food sources and their effects on human well-being is called NUTRITION. Nutrition science is the area of knowledge regarding the role of food in the maintenance of health. Nutrition Education is a systematically planned set of activities to improve the nutritional status of a population. It aims at developing personal skills and motivation to adopt healthy eating practices and increasing activities, awareness, enhancing people's motivation, and facilitating the ability to take action for improving nutritional status.

---

21. http://www.fao.org/fileadmin/user_upload/red-icean/docs/Nutrition%20Education_FAO_Concept%20note.pdf

Nutrition Education is one such systematically planned set of activities as an essential component to improve the nutritional status of a population and is crucial for the well-being of people in general. It aims at Information dissemination approach, which facilitates behaviours conducive to health and focuses on environmental change for sustainable development. Nutrition education can help children understand that diet is related to their health and can provide information on what food to eat for good health. It promotes access to a variety of nutritious food. It develops personal skills and motivation among children to adopt healthy eating practices. Scientists and health experts worldwide agree that well-nourished children are much more easily able to develop the cognitive and behavioural skills they need to reach their full learning potential. It also provides the basis for public health policies and to develop nutrition advisory services and nutrition education of the public thereby increasing participation in coordinated community nutrition programme to improve the nutritional status/level in the community.

Schools are an excellent setting for promoting lifelong healthy eating and improving long-term, sustainable nutrition security. Good nutrition is crucial for children's physical and mental development; schoolchildren are current, and future consumers and future parents; and are also an important link between school, home and community[22].

Most of us already connect nutrition with health. If we go one step further to connect health with educational goals, then; we will have effectively connected nutrition to academic performance. There is so much concern over test scores these days. However, if kids are not in a position to learn because they are hungry, or they do not get enough nutritious food at home, then schools that do not make the nutrition performance connection in the canteen/cafeteria end up undermining what they are trying to do in the classroom......Studies repeatedly link good nutrition to learning readiness, academic achievement, and decreased discipline and emotional problems. A hungry child is not equipped to teach.

Nutrition education is needed in all settings to ensure the holistic development of the children. Mothers should aware and practise some essential actions, e.g. healthy eating habits, breastfeeding exclusively up to six months, and then providing rich and nourishing complimentary food while continuing to breastfeed. Schoolchildren, at a critical age for forming good dietary habits, need to learn and enjoy a variety of vegetables and fruits. They should avoid too many sweets and sugary drinks and foods high in salt. People living with HIV and AIDS benefit from understanding that a good diet helps build resistance to infection. The focus cannot be too narrow: not

22. http://www.fao.org/fileadmin/user_upload/red-icean/docs/Nutrition%20Education_FAO_Concept%20note.pdf

only mothers but also husbands, families, the community and the professionals should advise them the need to understand that children's lives and futures depend on how they eat. Those in charge of children and youth, or caring for the sick also need nutrition education: families and teachers have to learn not only to eat well themselves but also to become sources of education[23]

Imparting Nutrition Education Effectively

There is already considerable knowledge and experience of what works in nutrition education for action. Practice and motivation are as valuable as information and understanding. Some repeatedly mentioned success strategies are:

- Hands-on experience
- Various kinds of modelling, including fictional stories, examples and cases
- Learning by experience, trial and error
- Maintaining activities over a long period
- Participation, dialogue and discussion
- Multiple channels and multiple activities
- Multi-sectorial collaboration.

Creating a supportive environment is also a key strategy. In schools, for example, unspoken but powerful nutrition messages can be embodied in food vendors' wares, hand washing practices, school meals, and snacks brought from home, the school garden, and teachers' eating habits as well as in classroom lessons. The schools provide nutrition education that will teach, encourage, and support healthy behaviours. On a wider scale, the government can act to create an enabling environment, for example by establishing standards for healthy school meals, insisting on accurate information and labelling, and putting restraints on food advertising aimed at children.[24]

The action-oriented model of nutrition education is still relatively little practised. One reason is lack of capacity. Few countries offer professional training in this field (in some it is unknown) and familiarity with behaviour change approaches is generally lacking. District and community development staff in health often has little training in nutrition and usually none at all in nutrition education. As a result, they believe that their job is simply to pass on information and advice, and this is what they do, often too little effect. The nutrition professions themselves often do not recognize the need for action-oriented nutrition education or promote it. Strong advocacy is needed to establish nutrition education in national policy and institutions, and there is a great

23. http://www.fao.org/fileadmin/user_upload/red-icean/docs/Nutrition%20Education_FAO_Concept%20note.pdf
24. http://www.fao.org/fileadmin/user_upload/red-icean/docs/Nutrition%20Education_FAO_Concept%20note.pdf

need for professional capacity to integrate effective nutrition education into health, agriculture, education and community services.

Schools and other education settings have long been considered a primary target to deliver nutrition education. School children are at the phase of life when they are acquiring habits that will last a lifetime; and children are an important link between school and home and community (Olivares et al., 1998).

As such, schools have probably received more attention as a specific setting for nutrition education than any other over the past 20 years. At the global level, the WHO's Global Strategy on Diet, Physical Activity and Health recommends that school policies and programmes support the adoption of healthy diets and physical activity (WHO, 2004). In 2008, to assist the Member States in implementing the Strategy at the country level, the WHO published a "School Policy Framework: Implementation of the Global Strategy on Diet, Physical Activity and Health '(WHO, 2008)'. The objective was to guide policy-makers at national and sub-national levels in the development and implementation of policies that promote healthy eating and physical activity in the school setting, as well as to recommend changes in the school food environment. For example, the guide recommends the inclusion of nutrition education in school policies and programmes, as a means of:

- Providing knowledge and skills about the relationship between a good diet, physical activity, and health.
- I am addressing the safe preparation of food and its consumption as an essentially positive and enjoyable aspect of life.
- I am allowing students to identify barriers to making healthy food choices and solutions to overcome the identified barriers.

Providing media and marketing literacy to students, especially related to food and non-alcoholic beverages. I am involving teachers in imparting health messages to students.

The WHO also hosts the Nutrition-Friendly Schools Initiative (NFSI), in partnership with a range of other international organisations to achieve the goal.

Nutrition education is an important way to encourage healthy eating, build good lifelong habits, and combat our country's malnutrition problem. Nutrition education can be offered as the after-school program also. It can support nutrition education by introducing children to new foods, especially fruits and vegetables, as well as reading recipes and preparing food through an interactive approach. It is easy for an after school program to add nutrition education to its activities. As the relationships among diet, health, and disease prevention have become clearer, nutrition education and the promotion of healthy eating behaviours and lifestyles continue to receive increased attention. In its broadest sense, nutrition education is "any combination of educational strategies designed to facilitate voluntary adoption of food choices and other food and nutrition-related behaviours conducive to health and well-being. Successful nutrition education uses a systematic approach and strategies that include a variety of activities to help the target group make behaviour changes.

Teachers being closer to their students can identify the needs, interests, habits and practices of the students. Thus it is easier to develop conducive provisions for the successful behaviour change communication programmes. As the students are in school for long hours, adequate time, intervention programmes for nutrition and health along with the involvement of the families, can be worked out effectively. Mid day meal programme in school has been implemented in many schools in India, but its effectiveness in terms of raising the nutritional status of children face various challenges. Sometimes the schools do not have enough open space or playground which restricts the physical activity of children in school.

There is a lack of facility to carry out proper impact studies of the nutritional interventions. It results in having a lack of data to provide guidelines for policy decisions for the nutrition education program. In the initial stage of children's life, the family plays a key role in the formation of food habits and choices. As they start going to school, influences other than family become important references due to the diversification of the environment. Their role models change from parents to teachers. Studies have proven that childhood food habits and influence children's growth and development. It has an impact on their health and risk factors as well as chronic diseases later in adulthood. Good nutrition in childhood goes a long way in maintaining their health and their increasing learning abilities. Thus nutrition education at school is the best strategy to prepare the children for the healthy nation.

Rules and plans made in schools about meals and physical activities are to be taught and followed collectively, so educating individuals and groups is very effective. School-based nutrition program should include the provision of meal in school so that children's food habits can be altered by guiding them for action and its importance. The locally available foods, relevance to culture, general socio-economic status is very important factors in evolving effective communication strategy for imparting nutrition education. Schools should take care of providing the foodstuff, which is very important nutritionally but not consumed due to unavailability or un-affordability, such as fruits, vegetables, milk etc. School-based nutrition education should teach simple food preparation, preservation and storage skills apart from imparting messages on nutrition. Very few schools have started restrictions on fast food items in school and parents are supposed to send them with home-made food. Nutrition experts should be in the loop of planning nutrition education through school curriculum and learning experiences. Adhocism as an approach to child health and nutrition programme should be avoided as this approach does not deliver the results despite spending considerable time, energy and funding into the programme. Nutrition experts also must continuously monitor the implementation of the programme collection of the database on the health status of children and come out with necessary suggestions for policy decisions at regular intervals.

Nutrition experts can also help in developing nutrition education modules for school teachers, children and their parents as well as health workers. It requires a public health approach too so that gradually all levels of education impart appropriate nutrition education. Nutrition education to children through school experiences must get a strong focus on the curriculum as well as health policies. In our country nutrition has been featuring in five-year plans but lack of planning, coordination among various concerned agencies/ departments and strategic planning for the implementation have been the hindrances in showing the results of the efforts. Poor nutrition and health contribute to India's substandard economic productivity. Enough attention is yet to be paid on nutrition education to children through school experiences. It is not given importance in the change process, whereas, it is the one upon which all others rely for success.

Looking at the nutrition and maternal and child health scenario in the country, nutrition and health education are central to the goal of helping students to prepare for healthy and productive lives. Programmes of iron supplementation, de-worming and supplementary food and so on have been implemented time and again. These have to be woven with a continuous nutrition education programme in schools so that a holistic approach can be achieved in sustaining children's health.

Phoebe Copp, Community Nutrition Adviser, California, pointed out five reasons to teach Nutrition Education in schools.

1. Students get excited about learning.
2. Students put nutrition education to the test in real-life situations.
3. The benefits of nutrition education reach far beyond the classroom.
4. Improve the quality of your students' education by teaching a topic left out of the standard curriculum.
5. Nutrition lessons provide essential education that can lead to more academic success.

Thus, the benefits of imparting nutrition education in schools are too valuable to pass up. From students making healthier choices to improved academic performance, nutrition education can benefit the whole school. When they go home, they transfer the information to the family and insist on making healthy food choices as they are educated about the difference between healthy and unhealthy foods. Their intake of fruits and vegetables also increases as a result of learning nutrition in schools. Teachers are role models for young children. They blindly follow what the teacher instructs.

Their indulgence in physical activity also increases as they learn the relationship between healthy food and physical activity in preventing dangerous illnesses.

School-based nutrition education should consider the needs and interests of the students, teachers and the school. Educational strategies include efforts to increase health awareness, communication and skill building. Previous literature reviews identified educational strategies directly relevant to a behavioural focus and theory-driven strategies among the elements conducive to successful programmes. Other features that contribute to gain effectiveness are the provision of adequate time and intensity for the intervention, involvement of families, particularly younger children, and incorporation of self-assessment and feedback in interventions for older children. The emphasis on environmental and behavioural factors in successful school-based physical activity and nutrition interventions highlights the importance of involving parents and other community members (Rodrigo and Aranceta, 2003).

Methodology for imparting nutrition education should not raise any issues in today's world of ICT. A wide variety of interesting media are available and accessible to everyone. More of participatory methodologies should be used in imparting nutrition education. Children should have the opportunity to get involved in finding out locally available nutritious foods, plan their menus, get first-hand experiences in cooking simple recipes, designing nutrition-related messages, graphics, slogans, jingles, etc. on important messages. Audiovisual media on various deficiency diseases and the effects of their long-term prevalence can be developed and used for teaching nutrition. Textbooks also should have enough pictures to impress upon their mind the effects of malnourishment so that they can associate it with the theory part of the book. Nutrition education should also include an understanding of where the food comes and how it is processed and supplied to the people.

Classroom discussions on students' food habits and practices, worksheets on nutrition-related facts and puzzles, keeping their food records, records of their food shopping, plays and role plays can be used effectively and creatively with a participatory approach. Students can be engaged in kitchen gardening, arranging exhibitions, attending workshops on physical activities, developing cooking skills, and so on. Modern media such as the internet, CD-ROM and the World Wide Web can be used with interactive features as well as for specific topics. Medical schools, nutrition departments, health departments, NGOs, parents can also join in a school-based nutrition programme to strengthen it and make it more fruitful. Together they can make sustained efforts by generating the resources, review the progress of the programme and take timely action.

Girls' health in India suffers much discrimination. They receive less attention as far as their food, medical care, recreation and opportunities for education and development are concerned. National development depends on the active participation of girls. Prevention is the key: nourish the children, educate them, and keep them healthy. Teaching nutrition must focus on this aspect to sensitise students on gender equality in health rights as national development process cannot afford less active participation of half of India's population. Special dietary needs of girls must be part of teaching nutrition. Nutrition for sports, illnesses, and during growth period must be taught in schools.

Teaching effective nutrition education requires training and capacity building of teachers to make the learning experiences more meaningful for the students. Content on nutrition is often too general and vague to be taken as an important one. Therefore, the role of teacher and methodology used in imparting nutrition education hold the key to its effectiveness. Teachers' capacity building in this subject should focus on behaviour change processes so that they can promote effective implementation of behaviour change learning experiences for students about their food habits. This component should be part of teachers' pre-service and in-service education. Adequate training of teachers contributes to their increased awareness and motivates teachers and educators to support healthy lifestyles. It can also contribute to enhancing teachers' self-efficacy.

Tools must be developed by schools to assess the effectiveness and efficiency of the nutritional interventions implemented by the school. The strategies used by schools should be participatory, creative, novel, inexpensive and widely disseminated. Food provided in schools should be palatable, tasty, nutritionally adequate, acceptable and consistent with classroom messages which provide a valuable opportunity for nutrition education. Schools should prioritize the essential elements of child health and nutrition services (e.g. by strengthening immunisation programmes and other preventive measures; and integrated approaches to clinical management of acute respiratory infections, malnutrition, diarrhoea and other major causes of a childhood illness) in their health and nutrition education programme. Many models of nutrition education have been tried out and are in practice. Schools have to decide the best possible and most suitable approach to their set up. The aim should not be lost in the process of making it suitable, i.e. it should not be a mockery or namesake programme.

These days mobile can offer many opportunities for behaviour change communication between students and school. Apps developed to give alerts related to nutrition and food selection as well as habit formation can work wonders in monitoring and evaluation of tracking of nutrition and health behaviour change in students and for action to be taken through software generated alerts. The information thus aggregated can facilitate communication and decision-making regarding the further teaching of nutrition and external interventions to the students. Schools are thus more easily able to impart timely preventive nutrition education to the student.

School-based nutrition education is an important component of comprehensive school health. Teaching nutrition to children throughout their educational experience is key to developing healthy eating habits. Nutrition concepts need to be reinforced throughout the year, and students can learn about food and nutrition as part of many subjects, including math, science, social studies, physical education, and health.

Also, nutrition education should extend beyond the classroom and needs to involve multiple channels of communications. Teachers, food service professionals, and family members all play a role in promoting life-long healthy eating habits. Therefore, nutrition education should be linked to the school food environment and at home. It improves health literacy, by learning about essential nutrients, the benefits of healthy eating, and safe food preparation; gain nutrition-related skills, such as understanding food labels, comprehending nutrition information, evaluating commercial food advertising as well as commercial advertising. Farm to school programmes has been made part of learning experiences in schools of some countries to impart effective and meaningful nutrition education. These kinds of first-hand experiences teach children about the food from the farm to the fork (Hard et al., 2015).

Connecting teaching of nutrition and school kitchen/canteen/cafeteria is very important. What is taught must be practised in the school itself. Habit formation consuming not so popular locally available nutritious foods must start at school. So that students relate theory and practice, and it serves as an excellent location to reinforce nutrition education messages. The canteen/cafeteria can act like a classroom where students learn healthy eating habits. As the home environment is extremely influential on a child's eating behaviours, parents should be oriented by schools to promote positive physical activity and eating habits. Schools can provide an orientation of nutrition education to parents in various ways.

Schools can and prepare a newsletter/pamphlet/folder/leaflet highlighting the importance of healthy eating physical activity for their wards and tips for a parent to use at home which should be in line with instruction in the school. The school can organise an exhibition, displays or an open house or a fair on nutrition education. These must include talks, demonstrations and workshops on healthy living by nutritionists and local health professionals. The school website can also promote nutrition education by having portal son nutrition and physical activity. It can also include healthy recipes, activities for families, and wellness information.

Schools should have bulletin boards, flannel boards, poster boards at important places in the school conveying messages on nutrition through various displays from time to time. School gardens serve as an excellent learning site to teach students about fruits and vegetables. Produce grown in the school garden can be incorporated into the school meal programme.

Research has also shown that printed, computer-tailored nutrition education is a more effective tool for motivating people to change to healthier diets than general nutrition education. New technology is providing more advanced ways of delivering tailored messages via the World Wide Web. It was also found that interactive, web-based computer-tailored education can lead to changes in determinants of behaviour. The tailored intervention was found more personally relevant and had a more subjective impact on people's opinions and intentions to change (Oenema. *et. al*, 2001).

Our country also needs to invest in education and training of teachers at various levels, health care professionals, policymakers, practitioners in understanding the importance and scope of nutrition education, imparting it effectively. Diploma and degree programmes in pre-school and school teachers' training must include this component as a core one in their syllabus. They should be trained to address lifestyle issues related to nutrition and physical activity behaviours of students. In order to address India's acute nutrition problems, dedicated education and training programmes in nutrition will need to be put in place. Resources need to be invested in curriculum revisions, rigorous training, and teaching research skills. To see meaningful and positive changes in the country's health profile, academic training and human resource generation needs to be complemented with political will, committed funds, equity, and multi-sectoral health promotion programmes.

The overview presented here illustrates how and why schools should include nutrition education. Schools cannot address the full range of health problems that challenge the children. However, they can serve to stimulate the children and parents to adopt good practices that have proved effective in improving children's nutritional status. Schools can develop partnerships with corporate, governments and private organisations to promote good food and health practices to large scale. These partnerships can also focus on training nutrition educators and curriculum framing. Thus, schools can serve as partners in nutrition mission of the country. Moving from good ideas on nutrition education in curriculum planning to action is not an easy task. It remains a challenge as our school systems are very rigid. It requires administrative will, planning and implementation as well as maintenance and continuance of nutrition education as an important part of the school system.

"The best preparation for good work tomorrow is to do good work today."

—Elbert Hubbard

References

1. Food and Agriculture Organisation of the United Nations. (2016). FAOSTAT Database. Rome, Italy: FAO. Retrieved 30th January, 2015, from http://faostat3.fao.org/home/E
2. Hard *et.al* (2015). The Importance of Nutrition Education in 2015. Child Nutrition Reauthorisation. Retrieved from:(www.tc.edu/tisch)
3. Oenema et al. (2001) Web-based Tailored Nutrition Education: Results of a Randomised Controlled Trial. Health Education Research. 16(6): 647-660.
4. Olivares, S., Kain, J., Lera, L., & Pizarro, F. (2004). The nutritional statue, food consumption and physical activity among Chilean school children: A descriptive study. European Journal of Clinical Nutrition, 58(9), 1278.
5. Phoebe Copp. Top 5 Reasons to Teach Nutrition Education in Your Classroom. Dairy Council of California. Retrieved from: www.healthy living.org
6. Rodrigo and Aranceta(2003) Nutrition Education in Schools: Experiences and Challenges. European Journal of Clinical Nutrition. 57.suppl. s82-s85.
7. World Bank. (2007) From Agriculture to Nutrition: Pathways, Synergies, and Outcomes. Washington. (web.worldbank.org)
8. World Health Organisation. (2004). WHO World Health Assembly adopts a global strategy on a diet, physical activity and health. In WHO World Health Assembly adopts a global strategy on a diet, physical activity and health.
9. Why Nutrition Education Matters. Retrieved from: www.fao.org/ag/humannutrition/nutritioneducation/en)

□

7

Protein an important Nutrient for Cognition and Brain Development of Children

—*Priyanka Kacker*

Abstract

Nutrition is important for body development and growth. Nutrients play an important role in brain functions too. It has been observed that the people respond to a stimulus as reaction time, i.e., in 2-3 seconds. However, the brain responds much faster in response to stimuli, i.e., 250-300 milliseconds. Some individuals are slow in giving a response, slow in following instructions and slow in cognitive processing. This slow processing is not because the person is mentally ill or mentally challenged. A study was done on children who were above average fluid intelligence and not suffering from any mental health issues as part of the research work. Initial data about food habits were taken where the protein diet was one of the major concerns. The research was divided into two groups, i.e., children taking high protein diet and children taking a low protein diet. ERP based research work was carried out, and it was found that the children who were taking high protein diet showed quick response to stimulus as compared to children taking low protein diet whose brain response was slow. For better brain functioning protein plays a vital role, which is scientifically accepted at the neuronal level.

However, through this study, it was found that to recognise a stimulus and to respond to it quickly, protein diet has a vital role to play. This will help in understanding slow learners in schools and colleges, age-based memory issues and infant brain development.

Introduction

It is a well-known fact that nutrients are the core elements for brain development and behaviour. Proper development and maturation of the brain are necessary for the acquisition of the full repertoire of integrated functions and behaviours that make us human. Approximately one billion cells communicate with each other through specialised interconnections. The actions of the brain underlie all behaviour ranging from the simplest acts like walking or eating to complex actions such as thinking, interacting or creating works of art (Mendoza, 2007). However, if a child is malnourished, then it hurts behavioural and intellectual development. It causes disorders of nutrition, most commonly affecting the nervous system (Mendoza, 2007). Approximately 150 million children worldwide are malnourished; which is an alarming number that our next generation is at risk of developing learning and behaviour problems. Various animal studies have shown that malnutrition can cause a decrease in brain volume, number of neurons, synapses, dendrites and reactive zones. After nutritional rehabilitation, although there was significant 'catch up' in brain weight and volume, there was a persistent reduction in the number of dendritic and synaptic spines and cortical cells. These structures are important in the cell–to–cell communications. The alterations in the hippocampus, which is associated with short term memory and cerebellum, which is responsible for fine motor control and balance, are permanent (Levitsky & Strupp, 1995). Attentional dysfunction, lack of concentration, impulsiveness, diminished ability to adapt to stressful situations, susceptibility to affective disorders like anxiety, and diminished motivations and exploratory behaviours are common problems observed among malnourished children. All these problems lead to impaired school performance and social and emotional development. The brain of a child is vulnerable during the time of rapid brain growth; the effect of malnutrition on brain development is experienced. Diatribe occurring at this time has significant negative effects on brain development, cognition, and behaviour, in turn, affects the development of the human brain and central nervous system.

The brain of a foetus undergoes a growth spurt during the third trimester. An infant's brain triples in size during the first year of life from 350 g to 1000 g and continues to develop rapidly during the first 2-3 years of life it reaches 80% of its adult weight. Also, a significant amount of brain construction happens at this time, wherein the fundamentals for intelligence, vision, and language are established. However, the groundwork for brain development begins at day one of conception. The prenatal period is the time when the organisation, neuronal differentiation, synaptogenesis, glial proliferation, biochemical differentiation of neurons, synthesis of neurotransmitters and myelination are taking place. If a fetal insult incurred from the 5th month of gestation onwards, it may cause mental retardation, Down's syndrome, autism, etc. (Hack, 1998).

Effects of protein-calorie or protein-energy malnutrition (PEM) and single nutrient deficiencies on brain development have been studied. Among children who were born small for gestational age, twelve longitudinal studies were conducted, and the children were evaluated at ages 9-17 years. Mild prenatal maternal undernutrition can also affect infant behaviour. When early preventive food supplementation trials were conducted among high-risk pregnant mothers in endemic areas in Mexico, Guatemala, and Bogota, Colombia, concurrent benefits were demonstrated in all the trials (Chavez & Martinez, 1982; Freeman, Klein, & Townsend Lechtig, 1980; Waber, 1981).

Vitamin and trace elements are also essential, and its deficiency can cause neurologic deficits. Deficiencies in certain micronutrients incurred during the prenatal period have been shown to cause specific neurologic deficits. These micronutrients are folic acid, iodine, iron, zinc, selenium, copper, magnesium, Vitamins A, C, D, E, B6 and B12 (Mendoza, 2007). Iodine deficiency is the most significant cause of irreversible mental impairment. Folic acid deficiency causes neural tube defects, i.e. meningocele and encephalocele; and orofacial clefts, i.e. cleft lips and palate. Iron deficiency anaemia is the most common nutritional deficiency worldwide; its highest prevalence is between 6-24 months of age. It hurts the infant's sleep-waking cycle and psychomotor and developmental maturation. Zinc is functionally an essential component of more than 200 enzymes that pervade all metabolic pathways. Zinc deficiency causes slowing and restriction of behaviour, lethargy, apathy and decreased growth rate. It is also associated with a compromised host-defence mechanics, thereby predisposing the child to recurrent infections. Pyridoxine or vitamin B6 is an essential cofactor in the developing central nervous system. Its deficiency in animals is associated with alteration in the glutaminergic neurotransmitter system, which is involved in memory and learning. Excess and deficiency of Vitamin A in the mother's diet during pregnancy have been shown to cause malformations of the fetal brain and hydrocephalus. Ground-breaking studies have shown an important neurodevelopmental benefit amongst breastfed infants. Results of studies show that school-age children have fewer neurological abnormalities, better school grades (Rogan & Gladen, 1993), better cognitive development up to 8 years of age (Lucas & Morley, 1992), and better scores in visual acuity up to 3 years of age. Breastfed infants also showed the same developmental advantage even among pre-term and small for gestational age babies (Lucas & Morley, 1992).

Brain development is maximum in the first two years of life, and for adequate functioning-minerals, vitamins, essential amino acids and essential fatty acids, including omega-3 polyunsaturated fatty acids are important (Black, Victoria, & Walker, 2013). The main substrate Glucose is utilised by the brain to offer energy for its functions.

At this age, the various vitamins are useful for brain activity like Vitamin B1 helps to produce energy by aiding in the utilisation of glucose by nervous tissue. It modulates cognitive function, Vitamin B9 preserves brain during its development and helps in maintaining memory, Vitamin B6 is involved in the synthesis of some neurotransmitters,

Vitamin B12 is involved in the synthesis of some neurotransmitters. It improves cognitive function, language function, as well as the functioning of factors related to the frontal lobe, Nerve endings in the brain, contains the highest concentration of vitamin C in the body after suprarenal glands, Vitamin D & its analogues. It helps in the prevention of various aspects of neurodegenerative diseases, Vitamin E Alpha-tocopherol actively works to protect nervous membranes, and Vitamin A helps to protect the functioning of rods and cones of the eye and preservation of vision especially night vision.

However, Protein has its role to play in brain development and functioning. The neurotransmitters permit brain cells to communicate with each other therefore in case of children; the developing, brain needs protein, or amino acids to make neurotransmitters. For example, the amino acid tryptophan makes the neurotransmitter serotonin, which helps the baby to sleep. In order to stay alert; the amino acid tyrosine makes norepinephrine. Infants need 9 to 11 grams of protein daily, toddlers need 13 grams of protein, and pre-schoolers need about 19 grams daily. Food and protein/energy supplementation are required for children who experience severe acute malnutrition, chronic malnutrition, and low birth weight tend to face other disadvantages that also affect brain development, such as poverty, poor housing and sanitation, poor healthcare, and less stimulating home environments, making it difficult to draw a causal link from observational studies. The results of randomised trials of maternal and child food supplementation, which provide stronger evidence of causation, are mixed (Table-1). Such trials that provided supplements to both mothers during pregnancy and children throughout the first two years of life showed the strongest evidence for long-term positive effects regarding cognition. In a large trial in Guatemala, pregnant women and their children up to the age of 7 years were provided with a milk-based high protein and energy drink with micronutrients or a low protein and energy drink with micronutrients. Children who received the high protein and energy drink had higher cognitive scores at 4-5 years of age, higher scores on tests of numeracy (math), knowledge, vocabulary, and reading achievement at 11-18 years of age54 and on reading and IQ scores (among women) at 22-29 years of age (Li H., Barnhart H.X., Stein A.D., et al., 2003) and a 46% increase in average wages (among men) at 26-42 years of age (Hoddinott, Malussio, & Behrman, 2008). While some of the effects on school-age performance were found in the late exposure group (after the age of 2 years), most of these effects were only found among individuals who began supplementation before the age of 2 or 3 years, including the effect on average wages.

In contrast, few long-term effects have been reported when supplementation was provided only to mothers or only to children, though some such trials have demonstrated short-term cognitive and motor effects (Table-1). Apart from the trial in Guatemala, only a trial in Jamaica (Walker, Chang, & Powell, 2005) conducted a longitudinal assessment at multiple time points throughout childhood and adolescence. Although the trial did not show long-term effects of the nutrition component of the intervention, the psychosocial stimulation component resulted in sustained effects on IQ, language, and reading ability up to 18 years of age (Walker, Chang, & Powell, 2005). The authors suggested that the lack of sustained effects of the nutrition component may have been because beginning supplementation sometime between 9 and 24 months was too late or because the supplements may not have been consumed exclusively by the children. They indicated that beginning supplementation at an earlier age or achieving higher compliance with supplement consumption may have resulted in more lasting effects (Walker, Chang, & Powell, 2005). Together, this evidence suggests that adequate nutrition during pregnancy and throughout infancy is necessary for optimal cognitive development. However, the most effective timing for nutritional supplementation is not yet precise, since few randomised trials have been conducted and even fewer have evaluated cognition and other outcomes in adolescence and adulthood (Prado and Dewey 2014).

Table-1: Food supplementation with micronutrients, protein, energy and it is the effect on brain development.

Study location	Intervention	Age at intervention	Age at assessment	Results
New York City (Rush, 1984)	High protein and energy drink with increased amounts of micronutrients versus moderate protein and energy drink with standard amounts of micronutrients	Maternal supplementation throughout pregnancy until birth	12 months	No effect was found on the BSID mental or motor scores at age 12 months, but children whose mothers had received the high protein/energy drink scored higher on two information processing measures (visual habituation and dishabituation) and one of five measures of play (length of play episodes).
Taiwan (Joos Pollitt, & Mueller, 1983; Hsueh & Meyer, 1981)	High protein and energy drink with micronutrients versus no protein, low energy drink with micronutrients	Maternal supplementation throughout pregnancy and lactation	Eight months	A positive effect was found on BSID motor but not mental scores.

			Five years	No effect on IQ or mental age (mental ability expressed in years of age by comparison with a norm reference group).
Guatemala (Pollitt, 1993; Li et.al, 2003; & Hoddinott et.al, 2008)	High protein and energy drink with micronutrients versus no protein, low energy drink with micronutrients	Maternal and child supplementation throughout pregnancy and until age seven years	11-18 years	Positive effects were found on tests of math and knowledge scores. Positive effects on vocabulary and reading achievement were found only in children who received supplementation before two years of age.
			22-29 years (women)	A positive effect was found on reading and IQ scores.
			26-42 years (men)	The high protein and energy drink resulted in a 46% increase in average wages.
Colombia (Waber et al., 1981; Super et al., 1991)	Families who were provided with food (e.g., oil, dried milk, and bread) versus families who did not receive food	Throughout pregnancy and until age three years	Three years	A positive effect was found on Griffith's Developmental Quotient.
			5-8 years	A positive effect was found on reading readiness but not arithmetic or knowledge.
Indonesia (Husaini, 1991; Pollitt et al., 1997)	Children in daycare centres who were provided with snacks containing protein and energy versus children in daycare centres not provided with snacks	Children between ages 6 and 20 months at enrolment for three months of intervention	9-23 months	A positive effect was found on BSID motor but not mental scores.

			8-9 years	A positive effect was found on a test of working memory but not on reaction time, recall, emotionality, vocabulary, or arithmetic
Indonesia (Pollitt et.al, 2000; Aitchison et.al, 2000)	High protein and energy milk plus micronutrient tablet (treatment 1) versus low protein and energy milk plus micronutrient tablet (treatment 2) versus low protein and energy milk plus placebo (control)	Children age 12 or 18 months at enrolment for 12 months of intervention	24 or 30 months	Positive effects of the two treatments versus the control were found on several measures of motor development and activity levels. An effect of the high protein and energy milk was found on one of several measures of cognitive development.
Jamaica (Gratham-Mc Gragor et.al, 1991; 1997; Walker et.al, 2000; Walker et.al, 2005;2007)	Stunted children assigned to supplementation with high protein and energy milk or psychosocial stimulation or both supplementation and stimulation versus non-stunted controls	Children age 9-24 months at enrolment for two years of intervention	33-48 months	A positive effect of supplementation was found on Griffith's Developmental Quotient as well as the locomotor and performance subscales
			7-8 years	No effect of supplementation on a battery of cognitive tests
			11-12 years	No effect of supplementation on a battery of cognitive tests
			17-18 years	No effect of supplementation on cognition or mental health

Source: Tabular Structure adopted from Prado and Dewey, 2014

Earlier researches emphasise the importance of micronutrients. The mid-day meals served in schools consists of vitamin and mineral rich food items. At home also, the emphasis is given on green leafy vegetables. However, one can not ignore the importance of protein, which is not only required for body development for bodybuilding but also brain development and functioning at various stages of life and must be consumed regularly but in limited quantity. An ERP based study shows that regular intake of protein helps in quicker response and better recognition as compared to low protein diet. The ERP is a time-locked to a specific event which is computed by averaging the brain activity in the electroencephalogram (EEG), for instance, an auditory, stimulus. These results in a waveform associated with the processing of that specific event. The ERPs found in such tasks have a distinctive waveform with clearly classifiable components, which are named as per their polarity and approximate latency, i.e., P100, N100, P200, N200, P300 etc. The P300 (also referred to as P3) component of the auditory ERP is a significant positive waveform that reaches a maximum at approximately 300 milliseconds after stimulus onset (figure 1). The amplitude is defined as the voltage difference between a pre-stimulus established baseline and the largest positive peak within a predefined latency window (Polich, 2007; Dinteren, Arns, Jongsma, & Kessels, 2014).

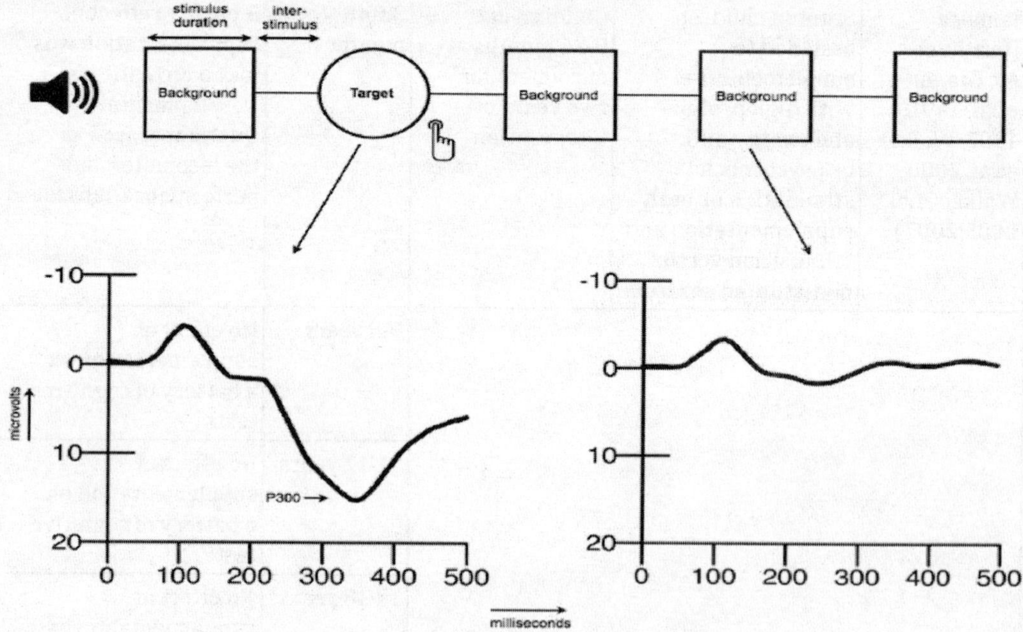

Fig. 1. Schematic overview of the oddball paradigm and an example of an ERP

Source: van Dinteren, Arns, Jongsma, & Kessels (2014)

The P300 is commonly elicited in signal-detection tasks. A typical signal-detection paradigm is the 'oddball' paradigm that was first used by Ritter and Vaughan (1969). In the auditory version, the participants were presented with two different tones that can be

30. Van Dinteren, R., Arns, M., Jongsma, M.L., & Kessels, R.P. (2014). P300 development across the lifespan: a systematic review and meta-analysis. PloS one, 9(2), e87347.
31. Waber D.P., Vuori-Christiansen L., Ortiz N., Clement J.R., Christiansen N.E., Mora J.O., Reed R.B. & Herrera M.G. (1981) Nutritional supplementation, maternal education, and cognitive development of infants at risk of malnutrition. American Journal of Clinical Nutrition 34, 807-813.
32. Walker S.P., Chang S.M., & Powell C.A. (2005) Effects of early childhood psychosocial stimulation and nutritional supplementation on cognition and education in growth-stunted Jamaican children: a prospective cohort study. Lancet; 366:1804-1807.
33. Walker, S.P., Chang, S.M., Powell, C.A., Simonoff, E., & Grantham-McGregor, S.M. (2007). Early childhood stunting is associated with poor psychological functioning in late adolescence and effects are reduced by psychosocial stimulation. The Journal of nutrition, 137(11), 2464-2469.
34. Walker, S.P., Grantham-McGregor, S.M., Powell, C.A., & Chang, S.M. (2000). Effects of growth restriction in early childhood on growth, IQ, and cognition at age 11 to 12 years and the benefits of nutritional supplementation and psychosocial stimulation. The Journal of paediatrics, 137(1), 36-41.

□

8

Malnutrition among Tribal Children: A Humanitarian Emergency

—Apoorva Laxman Patel

Abstract

'Nutrition' is one of the development issues of the nation. The investment in child health and development can be viewed not only as a desirable societal investment for the nation's future but also as the fulfilment of the rights of every child to 'survival, protection, and development'. The unacceptably high prevalence of malnutrition in our country implies the fact that we have deprived our children of their most elementary rights. Especially the tribal communities which constitute a major part of India are highly vulnerable to endemic problems like malnourishment, causing a high, degree of morbidity and mortality.

This mixed method research study was an attempt to explore the magnitude of malnutrition among tribal children, with a qualitative focus to find out the role/linkages of various factors & the effectiveness of nutrition interventions and several welfare programmes in addressing malnutrition. The study area was dominant tribal hamlets of Rewa district in Madhya Pradesh. These hamlets are regarded as the most malnourishment hit areas about associated morbidity. The population studied comprised of Kol, Gond and Khairwaar Tribes.

Anthropometric measurements were used to assess the nutrition status of children. The findings showed that 76% of children were malnourished as per 'MUAC measurement criteria for 6-60 months of children' and 54% were malnourished according to 'WHO Weight-for-Age standard growth criteria'. The study found that socioeconomic factors and health factors, along with traditional practices, contributed to, the poor nutritional status of children. Also, cultural beliefs practised in the community not only aggravate the situation of poor health but also cause a cycle of debt and mortgage for households.

Introduction

"We are guilty of many errors and many faults, but our worst crime is abandoning the children, neglecting the foundation of life. Many of the things we need can wait.

The child cannot. Right now is the time his bones are being formed, his blood is being made, and his senses, are being developed. To him, we cannot answer 'Tomorrow'... His name is 'Today'."

—*Gabriela Mistral, 1948*

Health, right from the womb, is an essential component of human development. The right to health is a fundamental part of our human rights and our understanding of a life of dignity (Gruskin, 2005). First articulated in 1946, Constitution of the World Health Organisation (WHO) preamble defines health as "a state of complete physical, mental and social well-being and not merely the absence of disease or infirmity". It further states that "the enjoyment of the highest attainable standard of health is one of the fundamental rights of every human being without distinction of race, religion, and political belief, economic or social condition (WHO. int, 1946)." The 1948 Universal Declaration of Human Rights also mentioned health as a part of the right to an adequate standard of living (Art. 25).

India's progress in many areas and march towards the global economic stage is visible in many forms. However, India shining and rambunctious success stories are often exceptions and against hard odds, which belies the fact that socio-economic, food and nutrition security remains an enormous challenge for an overwhelming majority of Indian households who struggle daily for existence. Hunger, nutrition security and malnutrition are the most severe of daily experiences.

Today is one of the biggest concern of developing countries growing deaths in under five children. The most neglected form of human deprivation is malnutrition, particularly among children. The first six years are the most crucial period in life. At this stage, the foundations for cognitive, social, emotional, physical or motor development and cumulative lifelong learning are laid. About four-fifths of a child's mental and physical growth takes place in the initial two years. By the end of the second year of life—critical brain structures are in place, and most of the growth of the human brain gets complete. During this time, the child should be given ample nutrition and care and the absence of which hampers the overall growth and development of the child.

Malnutrition (Srilakshmi, 2006) in all its forms increases the risk of disease and early death. Protein-energy malnutrition (PEM), for example, plays a major role in half of all under-five deaths each year in developing countries (Vir, 2015). There has been a large body of evidence presenting that the impact of prolonged malnutrition is irrevocable, past the child's first two-three years of life.

Growing up healthy is every child's right and for which Food and nutrition security is the central link. Thus, investment in child health and development can be viewed not only as a desirable societal investment for the nation's future but also as the fulfilment of the rights of every child to 'survival, protection, and development' and to achieve their full growth and potential. The United Nation (UN) estimates that 2.1 million Indian children die before reaching the age of five every year–four every minute-mostly from common preventable or easily treatable infectious illnesses such as diarrhoea, typhoid, malaria, measles and pneumonia; the risk of which occurs due to increased vulnerability of children because of malnutrition (Cohen, 2013). Thus, the risk of death for common childhood diseases is related to the degree of malnutrition.

It is a well-established fact that the prevalence of child under-nutrition in India is among the highest in the world; nearly double that of Sub-Saharan Africa, with grim repercussions of morbidity, mortality, productivity, and economic growth. Still today in developing countries like us, undernutrition remains a major problem. Malnutrition and food insecurity are widespread among disadvantaged populations, mainly residing in under-served areas such as remote, marginalised, rural, tribal, or slum areas. It has turned out death-defying owing to the threatening fact that we have deprived our children of their most elementary right to health and to sustain in life.

It is a major public health and nutrition challenges faced by many developing countries. What makes the situation more serious is that children under the age of six are the hardest hit victims of malnutrition.

Malnutrition is a major public health problem throughout the developing world and is an underlying cause of over half of the ten to eleven million children under six years of age who die each year of preventable causes. Worldwide there are about sixty million children with Moderate Acute Malnutrition (MAM) and thirteen million with Severe Acute Malnutrition (SAM). About 9% of Sub Saharan Africa and 15% of South Asian children have MAM, and about 2% of children in developing countries have SAM (Collins et al., 2006).

It affects all age groups, but it is especially common among the poor and those with poor access to health, education and adequate and safe water and sanitation facilities. More than 70% of children with protein-energy malnutrition (PEM) live in Asia, 26% live in Africa, and 4% in Latin America and the Caribbean (Chowdhury et al., 2005).

The World Bank estimates that India is one of the highest-ranking countries in the world for the number of children suffering from malnutrition (Mohanty, 2016). It had recognised malnutrition as the gravest health problem in the world. It is stated that malnutrition leads to maximum deaths among children; for instance, 6;0% of our chi, children who die of malaria, diarrhoea or pneumonia could have been saved if they were not malnourished.

'Malnutrition' is a common and widely used term to refer to suboptimal nutritional health (Semba & Bloem, 2008). In international health and this study also, the term 'malnutrition' generally refers to undernutrition[25] (condition of acute malnutrition or wasting[26], stunting, and underweight) rather than overnutrition (condition of obesity).

Research Objectives

The research is aiming to explore the situation of the nutritional health status of tribal children, and the whys and wherefores leading to aggravating situations instead of various measures undertaken. It also aims to find out the linkages of different factors or aspects of under-nutrition focusing on a tribal area in Madhya Pradesh (MP), what are its contributing factors, what are the effects of various goals or schemes of the state and interventions of non-governmental organisations. The objectives of this study can be listed as under:

To understand the socio-economic and demographic conditions of the study population.

To study the nutritional health status of pre-school tribal children.

To explore the linkages between different policy interventions (Schemes & Programmes) of Government.

To explore the effectiveness of programmes (policy interventions) in addressing the problem of malnutrition.

To evolve some recommendations helpful to improve the design and therefore, the effectiveness of the programs aimed at preventing malnutrition.

Materials and Methods

Madhya Pradesh is considered as the tribal heart of India, having the largest Scheduled Tribes (STs) population; comprising of 21.1% of the state population (15.31 million out of 72.62 million) (Dwivedi, 2016). Tribal communities, comprising a major part of the country's population, are highly vulnerable to endemic problems like malnourishment causing a high degree of morbidity and mortality. The Literature review shows that malnutrition and other deficiency disorders like anaemia are highly prevalent among the tribal communities. This is extremely relevant in the social context as in the long run; it has severe, repercussions related to the overall growth and development of the child to be a healthy citizen.

---

25. Undernutrition—An insufficient intake and/or inadequate absorption of energy, protein or micronutrients that in turn leads to nutritional deficiency.
26. Acute malnutrition or wasting is characterised by a rapid deterioration in nutritional status over a short period of time resulting into poor growth. In children, it can be measured using the weight-for-height or weight-for-age nutritional index or mid-upper arm circumference. It is further divided into two categories depending on the levels of severity as: moderate acute malnutrition (MAM) and severe acute malnutrition (SAM).

The high rate of Maternal Mortality Rate (MMR) and Infant Mortality Rate (IMR) along with the problem of malnutrition, is one of the major concerns of tribal health. MP tops the list with the highest IMR of 72, lowest life expectancy of 57.7 years in comparison to Indian average of 63.2 years (Moribund ICDS, 2009).

The child population (0-6 years) in MP is 14.53%, where the rural child population proportion is 15.48%, and the urban is 12.04% (Census, 2011). The trend of decline in the proportion of child population is greater in the rural areas as compared to its urban counterpart for both India and MP.

For the present research, the universe of the study is Rewa District. The study area was rural tribal dominant hamlets-Mainaha, Kakredi, Koni-Kureli, and Dhakra-Kotwa of Semariya and Jawa Block of Rewa district, M.P.; from where there had been subjective reports by media of suspected malnutrition or starvation deaths of children. The population studied comprise of Kol, Gond and Khairwaar Tribe.

Thirty-five respondents belonged to Semariya Block (16 of Mainaha and 19 of Kakredi), and 15 respondents belonged to Jawa Block (5 of Kureli and 10 of Dhakra-Kotwa) of Rewa dist.

A sample of 50 each-children aged between 1-6 years and their mothers (the main respondents) respectively, who are residing for more than the last six months were selected for the study. The sample size was taken by assuming the prevalence of under-nutrition of 45% with 10% allowable error and at 95% level of significance. All the children were selected randomly by a simple random sampling technique.

The study design adopted for the study is cross-sectional. The researcher used a mixed method approach design, i.e. used both, Quantitative and Qualitative methods for this study to get a complete view and build the linkages between different factors. The researcher engaged in mixed methods study to follow up with a quantitative study with a qualitative one to obtain more detailed specific information.

The interview schedule is used as a primary data collection tool for conducting this study. Data was collected using a pre-tested semi-structured interview schedule by house-to-house visit and mothers of infants were interviewed.

For collecting qualitative data-individual-based method like key informant interview was adopted

. An observation-based method like observations from the field visits ('observing people in their natural setting-as they live their everyday lives') was recorded, and group-based methods like focus group discussions were conducted with mothers in the community and as a documents based method—the existing data is used for data analysis. Case Study is a qualitative method of data collection & involves a careful and complete analysis of a limited event or condition & its inter-relationship. In this study case studies from the studied hamlets have been collected during interaction with the community.

The researcher visited Nutritional Rehabilitation Centres (NRC) at Jawa Block, Rewa district. For seeking supportive information, the researcher met with the local key people, medical social worker, the doctor in charge of NRC centre, an officer of Women & Children Welfare Department (*Baal Vikas Adhikari*), headmaster of village Govt. School, local leading newspaper reporters, leaders, and beauro chief.

For studying the nutritional status, the Quantitative data was collected using Anthropometric measurements like Mid-Upper-Arm Circumference (MUAC) and weight for Age (standard growth criteria of WHO); as they are statistically considerably associated with grades of malnutrition. MUAC is considered as a relatively simple measurement/index, but with a fixed cut-off, it ignores age-related changes. Evidence from the variously available study shows that MUAC is the best (in terms of age independence, precision, accuracy, sensitivity, and specificity) case– detection method for severe and moderate malnutrition and that it is also simple, cheap and acceptable. In this study, MUAC determined based on a fixed cut-off value is used as a proxy for low weight-for-height (wasting). It is an alternative measure of thinness which is used for children of 6-59 months, measured on the left upper arm, the best predictor of mortality and the Nutrition Rehabilitation Centers use it as criteria for admitting the child.

Therefore, Weight for age was also used as a criterion for the classification of grades of malnutrition. The children were weighed using a salter weighing machine after taking all the precautions and standardisation of the machine. According to the latest standard guidelines of WHO, the infants with the level of malnutrition—SAM, Malnourished, and Normal were identified.

CASE STUDY 1

A superstitious faith or helplessness!

A custom of pretense selling and purchasing the own child immediately after the birth of the baby prevails in the study area, in which a close female relative takes the child away from mother and demand money (which is given depending on the economic condition of the family) for giving the child's possession back to mother. This is followed as a lifesaving trick, which could be termed as a superstitious faith or as clearly presenting the picture of cruel circumstances and helplessness of the poor parents to save or protect their new born's life from disease/demise.

The families following this custom known as 'MOLA', are basically the ones where earlier children have not survived. Ramrati Bai of Mainaha hamlet had lost all her four children. Similar is the story of many other families too. Ramrati Bai says "What can be done in this situation where we do not have any facility or option and are thus only left with surrendering everything to fate and take help of some superstitious beliefs."

Another evident thing is that during all this process the baby is kept away from the mother, thus deterring her/him from the mother's first (colostrum) milk. As such this is the first step which proves to be fatal for life of the child, apart from lifetime name tagging as Mola child!.

CASE STUDY 2

The systems negligence: SNF of Adolescent Girls Distributed to Children; No recognition of demises as malnourishment deaths

Ankit (1 year)—Child of Sidhpal and Gudiya, had expired in the halfway while returning back to home from hospital. Before taking the child to hospital some treatment has been taken from traditional healer of the area as well. Ankit had fever and was admitted in hospital for three days after which also there was no improvement in his health. Sidpal then decided to bring the child back to home. He said that he also did not have any more money to stay further for treatment.

He told that while returning back Ankit was breathing heavily, but in the mid-way they could not return back. Sidhpal told that though the child was very weak, doctors themselves didn't take the decision of NRC admission nor did they suggest the family to do so. Another unfortunate thing is only after the newspaper reports of malnourishment deaths in both the areas of *Kakredi Panchayat*, the AWW face became visible.

First child of Sidhpal and Gudiya-Ramkali (4 years old), was also found moderately malnourished when examined using MUAC-anthropometric measurement. The mother told that she had not got vaccinations during her pregnancy, nor her children are given any vaccine. When asked about distribution of SNF from AWC, she says that it was never distributed before, just 2 days before the researcher's visit to the hamlet, two packets of SNF were being given by AWW. On checking the packets researcher found that those packets were for Adolescent Girls. The major concern is firstly no SNF is ever distributed and when it is given that too was not of pre-school kid.

CASE STUDY 3

Nanhi Bai and his son Ramprakash of Kakredi hamlet are busy these days collecting the scrap of '*Kahwa*' tree from the forest. They leave for these work in the early dawn and return at the late dusk. Both of them have gathered only 3 quintals of scrap after working for 10 days continuously which will be sold just for total of Rs.300 on the basis of its selling price being Rs.1/kg. This implies that the cost of 10 days hard labour of two people is just Rs. 300/-, i.e., Rs. 15 per person per day. This scrap of Kahwa tree is used for making an Ayurveda medicine for high blood pressure—'*Arjunarishta*'. The thekedaar comes to the village for taking this scrap and then sells it for Rs.50-60 per kg in the market. This case is not to mention here the economics of Kahwa's scrap but has altogether a different objective to put forth another sad story of our other half population. The actual thing is Nanhi Bai has agreed to read the sacraments at Basanan Mama Temple for the well-being and safety of her grandchildren and for this she is making efforts to collect every penny in all ways she can. Nanhibai says that there is still lot to add as the expenditure on this ritual will cost around Rs.1200.

Not only this, Nanhibai has also agreed to sacrifice a hen and a goat to her family god, which is to be done on the birth of "SON". But she says that after many efforts also she is not been able to gather this much amount to complete this promise of hers. And she says that its harms have also started to show up like child cries a lot, becomes aggressive, and is weaning day by day. He has anyways survived after many troubles. Her daughter-in-law yells in between saying that now her mother in law gets the nightmares of snake as she has not fulfilled her promise and because of this many times she has sleepless nights.

The actual story begins from here. Nanhibai has already lost her two grandchildren (of age 2.5 and 1.5 years). The actual reason she couldn't tell but said that they have become too weak and weaned. After which a girl—Priyanshi has born, who also survived the nearing death and then a boy—Luvkush is born and thus to save his life she has agreed for all those rituals.

Unheard Voices Surrendering Themselves to Delusions

Not limited to only Basanan Mama and Dulha Dev, but they have also followed the misbelief (*totka*) of selling and purchasing their son Luvkush. The custom is known as '*MOLA*'. All this may look a filmy story but it is the real story of Kakredi hamlet of Semariya Tahsil of Rewa district.

In this hamlet of 150 households, live either tribal or higher caste people. *Gond*, *Kol* and *Khairvaar* are tribal and Brahmin, Yadav and Thakur belong to higher caste. Nanhi Bai is Khairvaar. She just has an old, white ration card. Job card is their but is blank as no job has been given.

In such conditions, for survival they are working on a piece of land of Thakur. Nanhi Bai is living with her husband, son, daughter-in-law and two grandchildren in a small hut. When she was having her food, she didn't have *daal* on her plate with rice. On asking she said that it's been months from when they have not eat *daal*.

Her both grandchildren are severely malnourished to which she is considering as annoyance of Dulha Dev Baba. The actual reason of her grandson's weakness, weaning body is malnourishment. In this hamlet from last 5 years AWC has not opened. The AWW lives in the nearby hamlet. Recently, only after the deaths of children she has distributed the SNF packets for the first time. Luvkush and her mother Bitol has also not got any of the vaccination because no health worker visits the hamlet as according to the health dept. officials the area is dacoits infested so is left to God.

Here even today most of the deliveries take place at home as there is no means of transportation available. The only vehicle available is Milk van which serves as the Ambulance in emergency. The nearest hospital is at Ragauli village- 12kms away, where SHC has been inaugurated this month (October) only and other one is at Simariya—21kms and Siramur—30kms away.

After the deaths of children one after the other, the unaffected government system in hurry has done the face towards these hamlets but in the result the husband of AWW and members of SHG have knocked the doors of Aadiwasi households with guns and said that if anyone spoke anything in against than will be shot dead. The negligence of government and terror of powerful and higher class, leave nothing with the helpless villagers other than surrendering themselves to Dulha Dev and Basanan Mana. The resultant of all this is ever trapping cycle of poverty from which it's impossible for them to step out. Nanhi Bai and her family are even thinking to take some money on credit to anyhow save the life of their children.

Findings and Conclusions

Good nutritional health status gives the idea of progress and development of the country. Right to health is a fundamental of human rights for a life of dignity. Food and nutrition security is the central link of the right of every child to survival protection and development to achieve full growth and potential. Nutrition security is an important factor which contributes to further health, development and economic growth. The nutritional health is largely dependent upon factors like social, economic, environmental, agricultural, cultural, health and political. The unacceptably high prevalence of malnutrition in our country implies the fact that we have deprived our children of their most elementary rights. Especially the tribal communities which constitute a major part of India are highly vulnerable to endemic problems like malnourishment, causing a high, degree of morbidity and mortality.

Portrayal from quantitative indications and qualitative studies, this is an attempt to study the nutritional health status of tribal children, the magnitudes of child under-nutrition, its basic causes, the role of various factors influencing the nutritional status of tribal children and the effectiveness of the nutrition intervention and several other welfare programmes in addressing malnutrition.

The area of this research study is dominant tribal hamlets—Mainaha, Kakredi, Koni-Kureli, and Dhakra-Kotwa of Semariya and Jawa Block of Rewa District, MP, which are regarded as the most malnourishment hit areas about associated morbidity. The research sample study is based on 50 pre-school children.

The malnourishment deaths among pre-school tribal children have been high in these areas. A significant number of children fall in the category of severely acutely malnourished and at high risk of malnourishment and needs urgent attention and care to escape the trap of approaching bereavement. Malnourishment as the actual cause of death gets hardly assented, which further add to the problem instead of combating from it. Socio-economic, nutrition and food security is still a major challenge for these households who struggle daily for existence.

The population studied comprise of *Kol*, *Gond* and *Khairwaar* Tribe who follow Hindu religion. The majority of the respondents (mothers') were in the (lower) age group of 18-24 years, and the average age of marriage is 15-19 years. The respondents were all illiterate, and their spouses have also hardly attended primary school. Thus, Female illiteracy was found to be a strong determinant of child malnutrition, which is in line with results in earlier related literature.

Most of the people in the study area, work as daily wage labourers or agricultural workers. Some of them depend on the forest to manage their living. Many have to migrate in search of wage employment in nearby towns or neighbouring states. The substantial land holdings in the area belong to the upper caste community on which tribal people work as daily wage labourers.

People here have a joint family with an average family size of 5.5, with a minimum of three and a maximum of eight to ten members per household and all live in *kutcha* houses. The majority of the households are surviving on a very meagre amount of income.

This all factors directly influence the standard of living, expenditure, and food consumption pattern of households, the nutritional intake and health status of the family, and play the great role in health-seeking behaviour and practices, and availing medical facilities. This also brings out the fact that feudalism though not visible; prevailing in the area seems to have taken an additional toll and is responsible for the deteriorating conditions.

The physical conditions of water supply in studied areas are far from satisfactory. The majority of households use untreated water of open well as the main source of drinking water, which is not suitable for good health. Many of the households use hand pumps or *bawdi*. In summer when the water dries up, it is to be fetched from the river lying at a far distance from the houses or even have to use the drain water which often becomes the cause of illnesses. The hand pumps have been dug (at Koni-kureli) for the namesake but are not deep enough, so are of no use. Households do not have toilet facility and electricity connections also, and the oil lamps are the only source of light. Only Sarpanch's house had a solar light pole. Majority of the household does not own any asset.

Lack of integration of nutrition with safe drinking water, proper sanitation facility and hygiene issues, along with an invisible prevalence of caste and class power and politics seems to have to aggravate the situation.

The maximum respondents have had home deliveries and were not assisted by any trained health worker/Auxiliary Nurse Midwife (ANM) and owing to this fact another realities are that children have not been weighted at or after birth, the majority of children were not breastfed within one hour of birth. These reflect the poor availability, accessibility, and utilisation of Ante Natal Care (ANC) and Post Natal Care/post-partum check-ups (PNC) services.

Institutional delivery accounts for very few cases, and these women have the only breastfed their child within the first hour of birth. Thus, it can be said that if there is an expansion of institutional deliveries, it will lead to the encouragement of early initiation of breastfeeding.

There is a lack of awareness regarding the importance (nutritive value) of colostrum feeding. Ill-informed cultural practices, beliefs or behaviours are much prevalent, for instance, breastfeeding, after 3-6 days of birth. This show that maximum children are prohibited from colostrum milk and also the transitional milk which comes after colostrum, and thus gets deprived of first natural feed which provides antibodies to develop immunity and protect the new-born against diseases (like jaundice) as well as provides higher proteins for growth.

Another such cultural belief practised in the community is 'MOLA', Dulhadev, Baghaur Baba, Basanan Mama Katha; which not only aggravate the situation of poor health but also cause a cycle of debt and mortgage for households.

Generally, the child is breastfed till the age of around 1-2 years, and the complementary/solid food is introduced in child's diet after six months of age, only if child willingly eats; thereby left to the choice of the child rather than being a health need. The nutritious food like fruits, milk, egg, etc. is not at all the part of their daily diet due to inability to afford them. '*Kodo-Kutki*'–a type of cereal having tiny beans is given to the child mostly as supplement food.

The anthropometric measurements show that more than half of the studied children are malnourished. The average mean height and weight were far below the normal standards. They require an immediate reference for supplementation/ treatment and counselling and follow up for growth promotion and monitoring to come out from the trap of the cycle of malnutrition.

The health-seeking behaviour is very much affected by availability, accessibility, affordability, quality, etc. and thus is of important concern for health. There is no Primary Health Centre (PHC) or Sub Health Centre (SHC) in the village. The first line of treatment is usually the traditional healer *(Ojha)* as the majority believe it to be a good and cheap source and mostly prefer it because of easy accessibility. Majority of the people do not visit the doctor or hospital in case of children's illness mainly because of high travelling and treatment expenses, inaccessibility due to long distances of the PHC from home, the paucity of transport to the health centre, the attitude, and availability of health personnel. These are important issues, which have some definite impact on the health of children in these areas. This denotes the serious problems of physical access, affordability and the availability of many health care services in rural areas.

The household's do not have an immunisation card of their children. No nearby medical facility or service is available for providing immunisation and nor does any Anganwadi Worker (AWW), LHW or Multi-Purpose Worker (MPW) or any Health Worker ever visit for providing immunisation services in the hamlet. Some also do believe that after receiving the vaccination, the child gets, a fever or think that the child is too small to give vaccination; so are reluctant to visit a doctor for a vaccination.

The study brings out that the public health infrastructure is far from satisfactory, and shortfall of manpower is also a big problem, e.g., even after a considerably large no. of high-risk category/ SAM children in the block in need of urgent NRC admission, the shortage of beds at NRC often deter them from getting immediate treatment.

These also show that despite the tremendous advancement in the field of preventive and curative medicine, the health care delivery services in primitive tribal people are still poor and need to be strengthened in order to achieve the goal of Health for all in the country. Also, the illiteracy, of parents, their lack of knowledge about health-care services, their lower socio-economic status and accessibility to health services, etc. militate against the proper utilisation of health care services.

The study states that the status of AWCs, primary schools and schemes like Mid Day Meal (MDM) is despicable. They exist but are not adequately functional. The AWW has maintained no growth charts of children. Rarely the packets of Supplementary Nutrition Food (SNF) are distributed. Even children most vulnerable to malnutrition are neither registered at the AWCs and are not getting any substantial benefits of the scheme.

Though almost every household falls under the Below Poverty Line (BPL) category, no PDS facility is available or being utilised. Some of them do have BPL card or Antyodaya Anna Yojana (AAY) card, but they are unable to purchase their full quota of 35 kg per month. From PDS shops, the only 30kg ration is distributed (15kg-rice and 15kg-wheat). Half of them have the job cards made under Mahatma Gandhi National Rural Employment Guarantee Act (MNREGA), but most have not got any work.

Measures like NRHM appear to be disappointing because not even the Accredited Social Health Activist (ASHA) worker is aware of schemes like *Janani Suraksha Yojana*. Respondents have not got registered under any such scheme. No one has received any ANC and PNC check-ups or visits. There is no distribution of vitamin, iron, and iodine or IFA tablets in the village nor is the SNF properly provided. Other social security schemes like–old age and widow pension schemes are also absent.

It seems that addressing the underlying issues of food insecurity, unemployment, poor health, etc. to combat the problem of hunger and malnutrition among the Scheduled Tribe (ST) community at first place could prove to be instruments of change available before the state government. This requires a proper and simultaneous multisectoral provision of services, intervention, and implementation with political commitment.

The people of the area are still suffering from landlessness, lack of employment opportunities leading to migration, non-functional Govt. Schemes and non-operational Govt. Service delivery systems. In the context of specific child rights issues, there is a high incidence of drop out and low enrolment. The area has low birth registration, low immunisation rate and high incidence of malnutrition. Nutritional deficiencies have led to an increased number of underweight children.

Vertical health and family welfare programmes have shown very limited synergy at operational levels. As found out during the study, the administrative officials, policymakers, health department officials/personnel's and other government executives are confronted with difficulties because of poor demographic conditions, and presence of dacoits in few areas (like Mainaha)—making for them unreachable and challenging to address the prevalent problems. Surprisingly, (Mainaha) Sarpanch and people of the hamlet did not report of any such incidences of dacoit's terror at the time of research study. It could, therefore, be said that the actual growth story is about the silent growth of socio-economic insecurity, disparities, discrepancies, hunger.

The AWW/ANM/MPW or any other health workers also do not visit the hamlets. Only after the media and a civil society organisation highlighted the issue, the health department made a move under pressure to visit the hamlets and conducted a medical camp at Mainaha.

From the field study, it has become evident that the apparent reasons for mismatches are that the programmes face substantial operational challenges. There are many vertical programmes with poor targeting, accountability, and governance and poor convergence and synergy between the functioning of ministries and departments. Another problem is a very top-down approach is undertaken without sensitising the community and making them partners in planning and execution.

Apart from these factors, it was observed that the system of early marriage is still very much prevalent, which is also a significant cause of low-birth-weight baby. There is no family in the area that has not lost at least a single child. The fertility rate seems to be high because of the uncertainty of chances of survival than of having more hands to earn. Undernutrition is higher in children with short birth intervals and higher-order births. The youngest child in most of the houses is observed to be trapped in a cycle of malnourishment. The prevalence of malnutrition increased with increasing age group among infants. That is to say; the prevalence was significantly higher among infants more than six months of age. The infants more than six months of age are susceptible to malnutrition due to inappropriate weaning practices and improper nutritional supplementation.

The underlying causes of under-nutrition found the range from poverty, low levels of education, inaccessibility to health services, to huge disparities existing due to various factors -are worsening the situation. However, the study states malnutrition as the underlying cause of death is being perpetuated by existing social, economic, cultural, geographical and largely political factors.

Recommendations—A Way Forward

Based on the study, some probable, measures which can be taken up to address the issue improve the nutritional status of tribal children can be listed as below:

Developmental issues need to be addressed by addressing the basic needs like safe drinking water, proper sanitation, for health and hygiene, the road for easy conveyance, electricity facilities, etc., along with education and health awareness.

Ensuring food and nutrition security with socio-economic security is of utmost importance to achieve the goal of good nutritional health of all children.

It is seen that the presence of feudalism, caste, and class power politics is often the cause of landlessness, socio-economic insecurities, disparities, and discrepancies. Thus it is important to view child undernutrition as the individual biological manifestation of social, cultural, demographic, economic and political forces and the interplay of gender, caste, class, and household and community dynamics.

It is necessary to consider the specific circumstances of the poor while designing the interventions to address undernutrition.

It is recommended to Improve food and nutrient intake for adolescent girls, adult women, pregnant and lactating women; mainly to prevent anaemia through informal education and awareness campaigns.

The community should be made aware of some importance of timely initiation of breastfeeding within one hour of birth, exclusive breastfeeding during the first six months of life, timely introduction of complementary foods at six months, age-appropriate complementary feeding, adequate in terms of quality, quantity and frequency for children 6-24 months. It should also focus on appropriate weaning practices, safe handling of complementary foods and hygienic complementary feeding practices.

Reference, treatment, counselling, follow-up, growth promotion and monitoring, weight monitoring, etc., of children to prevent them from malnutrition and timely and quality therapeutic feeding and care for children with severe acute malnutrition is required to save the lives which are at high risk of death.

Timely and appropriate ANC and PNC services—check-ups and visits need to be ensured.

Training the primary health care workers/providers like AWW, ANM, Traditional Birth Attendant (TBA) and making them aware of malnutrition can help in early diagnosis and referral of the child for treatment, along with giving proper incentives and motivation can improve the health care services delivery.

The community women should be encouraged for registering their pregnancy at a nearby hospital and having institutional delivery for safe health of both mother and child.

Ensuring proper health infrastructure and health care delivery facilities and services, by the availability of Sub-health centre in each village can surely help to improve the health status of the population.

The working of the Anganwadi Centre, Mid Day-Meal—should be strengthened so that the proper distribution of supplementary nutrition food and take home ration can be ensured.

In the remote or backward areas like the study region, MNREGA creates hope for livelihood security. Awareness of the right to demand and get gainful employment and social security to live the life of dignity should be generated.

Better defining and refining the selection criteria of families below the poverty line and a host of essential interventions to improve nutritional security of these families can ensure the improved nutritional health status of children.

It is important to educate and aware women regarding the factors which affect the nutritional health status of the child such as early marriage, malnourished mother, low birth weight baby, high fertility rate, the birth of a child at short birth intervals, and higher-order births, etc.

The pre-school children, particularly those under two years of age who needs greater attention to survive and develop, should be now emphasised to prevent the occurrence malnutrition from the very beginning.

There is an urgent need to utilise the wealth of the existing data on widespread malnutrition for effective advocacy, to enable people to access their right to not only food security but nutritious food.

A specific value should be given for documenting starvation, malnutrition, both because it is a humanitarian emergency and because it may help to shake an otherwise complacent state and civil society into some action.

The changes are required to be brought in the perception of field staff and community about childhood illnesses, home-based care, and early referral.

There is a need to train and build the capacity of implementing agencies from local or lowest level to highest level of schemes and programmes like MDM, and to ensure that the stipulations under the schemes are adhered to and all norms are maintained.

The need is to redirect particularly the public investments in ICDS towards the younger children (0-3 years) and the most vulnerable population segments in those areas, particularly tribal, where the prevalence of undernutrition is higher.

There are a large number of Non-Governmental Organisations (NGOs) working in the field. To ensure the feasibility of different nutrition interventions and for strengthening the implementation of various schemes and programmes, collaboration with these non-governmental agencies or voluntary organisations, and funding agencies is required.

The understanding of the gaps in linkages and the areas affecting malnutrition can significantly help to improve the design and therefore, the effectiveness of the programs aimed at preventing malnutrition in our country.

There is a long way to go, and the result remains to be seen.

References

1. Census 2011, Child Population (0-6 Age Group), from http://censusmp.nic.in/censusmp/All-PDF/4childpopulation0-6-21.12.pdfAccessed on 12-03-2017
2. Chowdhury, F., Marufuzzaman, Md., Rashid, A., Nazmul, Md., Lt. Col. Azizul, & Khasru M. (2005). Protein Energy Malnutrition (PEM) With Rickets, J Medicine; 6: 30-32, from https://www.researchgate.net/publication/271208369_Protein_energy_malnutrition_with_RicketsAccessed on 05-04-2017
3. Cohen, P. (2013). Chapter 14–The capitalist holocaust 1914-2010. The Capitalist Holocaust, from https://thecapitalistholocaust.wordpress.com/2013/12/22/chapter-14-the-capitalist-holocaust-1914-2010/ Accessed on 12-04-2017
4. Collins, S., Sadler, K., Dent, N., Khara, T., Guerrero, S., & Myatt, M. et al. (2006). Key issues in the success of community-based management of severe malnutrition. From http://www.who.int/nutrition/topics/backgroundpapers_Key_issues.pdf Accessed on 4-04-2017

5. World Health Organisation, 1946. Constitution of the World Health Organisation, from https://www.who.int/governance/eb/who_constitution_en.pdf
6. Dwivedi, J., (2016). Indian, Tribal Ornaments; a Hidden Treasure, IOSR Journal of Environmental Science, from www.iosrjournals.org DOI: 10.9790/2402-1003020116 www.iosrjournals.org Accessed on 10-04-2017
7. Gabriela,M.(1948).SuNombreesHoy(HisNameisToday),http://14.139.60.114:8080/jspui/bitstream/123456789/691/4/Preface.pdf Accessed on 12-03-2017
8. Mohanty, A. (2016). Malnutrition: A curse for Odisha's Adivasi children-Adivasi Resurgence. Adivasiresurgence.com, from http://www.adivasiresurgence.com/malnutrition-curse-odisha-adivasi-children/Accessed on 18-03-2017
9. Moribund ICDS (a study on the ICDS and Child Survival issues in Madhya Pradesh). (2009). Vikas Samvad, from http://southasia.oneworld.net/Files/ICDS.pdf Accessed on 10-04-2017
10. Nazir, M. (2017). RIGHT TO HEALTH: A BASIC HUMAN RIGHT. International Journal of Legal Developments and Allied Issue, from http://ijldai.thelawbrigade.com/index.php/2017/05/24/right-to-health-a-basic-human-right/ Accessed on 12-04-2017
11. Semba, R., & Bloem, M. (2008). Nutrition and health in developing countries (1st ed.). Totowa, NJ: Humana Press, from https://www.researchgate.net/profile/Saskia_Pee/publication/226618419_Need_Efficacy_and_Effectiveness_of_Multiple_VitaminMineral_Supplements_for_Young_Children_and_Considerations_for_Programs/links/54ae8ac30cf2828b29ff0f95/Need-Efficacy-and-Effectiveness-of-Multiple-Vitamin-Mineral-Supplements-for-Young-Children-and-Considerations-for-Programs.pdf Accessed on 17-03-2017
12. Gruskin S. & Tarantola D. (2005). Perspectives on Health and Human Rights. New York: Routledge.
13. Srilakshmi, B. (2006). Nutrition Science, from https://books.google.co.in/books?id=f_i7j4_cMLIC&pg=PA2&lpg=PA2&dq=Accessed on 15-04-2017
14. Universal Declaration of Human Rights, 1948. (Article 25), from https://www.un.org/en/documents/udhr/
15. Vir, S. (2015). Public Health and Nutrition in Developing Countries (Part I and II). Google Books, https://books.google.co.in/books?id=Ykj7CAAAQBAJ&pg=PA292&lpg=PA292&dqAccessed on 28-03-2017

□

9

Nutritional Status of Primary School Going Children in Mumbai, India: A Case study

—*Niharika Rao and Aparajita Chattopadhyay*

Abstract

The study aims to understand the nutritional status of young school going children aged 6-9 years in the eastern part of Mumbai. It explores the role of socio-economic characteristics, food intake practice, daily routine and morbidity pattern of children in determining the nutritional status. Primary school going children require adequate nutrition for their healthy growth. The study assesses the levels and determinants of nutritional status of primary school children of grade 1st and 2nd . An exhaustive list of schools in the eastern suburb of Mumbai, India was prepared, and the schools were requested to permit the survey. Data was collected from 557 students of 1st and 2nd grade. Anthropometric measures like height and weight of children were measured using electronic machines. Height-for-age (Stunting), Weight-for-age (Underweight), Body Mass Index (BMI) were calculated to analyse the nutritional status. Nineteen percent of children are found to be stunted; about a quarter is having low BMI and 27 percent are underweight. Factors that have a significant negative impact on nourishment are the intake of baby tin milk, avoidance of breakfast, use of certain types of cooking oil, drinking of inadequate water, and childhood chronic diseases. Undernourishment is much more dependent on food habits and morbidity rather than socioeconomic factors. Provision of nutritious school breakfast, frequent intake of drinking water, the school-based de-worming programme can help to curb undernutrition among young children in India.

Introduction

Nutrition is a key element of development. Under-nutrition affects a large segment of the population in India. Reduction of child malnutrition is certainly the most desirable components of development (Handa, Ahamad, Kesari, & Prasad, 2008). Child under-nutrition is strongly associated with increased child mortality and morbidity, which hinders long-term physical growth, development of cognitive skills, and affects schooling attainment. In this context, our study aims to understand the nutritional status of school children aged 6-9 years and know their socio-economic characteristics, food-intake practice, daily routine and morbidity pattern.

Materials and Methods

Ethics: All the procedure necessary for carrying out the survey was taken from the selected school authorities. Full information, purpose, the confidentiality of the study was explained to teachers and students. After their verbal consent, we took up the survey.

Study Design: A list of schools in the eastern suburb of Mumbai (Deonar area) was prepared for the field survey and researchers visited for seeking permission from the authority. The survey was conducted in the selected few schools which gave consent to carry out the survey. Eleven schools were visited, out of which five schools permitted to do the study. All schools have the provision of serving a hot mid-day meal. However, mid-day meal distribution was not observed in any of the schools on the day of the survey.

The data were collected during April-May 2013, covering 557 students, out of which 271 were from 1st grade and 286 were from 2nd grade. Questionnaires for mothers were given to all students in grade 1st and second and were asked to return it within a specific period. The questionnaire contained sections like the background of children, characteristics of the school, parent's information, the prevalence of diseases, and daily routine of the child, food intake, and family environment. The height and weight of the students were measured in the school in the presence of a school teacher, using standard height measuring instrument and electronic weighing machine.

Statistics: Data were analysed using statistical software SPSS 20. Three grade indices of physical growth, namely; Height-for-age (Stunting/chronic under-nutrition), Weight-for-age (Underweight) and Body Mass Index (BMI, i.e. body weight according to height) were calculated. Definition of stunting, wasting and underweight as given by UNICEF are as follows: Stunting or low height for age is caused by long-term insufficient nutrient intake and frequent infections leading to delayed motor development, impaired cognitive function and poor school performance. Underweight is a combined measure of stunting and wasting, and it reflects overall nutrition. BMI is a measure of weight deficit about body mass. It is considered as an important indicator of malnutrition among adolescents. Nutritional measures were defined as Z-scores less than −2 (i.e., <2 SDs below the age-/sex-specific reference mean), whereas -3SD is an indication of severe undernourishment. Anthropometric data were analysed using the World Health Organisation's (WHO) grade growth reference tables of 2007. WHO provides growth reference data for children and adolescents aged 5-19 years. The z-scores for each index were used, and 3-grade indices were calculated. Undernutrition (below-2-grade deviation) and severe undernutrition (below -3-grade deviation) were calculated for each of the above indices by sex of the child. Significance of association between socioeconomic characteristics and child undernutrition is analysed. Three logistic regression models are developed to understand the determinants of stunting, underweight and low BMI.

Results: Basic characteristics of children are mentioned briefly in this section. Mean age of the students studying in grade 1 and 2 is seven years. Proportion of boys are 43.4 percent , and girls are 49.8 percent . The percentage of Hindus, General category and Marathi speaking students are highest in proportion compared to other groups. The main caretaker of 91.9 percent girls and 89.9 percent boys is a mother. The educational level of the parents is low. Only about 51.2 percent father and 46 percent of mothers studied till 10th grade. Majority of the fathers have their own petty business while working mothers do jobs in unorganised sectors. Sixty-eight percent of students live in 'one room kitchen house, i.e. a hall, a kitchen and toilet. Sixty percent of households reported that their average annual income is 50 thousand to 100 thousand rupees. About 53 percent of respondents said that they are satisfied with their total family earning. It is observed from our study population that on an average a child sleeps for 9.0 hours, watches television for 1.8 hours in a day and study for 3.0 hours. Usually, they play for 5 hours and spend 5 to 7 hours with time with their parents.

Thirteen percent oft of students consumed baby tin milk in younger days. For 15 percent , complementary feeding started before six months. Twenty-eight percent oft of children were fed through a bottle in early ages. Seventy percent usually eat breakfast that mainly includes milk and bread or *Chapati*-vegetable. When asked about three favourite food items, the majority supported for noodles, *dal-chawal/ chapati* (pulses and rice/wheat) and *dosa-meduvada* (food made up of a mixture of rice and pulses).

Level of Nutritional Status of Primary School Going Children

Four percent oft of students are severely stunted, 10.1 percent are severely underweight, while overweight students are negligible, i.e., only 0.9, percent. Proportion students underweight are more than proportion stunted (26.8% *vis a vis*18.5%) and while 23 percent of students has low BMI (22.8%), (Fig. 1).

Table-1 highlights the cross-classification of nutritional status. It shows that those students who are stunted, out of them 53.7 percent are underweight, and 30.7 percent have low BMI. Likewise, those students who are underweight, out of them 89.4

percent are stunted, and 75.6 percent have low BMI. Those students who are having low BMI, out of them 31.7 percent are stunted, and 46.8 percent are underweight. So, among underweight children, a large majority) is stunted, as well as has low BMI. The association of underweight with other two nutritional indices is the strongest.

Table-2 illustrates median and mean range of height and weight of children against the specified values of the WHO in the particulate ages. The mean and median range of height and weight for children, according to the WHO estimate, is around 115-133 cm and 20-28 kg respectively for children aged 6 to 9 years. While the mean and median heights of the total sample are 117.59 cm and 117.2 cm respectively, both are measuring marginally higher than the lowest limit of the WHO height specification. The mean and median weight of the study population is 19.7 kg, and 19.2 kg, respectively, both the values are lesser than the minimum mark of the WHO, i.e. 20 kg.

Table-3 shows the height and weight of children by boys and girls against the WHO values, according to age. For boys, the average height in centimetres is 114.7, and for girls, it is 113.7 at, age 6; indicating that both the values are below the WHO minimum mark of 115 cm. Likewise, for boys and girls of other ages, the observed values are calculated. It is worth noting that the deviation of values from the WHO minimum age specified value is increasing for either sex. Similarly, the average weight for 6 years old child according to the WHO value should be in between 20-22 k while the observed weights for boys and girls in each age are found below the lower limits of the WHO. Interestingly, the average observed weight deviates further from the WHO range with increasing age.

Undernutrition and Ailments

Morbidity is strongly associated with poor nutrition. The study reveals that primary school going students who suffered or suffering from any disease in last one month, tend to be more undernourished, mainly having underweight against those who were free from diseases during the last month (41%vis-a-vis 32%). Those students who keep on falling ill, tend to be more underweight (42%) and have low BMI (28%). The students who are suffering from any chronic ailment are more underweight and have low BMI compared to those who do not have any chronic ailment. Students who have not taken medicine for De-worming in the past six months are having lower BMI (23%) and underweight (39%) compared to those who consumed de-worming medicine.

Figure-2 shows the prevalence of the undernutrition by morbidities in the last month before the survey. Among the hose students who are having the problem of lack of appetite, among them, 50 percent are, underweight, 43 percent are stunted, and 29 percent have low BMI compared to undernutrition observed in other morbidities.

Determinants of Nutritional Status

In Table-4, three logistic regression models are developed to comprehend the determinants of under-nutrition, i.e. stunting, underweight and low BMI. Model-1 shows the coefficient of background characteristics of the student on undernutrition. Explanatory variables included are age, sex, type of schools, siblings, caste and religion, parent's educational levels, type of house and child's time utilisation. Model 2 explains the coefficient of food intake pattern along with background characteristics. Food intake pattern means characteristics of food intake during infancy—early childhood and current food habits. Consumption of baby tin milk, breastfeeding, complementary feeding, bottle feeding is early childhood feeding practices. While drinking adequate water, eating breakfast, the principal medium them of cooking is current food habits. In model 3, disease patterns are introduced in addition to background character and food intake pattern. Variables like disease in the last one month any chronic disease of the child, emotional comfort at home and consumption of de-worming medicine in the last six months the re-added in this model.

Among the background characteristics, three significant determinants of child nutrition are age, hours of sleeping and type of schools. With increasing age, all three parameters of undernutrition increases. Also, the coefficient values remain similar in three models, indicating that age per se has a strong effect on undernutrition even when all other variables are controlled. It also reveals that those children who remain undernourished at the beginning of primary schooling fail to catch up the standard height and weight with time. Increasing hours of sleeping helps marked improvement in body mass. It is found that one of the Marathi medium schools experiences2 times more chances of stunting and underweight as compared to the reference school.

Food intake and food pattern determine under-nutrition to a large extent. As observed, the consumption of the powder milk distinctly increases the chance of stunting and underweight of children. If food is regularly cooked in groundnut oil or oils other than refined oils, then the probability of the stunting is two times more compared to those cooking in refined oil (sunflower or soybean). Similarly, cooking food in 'other' oils (like mustard, *til* etc.) enhances the .probability of experiencing underweight and low BMI twice more compared to those households where cooking is done mainly in refined sunflower or soybean oil. However, this research has not explored the practice of reuse of oil or purchasing of loose oil from the open market. Drthe inking inadequate water (as perceived by mothers) has considerable bad impact on BMI. In model 3, the chance of having low BMI among those drinking inadequate water is 2-3 times more than those who are drinking adequate water. Not eating anything in breakfast and those who did not consume medicine for de-worming in the past six months are more likely to suffer from underweight. To elaborate, avoidance of breakfast increases the probability of experiencing underweight and low BMI 2.5 times and 3.8 times, respectively, against those who consume breakfast. Those who did not take medicine for de-worming in the past six months is two times more underweight compared to children who have administered the medicine. Chronic ailment enhances underweight substantially.

Discussions

Primary school going children require adequate nutrition for their healthy growth. The study assesses the levels and determinants of nutritional status of primary school children of grade 1st and second. Based on the above results, we propagate some pertinent discussions and policy measures:

Students belonging to morning schools can have breakfast break, as it is an essential component for proper growth. Many students come to school on an empty stomach. So, instead of giving a break in mid-day, it is essential to allow them to have food at the beginning school hours of the day. Breakfast provides the necessary energy for a day of learning and achievement. Research has shown many benefits of school breakfast, including academic achievement and improved behaviour (Murphy, 2007; Murphy, Pagano, Nachmani, Sperling, Kane, & Kleinman, 1998; Powell, Walker, Chang, & Grantham-McGregor, 1998; Vaisman, Voet, Akivis, &Vakil, 1996).In schools, a breakfast program can be made mandatory. In many African countries, vegetables and fruits given in school meals are cultivated in nearby areas while animals are raised in the communities. Thus, there is a steady supply of fresh food for school meals. A study by Morgan (Morgan, Warren, Lubans, Saunders, Quick, & Collins, 2010) shows that school gardens can impact positively on primary-school students' willingness to taste vegetables. '*Plumpy's nut*' the miracle food of Africa can also be introduced as breakfast in India

Safe drinking water is necessary to fight against malnutrition. However, the availability of safe water may not ensure the intake of adequate water. Consumption of drinking water in school may be encouraged by teachers after each class break. Children do forget to drink water unless they are obligated to do so. So a small instruction of the teacher can make a beneficiary health effect. Simple instruction of teacher along with the distribution of fortified milk at schools, can help to fight against the dual problem of food and liquid intake.

Treating children for worms improves school attendance, health, and long-run productivity. Primary School De-worming Project, a school-based de-worming program run in western Kenya proves that de-worming treatment is not only highly effective and inexpensive, it is easy to administer through public schools and brings benefits to children after treatment (Miguel & Kremer, 2004). Treated children experienced a range of health benefits and that these benefits spilled over to untreated schools and children. In 2011, the State Government of Bihar, India conducted a massive de-worming campaign, with technical assistance from DtW (De-worming the world) and policy support from J-PAL. In September 2011, the government announced that over 17 million school-aged children in the state were treated that year for intestinal worms (J-PAL Policy Bulletin, 2011). Along with de-worming, a growth evaluation of children in school can be done every year, and knowledge on nutrition can be imparted to children as well as their parents on 'School Nutrition Day'.

Baby formula is one of the significant determinants that increase the chance of being undernourished. Formula milk is a term that means a combination of foods that approximates the composition of mother's milk. Unfortunately, the commercial formula contains refined sugars, at times soy, powdered milk, some vitamins, preservatives, additives that have no place in the diet of a baby. Media and health providers can play a major role to make people understand about the content of formula milk and promote exclusive breastfeeding, avoidance of feeding formula milk and ideal varieties of complementary feeding.

Edible oil is an essential aspect of cooking and is used in most meals. Fortification of cooking oil and grain powder with vitamins and micronutrients is a strong strategy in many nations to sustain their progress in curbing malnutrition. Even in India, some large edible oil companies do have fortified oil with branded names. Directing millers and edible oil companies to produce fortified food grains and oil can help to fight against under-nutrition. Further research is needed to understand the impact of the type of cooking oil on undernutrition.

The success of the school food programme in India is a combined effort of the commitment of the governing authority, school management and involvement of the community people. Support in terms of provision of equipment, proper kitchen and dining hall, frequent invigilation and remuneration for excellent delivery is the need of the hour. Along with arrangement of nutritious and a variety of food, developing dependence on local area regarding food and beverage supply could lead to integrated development and a cleaner environment which help control diseases. School level de-worming, morning breakfast, and simple instructions of teachers regarding healthy habits to both children and parents could be a boon in handling undernutrition in India.

Conclusions

Policy to tackle the problems of child undernutrition has given adequate attention to children up to 6 years through Integrated Child Development Services. At the school level, serving of mid-day meal in government and semi-government schools are also playing a good role in tackling the problem of poor nutrition as well as school enrolment retention in India. However, many students are enrolled in private schools, especially in urban India. Therefore, the problem of under-nutrition cuts across socio-economic class. So, targeting only government or aided schools may not be enough to handle the problem of the mass. In this context, the study aims to understand the levels and determinants of nutritional status of primary school going children in the eastern part of Mumbai. Schools were selected according to the willingness to participate in the survey. Students of grade 1 and 2 ofthe selected five schools were interviewed. Out of 557 students (total sample size), about one fifth are stunted, and four percent are severely stunted; one-tenth are severely underweight, and 27 percent are underweight; 23 percent are with low BMI. A high proportion of underweight students is stunted, as well as having low BMI. The study clearly shows that at all observed ages, the average height and weight of the children are below the minimum value of height and weight as specified by the WHO. Also, the deviation observed from the WHO value increases with age, which indicates the failing of catch up process. Factors that significantly enhance under-nutrition are the intake of powder milk in early ages, regular cooking in certain variety of oil, non-consumption of breakfast, inadequate drinking of water and if the child is suffering from chronic illness. Also, it is seen that de-worming in past six months helps to enhance the nutritional status. Undernutrition is much more dependent on food intake habits and morbidity pattern rather than socioeconomic factors. Age shows a strong positive association with under-nourishment that increases with growing up of a child.

References

1. Handa, R., Ahamad, F., Kesari, K.K., & Prasad, R. (2008). Assessment of the nutritional status of 7-10 year of school going children of Allahabad district: A review. Middle-east journal of scientific research, 3(3), 109-115.
2. J-PAL Policy Bulletin. (2011). 'The Price is Wrong'. Cambridge, MA: Abdul Latif Jameel Poverty Action Lab.
3. Miguel, E., & Kremer, M. (2004). Worms: identifying impacts on education and health in the presence of treatment externalities. Econometrica, 72(1), 159-217.
4. Morgan, P.J., Warren, J.M., Lubans, D.R., Saunders, K.L., Quick, G.I., & Collins, C.E. (2010). The impact of nutrition education with and without a school garden on knowledge, vegetable intake and preferences and quality of school life among primary-school students. Public health nutrition, 13(11), 1931.
5. Murphy, J.M. (2007). Breakfast and learning: an updated review. Current Nutrition & Food Science, 3(1), 3-36.
6. Murphy, J.M., Pagano, M.E., Nachmani, J., Sperling, P., Kane, S., & Kleinman, R.E. (1998). The relationship of school breakfast to psychosocial and academic functioning: cross-sectional and longitudinal observations in an inner-city school sample. Archives of Pediatrics & Adolescent Medicine, 152(9), 899-907.

7. Powell, C.A., Walker, S.P., Chang, S.M., & Grantham-McGregor, S.M. (1998). Nutrition and education: a randomised trial of the effects of breakfast in rural primary school children. The American journal of clinical nutrition, 68(4), 873-879.
8. Vaisman, N., Voet, H., Akivis, A., & Vakil, E. (1996). Effect of breakfast timing on the cognitive functions of elementary school students. Archives of paediatrics & adolescent medicine, 150(10), 1089-1092.

Tables and Figures

Table-1: Cross-classification of Nutritional status among primary school going children

Nutritional status	Stunted	Underweight	Low BMI
Stunted	—	53.7	30.7
Underweight	89.4	—	75.6
Low BMI	31.7	46.8	—

**Source*: own calculation based on the primary sample collected for this research

Table-2: Observed and standard height and weight of the children

	Height in centimetres	Weight in Kilograms
Mean and Median range of Height and weight for children 6-9 as per WHO norm	115-133	20-28
Mean	117.6	19.7
Median	117.3	19.2
Minimum	100.0	13.0
Maximum	135.2	40.3

**Source*: own calculation based on the primary sample collected for this research

Table-3: Height and weight of children by sex according to age

Age	Height (cm)				Weight in kg			
	Boys	Girls	Total	WHO range of height	Boys	Girls	Total	WHO range of weight
6	114.7	113.7	114.2	***115-120***	18.8	17.9	18.4	***20-22***
7	118.8	116.8	117.8	***121-126***	20.1	19.2	19.7	***23-25***

8	121.3	120.0	120.7	***127-131***	21.0	20.7	21.0	***26-27***
9	120.7	122.4	121.3	***132-138***	20.2	21.4	20.3	***28-31***

Source: own calculation based on the primary sample collected for this research

Table-4: Binary logistic regression analysis showing the determinants of Nutritional status

	Stunted			**Underweight**			**Low BMI**		
Background characteristics	Model 1	Model 2	Model 3	Model 1	Model 2	Model 3	Model 1	Model 2	Model 3
School (English Medium School ®)									
English Medium School -1	0.459 (.484)	0.444 (.502)	0.48 (.549)	0.779 (.410)	0.234 (.197)	0.333 (.388)	0.98 (.978)	0.379 (.397)	0.545 (.597)
Marathi Medium School -1	0.726 (.410)	0.83 (.663)	0.872 (.756)	1.032 (.911)	0.922 (.807)	1.297 (.464)	0.823 (.566)	0.821 (.613)	0.901 (.798)
English Medium School -2	0.872 (.684)	0.664 (.283)	0.618 (.250)	2.382** (.033)	0.874 (.665)	1.117 (.745)	1.137 (.682)	0.793 (.513)	1.08 (.841)
Marathi Medium School -2	3.203*** (.007)	2.502* (.069)	2.455* (.102)	0.801 (.286)	1.905 (.167)	2.398* (.094)	0.714 (.483)	0.55 (.289)	0.623 (.439)
Age (C)	1.059*** (.000)	1.061*** (.000)	1.052*** (.001)	1.036* (.001)	1.037*** (.003)	1.036*** (.008)	1.024** (.050)	1.023* (.094)	1.034** (.025)
Father's education (Primary/illiterate ®)									
SSC pass	1.216 (.619)	1.278 (.568)	1.039 (.932)	0.798 (.469)	0.687 (.273)	0.547 (.103)	0.857 (.652)	0.601 (.191)	0.572 (.196)
12th pass/ Graduate	1.597 (.130)	1.845** (.077)	1.659 (.152)	0.976 (.992)	1.059 (.831)	0.934 (.814)	0.898 (.693)	0.796 (.456)	0.682 (.239)
Child sleeps in day and night (hours)(C)	1.331 (.273)	1.355 (.291)	1.25 (.460)	1.129 (.572)	1.217 (.404)	1.364 (.223)	.666* (.084)	.616* (.069)	0.748 (.307)
Whether Child had powder milk (Yes ®)									
No		.506* (.076)	.443** (.041)		0.74 (.345)	.563* (.091)		0.978 (.952)	0.874 (.726)

Principal medium of cooking Refined (Sunflower/ Soybean ®)									
Groundnut		2.180** (.012)	2.266** (.013)		1.398 (.188)	1.636* (.072)		1.469 (.188)	1.528 (.174)
Others (mustard, til etc.)		2.782** (.017)	2.802** (.023)		2.065** (.046)	2.372** (.029)		2.183* (.052)	2.211** (.066)
Does child drink adequate water (Yes ®)									
No		1.181 (.667)	1.308 (.515)		1.549 (.178)	1.317 (.436)		2.641*** (.005)	2.395** (.018)
Whether eats breakfast (Yes ®)									
No		1.734 (.269)	1.99 (.194)		1.833 (.157)	2.470** (.060)		4.076*** (.001)	3.753*** (.006)
A child suffering from chronic disease (Yes ®)									
No			1.338 (.431)			.589* (.073)			0.582 (.102)
Any medicine for Deworming (Yes ®)									
No			0.923 (.834)			2.063** (.029)			1.463 (.305)
Constant	0.002	0.003	0.007	0.028	0.045	0.066	0.051	0.164	0.101
R-Square	0.106	0.139	0.127	0.064	0.09	0.131	0.032	0.097	0.112
N		375			375			375	

C—Continuous, ®—Reference category, **—5percent level of significance, ***—1 percent level of significance p<0.05. The values in brackets are P value.

Source: own calculation based on the primary sample collected for this research

Note: (Sex, Age gap between child and elder brother/sister, Total family members, Religion, caste, Type of housing, Child watch TV (hrs.), Whether child was breastfed, Age at which child started eating food/drinking other than milk, Whether child was bottle fed, Child suffered/suffering any disease in last 1 month, Last time ill, Does child has emotional comfort at home are the variables which were also controlled in the model but are not shown in the above table due to their insignificant effect on Dependent variable.)

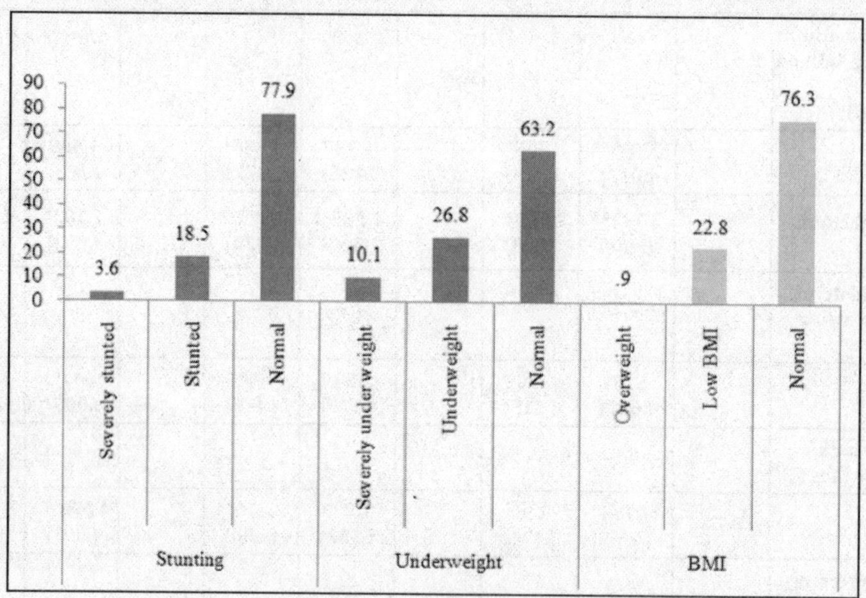

Fig. 1: Nutritional status of Primary school children

**Source*: own calculation based on the primary sample collected for this research

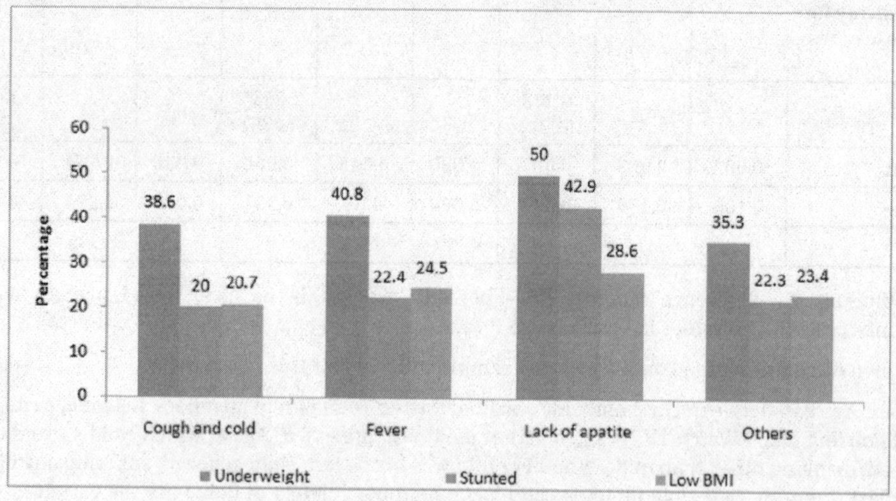

Fig. 2. Prevalence of malnutrition by Morbidities

**Source*: own calculation based on the primary sample collected for this research

10

Parental Child Marriages and Childhood Undernutrition in India: A Cross-spousal Analysis Using a Nationally Representative Data

—Praveen Kumar Pathak and S.V. Subramanian

Abstract

Under-nutrition is a major health burden among children and women in India. The risk on childhood under-nutrition is perpetuated through the operation of an array of risk factors including nutritional, socioeconomic and environmental characteristics. A few studies have attempted to establish causal linkages between childhood under-nutrition and maternal child marriages. However, there is no clear understanding of the plausible association between parental child marriage and childhood under-nutrition in India. The objective of the present study was to examine the influence of parental child marriages (marriage below legal ages) on childhood nutritional status in India. The study population was a nationally representative cross-section sample of singleton children (n=16756) who were aged 0 to 59 months from the 2005-2006 Indian National Family Health Survey. Modified logistic regression models that account for multistage survey design and sampling weights were applied to estimate the association between parental child marriages and childhood under-nutrition. The outcome measures were child underweight and stunting; parental child marriages (<18 years among mothers &<21 years among fathers) was the primary exposure variable.: In the mutually adjusted regression models, we do not find any significant association between parental childhood marriage and child underweight [underweight OR: 1.06 (95% CI: 0.98-1.15) and 1.03 (95% CI: 0.94-1.12) for early married mothers and fathers respectively]. However, in case of child stunting, we found children born too early married mothers were significantly more likely to be stunted [stunting OR: 1.11 (95% CI: 1.03-1.21)] than their counterparts. However, we do not find any significant association of childhood stunting with early married fathers [stunting OR: 1.07 (95% CI: 0.98-1.17)]. The null findings between the association of parental child marriage and childhood underweight indicate that early age at marriage of parents may not explain childhood under-nutrition in India

Introduction

Globally close to 207 million children suffer from under-nutrition (including both stunting and wasting), and another 3 million children die annually due to underlying factors related to poor and insecure nutrition (UNICEF, WHO, World Bank Group, 2017; IFPRI, 2016; Black et al., 2013). Despite concerted efforts leveraged by national and global agencies to meet nutrition-related targets vowed under the Millennium Development Goals (MDGs) framework (i.e. 2010 to 2015); tremendous inequalities in the childhood under-nutrition still persists along varied axes of geographies, economic status, educational attainment, rural-urban context, gender asymmetry, and racial/ethnic divide, among the others (Alderman and Heady, 2017; Smith and Haddad, 2015; World Bank, 2013; Barros et. al., 2010; Van de Poel et al., 2008;Fost, 2006). Evidence suggests that nutritional deprivation in the early childhood triggers irreparable damage to the cognitive skills, poor educational outcome, low economic productivity, and heightened risk of contracting chronic disease over the life course, thus blighting potential human resources of future communities and societies (Black et al., 2013; de Onis, Blossner, and Borghi, 2012; Black et al., 2008; Grantham-McGregor et al., 2007).

Among the world regions in 2016, South Asia and Africa together accounted for 162 million (little above three-fourth of the world total) undernourished children globally (UNICEF/WHO/World Bank Group, 2017). India disproportionately accounts for the sizeable burden related to poor maternal and child nutritional/health indicators in the region (Akseer et al., 2017). Previous studies on the predictors of child nutrition in India have employed an array of economic, social, cultural, gender/women empowerment, nutritional intake, agricultural systems, climatic variations, environmental, health practices, health systems, and governance perspectives to explain and, or identify potential risk factors amenable for effective programmatic design and policy intervention (Kim et al., 2017; Shankar et al., 2017; Corsi, Mejia-Guevara, and Subramanian, 2016; Cavatorta, Shankar, and Flores-Martinez, 2015). Few studies have also examined the plausible association between early marriage, teenage motherhood, and its linkages with child health/under-nutrition in the Indian context (Vir, 2016; Hall et al., 2015; Prakash et al., 2011; Raj et al., 2010). These studies attempted to highlight the role of women agency, decision making prowess, bargaining power and its protective effect on the child health/nutritional status. However, they have also underscored that early entry into wedlock and resultant early childbearing predisposes heightened risk of poor health and under-nutrition for both children and mother (Raj et al., 2010; Prakash et al., 2011). Here an inherent assumption seems to be the fact that early age at marriage of women is in some sense a proxy for some unobservable individual/household characteristics—potentially correlated with the limited negotiating agency in household decision making, low education, and poor socio-economic status. This perhaps could lead to a plausible association between early age at marriage of women and poor nutritional status of children. However, to what extent such association is genuinely causal appears intuitively problematic based on cross-sectional data as reported elsewhere. In order to advance the knowledge on yet unsettled debate on the linkages between early age at marriage of parents and child under-nutrition. We test the plausibility of any causal association by comparing the paternal and maternal early age at marriage (referred hereafter as 'child marriage of mother: married below 18years of age vs. adult marriage of mother: married above 18 years of age'; 'child marriage of father: married before 21 years of age vs. adult marriage of father: marriage after 21 years of age'). It also includes the nutritional outcome of children, net of the salient demographic, socioeconomic, nutritional characteristics of parents, and contextual factors. We hypothesise here that paternal age at marriage is not associated with offspring nutritional status, considering linkage of offspring nutritional status with the subjugated status of women perpetuated through maternal child marriages. In other words, any significant association of paternal child marriage with offspring nutritional status shall challenge/contest any causal association of maternal child marriage and offspring nutritional status.

Methods

Data Source: The data for the present study came from the 2005-06 National Family Health Survey (NFHS) conducted in India (IIPS & Macro International, 2007). The 2005-06 NFHS, the equivalent of the Demographic and Health Surveys (DHS), was conducted to provide representative information at the national and state level on various population and health indicators, with special emphasis on maternal and child health outcomes. The target population for the 2005-06 NFHS was women aged 15 to 49 years, men aged 15 to 54 years and children aged 0-59 months.

The 2005-06 INFHS adopted a multistage stratified sample survey design across all the 29 states of India for the selection of eligible respondents. In each state, populations were stratified by urban and rural area of residence, and the sample size at the state level was proportional to the size of the state's urban and rural populations. The rural sample was obtained through a selection of primary sampling units, which were villages or village clusters, based on a probability proportional to population size, followed by a random selection of households. In urban areas, at the first stage, wards were selected with probability proportional to population size sampling, followed by a random selection of one census enumeration block within the sample ward, followed by a random selection of households. Within the urban and rural households, all women between ages 15 to 49 years across all 29 states of

India who resided the previous night in the household were eligible to participate in the survey. However, all men between ages 15-54 years who resided the previous night in sample households were eligible respondents in seven states, namely Andhra Pradesh, Karnataka, Maharashtra, Manipur, Nagaland, Tamil Nadu, and Uttar Pradesh, particularly to generate HIV prevalence estimates. In the remaining 22 states, all men between age 15-54 years were eligible respondents in less than half (38%) of sample households. The first phase of data collection (covering 12 states) took place from November 2005 to May 2006, and the second phase of data collection (covering the remaining 17 states) took place from April to August 2006.

A total of 131 596 women and 85373 men were eligible (based on the age cut-offs) for participation in the survey from a random sample of 116 652 households. Of the 131 596 eligible women, 124 385 women participated in the survey yielding a response rate of 94.5%. Of the 85373 eligible men, 74369 men participated in the survey yielding a response rate of 87.1%. The response rate for eligible women varied from 90% to 99% between states, and was 93.3% and 95.5% in urban and rural areas, respectively. While for the eligible men, the response rate varied from 76% to 98% between states, and was 84.6% and 89.9% in urban and rural areas, respectively. Of the interviewed eligible respondents, 87925 women and 40574 were currently married at the time of the survey.

Study Population and Sample Size

The analyses in the present study were based on the representative, cross-sectional 2005-2006 Indian National Family Health Survey (INFHS) of 16756 singleton children (0-59 months old) in 29 Indian states which account for almost 99 percent of the country's population. We imported the information of father's height and weight from the couple's file and merged the same into the children's file of the NFHS for analysis. After excluding children whose father was either not interviewed, or with missing information of father's height, weight and education; mother's height, weight, pregnant mothers; dead children, flagged/missing cases of children height/ weight, and religion, the final analytical sample consisted of 16756 singleton children.

Outcome

The nutritional status of children in the present study has been measured using anthropometric data on height and weight directly collected in the 2005-2006 NFHS (IIPS & Macro International, 2007). Using the z-score values of anthropometric data following the World Health Organisation child growth standards (WHO, 2006), two outcomes variables were devised: i) stunting (low height-for-age using z-score of less than -2 SD); ii) underweight (low weight-for-age using z-score of less than -2 SD).

Exposure

The main exposure variable in the present study is parental age at marriage. Information of age at marriage of mother and father of the index child has been used to construct the following two exposure variables: 1) maternal age at marriage (adult marriage of mother>=18 years=0; child marriage of mother<18 years=1); 2) paternal age at marriage (adult marriage of father>=21 years=0; child marriage of father<21 years=1).

Covariates

The present study included salient demographic, socioeconomic, nutritional characteristics of parents, and contextual factors to investigate its association with childhood under-nutrition in India (Corsi, Mejia-Guevara, and Subramanian, 2016; Bhutta et al., 2008; 2013; Black et al., 2008; 2013). Demographic characteristics included age of child (<11 months; 12-23 months; 24-35 months; 36-47 months; 48-59 months); sex of the child (male; female); mother's age at birth of index child (<18 years; 18-20 years; 21-24 years; 25-29 years; >=30 years); father's age at birth of index child (<18 years; 18-20 years; 21-24 years; 25-29 years; >=30 years) ; multiparous birth (singe birth; multiple birth). Socioeconomic characteristics included education of mother (no education; primary; secondary & above); education of father (no education; primary; secondary & above); access to antenatal care (no, yes); religious affiliation (Hindu, Muslims, Others). Nutritional characteristics included the body mass index (measured through height in meter square divided by weight in kilograms) of the mother (continuous); body mass index of the father (continuous). Contextual characteristics included the place of residence (mega city; large city; small city; large town, small town; rural); region as per NFHS scheme (north; central; east; northeast; west; south).

Analysis

Descriptive characteristics of the study population and outcome variables were presented using weighted percentages. Association between parental child marriages and selected child/parental demographic characteristics was examined using the Chi-square test for categorical variables, and Student-t-test for continuous variables. Scatter plot was generated to depict the association between parental mean age at marriage with child under-nutrition (measured through underweight, severe underweight, stunting, and severe stunting). Pearson's correlation coefficients were also estimated to identify the degree and direction of the association between parental mean age at marriage and child under-nutrition across states in India.

Mutually adjusted multiple logistic regression models (six sets) were separately fitted to examine the association of parental child marriage with outcome variables i.e. underweight and stunting. For instance, in order to predict underweight children, the first regression model adjusted for maternal child marriage; second model adjusted for paternal child marriage; third model mutually adjust for both maternal and paternal child marriage; fourth model adjusts for maternal child marriage along with demographic, socioeconomic, nutritional characteristics of parents and contextual factors; fifth model adjusts for paternal child marriage along demographic, socioeconomic, nutritional characteristics of parents and contextual factors; sixth model mutually adjusts for both maternal and paternal child marriages along with demographic, socioeconomic, nutritional characteristics of parents and contextual factors. Results were reported as unadjusted and adjusted odds ratios with 95% confidence interval to assess statistical stability of the associations.

Ethical Review

The 2005-06 NFHS was conducted under the scientific and administrative supervision of the International Institute for Population Sciences, (IIPS) Mumbai, India. The IIPS is a regional centre for teaching, training and research in population studies, and is associated with the Ministry of Health and Family Welfare, Government of India. The institute conducted an independent ethics review of 2005-06 NFHS protocol. The ORC Macro institutional review board also approved data collection procedures. Trained interviewers obtained verbal informed consent from all participants before implementing the interview/survey and administering tests.

Results

Descriptive Analysis

Socio-demographic characteristics of parents by their age at marriage

Descriptive socio-demographic characteristics of birth to married mothers by their age at marriage (child marriage mothers and adult marriage mothers) have been presented in **Table-1**. It may be observed that overall majority of births among child marriage mothers had relatively low access to antenatal care, predominantly residing in the rural areas, largely concentrated in the Central and Eastern regions of India, disproportionately coming from the economically poor households, high prevalence of teenage motherhood, massive illiteracy, and poor nutritional status.

On the contrary, births among adult marriage mothers had relatively better access to antenatal care, largely concentrated in the Western and Southern regions of India, coming from the economically better-off household, low prevalence of teenage motherhood, higher literacy rates and recorded overall better nutritional status. On the other hand, **Table-2** presented socio-demographic characteristics of birth to married father by their age at marriage (child marriage fathers and adult marriage fathers). It also consistently depicts limited access to antenatal care, higher prevalence of teenage fatherhood, low education, poor economic status, and poor nutritional status among child marriage fathers than their counterparts.

Association of child under-nutrition by parental age at marriage and age at birth

Figure 1 and 2 present a generalised overview of the crude association between parental mean age at marriage and child under-nutrition measured through underweight, severe underweight, stunting, and severe stunting across states in India. Data confirmed a strong negative association between parental mean age at marriage and child under-nutrition status. For instance, the association between maternal mean age at marriage and child under-nutrition varied from -0.78 (stunted) to -0.63 (severely underweight). On the other hand, the association between paternal mean age at marriage and child under-nutrition range between -0.79 (stunted or severely stunted) to -0.58 (severely underweight).

Data presented in **Table-3** shows the differentials in the prevalence of underweight and stunting among children (0-59 months old) across parental age at marriage and age at birth in India. It was noted that overall, about 46 percent children were underweight, while, 41 percent children were stunted in India. However, there were marked variations in the prevalence of underweight and stunting among children by the parental age at marriage and age at birth. For instance, the prevalence of underweight was relatively higher among children born to child married mothers (got married before 18 years) than their counterparts. On similar lines, the prevalence of underweight was relatively higher among children born to child married fathers (got married before 21 years).

On the other hand, there were striking differentials in the prevalence of underweight across the parental age at birth. For instance, children born to mother and father less than 20 years of age had on the average higher prevalence of underweight than their counterparts. The same pattern was true in case of stunting as well. Children born to parents experienced child marriage, and teenage parenthood recorded the higher prevalence of stunting than their counterparts.

Multivariate Analysis

The result from the previous section suggests marked differentials in the prevalence of underweight and stunting rates among children across parental age at marriage. However, such a crude association could be spurious. Therefore, in order to understand the more refined association between childhood under-nutrition and parental age at marriage, we used adjusted logistic regression model, considering the dichotomous nature of the dependent variables (underweight=1; otherwise=0; stunted=1; otherwise=0) (Retherford and Choe, 1993). We fit six panels of logistic regression models (separately for underweight and stunting) to examine the influence of exposure on the outcome variables, net of the effect of covariates (**Table-4**). In the case of underweight children, it may be observed from Model-1 that maternal age at marriage had a statistically significant association with underweight children. For instance, children born to mothers who were child brides were 69 percent more likely to be underweight than their counterparts.

Similarly from Model-2, it may be seen that paternal age at marriage had a statistically significant association with underweight children. Children born to fathers who were child grooms were 58 percent more likely to be underweight than their counterparts. In mutually adjusted Model-3, an association of maternal and paternal child marriage seems to have a statistically significant and positive association with underweight children. Model-4 and Model-5 separately adjusted for the demographic, socioeconomic, nutritional and contextual factors over the effect of maternal and paternal child marriage, respectively. In mutually adjusted Model-6, the effect of maternal and paternal age at marriage dissipates away once other covariates are controlled for. This suggests that there exist no statistically significant association between parental child marriage and underweight children in the Indian context.

We further examine the association of parental child marriage with stunting (**Table-3**). In the final regression model (Model-6), it may be noted that children born to mothers who were child brides had a statistically significant and positive association with stunting. For instance, children born to mother who was child brides were 11 percent more likely to be stunted than their counterparts. However, we do not find any statistically significant association of paternal child marriage with the likelihood of stunting.

Discussion

The present study attempts to understand the association between parental child marriages and child under-nutrition in India. Our finding suggests that paternal child marriage had a statistically null association with underweight and stunting among children (0-59 months) in India. On the other hand, maternal child marriage had a statistically significant and positive association with stunting, whereas, a null association was found with underweight among children (0-59 months) in India. These results suggest that after accounting for the paternal child marriage, the association of maternal age at marriage with child under-nutrition potentially nullifies (particularly for underweight). It further adds to the ongoing debate to the linkages between parental child marriage and child under-nutrition. Most of the existing studies have only factored into the influence of maternal child marriage and found a statistically significant association with child under-nutrition. Our results perhaps suggest that ignoring the effect of paternal child marriage overestimate the true effect of maternal child marriages. It further suggests that in the absence of information on the paternal child marriages, drawing any inference about maternal child marriage could be an exaggeration.

Our findings also confirmed the strong association of teenage parenthood, lack of access to antenatal care, poor parental nutritional status, multiparous birth, rural residence, geographical region, poor economic status and low education with a heightened risk of underweight and stunting among children in India. These finding also echo the results from some of the previous studies that focused upon addressing both the upstream and downstream drivers of child under-nutrition in developing countries (Kim et al., 2017; Black et al., 2013; Black et al., 2008). These social interventions are critical considering the important role of nutrition, both as an input and outcome, which will shape the progress of the global community towards achieving Sustainable Development Goals by 2030.

References

1. Akseer, N., Kamali, M., Arifeen, S.E., Malik, A., Bhatti, Z., Thacker, N., Maksey, M., D'Sliva, H., da Silva, I.C., Bhutta, Z.A. (2017). Progress in maternal and child health: how has South Asia fared? British Medical Journal, 357.doi: 10.1136/bmj.j1608
2. Alderman, H., Headey, D.D., (2017). How important is parental education for child nutrition? World Development 94, 448-464.
3. Barros, F.C., Victora, C.G., Scherpbier, R., Gwatkin, D. (2010).Socioeconomic inequalities in the health and nutrition outcome in low-and-middle income countries. Revista de SaúdePública, 44, 1-16. doi.org/10.1590/S0034-89102010000100001
4. Bhutta, Z.A., Ahmed, T., Black, R.E., Cousens, S., Dewey, K., Giugliani, E., ...Shekar, M. (2008).What works? Interventions for maternal and child under-nutrition and survival. Lancet, 371, 417-440.
5. Bhutta, Z.A., Das, J.K., Rizvi, A., Gaffey, M.F., Walker, N., Horton, S.,... Black, R.E. (2013) Evidence-based interventions for improvement of maternal and child nutrition: what can be done and at what cost? Lancet, 382, 452-477.
6. Black, R.E., Victora, C.G., Walker, S.P., Bhutta, Z.A., Christian, P., de Onis, M., ...Uauy, R. (2013). Maternal and child under-nutrition and overweight in low-income and middle-income countries. Lancet, 382, 427-451.
7. Black, R.E., Allen, L.H., Bhutta, Z.A., Caulfield, L.E., de Onis, M., Ezzati, M., ... Rivera, J., (2008). Maternal and child under-nutrition: global and regional exposures and health consequences. Lancet, 371, 243-260.
8. Cavatorta, E., Shankar, B., Flores-Martinez, A. (2015). Explaining cross-state disparities in child nutrition in rural India. World Development, 76, 216-237.
9. Corsi, D.J., Mejia-Guevara, I., Subramanian, S.V. (2016).Risk factors for chronic under-nutrition among children in India: Estimating relative importance, population attributable risk and fractions. Social Science and Medicine, 157, 165-185.

10. Dennis, M., Blossner, M., Borghi, E. (2012). Prevalence and trends of stunting among pre-school children, 1990-2020. Public Health Nutrition, 15, 142-148.
11. Fosto, J.C., (2006). Child health inequities in developing countries: differences across urban and rural areas. International Journal for Equity in Health, 5, nine doi.org/10.1186/1475-9276-5-9
12. Grantham-McGregor, S., Cheung, Y.B., Cueto, S., Glewwe, P., Richter, L., Strupp, B.(2007). Developmental potential in the first five years of children in developing countries. Lancet, 369, 60-70.
13. Hall, C.H.D., Sachdev, H.S., Osmand, C., Restrepo-Mendez, M.C., Victora, C., ...Richter, L.M., (2015). Association between maternal age at birth and child and adult outcomes in the offspring: a prospective study in five low-income and middle-income countries (COHORTS Collaboration). Lancet Global Health,3,e366-e377. doi.org/10.1016/S2214-109X(15)00038-8
14. International Food Policy Research Institute. (2016). Global Nutrition Report 2016: From Promise to Impact—Ending Malnutrition by 2030. Washington, DC. Retrieved from http://ebrary.ifpri.org/utils/getfile/collection/p15738coll2/id/130354/filename/130565.pdf Accessed on 12-06-2017
15. International Institute for Population Sciences (IIPS) & Macro International. (2007). National Family Health Survey (NFHS-3), 2005-06: India, Volume I. Mumbai: IIPS.
16. Kim, R., Mejia-Guevara, I., Corsi, D.J., Aguayo, V.M., Subramanian, S.V. (2017) Relative importance of 13 correlates of child stunting in South Asia: Insights from nationally representative data from Afghanistan, Bangladesh, India, Nepal, and Pakistan. Social Science and Medicine, 187, 144-154.
17. Prakash, R., Singh, A., Pathak, P.K., Parasuraman, S. (2011). Early marriage, the poor reproductive health status of mother and child well-being in India. Journal of Family Planning and Reproductive Health Care, 37, 136-145. doi: 10.1136/jfprhc-2011-0080
18. Raj, A., Saggurti, N., Winter, M., Labonte, A., Decker, M.R., Balaiah, D., Silverman, J.G. (2010). The effect of maternal child marriage on morbidity and mortality of children under 5 in India: a cross-sectional study of a nationally representative survey. British Medical Journal, 340, b4258. doi:10.1136/bmj.b4258
19. Retherford, R.D., Choe, M.K. (1993) Statistical models for causal analysis. New York: John Wiley & Sons, Inc.
20. Shankar, B., Agrawal, S., Beaudreault, A.R., Avula, L., Martorell, R., Osendarp, S., Prabhakaran, D., Mclean, M.S. (2017). Dietary and nutritional change in India: implications for strategies, policies, and interventions. Annals of The New York Academy of Sciences, 1395, 49-59.
21. Smith, L.C., Haddad, L. (2015). Reducing child malnutrition: past drivers and priorities for the post-MDG agenda. World Development, 68, 180-204.
22. United Nations Children's Fund, World Health Organisation, World Bank Group. (2017) Levels and trends in child malnutrition.UNICEF/WHO/World Bank Group-Joint Child Malnutrition Estimates 2017 editionRetrieved fromhttp://www.who.int/nutgrowthdb/jme_brochoure2017.pdf?ua=1 Accessed on 22-08-2017

23. Van de Poel, E., Hosseinpoor, A.R., Speybroeck, N., Ourti, T.V., Vega, J. (2008). Socioeconomic inequalities in malnutrition in developing countries.Bulletin of the World Health Organisation, 86.282-291.
24. Vir, S.C. (2016) Improving women's nutrition imperative for rapid reduction of childhood stunting in South Asia: coupling of nutrition-specific interventions with nutrition-sensitive measures essential. Maternal and Child Nutrition, 12 (S1), 72-90.
25. World Bank. (2013). Improving nutrition through multisectoral approaches. Washington, DC: World Bank. Retrieved from http://documents.worldbank.org/curated/en/625661468329649726/pdf/75102-REVISED-PUBLIC-MultisectoralApproachestoNutrition.pdf Accessed on 02-08-2017
26. World Health Organisation (WHO) (2006) WHO Child Growth Standards: Length/height-for-age, Weight-for-age, Weight-for-length, Weight-for-height and Body Mass Index-for-age: Methods and Development. World Health Organisation, Geneva.

Table-1: Demographic indicators for births in the past five years to married women in India by maternal age at marriage. Data are % (n) or Mean (SD)

	Total births (n=16756)		Births to child marriage mother (n=8738)		Births to adult marriage mother (n=8018)		P for the difference in demographics by maternal age at marriage
The current age of the child							P<0.001
0-11	18.55	3161	18.01	1445	19.30	1716	
12-23	18.92	3225	18.09	1469	20.09	1756	
24-35	19.67	3359	19.56	1577	19.82	1782	
36-47	20.62	3418	21.50	1725	19.38	1693	
48-59	22.24	3593	22.84	1802	21.41	1791	
Sex of child							P=0.996
Male	53.67	8849	53.29	4233	54.20	4616	
Female	46.33	7907	46.71	3785	45.80	4122	
Antenatal care							P<0.001
Yes	57.14	9900	52.00	4239	64.31	5661	
No	13.68	1966	17.22	1260	8.72	706	
Unknown	29.19	4890	30.78	2519	26.96	2371	
Area of residence							P < 0.001
Mega city	2.18	806	1.21	242	3.54	564	
Large city	7.37	2658	4.94	955	10.78	1703	

Small city	7.54	971	5.66	399	10.16	572	
Large town	1.58	472	1.21	178	2.09	294	
Small town	10.59	2102	8.99	825	12.81	1277	
Rural	70.74	9747	77.98	5419	60.61	4328	
Region of residence							P<0.001
North	8.48	1811	8.19	825	8.89	986	
Central	33.68	4270	38.04	2554	27.59	1716	
East	14.68	1610	16.75	1023	11.78	587	
Northeast	2.88	3421	2.16	1195	3.90	2226	
West	15.22	2087	13.59	873	17.49	1214	
South	25.06	3557	21.27	1548	30.36	2009	
Wealth Index							P<0.001
Poorest	21.39	2473	28.05	1818	12.09	655	
Poorer	21.6	3046	26.06	1907	15.37	1139	
Middle	21.66	3657	23.02	1948	19.75	1709	
Richer	19.66	3936	15.98	1599	24.81	2337	
Richest	15.68	3644	6.89	746	27.98	2898	
Religion							P<0.001
Hindu	81.41	11751	82.42	5912	80.00	5839	
Muslim	13.94	2412	14.64	1293	12.96	1119	
Other	4.65	2593	2.93	813	7.04	1780	
Mother's age at birth							P<0.001
<18 y	6.21	824	10.63	822	0.02	2	
18-20 y	20.75	3065	26.88	2181	12.17	884	
21-24 y	33.15	5408	29.62	2404	38.10	3004	
25-29y	25.22	4616	19.99	1586	32.53	3030	
30y+	14.67	2843	12.88	1025	17.18	1818	
Mean age of mother (SD)	24.04 (5.18)		23.09 (5.35)		25.36 (4.62)		P<0.001
Maternal education							P<0.001
No formal	45.93	6239	58.64	4251	28.15	1988	
Primary	14.11	2369	15.7	1364	11.89	1005	
Secondary+	39.96	8148	25.66	2403	59.96	5745	
Mean BMI of the mother (SD)	19.84 (3.36)		19.29 (2.81)		20.22 (3.64)		P<0.001

Source: Author's calculation from the third round of National Family Health Survey (2005-2006) data.

Table-2: Demographic indicators for births in the past five years to married men in India by paternal age at marriage. Data are % (n) or Mean (SD)

	Total births (n=16756)		Births to child marriage father (n=5536)		Births to adult marriage father (n=11220)		P for the difference in demographics by paternal age at marriage
The current age of the child							P<0.020
0-11	18.86	3161	18.68	1034	18.96	2127	
12-23	19.25	3225	18.10	1002	19.81	2223	
24-35	20.05	3359	19.74	1093	20.20	2266	
36-47	20.40	3418	21.37	1183	19.92	2235	
48-59	21.44	3593	22.11	1224	21.11	2369	
Sex of child							P=0.195
Male	53.67	8849	53.77	2963	53.60	5886	
Female	46.33	7907	46.23	2573	46.40	5334	
Antenatal care							P<0.001
Yes	57.14	9900	48.82	2764	62.94	7136	
No	13.68	1966	19.48	994	9.63	972	
Unknown	29.19	4890	31.70	1778	27.43	3112	
Area of residence							P<0.001
Mega city	2.18	806	0.89	123	3.08	683	
Large city	7.37	2658	4.69	607	9.25	2051	
Small city	7.54	971	4.18	220	9.88	751	
Large town	1.58	472	1.25	98	1.81	374	
Small town	10.59	2102	7.52	503	12.73	1599	
Rural	70.74	9747	81.47	3985	63.25	5762	
Region of residence							P<0.001
North	8.48	1811	9.52	660	7.76	1151	
Central	33.68	4270	46.95	2167	24.43	2103	
East	14.68	1610	15.87	657	13.85	953	

Northeast	2.88	3421	1.64	817	3.75	2604	
West	15.22	2087	9.79	452	19.00	1635	
South	25.06	3557	16.23	783	31.21	2774	
Wealth Index							P<0.001
Poorest	21.39	2473	30.09	1359	15.33	1114	
Poorer	21.60	3046	27.81	1407	17.27	1639	
Middle	21.66	3657	22.23	1331	21.26	2326	
Richer	19.66	3936	14.31	1015	23.39	2921	
Richest	15.68	3644	5.56	424	22.75	3220	
Religion							P<0.001
Hindu	81.41	11751	82.51	4037	80.65	7714	
Muslim	13.94	2412	14.76	869	13.37	1543	
Other	4.65	2593	2.74	630	5.98	1963	
Father's age at birth							P<0.001
<18 y	0.36	50	0.87	50	0.00	0	
18-20 y	3.51	479	8.52	475	0.02	4	
21-24 y	17.75	2683	29.14	1650	9.80	1033	
25-29y	34.01	5543	30.46	1691	36.49	3852	
30y+	44.37	8001	31.02	1670	53.68	6331	
Mean age of father (SD)	29.33 (5.92)		27.32 (6.05)		30.73 (5.40)		P<0.001
Paternal education							P<0.001
No formal	23.58	3285	32.31	1649	17.49	1636	
Primary	18.74	2942	21.38	1193	16.90	1749	
Secondary+	57.68	10529	46.31	2694	65.61	7835	
Mean BMI of the father (SD)	20.50 (3.35)		19.77 (2.89)		21.01 (3.54)		P<0.001

Source: Author's calculation from the third round of National Family Health Survey (2005-2006) data.

Table-3: Prevalence of underweight and stunting among births in the past five years by married couples age at marriage and age at parenthood in India. Data are % (n)

Infant/child health indicators	Underweight	P value	Stunting	P value
Total (n=16756)	45.7 (6822)		41.4 (6271)	
Maternal age at marriage		P<0.001		P<0.001
Child marriage (<18y)	49.9 (3793)		46.4 (3537)	
Adult marriage (>=18y)	39.9 (3029)		34.4 (2734)	
Paternal age at marriage		P<0.001		P<0.001
Child marriage (<21y)	51.2 (2666)		48.3 (2529)	
Adult marriage (>=21y)	41.9 (4156)		36.7 (3742)	
Maternal age at birth		P<0.001		P<0.001
<18 y	54.5 (421)		50.8 (410)	
18-20 y	46.2 (1341)		42.3 (1215)	
21-24 y	43.5 (2165)		39.4 (1989)	
25-29y	44.7 (1778)		40.2 (1620)	
30y+	47.9 (1117)		43.0 (1037)	
Paternal age at birth		P<0.001		P<0.001
<18 y	47.0 (23)		53.8 (27)	
18-20 y	54.6 (236)		51.3 (233)	
21-24 y	48.4 (1211)		43.8 (1129)	
25-29y	44.1 (2228)		41.1 (2070)	
30y+	45.2 (3124)		39.9 (2812)	

Source: Author's calculation from the third round of National Family Health Survey (2005-2006) data.

Table-4: Adjusted odds ratio predicting underweight and stunting among births 0-59 months, India, 2005-06

Covariates	Underweight					
	Model-1	Model-2	Model-3	Model-4	Model-5	Model-6
Mother's age at marriage						
>=18y	1	—	1	1	—	1
<18y	1.69a (1.59-1.80)		1.53a (1.43-1.64)	1.11a (1.03-1.20)		1.06 (0.98-1.15)

Father's age at marriage						
>=21y	—	1	1	—	1	1
<21y		1.58a (1.48-1.69)	1.34a (1.25-1.44)		1.14a (1.05-1.23)	1.03 (0.94-1.12)
			Stunting			
	Model-1	**Model-2**	**Model-3**	**Model-4**	**Model-5**	**Model-6**
Mother's age at marriage						
>=18y	1	—	1	1	—	1
<18y	1.73a (1.63-1.85)		1.53a (1.43-1.64)	1.17a (1.08-1.26)		1.11a (1.03-1.21)
Father's age at marriage						
>=21y	—	1	1	—	1	1
<21y		1.68a (1.57-1.80)	1.43a (1.33-1.53)		1.22a (1.13-1.32)	1.07 (0.98-1.17)

Note: Author's calculation from the third round of National Family Health Survey (2005-2006) data.

a-P < 0.001; b-P < 0.05.

- Model 1 shows the unadjusted effect of maternal age at marriage;
- Model 2 shows the unadjusted effect of paternal age at marriage;
- Model 3 shows the unadjusted mutual effect of maternal and paternal age at marriage;
- Model 4 is adjusted for age of the child, sex of the child, whether the child had multiparous birth, area of residence (urban vs. rural), national region, religion, maternal age at birth, maternal education, and maternal body mass index (BMI);
- Model 5 is adjusted for age of the child, sex of the child, whether the child had multiparous birth, area of residence (urban vs. rural), national region, religion, paternal age at birth, paternal education, and paternal body mass index (BMI);
- Model 6 is adjusted for age of the child, sex of the child, whether the child had multiparous birth, area of residence (urban vs. rural), national region, religion, maternal and paternal age at birth, maternal and paternal education, maternal and paternal body mass index (BMI);

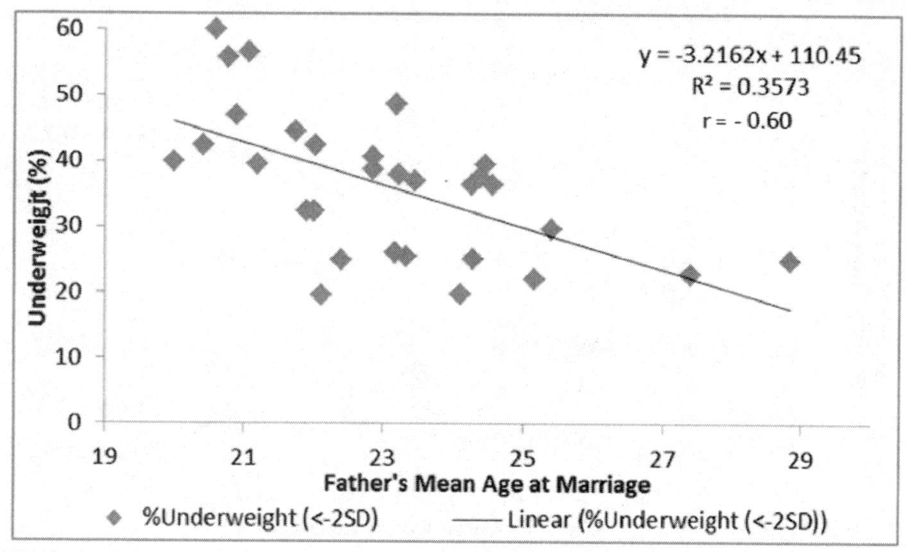
y = -3.2162x + 110.45
R^2 = 0.3573
r = - 0.60
Underweigjt (%)
Father's Mean Age at Marriage
%Underweight (<-2SD)
Linear (%Underweight (<-2SD))

[A]

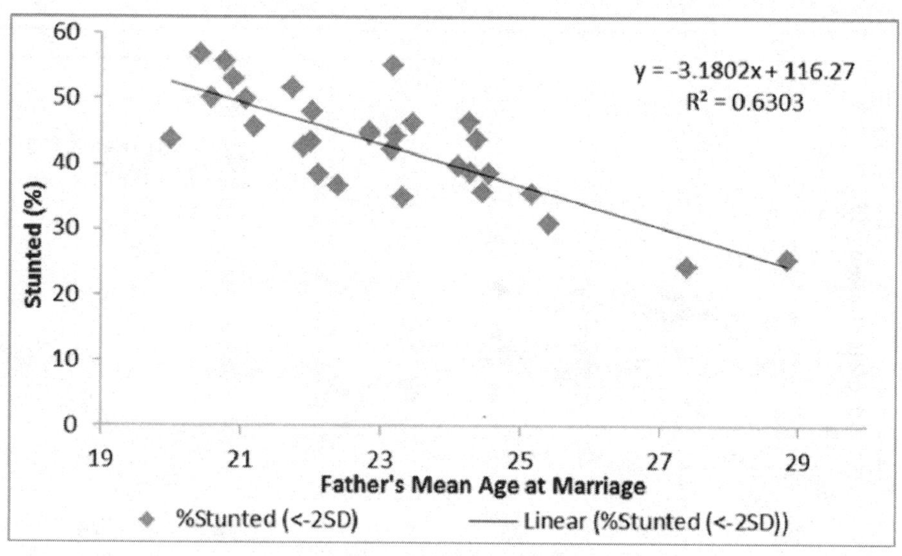
y = -3.1802x + 116.27
R^2 = 0.6303
Stunted (%)
Father's Mean Age at Marriage
%Stunted (<-2SD)
Linear (%Stunted (<-2SD))

[B]

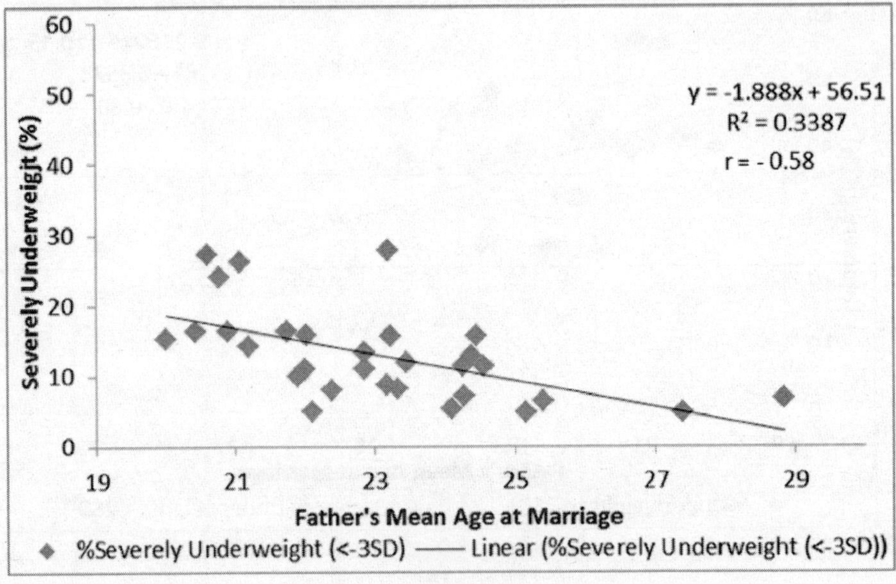

[C]

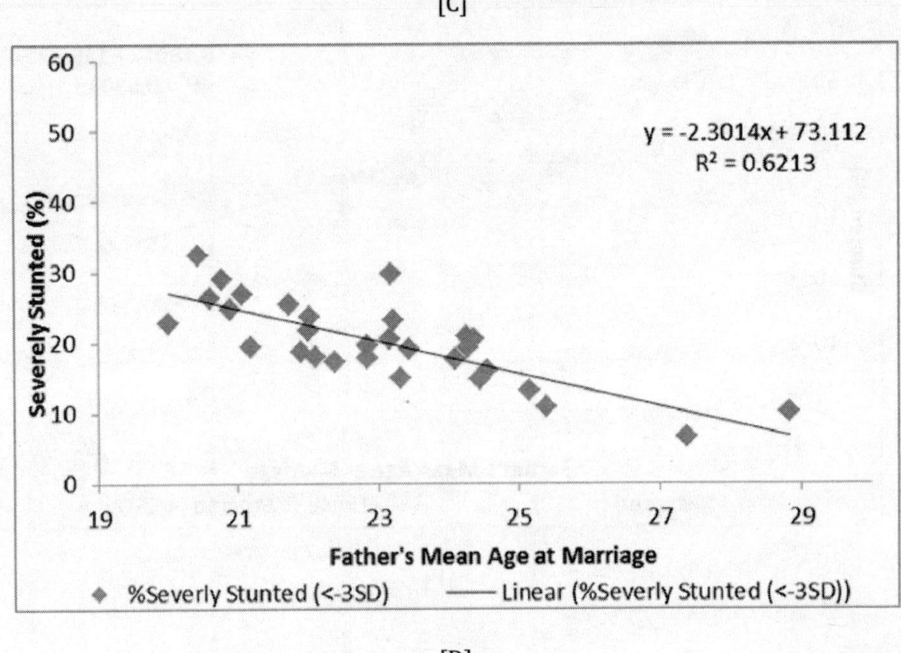

[D]

Source: Author's calculation from the third round of National Family Health Survey (2005-2006) data.

Figure 1: Association between father's mean age at marriage and nutritional status of children (0-59 months) across states in India, 2005-2006.

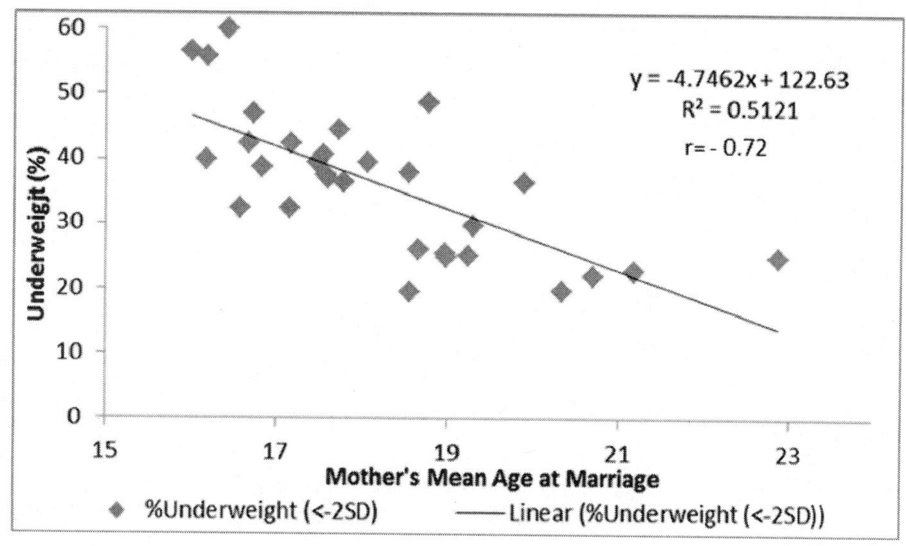
y = -4.7462x + 122.63
R² = 0.5121
r= - 0.72
Underweigjt (%)
Mother's Mean Age at Marriage
%Underweight (<-2SD)
Linear (%Underweight (<-2SD))

[A]

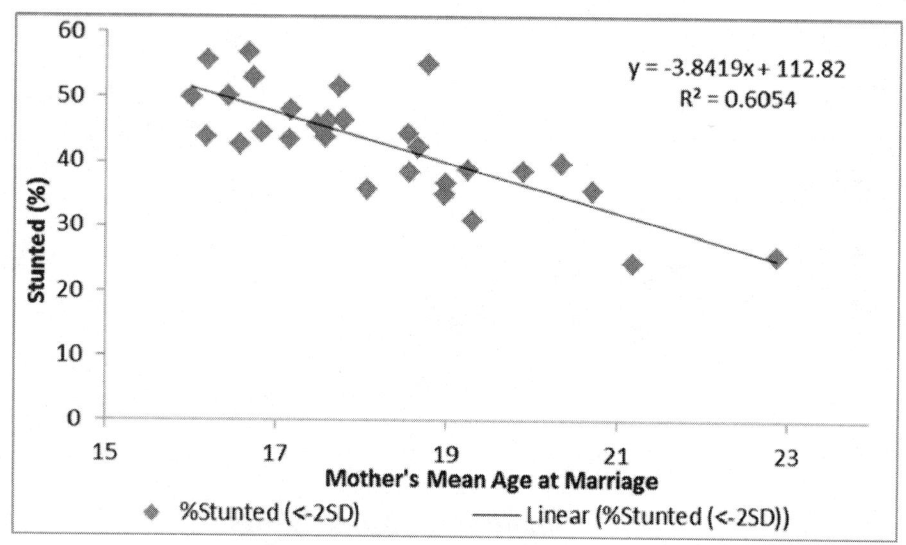
y = -3.8419x + 112.82
R² = 0.6054
Stunted (%)
Mother's Mean Age at Marriage
%Stunted (<-2SD)
Linear (%Stunted (<-2SD))

[B]

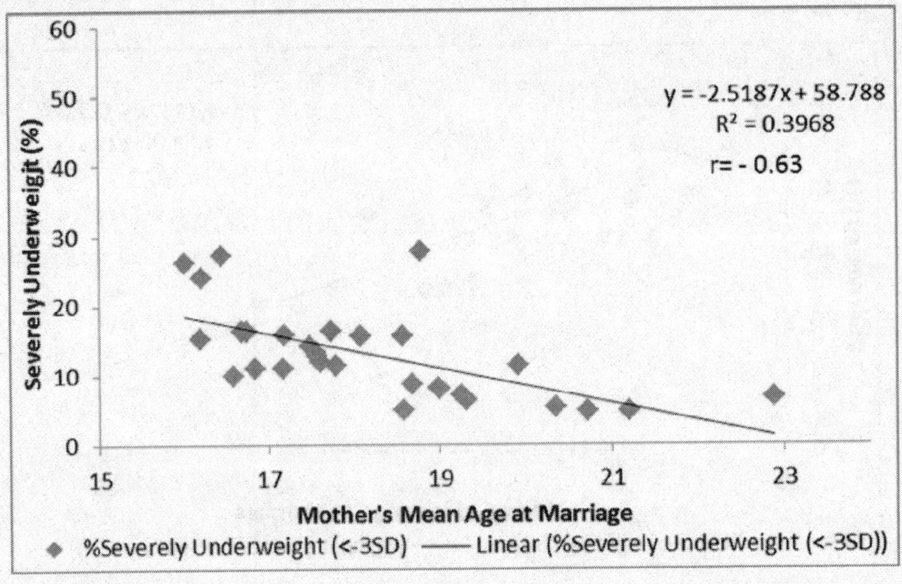

[C]

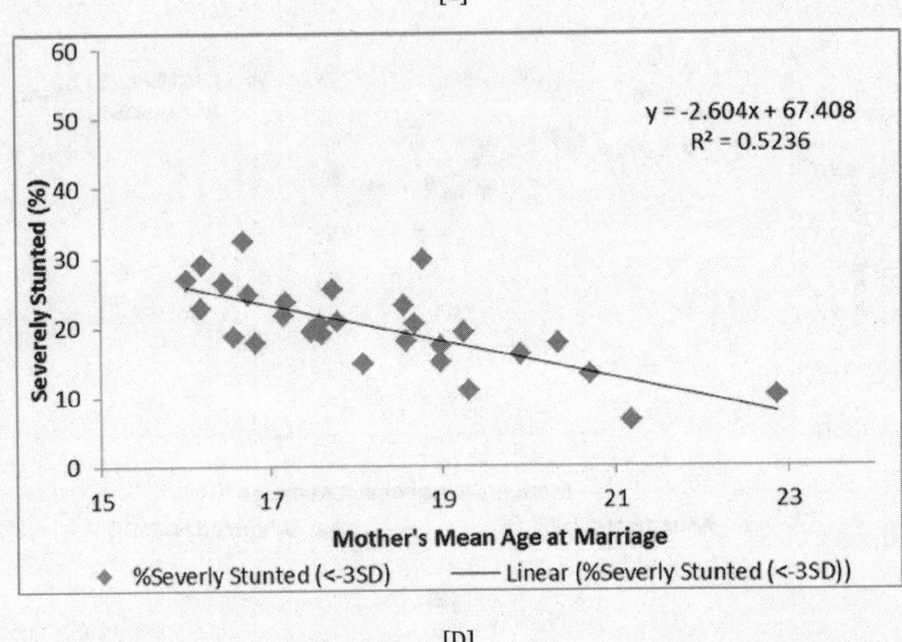

[D]

Source: Author's calculation from the third round of National Family Health Survey (2005-2006) data.

Figure 2: Association between mother's mean age at marriage and nutritional status of children (0-59 months) across states in India, 2005-2006.

11

Nutritional Awareness, Feeding Practices and Nutritional Status among U5-Children in India

—Mukesh Ravi Raushan and Rajesh Raushan

Abstract

Malnutrition is considered a major health problem, especially in developing countries contributing to poor child growth and development to high morbidity and infant & child mortality. The evidence demonstrates that not just food shortage but feeding practices are believed to be the most important for child malnutrition other than knowledge and awareness among mothers. Hence, the study posed to investigate the nutritional awareness and dietary diversity, followed by a causal relationship between dietary diversity and nutritional outcomes among children in India. This study utilises data from the National Family Health Survey: 2005-06 (NFHS-3) considering the youngest child living with the women. The nutritional health status measured along with wasting (weight-for-height). Dietary diversity was assessed by constructing the composite score of dietary diversity, named as Complementary Food Diversity Score (CFDS) based on WHO-IYCF model.

The study revealed that only 40 percent mothers were aware of the food provided to their children during the infancy, ranges from a highest of around 82 percent among mothers in Tamil Nadu to lowest of only 14 percent in Bihar. Notably, mothers from North Indian states were having very poor to poor knowledge about nutrition compared to mothers from south Indian states. Only 28 percent of children had consumed four and more food. Interestingly, there is no clear north-south disparity pattern found in food diversity for children. Accessibility of food found more among urban children. The impact of education on the place of the residence revealed a significant association with CFDS. Along the economic scale, the poorer households were found at greater risk to give less diversified recommended food than the richer households. The result shows that staple food was very much prevalent among Indian as it was very hard to differentiate between poor and rich, but the animal and milk product food were more prevalent among richer than poorer.

The study demonstrated that the child who consumed milk product food were less likely to be malnourished than their counterparts who did not consume. Notably, as the score gets improved the risk for malnutrition among children decreases simultaneously. Overall, the CFDS and frequency of the food given to the child, both were found negatively associated with the child malnutrition in India. Hence study concludes that increasing nutritional awareness on complementary dietary diversity may be one of the major ways to reduce the poor nutritional status and adverse health outcomes at infancy and young age among children in India.

Introduction

Nutrition during the first five years have a greater impact not only on growth and morbidity during childhood but also acts as a determinant of nutritional status during adolescent and adult life. Malnutrition is considered a major health problem, especially in developing countries, contributing to high infant and child mortality (Black et al., 2008; Victoria et al., 2008). The global nutrition report, 2016 revealed that 44 percent of the countries (57 out of 129) now experiencing very serious level of both malnutrition and adult overweight & obesity. Malnutrition is responsible for nearly half of all deaths of children under age 5 and, together with poor diets, is a major driver of the global burden of disease. At least 57 countries experience serious levels of both undernutrition, including stunting and anaemia, and adult overweight and obesity (IFPRI, 2016). Although progress has reduced the burden of underweight children, still one in seven children are underweight at the global leve, and south Asia has the highest burden of underweight children with approximately one in three children still affected. Whereas, one in four children have stunted growth in 2013(UN, 2015).The prevalence of underweight and stunted children in India is amongst the highest in the world, and nearly doubles that of Sub-Saharan Africa with dire consequences for mobility, mortality, productivity and economic growth (Gragnolati et al., 2005). Still, 38 percent and 36 percent children under five years of age are underweight and stunted, whereas only around 10 percent of children aged 6-23 months are receiving adequate diets (MoHFW, 2017).

Several studies revealed that malnutrition during childhood leads to poor child growth and development(Grantham-McGregor et al., 1991; Walker et al., 2005) on the one hand and a higher incidence of morbidities and mortalities on the other hand (Walker et al., 2007). Malnourished children tend to have more severe diarrhoea episodes and associated growth faltering (De Onis & Blossner, 2003; Lutter et al., 1989; Tomkins & Watson, 1989). The income, poverty and mother's education are recognised as being the strongest factors that mark child nutrition (Glewwe, 1999). However, there is also evidence that intra-household relations, particularly those which rely on gendered social and cultural norms, mediate aspects of child health and nutrition and impact on infant and child mortality (Dyson & Moore, 1983). The evidence demonstrates the strong link of women's education with child survival and nutrition as it increases mother's mobility outside the community, the accessibility of health care and their ability to negotiate health systems effectively, as well as increase their knowledge, skills and responsiveness to learned experience to feed and nourish their child (Glewwe, 1999). Although the problem of malnutrition, as believed by a nutritionist, is multifaceted not just related to food shortage feeding practices to be the most important for child nutrition (Brown et al., 1989).

Efforts to quantify child feeding practices have been limited due to methodological issues (Ruel & Menon, 2002). Most of the studies about child feeding practices and nutrition outcome has focused on single behaviour like on exclusive breastfeeding, the timing of introduction of complementary food, duration of breastfeeding etc. (Cohen et al., 1994; Sidney et al., 2016). It was Ruel and Menon (2002), who first attempted to create a composite age-specific feeding index to understand its association with child nutrition mainly for the Latin American countries. Even after, a few research studies have been carried out on child feeding practices and nutritional outcomes. The World Health Organisation provided guidelines for child feeding practices in 2008. Despite there have been a very few studies which attempted to construct a composite index of feeding practices, even in India. Therefore, the present study tries to understand the mother's nutritional awareness and the role of child feeding practices on child nutritional outcome using a composite child feeding index.

Hence, the prime objectives of this paper are a) to assess the nutritional awareness among women in India and their regional variation; b) to analyse variability in dietary diversity among Indian children; c) to examine the causal relationship of dietary diversity and nutritional outcomes among children in India.

Data and Methods

Data under Study

This study utilises data from National Family Health Survey, 2005-06 (NFHS-3), designed to provide estimates of important indicators on family welfare, maternal and child health, and nutrition in India (IIPS & Macro, 2007). This survey is the Indian version of Demographic and Health Survey (DHS), conducted worldwide and considered as one of the most robust data sources in India. The two-stage sample design in most rural areas and three-stage sample design in most urban areas were adopted for selecting the households. Hence study focuses on infant and young children aged 0-59 months (μ = 29.54; SD = 17.21) from the selected households during the survey (IIPS & Macro, 2007).

Methodology

The study included the youngest child living with women. Though the analysis was done on the youngest child of 0 to 59 mont; it is important to note that for the children below five months it is not advisable to give any complimentary food. The dietary diversity score and all the complementary food given to the youngest child was separately analysed, and it was found that only 0.01 percent children whose age was below five months consumed any complementary food. Therefore, to increase the reliability of the analysis with other covariates, the children of all ages were analysed. The crude association between complementary foods given to the indexed child was assessed by the chi-square test for association. Nutritional awareness was measured on mothers of all children (N=51555) ranging from zero to 59 months. Consumption of all seven recommended food and nutritional status of the child was analysed by binary logistic regression analysis.

Outcome Variable

The nutritional health status among children is assessed using an anthropometric tool called wasting (weight-for-height). Wasting represents the failure to receive adequate nutrition in the period immediately preceding the survey and may be the result of inadequate food intake or a recent episode of illness-causing loss of weight and the onset of malnutrition. Epidemiological evidence suggests that the first response to a nutritional and infectious insult is weight loss (wasting), followed by retardation in linear growth (stunting) (Grantham-McGregor et al., 1991; Walker et al., 2005). If the insult persists, children will cease to grow in height and will lose weight, thus augmenting the process of wasting.

The children whose Z-score is below minus two standard deviations (-2SD) from the median of the reference population were considered wasted for their height and were acutely malnourished. To assess the nutritional status of children concerning the reference population, Z-scores (standard deviation scores) are employed. Z score is defined as:

Z-score = (Observed Individual Value–Median Value of Reference Population)/ (Standard Deviation of Value in Reference Population)

Feeding Practices among 0-59 Months Children

For exploring the malnutrition among children on indicator mentioned above i.e., Wasting, food consumption behaviour has assessed for the youngest child in each of the sampled households by interviewing his/her mother if the child had consumed food items recommended by WHO for better nutritional status among children globally. World Health Organisation categorised seventeen types of food items into seven recommended complementary food types(WHO, 2008). On the line, the 17 food items have categorised into seven food groups according to the WHO IYCF model and can be understood as follows:

1. Staple foods group included four items (bread, rice, noodles, or other grains; white potato/yam, manioc, cassava, or another tuber; commercial baby cereal; and porridge);
2. Animal source foods group included five items (beef, pork, lamb, goat, rabbit or deer; chicken, duck or other birds; liver, kidney, heart or other organs; eggs; and fish or shellfish);
3. Milk products group included two items (tinned/powder or fresh milk; and baby formula);
4. Green leafy/orange colour vegetable group included two items (dark green leafy vegetables; and pumpkin, carrots, squash, or sweet potato)(Gleaves);
5. Pulses group included 1 item (beans, peas, or lentils);
6. Oils/fats group included 1 item (oils, fats, and butter); and
7. Seeds group included 1 item (nuts) (WHO, 2008).

The dietary diversity was assessed by constructing the composite score of dietary diversity and named as Complementary Food Diversity Score (CFDS). The Cronbach alpha for this index was found to be acceptable (alpha = 0.77). The dietary diversity score ranged from 0 to 17. Since the score above 10 comprised just one percent , therefore, the score above ten were clubbed into ten. Additionally, the number of times food consumed by the child were also assessed to investigate the dietary diversity with the frequency of food consumed by child day before the survey conducted in respective areas. Normally, it was expected that children had been consumed food items for at least three times prior to the survey day.

Nutritional Awareness, Feeding Practices and Explanatory Variables

Along the line to understand the causal relationship of nutritional awareness and feeding practices in India, nutritional awareness assessed whether women with nutritional awareness have a more significant impact on food diversity index or not? The nutritional awareness may propagate that the woman having any one type of exposure of advice received (either during antenatal care women received advised on pregnancy nutrition or during pregnancy received health and nutrition education or when breastfeeding received health and nutrition education) may have better dietary diversity for their children compared to the one who has not been received it.

For explaining variables of feeding practices on the one hand and nutritional awareness, on the other hand, was concerned, mother's educational attainment (single years of schooling and categorised, both) for awareness about child nutrition followed by feeding practices, household economic status using wealth quintile (into five categories) as a proxy, partner' work status for availing the food items, caste and place of residence as exclusion and deprivation on accessing various food items, religion as one way of food consumption behaviour and mother's body mass index to link it with child nutritional health at first sight. Moreover, along with the demographic factors; Mother's age at first birth and birth order has considered under the study.

Results of the Study

State Level Variation in Nutritional Awareness among Mothers of 0-59 Months Children.

Nutritional awareness among Mothers of children under five years of age is measured at the state level before moving on feeding practices through food diversity based on WHO standards. Table-1 shows that only 40 percent mothers were at the ware of the food provided to their children during the infancy which ranges from a highest of around 82 percent among mothers in Tamil Nadu to lowest of only 14 percent in Bihar. Notably, mothers from North Indian states are having very poor to poor knowledge about nutrition compared to mothers from south Indian states. North-eastern states were lying close to North Indian states on the awareness about child nutrition. Moving on food diversity, it has been assessed on dietary diversity scores four and above. Table-1 revealed that only of 28 percent children had consumed four and more food items the recommended by the World Health Organisation. State level variation shows found the highest of 56 percent and 55 percent in Kerala, Goa and West Bengal to only 9 percent in Rajasthan followed by 12 percent in Andhra Pradesh. Interestingly, there is no clear north-south disparity pattern found on food diversity for children.

Table-1: Nutritional Awareness among Mother of Children 0-59 Months in India (%)

States	Nutrition Awareness		CFDS (4+)	
	%	N	%	N
Tamil Nadu	82.14	1735	28.79	1023
Kerala	76.20	1017	56.19	610
Goa	72.26	988	54.98	574
Andhra Pradesh	66.10	2292	12.17	1138
Karnataka	65.56	2188	31.16	1166
Sikkim	61.30	653	49.94	358
West Bengal	58.29	2368	54.95	1215
Delhi	56.86	1251	34.11	681

Maharashtra	54.80	3038	16.47	1458
Himachal Pradesh	54.79	995	53.64	521
Orissa	53.42	1781	47.7	949
Gujarat	52.10	1571	25.18	851
Chhattisgarh	50.23	1592	31.31	808
Tripura	50.09	639	42.25	321
Punjab	47.27	1307	23.1	621
Mizoram	45.62	848	27.58	420
Jammu and Kashmir	44.65	1226	31.14	676
Manipur	43.94	1912	49.3	1118
Meghalaya	42.50	1093	30.73	557
Madhya Pradesh	38.79	3016	19.47	1582
Haryana	35.58	1256	14.09	627
Jharkhand	35.10	1657	30.98	954
Assam	33.52	1532	28.6	704
Uttaranchal	30.31	1228	35.87	652
Rajasthan	27.38	2023	8.9	977
Arunachal Pradesh	23.19	870	22.36	471
Nagaland	20.69	2108	31.89	1217
Uttar Pradesh	16.81	7051	23.35	3756
Bihar	14.79	2320	31.86	1294
India	40.09	51555	27.7	27299
Source: Authors' calculation based on NFHS-3 (2005-06) round data				

Dietary Diversity and Food Frequency among 0-59 Months Children

Table-2 shows that the household's affordability for CFDS four & above as well as food frequency three & above on selected demographic and socio-economic characteristics for children under the study. Mother's age at first a birth having greater impact on dietary diversity for their children as it was found only 26 percent among women who delivered at age less than 19 years for the first time which founded increased with higher age of women at first birth. Dietary diversity also found decreases with increasing birth order. Accessibility of food shows that more children from urban areas received diversified food compared to the rural areas. The child whose mother was educated receiving more complimentary food than their counterparts and also the frequency of the food consumed was higher as 30 percent children whose mother were highly educated were receiving food three or more times compared to about 16 percent among not educated mothers. The impact of the education with the place of residence was found to be significantly associated with the CFDS in India. The pattern of CFDS of children was significantly increasing as the education of the mother increases, but it is interesting to note the degree of performance was lower in rural India than their counterpart from urban (Figure 1).

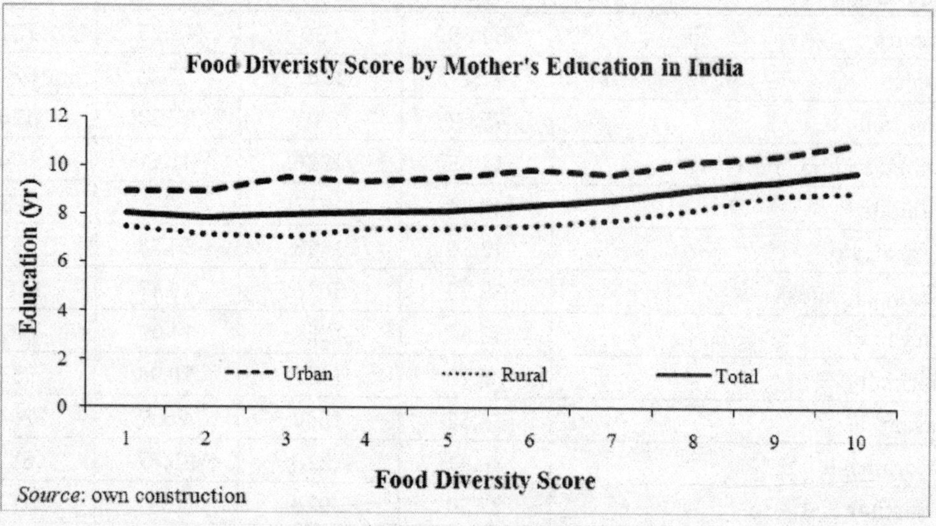

Fig. 1: Rural-Urban Differential in Dietary Diversity with Mother's Year of Schooling in India

Source: Authors' construction based on NFHS-3 (2005-06) round data

Further, the poorer households were found at greater risk to feed their children with greater food diversity. The household's dietary diversity with four or more was found much high among richer than their counterpart as about only 23 percent mothers from poor household reported giving their children four or more types of complementary food as compared to about 37 percent among mothers from richer households. More or less food frequency for three & more time followed the same pattern, However, along the caste line, more children among better off caste were receiving four and more complimentary food compared to the children from the rest of the caste groups. On religiȯn, more Muslim children receiving complementary food compared to Hindu children but on several times receiving for the d is found the opposite (P<0.001).

Table-2: Children Dietary Diversity and Food Frequency by Demographic and Socio-Economic Characteristics in India: 2005-06

Covariates	Dietary Diversity (4+)			Food Frequency(3+)		
	%	Chi2	Pr.	%	Chi2	Pr.
Mother's Age at First birth						
<19	26.34	197.27	0.001	16.77	129.82	0.001
20-24	28.11			18.45		
25-29	36.91			23.12		
30+	36.96			27.92		
Birth Order						
1	28.85	94.2	0.001	17.23	17.47	0.001
2	29.66			18.68		
3	26.69			18.12		
4+	23.52			17.49		
Residence						
Urban	30.83	75.65	0.001	20.73	75.36	0.001
Rural	26.62			16.94		
Mother's Education						
No education	22.71	600.89	0.001	15.72	294.45	0.001
Primary	28.29			16.64		
Secondary	32.84			19.51		
Higher	43.09			30.1		
Wealth Quintile						
Poorest	22.81	449.48	0.001	15.58	249.3	0.001
Poorer	26.33			16.36		
Middle	26.41			16.66		
Richer	30.62			18.63		
Richest	36.50			24.73		
Partner's Working Status						
Not Working	25.50	3.58	0.001	13.36	0.19	0.667
Working	27.69			17.96		
Caste						
SC	25.87	154.89	0.001	17.66	42.6	0.001
ST	22.93			16.08		

OBC	25.90			17.42		
Others	32.86			19.58		
Religion						
Hindu	26.99	36.57	0.001	18.05	62.15	0.001
Muslim	29.24			16.57		
others	33.2			20.78		
Sanitation Facility						
Improved	34.49	411.56	0.001	22.39	186.25	0.001
Not improved	23.34			15.97		
Source: Authors' calculation based on NFHS-3 (2005-06) round data						

Table-3 shows the proportion of seven types of recommended food consumed by the children in the last 24 hours the before the survey. This is examined on selected covariates to understand the differentials in consumption of those food items by children. Economically, poorer households were at greater risk to providing less diversified recommended food than the richer as the mean of the CFDS is found 4forthe children belonged to richest households compared to 3 for children from poorest households. The result shows that the staple food was very much prevalent among Indian as about it was very hard to differentiate for poor and rich, but the animal and milk product food were more prevalent among richer than the poorer. Further, women with a higher level of education and residing in urban areas were more affluent to provide diversified complementary food to their children compared to their counterpart. Region-specific analyses report that the animal products were more prevalent within south region of the country followed by north-east and is observed least in central India, whereas the milk product was more prevalent in the north region followed by the south.

Table-3: Food Consumed by Children in the Last 24 Hours on Selected Covariates in India: 2005-06

Covariates	N	% the consumed in the last 24 hours							Food Variety Score	
		Staple	Animal	Milk	Gleaf	Pulse	Oil	Seed	Mean	CV
Wealth Index										
Poorest	9200	98.79	10.97	23.73	27.96	7.32	7.82	1.94	3.22	0.58
Poorer	9571	98.63	12.60	32.00	30.48	8.68	9.27	3.28	3.42	0.60
Middle	10659	98.45	15.61	36.41	28.65	9.71	9.87	4.04	3.42	0.64

Richer	11300	98.62	19.35	43.32	31.89	12.33	10.83	5.54	3.68	0.67
Richest	10825	99.46	24.13	48.54	37.79	14.00	13.12	8.78	4.02	0.63
Residence										
Urban	19483	98.87	20.88	40.44	32.79	12.11	11.42	6.38	3.66	0.65
Rural	32072	98.72	13.87	33.38	30.09	9.22	9.32	3.57	3.44	0.62
Mother's Education										
No Education	21057	98.49	10.89	29.33	27.89	7.87	8.43	2.75	3.22	0.59
Primary	7476	98.78	15.73	35.01	30.13	9.42	9.35	3.55	3.53	0.62
Secondary	19102	99.03	21.54	42.2	33.93	12.21	11.51	5.8	3.76	0.65
Higher	3919	99.53	26.59	50.54	41.93	18.3	15.24	12.27	4.49	0.61
Region										
North	9286	99.54	11.2	46.12	28.14	8.5	8.7	5.21	2.91	0.76
NE	17781	98.34	19.77	30.46	34.8	10.97	10.49	3.49	4.17	0.53
East	1571	98.52	10.91	41.8	32.17	8.47	6.84	3.14	3.30	0.60
West	4026	99.23	17.89	27.68	24.38	5.24	3.42	3.27	2.71	0.76
Central	11659	98.76	8.16	35.04	28.76	11.12	10.56	4.46	3.26	0.57
South	7232	98.8	26.05	36.88	32.11	9.86	12.38	5.48	3.53	0.71

Note: Seven types of food as recommended by WHO; Milk: food of milk product; Gleaf: green leafy vegetables
Source: Authors' calculation based on NFHS-3 (2005-06) round data

Dietary Diversity and Growth Pattern among Children

Growth pattern along the line of notional intake and their quick response has been examined on wasting under the study. First, it has been examined on recommended seven types of complementary food types followed by CFDS and frequencies of food per day. Table-4 shows the result of binary logistic regression on wasting with WHO seven types of recommended food for children in India. The result suggests that child who consumed the milk product food (OR: 0.87, $p < 0.0001$) were less likely to be malnourished than their counterparts who did not consume, whereas, in case of other food items as the child who consumed food product of seed (OR: 0.75, $p < 0.0001$) were less likely to be malnourished than those who did not. The nutritional status among children was negatively associated with the protein containing complementary food given the child as that child who received pulse in last 24 hours were less likely to be wasted (OR: 0.87, $p < 0.00001$) as compelled to the reference category. This estimate was done on 95 percent confidence interval, meaning that this estimate was 95 percent certain that the true population value as it might be estimated from a much larger study (Neyman, 1937).

Table-4: Results of Logistic Regression on Child Wasting in the India along the WHO Recommended Complementary Food

Complementary Foods	Wasting	OR	Std. Err.	95% CI	
				Upper	Lower
Staple	No				
	Yes	1.13	0.214	0.776	1.636
Animal	No				
	Yes	0.96	0.047	0.875	1.058
Milk	No				
	Yes	0.87***	0.038	0.799	0.948
Gleaf	No				
	Yes	0.87***	0.039	0.799	0.951
Puls	No				
	Yes	0.83**	0.062	0.714	0.959
Oil	No				
	Yes	0.77***	0.049	0.676	0.868
Seed	No				
	Yes	0.75**	0.083	0.606	0.936
	Intercept	0.29	0.054	0.198	0.414
Log pseudo likelihood		–12930.887			
Intercept Model					
Log pseudo likelihood		–22739.51			

*** : Significant at 1 percent level; **Significant at 5 percent level.
Note: Milk: food of milk product; Gleaf: green leafy vegetables
Source: Authors' calculation based on NFHS-3 (2005-06) round data

Table-5 shows that the child whose CFDS were reported to be two were less likely to be wasted (OR: 0.75, p<0.0001) as compared to reference category of score but as the score gets improved the risk for malnutrition among children in India decreases, for instance, the children whose CFDS was zero were about two times more likely to be wasted as compared to that child whose CFDS was 8 or more. The CFDS and the frequency of the food given to the child; both were negatively associated with the child health outcome. The less likelihood of wasted child was reported among those who were fed two or more times in last 24 hour, and the risk of being wasted was observed to be half among those who were fed six times (OR: 0.55, p<0.0001) in last

24 hour before the survey. The estimate was retested with linear regression and found that as CFDS was negatively associated as the 10 percent change in food diversity the expected change in the child nutritional health outcome decreased with one percent, whereas as the frequency to feed the child increases by 10 percent, the expected change in child health outcome in terms of wasting decreases by 2 percent when place of residence, mother's education, religion and birth order were controlled. The result from the regression analysis shows that the p-value of the F-test of the overall model is statistically significantly estimated.

Table-5: Result of Logistic Regression for Wasting on Dietary Diversity and Food Frequency among 0-59 Months Children in India

	Wasting					
CFDS	**N**	**%**	**OR**	**95% Class Interval**		
				p	**Lower**	**Upper**
0	8806	24.61				
1	4432	23.27	0.94	0.231	0.84	1.04
2	3947	19.69	0.75	0.0001	0.66	0.84
3	4100	19.58	0.73	0.0001	0.65	0.83
4	3139	20.21	0.77	0.0001	0.67	0.87
5	2383	19.49	0.74	0.0001	0.64	0.86
6	1708	17.53	0.67	0.0001	0.56	0.80
7	1160	14.7	0.57	0.0001	0.45	0.72
8	750	14.13	0.55	0.0001	0.41	0.75
9	462	14.17	0.57	0.008	0.38	0.86
10	741	13.94	0.61	0.004	0.43	0.85
Linear Model			Coeff.			
			-0.010	0.0001	-0.012	-0.008
Food Frequency						
0	4445	30.83				
1	1597	24.26	0.76	0.0001	0.64	0.90
2	5336	21.92	0.64	0.0001	0.57	0.72
3	5417	21.33	0.62	0.0001	0.55	0.70
4	2330	22.13	0.66	0.0001	0.56	0.77
5	1084	21.65	0.66	0.0001	0.53	0.83

6	423	18.49	0.55	0.0001	0.38	0.79
7	595	18.15	0.59	0.0001	0.42	0.84
Linear Model			Coeff.			
			−0.02	0.0001	−0.02	-0.01
Note: CFDS: Complementary food diversity score; residence, mother's education, religion and sex of child were controlled.						

Source: Authors' calculation based on NFHS-3 (2005-06) round data

Conclusion

The study aimed to understand regional variation in nutritional awareness, dietary diversity and nutritional health among children of 0-59 months in India. For nutritional status, an appropriate indicator of nutrition, i.e., wasting is considered. For considering wasting as an outcome having worth importance that wasting represents the failure to receive adequate nutrition in the period immediately preceding the survey. Epidemiological evidence suggests that the first response to a nutritional and infectious insult is weight loss (wasting), followed by retardation in linear growth(Grantham-McGregor et al., 1991; Walker *et al.*, 2005).

Hence, relying on the robust data available in the is regard, the study found that nutritional awareness in much higher in south Indian states and less in North Indian states with lowest in Bihar and Highest in Tamil Nadu. Moving on food diversity for children, no clear pattern was the observed at the state level. At demographic front; mother's age at first bias rth having greater impact on dietary diversity as younger mother found very low on CFDS as compared to the mothers delivered at higher er age for the first time. As having more children may direct the competition among them for the food, and it was tried to examine through the childbirth order, and it is found higher birth order receiving less number of diversified food.

Accessibility of food shows that more children from urban areas received diversified food compared to the rural areas. The impact of educate action with h the place of the residence revealed significant association with the CFDS in the country as increasing mother education increases diversity in complementary food. It is interesting that to note that the degree of performance was lower in rural India than their counterpart from urban. Along the economic scale, the poorer households were found at greater risk to give less diversified recommended food than the richer households. The result shows that staple food was very much prevalent among Indian as it was very hard to differentiate between poor and rich, but the animal and milk product food were more prevalent among richer than poorer.

The result from logistic regression revealed that the child who consumed milk product food were less likely to be malnourished than their counterparts who did not consume. Whereas, nutritional status among children was negatively associated with protein containing complementary food given to the child as that child who receive the d pulse in the last 24 hour were less likely to be wasted. It is also found that the child whose CFDS were even two are found less likely to be wasted compared to whose CFDS as zero. Notably, as the score gets improved the risk for malnutrition among children decreases simultaneously. Overall, the CFDS and frequency of the food given to the child, both were found negatively associated with the child nutritional outcome in India. Hence, increasing nutritional awareness of complementary dietary diversity may be one of the major ways to reduce the poor nutritional status and adverse health outcomes at infancy and young age among children in India.

References

1. Brown, K.H., Black, R.E., Lopez de Roman, A.G., & Creed de Kanashiro, H. (1989). Infant Feeding Practices and Their Relationship with Diarrhea and Other Diseases in Huascar (Lima), Peru. Pediatrics, 83, 31-40.
2. Cohen, R.J., Brown, K.H., Canahuati, J., Rivera, L.L., & Dewry, A.G. (1994). Effects of Age of Introduction of Complementary Foods on Infant Breast Milk Intake, Total Energy Intake, and Growth: A Randomised Intervention Study in Honduras. The Lancet, 344, 288-293.
3. De Onis, M., & Blössner, M. (2003). The World Health Organisation global database on child growth and malnutrition: methodology and applications. International journal of epidemiology, 32(4), 518-526.
4. Dyson, T., & Moore, M. (1983). On Kinship Structure, Female Autonomy, and Demographic Behaviour in India. Population and Development Review, 9(1), 35-50.
5. Glewwe, P. (1999). Why Does Mother's Schooling Raise Child Health in Developing Countries? Evidence from Morocco. The Journal of Human Resources, 34(1), 124-159.
6. Gragnolati, M., Shekar, M., Gupta, M.D., C., B., & Lee, Y. (2005). India's undernourished children: A call for reform and action. Washington, DC: The International Bank for Reconstruction and Development & The World Bank.
7. Grantham-McGregor, S.M., Powell, C.A., Walker, S.P., & Himes, J.H. (1991). Nutritional supplementation, psychosocial stimulation, and mental development of stunted children: The Jamaican study. The Lancet, 338, 1-5.
8. IFPRI. (2016). Global Nutrition Report, 2016.Washington DC: International Food Policy Research Institute.
9. IIPSandMacro.(2007).NationalFamilyHealthSurvey(NFHS-3),2005-06:IndiaVolumeI. Mumbai: International Institute for Population Sciences & Macro International.
10. Lutter, C.K., Mora, J.O., Habicht, J.P., Rasmussen, K.M., Robson, D.S., Sellers, S.G., ... Herrera, M.G. (1989). Nutritional supplementation: effects on child stunting because of diarrhoea. The American Journal of Clinical Nutrition, 50(1), 1-8.

11. MoHFW. (2017). India Fact Sheet: National Family Health Survey (NFHS-3), 2015-16. Mumbai: International Institute for Population Sciences.
12. Ruel, M.T., & Menon, P. (2002). Child feeding practices are associated with child nutritional status in Latin America: innovative uses of the demographic and health surveys. The Journal of Nutrition, 132(6), 1180-1187.
13. Sidney, K., Salazar, M., Marrone, G., Diwan, V., Decosta, A., & Lindholm, L. (2016). Out-of-pocket expenditures for childbirth in the context of the Janani Suraksha Yojana (JSY) cash transfer program to promote facility births: Who pays and how much? Studies from Madhya Pradesh, India. International Journal for Equity in Health, 15(1). https://doi.org/10.1186/s12939-016-0362-4
14. Tomkins, A., & Watson, F. (1989). Malnutrition and Infection: A Review. Nutrition Policy Discussion Paper No. 5.
15. UN. (2015). The Millennium Development Goals Report, 2015. New York: United Nations.
16. Walker, S.P., Chang, S.M., Powell, C.A., & Grantham-McGregor, S.M. (2005). Effects of early childhood psychosocial stimulation and nutritional supplementation on cognition and education in growth-stunted Jamaican children: Prospective cohort study. The Lancet, 366, 1804-1807.
17. Walker, S.P., Wachs, T.D., Gardner, J.M., Lozoff, B., Wasserman, G.A., Pollitt, E., et al. (2007). Child development: Risk factors for adverse outcomes in developing countries. The Lancet, 369, 145-157.
18. WHO. (2008). Indicators for Assessing Infant and Young Child Feeding Practices: Conclusions of a Consensus Meeting held 6th-8th November, 2007 in Washington D.C., USA. Geneva: World Health Organisation.

□

12

Nutrition and Health Status of Construction Workers' Children in Gujarat: An Empirical Study of Gandhinagar

—Manoj K. Sahoo and D. Sriram

Abstract

*Nutrition and health status of children in India has remained a matter of concern—despite all-round economic achievements in the country. The children of construction workers face special challenges towards ensuring access to proper nutrition and health facilities. Construction workers' children in Gujarat, despite the state government's numerous facilities regarding health and nutrition care available to them, face some challenges in real access and avail the ability on the ground. The government of Gujarat, in order to provide social security benefits to the workers, implemented the Unorganised Workers Social Security Act 2008. The workers are provided with the Smart Card or identity card so that they can avail the benefits of the schemes such as Balwadi/*Anganwadi *for children to provide nutritious food at the construction sites, maternity benefits and free treatment at the government hospitals. The Gujarat Building and Construction Welfare Board has implemented schemes like hostel facility, temporary housing facilities at the worksites, Shramik Sahay Suvidha—a helpline facilities for any problem including health problems of the construction workers, medical aid in major disease under Mukhyamantri Amrutam Yojana and Mukhyamantri Amrutam Vatsalya Yojana for mother and child and so on. The present study attempts to assess the implementation of the above policies empirically and tries to address the issues of on-ground access and availability of the facilities to the construction workers' children related to their health and nutrition. The study covered fifty children from ten construction sites in and around the capital city of Gandhinagar in Gujarat. It is found from the study that the construction workers' children in the study area avail polio vaccine facilities regularly and medicine and treatment facilities for normal health problems like fever, cough and cold, diarrhoea etc. However, other vaccinations for the children and nutritional benefits like iron supplements, milk, Anganwadi meals have potential for improvements.*

Introduction

Nutrition and health status of children in India has remained a considerable matter of concern despite significant improvement in growth and development in the human resource parameters in the country. Gujarat has and is growing at a faster pace in the last decades, but its health and nutrition parameters have to improve in order to better than the country average. The construction activity as an occupational category falls in the informal sector, which is unorganised. Despite numerous safeguards made available by the central and state governments, the construction workers and their children face considerable challenges towards access to proper nutrition and health facilities. This occurs due to the presence of a sizeable proportion of migrant workers in this sector, as they quite often do not have proper entitlement to the social welfare benefits provided by the state governments at their workplace or the place of destination of the migrant workers. Because of this nature of construction activity, this sector falls in the vulnerable occupational the category of the migrant-dominated informal sector.

The migrant construction workers are mostly temporary or circular migrants. Moreover, they do not necessarily settle in their place of destination for long periods. Due to their temporary nature of stay at the work-site, they are often denied from the basic social services and benefits that are generally available to the native locals. Due to this, the family members of the construction workers face special challenges in matters of access to nutrition and health services, especially their women and children. Construction workers' children in Gujarat are no different as despite state government has provisioned numerous facilities in health and nutrition car; they face considerable challenges in real access and availability on the ground.

Children as Part of Inclusive Growth

India's Eleventh Five Year Plan (2007-12) included children as part of its inclusive growth strategy, as a significant the portion of the population is children below 18 years. Thus children were recognised as the future growth component of the nation, and hence realisation of their full potential is critical for India's sustained economic growth and enhancement of human development. However, access and coverage of health services to all the children have remained unfulfilled, and millions of children still have to face basic challenges related to health and survival (Sahoo, 2008). India's public health system is under-funded so that about 9 out of 10 patients do not have access to a government doctor and more than eighty percent of all private health expenditure is out of own pocket (The 11th FY Plan). Though India has made progress in living conditions in many respects in the South Asian region in last two decades (Dreze & Sen, 2013), in terms of infant mortality rate (IMR: 57) and the life expectancy at birth (64 years), it is far behind China.

Moreover, one-fourth of India's population is especially disadvantaged due to prevalent social inequalities and thus has significant levels of income-poverty and human development. Poverty and disenfranchisement of basic access to health services become even further challenging for women, and girls, thus making their struggle for survival harsh. Hence, the 11th Five Year Plan recognised that a critical part of India's workforce needs improvement in quality and thus necessitates investments in its education, health, nutritional level, and its skills. It also recognises the importance of creating social protection for these children. In this matter, the protection to the construction workers' children is utmost important as they are most vulnerable among the rest in terms of uncertainties of livelihood, a vulnerability in health and access to basic nutrition.

The vulnerability of Migrant Children to Health and Nutritional Deficiency

As per the National Urban Health Mission Draft 2008, in India, 47.1 percent of children face under-nutrition among the migrant workers' children, compared to urban children's 32.8 percent and rural children's 4. Moreover, 28 percent of migrant children were severely stunted, and urban migrant children had higher under-five mortality rate (U5MR). The National Rural Health Mission (NRHM) was framed by the Indian government to ensure states make full utilisation of public health facilities and use health care services available in remote and disadvantaged regions. NRHM provisioned health care, and nutrition facilities thus must be available to the construction workers' children. The National Health Policy, 2002, was formulated to encourage private investments to increase the availability and coverage of health services by integrated and evenly spread network of speciality and super-speciality health services. The National Population Policy, 2000 envisioned a partnership between non-government voluntary organisations (NGOs) and private organisations, including corporate houses in order to upgrade health care services in the country.

Latest World Development Indicators data reveals that India has one of the world's highest levels of children with malnutrition–double that of Sub-Saharan Africa (World Bank, 2017). India ranks 67 among the 80 countries in the Global Hunger, Index 2011, indicating the worst hunger situation. 44% of under-5 children in India are underweight, while 72% of infants have anaemia. Poor, slum dwellers and backwards communities specifically suffer from diarrhoea and related deaths in the five Indian states, reaching 2 million people including over two lakh children. India's above initiatives and investment in child malnutrition programmes have final only led to a substantial al fall in several underweight and stunted children. By 2014, India had 14.5 million fewer stunted children, and over 72 % of infants below six months were breastfed. UNICEF finds that by 2011, more than one-third of under-5 deaths globally were due to under-nutrition. Moreover, about 20% of under-5 children in India were wasted, 43% were underweight, and 48% stunted (UNICEF, 2011).

India continues to be ranked lowly 97 among 118 developing countries by the 2016 Global Hunger Index (GHI)—reflecting the widespread prevalence of hunger in the country (GHI, 2016). The 2016 GHI estimates 15 percent of India's population as undernourished-with about 15 percent of under-5 children as 'wasted' and a significant 39 percent of children as 'stunted'. This denotes a challenging situation of inadequate nutritional intake in the country. The under-5 mortality rate is 4.8 percent at present in India, indicating precarious consequences of insufficient nutrition and poor access to health services.

Construction workers' children, are, however, especially disadvantaged because of the nature of their migration along with their families to the workplace destinations. They become forced to leave schools, loss education; do not have access to healthcare, safety, proper nutrition and developmental needs. They experience hard economic and social conditions due to limited opportunity to diversify their parents' livelihoods, risk of becoming malnourished and non-availability of formal and informal social safety nets for their support, including difficulties in accessing public services and welfare UNICEF (2008). They are left, unattended, thus potentially becoming vulnerable to trafficking and abuse. They become part of child labour and exploitation in the end. Local authorities fail to include the migrant construction workers' children in basic access to health, nutrition, education and other services available from *anganwadis*, schools and hospitals. The migrant workers' families face numerous challenges at the work sites outside their states. Moreover, they do not have any official documents of local identity to get access to basic public goods and services like PDS, medicine or health services.

Construction sites not being children and women-friendly, the children face health and life risks, even more, risks are faced by girl children. Construction sites, in many cases, do not provide proper shelter, drinking water, toilet, crèche or other facilities for children. Women workers being subject to discrimination, less wage, exploitation and abuse, their ability to take care of their the children at the workplace severely gets curtailed leading to children facing health risk and malnutrition. Smaller children of 0-3 years of age become more vulnerable as their mothers do not get breastfeeding and health care breaks at the construction sites. These children more often do not get proper health, nutrition and immunisation facilities leading to severe malnourishment, illness and mortality. Children of 6-14 years, devoid of schooling, lose their nutritional entitlements from Mid day-meals and health facilities from schools like medicines, health check-ups, vitamins and iron tablets etc.

Migrant construction workers' lack of identity, breakdown of their village and traditional community support networks due to migration, often deprive their children of basic health and nutrition. In 1996, the Government of India specifically for the welfare and protection of construction workers, passed the Building and Other Construction Workers' Act. This Act imposed access of 1-2% of project turnover, to fund welfare programs for construction workers and their children.

Construction Workers' Migration: Gujarat

The NCPCR-2014-15 study found the major reasons of migration among the informal workers including construction workers in Gujarat to be lack of work opportunities back home (67.6%), better wage rates (71.2%), better chance of getting work at destination (53.8%), financial crisis/ repayment of debt (29.5%) and natural disaster (1.7%). The study found a pattern in the lean months when work is not available for the migrant workers, which had a high share of short-term migrants. 78% of brick kiln workers, 50% of agricultural labourers and 40% of construction workers had reported peak monsoon months of July and August as the lean months. The NCPCR study also had revealed that the majority of migration among the construction workers was rural to urban migration (72%).

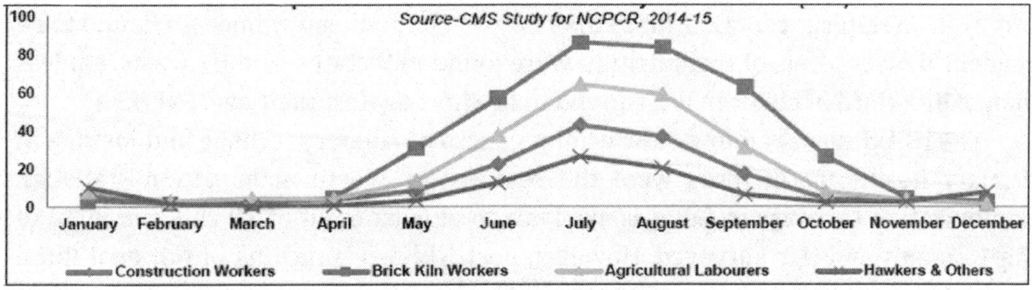

Chart 1: Lean Months of Informal Workers when Availability of work is Less (%)

Nutrition and Health Status of Children in India & Gujarat

Beginning the year 2000, countries throughout the world under the United Nations Millennium Declaration embarked on a global partnership to achieve eight targets by 2015 known as Millennium Development Goals (MDGs) which finally led to reduction of the number of persons living in extreme poverty by more than half since 1990, and decline in the proportion of undernourished people in the developing regions by almost half. Likewise, globally, the under-5 mortality rate has declined by more than half, and maternal mortality is reduced by 45 percent. (UNDP, 2014) In tackling child under-nutrition, the crucial importance of nutrition during the critical 1,000-day (pregnancy plus first two years) of the child's life is well recognised. The

World Health Assembly has adopted a new target of reducing the number of under-5 stunted children by 40% by 2025 (UNICEF, 2013; WHO 2014).

The number of children in India below 15 years has decreased in the last decade. The 4th National Family Health Survey 2015-16 (NFHS-4) puts India's current Infant mortality rate (IMR) at 37 per 1000 live births with 13 states and 2 UTs with IMR level less than 51. Data from the past NFHS surveys show a gradual declining trend in both IMR and under-5 child mortality rate (CMR) in the country. However, India still lags in these statistics compared to not only high-income countries but also many low and middle-income countries like Sri Lanka whose CMR was as low as 10 in 2015. India is also lagging in terms of gender health parameters. National Family Health Survey 2015-16 (NFHS-4) also showed sex ratio in 11 states at 985 females per 1,000 males in 2015-16 vis-a-vis 1000 females per 1000 males in 2005a 06 showing a disturbing trend of decline in sex ratio. (NHFS-4).

Child nutrition, stunting and underweight data in India also reflect significant undernourishment. NFHS–4 data had revealed a decline in under-5 child stunting from 43% to 32% and under-5 underweight from 39% to 29%. However, the entire country was not free from wide regional differences with poor levels of health and nutrition. Poor nutrition, despite found to be less prevalent in the latest NFHS-4 survey in all states except Goa, more than 50% of children and women are found to be anaemic. Lower levels of malnutrition were found in 9 states, and UTs, wherein less than of one-third of children were found to be short against their age. (NFHS-4)

The NFHS surveys found slow economic growth, dietary lacunae and inefficient primary healthcare in India were the reasons for worse malnutrition statistics. Immunisation coverage in full was available to at least 6 out of 10 children in 12 of the 15 states and UTs surveyed. However, post-NFHS-3 launching of National Rural Health Mission showed improvements in public health in the country with progress in immunisation coverage in many states, including Gujarat.

There is a reduction in maternal mortality rates (MMR) also due to improvement in healthcare, institutional delivery, nutritional supplements and cash incentives under the Janani Suraksha Yojana (JSY) since 2005. Institutional birth is more than 90% in 8 of the 15 states in the country, thus aiding in post-natal care and reduction of IMR and MMR rates. However, half of the women are still anaemic in 11 of the 15 states found by NFHS survey. One improvement in total fertility rate (the number of children born per woman) declining from 2.1 to 1.8 children per woman is an indicator which has strong potential for betterment children's health as better availability in the share of nutrition, healthcare and attention time by the mother. However, the NHS-4 finds the increasing cost of healthcare in public health facilities; for example, despite free-cashless services for pregnant women and newborns, under *Janani-Shishu Suraksha*

Karyakram, the range of delivery costing a public health facility was between Rs. 1,258 (Andaman & Nicobar) and Rs. 7,772 (West Bengal) for a delivery. (NFHS-4)

The Global Nutrition Report (GNR) 2016 reveals the number of under-6 Severe Acute Malnutrition (SAM) children at more than 1.45 lakh in Gujarat. Gujarat has about 10.1% children as 'severely underweight', 33.6% underweight, 18.3% severely stunted and 41.6% stunted as found by UNICEF's Rapid Survey on Children (RSOC-2015), a national sample survey of over 1 lakh households including 90,000 children of 0-4 years. Severely underweight children's share was 11.3% in rural and 8.2% in urban areas. Among scheduled tribes, severely underweight children's share was 13.8%.

It should be noted that the ratio of stunted children in Gujarat at 41.6% was more than the national average of 38.80% in India. Gujarat's share of underweight children is relatively preponderant to the country's average of 29.4%. To prevent this malnutrition situation, Gujarat state is taking serious efforts and is running an anti-malnutrition campaign named *'Kuposhan Mukt Gujarat Maha Abhiyan'* since 2015.

Government Surveys and Schemes on Health and Nutrition

Since the early 1990s, several prominent nutrition surveys are launched in India to assess the health attainment and nutritional levels of its population:

National Family Health Surveys (NFHS)—four rounds—1992-1993, 1998-1999, 2005-2006 and 2015-16.

District-Level Health Surveys (DLHS)—four rounds—1998-99, 2002-2004, 2007-08, and 2012-13.

Annual Health Surveys (AHS)— three rounds—2011, 2012 and 2013.

UNICEF's Rapid Survey on Children (RSOC)—2015, and

HUNGaMA Survey by Nandi Foundation—2011.

Though India has reaped benefits from these schemes and surveys and its health, statistic, have improved significantly over the decades, a note of caution here. Due to non-standardisation and wide variations in coverage and frequency of data collection, results from these surveys overlap and lack suitable comparability. Thus framing target-based health and nutrition policy in India and state levels become complicated, leading to delays and faulty planning and wastage of resources.

However, there are several health and nutrition schemes in the country and run by the state and local governments. Most important among them are Indian government's ICDS *(Integrated Child Development Scheme)* launched since 1975 to take care of health and nutrition of mothers and children (Adhikari and Bredenkamp, 2009; WCD, 2014). It is the prominent government program in the country for children's right to access adequate food mandated by the Convention on the Rights of the Child and the Universal Declaration of Human Rights at the international level and ensured by the National Food Security Act, 2013, at the national level. (Sinha, 2016; UN General Assembly, 1989). The Government of India's other prominent programmes is the *Mid Day Meal Scheme, National Rural Health Mission* (NRHM) and the popular cereals-allocating *Public Distribution System*. The *National Nutritional Anaemia Prophylaxis Programme, 1970* was initiated to supplement iron and folate tablets to the1-5 age group kids, anaemic youths, expecting women and lactating mothers.

Other health programmes by Government of India like *Janani Suraksha Yojana* (JSY)—for safe motherhood for poor women under NRHM to reduce, maternal, neonatal mortality by institutional delivery and *Rashtriya Swasthya Bima Yojana*: cashless health insurance cover of Rs. 30 thousand per family per year at just Rs. 30 premium is available to the construction workers families.

The government of Gujarat implemented the Unorganised Workers Social Security Act 2008 in order to provide social security benefits to the workers. The workers are provided with the Smart Card or identity card so that they can avail the benefits of the schemes such as Balwadi/Anganwadi for children to provide nutritious food at the construction sites, maternity benefits and free treatment at the government hospitals. The Gujarat Building and Construction Welfare Board has implemented schemes like hostel facility, temporary housing facilities at the worksites; *Shramik Sahay Suvidha*—a helpline facilities for any problem including health problems of the construction workers; medical aid in critical diseases under *Mukhyamantri Amrutam Yojana* and *Mukhyamantri Amrutam Vatsalya Yojana* for mother and child and so on.

Parallel health schemes available at the state level from the Gujarat government are, *Swasthya Bima Yojana*: cashless health cover up to Rs. 30 thousand for unorganised BPL workers and their family;*Chiranjeevi Yojana:* free maternity services to BPL or tribal women (including delivery facilities, investigation & medication); *Bal Sakha Yojana:* free neonatal & intensive care to all newborns of BPL mothers; and *Mukhya Mantri Amrutam Yojana:* medical care to BPL families (with Rs. 2 lakh sum assured per family p.a.) for treatment of critical diseases like—cardiovascular, neurosurgeries, burns, polytrauma, cancer, kidney and neonatal diseases.

Literature Review

A study by UNICEF-CMS (2012) on the immunisation status of the children of migrant families conducted in five states of India found that the percentage of migrant children in the age group of 3-6 years going to Anganwadi Centres (AWCs) was quite small. Only one out of every three children of the migrant families was enrolled in schools at the destination. These out of school children, later on, add to the unorganised workforce in the country, often in the domestic works sector, which is not duly recognised as a working category.

The report of the National Commission for Enterprises in the Unorganised Sector (2007) estimates that out of 4 million domestic workers in the unorganised sector, women, girls and children constitute 92 percent, and out of that 20 percent were under 14 years of age.

National Commission for Protection of Child Rights (NCPCR, 2015) study *Status Report on School Participation and Availing of Health & Nutrition Services for Children of Migrant Labourers* makes an assessment of access of educational, health and nutritional services to migrant workers' children in rural and urban destination locations in six high in-migration states across India viz. Delhi/NCR, Gujarat, Karnataka, Maharashtra, Punjab and West Bengal. This study included four types of informal-unorganised occupational categories—Agriculture labour, Brick Kiln worker, Construction worker and hawkers & others. The study finds that the Anganwadi Centre was about one kilometre away from the place of residence on an average, but two-third of the migrant workers were not availing the services at AWC at the worksite destination. Moreover, workers were aware of certain key facilities like supplementary nutrition (53%) and children's pre-school education (40%). The awareness in other services like immunisation facility, Iron Folic Acid tablets was comparatively low. The visit of health workers to the worksites was found to be to about 65 percent of migrant households. However, in majority of cases (more than 90%), the health functionaries' visits were for mostly administering Polio vaccines. In terms of health facility awareness, more than 80 percent of workers' households were yet to know about Mother and Child Protection (MCP) Card. Among the MCP-aware families, 85 percent had one card in the family. This awareness was found to be relatively higher in Maharashtra and Karnataka (about 35%). (NCPCR, 2015)

The 12th Five Year Plan (2012-17), Planning Commission, Government of India, mentions in clear terms about the non-availability of basic facilities at work sites like sanitation and crèche facilities. Moreover, informal sector workers have poor information and access to health services about contraception, pre and postnatal care, and so on, which leads to poor conditions of sexual and reproductive health. Poor worker families are vulnerable to worsening poverty in times of inability to work due to health problems or inability to afford expensive healthcare. Women's wages are generally lesser than men, and they have to work under extremely hostile conditions during pregnancy or breastfeeding. This, itself, may result in lack of better nutrition and consequent health problems to their children. In addition to this, lack of official identify at destination places, absence of ration/voter card, health or insurance card limits the working families' access to health and nutritional services.

National Urban Health Mission Draft (2010), reveals that migrant communities have to face poorer maternal and infant health conditions compared to non-migrant populations. Antenatal care coverage, access to MNCH facilities remains poor among the migrant worker families. Other common health problems faced by them are lack of immunisation coverage, higher prevalence of low birth weight, anaemia and considerable malnutrition among the children.

A study on health and nutritional status of Migrant Labourers in Himachal Pradesh (Bhatia, Agarwal, Neena, Mehla, Makhijani, 2014) found the migrant children's nutritional status to be worst among all the urban groups and it was found to be even poorer than rural average. Urban migration had not helped them to escape from poverty and under-nutrition. High prevalence of malnutrition among children was found to be due to faulty infant feeding and proper child care practices, inadequate food and health security, higher prevalence of infections and parasites, unhygienic environmental conditions and absence of awareness and knowledge about food and nutrition requirements.

D.B. Research Centre, Mumbai in a national study (Mathew, 2017) on the children of migrant construction workers from six cities, Delhi, Mumbai, Pune, Ahmedabad, Bangalore and Kochi, revealed the magnitude of vulnerability in education, health, nutrition and security. Moreover, it discovered the inadequacies in their living conditions, sanitation and child care services. Major factors were also found to be unaddressed by the government like gender disparity in wages, addiction of parents to substances and vulnerability of girl children. Majority of workers had possession of Aadhar, Ration and Voter IDs, but entitlement and access to PDS food, health and educational services were yet to be realised. Mandatory registration of construction workers and holding health camps on construction sites would help a lot to the migrant worker families.

Chawda, Modi and Kosambiya (2013) studied the health status of construction workers' children with the help of anthropometric measurements. The study found 67.2% of children as underweight; 28.4% wasted and 49.3% stunted. All mothers had a belief that mother's milk was good for baby for the first few months, but only a low 11% of them were providing breastfeeding. Mothers also understood about the importance of complementary feeding, balanced diet and vaccination. However, mothers were unable to practice their childcare knowledge due to fear of wage loss, lack of proper living facilities and pressure of labour contractor.

Financial inclusion is crucial for availability and access to adequate nutrition and health services primarily for the workers in the informal and unorganised sector. Sahoo and Gomkale (2015) in a study on the state of financial inclusiveness in the unorganised sector of Gujarat (covering 100 unorganised workers) found that access to credit for women in the informal, as well as formal sources, was not very high in Gujarat in 2015, especially in the Gandhinagar district. Out of those who had availed credit from the informal sources, 72 percent were males, and only 28 percent were females in the sample. Likewise, in the formal sources, out of those who had availed credit, two-third were males, and only one-third were females. This again suggests the comparatively insufficient level of access to credit for the women and their vulnerability in survival.

Bajaj and Sharma (2016) found the involvement of voluntary organisation, like New Delhi-based Mobile Crèches, in providing early childhood care and educational services to the children of construction workers. There was a three-way partnership model in place as the voluntary organisation made efforts to persuade construction firms to support children's services and train other NGOs to provide those services.

Sriram and Sahoo (2015) advocate public-private partnership model and enhanced public investment for creating health infrastructure, along with incentivising PPP projects with private collaboration in health infrastructure. Moreover, they build a case for health service delivery through the participation of CSR activity by industrial houses like donating drugs for critical and chronic diseases like HIV-AIDS, cancer, malaria, TB, and so on. Apart from mine-townships, Industrial Houses should partner with government in adopting at least one health centre in those areas and contribute to developing health infrastructure and medical facilities.

Sriram (2014) makes a case for effective implementation of public health services programmes like *Chiranjeevi Yojana* of the Gujarat government by the public-private-partnership model. This programme showed that poor women accustomed to deliveries at home would rapidly change their behaviour if perceived good quality services are accessible, free of cost and within a reasonable travelling distance.

Research Methodology

The present study focuses on one of the most vulnerable occupations in the informal sector-that is the construction sector. To understand the nutrition and health status of construction workers' children in Gujarat the empirical study is conducted on one of the rapidly growing and urbanizing area of Gujarat—i.e. the Gandhinagar city limits which is the capital city of Gujarat. The study area covers ten construction sites from Gandhinagar—particularly from the urban locations of Gandhinagar city. A total of 30 households were surveyed for the present study covering a statistically significant sample of 50 children (comfortably beyond the small sample threshold of 30 sample sizes) from the age group of 0-14 years. In India, working population group is defined by Census as 15-59 years, and Indian labour law considers labour below 14 years of age as child labour; hence technically up to 14 years aged are considered as children for the present study (Table-1).

The sampling technique executed for the present study is 'purposive sampling method'—generally used in case the information about the targeted population is unavailable from other sources and hence, the particular persons, settings or events are deliberately chosen. The eligible respondents are selected from the settlements spread in and around various construction sites scattered in the urban locations of Gandhinagar. The occupational sites are personally visited after identification, and the heads of the construction workers' families are selected as targeted respondents for executing the survey. To capture construction workers families' experience and awareness on children health and nutrition issues, data collection method adopted is a combination of quantitative and qualitative ones. Hence, to capture these aspects, the survey implemented two techniques, structured questionnaire and in-depth interviews (IDIs). The quantitative data was collected with the help of household level survey schedules, and the qualitative data was collected by executing in-depth interviews with the respondents.

The data collection in all the construction sites was conducted over two weeks in February 2017 with the suitable engagement of trained in-house research scholar. To facilitate the survey, the study tools were first developed in English and then translated into local Gujarati language, which was spoken out by the investigator to the targeted respondents in the local language. Finally, data and information complied in English with a suitable translation. With suitable scrutiny and check for errors, data entry was done with the help of SPSS software, and then quantitative data was tabulated in the form of suitable frequency tables and cross-tabulations. Appropriate statistical tools were implemented to analyse the data and. Qualitative data was analysed, and the relevant information was derived and reported with the help of qualitative data analysis tools and qualitative analysis reporting.

Sample Survey Information

The study area in the present study covered ten construction sites from Gandhinagar-particularly from the urban locations of Gandhinagar city, particularly in and around Raisin village area. A total of 30 households were surveyed for the present study covering a statistically significant sample of 50 children (comfortably beyond the small sample threshold of 30 sample sizes) from the age group of 0-14 years. Out of 30 households, 26 families (87%) were from Gujarat (Dahod district), and rest 4 (13%) were migrant families from Rajasthan (Dungarpur district). Migration status of construction workers was of two types: intra-state and interstate. Actual children surveyed were in the age group 0-11 years as per availability in the sample. The survey period was Dec 2016-Jan, 2017 (see Table-1).

Table-1: Summary of Survey on Children of Construction Workers in Gandhinagar

Location & Survey Period	Respondents	Total Construction Sites surveyed	Total families surveyed	Children surveyed (Sample Size)	The age group of children	Migration status of construction workers
Gandhinagar (Dec 2016-Jan 2017)	Mothers of the children	10	30	50	0-11 years (actual)	Intra-state and inter-state migration
Village: Raisan District: Gandhinagar		Nature of Construction: Residential & commercial buildings	26 families from Gujarat (87%) and four from Rajasthan (13%)		Intended coverage 0-14 years	Migrant from 2 districts: 1 each from Gujarat (Dahod) & Rajasthan (Dungarpur)

Source: Oswn primary survey.

Data Analysis and Findings

The sample surveyed covered 30 construction workers households. The average family size turned out to be 4.83. A total number of children covered in the survey was 50 consisting of 22 boys and 28 girls, with a ratio of boys to girls at 0.79. An average number of children per family surveyed turned out to be 1.67. Total children were divided into two groups: of age groups 0-6 years and 6-14 years. There were 23 children (boys-13, girls-10) in age groups 0-6 years (46% of the sample) and 27 children (boys-9, girls-18) in the age group 6-14 years (54% of the sample). Mean a number of children per family in the age group 0-6 turned out to be 1.2 (out of 19 families) and mean number of children per family in the age group 6-14 turned out to be 2.45 (out of 11 families).

Table-2: Average Family Size, Children and Age Group of Construction Workers

No. of Households Surveyed	Average Family Size	Total No. of children	Average no. of children per family	The ratio of boys to girls	Children in the Age group (0-6)	Children in Age group (6-14)	Mean Children Per family (0-6)	Mean Children Per family (6-14)
30	4.83	50 [boys-22, girls-28]	1.67	0.79	23 [boys-13, girls-10]	27 [boys-9, girls-18]	1.2 [out of 19 families]	2.45 [out of 11 families]

Source: Own primary survey.

The present study involved a survey on three aspects to assess the health and nutritional scenario of the children of construction workers in Gandhinagar: 1. Nutritional status of the children, 2. Health Status of the children, and 3. Awareness among construction workers about children's health. The nutritional status of the children of construction workers was assessed based on five parameters: 1. Attendance in school (3-14 age), 2. Attendance in Anganwadi (0-6 age), 3. Regularity in taking milk, 4. Regularity in taking three meals a day and 5. Intake of iron folic acid tablets. Each of these parameters is constructed as binomial response variables with yes or no response, followed by an in-depth interview for exploration into these parameters.

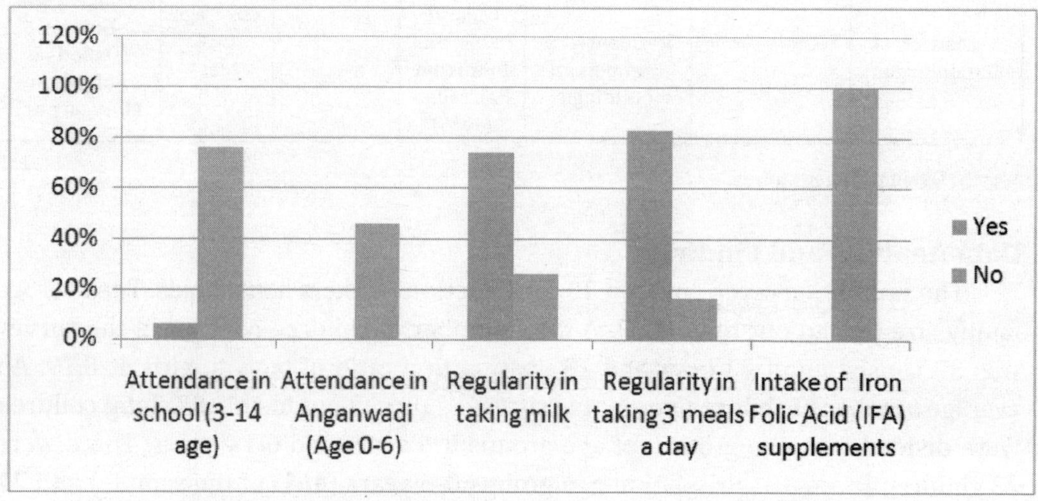

Chart-2: Nutritional Status of Children of Construction Workers

Source: Based on Table-3, from own survey.

It was found that only 6% of the children were attending schools at the place of construction destination in the age group 3-14. Three years is included in this group to capture some pre-school attendance. However, attendance in anganwadis is meant for 0-6 years of age group. So there may be overlapping in total percentages. 46% of all children were in the 0-6 age group, and none of them was attending Anganwadi in construction sites of Gandhinagar. Total attendance in school and Anganwadi of all children of surveyed construction workers was a meagre 6% only. This reveals lack of proper nutrition availability to these children from the school sources like mid-day-meals and Anganwadi sources provided in Gujarat like AWC food—breakfast, noon meal, carry-away *laddu* etc. (see Chart 2 and Table-3).

Table-3: Nutritional Status of Children of Construction Workers

Nutritional Parameters	Yes	No	In-depth Exploration on Nutritional Availability
Attendance in school (3-14 age)	6%	76%	Mi-Day-Meal
Attendance in Anganwadi (Age 0-6)	0%	46%	AWC food—breakfast, noon meal, carry away *laddu*
Regularity in taking milk	74%	26%	Mothers' milk and self-purchased
Regularity in taking three meals a day	83.3%	16.7%	Mostly bajra roti and curry. Rice-dal, jowar sometimes. No sufficient vegetables.
Intake of Iron Folic Acid (IFA) supplements	0%	100%	Seasonal fruits twice a week distributed by the state government

Source: Own primary survey. Percentage figures are out of all children.

Regularity in taking milk was high 74 percent of children, but some 26 percent were not getting milk regularly, which can have potential nutritional deficiency among them. Moreover, the source of milk was mothers' milk and self-purchased packaged or local milk from the market and vicinity, devoid of any freely distributed milk from the state government and local authorities. Likewise, about a very high 83% of children had regular access to three meals a day, and only 17% lacked this. Meals for these children were mostly *bajra roti* & curry, and sometimes rice-*dal*. Lack of sufficient vegetables and fruits indicated that their meals were not much diversified and lacked sufficient minerals. Seasonal fruits, however, were found to be distributed twice a week by the state government to the working families, which can supplement some nutritional availability for the children. However, an important supplement like iron-folic acid tablets, which should have been distributed by the anganwadis or local health officials, was not found to be distributed to the construction workers and their children during the survey period. This can bear considerable implication the n growth of these children with the likelihood of stunting for their age (see Table-3).

Health Status of Children of Construction Workers in Gandhinagar was assessed by collecting data on seven parameters. These are 1.Availability of health benefits from local or state governments; 2. The regularity of visit of Health workers; 3. Availability of benefits from AWCs on site; 4. Availability of benefits from AWCs off-site at the native place; 5. The regularity of vaccination on site; 6. The regularity of vaccination off-site (at the native place) and 7. Presence of any disease or health problem in children (see Table-4). Primary part of these responses was binomial in the form of yes or no, followed byan in-depth interview for exploration into these parameters. About a majority 93 of workers surveyed said health benefits were available of from local or state governments in the form of medicines, health check-up, visit of health workers and so on. All workers surveyed said that health workers were regularly visiting their construction sites—once in a week every Thursday in Gandhinagar.

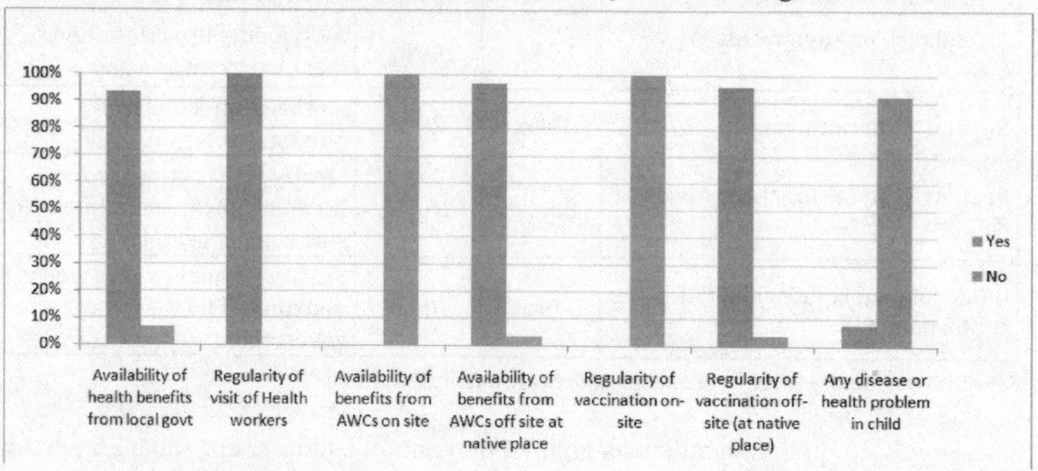

Chart 3: Health Status of Children of Construction Workers in Gandhinagar

Source: Own primary survey. Based on Table-4.

On-site availability of benefits from Anganwadi centres (AWCs) however, was not found for the construction workers' children during the survey period. Non-attending anganwadis by the workers' children and non-visit of AWC worker to the construction site could lead to a double disadvantage, as found in the survey, for lack of on-site availability of food, medicines or nutritional supplements. This indicates that AWCs are relatively immobile in their activities. However, the same workers agree that (97%) benefits like milk, cereals, health care facilities etc. are available from the AWCs in their native place. As the workers do not visit the Anganwadi centres in the local area in and around the construction sites in Gandhinagar, it could not be ascertained whether health and nutrition benefits would have been available for the children of these migrant workers. Likewise, regular on-site vaccination was not found during the survey period, which, however, was mostly available off-site at the workers' native place (96%). Off-site vaccines were commonly that of Polio, BCG etc. Major health problems, however, were absent in the children of the surveyed construction workers in Gandhinagar. Only a minuscule 8% had common health problems of flu, cough and cold (see Chart 3).

Table-4: Health Status of Children of Construction Workers in Gandhinagar

Health Parameters	Yes	No	In-Depth Explorations
Availability of health benefits from local or state governments	93.3%	6.7%	Medicines, health check-up, visit of health workers
The regularity of visit of Health workers	100%	0%	Once a week on every Thursday
Availability of benefits from AWCs on site	0%	100%	Neither children go to AWCs nor any worker from AWC visits them
Availability of benefits from AWCs off-site at native place	96.7%	3.3%	Milk, cereals, health care facilities
The regularity of vaccination on site	0%	100%	No on-site vaccination at all
Regularity of vaccination off site (at native place)	96%	4%	Polio, BCG etc. vaccination given
Presence of any disease or health problem in child	8%	92%	Flu, cough and cold are common

Source: Own primary survey.

Construction workers' awareness about child health was assessed by collecting observations on four binomial response parameters viz.-1. Awareness about vaccinations other than polio (like BCG, measles etc.); 2. Awareness about ICDS or any other Government scheme; 3. Awareness about Mother and Child Protection Card (*Mamta Card*) and 4. Awareness about the *Mukhyamantri Amrutam* health scheme. These health awareness parameters were related to child health protection schemes available to the worker's families and their children under some popular central and state government programmes and schemes. The outcome from the survey revealed that only a small about 13% of the workers were aware of vaccinations other than polio (like BCG, measles etc.) and further smaller 10% had awareness about ICDS or any other government scheme which caters to children's healthcare and nutrition (see Table-5).

However, a significant 26.7% construction workers surveyed in Gandhinagar had awareness about Mother and Child Protection Card called *Mamta Card*, signifying its increasing popularity and possibly easy availability to the bottom strata of the work force. However, these workers were not all aware of the Gujarat government's *Mukhyamantri Amrutam Yojana* health scheme meant for them (see Table-5).

Table-5: Child Health Awareness in Construction Workers of Gandhinagar

Awareness Parameters	Yes	No
Awareness about vaccinations other than polio (like BCG, measles etc.)	13.3%	86.7%
Awareness about ICDS or any other Government scheme	10%	90%
Awareness about Mother and Child Protection Card (*Mamta Card*)	26.7%	73.3%
Awareness about *Mukhyamantri Amrutam Yojana* health scheme	0%	100%

Source: Own primary survey.

Discussion and Implications

Construction workers' children in Gujarat, despite the state government's numerous programmes and facilities regarding health and nutrition care available to them, face several challenges in real access and implementation on the ground. The empirical evidence from the present study suggests that a step forward is required to identify the challenges related to maternal and child health as faced by the families of the construction workers and further reinforce existing policies to ensure better access to health care benefits by the migrant workers. It is found from the study that the construction workers' children avail polio vaccine facilities regularly and medicine and treatment facilities for normal health problems like fever, cough and cold, diarrhoea etc. However, other basic vaccinations and nutritional benefits like iron supplements, milk and Anganwadi-meals are required to be made available to them regularly.

Thus, to improve on this scenario, the central and state governments needs to intervene and focus on local ground level on promoting health and nutrition level of workers children by encouraging good quality diverse diets. Global Nutrition Reports have highlighted the importance of incorporating millets and fortified foods in midday meals to control the problem of hidden hunger resulting from micronutrient deficiency. Millets have higher nutrient levels compared to cereals; a fact should be kept in mind while designing any targeted nutritional policy. It is heartening to see that millets like bajra, jowar form part of migrant workers in Gujarat, which can be further supplemented with fortification to enhance the availability of the nutrients present in staple meals.

Awareness levels about the health and nutritional rights available to the workers in general and the construction workers in particula are not sufficient enough to guarantee them protection from denials at non-native destinations for the migrant workers. Hence, there is an urgent need to strengthen the health and nutrition schemes like ICDS in all states, and particularly those states having a notable proportion of anaemic, underweight and stunted children. The study also identified the existence of problems like insufficient involvement of AWCs beyond their physical boundaries. This has to be taken care of urgently with local participation from the state government and health officials. Visiting health workers or Accredited Social Health Activists (ASHA) workers should function both as complete health-cum-nutrition workers and AWCs should coordinate with them in distributing milk, nutrition, PDS items, nutrition supplements, medicines etc.

Prioritisation of targeted health and nutrition care for the most vulnerable even within the migrant worker's children is another area of intervention which should be looked into by the policy planners at the central and state levels. Programmes like ICDS should provide adequate health and nutrition care through its AWC networks for the migrant children of construction workers of especially in the age group 0-6. These children are most vulnerable, particularly, the under-3 ones when timely access and availability of adequate health care and nutrition is denied to them.

Another major issue is about awareness and ownership of Mother and Child Protection Card or *Mamta Card*, which is a smart card for accessing all free health services for the pregnant women, young mothers and women. The study revealed a large proportion of workers (more than 73%) had no idea about it, suggesting a lack of ownership also and non-availability of health services to them instead of it.

Conclusion

Construction workers' children, being migrant, are the most vulnerable ones in terms of accessing their rights on health and nutrition. Gujarat has to proactively work to tackle the issue of malnutrition and ensure adequate provision of nutrition and health facilities to the most vulnerable children. Other prominent areas requiring intervention in Gujarat are enhancing access to ante-natal care, reducing high anaemic conditions among women, and improving immunisation for the overall children, especially for the disadvantaged ones. Coupled with this, it has to devise policies and programmes to the targeted intervention of acutely vulnerable sections of its people like the informal workers and their families in general, including the construction workers' children. Standardisation of health and nutrition surveys at the national, state or even at the local levels will go a long way in designing specific health and nutritional targets, which are achievable in time bound manner. Regular assessment and monitoring the target health and nutrition parameters with proper prioritisation of the vulnerable sections like construction workers' children at both the on-site and off-site (native place) will help effective attainment of health and nutrition levels and reduction in mortality and nutritional deficiency. Compulsory introduction and effective utilisation of health smart cards like *Mamta cards* to the construction workers families by the Central government with all-India validity at state and local level health centres will go a long way in access of health services for the vulnerable and migrant sections at the bottom.

References

1. Adhikari, S.J. and Brendenkamp, C. (2009). Monitoring for Nutrition Results in ICDS: Translating Vision into Action. IDS Bulletin, 40(4), 70-77.
2. Bajaj and Sharma, (2016)., 'Scaling-up Early Childhood Centres for Migrant Construction Workers' Children in India', Early Childhood Matters, pp 74-79. Retrieved on 20th May, 2017 from https://bernardvanleer.org/ecm-article/scaling-early-childhood-centres-migrant-construction-workers-children-india/
3. Bhatia A., Agarwal P, Neena E., Mehla A., & Makhijani N. (2014). Assessment of Health, Hygiene and Nutritional Status of Migrant Labourers: Scientific Intervention and Community Participation (With a special focus on Migrant Labourers in Himachal Pradesh). Retrieved on 17th May, 2017 from http://www.iitmandi.ac.in/istp/projects/2014/reports/Group%2005%20Health%20Nutrition.pdf
4. Chawada, B.L., Modi, A., Kantharia, S.L., Rao, S., & Kosambiya, J.K. (2013). Exploring health status and care practices among children of female workers in the unorganised sector. International Journal of Medicine and Public Health, 3(1).
5. Dreze, J. & Sen, A. (2013). An Uncertain Glory: India and its Contradictions. Penguin: London, England.
6. Government of India, (2000). National Population Policy, 2000. National Commission on Population, New Delhi, Ministry of Health and Family Welfare. Retrieved on 12th May, 2017 from http://mohfw.nic.in/sites/default/files/26953755641410949469%20%281%29.pdf
7. International Food Policy Research Institute. (2016). Global Nutrition Report 2016: From Promise to Impact: Ending Malnutrition by 2030. Washington, DC.
8. Mathew S. (2017). Working for the Rights of Children of Migrant Construction Workers (BIS #5037). Retrieved on 22nd May, 2017 from http://Bismumbai.Blogspot.In/2017/01/Bis-5037-Working-For-Rights-Of-Children.Html
9. National Commission for Enterprises in the Unorganised Sector. (2007) Report on Conditions of Work and Promotion of Livelihood in the Unorganised Sector, Government of India, retrieved on 22nd May, 2017 from http://dcmsme.gov.in/Condition_of_workers_sep_2007.pdf National Family Health Survey IV, Government of India. Retrieved on Jun 14, 2017, from http://www.nfhsindia.org/NFHS-Data/
10. NCPCR (2015) Status Report on School Participation and Availing Health and Nutrition Services for Children of Migrant Labourers, National Commission for Protection of Child Rights. Retrieved on 20th May, 2017 from http://ncpcr.gov.in

11. National Urban Health Mission Draft (2010). Ministry of Health and Family Welfare, Government of India. Retrieved on 22nd May, 2017 from www.mumbaidp24seven.in/reference/UH_Framework_Final.pdf.
12. Rapid Survey on Children, 2015, Ministry of Women and Child Development, Government of India. Retrieved on 24th May, 2017 from http://wcd.nic.in/sites/default/files/State%20RSOC.pdf
13. Sahoo M.K. and Gomkale, M. (2015) 'Financial Inclusion in India: An Empirical Study of Unorganised Sector in Gujarat', Information Management and Business Review. 7, (5), 6-17.
14. Sahoo, M.K. (2008) 'An Exploration into Dimensions of Growth and Backwardness in India', Parikalpana, KIIT Journal of Management, 5(1 & 2).
15. Sinha, A., 2016. Rapid Assessment of Integrated Child Development Scheme in Delhi. Institute for Human Development. New Delhi: India. Retrieved on 20th May, 2017 from http://www.ihdindia.org/hdidelhi/pdf/icds_report.pdf
16. Sriram, D., & Sahoo, M.K. (2015)., 'Alternative Service Delivery in Indian Health Sector: Neglected Areas in PPP Projects', Journal of Governance and Public Policy, 5 (2): 2-9.
17. Sriram, D., (2014). 'Public-Private Partnership in Safeguarding Maternal Mortality and Neonatal Health: The Gujarat Model (Chiranjeevi Yojana)', Public Affairs and Governance, 2(1), 93-102.
18. Planning Commission. Twelfth Five Year Plan 2012-17. Government of India. Retrieved on 14th May, 2017 from http://planningcommission.gov.in/plans/planrel/12thplan/welcome.html
19. Planning Commission, Eleventh Five Year Plan 2007-12. Government of India. Retrieved on 14th May, 2017 from http://planningcommission.gov.in/plans/planrel/fiveyr/11th/11default.htm
20. UN General Assembly (1989), Convention on Rights of the Child, United Nations, Treaty Series1577, 3 retrieved on 18th May, 2017 from http://www.ohchr.org/EN/HRBodies/CRC/Pages/CRCIndex.aspx
21. UNDP, (2014). Millennium Development Goals. United Nations Development Programme. Retrieved on 15th May, 2017 from http://www.undp.org/content/undp/en/home/ mdgoverview.html
22. UNICEF, (2013). Improving Child Nutrition: The Achievable Imperative for Global Progress. UNICEF. New York: USA
23. UNICEF-CMS. (2012), Migration-Threat to Polio Eradication, Centre for Media Studies (CMS), New Delhi. Retrieved on 29th May, 2017 from www.iple.in/documents/download/3492
24. UNICEF, (2011). The Situation of Children in India. United Nations Fund for Children, India Retrieved on 15th May, 2017 from http://unicef.in/Uploads/Publications/Resources/pub_doc36.pdf
25. UNICEF, (2008). UNICEF and Nutrition Security in the Crises of Food. UNICEF. Retrieved on 15th May, 2017 from http://www.unicef.org/eapro/media_9065.html

26. WCD, (2014). Integrated Child Development Scheme (ICDS). Ministry of Women and Child Development. India. Retrieved on 19th May, 2017 from http://icds-wcd.nic.in/icds/icds.aspx
27. WHO, (2014). Global Database on Child Growth and Malnutrition: India. World Health Organisation.
28. Retrieved on 25th April, 2017 from http://www.who.int/nutgrowthdb/database/countries/ind/en
29. World Bank. (2017). World Development Indicators., Retrieved on 24th May, 2017 from http://data.worldbank.org/data-catalog/world-development-indicators
30. International Food Policy Research Institute. (2016). Global Hunger Index: Getting to Zero Hunger. Retrieved on 20th July, 2017 from http://www.ifpri.org/publication/2016-global-hunger-index-getting-zero-hunger
31. International Food Policy Research Institute. (2011). 2011 Global Hunger Index, The Challenge of Hunger: Taming price spikes and excessive food price volatility. Retrieved on 24th May, 2017 from http://www.ifpri.org/publication/2011-global-hunger-index

□

13

Reasons to Review, Reflect and Restructure ICDS: A Case from Rajasthan

—*Neetu Purohit and Dipti Govil*

Abstract

The paper aims to highlight the functioning of the ICDS programme with a focus on supplementary nutrition and growth monitoring. An observational descriptive study was conducted as part of the periodical assessment of ICDS services in the state of Rajasthan. For over 6 months, a total of 488 AWCs from all blocks of 33 districts of the state were observed and 482 AWWs were interviewed. Also, a total of 2442 beneficiaries, including mothers of 6 months to 6 years old children, pregnant and lactating women, were interviewed from the catchment area of those AWCs. Verbal consent was taken from the participants of the study. Data were analysed using SPSS, and bivariate and binary logistic regression analysis were carried out. The mean age of interviewed AWWs was 37 years; three percent were not literate, and another 19.3%studied up to the seventh standard. A hot meal and morning snacks were served at 82% and 35.5%AWCs respectively. RTE was received by 89.4%mothers of children aged six months to 3 years, whereas 57.3% of these mothers were informed about the quantity to be consumed. Nearly 50% of AWCs had functional weighing machine and salter scale. Eight percent AWWs had complete job clarity, and 17.5% and 19.4% AWWs could weigh and plot child correctly while using weighing machine and salter scale respectively. Less than one-third of children were weighed at the recommended time interval. The binary logistic regression analysis has shown the result in both expected and unexpected direction. AWWs who were not completely aware of their roles and responsibilities were less likely to weigh and inform the nutritional status of the child to the mother as compared to their counterparts. AWWs with partial or poor job clarity were more likely to educate mothers about the amount of RTE to be consumed by the child. The findings suggest for adopting a holistic convergence approach, which encompasses availability of supplies and equipment, knowledge and competency of the worker and accountability towards beneficiaries by providing the right services in the right manner so that the problem of malnutrition could be addressed.

Introduction

Malnutrition is a serious public-health problem (IFPRI, 2014) that has been linked to a substantial increase in the risk of mortality and morbidity (Blössner and de Onis, 2005). In every three persons, one person is malnourished in one form or another (IFPRI, 2015) Malnutrition and diet are by far, the most significant risk factors responsible for the global burden of disease in the current times (Forouzanfar et al., 2015). Among children, about 45% of deaths of children under age five are associated with malnutrition (Black et al., 2013).

The importance of improved nutrition cannot be overemphasised. It is not only the platform for progress in health, education, employment, and poverty but also plays a role in female empowerment and inequality reduction. Nutrition is also the key in the physical, mental and emotional development of children. Hence, much emphasis needs to be given to provide proper nutrition, particularly in the formative years of life (Kumar et al., 2010).

Status of Nutrition in India

The 2016 Global Hunger Index (GHI) reveals substantial progress in hunger reduction for the developing world. The 2000 GHI score for developing world was 30.0, which recorded a decrease of 29% in 2016 GHI (score21.3) (von Grebmer, 2016). Underlying this improvement are reductions in each of the GHI indicators, i.e., the prevalence of undernourishment, stunting, wasting, and mortality among children, for each country, which forms the basis of country-level GHI score. India's rank on GHI also showed improvement as the score declined to 28.5 in 2016 from 46.4 in 1992 (von Grebmer, 2016).

At this juncture, the pertinent question arises about the adequacy of efforts to address malnutrition. Are our manner and pace of efforts to address malnutrition relevant and justified? As one considers the MDGs (to be achieved by 2015) and current SDGs (to be achieved by 2030), it is realised that the expected achievements are far away from the reach and the implementation mechanism needs to be reviewed. Between 1990 and 2015, Millennium Development Goal 1 (target 2) aimed to halve the proportion of people who suffered from hunger as measured by the prevalence of under-weight among under-5 children (Park, 2011). India's Country Report on Millennium Development Goals of 2015 concluded that efforts to achieve Target 2 were not very successful (MoSPI, 2015). It elaborates that in 1990, to meet the target, the proportion of underweight children should have decreased from 52 percent in 1990 to 26% by 2015. Moreover, the National Family Health Survey-4 showed a decline of 3 percent point in the proportion of underweight children below three years between 2005-6 (43%) and2015-16 (35.7%) (IIPS and ICF, 2017). This indicated that India was falling short of the target of 26% (MoSPI, 2015). The report was published before the release of NFHS 4 factsheet. The proportion of underweight children was3 6.7% for Rajasthan (IIPS and ICF, 2017a), which was much higher than the expected level.

Malnutrition is a complex issue and has multiple dimensions. Hunger is a tightly associated dimension of malnutrition. Micronutrient deficiency and malnutrition are the natural results if a substantial proportion of the people, including children, does not have enough to eat. In recognition of this fact, a notable achievement, which needs mention, is passing of the National Food Security Act, 2013 by the Parliament on 10th September, 2013. The objective of the Act was to provide food and nutritional security in human life cycle approach, by ensuring access to adequate quantity of quality food at affordable prices to people to live a life with dignity (MCA, 2016).

A year later, in September 2014, the UN General Assembly decided that the Report of Open Working Group on Sustainable Development Goals would be the primary basis for integrating the SDGs into the post-2015 development agenda. The proposed SDGs aimed to "end hunger, achieve food security and improved nutrition, and promote sustainable agriculture." Under this, it targeted to end all forms of malnutrition by 2030, including achieving the internationally agreed targets on stunting and wasting in children under five years of age 2025 (UN-DESA/DSD, 2014). The problem of malnutrition; therefore, is being addressed both by supplementary nutrition and by ensuring food security. As per the opinion of experts, despite the interventions, this target appears to be far-fetched. Although the decline in India's child under-nutrition rates has accelerated since 2006, these faster developments are still well below the rates of progress needed to achieve global nutrition targets (IFPRI, 2016). Given the current situation of malnutrition in India and the goals to be achieved, it is imperative to reflect on one of the most extensive child development programs, called Integrated Child Development Services (ICDS).

About ICDS

Integrated Child Development Services (ICDS) was introduced in 1975. The program started in a phased manner but gradually covered the entire country and is presently being implemented in all states of India. The roots of the ICDS program are embedded in the problem of malnutrition, particularly child malnutrition. Since the needs of a young child cannot be addressed in isolation from those of her mother, the program also extends its services to adolescent girls, pregnant women, and nursing mothers to achieve its objective. The objectives of the scheme area (a) to improve the nutritional and health status of children in the age group 0-6 years; (b) to lay the foundation for proper psychological, physical and social development of the child; (c) to reduce the incidence of mortality, morbidity, malnutrition and school dropout. Other objectives were (d) to achieve effective coordination of policy and implementation amongst the various departments to promote child development; (e) and to enhance the capability of the mother to look after the normal health and nutritional needs of the child through proper nutrition and health education.

In this endeavour, ICDS offers a package of six services, viz., Supplementary Nutrition (SN), Pre-school non-formal education, Nutrition & health education, Immunisation, Health check-up and Referral services. ICDS services are provided through a network of ICDS centres, known as Anganwadi Centres (AWC) at the village level. The program has a dedicated human resource structure, starting with the Department of Women and Child Development at the state level, and decentralised through the workers, i.e., Anganwadi worker (AWW) and Sahayika (Helper) at Anganwadi Centres (AWC).Of all the services offered, two functions, which are critical for achieving the expected results in addressing malnutrition, are supplementary nutrition and growth monitoring (MoWCD, 2015).

Supplementary Nutrition

Supplementary feeding support is provided for 300 days a year to children below the age of 6 years and pregnant and nursing mothers to bridge the calorie gap that exists in disadvantaged communities and to control nutritional anaemia. Beneficiaries of service under which supplementary nutrition is served or distributed include, baby mix for six months to 3 years old child, hot meal for 3 to 6yearold at AWC, Take Home Ration (THR) for pregnant and lactating women and adolescent girls.

Growth Monitoring

Since under-nutrition is a function of both food deprivation and disease, anthropometric indices can serve as proxies for evaluating the prevalence of under-nutrition among children. Hence regular growth monitoring is crucial in arresting growth faltering and consequently malnutrition (Anwar et al., 2013).

The paper attempts to review and reflect on the functioning ofthe ICDS programme with the sole focus on supplementary nutrition and growth monitoring. The paper focuses on the limitations and suggests measures, which could go a long way in altering the situation and progressing towards health and nutrition.

Methodology

A descriptive and observational study was conducted in all regions of Rajasthan to know the status of services provided under ICDS. The data were collected at multiple levels and from numerous stakeholders. The data collection was a part of a periodical assessment to assess the reach and quality of ICDS program in Rajasthan.

Selection of AWC

The state of Rajasthan has seven administrative divisions, i.e., Ajmer, Bikaner, Bharatpur, Jaipur, Jodhpur, Kota, and Udaipur. To provide periodical assessment in a streamlined manner, we assessedthe selected number of AWCs from each of the administrative division every month. List of all regular AWCs was procured from each of the districts. From each administrative division, one district was randomly selected. Two AWCs were further randomly chosen from each of the blocks of everychosen district. In this way, each month seven districts were surveyed, and over a period of six months, all 33 districts were included.

Sample Size

The data was collected from 488 AWCs forover six months, which ensured representativeness of 33 districts of Rajasthan. A total of 482 AWWs were covered under the study. At some places, AWWswas not found, and in her place, ASHA or Sahayika was found to be managing the centre. In such a case, only observation and community interviews could be conducted. From the catchment area of each AWC five beneficiaries (mothers of 6 months to 6 year, children, pregnant and lactating women) were contacted and interviewed. For recipients of the services, a list of households was obtained from AWW and respondents were selected using systematic random sampling from each category. In tota, 2442 beneficiaries of the services were interviewed.

Tools of the Study

An observation checklist for AWC to observe the activities conducted on the day of the visit, an interview schedule for AWW to assess her knowledge and competency and review of records to know the amount of work done by AWW were the tools used to collect data on all the required parameters from AWW and AWC. Also, beneficiaries of the services, i.e., mothers of children under six years were contacted and interviewed to know their knowledge and practices for addressing malnutrition using household survey approach.

Ethical Considerations

Verbal consent was taken from the participants of the study. All the participants were informed of their right to withdraw from the study at any point in time. The participants have ensured the privacy and confidentiality of the information provided by them.

Analysis

The analysis presents the profile of the AWWs. Also, the status of services provided by AWW, the state of supplies and logistics (SNP packets, availability and functionality of weighing machine, growth charts), knowledge and competency of AWW and community perception on the services are presented. Binary logistic regression was conducted to know if the status of services differed by the age, education, experience, training status, knowledge, and competency of AWW. Data were analysed using SPSS, version 18.

Results

The paper has considered the services directly related to the problem of malnutrition, which could play a vital role in addressing it. The distribution of supplementary nutrition and growth monitoring services are analysed in detail concerning service delivery, supply and equipment for services delivery, knowledge, and competency of AWW, and community perception on the status of services.

Profile of the AWW

Table-1 shows that of 482 interviewed AWWs, around one fourth (22.4%) were less than 30 years of age. Bikaner was the only region, where this proportion was more than one third (34.9%). Next to it was Jaipur region, where 30.6% of the AWWs were less than 30 years of age. Since the nature of AWW entails fieldwork, age can be an important factor affecting the delivery of services. More than one-third (37.2%) of the AWWs were above 41 years of age. While the proportion of AWWs in the age bracket of 41 and above was lowest in Jaipur (21.4%), it was almost twice in Ajmer and Kota region. Nearly 90% of interviewed AWWs were married, and the married proportion was virtually the same across regions except for Jodhpur, where 23.5% of the AWWs were single. About 95% of AWWs professed Hinduism. As far as caste distribution is concerned, 25.3% belonged to SC/ST and 39.8%were OBC. Bikaner region had the lowest proportion of SC/ST AWWs, and Bharatpur (33.3%) and Udaipur (34.4%) had the highest percentage.

In Rajasthan, the majority of the interviewed AWWs were literate. Overall, 32.4% reported to have attained class 8th education, and as much as 55.6% of AWWs of Bharatpur reported class 8th as their educational qualification. Of the total AWWs, 23.7% had 0-4 years of work experience, and 25.7% had more than 15 years of work experience. Kota region had the highest proportion of AWWs with 0-4 years of experience (30.2%), and more than one-third AWWs of both Ajmer and Udaipur region had work experience of more than 15 years. In all the regions of Rajasthan, more than 60% AWWs received training in the last three years except Jaipur.

Table-1: Sample Profile of AWWs covered under the study in seven administrative regions of Rajasthan, 2011

Background Characteristics	Region							Rajasthan
	Ajmer	Bikaner	Bharatpur	Jaipur	Jodhpur	Kota	Udaipur	
N	78	43	45	98	85	43	90	482
Mean Age	38.4	37.1	38.0	33.7	39.7	36.4	36.5	37.0
Age Group								
Less than 30	16.7	34.9	17.8	30.6	15.3	20.9	22.2	22.4
30-39	37.2	25.6	42.2	48.0	35.3	39.5	46.7	40.5
40-49	37.2	18.6	28.9	17.3	35.3	32.6	20.0	26.8
50 and highest	9.0	20.9	11.1	4.1	14.1	7.0	11.1	10.4
Marital status								
Married	91.0	100.0	91.1	93.9	76.5	95.3	87.8	89.6
Not Married	9.0	0.0	8.9	6.1	23.5	4.7	12.2	10.4
Religion								
Hindu	96.2	88.4	88.9	96.9	96.5	95.3	96.7	95.0
Others	3.8	11.6	11.1	3.1	3.5	4.7	3.3	5.0
Caste								
SC/ST	15.4	11.6	33.3	27.6	23.5	27.9	34.4	25.3
OBC	47.4	62.8	31.1	40.8	43.5	32.6	25.6	39.8
General	37.2	25.6	35.6	31.6	32.9	39.5	40.0	34.9
Education								
Not Literate	1.3	0.0	0.0	0.0	11.8	0.0	4.4	3.1
less than 8 std.	23.1	16.3	8.9	7.1	40.0	14.0	18.9	19.3
8 std.	21.8	27.9	55.6	30.6	32.9	34.9	32.2	32.4
9-12 std.	41.0	32.6	28.9	49.0	10.6	37.2	33.3	33.6
Above 12 std.	12.8	23.3	6.7	13.3	4.7	14.0	11.1	11.6
Work experience								
0-4 years	24.4	23.3	20.0	27.6	15.3	30.2	25.6	23.7
5-10 years	23.1	32.6	20.0	43.9	29.4	39.5	28.9	31.5
11-15 years	19.2	14.0	31.1	21.4	23.5	14.0	11.1	19.1
> than 15 years	33.3	30.2	28.9	7.1	31.8	16.3	34.4	25.7

Received last training								
0-1 years	29.5	46.5	40.0	27.6	34.5	60.5	27.8	34.9
2-3 years	37.2	27.9	20.0	23.5	23.8	11.6	25.6	25.2
4-5 years	14.1	16.3	13.3	20.4	22.6	16.3	28.9	20.0
> than 5 years	19.2	9.3	26.7	28.6	19.0	11.6	17.8	20.0
Job Clarity								
Complete	11.5	0.0	0.0	1.0	0.0	7.0	26.7	7.7
Partial	67.9	81.4	51.1	70.4	65.1	86.0	56.7	67.1
Poor	20.5	18.6	48.9	28.6	34.9	7.0	16.7	25.2

Source: Authors calculation

Job responsibilities of AWW entail 21 activities; the most important activities/duties are 1) distribution of supplementary nutrition, 2) assistance in immunisation services, 3) growth monitoring, 4) early childhood education, 5) health check-ups, 6) referral services and 7) nutritional & health education. As part of the interview, AWWs were asked about the activities they were required to perform. The spontaneous responses of AWWs were used to measure job clarity. All those who were able to list all seven responsibilities were considered having complete job clarity, those who listed 3-6 responsibilities were considered to be having partial job clarity and less than that were considered as having poor job clarity. Table-1 shows that only 7.7% of the AWWs had complete job clarity.

Status of services, supplies, and equipment at AWC

Table-2 shows the state of services provided at AWC; it's quality and quantity. This information is based on the observation of services offered on the day of the visit to AWC. The table reveals that overall in 35.5% AWCs morning snacks were served, and 22.1%AWCs provided the snacks in the right amount. In Bharatpur and Jodhpur, only one-fourth of AWCs (26% each) served morning snacks on the day of the visit. None of the centres in Bharatpur and Udaipur served morning snacks in the right amount.

Similarly, while the hot meal was served at 82% of the total AWCs visited, only one-fourth AWWs served a hot meal in the right amount. As far as quality is concerned, 34.3%centres did not provide the prescribed balance of the ingredients in a hot meal. Either, hot meal contained only rice or more rice and fewer pulses or had no oil.

Concerning the supply, 72.9% of centres reported having a regular supply of RTE and 93% centres reported to be receiving a supply of hot meal from SHGs. In Bharatpur and Jaipur, about 47.8% and 57.6% centres respectively reported regular supply for

RTE. Around 67% of the centres had RTE packets with them on the day of the visit. At all such places, two packets of each type (as per weight) of RTE were randomly weighed to know if the amount in the packets varied with the marked weight. At 76.1% of the visited centres, the measured weight of the RTE packet matched with written weight. In Bharatpur, only 54% of centres were found to have RTE packets where actual weight matched correctly with written weight.

Availability and functionality of weighing and salter scale are crucial in an AWC. It was found that weighing machine and salter scale was not available at 22.1% and 28.1% of the visited AWCs respectively. In the remaining places, about 54% of centres had a functional weighing machine. Functional salter scales were also available in half of the visited centres (50.6%). It indicates that at half of the centres, growth monitoring services could have been affected.

At one-third of the AWCs growth monitoring charts were not available, whereas, at another 34.6% centres, AWWs did not fill the available chart. The situation was worse in Jodhpur where at 29%AWCs, growth monitoring charts were not available and at 56% AWCs, charts were available but not filled.

Table-2: Percent distribution of status of services, supplies, and logistics in AWCs in Rajasthan, 2011

Variables	Region							Rajasthan
	Ajmer	Bikaner	Bharatpur	Jaipur	Jodhpur	Kota	Udaipur	
N	***78***	***43***	***46***	***99***	***86***	***44***	***92***	***488***
Morning snacks provided at AWC	47.4	34.9	26.1	35.4	25.6	29.5	42.4	35.5
N	***37***	***15***	***12***	***35***	***22***	***13***	***39***	***173***
Morning snacks served in right amount	27.0	100.0	0.0	20.0	14.3	23.1	0.0	22.1
N	***78***	***43***	***46***	***99***	***86***	***44***	***92***	***488***
Hot Meal Provided at AWC	93.6	67.4	91.3	77.8	72.1	81.8	88.0	82.0
N	***73***	***29***	***42***	***77***	***62***	***36***	***81***	***400***
Hot Meal Served in right amount	23.3	96.6	14.3	15.6	25.8	33.3	11.1	25.0
Seating arrangement of children as per nutritional status during hot meal	12.3	6.9	0.0	15.6	0.0	2.8	48.1	15.8
Quality of hot meal								
Edible	64.4	100.0	64.3	57.1	53.2	75.0	69.1	65.8

Edible with imbalanced ingredients	35.6	0.0	35.7	42.9	46.8	25.0	30.9	34.3
N	***78***	***43***	***46***	***99***	***86***	***44***	***92***	***488***
Regular Supply of RTE meal at AWC	82.1	62.8	47.8	57.6	75.6	79.1	93.5	72.9
Regular Supply of Hot meal at AWC	96.2	88.4	93.5	81.8	96.5	97.7	98.9	93.0
Availability of RTE at AWC	74.4	58.1	52.2	79.8	59.3	52.3	71.7	66.8
N	***58***	***25***	***24***	***79***	***51***	***23***	***66***	***326***
Correct weight of RTE packet	72.4	92.0	54.2	88.6	82.4	78.3	60.6	76.1
N	***78***	***43***	***46***	***99***	***86***	***44***	***92***	***488***
Weighing Machine								
Not available	24.4	27.9	19.6	31.3	23.3	18.2	9.8	22.1
Available and Functional	56.4	60.5	52.2	45.5	51.2	56.8	58.7	53.7
Available but Non-Functional	19.2	11.6	28.3	23.2	25.6	25.0	31.5	24.2
Salter Scale								
Not available	20.5	37.2	23.9	29.3	36.0	18.2	28.3	28.1
Available and Functional	62.8	48.8	39.1	55.6	39.5	61.4	46.7	50.6
Available but Non-Functional	16.7	14.0	37.0	15.2	24.4	20.5	25.0	21.3
Growth Monitoring Chart								
Not available	29.5	30.2	54.3	43.4	29.1	20.5	21.7	32.4
Available and Filled	46.2	65.1	19.6	13.1	15.1	45.5	45.7	33.0
Available but Not Filled	24.4	4.7	26.1	43.4	55.8	34.1	32.6	34.6

Source: Authors' calculation

Table-3: Percent distribution of AWWs by knowledge and competency, Rajasthan, 2011

Indicators	Region							Rajasthan
	Ajmer	**Bikaner**	**Bharatpur**	**Jaipur**	**Jodhpur**	**Kota**	**Udaipur**	
Reported Correct amount of Supplementary Nutrition for (N)	***78***	***43***	***45***	***98***	***83***	***43***	***90***	***480***

Children 6 months to 3 years	79.5	55.8	95.6	81.6	62.7	79.1	76.7	75.8
Malnourished children 6 month to 3 years	26.9	41.9	22.2	38.8	20.5	30.2	33.3	30.6
Children 3 years to 6 years	41.0	18.6	53.3	55.1	19.3	41.9	47.8	40.6
Malnourished children 3 to 6 years	29.5	27.9	20.0	37.8	18.1	14.0	18.9	24.8
Pregnant woman	84.6	74.4	84.4	75.5	69.9	86.0	61.1	75.0
Lactating woman	83.3	72.1	84.4	75.5	69.9	86.0	61.1	74.6
Correct knowledge on weighting a child (N)	***78***	***43***	***45***	***98***	***85***	***43***	***90***	***482***
0-1monthold baby-per week	23.1	32.6	26.7	35.7	23.5	60.5	22.2	30.1
1-3yearold child-per month	75.6	74.4	84.4	77.6	49.4	90.7	90.0	76.1
3-6yearold child-per quarter	52.6	51.2	46.7	69.4	25.9	62.8	50.0	51.0
Salter Scale-AWW could (n)	***49***	***21***	***18***	***55***	***34***	***27***	***43***	***247***
Weigh child correctly	49.0	90.5	33.3	14.5	26.5	66.7	62.8	44.9
Weight and plot correctly	18.4	57.1	11.1	12.7	11.8	22.2	18.6	19.4
Weighing Machine-AWW could (n)	***47***	***26***	***26***	***49***	***44***	***25***	***58***	***275***
Weigh child correctly	72.3	76.9	46.2	30.6	15.9	60.0	58.6	49.8
Weight and plot correctly	14.9	57.7	7.7	12.2	9.1	28.0	12.1	17.5

Source: Authors' calculation

Knowledge and Competency of AWW

Table-3 throws light on the knowledge and competency status of AWW concerning the distribution of supplementary nutrition, time of weighing of the beneficiaries and competency in using weighing and salter scale and plotting on the growth chart. While three fourth of the AWWs were aware of the amount to be given to the children between aged six months to 3 years old, less than one third knew about the amount to be provided in case of a malnourished child. The knowledge on the correct amount of hot meal to be provided per child (80 gms) was present among 40.6% of the AWWs. One-fourth of the interviewed AWWs were aware of the amount to be provided in case of 3 to 6years malnourished child. Further, table 3 shows that around three fourth of the AWWs were aware of the THR to be given to pregnant and lactating women.

The knowledge of AWW for the interval in which a child has to be weighed was found to be varying. While less than one-third of AWWs (30.1%) reported that from birth to the first month, a child has to be weighed per week; around 76.1%said that a child up to three years should be weighed every month. Half of the AWWs reported that a child in the age group of 3 to 6 years should be weighed every quarter.

Competency of AWW was assessed for using the weighing and salter scale. This was done only at those centres where the weighing machine or salter scale was available and functional; hence, the number of AWWs who could be assessed were reduced to less than 300. Of those who were evaluated, it was found that 44.9% and 49.8% of AWWs could correctly weigh child while using salter and weighing machine respectively. However, this number reduced further as only 19.4% and 17.5% of AWWs were able to both weigh and plot correctly on growth chart using salter and weighing machine respectively.

Community Perspective on Services Provided by AWW

Supplementary Nutrition' provided under the ICDS program, only supplements the main diet, which ideally is available at the household level. An AWW is supposed to inform beneficiaries about the quantity and the method of consuming supplementary nutrition. Table-4 shows that around 89% of the mothers reported having received RTE. However, 57.3% of these mothers with childup to age three years, did not receive information about the correct amount to be consumed.

Around 31% of the mothers reported that their child was weighed every month, and of this, 68.7%were informed of the nutritional status of the child. In Jodhpur and Jaipur region, only 15.8% and 20.6% of children were weighed every month respectively. Similarly, 71.4% of children aged 3 to 6 years received a hot meal and ate it at AWC. About one-third of the mothers reported that their children were weighed every quarter, and of this, almost all were informed of the nutritional status.

Table-4: Percent distribution of mothers, pregnant and lactating women on the status of services received by AWW, Rajasthan, 2011

Variables	Region							Rajasthan
	Ajmer	Bikaner	Bharatpur	Jaipur	Jodhpur	Kota	Udaipur	
Children aged six months to 3 years								
N	***194***	***105***	***142***	***223***	***146***	***95***	***190***	***1095***
Received RTE for child	86.6	82.9	79.6	93.7	94.5	87.4	95.3	89.4

Knowledge on amount of RTE to be consumed (n)	***168***	***87***	***113***	***209***	***138***	***83***	***181***	***979***
Not received information	49.4	12.6	76.1	48.3	64.5	66.3	75.1	57.3
Received information and gave correct response	5.4	11.5	4.4	2.9	0.0	1.2	3.9	3.9
Received information but gave wrong response	10.7	40.2	13.3	2.4	2.2	6.0	5.5	9.3
Received information but can't remember	34.5	35.6	6.2	46.4	33.3	26.5	15.5	29.5
Weight measured*(N)*	***194***	***105***	***142***	***223***	***146***	***95***	***190***	***1095***
Not measured	49.5	40.0	56.3	47.5	72.6	40.0	46.3	50.8
Measured not in last month or do not remember	12.9	20.0	15.5	31.8	11.6	18.9	15.3	18.5
Measured every month	37.6	40.0	28.2	20.6	15.8	41.1	38.4	30.7
N	***97***	***63***	***62***	***113***	***38***	***55***	***102***	***530***
Nutritional status informed to mother	82.5	98.4	91.9	21.2	44.7	72.7	82.4	68.7
Children aged 3 to 6 years								
Received hot meal and ate at AWC *(N)*	***159***	***89***	***115***	***156***	***123***	***85***	***178***	***905***
Did not receive Hot Meal	11.9	14.6	10.4	14.1	4.1	37.6	3.9	12.2
Received hot meal and ate at AWC	77.4	79.8	62.6	71.2	59.3	36.5	92.7	71.4
Received hot meal and brought at home	10.7	5.6	27.0	14.7	36.6	25.9	3.4	16.5
Weight measured *(N)*	***147***	***88***	***108***	***138***	***120***	***55***	***176***	***832***
Not measured	63.3	55.7	61.1	60.9	73.3	54.5	51.7	60.2
Measured not in last three months	4.1	5.7	4.6	13.0	14.2	1.8	5.1	7.3
Measured every three months	32.7	38.6	34.3	26.1	12.5	43.6	43.2	32.5
N	***48***	***34***	***37***	***36***	***15***	***24***	***76***	***270***
Nutritional status informed to mother	100	100	97.3	100	100	100	100	99.6
Pregnant and Lactating women								
N	***100***	***56***	***78***	***131***	***75***	***57***	***91***	***588***

THR received	94.0	91.1	85.9	95.4	86.7	94.7	97.8	92.7
N	***94***	***51***	***67***	***125***	***65***	***54***	***89***	***545***
AWW informed amount to be eaten	21.0	67.9	16.7	6.1	1.3	5.3	13.2	16.3
N	***21***	***38***	***13***	***8***	***1***	***3***	***12***	***96***
Respondent stated correct amount	9.0	32.1	6.4	1.5	0.0	0.0	8.8	7.1

Source: Authors' calculation

About 93% of the lactating and pregnant beneficiaries reported receiving THR. However, only 16.3% were informed about the amount to be consumed, and only 7% of these women could correctly state the amount to be consumed. This indicates that the intake necessary to supplement the diet is probably not consumed expectedly.

Determinates of services of AWW

Binary logistic regression was applied to know the determinants of services provided by AWW. Two aspects of service delivery (from a community perspective) were considered as the dependent variable for analysis. One of the dependent variables referred to AWW distributed RTE and informed mothers of 6 months to 3 years old children about the amount of RTE. Another variable was the weight of the child (6 months to 6 years) was measured, and nutritional status was informed to the mother. Background characteristics, place of operation, job clarity, knowledge and competency of AWW were regressed with these two aspects of services, known to affect the nutritional outcomes of the recipient. The independent variables were of both continuous and categorical nature. The continuous variables were age, education; work experience, last training and remaining variables were categorical

Table-5 shows that with an increase in educational attainment by one year, there was a 6% increase in the likelihood of AWW distributing RTE and informing mothers for the amount of RTE to be consumed. The table further shows that compared to those who had complete job clarity, AWWs with partial and poor job clarity were four and five times respectively, more likely to be informing the mothers about the amount of RTE to be consumed by the child. Compared to the Ajmer region, AWWs of Bikaner region were almost four times more likely to have distributed and informed mothers about RTE. AWWs who could not report the correct amount of RTE to be given to children were more likely to educate mothers about the amount of RTE than AWWs who know exact amount. Many of these findings are not in the desired direction. The model showed a 16.4% variation.

In the second model, except work experience and last training, all the variables were significantly associated with dependent variables. With the increase in one year of age of AWW, a 4% increase in the likelihood of measuring the weight and informing mothers about the nutritional status of the child was observed. Similarly, with one year of improvement in education, the chances of weight monitoring and sharing of nutritional status by AWW increased by 10%. Compared to the Ajmer region, AWWs of Jaipur and Jodhpur region were less likely to weigh and inform mothers about the nutritional status of the child. AWW with poor job clarity were 43% less likely to weigh and tell the nutritional status of the child to the mother. Similarly, AWWs who were competent in weighing and plotting the chart had 88%higher chances of weighing and sharing the nutritional status with the mother than AWW with no competency. The model showed a 13.9% variation.

Table-5: Determinants of Services provided by AWWs in Rajasthan: Binary Logistic Regression Analysis

Characteristics of AWW	AWW distributed RTE and informed mothers of 6months to 3 years old children about the amount of RTE			Weight was measured, and Nutritional Status was informed to Mother		
	OR	95% C.I.		OR	95% C.I.	
		Lower	Upper		Lower	Upper
Age	1.018	0.996	1.040	1.037	1.017	1.058
Education	1.059	1.005	1.117	1.105	1.053	1.158
Work Experience	1.005	0.977	1.035	1.013	0.987	1.038
Last Training	0.972	0.928	1.018	1.004	0.964	1.046
Job Clarity						
Complete®						
Partial	4.439	2.164	9.102	0.693	0.437	1.100
Poor	5.978	2.775	12.877	0.566	0.326	0.983
Administrative Regions						
Ajmer®						
Bikaner	3.942	1.992	7.799	1.044	0.654	1.664
Bharatpur	0.235	0.132	0.417	0.885	0.552	1.417
Jaipur	0.837	0.539	1.302	0.260	0.163	0.415
Jodhpur	0.444	0.266	0.739	0.271	0.159	0.462
Kota	0.410	0.231	0.728	1.164	0.716	1.890
Udaipur	0.348	0.215	0.563	1.361	0.934	1.982

Knowledge of AWW on the amount of RTE for childrensix months-3 years						
Not reported correct amount®						
Reported correct amount	0.614	0.427	0.881			
Competency of AWW on weighing and plotting						
Not competent®						
Competent				1.882	1.345	2.634
Constant	0.131			0.067		

Source: Authors own calculation

Discussion

Init is Economic Survey 2015-16, India's Ministry of Finance has devoted a chapter on malnutrition. This chapter highlighted that relatively low-cost maternal and early-life health and nutrition programs offer very high returns on investment" (MoF, 2016). ICDS is one such relatively low cost maternal and early-life health and nutrition programs, and its review will help us in identifying the prerequisites for ensuring returns in investing in ICDS. The findings of the paper are expected to enable reflection and need for restructuring to improve the status of the services provided under ICDS.

The window of opportunity of correcting malnutrition lies in the initial two years, and hence, the first two years are most crucial (Barker, 2007, Prentice et al., 2013). The results from our study show that 89% of the mothers of children aged six months to 3 years received RTE, 57% of these mothers were not informed about the quantity required to be consumed by the child. Similarly, while supplementary nutrition (hot meal) was distributed at more than 80% of the visited AWCs, the proportion falls to merely one third for morning snacks. In some regions, at none of the visited AWCs, RTE was provided in the right amount. The issue, which emerges, is that the daily recommended quantity of supplementary nutrition is unable to reach the children, who were eligible for the supplements either because of not adhering to distribution norms or not informing mothers who would be feeding the children. This would adversely affect the nutrition status, given that all other things are controlled.

Literature reports that growth assessment best defines the health and nutritional status of children because disturbances in health and nutrition regardless of their aetiology invariably affect child growth, growth monitoring at regular interval is, therefore, a key to identify growth faltering and a window to correct it (De Onis M. et al., 1993). However, our study found that less than one-third of the children were weighed at the recommended time intervals for children among both age group, i.e., six months to 3 years and 3 to 6 years. It also needs recognition that at some places, services could not be delivered due to unavailability of weighing machine and salter scale.

Education is playing an essential role in determining the status of the services, however, at three percent of AWCs, AWWs were illiterate, and another 19% had less than class 8th education. Providing posting to an AWW who is not fulfilling the eligibility criteria was permissible only when there was no educated woman in the entire catchment area; with the spread of education, a fresh review is required so that qualified women are posted as AWWs.

Regression results have shown relations in both expected and unexpected direction. One of the results indicated that less aware AWWs and AWWs with partial and poor job clarity were more likely to provide RTE and inform others about quantity to be consumed. This is somewhat not understandable, as opposed to the expectation. However, for the second dependent variable, weighing of the child and informing the nutrition status to the mother, results are in the expected direction as AWWs competent in weighing and plotting were more likely to be performing this. The above-unexpected result could, however, be understood by the fact that of all the services provided by AWW, distribution of supplementary nutrition is the most known service. Hence, irrespective of knowledge/job clarity, services related to this component are discharged, not necessarily in the expected manner. For weighing and plotting, AWW needs to know the skill, and therefore, the competent AWWs were more likely to execute it.

Literature has documented that proper training improves AWWs' performances (Halder et al., 2001) and inadequate training of AWWs may be the reason for the poor performance of AWCs (Datta et al., 2010). It was, however, interesting to note that the training of the AWW, which is so fervently promoted, had failed to show any significant association with both the dependent variables in this study. This finding needs attention and appropriate corrective measures so that training initiatives could bear desired results.

The burden of undernutrition among under-five children has not changed much even though various intervention programs are in operation in India (Sahu et al. 2015). It is entirely expected if literature reports the success of the ICDS program in tackling maternal and childhood problems as a matter of concern (Agarwal et al., 2000). The implementation bottlenecks probably restricted ICDS to make an expected dent on the problem of malnutrition. The findings of our study also indicate about the worrisome state of services.

Despite, many lacunae in the functioning of the scheme, ICDS have always been lauded for its remarkable conceptualisation, and hence, efforts are required to restructure implementation of ICDS regarding the delivery of quality services. AWWs under ICDS have become workers of umbrella program having multiple functions. The need is to ensure that their primary functions of addressing malnutrition do not get compromised or lost. The program needs to be implemented with the intent of individualised attention and expected outcomes as the drivers of better health rather than an activity-based generalised routine process. A holistic convergence approach which encompasses availability of supplies and equipment, knowledge and competency of the worker and accountability towards beneficiaries by providing the right services in the correct manner can make a dent into the problem of malnutrition.

Funding Support

We express our heartfelt gratitude to UNICEF, State Office for funding and department for necessary support in conducting the periodical assessment of ICDS services in 2011.

References

1. Agarwal, K.N., Agarwal, D.K., Agarwal, A., Rai, S., Prasad, R., Agarwal. S., Singh, T.B. (2000). Impact of the Integrated Child Development Services (ICDS) on maternal nutrition and birth weight in rural Varanasi. Indian Pediatrics, 37, 1321-1327.
2. Anwar, F., Gupta, M.K., Prabha, C., Srivastava, R.K. (2013). Malnutrition among rural Indian children: an assessment using the web of indices. International Journal of Public Health and Epidemiology, 2 (4), 078-084.
3. Barker, D.J.P. (2007). Introduction: The Window of Opportunity. The Journal of Nutrition, 137(4), 1058-1059.
4. Black, R.E., Victora, C.G., Walker, S.P., Bhutta, Z.A., Christian, P., de Onis, M., Ezzati, M., Grantham-McGregor, S., Katz, J., Martorell, R., Uauy, R. (2013). Maternal and child undernutrition and overweight in low-income and middle-income countries. Lancet, 382(9890), 427-451.
5. Blössner, M., de Onis, M. (2005). Malnutrition: quantifying the health impact at national and local levels. Geneva, World Health Organisation, 2005. (WHO Environmental Burden of Disease Series, No. 12).
6. Datta, S.S., Boratne, A.V., Cherian, J., Joice, Y.S., Vignesh, J.T., Singh, Z. (2010). Performance of Anganwadi centres in an urban and rural area: a facility survey in Coastal South India. Indian Journal of Maternal and Child Health, 12(4), 1-9.
7. De Onis, M., Monteiro, C., Akre, J., Clugston G. (1993). The worldwide magnitude of protein-energy malnutrition: an overview from the WHO Global Database on child growth. Bulletin of the World Health Organisation, 71(6), 703-712.

8. Forouzanfar, M.H., Alexander, L., Anderson, H.R., Bachman, V.F., Biryukov, S., Brauer, M., & Cohen, A. (2015). GBD 2013 Risk Factors Collaborators. Global, regional, and national comparative risk assessment of 79 behavioural, environmental and occupational, and metabolic risks or clusters of risks in 188 countries, 1990-2013: a systematic analysis for the Global Burden of Disease Study 2013. Lancet, 386(10010), 2287-2323.
9. Halder, A., Ray, S., Biswas, R., Biswas, B., Mukherjee, D. (2001). Effectiveness of training on infant feeding practices among community influencers in a rural area of West Bengal. Indian Journal of Public Health, 45(2), 51-56.
10. IFPRI (International Food Policy Research Institute). (2014). Global Nutrition Report 2014: Actions and Accountability to Accelerate the World's Progress on Nutrition. Washington, DC.
11. IFPRI (International Food Policy Research Institute). (2015). Global Nutrition Report 2015: Actions and Accountability to Advance Nutrition and Sustainable Development. Washington, DC.
12. IFPRI, (International Food Policy Research Institute). (2016). Global Nutrition Report 2016: From Promise to Impact: Ending Malnutrition by 2030. Washington, DC.
13. vonGrebmer, K., Bernstein, J., Nabarro, D., Prasai, N., Amin, S., Yohannes, Y., Sonntag, A., Patterson, F., Towey, O., Thompson, J. (2016). 2016 Global hunger index: Getting to zero hunger. Bonn Washington, DC and Dublin: Welthungerhilfe, International Food Policy Research Institute, and Concern Worldwide. http://dx.doi.org/10.2499/9780896292260
14. International Institute for Population Sciences (IIPS) and ICF (2017).National Family Health Survey (NFHS-4), 2015-16: India. Mumbai: IIPS. Retrieved from http://rchiips.org/NFHS/NFHS-4Reports/India.pdf
15. International Institute for Population Sciences (IIPS) and ICF (2017a). National Family Health Survey (NFHS-4), India, 2015-16: Rajasthan. Mumbai: IIPS. Retrieved from http://rchiips.org/NFHS/NFHS-4Reports/Rajasthan.pdf
16. Kumar, A., Kamath, V.G., Kamath, A., Rao, C.R., Pattanshetty, S., Sagir, A. (2010). Nutritional status assessment of under-five beneficiaries of Integrated Child Development Services program in rural Karnataka. Australian Medical Journal, 3(8), 495-98.
17. MCA(Ministry of Consumer Affairs, Food and Public Distribution) (2016). National Food Security Act (NFSA), 2013. Department of Food and Public Distribution, Government of India. Retrieved from http://dfpd.nic.in/nfsa-act.htm.
18. MoF (Ministry of Finance). (2016). Mother and Child. India. It is retrieved from: http://indiabudget.nic.in/es2015-16/echapvol1-05.pdf.
19. MoSPI (Ministry of Statistics and Programme Implementation). (2015). Millennium Development Goals-India Country Report, 2015. Central Statistics Office, Social Statistics Division, Government of India, New Delhi. Retrieved from http://mospi.nic.in/sites/default/files/publication_reports/mdg_2july15_1.pdf.
20. MoWCD (Ministry of Women and Child Development) (2015). Annual Report 2014-15. Government of India. Retrieved from http://wcd.nic.in/sites/default/files/AR2014-15.pdf

21. Park, K., (2011). Park's Textbook of Preventive and Social Medicine, 21st edition. Jabalpur, Bhanot Publications, (830-1).
22. Prentice, A.M., Ward, K.A., Goldberg, G.R., Jarjou, L.M., Moore, S.E., Fulford, A.J., Prentice, A. (2013). Critical windows for nutritional interventions against stunting. The American Journal of Clinical Nutrition, 97(5), 911-918. http://doi.org/10.3945/ajcn.112.052332
23. Sahu, S.K., Kumar, S.G., Bhat, B.V., Premarajan, K.C., Sarkar, S., Roy, G., Joseph, N. (2015). Malnutrition among under-five children in India and strategies for control. Journal of Natural Science, Biology, and Medicine, 6(1), 18-23. http://doi.org/10.4103/0976-9668.149072
24. UN-DESA/DSD (2014). SDG 2: End hunger, achieve food security and improved nutrition, and promote sustainable agriculture. Retrieved from https://sustainabledevelopment.un.org/?page=view&nr=164&type=230.

□

14

Challenges and Scope of Mid day Meal intervention: A Systematic Literature Review

—*Shachi Barot and Dr. Ritu Sharma*

Abstract

Indian constitution makers have framed plenty of provisions for the protection of children in Independent India. Indian constitution provides that the state shall direct its policy towards ensuring "that children are given opportunities and facilities to develop in a healthy manner and condition of liberty and dignity and that childhood and youth are protected against exploitation and moral material rejection" (Col., Article-39). This Directive positions that children deserve as the highest priority in national apprehension of the fundamental rights and the special provisions for those most vulnerable to discrimination and exclusion. Through a systematic literature review of the article, annual reports, policy guidelines, news and review and assessment reports by government and authorised agencies, this paper attempts to understand the challenges and scope of Mid Day Meal scheme on in Indian context.

Background

India, a country with 472 million children (Status of Children in Urban India, 2016). Also, children between 0-18 years represent 39 percent of the country's total population. An analysis of the National Institute of Urban Affairs on age-wise distribution reveals that 29.5 percent of children are aged between 0-5 years, 33 percent are aged between 6-11 years, 16.4 percent are 12-14 years group and 21 percent belong to 15-18 years age group respectively (Status of Children in Urban India, 2016). The majority of India's children (73 percent) reside in rural areas (Ministry of women and child development, 2016).

The level of a child under nutrition remains unacceptable throughout the world, with 90 percent of the developing world's chronically undernourished (stunted) children living in Asia and Africa. Detrimental and often undetected until severe, under nutrition undermines the survival, growth and development of children and women, and diminishes the strength and capacity of nations. With persistently high levels of under nutrition in the developing world, vital opportunities to save millions of lives are being lost, and many more millions of children are not growing and developing to their full potential. Nutrition is a core pillar of human development and concrete, large-scale programming not only can reduce the burden of under nutrition and deprivation in countries but also can advance the progress of nations (Mukharjee, 2017). For the protection of children in Independent India, the Constitution of India (CoI, Article-39) provides that the State shall direct its policy towards ensuring "that children are given opportunities and facilities to develop in a healthy manner and conditions of liberty and dignity and that childhood and youth are protected against exploitation and moral and material abandonment" (CoI, Article-39). This Directive undoubtedly places children as worthy of the highest priority in the national realisation of the Fundamental Rights and the special provisions for the one who are exposed to discrimination and exclusion.

Indian policymakers have notably framed national mandate for what must be done, through policy, law, planning, and practical programming, with the awareness and clarity on the required resources of knowledge and skills, time and attention, material and financial support, and dedicated practical effort to reach all children, during childhood.

Health should be viewed as not merely the absence of disease but as a state of complete physical, mental and social well-being. (World Health Organisation, 2014) The determinants of good health are access to various types of health services and an individual's lifestyle choices, personal, family and social relationships.

Policies and Laws related to Child in India

Indian Government has identified International values and became signatory with Universal Declaration of Human Rights from 1948, and inspired the UN General Assembly to Declare an International Year for the Child in 1979. It acceded to the UN Convention on the Rights of the Child (UN CRC) in 1992. Apart from other rights, Article 24 (1) & (2) of CRC, 1992 specifically provisioned that:

1. States Parties recognise the right of the child to the enjoyment of the highest attainable standard of health and facilities for the treatment of illness and rehabilitation of health. States Parties shall strive to ensure that no child is deprived of his or her right of access to such health care services. 2. States Parties shall pursue full implementation of this right and, in particular, shall take appropriate measures: (a) To diminish infant and child mortality; (b) To ensure the provision of necessary medical assistance and health care to all children with emphasis on the development of primary health care; (c) To resist disease and malnutrition, including within the framework of primary health care, though, inter *alia*, the application of readily available technology

and through the provision of adequate nutritious foods and clean drinking-water, taking into consideration the dangers and risks of environmental pollution; (d) To ensure appropriate pre-natal and post-natal health care for mothers; (e) To ensure that all segments of society, in particular parents and children, are informed, have access to education and are supported in the use of basic knowledge of child health and nutrition, the advantages of breastfeeding, hygiene and environmental sanitation and the prevention of accidents; (f) To develop preventive health care, guidance for parents and family planning education and services. These acts of accession and ratification stand as treaty obligations which India has undertaken to fulfil. (CRC, 1992)

With affiliation to the UN CRC, India has significantly affirmed its recognition of children in the development route of the country as human beings with distinct and absolute rights rather than as passive objects of care and charity. Children's rights were the global agenda in the UN General Assembly's special session (UNGASS) in May 2002. India accepted the resulting 'World Fit for Children' decisions without reservations and pledged to take positive steps to address the major gaps identified in terms of securing all rights of children. The Government has subsequently taken several significant measures to achieve these aims. (Ministry of women and child development, 2016)

The National Policy for Children (NPC) implementation in 1974 one of the first and wide-ranging initiation by Government, and followed up with Integrated Child Development Services (ICDS) programme, 1975 for early childhood care, immunisation scheme till 1978 to prevent children from preventive deadly diseases, and taking on Child Labour (Prohibition and Regulation) Act from 1986. Then after National Action Plan was framed, and implemented in 1979, 1992, 2005 and finally in 2016.

Indian Government also have acknowledged variety of legislation like Juvenile Justice Care and Protection Act, (2000), and amended Juvenile Justice (Care and Protection) Act (2015), extension with National Commission for the Protection of Child Rights (NCPCR), Prohibition of Child Marriage Act (2006), Right to Education for free and compulsory for children (2009), Protection of Children from Sexual Offences (POCSO) Act (2012), and Child Labour (Prohibition and Regulation Amendment Act, 2016.

Also it has been observed many schemes and programmes for infants and young children in which National policy for children (NPC) in 2013 and Integrated child development scheme (ICDS) in 1975, Sarva Shiksha Abhiyan (SSA) in 2000, National Health Mission (NHM) 2005 and Child Protection Services formerly run as Integrated Child Protection Scheme (ICPS) 2009 are major milestones, Its primary focused on health, nutrition, education and protection of lives and growing up fit and safe. (Ministry of women and child development, 2016)

By following to NPC 2013, National Food Security Act and the Swachchh Bharat Mission (SBM, 2014), National Skill Development Mission (NSDM, 2015) widely appreciated and accepted *Beti Bachao, Beti Padhao* in 2015 has successfully implemented by the Government. The National Nutrition Mission aimed to malnutrition in children, pregnant and feeding mothers. (Ministry of Women and Child Development, 2016)

The National Plan of Action for Children spells key issues and concerns about children's right to survival, health, nutrition, education, dignity, protection and participation. (National Plan of Action for Children, 2016)

Outline of Mid Day Meal Scheme

On 2nd October, 1975, the Government of India is addressing malnutrition among mothers and children via an integrated approach under the Integrated Child Development Scheme (ICDS) for a better and effective impact. The scheme suggests six services which are essential for child development, *i.e.,* supplementary nutrition, health check-up, immunisation, referral services, pre-school education and health and nutrition education through the platform of Anganwadi Centre. (ICDS. 2017)

Mid Day Meal in schools has had a long history in India. In 1925, a Mid Day Meal Programme was introduced for disadvantaged children in Madras Municipal Corporation. By the mid-1980s three States viz. Gujarat, Kerala and Tamil Nadu and the UT of Puducherry had universalised a cooked Mid Day Meal Programme with their resources for children studying at the primary stage. By 1990-91 the number of States implementing the mid-day meal programme with their resources on a universal or a large scale had increased to twelve states. (ATMDMS)

Ministry of Education, Government of India, has been running one of the World's budgets of largest food assistance program with the object of enhancing enrolment in schools, retention, attendance and simultaneously improve nutritional standards among children. The Union Budget of 2018-19, Rs. Ten thousand five hundred crores allocated for MDM, which has seen 500 crores increase over 2017-18.

Malnutrition plays important role in increase in Higher mortality rate, disability, life-threatening diseases among the children. The safe and caring environment with three other factors majorly influence nutrition level in children. They are food, Health and Care, Water and Sanitation. (Improving Child Nutrition, 2013)

Nutrition in children, measured in terms of the prevalence of stunting, wasting, and underweight, show that India has much to achieve in this field. The recently published India Health Report on Nutrition 2015 (Raykar, 2015) notes that despite significant growth in India's GDP; the nutritional status of children has not enhanced at the same pace.

According to the survey of (The Rapid Survey on Children (RSOC) 2013-14), Ministry of Women and Child Development and UNICEF shows considerable improvement in nutrition level of children under five years of age in comparison to 2005-06; but it remains very high. The stunting has reduced from 48 percent (2005-06) to 38.7 percent (2013-14). Underweight and wasting have reduced from 42.5 percent to 29.4 percent in 2005-06 and from 19.8 percent to 15 percent in 2013-14. Around 4.6 percent of children in the age group 0-59 months were found to be severely wasted. (National Plan of Action for Children 2016)

Mid Day Meal Scheme aimed to:

- avoid classroom hunger
- increase school enrolment
- increase school attendance
- improve socialisation among castes
- address malnutrition and
- empower women through employment

On 28th November, 2001, in the case People's Union for Civil Liberties Vs Union of India & Ors, Supreme Court of India passed an order stating:

"We direct the State Governments/Union Territories to implement the Mid Day Meal Scheme by providing every child in every Government and Government assisted Primary School with a prepared mid-day meal."

The Hon'ble Supreme Court of India in its direction has linked the feeding programme of the children to quality education programme of Government. This was done to ensure that a lesser number of children go to bed hungry. This resulted in encouraging the poor family to enrol their children in government schools and thereby enable them to guarantee at least one meal a day.

The Mid Day Meal scheme is a well-intentioned programme. Government of India has attempted to address the fundamental problems of health, education, and overall development of children in the country by implementing programme all over the country. It provides children with at least one nutritionally adequate meal a day. This program is known to lead to higher attention spans, better concentration, and improved class performance. School meal program also provides parents with a strong incentive to send children to school, thereby encouraging enrolment and reducing absenteeism and dropout rates. It supports health, nutrition, and education goals and consequently will have a multi-pronged impact on a nation's overall social and economic development. (MDM-AP, 2014-15)

Outreach and Development in Mid Day Meal

The National Programme of Nutritional Support to Primary Education (NP-NSPE) was launched as a Centrally Sponsored Scheme on 15th August, 1995, initially in 2408 blocks in the country. By the year 1997-98, the NP-NSPE was introduced in all blocks of the country. It was further extended in 2002 to cover not only children in classes IV of Government, Government aided and local body schools, but also children studying in EGS and AIE centres. Central Assistance under the scheme consisted of free supply of food grains @ 100 grams per child per school day, and subsidy for transportation of food grains up to a maximum of Rs 50 per quintal. (NP-NSPE)

In September 2004 the scheme was revised to provide cooked mid-day meal with 300 calories and 8-12 grams of protein to all children studying in classes I–V in Government and aided schools and EGS/ AIE centres. In addition to free supply of food grains, the revised scheme provided Central Assistance for (a) Cooking cost @ Re 1 per child per school day, (b) Transport subsidy was raised from the earlier maximum of Rs. 50 per quintal to Rs. One hundred per quintal for special category states, and Rs. 75 per quintal for other states, (c) Management, monitoring and evaluation costs @ 2% of the cost of food-grains, transport subsidy and cooking assistance, (d) Provision of mid-day meal during summer vacation in drought-affected areas. (NP-NSPE)

In July 2006 the scheme was further revised to provide assistance for cooking cost at the rate of (a) Rs. 1.80 per child/school day for States in the North Eastern Region, provided the NER States contribute Rs. 0.20 per child/school day, and (b) Rs. 1.50 per child/ school day for other States and UTs, provided that these States and UTs contribute Rs. 0.50 per child/school day. (NP-NSPE)

In October 2007, the scheme was further revised to cover children in upper primary (classes VI to VIII) initially in 3479 Educationally Backwards Blocks (EBBs). Around 1.7 crore upper primary children were included by this expansion of the scheme. From 2008-09 i.e. w.e.f 1st April, 2008, the programme covers all children studying in Government, Local Body and Government-aided primary and upper primary schools and the EGS/AIE centres including Madrasa and Maqtabs supported under SSA of all areas across the country. The calorific value of a mid-day meal at an upper primary stage has been fixed at a minimum of 700 calories and 20 grams of protein by providing 150 grams of food grains (rice/wheat) per child/school day. (NP-NSPE)

From the year 2009 onwards the following changes have been made to improve the implementation of the scheme:

Food norms have been revised to ensure balanced and nutritious diet to children of the upper primary group by increasing the number of pulses from 25 to 30 grams, vegetables from 65 to 75 grams and by decreasing the quantity of oil and fat from 10 grams to 7.5 grams.

8.41 crore in Primary and 3.36 crore Upper Primary children i.e. a total of 11.77 crore children were estimated to be benefited from MDM Scheme during 2009-10. 11.04 Crore children were covered under MDM Scheme during 2009-10. During 2010-11, 11.36 crore childreni.e. 7.97 Cr. children in primary and 3.39 Cr. children in the upper primary had been covered in 12.63 lakhs institutions. During 2011-12 total coverage of children against enrolment was 10.52 Crore (i.e. Primary-7.71 crore and Upper Primary 3.36 crore children). During 2012-13, 10.68 Cr. children (Elementary level) had been covered in 12.12 lakh Schools. 10.45 Cr. children were covered in 11.58 lakh Schools during 2013-14. (Mid Day Meal Scheme, PIB, 2017)

Mid Day Meal Scheme-Structure Implemented

The Mid day Meal is provided to children studying in class's I-VIII of eligible schools in the States/UTs as per the following norms: (Ministry of HRD, 2016):

S. No.	Items	Quantity per day/ child	
		Primary	Upeer Primary
1.	Foodgrain (Rice/ Wheat)	100 gm	150 gm
2.	Pulses	20 gm	30 gm
3.	Vegetables (leafy also)	50 gm	75 gm
4.	Oil & Fat	5 gm	7.5 gm
5.	Salt & Condiments	As per need	As per need

Source: Ministry of HRD, 2016

The State/UT-wise details of the number of incidents of serving substandard/ contaminated mid-day meal reported from various States/UTs during the last three years are given at Annexure-II.

The Government has adopted an elaborate monitoring mechanism at Central, State and District levels to check the quality, safety and hygiene of Mid Day Meals. The formation is like as follows:

At national level, an Empowered Committee, headed by Minister of HRD, a National level Steering-cum—Monitoring Committee (NSMC) and Programme Approval Board (PAB), both headed by Secretary (School Education & Literacy), evaluate the performance of each State in implementation of the Scheme and suggest measures for its smooth and effective implementation.

At the State level, a State level Steering–cum-Monitoring Committee headed by the State Chief Secretary and,

At District Level, a District Level Committee under the Chair person ship of senior-most Member of Parliament of Lok Sabha, of the district monitors the implementation of the scheme in the concerned District.

Besides, at local level Gram Panchayats/ Gram Sabhas, member of Village Education Committees (VECs), Parent Teacher Associations (PTAs), School Management Committees (SMCs) are required to monitor the regularity and wholesomeness of the mid-day meal served to children, cleanliness in cooking and serving of the mid day meal, timeliness in procurement of good quality ingredients, fuel, etc., implementation of varied menu and social and gender equity on a daily basis.

Mid Day Meal Scheme-Incidences Reported (Govt. Data)

Number of an incident of serving substandard/contaminated mid-day meal reported during the last three years: (Ministry of HRD, 2016):

		Poor Quality				Total
S.No.	**State/UT**	**2013**	**2014**	**2015**	**2016**	
1.	Andhra Pradesh	0	2	0	1	**3**
2.	Arunachal Pradesh	0	0	0	0	**0**
3.	A & N Island	0	1	0	0	**1**
4.	Assam	0	0	1	2	**1**
5.	Bihar	5	9	7	2	**23**
6.	Chandigarh	0	0	1	0	**1**
7.	Chhattisgarh	1	3	1	1	**6**
8.	Delhi	1	2	6	0	**9**
9.	Gujarat	0	1	1	0	**2**
10.	Goa	0	0	1	0	**1**
11.	Haryana	1	1	0	1	**3**
12.	Himachal Pradesh	0	0	1	0	**1**
13.	J & K	0	0	0	1	**1**
14	Jharkhand	1	3	2	2	**8**
15	Karnataka	1	3	0	0	**4**
16.	Kerala	0	0	0	0	**0**
17.	Madhya Pradesh	0	3	3	0	**6**
18.	Maharashtra	0	2	5	2	**9**
19.	Odisha	3	4	2	1	**10**
20.	Punjab	0	0	0	1	**1**
21.	Rajasthan	2	0	0	0	**2**

22.	Tamil Nadu	1	0	0	0	**1**
23.	Telangana	0	1	0	0	**1**
24.	Tripura			1		**1**
25.	Uttarakhand	0	0	0	0	**0**
26.	Uttar Pradesh	1	6	13	5	**25**
27.	West Bengal	1	0	1	2	**4**
	Total	**18**	**41**	**46**	**19**	**124**

(Table Ministry of HRD, 2016)

Past Research Findings on Mid Day Meal

Some significant researches have been done till date on Mid Day Meal Scheme conducted by independent agencies and reported that Mid Day Meal programme is a visible programme and has helped in increase in attendance and enrolment of children particularly girls. They also reported that there is an increase in retention, learning ability and achievement as well as greater social equity among caste, creed, sex and gender groups in the schools. (Research Findings on Mid Day Meal)

The main research findings of the Ministry of Human Resource Development about Mid Day Meal Scheme (1999-2014) suggested:

(i) Research findings (2010) of Pratichi trust of Prof. Amartya Kumar Sen: Unlike many other Government programmes, implementation of MDM has been a success throughout the country. Though the quality of food needs to be improved, it must be said that with the active participation of the beneficiaries, it has become a community programme. The quick response of the state administration in amending the shortcomings indicates that the administration is gradually becoming aware of this (Pratichi Trust, 2010).

(ii) The major findings of the Public Report on Basic Education Report indicated that 84% of households reported that the children get cooked mid-day meal in schools and children enjoy a varied menu. Good practices like washing hands before eating, & after eating are imparted in the schools. Incentives like MDM have contributed to improving enrolment rates. (PROBE)

(iii) Mid Day Meal Scheme in Madhya Pradesh by National Institute of Public Cooperation & Child Development, Indore has reported that MDM has shown marked improvement in enrolment pattern of children in primary schools. Mid Day Meal Scheme undoubtedly resulted in increased school attendance and retention of children in schools for a longer period. The Scheme has played a crucial role in reducing drop out ratio, especially among girls. Parents viewed that the midday meal had reduced the burden of providing one-time meal to their children and considered it as a great support to their families. Teachers opined that mid-day meal aided in active learning of children, which indirectly improved their academic performance. The Scheme has played a significant role in bringing social equity among all the sections of society. (Ministry of HRD, 2013)

(iv) An empirical study conducted on Mid Day Meal scheme in Khurda district of Orissa revealed that cooked mid-day meal has increased socialisation among the children and helped in increasing enrolment and afternoon session attendance. MDM has created new employment opportunities for underprivileged sections. (Ministry of HRD, 2013)

(v) Annual Status of Education Report (ASER) 2010 reported that in 83.4% schools served MDM on a day of visit and almost same percent of schools (81.3%) schools had kitchen sheds for cooking mid-day meal. Vastly improved availability of mid-day meals had contributed to the increase in enrolment. (ASER, 2010)

(vi) Supreme Court Commissioners undertake an extensive review of various welfare schemes through field visits. They have observed that the MDM is widely acknowledged as one of the most successful schemes of GOI. Increase in enrolment and attendance of children in primary schools has been noticed after the introduction of MDM. (Research Findings on Mid Day Meal)

(vii) Performance audit (2011) conducted by Centre for Environment and Food Security on food security schemes in Orissa and Uttar Pradesh; The sample survey in 130 villages spread over 12 districts of Orissa and Uttar Pradesh (Bundelkhand) was carried out and reported that performance of the MDM scheme is far better in Orissa in comparison with the Uttar Pradesh. An overwhelming 86.7 percent of Orissa's children were getting a second best category of MDM (regular but inadequate and unsatisfactory meal), only 51.8 percent of children in UP were getting a regular but inadequate and unsatisfactory meal in their schools. (Ministry of HRD, 2013)

(viii) A few NGOs have solicited local women's groups to do the cooking with some success. Research from the non-profit organisation; Akshaya Patra, works for the government to implement the program, states that the meal scheme has led to "increased enrolment in schools, increased attendance in schools, improved performance of students in class in terms of better attention span and academic progress, and improved nutritional status of students." (Lentz-Marino, 2014)

(ix) Another study by Farzana Afridi of Syracuse University and the Delhi School of Economics claimed that the program has "reduced the daily protein deficiency of a primary-school student by 100 percent, the calorie deficiency by almost 30 percent and the daily iron deficiency by nearly 10 percent." (Lentz-Marino, 2014)

Planning Commission (2010)

Performance Evaluation of Cooked Mid Day Meal Scheme-study conducted by Programme Evaluation Organisation of Planning Commission (2010): (PEO Report, 2010).

The highlights of the Study conducted by the Planning Commission are as under:

(i) The Cooked Mid Day Meal Program has been successful in addressing classroom hunger in sample schools.

(ii) Cooked Mid Day Meal is reported to have created a platform for children of all social and economic backgrounds to take meals together, thereby facilitating achieving the objective of social equity.

(iii) It has also been observed that the programme has resulted in the diversion of the attention of teachers and students on activities related to it, rather than towards teaching and learning activities, which results in loss of studies.

(iv) In general, a visible shortage of basic infrastructural facilities and manpower (that are crucial for the success of the Cooked Mid Day Meal programme) were noted.

(v) Most of the states, it was observed, did not follow the guidelines of Government of India to deliver food grains at the school point by PDS dealer, thereby resulting in the leakage of food grains. There have been instances where, due to long supply chain, food grains supplied got adulterated and pilfered.

(vi) While Cooked Mid Day Meal Scheme seems to have contributed to an increase in the attendance in schools across the country, it does not seem to have any significant impact on fresh enrolments in sample schools. (PEO Report, 2010)

Mid day Meal Scheme and past setbacks

Mid day meal program is to assist 120 million children every day, and undoubtedly such a mass scale scheme may suffer from organisational problems (Lentz-Marino, 2014).

Some of the more precise problems related to MDM implementations are as follows:

- Delayed payments, poor food quality, snakes and worms in the food, cooks not receiving pay and food not being delivered or being wasted. (Lentz-Marino, 2014)
- It is also a difficult challenge to deliver food to rural areas. Roads are not paved, and the infrastructure is lacking. Even if food makes it to these remote

areas, kitchens to cook the food in are not available within the schools. (Lentz-Marino, 2014)

- Lack of kitchen halls for cooking mid-day meal in schools is posing a serious threat to the health of children. The food many schools lack drinking water facility, gas connection, compound wall, toilets, electricity and other necessary infrastructure facilities. (Gopal, 2013) Part of the problem is poor infrastructure. Thousands of schools in India do not even have their buildings and are run from community centres with no storage facilities. The kitchen was a pile of bricks and charcoal in a corner outside the classroom and parents said, due to lack of storage facility, the ingredients for lunch had to be brought in every day. (Banerji, 2013)

Supreme Court Commissioners are monitoring all welfare Schemes of the Central Government, including the Mid Day Meal Scheme. They have monitored seven States viz. Assam, Bihar, Jharkhand, Madhya Pradesh, Nagaland, Orissa and West Bengal during 2010-11. The main recommendations of the reports are as under: (Lentz-Marino, 2014)

(a) The midday meal should be expected to cover all children in the school going age irrespective of whether they are enrolled in school. The location of the meal served can continue to be the school; this might further encourage those out of school children to join schools.

(b) The provision for cooking costs under the midday meal should be increased based on the Price Index developed for Mid Day Meal Scheme to counter the effect of inflation.

(c) Proper infrastructure for mid-day meals should be mandatory, including cooking sheds storage space, drinking water, ventilation, utensils etc.

(d) Mobilisation for kitchen garden in school premises should be encouraged.

(e) Priority should be given to disadvantaged communities (especially *Dalits* and *Adivasis*) in the appointment of cooks and helpers. All cooks and helpers should be paid not less than the statutory minimum wage.

(f) Midday meal should be linked with nutrition education and related educational activities. State Government should be encouraged to adept their textbooks for this purpose, as the NCERT has already done for some textbooks.

(g) Nutritious items such as eggs and green vegetables should be provided regularly.

(h) Community participation in the monitoring of Mid day meal should be strengthened, particularly to prevent corruption and ensure quality.

(i) Mid day meal should be integrated with school health services, including immunisation, de-worming, growth monitoring, health check-ups and micronutrient supplementation.

(j) Grievance redressal mechanism must be within easily reachable distance of complainant and should, therefore, be decentralised to *Panchayat* level. It could also consist of mobile camps that reach out to each village. (PEO Report, 2010)

Way Forward

Since 1947, India has made significant progress in human development. The future of society depends on the quality of life of the children. Nutritional needs change throughout life, depending on genetics, rate of growth, activity and many other factors. Nutritional status is the condition of health of the individual as influenced by the utilisation of nutrients. Nutritional needs also vary from individual to individual. (Mehrotra, 2011)

The National Programme of Nutritional Support to Primary Education (NP-NSPE) was launched as a Centrally Sponsored Scheme on 15th August, 1995 to enhance enrolment, retention and attendance and simultaneously improve nutritional levels among children. It is also visualised that such a meal would promote friendship and feeling of brotherhood among the children belonging to diverse caste, colour and creed. This is the world's greatest governmental programme of food distribution eventually catering to a crore of children come for study to school. (James, 2013)

Problems related to scheme implementation must be addressed by incorporating roles of key stakeholders like Parents, *Panchayats* and local authorities. More rigorous auditing can be considered as an immediate action to ensure the objectives of the schemes are met at all the levels.

Children have the right to get the highest attainable health according to human rights law. This right further requires proper food and nutritious food. Mid Day Meal is one of those kinds of noble attempts of Government of India. More rigorous measure has to be chosen to ensure the fulfilment of this objective. Three-pronged approaches which includes responsibility, accountability and timely audit is recommended to ensure Mid day meal scheme success beyond the philanthropic movement by the government.

References

1. About the Mid Day Meal Scheme (ATMDMS), Retrieved from http://www.mdm.nic.in/aboutus.html
2. Annual Status Of Education Report 2010, Retrieved from http://img.asercentre.org/docs/Publications/ASER%20Reports/ASER_2010/ASERReport2010.pdf

3. Banerji A. & Kotoky A., (2013), Poor quality and bad management: India ignored warnings in the free meal programme, Reuters: South Asia News, Retrieved from http://in.reuters.com/article/bihar-mid-day-meal-warnings-idINDEE96K04D20130721
4. Constitution of India (1950); Article 39
5. Convention on the Rights of the Child, Adopted and opened for signature, ratification and accession by General Assembly resolution 44/25 of 20th November, 1989, Retrieved from http://www.ohchr.org/EN/ProfessionalInterest/Pages/CRC.aspx
6. Gopal, M. V,(2013), Problems In Execution of Mid Day Meal Scheme. The Hans India. Retrieved from http://www.thehansindia.com/posts/index/North-Telangana/2013-08-30/Problems-in-execution-of-mid-day-meal-scheme-/70620
7. Improving Child Nutrition (2013). The achievable imperative for global progress, the United Nations Children's Fund (UNICEF). UNICEF. Retrieved from: www.unicef.org/publications/index.html
8. Integrated Child Development Services (ICDS) Scheme, Retrieved from http://icds-wcd.nic.in/icds/icds.aspx
9. James, G., (2013). Fighting 'Classroom Hunger'—Achievements of 'Mid Day Meal Scheme' Retrieved from http://yojana.gov.in/mid-day-meal-scheme.asp
10. Lentz-Marino, E., (2014). Problems With Mid Day Meal Scheme in India 2014, HUMANITY, POLITICS & YOU, BORGEN Magazine. Retrieved from: http://www.borgenmagazine.com/problems-mid-day-meal-scheme-india/
11. Lessons learned from India's midday meal scheme for school children (2014). Retrieved from: https://www.theguardian.com/global-development/2014/aug/11/india-midday-meal-scheme-schoolchildren
12. Ministry of Human Resource Development, Department of School Education & Literacy, Lok sabha, unstarred question no.2056, to be answered on 28.11.2016, Government of India, Retrieved from http://164.100.47.190/loksabhaquestions/qhindi/10/AU2056.pdf
13. Ministry of Women and Child Development (2016), Child Welfare-I Section, National plan of action for children, Government of India. New Delhi. Retrieved from: http://wcd.nic.in/sites/default/files/National%20Plan%20of%20Action_0.pdf
14. Mid Day Meal, Andhra Pradesh write-up, 2014-15, Retrieved from http://www.mdm.nic.in/Files/PAB/PAB201415/Andhra_Pradesh/1_AWPB%202014-15writeup.pdf
15. Mid Day Meal Scheme (2016). Retrieved from: http://mhrd.gov.in/mid-day-meal
16. Mid Day Meal Scheme (2017), PIB, Retrieved from http://pib.nic.in/archieve/flagship/bkg_mdm1.pdf
17. National Plan Of Action For Children, 2016, Ministry Of Women And Child Development Government Of India, Retrieved from http://wcd.nic.in/sites/default/files/National%20Plan%20of%20Action_0.pdf
18. Mehrotra Monika, Arora Santosh, And Nagar Veenu (2011), Nutritional Health Status of Primary School Children A study in Bareilly District, Indian Educational Review, Vol. 48, No.1, January 2011, http://mdm.nic.in/Files/Initiatives%20&%20Case%20Studies/Nutritional_Health.pdf

19. The National Programme of Nutritional Support to Primary Education (NP-NSPE), Retrieved from http://mdm.nic.in/Files/Initiatives%20&%20Case%20Studies/CMDM%20Report.pdf
20. UNICEF-Nutrition, available at http://unicef.in/Story/1124/Nutrition#sthash.AKmawChM.dpuf
21. Ojha Anjali, (2013). Lack of Monitoring, corruption plague mid-day meal scheme. DNA, Daily news and analysis. Retrieved from: http://www.dnaindia.com/india/comment-lack-of-monitoring-corruption-plague-mid-day-meal-scheme-1866691
22. Performance Evaluation of COOKED MID-DAY MEAL (CMDM), PEO Report No.202, 2010, Retrieved from http://planningcommission.nic.in/reports/peoreport/peoevalu/peo_cmdm.pdf
23. Pratichi Trust, (2010). Mid Day Meal: The Mid day Meal Programme in Urban Primary and Rural Upper Primary Schools in West Bengal, New Delhi.
24. Probe Team (1999), Research Findings on Mid Day Meal, Public Report on Basic Education in India, Oxford University Press, Retrieved from http://mdm.nic.in/Files/OrderCirculars/Findings_of_Research_studies.pdf.
25. Raykar, N., Majumder, M., Laxminarayan, R., & Menon, P. (2015). Indian Health Report: Nutrition 2015, Public Health Foundation of India, New Delhi. Retrieved from: http://www.transformnutrition.org/wp-content/uploads/sites/3/2015/12/INDIA-HEALTH-REPORT-NUTRITION_2015_for-Web.pdf
26. Research Findings on Mid Day Meal, Retrieved from https://educheer.com/essays/research-findings-on-mid-day-meal/
27. Status of Children in Urban India Baseline Study (2016). National Institute of Urban Affairs. Retrieved from: www.niua.org
28. Times of India (2016), Dead lizard in midday meal: 60 students fall sick, Retrieved from http://timesofindia.indiatimes.com/city/erode/dead-lizard-in-midday-meal-60-students-fall-sick/articleshow/56168280.cms
29. Union Budgetary Allocation, Retrieved from http://mdm.nic.in/union%20budgetary.html
30. World Health Organisation, (2014).Twelfth General Programme of Work 2014-2019, Not merely the absence of disease, Retrieved from www.who.int/about/resources_planning/twelfth-gpw
31. Biswamoy Mukharjee, Nutrition is a core pillar of human development, 2017, https://news.webindia123.com/news/Articles/India/20170903/3180000.html

□

15

Developmental Programmes, Under Nutrition and Developmental Progress of Young Children (<6 Years): Time to Change

—*Vanisha S. Nambiar and Tanya Khanna*

Abstract

The all India Poverty Head Count Ratio (PHCR) estimate was 47.8% in 199, which is 2011-12, was 21.9%, indicating that India had already achieved the MDG target well ahead of time. However, despite its existence in India since 1975, Integrated Child Development Services (ICDS), the welfare programme of the Indian Government which aims to provide supplementary nutrition, preschool education and basic health care, intends to fight malnutrition and improve overall development among children, the recent RSOC reports, (2013-14) reveal that among 0-59 months old children in India, 39% are stunted, 17% severely stunted, 15% wasted, 5% severely wasted, 29% underweight and 10% are severely underweight indicating several other aspects are involved in controlling child health and nutrition. The recent Child Development Index (CDI) also indicates a poor score of South Asia (26.4), which is largely contributed by India. Thus, it is important that along with economic growth in India, it is time to relook into our developmental programmes and policies and alter motoring and surveillance systems, thereby translating into reduced child deprivation.

Introduction

The world has made significant progress since setting the Millennium Development Goal to halve poverty and hunger between 1990 and 2015. Despite progress, 800 million people still go to bed hungry every night, and an even greater number live in poverty (Townsend, 2015). It has been recently estimated that in developing nations, 200 million children (roughly 39%) under age five are not reaching their developmental potential because poverty, malnutrition, high rates of infection, lack of stimulation and education and instability in the home have negative effects on child development (Chilton, Chyatte, & Breaun, 2007). Higher levels of economic growth in the region are not widely translating into reduced child deprivation or improving young child's development and learning potential. Children raised in food insecure households are at increased risk for academic and socio-emotional difficulties (Engle & Black, 2008). The optimal nutritional status can be achieved when every child has access to affordable, diverse, nutrient rich food, appropriate maternal and child care practices, a healthy environment including safe drinking water, good hygiene and sanitation practices and adequate health services. These factors directly determine the nutrient intake and the presence of morbidities. The interaction between these factors creates a potentially lethal cycle of worsening illness and deteriorating nutritional status (UNICEF, 2013).

Food Insecurity and Child Growth and Development—Current Scenario in India

The Food and Agricultural Organisation (FAO, 2006) states that food security emerges when all people at all times have physical and economic access to sufficient, safe and nutritious food to meet their dietary needs and food preferences for an active and healthy life. Food security has three important and closely related components, which are the availability of food, access to food, and absorption of food. Results of across-sectional study revealed that household food availability and accessibility results in better food utilisation. A poor picture of household food security is mainly due to low dietary diversity, less income, poor road condition and very high incidence of undernutrition/wasting among children. Practices such as child feeding, health care and hygiene also lead to better nutritional outcomes (Saha & Nambiar, 2017). Food security is thus a multi-dimensional concept and extends beyond the product availability, and demand for food. There has been a definite and significant paradigm shift in the concept of food security from mere macro level availability and stability to micro level household food insecurity, and also from an assessment of energy intake to measures and indicators of malnutrition (Ittyerah, 2015).

According to the FAO's food security report, micronutrient and Vitamin A deficiency were the prime determinants to child health and nutrition in India (FAO, 2015). It is increasingly being recognised that food security and nutrition are foundations for development. Nutritional status of children was used as one of the key indicators for poverty reduction in the framework of the Millennium Development Goals (MDGs). This reflects the insight that policies, programmes and processes to improve nutrition outcomes have a role to play in poverty reduction and global development (UNSNC, 2004). The main determinants of food insecurity in India today are the shrinking of agrarian and informal sector incomes and poverty. (Chakravarty

& Dand, 2005). In the MDGs, Hunger and Poverty were lumped together in MDG1–as if solving one would solve the other. So much has been learned about nutrition since that time, and the SDGs treat the issue of poverty separately from Food and Nutrition Security as SDG1 and SGD2 (SDGs, 2015).

Child growth and development: Globally approximately 162 million children under the age of 5 years are affected by stunting and 52 million children are severely wasted, and nearly half (48%) of the world's stunted children live in South Asia (WHO, 2012). About one-quarter of children under age five are stunted. Further, an estimated 101 million children under five years of age were underweight, or approximately 16% of children under 5—the children who suffer from wasting face a markedly increased risk of death. According to the latest available data, 52 million or 8% children under five years of age were moderately or severely wasted and more than 29 million children under 5, an estimated 5%, suffered from severe wasting (WHO, UNICEF, World Bank, 2012). Globally around 69 lakh children (6.9 million) died in the year 2011 before reaching their first birthday with five countries *viz.* India, Nigeria, Democratic Republic of Congo, Pakistan, and China collectively accounting for half of these deaths. India alone accounted for about 20% of these deaths. Similarly, India carries the highest share of neonatal deaths in the world, with around 30% of the global neonatal deaths (WHO, UNICEF, World Bank, 2012). The global child mortality rate (under-five mortality rate) decreased by 41.3% (from 87 in 1990 to 51 per thousand live births in 2011) but at a faster pace in India, i.e. by 46.5% (from 114 to 61 per thousand live births during the same period). Furthermore, the global neonatal mortality rate (NMR) decreased by 31% (from 32 in 1990 to 22 in 2011) and at a similar pace in India, i.e. by 32% (from 47 to 32 during the same period) (Planning Commission, 2012-17). According to RSOC 2013-14 report, among 0-59 months old children in India, 39% are stunted, 17% severely stunted, 15% wasted, 5% severely wasted, 29% underweight and 10% are severely underweight. India has made progress towards the international hunger targets, but it still has the second-highest estimated number (194.6 million) of undernourished people in the world (Ministry of Women and Child Development, 2013-14). The all-India Poverty Head Count Ratio (PHCR-percentage below the national poverty line) declined by 15 percentage points from 37.2% in 2004-05 to 21.9% in 2011-12. The percentage of people below the national poverty line has already narrowed down to a level less than half of its position in 1990, in 2011-12 itself, at all India level and for rural and urban areas, ahead of the MDG target year of 2015. Children are the worst sufferers of poverty and malnourishment among children is a significant indicator of food insecurity (Ministry of Statistics and Program Implementation, 2015).

In India where a very few children with developmental delays are identified before starting school, by which time significant delays already might have occurred, and opportunities for treatment might have been missed, the prevalence of developmental delay in children under 2 years of age is 1.5-2.5% (Nair et. al, 2009, Poon, et. al, 2010).

Various Indices for Assessing Food Security and Child Growth and Development

The Human Development Index (HDI) is a summary measure of achievements in key dimensions of human development: a long and healthy life, access to knowledge and a decent standard of living. The HDI is the geometric mean of normalised indices for each of the three dimensions. The HDI is based on a cut off point defined by a level of income regarded as adequate for a reasonable standard of living and a reasonable fulfilment of human capabilities (Human Development Report, 2015).

The Global Hunger Index (GHI) is designed to inform the state of hunger globally in a comprehensive way. It highlights the successes and failures in the progress of hunger reduction and provides information on the drivers of hunger. To capture the multidimensionality of FNS, the GHI combines four component indicators into one index: undernourishment, child wasting, child stunting, and child mortality (International Food Policy Research Institute, 2014). The GHI is used to rank 120 developing countries, which are assigned to five categories based on arbitrarily selected cut-off points: low (≤4.9), moderate (5.0-9.9), serious (10.0-19.9), alarming (20.0-29.9), and extremely alarming (≥30) (Masset, 2011) (Grember et. al, 2011).

The Global Food Security Index (GFSI) considers the core issues of affordability, availability, and quality & safety across a set of 113 countries. Its main objective is to create a quantitative approach to evaluating the dynamics of food systems and the ability of countries to feed their populations. The index is a dynamic quantitative and qualitative benchmarking model, constructed from 28 unique indicators, that measures these drivers of food security across both developing and developed countries (Food Security Index, 2016). These indicators reflect not only food availability, but food access (e.g., food consumption as a proportion of total household expenditure, the proportion of the population living under or close to the global poverty line, food prices) and diet quality (e.g., dietary availability of micronutrients)[27]. The GFSI is recalculated quarterly based on shifts in food price data (Jones et al., 2013).

27. https://foodsecurityindex.eiu.com/

Table-1: India's Rank in Various Global Indices of Development

S. No.	Index	Rank	Agency, Year
1	HDI	130/188	UNDP, 2015
2	GHI	80/104	IFPRI, 2014
3	Global Food Security Index	75/113	EIU & Dupont, 2016

Source: UNDP, 2015; IFPRI, 2014 and EIU & Dupont, 2016

Underweight among children under five is used extensively as an indicator of food insecurity. Anthropometric assessment is one of the most widely used methods for assessment of nutritional status both at the community level and for the individuals because of the relative ease and reproducibility of measurements, availability of standards based on normal population for comparison and demonstrated an association between abnormal measurements and clinical illnesses. Height is influenced by genetic and environmental factors, including dietary intake and stunting reflects the cumulative impact of past undernutrition (Ramachandran, 2013).

The ***WHO Child Growth Standards*** are widely used to assess growth in children. The three most commonly used anthropometric indices to assess their growth status are weight-for-height, height-for-age and weight-for-age. Low weight for height (wasting or thinness) is often associated with acute starvation and severe disease and may also be the result of a chronic unfavourable condition. Provided there is no severe food shortage, the prevalence of wasting is usually below 5%, even in poor countries. A prevalence exceeding 5% is alarming. On the severity index, prevalence between 10-14% are regarded as serious, and above or equal 15% as critical. Low height-for-age (stunting) reflects a process of failure to reach linear growth potential as a result of suboptimal health and nutritional conditions. High levels of stunting are associated with poor socioeconomic conditions and increased risk of frequent and early exposure to adverse conditions such as illness and inappropriate feeding practices. Weight-for-age reflects body mass relative to chronological age. It is influenced by both the height of the child (height-for-age) and his or her weight (weight-for-height), and its composite nature makes interpretation complex (WHO, 2009).

The ***Child Development Index (CDI)*** is made up of three indicators of three areas of child well-being: Health, Nutrition and Education. The Child Development Index shows that, globally, from 1990 to 2006, children's well-being has improved by about 34%. *South Asia* made less progress compared with these other regions—a 32% improvement. The regional performance of South Asia has been on a descending scale as India accounts for almost three-quarters of all the children in this region).[28]

28. https://hetv.org/resources/child-development-index.pdf

Economic growth averaged around 7% annually from 2000 to 2006, which indicates a progressive approach. However, the child malnutrition indicator displayed limited progress, which fell by only 14%. Nearly half of all children under five in India are underweight, representing 40% of the world's malnourished children, thereby attributing to South Asia's poor performance (The Child Development Index, 2008).

Global Developmental Delay (GDD) is the "significant delay in the acquisition of milestones or skills in two or more domains of development observed in a child" (Gross and fine motor, language, cognitive, personal/social interactions and activities of daily living) (American Academy of Neurology).

The commonly used ***developmental assessment tools*** that are used in India are Baroda Developmental Screening Test, Trivandrum Developmental Screening Chart, Developmental Assessment Scale for Indian Infant, Indian Adaptation of Vineland Social Maturity Scale and Indian adaptation of Stanford Binet Test.

Various Programs of Govt. of India To Improve Food Security, Child Growth And Development

The Government has accorded high priority to the issue of malnutrition in the country and is implementing several schemes/programmes under different Ministries/Departments through State Governments/UT Administrations under multi-sectoral approach for accelerated action on the determinants of malnutrition in targeting nutrition in schemes/programmes of all the sectors. The schemes/programmes include the Integrated Child Development Services (ICDS), National Health Mission (NHM), National Policy on Early Childhood Care and Education (ECCE), Mid Day Meal Scheme (MDM), Rajiv Gandhi Schemes for Empowerment of Adolescent Girls (RGSEAG) namely SABLA, Indira Gandhi Matritva SahyogYojna (IGMSY) as direct targeted interventions. Besides, indirect multi-sectoral interventions include Targeted Public Distribution System (TPDS), Mahatma Gandhi National Rural Employment Guarantee Scheme (MGNREGS), Swachh Bharat Abhiyan, National Rural Drinking Water Programme etc. Newborn and Child Health interventions include Facility Based Newborn Care (FBNC) under which Janani Shishu Suraksha Karyakram (JSSK) and Navjaat Shishu Suraksha Karyakram (NSSK) are being implemented. All these schemes address one or other aspect of nutrition (Ministry of Women and Child Development)[29]

The specific interventions targeted towards the vulnerable groups of children below 6 years include the programmes of Ministry of Women and Child Development-the Integrated Child Development Services (ICDS) Scheme which provides a comprehensive package of services encapsulating integrated provisions for health,

29. http://www.wcd.nic.in/

nutrition and stimulation to support cognitive; physical, motor, emotional and socio-personal development (WCD, 2017[30]; Lokshin, Gupta, Gragnolati, &Ivaschenko, 2005).

Among the several steps undertaken by the Government of India to increase productivity of agriculture[31] schemes such as Rashtriya Krishi Vikas Yojana (RKVY), National Food Security Mission (NFSM), Development and Strengthening of Infrastructure facilities for Production and Distribution of Quality Seed, National Horticulture Mission (NHM), Rainfed Area Development Programme (RADP), Integrated Scheme of Oilseeds, Pulses, Oil Palm and Maize (ISOPOM), Gramin Bhandaran Yojana are prominent. Also, Government has also improved the availability of farm credit; implemented debt waiver; introduced better crop insurance schemes; increased Minimum Support Price (MSP), improved marketing infrastructure, etc. [32]Further, in order to provide food security to the people by ensuring availability of food at affordable prices, the Government has enacted the National Food Security Act, recently. The National Food Security Act is a historic initiative for ensuring food and nutritional security to the people. It gives the right to the people to receive an adequate quantity of foodgrains at affordable prices (Karhad, 2014).

Strategies to Improve the Scenario of Child Growth and Development in India

Early child development (ECD) is the foundation of human capital formation; has the highest rate of return in economic development and is the most cost-effective way to reduce poverty and to foster economic growth. Concerns have been raised that beginning an ECD program at age 3 is too late, especially for children who are considered at high risk. Furthermore, neuroscience shows that when a child receives an intervention as an infant or toddler, the brain is more receptive than when the intervention is delivered at ages 3 and 4 (Young & Richardson, 2007).

Malnutrition, especially undernutrition in the Indian population (rural, tribal or urban) can be attributed mainly to ignorance. Therefore, efforts should be made to educate the population and coordinate with nutrition-specific interventions. This alone can enhance their domestic production, dietary diversity, frequency of healthy food consumption patterns and in turn, improve their nutritional status. For rural communities, promotion of Agri-Nutri-Health concept individually as well as through existing government programme is the need of the hour to improve food security in respect to address the persistent undernutrition (Saha and Nambiar, 2017).

30. http://www.wcd.nic.in/,
31. http://agriculture.gov.in/)
32. https://indolinkenglish.wordpress.com/tag/agriculture/page/11/

There is growing recognition that investments in early education, maternal-child attachment and nurturance, and more creative nutrition initiatives are critical to helping break the cycle of poverty (R. Prakash Upadhyay, 1st December, 2011).

An educational intervention implemented based on locally accessible, affordable and acceptable resources in the rural areas in West Bengal showed that the intervention improved caregivers knowledge, food selection, responsive feeding, IYCF practices and hygiene behaviours as well as children's physical growth (Saha et al., 2015). Breastfeeding and appropriate complementary feeding are essential to ensure the healthy growth of infants and young children (Léon Carva *et al.* 2002). Appropriate practices and key nutrient-dense local foods need to be highlighted and promoted in this district to maximize the potential growth and development of all children. Adequate nutrition is not enough to promote optimal child development. Child development is related to parental education and is also dependent upon cognitive stimulation, sensitivity and responsiveness, and attachment with the caregiver (Shonkoff, 2003). Interventions to improve infant-feeding hold the promise of reducing malnutrition among these children. The success of training in communication and counselling skills among health workers as well as care givers in improving the nutritional status of young children is also necessary.

Research shows that early intervention treatment services can greatly improve a child's development. Early intervention services help children from birth through 3 years of age learn important skills. Services include therapy to help the child talk, walk, and interact with others (HCS Learning Centre, 2015). Early intervention can be very specific depending on the nature and severity of developmental delay (Rapee, 2013). Co-occurring risk factors such as stunting and lack of stimulation should be addressed together for maximum effects, such as combining nutrition, responsive child feeding, and child-stimulation interventions (Campbellet al., 2002). Cognitive caregiving stimulation is one of four key factors in need of urgent intervention in developing countries (Walker et al., 2007).

Transforming the Integrated Child Development Scheme (ICDS) into an intervention that effectively combats undernutrition will yield huge benefits for India, both in terms of human development and economic returns. The focus should be on those ICDS components that directly address the most important causes of undernutrition in India (sensitive nutrition interventions), specifically improving mothers' feeding and caring behaviour, improving household water and sanitation, strengthening the referral to the health system and providing micronutrients (Lokshin et al., 2005). Besides the existing response to malnutrition in India (food-based interventions), emphasis on schemes addressing the other determinants of malnutrition has to be made. The World Bank suggests to focus on the girl child and provide more funding for the poorest and most undernourished states of India (Young & Richardson, 2007).

Due to a shortage of trained early intervention tool professionals in India or available professionals are situated in big towns and cities, the developmentally delayed population in the rural communities have been neglected. Thus, in rural and more disadvantaged areas of India, supervision of trained professionals is required along with an easy, comprehensive and time efficient tool to measure the progress of a child who is receiving the intervention (Das & Singh, 2013, Lakhan et al., 2013). This promotion of development and expansion of ICDS programme to support early child development can be done by maximizing the quality of early child development programmes, promoting multi-sectoral integration and prioritising monitoring and assessment (Engle et al., 2011).

Innovations are required to strengthen the public distribution system to curb the inclusion and exclusion errors and increase the range of commodities for people living in very poor conditions. It is essential that the government puts forth action plans to increase domestic food grain production, raise consumer incomes to buy food and make agriculture remunerative (Lakshminarayanan, 2011).

Six common interventions that are both scalable and significantly improve child health and nutrition identified as under:

- To create sustainable ways of ensuring that communities are more educated about home-based care practices as well as more proactive in their health-seeking behaviour.
- To ensure a systemic shift in prioritising child health and nutrition within the public system.
- To create a policy environment that is in tune with the realities of urban slums, and thereby enables effective implementation of the policy.
- To link communities with the appropriate points in the public healthcare system and thereby better leverage the existing system without overburdening hospitals.
- To inform policy, create successful pilots and be the basis for roll out and scaling up of government schemes.
- To provide child health and nutrition services in marginalised slum communities where the public healthcare infrastructure is inadequate or ineffective (Dasta & Piramal, 2011).

Poverty alleviation programmes need to be re-oriented, and focus needs to be shifted to the workers in the informal sector by providing decent wages and healthy working conditions. It should be ensured that nutritional objectives should be an integral part of all the poverty alleviation programmes (Upadhyay & Palanivel, 2011).

Conclusion

It is imperative that the archaic policies need to be reframed and implemented seriously in order to improve living conditions, which will subsequently alleviate poverty. Interventions should focus on the first thousand days in order to reduce the risk of undernutrition and developmental delay. Community-based approaches need to be adopted, which should be facilitated by effective policy implementation. In order to ensure food security and development, the government can take requisite steps to ensure progress in industrial as well as agricultural sectors.

References

1. American Academy of Neurology. Testing for the cause of Global Developmental Delay. Retrieved from: http://tools.aan.com/professionals/practice/guidelines/guideline_summaries/Global_Devlopmental_Delay_Patients.pdf
2. Bornstein, M.H., (2006). Parenting Science and Practice. Handbook of Child Psychology, (4) pp: 893-949. New York: Wiley.
3. Campbell, F.A., Ramey, C.T., Pungello, E., Sparling, J., & Miller-Johnson, S. (2002). Early childhood education: Young adult outcomes from the Abecedarian Project. Applied Developmental Science, 6(1), 42-57.
4. Chakravarty, S. &Dand, S.A. (2005). Food Security in India: Causes and Dimensions. Indian Institute of Management, Ahmedabad, Research and Publication Department.
5. Chilton, M., Chyatte, M., & Breaux, J. (2007).The negative effects of poverty & food insecurity on child development. Indian Journal of Medical Research, 126(4), 262.
6. Das, A., & Singh, A. (2013). Training needs of secondary regular education teachers to implement inclusive education in Delhi, India. In Society for Information Technology & Teacher Education International Conference (Vol. 2013, No. 1, pp. 5003-5003).
7. Dasra&Piramal (2011).Nourishing our future, tackling child malnutrition in urban slums.
8. Economic Intelligence Unit (2016).Global Food Security Index 2016. Retrieved from: http://foodsecurityindex.eiu.com/
9. Engle, P.L., & Black, M.M. (2008). The effect of poverty on child development and educational outcomes. Annals of the New York Academy of Sciences, 1136(1), 243-256.
10. FAO, (2006).Policy briefs. Agricultural and Development Economics Division: Food Security Programme: http://www.foodsecinfoaction.org/
11. FAO, (2015).State of Food Insecurity in the World. Retrieved from: http://www.fao.org/publications/sofi/en/
12. Government of India (2013).Twelfth Five Year Plan.Planning Commission.Retrieved from: http://planningcommission.gov.in/plans/planrel/12thplan/pdf/12fyp_vol3.pdf
13. Grebmer et al., (2011). 2011 Global hunger index: the challenge of hunger: Taming price spikes and excessive food price volatility. (1st ed.). Bonn: Welthungerhilfe.

14. HCS Learning Centre (2015). Retrieved from: http://asimplechoicehcs.com/learning-center/intellectual-disability/
15. Human Development Report Office (2015). Sustaining Human Progress: Reducing Vulnerabilities and Building Resilience. United Nations Development Programme.
16. International Food Policy Research Institute (2014). Global Hunger Index: The Challenge of Hidden Hunger Report, 2014. Washington D.C.
17. Ittyerah, A.C. (2013). Food security in India: issues and suggestions for effectiveness. Indian Institute of Public Administration, New Delhi.
18. Jones, A.D., Ngure, F.M., Pelto, G., & Young, S.L. (2013). What are we assessing when we measure food security? A compendium and review of current metrics. Advances in Nutrition: An International Review Journal, 4(5), 481-505.
19. Karhad, B.D., (2014). Food Security in India: Issues and measures. Indian Journal of Applied Research, 4(4), 26-29.
20. Lakhan, R., Mario, A., Qureshi, F.N., & Hall, M.L. (2013). Early intervention services to children with developmental delay in poor resource settings in India. Nepal Journal of Medical Sciences, 2(2), 149-155.
21. Lakshminarayanan, S., (2011). Role of government in public health: Current scenario in India and future scope. Journal of Family and Community Medicine, 18(1), 26.
22. Léon-Carva N., Lutter C., Ross J. & Martin L. Quantifying the Benefits of Breastfeeding: A Summary of the Evidence. PAHO (Pan American Health Organisation): Washington, DC. 2002.
23. Lokshin, M., Das Gupta, M., Gragnolati, M., &Ivaschenko, O. (2005). Improving child nutrition? The integrated child development services in India. Development and Change, 36(4), 613-640.
24. Masset, E., (2011). A review of hunger indices and methods to monitor country commitment to fighting hunger. Food policy, 36, S102-S108.
25. Ministry of Statistics and Program Implementation (2015).Millennium Development Goals India Country Report 2015.Government of India. Retrieved from: http://mospi.nic.in/Mospi_New/upload/mdg_26feb15.pdf
26. Ministry of Women and Child Development (2013-14). Rapid Survey on Children—RSOC.Government of India. Retrieved from: http://wcd.nic.in/sites/default/files/RSOC%20National%20Report%202013-14%20Final.pdf
27. Ministry of Women and Child Development.Towards a New Dawn-.Government of India.Retrieved from: http://motherchildnutrition.org/resources/pdf/mcn-the-governments-efforts-to-fight-malnutrition.pdf
28. Nair, M.K.C., George, B., Padmamohan, J., Sunitha, R.M., Resmi, V.R., Prasanna, G.L., & Leena, M.L. (2009). Developmental delay and disability among under-5 children in a rural ICDS Block. Indian Pediatr, 46(Suppl 1), s75-8.
29. Nutrition, I.C. (2013). The Achievable Imperative for Global Progress New York. NY United Nations Children's Fund.
30. Pelto G.H., Santos I., Gonçalves H., Victora C., Martines J., Habicht J.P. Nutrition counselling training changes physician behaviour and improves caregiver knowledge acquisition. J Nutr. 2004; 134(2): 357-362.

31. Poon, J.K., Larosa, A.C., & ShashidharPai, G. (2010). Developmental delay: timely identification and assessment. Indian paediatrics, 47(5), 415-422.
32. Ramachandran, P. (2013). Food & nutrition security: Challenges in the new millennium. The Indian journal of medical research, 138(3), 373.
33. Rapee, R.M., (2013). The preventative effects of a brief, early intervention for preschool-aged children at risk for internalising: follow-up into middle adolescence. Journal of Child Psychology and Psychiatry, 54(7), 780-788.
34. Saha C., RoyChowdhary A., Nambiar V.S. (2015). Effect of personalised counselling as a tool for behaviour change communication for improving the nutritional status and IYCF practices of children(0-5years) in under five clinics and day care centre, south 24 Parganas, West Bengal. International Journal of Food and Nutritional Sciences, 4 (3): 1-11.
35. Saha C. & Nambiar V.S., (2017). Can food availability and accessibility result in better food utilisation? A cross-sectional study on food security indicators to address the persistent undernutrition in rural Vadodara. International Journal of Applied Biology and pharmaceutical technology, 8 (3): 36-42.
36. Save the Children (2008) The Child Development Index: Holding governments to account for children's well-being. Save the Children. Retrieved from: https://hetv.org/resources/child-development-index.pdf
37. Roy S.K., Fuchs G.J., Mahmud Z., Ara G., Islam S., Shafique S. et al. Intensive nutrition education with or without supplementary feeding improves the nutritional status of moderately-malnourished children in Bangladesh. J Health PopulNutr. 2005; 23(4): 320-330.
38. Saloojee H., De Maayer T., Garenne M., Kahn K. What's new? Investigating risk factors for severe childhood malnutrition in a high HIV prevalence South African setting. Sc and J. Public Health Suppl. 2007; 69: 96-106.
39. SGDs (2015).Sustainable development Goals. http://www.undp.org/content/undp/en/home/sustainable-development-goals.html
40. Shonkoff, J.P. (2003). From neurons to neighbourhoods: old and new challenges for developmental and behaviouralpediatrics. Journal of Developmental & BehavioralPediatrics, 24(1), 70-76.
41. Townsend, Robert. 2015. Ending poverty and hunger by 2030 : an agenda for the global food system. Washington, D.C. : World Bank Group. http://documents.worldbank.org/curated/en/700061468334490682/Ending-poverty-and-hunger-by-2030-an-agenda-for-the-global-food-system
42. UNSCN (2004).5th Report on the world nutrition. Nutrition for improved development outcomes. Geneva.
43. UNICEF, New York; WHO, Geneva; The World Bank, Washington, DC; (2012) Levels and trends in child malnutrition: UNICEF-WHO-The World Bank joint child malnutrition estimates. (UNICEF, New York; WHO, Geneva; The World Bank, Washington, DC
44. Upadhyay, R.P., & Palanivel, C. (2011).Challenges in achieving food security in India. Iranian journal of public health, 40(4), 31.

45. Walker, S.P., Wachs, T.D., Gardner, J.M., Lozoff, B., Wasserman, G.A., Pollitt, E., ...& International Child Development Steering Group. (2007). Child development: risk factors for adverse outcomes in developing countries. The lancet, 369(9556), 145-157.
46. WHO (2009). WHO Child Growth Standards: Growth velocity based on weight, length, and head circumference: Methods and development. WHO Multicentre Growth Reference Study Group. Geneva.
47. WHO (2012). Trends in Maternal Mortality from 1990 to 2010. WHO, UNICEF, UNFPA and The World Bank Estimates. Retrieved from: http://apps.who.int/iris/bitstream/10665/44874/1/9789241503631_eng.pdf
48. Young, M.E., & Richardson, L.M. (Eds.). (2007). Early child development from measurement to action: a priority for growth and equity. World Bank Publications.

□

16

Conceptualising the Components of Pregnancy-Specific Stress through Qualitative Investigation among Pregnant Working and Non-Working Women in the Indian Context

—*Urmila Rani Srivastava, Pooja Sahu, and Madhu Jain*

Abstract

Pregnancy is an event that changes many perspective of women's life, and researchers have consistently shown that stress during pregnancy can have an extensive number of maternal as well as neonatal adverse effects. The study was conducted in two stages. Semi-structured interview was conducted for stage 1 (n=24) of the study at the third trimester of pregnancy. Data collection and analysis occurred concurrently to identify the key themes of the study. In stage II, all emerged themes and subthemes were given to another sample of working (n=35) and non-working (n=35) women. Nine major themes, along with their subthemes, had emerged from the analysis of stage I of the study. Analysis of stage II of the study revealed that the emerged themes were highly stressful for pregnant working and non-working women. The findings of the present study revealed that to get individual solution for pregnant women should be aware of the importance of psychosocial correlates of maternal health and well-being. This study is an important addition to the existing literature on pregnancy-specific stress and has the potential to provide useful information for clinicians and practitioners.

Introduction

Pregnancy is an event that changes many perspective of women's life. During pregnancy, a woman prepares mentally for permanent life changes and new responsibilities after the birth of the infant. Pregnancy-specific stress can be described as maternal fear or anxiety related to pregnancy outcomes and the experience of the labour, the ability to care of a new infant and the health and well-being of the infant (Dunkel-Schetter, & Lobel, 2012; Rini, Dunkel-Schetter, Wadhwa, Sandman, 1999).

Pregnancy-specific stress is defined as "the imbalance that a pregnant woman feels when she cannot cope with demands, which is expressed both behaviourally and physiologically" (Ruiz & Fullerton, 1999). It is well documented that stress during pregnancy can have an extensive number of maternal as well as neonatal adverse effects.

Pregnancy-specific stress may be a more powerful contributor to birth outcomes than general stress. This is a promising area for research on these adverse birth outcomes, because it may be possible to intervene with women who have high levels of pregnancy-related stress and relieve some of their worries and concerns, thereby reducing pre-term birth and low birth weight. Pregnant women experience stress originating from a variety of pregnancy-specific issues, including physical symptoms and changes, physiological, social and emotional changes, financial demands, parenting concerns, changes in relationships with significant others or relationship strains, bodily changes, changes in body image, medical problems, anxiety about labour and delivery, concerns about birth, parenting competency and concerns about the baby's health (Alderdice & Lynn 2011; Furber, Garrod, Maloney, Lovell & McGowan 2009; Lobel et al., 2008;Yali & Lobel 1999).

Thus, it is noticeable that pregnancy itself presents unique psychological and social challenges and measuring stress during pregnancy is relatively an unrecognised methodological issue (Dipietro, Ghera, Costigan & Hawkins, 2004; Goldenberg & Gotlieb, 2002; Rini et al., 1999). Thus, failure to measure pregnancy-specific stress can underestimate maternal distress. Pregnancy-specific measures have not been commonly included in studies on birth outcomes related to pre-term delivery and low birth weight (Dipietro et al., 2004; Geller, 2004).

In general, many studies have used Life Events Inventory (Cochrane, and Robertson, 1973), General Health Questionnaire (GHQ) (Schmitz, Kruse & Tress, 1999) to measure stress and such instruments measured general stress only which is not sufficient for measuring pregnancy-specific stress. Few studies have used a qualitative approach in investigating the experience and attitude of the women, especially during their pregnancy. While there has been increasing research interest in pregnancy-specific stress of women, few studies have yielded detailed insights into the views and experience of pregnant working and non-working women. Therefore there is a need to identify dimensions of pregnancy-specific stress among pregnant working women and non-working women in the Indian context. With this background, the major objectives of the study were:

To identify the components of stress during the **third trimester of** pregnancy among working and non-working Indian women.

To gather a list of stressors from pregnant women asking about 'difficulties' or stressful situation.

The qualitative approach described in this study aimed to explore the views and experiences of during their entire course of pregnancy using a flexible and responsive approach. The texts were indexed and mapped based on recurring themes.

The inclusion-exclusion criteria of the participants that were taken into consideration for both the stages of the study were as follows:

The inclusion criteria of the pregnant women were included in the study are:

1. The age of pregnant women between 20-35 years.
2. Married or in a stable relationship at the time of recruitment.
3. Conception achieved normally.
4. Able to read, write and understand Hindi or English language easily.
5. The sample included women in the early third trimester of pregnancy (28-30 weeks of gestation) with single intrauterine pregnancy.

The exclusion criteria of participants were:

Women were excluded from the study if they are not fluent in English or Hindi language.

Women using drugs or using medication with the risk for the fetus were excluded.

Women with major physical, social or psychosocial complications of the pregnancy (such as spontaneous abortion, vaginal bleeding, hypertensive disorders, and gestational diabetes) were excluded from the study.

Women with chronic hypertension, chronic diabetes mellitus, cardiopathy, actively-treated epilepsy or thyroid disease or as being at risk for congenital malformation were excluded from the study.

Women who had a prior miscarriage or having undergone infertility treatment were excluded from the study.

Plan of the Study

This study was conducted in two stages.

Stage 1 of the study

The aim of stage I of the study was to increase the understanding that how working and non-working women experience Pregnancy Specific Stress by using their own words as a starting point and to indicate ways in which practice and care might be improved. This study identified the components of pregnancy-specific stress by capturing the personal perspective and experiences of pregnant women during their third trimester of pregnancy. The results of this stage I of the study were utilised in developing initial categories and overarching themes about pregnancy-specific stress.

Methods

Sample and Procedure

Initially, 60 pregnant women in the third trimester in the pregnancy were contacted out of which 24 were eligible for the study. Out of these 24 participants, 15 were non-working, and nine were working. The age range of the participants was 20-35 years with singleton and low-risk pregnancy. They were recruited from Sir Sundar Lal Hospital, IMS, BHU, Varanasi. The researcher contacted the participants personally and described the aims and designs of the study. A semi-structured questionnaire which contained more detailed questions about women's views and stressful experiences during their pregnancy was given individually to each participant. The aim was to obtain a detailed exploration of women's view is using a flexible and responsive approach. Subjects self-report was a major source of information. Specifically, the following open-ended questions were used in the study.

How do you feel about your pregnancy?

How are things going on with your pregnancy?

Has your lifestyle changed with pregnancy?

What is your understanding about stress related to pregnancy?

How pregnancy made things difficult for you?

How is the relationship between the pregnant women and her family, peer and significant others characterised?

Are there economic and other environmental factors that is characterised as stressful to pregnant working and non-working women during pregnancy?

Has pregnancy changed your career or job-related goals?

Do you have any other issue related to pregnancy?

The questionnaire also comprised of various sections that include eliciting data about basic demographic details such as age, education, occupation, the structure of the family, income, parity, smoking, drinking, previous history of pregnancy and other medical problems during pregnancy. Informed consent was taken from the women before the interviews; their personal history was kept confidential. Participants were encouraged to discuss issues which in their opinion were most relevant to pregnancy distress. The intention was to obtain the experiences related to stress felt by pregnant working and non-working women since it is well known that psychological distress is often poorly recognised by clinicians (Gilbody, House & Sheldon, 2005). The collection of the data continued until no new dimension of pregnancy-specific was identified. Further, the content of the questionnaire was also utilised as a base to generate discussion on with probing to gain further understanding of experience during pregnancy.

Ethical issues: The approval for the study was obtained from the Research Governance Procedure followed at the study site of Institute of Medical Sciences (IMS) BHU Varanasi (UP) India. Written permission was obtained from the medical superintendent of IMS BHU.

Data Analysis

The research team organised data into categories that reflected symbolic domains of meaning, and within domains, relational patterns, and finally overarching themes. These themes and subthemes emerged from the information provided by both of the group working and non-working pregnant women.

The text responses to these questions were analysed qualitatively using thematic analysis, with initial codes then being used to create higher order categories (Carter, 2004). Coding was done to identify recurring themes, words, or ideas integral to the perception of stress with the intent to summarize categories of data described by the participants. The categories were refined in the course of reading and re-reading and continuously checking the data for counter-examples and alternatives. With each re-reading, new insights occurred, and it became possible to make associations and connections between different aspects of the data Dyer, Abrahams, Moekoena & Van-der Spuy, 2004; Peddie, van Teijlingen & Bhattacharya, 2005). The process was repeated with each set of responses. Quotations are used to illustrate the themes generated by the analysis, and to support the interpretations made (Henwood & Pidgeon, 1992). The research team regularly met to review the range of data, inspected contradictory data, and concerned about the possibility of symbolic meaning or social desirability underlying apparent discrepancies.

Researcher's notes and memos were kept throughout the fieldwork and coding of the data. Given that the present study was exploratory; all issues raised by any of the participants were treated as potentially important to inform future exploration using quantitative methodology.

Table-1: Major Themes and Sub-themes emerged in the study along with illustrative quotes in participants own words

S. N.	Major Themes	Sub-themes	Illustrative quotes
1.	Feeling regarding conception and pregnancy	1. Pleasurable feelings 2. Apprehensive about some miss-happening or problem during pregnancy	"Feelings of being pregnant make me happy, a good motivational point to know more about pregnancy and related experiences." "I am delighted to be pregnant and feel that God blessed us that we were able to conceive." "For me, pregnancy requires constant attention for the developing baby—I always fear that I will slip from the stairs or I will fall and my baby will be hurt. I try to take my mind off of these thoughts."
2.	Fear of medical testing, labour and delivery	Fear of medical testing	"The procedures of medical testing for ultrasound and HIV test terrify me. Earlier during blood tests or ultrasound, I became so nervous that my blood pressure tended to shoot up drastically". "the treatment and medical testing are physically very hard and almost emotionally unbearable."
		Fear about the mode of delivery	"I never think about my baby delivered through caesarean section. I want an easy and safe delivery."
		Excessive pain during delivery	"My labour will be prolonged and painful this mere thought frightens me." "I am in my third trimester of pregnancy, and am terrified of giving birth and the pain! I'm so excited, but very nervous". "I wanted a baby 'so' badly, and then once I got pregnant, I was scared to the process of the birth and pain delivery. I never told this to my husband, only my mother knew about it. As the time of delivery is reaching, I am more fearful about the process of delivery and pain".
		Apprehensive about receiving good medical care and management	"Unhygienic conditions are prevailing everywhere. I am anxious about medical care and facilities which I will be getting during delivery."

3.	Worries about the baby's sex physical appearance and health	Fear about the sex of the baby	"My mother-in-law and other family members deeply wish a male child. I do not know how they will react if I deliver a girl child".
		Fear of premature child birth	"I am always concerned about labour and child birth. Most of the time, I am preoccupied with thoughts related to the premature or unhealthy baby. —I do not want to do anything that is going to harm the baby".
		Physical appearance and health of the baby (baby may not be attractive and normal)	"The day I came to know that I am pregnant, I wish that my baby about a healthy and cute baby." "I am expecting my first child in about a month. From almost the beginning, I have had much anxiety about the baby's appearance and health. I've tried hard to not worry about these things but could not succeed." "A friend of mine had terrible results after delivery. Her baby born with a severe birth defect. Now, when I try to reassure myself that our baby will be OK, I have difficulty in reconciling that with their experiences."
		Movement of the baby	"I am always alert about the movements of the foetus. I am scared when not I feel the movements properly".
4	Financial stress due to pregnancy	Perceived financial pressure after delivery	"Our financial condition is not very sound. How I will manage my pregnancy, and other expenditures after delivery are big questions in front of me"
		Financial pressure on medical testing during pregnancy	My husband is in a private job. He has joined recently. Heavy expenditure on testing and medicines is creating lots of problems in my family. We are bound to curtail our other important expenditures."
5	Discomforts related to pregnancy-specific physical changes and symptoms	Work getting late due to pregnancy	"As I wake up in the morning, all my routine activities are getting late. I feel lots of exhaustion and morning sickness. For a prolonged period I am not able to do anything—I feel difficulty in performing even very simple tasks such as making tea or some other household chores."
		Difficulty in performing routine work due to pregnancy	"I am so heavier and bigger, and it is harder even to move, and everything has become very uncomfortable for me. I feel uneasiness all the time." "Physical symptoms of pregnancy irritate me and cause difficulties in my day to day work."

		Difficulty in performing a task such as bending, prolonged standing or sitting	"With the ongoing months of pregnancy, I am feeling difficulty in bending, standing straight for a prolonged period."
		Psychological and mood changes during pregnancy	"My mood gets very upset when I find difficulty in performing routine work."
		Lack of sound sleep	"Sleep has become a problem for methis days—many times I feel that I have not slept the whole night."
6.	Parenting concerns	Lack of discussion about baby related issues with husband and family members	
		Doubt about adequate nurturing of the infants leading to stress	"Of course, I become very upset and in floods of tears that how I grow up my baby. "When I first came to know that I am pregnant, I was very excited. Then, I kept asking myself if I could properly handle the baby or not."
7.	Lack of family and partner support during pregnancy		"Women do need much support during pregnancy. However, I am not fortunate enough. My husband used to say that you are just pregnant, not ill. He considers my problem as very normal features of pregnancy." "My pregnancy is easy for me because my mother and husband are helping me. They take care of me very much and also considerate about my worries. Support from my husband dilutes my problems." "My husband is very busy. I have to do it all alone and do not feel supported."
8.	Changes in the life style of self		"Cannot go out in the night time. Cannot do the things I used to perform when I was not pregnant. I do not have the freedom to go as I wish." "One of my best friends said that Ihad been changed during pregnancy. I lack my social circle and interaction".
9.	Career-related stressors	Continuation and maintaining of job and career after delivery	"I am conscious that I will have to put more effort into reviewing my career after this baby is born." "I am also career oriented and cannot imagine what it is going to be like not being at work."

		Difficulty in accommodating job and family responsibilities after delivery	"How can I be able to make a balance between work and family responsibilities will become a great challenge for me after delivery". "I and my husband both were working even when I was not pregnant: I found difficulty in accommodating work and family responsibilities. Now I am pregnant—I will get maternity leave for six months. I am apprehensive about what will happen when the maternity leave is over."
		Stress related to availing good day care or baby sitter	"For a working lady, day care or baby sitter is the need the hour. My main worry is how will I search good day care or baby sitter for my baby after it comes?"

Source: Author's results from the analysis

Stage 2 of the study

In order to get a broader view of the themes which emerged during the stage, I of the study were presented to another matched sample of pregnant women during their third trimester of pregnancy. Women were asked to read each theme and subtheme carefully and appraise on a three-point rating scale (Little or Low stress, Normal stress, and High Stress). They were asked to rate how severe each item has been for them. Thus, the stage-2 of the study was consistent with a complimentary approach in which qualitative and quantitative data were integrated during the later phases of analysis.

Sample Description

The sample of Stage 2 of the study was also recruited from Sir Sundar Lal Hospital, IMS, BHU, Varanasi and included seventy pregnant women out of which thirty-five were non-working and thirty-five women were working.

Table-2: Characteristics of the Sample of Stage 2 of the study (N=70)

Sample Description	Frequency	% of frequency
Age Group		
18-21	11	15.71
22-26	27	38.57
27-31	21	30.00
32-35	11	15.71

Type of Family		
Joint	47	67.14
Nuclear	23	32.86
Education		
0-8	8	11.42
10-12	19	27.42
Graduate	36	51.43
Post Graduate	7	10.00
No. of Previous Pregnancy		
0	36	51.42
1	21	30
2	10	14.28
3+	3	4.28

Source: Author's calculation

Table-3: Response of the participants (N=70) of stage-2 of the study on Major and Sub-dimensions emerged during the interview of working (n=35) and non-working (n=35) pregnant women

Themes/Sub-themes			Percentage of the women who mention the theme as-		
S.N	**Major themes**	**Sub-themes**	**Low stress**	**Normal stress**	**High stress**
1.	Feelings regarding conception and pregnancy	Pleasurable feelings	58 (82.86%)	10 (14.28%)	2 (2.86%)
		Apprehensive about some miss-happening or problem during pregnancy	4 (5.71%)	5 (7.14%)	61 (87.14%)
2.	Fear of medical testing, labour and delivery	Fear of medical testing	10 (14.29%)	18 (25.71%)	42 (60%)
		Fear about mode of delivery	15(21.43%)	5 (7.14%)	50 (71.41%)
		Excessive pain during delivery	30 (42.86%)	10 (14.29%)	30 (42.86%)
		Apprehensive about receiving good medical care and management	10 (14.28%)	25 (35.71%)	35 (50%)
3.	Worries about baby's sex, physical appearance and health	Fear about the sex of the baby	10 (14.29%)	18 (25.71%)	42 (60%)
		Fear of premature child birth	15 (21.42%)	20 (28.57%)	40 (57.14%)
		Physical appearance and health of the baby (baby may not be attractive and normal)	11 (15.71%)	17 (24.29%)	42(60%)
		Movement of the baby	8 (11.43%)	20 (28.57%)	42(60%)

4	Financial stress due to pregnancy	Perceived financial pressure after delivery	7(10%)	18(25.71%)	45 (64.28%)
		Financial pressure on medical testing during pregnancy	8 (11.43%)	20 (28.57%)	42(60%)
5.	Discomforts related to pregnancy-specific physical changes and symptoms	Work getting late due to pregnancy	5 (7.4%)	40 (57%)	25 (35.71%)
		Difficulty in performing routine work due to pregnancy	25 (35.71%)	28 (40%)	17(24.29%)
		Difficulty in performing a task such a bending, prolonged standing or sitting	11 (15.71%)	9 (12.85%)	50 (71.42%)
		Psychological and mood changes during pregnancy	15(21.43%)	17(24.29%)	38 (54.29%)
		Lack of sound sleep	20(28.57%)	25 (35.71%)	25 (35.71%)
6.	Parenting concerns	Lack of discussion about baby related issues with husband and family members	15 (21.43%)	19 (27.14%)	36 (51.42%)
		Doubt about adequate nurturing of the infants leading to stress	11(15.71%)	14(20%)	45(64.28%)
7.	Lack of family and partner support during pregnancy		5 (7.14%)	2 (2.86%)	63 (90%)
8.	Changes in life style of self		10(14.29%)	20(28.57%)	40 (57.14%)
9.	Career related stressors	Continuation and maintaining of job and career after delivery	7(20%)	5(14.29%)	23 (65.71%)
		Difficulty in accommodating job and family responsibilities after delivery	4(11.43%)	5(12.85%)	26(75.71%)
		Stress related to availing good day care or baby sitter	17(48.57%)	7(21.43%)	11(30%)

Source: Author's calculation

Results of Qualitative and Quantitative Analyses

During the stage I of the study, the researcher analysed 216 text messages written by 24 pregnant women during their third trimester of pregnancy. A total of nine major themes encompassing 22 subthemes were extracted from these data Table-2). During Stage 2 of the study, the themes were presented to another matched sample of pregnant women during their third trimester of pregnancy. Women were asked to read each theme and subtheme carefully and appraise on a three-point rating scale

(Little or Low stress, Normal stress, and High Stress). The most important themes that emerged from the qualitative analysis of stage 1 of the study and their quantitative interpretations at stage 2 of the study were as follows.

Theme-1 Feelings regarding conception and pregnancy

The first major theme that emerged from many women's responses was feelings regarding conception and pregnancy and further encompassed two major subthemes-pleasurable feelings and experiences during pregnancy and apprehension about some miss-happening or problem during pregnancy. The results of the quantitative analysis also revealed that 87% of the participants reported the feelings of high stress about some miss-happening or problem during pregnancy, while pleasurable feelings were regarded as an indicator of low or moderate stress by the majority of women. In their written messages, the pregnant women described their pleasant emotions related to their pregnancy. This was characterised by establishing a bond with the baby. While for some mothers, the sense of general feelings of stress related to a pregnancy, and related to a new life as a mother. Most of the pregnant women were afraid that involving any physical activity may have a harmful effect on their fetus. They revealed that involving any physical activity may have a harmful effect on their baby. On the one hand, the majority of the women reported pregnancy as a pleasurable experience and considered it as an important positive life event that transitioned them into adulthood and provided an opportunity for personal growth. They also expressed satisfaction and joy when they became aware of their pregnancy (Pop et al., 2011).

Theme-2 Fear of Medical Testing, Labour and Delivery and hospitalisation

The second major theme which has been emerged from the analysis is fear of medical testing, labour and delivery, which was further divided into four subthemes (Table-3). All these themes were appraised as highly stressful by the majority of the women during pregnancy and consistent with the previous research (Table-3). Nearly all the participants exhibited fear from medical testing, pain and caesarean mode of delivery.

In the Indian context, mostly the women and their family primarily focused on normal delivery because of complications and heavy expenditure incurred in caesarean delivery. Most of the pregnant women also tend to worry about medical testing and seeking good medical care during pregnancy. They also spoke of feeling dissatisfaction about the facilities in the hospital. Approximately half of the respondents indicated that there were no ways in which their fear of hospitalisation and management has been improved.

Theme-3 Worries about Baby's Sex, Physical Appearance and Health

The third major theme was related to worries about the sex of the baby, physical appearance and health of the baby. Under these four subthemes were identified, such as fear about the sex of the baby, fear about premature delivery, the physical appearance of the baby and movements of the baby. In answering the question about stress and worries during pregnancy, mostly the participants wished the male child to avoid probable negative reactions of their in-laws and other family members. Although, a very limited number of women showed their concern about the sex of the baby however, they perceived it as 'natural' and 'gift of God'. The institution of gender roles is started right after the birth of boys and girls. While boys are showered in love and affection and taught to be outgoing, receive better healthcare, and respected, girls are encouraged to be more introverted and be homely. A common Hindu wedding blessing given amongst Indian women is "May you be the mother of a hundred sons". Thus, the desire to have a male child was a subtheme exclusively reported by some of the Indian women. In India, there is always a sex preference for male because daughters are seen as an expense due to the traditions of paying dowries when daughters marry. Some researchers also found that some pregnant women were very much concerned about the birth of a girl child (Kazi, Fatmi, Hatcher, Niaz & Aziz, 2009). It is clear from the above discussion that male and female children are often treated differently, with girls regarded as less valuable in some families leading to foetal sex determination and selective sex abortion by a medical professional.

The second subtheme was found the fear of premature childbirth. Many studies also reported in their study that women were especially worried about pre-term delivery (Alderdice & Lynn, 2011; Wang, Faan & Billings, 2011;Yali & Lobel, 1999). The third subtheme emerged Physical appearance and health of the baby (baby may not be attractive and normal). Participants discussed that the health of the baby is the most concerning issue for them. Many studies also focused that health and physical appearance of the baby is major stress factor for pregnant women (Alderdice & Lynn, 2011; Di Pietro et al., 2004; Melender, 2002; Wang, et al., 2011). Movement of the baby was forth subtheme emerged in the present study, which was felt by many of the participants (Di Pietro et al., 2004).

Theme-4 Financial stress due to pregnancy

The fourth theme, which has been emerged in the study was financial pressure during pregnancy and after delivery included two subthemes (Table-3). Both these subthemes were rated as highly stressful by 60% of the participants. These findings are consistent with a number of previous studies (Green, Kafetsios, Statham, & Snowdon, 2003; Petersen, Paulitsch, Guethlin, Gensichen & Jahn 2009; Pop et al.,

2011; Somerville et al., 2014). In the Indian context, due to heavy expenditure, nearly all participants showed fear about the caesarean mode of delivery.

Theme-5 Discomforts Related To Pregnancy Specific Physical Changes and Symptoms

The fifth theme that emerged in the study is related to discomforts related to pregnancy-specific physical changes and symptoms with five important subthemes (Table-3). A handful of research has shown that the most common complaint in a group of low-risk women was 'normal discomforts of pregnancy (Di Pietro et al., 2004; Somerville et al., 2014). In many accounts, the impact of pregnancy discomforts on their well being was evident to the women themselves. The participants were aware of and generally gave importance to a 'healthy diet' for being physically active during pregnancy. Women reported that weight gain during pregnancy, causing difficulties in performing even the normal routine work. Personal health problems related to pregnancy were most frequently cited during pregnancy included sickness, morning sickness and dizziness. Many participants discussed that due to the increase in abdomen, they feel lots of problems in bending, prolong standing and sitting. This problem rose, especially in the third trimester of pregnancy. Participants expressed these changes in terms of "uneasiness, tiring, and exhausting and approximately physically unbearable".

Furthermore, some women also commented about their mood swings up and down and emotional sensitivity. Women also spoke of the impact of sleep deprivation on their health.

In conclusion these results revealed that women were most stressed about the difficulty in performing a task such as bending, prolonged standing or sitting and psychological and mood changes during pregnancy. While work getting late due to pregnancy and difficulty in performing routine work were two subthemes reported as moderate stress by the majority of the women. Some participants also commented about sound sleep (DiPietro et al., 2004).

Theme-6 Parenting Concerns

The sixth major theme emerged was related to parenting concerns, which further included two subthemes (table-3). The findings implicated that pregnancy and parenthood were considered as advantageous from a developmental perspective. However, some participants also reported their doubts about appropriate parenting concerns. These participants have also illustrated how certain difficult life situations make parenting problematic and difficult. Women who had their first pregnancy were seemed more worried about the proper nurturing of their baby.

Theme-7 Family and partner support during pregnancy

Seventh major themes emerged in the present study was family and partner support during pregnancy. Nearly all women spoke of an increased need for emotional and instrumental support from their partners and other family members. Further unavailability of social support was identified by many participants as major cause of pregnancy-specific stress. The support of their partner and family was also central in making the process of pregnancy easy for many women in terms of access to psychological services have assisted them in the course of their pregnancy. Participants who get support from their family and husband feel no stress about their pregnancy, but participants who did not get any type of support feel more stress. Women recognised that partners and family members often suggested, encouraged or facilitated, accessing additional support. Likewise, working women also discussed stress related to their workplace and support provided by their colleagues during pregnancy.

Theme-8 Changes in the life style of self

The eighth major theme that emerged in this study was changes in the life style of self. The antenatal period was often viewed as an opportunity to make positive lifestyle changes but formed some women; it becomes a reason for changes in their lifestyle. In their written messages, some participants were concerned about how they will manage their other outgoing, meeting with close family members. In many accounts, the impacts of changed lifestyle on their well-being were evident to the women themselves.

Theme-9 Career related stressors

Career-related stressors were the ninth and the last theme emerged from the data obtained from the group of working women (n=35) subdivided into three subthemes (table-3). Work was an issue for pregnant working women and their partners. Regarding career-related issues, some women were very serious about how they will manage their job after delivery. In describing how pregnancy changes their career and related goals, some women mentioned arousal related to work and family conflict. For the smooth progression of job and career, some working women who had nuclear family expressed an overwhelming desire for the baby sitter.

During a discussion with the participants, it was found that the participant who lives in a joint family feel very low or little stress as a comparison to who live in a nuclear family because in joint family women do not need to search baby sitter or day care. In conclusion, this study sought to explore the characteristics of stress specially experienced during pregnancy, and the results strongly reflect the findings of previous research, adding to their strength and transferability.

Discussion

The major objective of the present study was to identify the components of stress during pregnancy separately among working and non-working Indian women and to gather a list of stressors from pregnant women asking about 'difficulties' or stressful situation. This qualitative study has lent us some useful insights about features and components of pregnancy-specific stress in a sample of pregnant working and non-working women in the Indian context during their third trimester of pregnancy.

This study was conducted in two stages. The aim of stage I of the study was to identify the components of pregnancy-specific stress by capturing the personal perspective and experiences of pregnant women during their third trimester of pregnancy. While the stage II of the study was quantitative and concerned with the results of qualitative analysis of stage, I of the study revealed nine major themes along with their subthemes. These results strongly supported past research evidence (Alderdice & Lynn, 2011; Di Pietro et al., 2004; Melender, 2002; Pop et. al., 2011; Somerville et. al., 2014; Wang, et al., 2011;Yali & Label, 1999) The participants of the study frequently endorsed that having a baby is much more expensive nowadays. The medical bills mount for diagnostic testing and prenatal care, baby supplies, and other long term future financial concerns such as saving for the child's education, monetary pressure was major source of experienced stress. This finding is similar to the study of Yali and Lobel (1999) and Pop et al., (2011) who also reported that women were especially worried about pre-term delivery, physical symptoms, and labour and delivery, concern about financial issues and least concerned about changes in their relationship with and becoming attached to the newborn.

In a study on the development of an instrument for measuring stress during pregnancy among women, Wang et al., (2011) have reported four major factors of stress during pregnancy about concerns about baby and delivery, baby and post delivery, body image and career and lifestyle. These results strongly suggested that all these themes should be taken into consideration in understanding the nature of pregnancy-specific stress.

Although this study is supported by numerous stress and pregnancy research (Dunkel-schetter & Tanner, 2012; Mulder, et al., 2002), a key finding unique to this study is women's stressful perceptions about the sex of the baby. Wanting a male child emerged as an important predictor of pregnancy-specific stress in the South Asian context (Winkvist & Akhtar, 2000; Kazi, Fatmi, Hatcher, Niaz & Aziz, 2009). In a study on Pakistani women, Kazi et al., (2009) have also reported a concern about giving birth to a girl child as one of the major issues of stress for pregnant women. These findings demonstrated that the influence of Indian culture as the value placed on the gender of the child, the influence of family members and their socio-economic status and economic conditions of future motherhood. The influence of boy preference, much reported in South Asia (Patel, Rodrigues & De Souza, 2002; Winkvist & Akhtar, 2000) was confirmed in this qualitative investigation. In the Indian social system, the girl child has frequently been cited as a heavy economic drain on the family. This was partly due to the perception that most girls would ultimately be married and would not contribute economically to the family. Further, dowry payments made at the time of marriage is also a leading reason for boy preference.

The sixth critical theme and sub-theme about pregnancy-specific stress emerged in this qualitative investigation was discomforts related to pregnancy-specific physical changes and symptoms. The hormonal and physical changes of pregnancy result in enormous changes in a woman's body. The quantitative results revealed that difficulty in performing the routine task was endorsed as moderate stress and subthemes related to performing difficult tasks, Psychological and mood changes during pregnancy, and lack of sound sleep were endorsed as high stress by the majority of participants. A handful of past research has confirmed these Findings (Alderdice & Lynn, 2011; Di Pietro et al., 2004).

The 6th, 7th, and eighth theme emerged in the present study were related to Parenting concerns (lack of discussion about baby related issues with husband and family members, and doubt about adequate nurturing of the infants), lack of family and partner support, and changes in life style of self. All these themes were endorsed as highly stressful by the majority of participants. These themes are consistent with the reported dimensions of pregnancy-specific stress by (Di Pietro et al., 2004). These findings can be explained by the fact that Indian families today are facing lots of changes in their structure because of a decline in joint or extended families. Some of the husbands were unaware that their wives are alone carrying the burden of child birth. New mothers often stress over the many issues of parenting that they never concerned about before the pregnancy. Issues such as giving emotional bonding, providing care for an infant, finding a babysitter, the process of schooling, and their readiness to become a mother can easily cause mental stress during pregnancy.

Another most common reason for stress during pregnancy was the lack of family and partner support. Regarding social support, the women emphasised the need for providing quality care by spouse and family member. Women in this study felt at times isolated and expressed a wish for more support from peers and professionals. The findings collobrate with the results of Badr, Abdallah & Mahmoud, (2005) and Rondo et al., (2003). These authors have also found that lack of social support increase stress during pregnancy and predict IUGR and LBW.

It has been proposed that providing emotional and instrumental support, are protective by buffering the impact of life stress on the emotional well-being of the mother (Glazier, Elgar, Goel & Holzapfel, 2004). Overall, the evidence suggests that pregnant women need the support of family members, friends, and health professionals.

Pregnant women experience social and lifestyle changes during pregnancy as well. During pregnancy, it is common for a pregnant woman to develop a renewed motivation to look after her body for her baby. Caring for a new baby requires a sacrifice of sleep, expenses, and time. This often involves a few lifestyle changes during pregnancy. The lifestyle changes required in pregnancy means that activities such as drinking or smoking are no longer an option, and the extra rest needed in pregnancy can cut back on the energy available for time spent with friends; go out in the night time, and social circle and interaction.

Although, these social and lifestyle changes are necessary to stay healthy during pregnancy, but they are sometimes perceived as obstacles to their social life and interaction. Hence, the high-stress levels that come with anticipating the new baby can make it difficult to enjoy extracurricular activities. In the present study the majority of the participants expressed that they had previously been engaged in many social activities, and it was a shocking change to be unable to participate in many extracurricular activities suddenly. These results corroborate with the findings of Alderdice and Lynn (2011), who also suggested that pregnant women felt stressed about their changing relationship with other people due to pregnancy. Likewise, Wang et al. (2011) opined that pregnant women often feel stressed due to changes in their living pattern. Career-related stressors were the ninth, and the last theme emerged from the data obtained from the group of working women (n=35). In the present study, the majority of the participants of the study belong to middle reproduce age who often give topmost priority to their career-related issues. During these years the women may be juggling family, home and career responsibilities with resulting increases instress-related condition. In addition to the pressure associated with starting, developing and maintaining a career before delivery, a mismatch in expectations, feeling undervalued, discriminated and frustration in attaining a sense of achievement are common 'career' related stressors during and after pregnancy.

In conclusion, results showed that pregnant working women were highly concerned about career-related issues during pregnancy.

Contributions and Implications of the Study

To our knowledge, the current paper is among the first to report about pregnancy-specific stress issues in the Indian context, which was gathered through close interaction with pregnant women. The combination of qualitative and quantitative research method in the present study provided a richer description of the dimension of stress during pregnancy. The current study's key strength relates to the fact that the themes and subthemes originated from direct consultation with pregnant working and non-working women. The integration of the qualitative and quantitative research and involvements of both pregnant working and working women are the methodological strength of the study. All the above-mentioned themes emerged in the study indicated that pregnancy-specific stress is not an individual construct and can be differentiated into different components as evident in our data. The themes emerged in this study could be used by the gynaecologist to identify women with psychosocial problems and stress during pregnancy and the potential areas of counselling for pregnant women to prevent their stress during pregnancy. Awareness about pregnancy-specific stress may allow clinicians to be sensitive to such stresses, educate women regarding potential stresses, and normalize such worries and stresses.

Limitations and Future Research Suggestions

The major limitation was that the study was conducted only one point of time (i.e. third trimester) in pregnancy, leading to the possibility of variations in responses at different times. The term of gestation at which the women were assessed in the present study varied between 28 and 40 weeks. One may argue that the scores on the themes and subthemes that emerged in the present study are trimester specific, which would, in turn call for future research to validate the results of the present study. Another important limitation of the study was the small sample size. However, this is unlikely to compromise the quality of findings as the sample included as wider range of socio-demographic characteristics in both stage-1 and stage-2 of the study and various occupational categories are included in stage-2 of the study.

Some researchers have argued that analysis of open-ended responses to written questionnaires is not conventional qualitative research method (Pope & Campbell, 2001). To avoid this limitation, the research team of the study regularly met to review the range of data, inspected contradictory data, and concerned about the possibility of symbolic meaning or social desirability underlying apparent inconsistencies. Further, the researcher team have kept notes and memos throughout the fieldwork and coding of the data. Taking into consideration the findings of the present study it is recommended that further discussion or structured intervention should be done with low-risk women about diet, physical symptoms in pregnancy, psychological and emotional changes, awareness about labour and birth might provide the support that could prevent or reduce experiences of stress during pregnancy

Conclusion

In conclusion, the nine overarching themes offered a novel conceptual, analytic framework for pregnancy-specific stress. The recognition that stresses during pregnancy may be associated with adverse pregnancy outcomes; therefore managing psychological stress may affect the course of current pregnancy as well as health and well being of the women. These findings revealed that to get individual solution for pregnant women should be aware of the importance of psychosocial correlates of maternal health and well being. In understanding this qualitative analysis, the aim was to understand better the perspectives of pregnant working and non-working women who have experienced pregnancy-specific stress and categorised some of their psychological and practical needs. Focusing on intervention to support pregnant working women's family decrease social isolation and empower these women to pursue career goals may decrease the career-related stress.

This study is an important addition to the existing literature on pregnancy-specific stress and has the potential to provide useful information for clinicians and practitioners.

References

1. Alderdice, F., & Lynn, F. (2011). Factor structure of the prenatal distress questionnaire. Midwifery. 27, 553-559.
2. Badr, L.K., Abdallah, B., & Mahmoud, A. (2005). Precursors of pre-term birth: comparison of three ethnic groups in the middle east and the United States. J. obstetgynecol neonatal nur. 34, 444-452.
3. Carter, B. (2004). How do you analyse qualitative data? In Lavender, T., Edwards, G. & Alfirevic, Z. (eds) Demystifying Qualitative Research in Pregnancy and Childbirth. MA Healthcare, Salisbury 87-108.
4. Cochrane, R., & Robertson, A. (1973). The life events inventory: A measure of the relative severity of psycho-social stressors. Journal of Psychosomatic Research. 17, 135-140.
5. Di Pietro, J.A., Ghera, M.M., Costigan, K., & Hawkins, M. (2004).Measuring the ups and downs of pregnancy stress. J. Psychosom Obstet Gynecol, 25, 189-201.
6. Dunkelschetter, C., lobel, M. (2012). Pregnancy and birth: a multilevel analysis of stress and birth weight. In: Revenson, T.A., Baum, A., Singer, J., editors. Handbook of Health Psychology. 2nd ed. London: Psychol. Press.
7. Dunkel-Schetter, C., & Tanner, L. (2012). Anxiety, depression and stress in pregnancy: implications for mothers, children, research, and practice. Current Opinion in Psychiatry, 25, (2), 141-148.
8. Dyer, S.J., Abrahams, N., Moekoena, N.E. & Van-der Spuy. (2004). 'You are a man because you have children': experiences, reproductive health knowledge and treatment-seeking behaviour among men suffering from couple infertility in South Africa. Hum Reprod 19(4), 960-697.
9. Furber, C.M., Garrod, D., Maloney, E., Lovell, K. & McGowan, L. (2009). A qualitative study of mild to moderate psychological distress in pregnancy. International journal of nursing studies. 46 (5), 669-677.

10. Geller, P.A. (2004). Pregnancy as a stressful life event. CNS Spectrum, 9, 188-197.
11. Gilbody, S., House, A.O., & Sheldon, T.A. (2005). Screening and case finding instruments for depression. Cochrane Database Syst Rev, 4: CD002792.
12. Glazier, R.H., Elgar, F.J., Goel, V., &Holzapfel, S. (2004). Stress, social support, and emotional distress in a community sample of pregnant women. J. Psychosom Obstet Gynaecol, 25, 247-255.
13. Goldenberg, R.,&Gotlieb, S. (2002). Social and psychological factors and pregnancy outcome. In: Cherry S, Merkatz I, eds. Complications of pregnancy: Medical, surgical, gynecologic, psychosocial, and perinatal. Baltimore: Williams & Wilkins, 1991:80-96.
14. Green, J., Kafetsios, K., Statham, H.,&Snowdon, C. (2003). Factor structure, validity and reliability of the Cambridge Worry Scale in a pregnant population. J Health Psychol, 8(6), 753-64.
15. Henwood, K.L., & Pidgeon, N.F. (1992). Qualitative research and psychological theorizing. Br. J. Psychol 83, 97-111.
16. Kazi, A., Fatmi, Z., Hatcher, J., Niaz, U., &Aziz, A. (2009). Development of a stress scale for pregnant women in the South Asian context: the A-Z Stress Scale. East Mediterr Health J., 15(2), 353-61.
17. Lobel, M., Cannella, D.L., Graham, J.E., De Vincent, C., Schneider, J., & Meyer, B. (2008). Pregnancy-specific stress, prenatal health behaviours and birth outcomes. Health Psychology 27, 604-615.
18. Melender, H. L, (2002). Experiences of fears associated with pregnancy and childbirth: A study of 329 pregnant women. Birth. 29, 101-111.
19. Mulder, E., Robles de Medina, P., Huizink A., Van den Berg, B., Buitelaar, J., &Visser, G. (2002). Prenatal maternal stress: Effects on pregnancy and the (unborn) child. Early Hum Dev. 70, 3-14.
20. Patel, V., Rodrigues, M. & De Souza, N. (2002). Gender, poverty and post-natal depression: a cohort study from Goa, India. American Journal of Psychiatry, 159, 43-47.
21. Peddie, V.L., van Teijlingen, E., & Bhattacharya, S. (2005) A qualitative study of women's decision-making at the end of IVF treatment. Hum Reprod 20 (7), 1944-1951.
22. Petersen, J.J., Paulitsch, M.A., Guethlin, C., Gensichen, J., & Jahn, A. (2009). A survey on worries of pregnant women-testing the German version of the Cambridge Worry Scale. BMC Public Health, 9:490 doi:10.1186/1471-2458-9-490.
23. Pop, V.J.M., Pommer, A.M., Pop-Purceleanu, M., Wijnen, H.A.A., Bergink, V., & Pouwer, F. (2011). Development of the Tilburg Pregnancy Distress Scale: the TPDS. BMC Pregnancy and Childbirth, 11:80. (http://www.biomedcentral.com/1471-2393/11/80).
24. Pope, C. & Campbell, R. (2001). Qualitative research in obstetrics and gynaecology. Br. J. Obstet Gynecol 108, 233-237.
25. Rini, C.K., Dunkel-Schetter, C., Wadhwa, P.D., & Sandman, C.A. (1999). Psychological adaptation and birth outcomes: the role of personal resources, stress, and socio-cultural context in pregnancy. Health Psychol, 18, 333-45.

26. Rondo, P.H., Ferreira, R.F., Nogueirra, F., Ribeiro, M.C., Lobert, H., & Artes, R. (2003). Maternal psychological stress and distress as predictors of low birth weight, prematurity and intrauterine growth retardation. Eur. J. Clin. Nutr. 57 (2), 266-72.
27. Ruiz, R., & Fullerton, J. (1999). The measurement of stress in pregnancy. Nursing and health sciences. 1, 19-25.
28. Schmitz, N., Kruse, J., & Tress, W. (1999). Psychometric properties of the general health questionnaire (GHQ-12) in a German primary care sample. Acta psychiatr scand. 100, 462-468.
29. Somerville, S., Dedman, K., Hagan, R., Oxnam, E., Wettinger, M., Byrne, S., Coo, S., Doherty, D., &Page, A.C. (2014). The Perinatal Anxiety Screening Scale: development and preliminary validation. Archives of Women's Mental Health, DOI: 10.1007/s00737-014-0425-8.
30. Wang, F.J., Faan, R.N., & Billings, A.A. (2011). Instrument Development for Measuring Stress during Pregnancy among Women in Beijing, China. A southern online journal of nursing research. 11,
31. WHO. (2002). Safe motherhood: A newsteller of worldwide activity. Issue 28 (1).
32. Yali, A.M., & Lobel, M. (1999). Coping and distress in pregnancy: an investigation of medically high-risk women. Journal of Psychosomatic Obstetrics & Gynecology. 20 (1), 39-52.

□

17

Improving Health Outcomes across the Life Cycle Continuum by Focusing on Adolescent Girls

—*Manisha Chandra*

Abstract

Adolescence is the most important phase of the life cycle. It is marked by rapid physical, cognitive, emotional and social changes. During this time onset of health-related behaviours and conditions is seen, which affects not only this phase but has implications in the later years of the life cycle. Therefore, if investments are made in educating the adolescents on health and nutrition related issues then the disease burden which manifests in the population in the form of undernutrition, anaemia, obesity and other health issues of vital importance can be curbed. From these varied issues of importance, this article identifies and discusses the lessons learnt in adolescent programming, which may contribute to positive health and nutrition outcomes through nutrition and health education. It is envisioned that the initiatives are taken up by ICDS, Gujarat would help make a framework which would help in initiating programmes for adolescent girls at the Anganwadi level by involving both the Anganwadi worker and adolescent girls.

In this article, it emerges out that weekly educative sessions helped in initiating the adolescent programme at the Anganwadi while the peer educator approach helped in providing information to the girls in the most acceptable way. The campaign approach named Kishori Jagrut Abhiyan provided an impetus to the issues of adolescent girls among the community stakeholders through creative activities by providing correct scientific information. The success of the approach can be witnessed in the form of increased awareness and more and more number of Anganwadi conducting this campaign. The strength of this article being, it draws the framework of improving health and nutrition programmes for adolescent girls from the field experiences gathered by the ICDS functionaries at the grass root level.

Introduction

Evidence shows that up to 45% of skeletal growth, 15 to 25% of adult height (Rees and Christine, 1989) and up to 37% of total bone mass accumulation (Key and Key, 1994) takes place during adolescence. Thus, reflecting increased demand for proper nutrition, consequently, making them an ideal target for nutrition and health education programmes. Improving nutrition practices among adolescent girls have long term benefits like increased pre-pregnancy weight and body stores of nutrients, thus contributing to improved future pregnancy and lactation outcome, improved iron status with reduced risk of anemia in pregnancy, low birth weight, maternal morbidity and mortality and improved foliate status, with reduced risk of neural tube defects in the newborn and megaloblastic anemia during pregnancy. Apart from improving reproductive health, it is also important to improve the health of adolescent girls for their well-being as *'Individuals'*.

On the other than, if we analyse the process of administering food, it is commonly seen that for young children parents decide their diet whereas among adults the diet-related behaviour gets formed and is difficult to modify. As adolescence is a transition period between childhood and adulthood, it provides an opportunity to educate and inform them to prevent nutrition-related problems. Therefore, it is an appropriate time to provide health promotion programmes so that they understand the importance of healthy eating and make correct food choices.

To provide nutrition and health education mechanisms through adolescent reproductive and sexual health clinics, schools and peer educators have been explored, but approaches with community stakeholders like Anganwadi worker is yet to be investigated. Therefore, an attempt was made under the Integrated Child Development Scheme (ICDS), Gujarat to revitalize the existing programmatic framework of Sabla and Kishori Shakti Scheme and impart nutrition, health and life skill education to girls by actively engaging them into creative and simple activities where they could learn through the approach of learning with the active support of Anganwadi worker. Anganwadi workers were provided adequate knowledge about the information and method to be used for providing information to adolescent girls.

Global Scenario

Good adolescent health generates a 'triple dividend' as it enhances optimal growth, has an impact across the life course and provides a healthy start to life for the next generation (Patton et al., 2016). Therefore, making adolescents as an integral part of public health programming is vital.

Globally, in 2012, there were 1.2 billion adolescents in the world–defined as young people between the ages of 10 and 19 years. A vast majority of adolescents

(90%) live in low- or middle-income countries. Iron deficiency anaemia is the third most important cause of lost disability-adjusted life years(DALYs) in adolescents worldwide at 3%, after alcohol and unsafe sex (Sawyer et al., 2012). In some countries, as many as half of all adolescents are stunted (Black et al., 2013), which means their physical and cognitive development has been restricted because of inadequate nutrition. The first 1,000 days of life–from the start of the mother's pregnancy to the child's second birthday–are critical for healthy development. Therefore, the majority of nutrition policies and interventions are targeted towards them. The Lancet (2013) series also confirms the same fact and identifies adolescents as a key neglected group in current research and programming. Research, practical experiences, policies and programmes to support adolescent health and nutrition need more focus.

The Situation in India and Gujarat

According to NFHS-4 (2015-16), 53% of women of reproductive age are anaemic and 22.9% are underweight in India as against 55% anaemic women and 27.7% underweight women in Gujarat. It is noted that the efforts are on the way in the form of intervention measures like providing supplementary nutrition. Such high rates of anaemia and underweight can be contributed to inadequate knowledge about the nutritional requirement and faulty nutrition practices at the household level. Therefore, the need of the hour is to provide nutrition and health education to adolescent girls. Experiences of programme implementation show that 'how' the adolescent girls are covered and 'what' is the effectiveness of nutrition and health programme which caters to them is almost unknown. It is also seen that when preferences of adolescent girls are asked on designing health and nutrition programmes, a clear view is difficult to obtain. Therefore, planning need based interventions for this group of the population becomes an arduous task.

Gujarat Initiative

Under Integrated Child Development Scheme (ICDS), programmes for adolescent girls have been formulated and implemented through various schemes like Rajiv Gandhi Scheme for Empowerment of Adolescent Girls (Sabla) and Kishori Shakti Yojana (KSY). The focus on improving the health and nutrition status of adolescent girls by providing commodities like Supplementary nutrition and Iron Folic Acid (IFA) tablet was seen on the ground. The uptake of Supplementary nutrition programme by girls was good, but consumption of IFA tablets was minimal. On the other side, field visits and periodic reviews revealed that Nutrition and Health Education sessions were rarely conducted. It was observed that knowledge of Anganwadi workers on issues of adolescent girls was inadequate. It was noticed that Anganwadi workers and all other ICDS functionaries had a concern to work for adolescent girls but were not aware of 'how' it could be done. Therefore, incessant improvements in programming became an integral part of ICDS in the last two years with the underlying assumptions being:

Programs to prevent and control anaemia and undernutrition have been constrained due to unavailability of effective and practical interventions. Therefore, revisions in programming which are more community friendly, acceptable, simple and do-able can be explored, keeping in mind the stakeholders and target audience.

Anaemia and undernutrition can be prevented at a low cost by providing information through community stakeholders.

Capacities of Anganwadi workers in providing clear and specific messages to prevent anaemia and undernutrition can be built using technology.

Strategies

1. Developed theme based, weekly educative sessions: Considering this scenario, ICDS Gujarat took an initiative of exploring methods by which at-least one weekly session on health, nutrition and life skill education gets conducted at the Anganwadi. It was also believed that when adolescent girls would approach the Anganwadi centre for weekly sessions they would be provided IFA tablets for consumption under the direct supervision of Anganwadi workers thereby, strengthening the National Iron Plus Initiative (NIPI). Hence, considering the dual benefits, educative sessions were articulated on the following themes:

Nutrition and Health Education session

Adolescent Reproductive and Sexual Health and Child care

Life skill Education Communication

Accessing Public services

Legal awareness

Along with the themes, month wise timetable was provided to the field level functionaries wherein week-wise subthemes or topics to be conducted were suggested.

Training were imparted till the Mukhya Sevika level, and they were instructed to train Anganwadi worker for one day. It was witnessed that health and nutrition session started at the Anganwadis, but the worker had to call the girls for the session. This sometimes resulted in low turnout and participation.

Table-1: Theme based Weekly Sessions

Theme based weekly sessions under Sabla and Kishori Shakti Yojana						
		1st week of the month	2nd week of the month	3rd week of the month	4th week of the month	A 5th week or as per availability
S. No.	Month	Nutrition and Health Education (NHE)	Adolescent Reproductive and Sexual Health (ARSH)	Life Skill Education	Legal awareness	Visit Public Institutions
1	January	Understanding self and orientation on Sabla/KSY scheme	Understanding the process of growing up	Effective Communication	Correct age of marriage	Bank
2	February	Anaemia	Process of Menstruation and menstrual hygiene	Decision making	Dowry and introduction about the Dowry Prohibition Act	Health Center
3	March	Importance of Vitamin A	importance of IYCF practices	Leadership	Domestic Violence Act-2002	School/ College
4	April	Importance of IFA	Importance of IYCF practices	Home management	First Information Report(FIR)	Police Station
5	May	Deworming	Role of a balanced diet during adolescence period	Rights of adolescent girls	Rape and what to do in case of rape	Cottage or small industry
6	June	BMI and its significance	Deficiencies due to inadequate food intake	Introduction to domestic violence	Right to education	NGO
7	July	Correct methods of cooking	Family Planning methods and their use	Self-defence	Right to vote	District Panchayat Office
8	August	What is a Balanced diet?	Immunisation of mother and children	Importance of Yoga	PCPNDT	E-ticketing centre (any travel agency)
9	September	Personal hygiene	Importance of MCP card	Stress and its management		Post office

10	October	The correct way of washing hands	Reproductive Tract Infections(RTI)			Visit SevaSetu
11	November	First Aid	Sexually Transmitted Diseases(STDs)			Visit Gram Panchayat
12	December	Introduction to Government programmes on health and nutrition	Addiction			

Source: By the Author and team ICDS.

Benefits of Weekly Sessions

Previously, age-disaggregated report of services provided to the school and non-school going girls were not available while currently the type of information and services provided to girls can be known easily and as depicted in table 2.

Table-2: Age-disaggregated data of services provided to adolescent girls through Anganwadi

Category	Enrolled Girls	Girls provided SNP	% of girls provided SNP	Girls provided NHE	% of girls provided NHE	Girls provided ARSH and FW	% of girls provided ARSH and FW
OOS AG (11-14 years)	301737	226332	75	147629	49	98137	33
OOS AG (15-18 years)	380131	369829	97	267243	70	189774	50
SG (15-18 years)	591805	418418	71	224443	38	172960	29
Total	**1273673**	**1014578**	**80**	**639315**	**50**	**460871**	**36**

Source: MPR August 2017
OOSSG-Out of school adolescent girls

Distribution and consumption of IFA (table 3 show improvement: Previously, the data of IFA distribution was available but was not accurate, whereas information about IFA consumption was not available. A marked improvement is witnessed in reporting of this indicator from the past year.

Table-3: Age-disaggregated data of IFA provided to adolescent girls through Anganwadi

Category	Enrolled Girls (A)	Girls provided IFA (B)	% of Girls provided IFA(B/A)	Girls consuming IFA (C)	%of girls consuming IFA (C/B)
OOS AG (11-14 years)	301737	196625	65	187730	95
OOS AG (15-18 years)	380131	254757	67	223321	87
SG (15-18 years)	591805	334150	56	292172	87
Total	1273673	785532	61	703223	89

Source: MPR August 2017

Training of Peer educators: In a similar vein, peer educators were also trained so that the information on health and nutrition issues reaches the adolescent girls most acceptably. Adolescent girls with good communication and leadership skills were selected as Peer educators by Anganwadi workers. The training was given by 8 Non-Governmental Organisations (NGOs), and 73132 girls were trained as peer educators across Gujarat in 4 months. The outcome was peer educators started communicating and sharing correct information on topics which were not discussed earlier. The interventions were monitored rigorously through field visits, but it was observed that knowledge gap both at the level of Anganwadi worker and beneficiary persisted.

Kishori Jagrut Abhiyan: In order to fill up the knowledge gap, a five-phased campaign called '*Kishori Jagrut Abhiyan*' was formulated from the month of 'August 2017 to December 2017'. A short study was also conducted with the adolescent girls before the campaign on factors that governs food choices and food intake among 16 rural adolescent girls by using Semi-structured interviews. Data were analysed using 'Thematic Coding Analysis'. Critically, analysing further, family, society, community groups, religion and culture form the environment of an individual which either encourages or obstructs the behaviour of an individual. Therefore, holistic understanding and subsequently suitable interventions on multiple factors affecting food choices and food intake among young women were explored. It was observed that during fasting nothing was eaten, and the intake of certain foods was restricted during 'Menarche'. Hence, indicating culture and religion as barriers to food intake. Limited income (Norhasmah et al., 2010) was an important factor in determining food choices. Community stakeholders have influenced in improving nutrition practices (Nandi and Schneider, 2014). Hence, it shows that social support promotes behaviour change. It is seen that compliance of IFA was good when health benefits were encountered while it was reduced at times due to bad taste and other side effects. This shows a need to strengthen efforts about health education.

To execute the robust campaign planning was done. The nucleus of planning being an organisation of health, nutrition and life skill education sessions in a creative way where adolescent girls were involved in activities which interest them. To ensure participation of adolescent girls, proper planning and implementation were ensured at each level i.e. from the state level to the Anganwadi level. Equal importance was given to summarizing the session with correct information by Anganwadi workers. 'Kishori Jagrut Abhiyan' turned out to be a 'Behaviour Change Communication exercise' which led to increased attendance of adolescent girls at the Anganwadi, and an increased knowledge on the issues of health and nutrition. All these indicators can improve health outcomes of the population.

Phase-wise details of the campaign are summarised below:

Kishori Diwas: Magnitude of the problem was understood through a baseline survey, whereas the results of endline survey would show the impact of health and nutrition on the health status of girls. Health Screening of adolescent girls was called as 'KishoriDiwas', where haemoglobin was estimated using Sahlis haemoglobinometer, and BMI was measured using ICMR tool having four zones red (under-nutrition), green (Normal), orange (overweight) and pink (obese) denoting different zones of over and under-nutrition.

On the day of '*Kishori Diwas*', anganwadi workers had mobilised all the adolescent girls of the community at the Primary Health Center or the Anganwadi centre. Haemoglobin estimation was conducted with the active support of ANM/Staff nurse/lab technician. It was observed that the names of every girl were maintained in the register where haemoglobin status and BMI was recorded for every girl very accurately. It was seen that girls were curious to know their haemoglobin status, and if found low, they tried to find out how it could be restored to normal. It was evident that the LT/ANM/Staff nurse sensitised the girls about having a balanced diet and the importance of eating green leafy vegetables.

Therefore, active participation of girls was seen at *Kishori Diwas* marked by interpersonal communication by the health functionaries. In a similar vein, Anganwadi workers were instructed to line list severely anaemic girls so that focused interventions could be designed for them.

Previously, health screening was not a part of the programme activities under Sabla and KSY, but through this campaign, it was mandatory to measure BMI and haemoglobin of adolescent girls. Out of 1273673 enrolled girls in 33 districts (data not received from Chota Udepur, Rajkot and Panchmahal, three districts), BMI of 860593 girls (67%) and haemoglobin of 729219 girls(57%) was measured in the first phase.

Nutrition Education

After preliminary health screening, from second phase onwards girls were provided nutrition, health and life skill education through activity-based learning. **Girls were engaged in creative activities, games and competition which interest them for facilitating scientific learning.** Girls were kept involved through different activities like toran making where predesigned messages on nutritious food and anaemia were provided to them.

'Toran' were made by adolescent girls at the anganwadis that deals with topics related to anaemia; its causes, prevention by consuming a healthy diet and health benefits by consumption of cereals, pulses, vegetables, fruits and milk. The outcome of this activity was, girls discussed among themselves the topic they had to choose for making torans, i.e. anaemia or undernutrition. After selecting the topic, girls discussed the design of toran and then wrote the messages. **The entire process was discussion driven.**

After completing the toran making exercise, girls made a salad from fruits, vegetables and sprouts which they had brought from their homes. The Anganwadi worker had instructed the adolescent girls beforehand to get one fruit or vegetable or any sprouts from their home on the day of the activity. Locally available nutritious fruits and vegetables like banana, pomegranate, *sapota* (chiko), papaya, apple, guava, cucumber, carrot, beet root, radish, lady finger and sprouts of *moong*, *math*, *chana* (chick peas) and *rajma* (kidney beans) dominated the platter.

Apart from this, adolescent girls also adorned the Anganwadi with symbol of ICDS through *rangoli* made of rice and wheat grains or from vegetables. At many places, green leafy vegetables like pumpkin, ridge, bottle and bitter gourd, spinach and than dalja were also displayed. It was seen at many places that Toran made by adolescent girls were displayed at the entrance of anganwadi centre and were also used to educate beneficiaries.

The session was summarised by highlighting the significance of nutritious food during adolescence and deficiencies in the absence of proper diet.

Health Education

The health education session was marked with a competition called as 'Sukanya award' which was given to adolescent girls who were neat and tidy and had knowledge about the scheme, were aware of the benefits of IFA consumption. Parameters for assessing health and hygiene, knowledge regarding a scheme for adolescent girls was set and given to Anganwadi workers.

The winners were chosen and felicitated by giving a certificate called 'Sukanya Award'. The award inculcated a habit of maintaining personal hygiene. After the competition, quiz on various topics of health was conducted. Questions on the session of nutrition education were also recapitulated. The girls were enthusiastically participating in all the activities and were able to answer the questions confidently. The reason is contributed to their participation and learning during the nutrition education session. The session was summarised by highlighting the importance of personal and menstrual hygiene and growing up during adolescence.

" I am organising programmes for adolescent girls since long. In the past, I had to call adolescent girls to come at the Anganwadi but after the campaign, the girls themselves ask me about the sessions. They are enthusiastic about the activities and have learnt many new things through these interesting activities".

Anganwadi Worker-Jadav J.P., AWC: Mendarda, Code No.10., District: Junagadh

---

Life Skill Education

The phase of life skill education was marked by a game called 'passing the parcel' where customised messages on life skill education were formulated and provided to Anganwadi centres. The girls read aloud the messages on life skill education in their group. It was seen that adolescent girls understood the complex issues of emotions, decision making and problem-solving effortlessly. In between the session, Anganwadi workers were linking the life skills with the practical situations which arise in the life of adolescent girls and the way life skills help them in overcoming it. The session was summarised by the Anganwadi worker in the end.

The outcome of the campaign on knowledge of adolescent girls:

The effectiveness of the campaign can be measured by increased attendance and number of anganwadis conducting the campaign. Improvement in the knowledge level is also shown below:

(i) Increased attendance of girls:

It can be observed that in the phase of nutrition education, sessions were conducted in 66% anganwadis while 69% anganwadis conducted heath education session. The participation of adolescent girls also shows an increase during the nutrition and health sessions. On an average, 67.5% of girls attended the sessions.

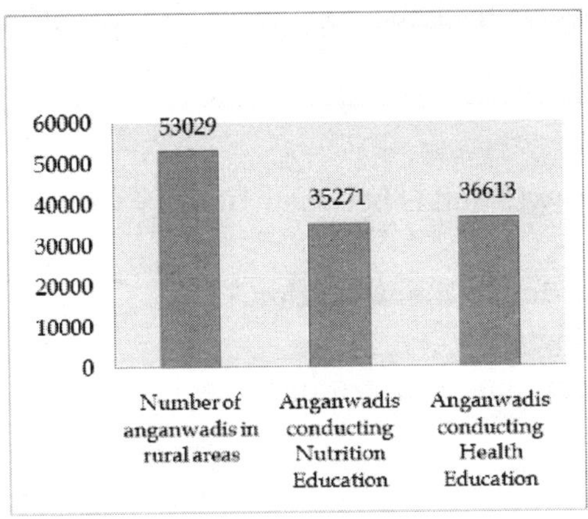

Report of 27 out of 33 districts.

Fig. 1. Number of anganwadis conducting education sessions

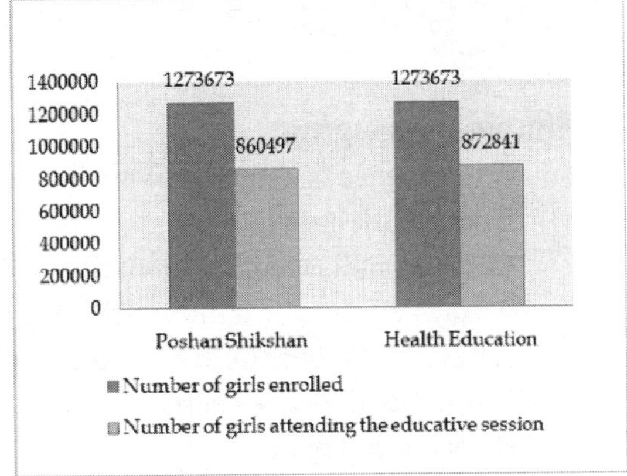

Report of 29 out of 33 districts

Fig. 2. Number of girls enrolled Vs attending educative sessions

Impact on Knowledge

Pre and post-test were conducted before and after the session for 250 beneficiaries. It was observed that awareness of health and nutrition issues increased during the session. The findings have been presented below:

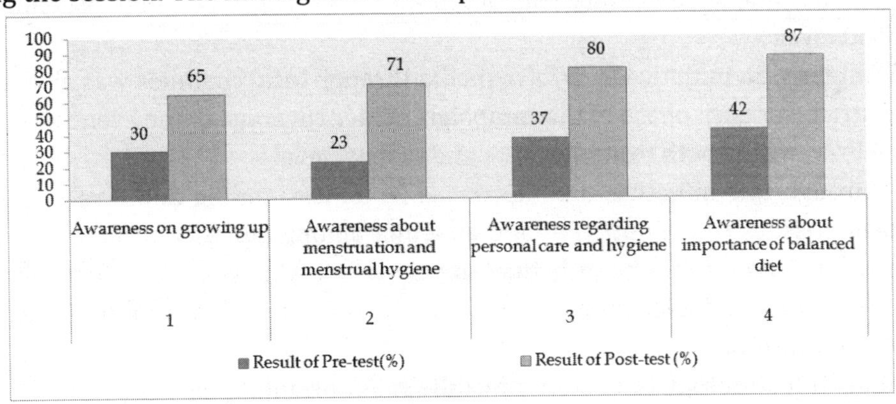

Fig. 3: Increase in the awareness of health and nutrition issues during sessions

Steps that led to the success of the campaign:

It was a need-based campaign, creatively designed and was very simple to understand.

Simple messaging

Adolescence is a period of maximum growth and is between 10 to 19 years

Take a bath daily.

Cut your nails weekly. Maintain hygiene during menstruation.

Always wash your hands with soap and water.

A balanced diet should be taken to prevent under-nutrition.

Proper food intake keeps away diseases.

Eat seasonal fruits.

Citrus fruits improve immunity and help in iron absorption.

Take IFA tablet once a week and take deworming tablets provided every six months at the Anganwadi centre.

Calorie and protein-rich foods should be taken to support the growth spurt

For proper and smooth implementation of the campaign minute to minute planning of all activities was done and provided to the anganwadi worker.

For an unbiased view evaluation by UNICEF was conducted and for generating mass awareness, documentary was prepared by the State level and disseminated at the field level.

Similarly, an initiative to involve media through local channels was also taken by the districts for each phase of the campaign. Wider coverage of the event was done by use of Print media both from the State and district level.

Through this initiative, a comprehensive understanding and awareness about managing issues of malnutrition and anaemia among adolescent girls by involving them were created. Consequently, the campaign led to a 'movement' which enlightened the young girls and kept them involved in the process of learning on issues which affect their health.

Use of technology in capacity building: For orienting the ICDS functionaries at ground level who interact continuously with the community, a process of continuous learning about the campaign was initiated through Satellite Communication (SATCOM) through Bhaskaracharya Institute For Space Applications and Geo-Informatics (BISAG). Before the commencement of each phase, SATCOM sessions were conducted for generating awareness and imparting clarity about the campaign to all the ICDS functionaries. In the later sessions, adolescent girls were also made a part of SATCOM so that they also understand the importance of this campaign. Orientations through

SATCOM minimised information loss. Positive feedbacks during SATCOM suggested that the Campaign was well accepted among stakeholders and beneficiaries.

Apart from this WhatsApp was also used as a method of exchanging information by the district functionaries. This led to the sharing of ideas actively by the district teams on the problems encountered and possible solutions for conducting weekly sessions and campaign. Above all, WhatsApp group also helped in guiding the State level to the district teams, and this helped in providing timely instructions in order to conduct the programme efficiently. Some of the good videos shared by the districts would also be used for educating adolescent girls in the future.

The important building blocks of the campaign were dynamic leadership and availability of funds from the ongoing Government programme. As a result, ICDS was able to deliver health and nutrition-related services with equity and provide information to those who needed it the most. Secondly, the system became responsive and accountable to conduct the campaign, thereby, improving health outcomes among girls.

Convergence with allied departments like the Department of Health and Family Welfare ensured proper implementation of health screening and strengthened the coordination among community level stakeholders like ANM/Lab technician/FHW and Anganwadi worker.

Project Replicability

The project is functional in all districts of Gujarat. It has been initiated by the Government and is in partnership with other government departments and agencies like UNICEF and Nutritional International (NI). Further, government based programme funding through SABLA and Kishori Shakti Scheme (KSY) has been used in the programme. This makes the project sustainable.

The programme can be replicated by the other States of India as it is simple to execute. Apart from this, through these initiatives, a lot of qualitative and quantitative information is generated, prudent utilisation of which would depend on the discretion of decision makers.

The preliminary health screening conducted during the campaign provided a baseline data on the magnitude of anaemia and undernutrition whereas the end-line screening will provide an understanding that is there a change witnessed in the health and nutrition status of adolescent girls after providing accurate information.

Name wise list of anaemic and undernourished beneficiarie, which will be useful in planning focussed interventions will now be available.

Looking at the dearth of academic literature on health and nutrition aspects of adolescent girls, findings of the programme can be used to influence research and policy.

Information sharing with stakeholders and academic institutions would provide new and creative ideas that would help in designingneed-based programmes for adolescent girls. Thus, the way forward for Gujarat in nutrition and health programming would be focussed more towards exploring new ways to reach adolescent girls directly. Constructive use of SATCOM to address this age group under the guidance of experts will be of foremost importance.

Challenges and ways to overcome them:

System thinking framework (WHO, 2009) helped in identifying the key blocks and challenges to implement the programme.

Capacity building: Capacity building of field functionaries is a challenge which will be overcome by using technology. Furthermore, formulation of a training module for Anganwadi workers having detailed chapters on nutrition, health and life skill education aspects of adolescent girls is also underway. On the other hand, educative training kits will be procured for 53029 anganwadis through funds allocated by the Government of India and Government of Gujarat.

Continuous Involvement of adolescent girls: It is a critical challenge which will be overcome by using SATCOM by weaving it in the form of a programme called 'SAMVAD'. The programme will initiate direct dialogue with adolescent girls. Apart from this, ICDS professionals will need to set a common goal of informing and engaging with adolescent girls continuously. Anganwadi workers will have to integrate educative activities for adolescent girls in their routine work.

Monitoring and Evaluation: Regular monitoring of programme and supportive supervision is identified as an important challenge which will be overcome by involving not only the State level teams but also district and block level teams. An online portal (http://esabla.gipl.in) has been developed to maintain the data of initiatives taken up. It will be made operational. For ensuring data quality, mentoring support will be provided regularly to the field level functionaries.

Community Participation: Awareness generation on the issues of adolescent girls among parents and decision-makers is a challenge which will be overcome by involving them in the SATCOMs, which will be organised for adolescent girls.

Creation of learning organisations: Managing and coordinating partnerships, fostering ownership of the programme is a foreseen challenge. The system is evolving continuously; health and nutrition problems are also transforming. Hence, it will be a challenge to create learning organisations which create an organisational culture that continuously identifies knowledge gaps in practice, processes and ensures simultaneous action to fill the gaps. For identifying the challenges, third-party evaluation will be taken up. Findings of which will help in developing new strategies and reinforcement of concepts which are required for improving health outcomes.

Leadership: Continuity of programme at the same pace is envisaged as another challenge. Presently, the programme could flourish because of strong leadership and continuous handholding. Therefore, it is assumed that strong leadership is essential for sustaining the programme.

Research studies: There is a dearth of research studies on health and nutrition aspects of adolescent girls which will be overcome by involving research organisations, academicians and educational institutes.

Recommendations

Focused efforts should be directed towards improving nutrition and health education.

It is important to reach adolescent girls through activity-based learning methods, interactions and discussions.

Programmes should be designed for the adolescent as a separate category as commonly they are either included with children or with mother. Similarly, recurrent monitoring and evaluation of programmes focusing on adolescent girls should be formulated.

Context-specific strategies for anaemia and undernutrition should be framed.

Counselling of girls on health and nutrition through peer educators or community level stakeholders like Anganwadi worker will help in initiating a dialogue between them. Focused approach on IFA consumption can also be initiated in this way.

Initiate kitchen garden through adolescent girls in the anganwadi centre and at home.

Improve understanding of anaemia among adolescent girls by highlighting future health consequences.

Strengthen prevention, control and treatment activities for adolescent anaemia by implementing the National Iron Plus Initiative Programme.

In conclusion, the involvement of Anganwadi workers can be improved by framing a systematic programme where all activities are indicated properly. Participation of adolescent girls also increases if activities are provided to them in a simple manner. The initiative by ICDS, Gujarat is an attempt to prioritize the issues of adolescent girls in Public Health programming and in making them aware of their health and nutrition issues. This will have implications on improving the next stages of life course and will be visible in improved health outcomes of the future generation.

List of Abbreviations

S. No.	Abbreviation	Full form
1	ICDS	Integrated Child Development Services Scheme
2.	IEC	Information, Education and Communication
3.	SATCOM	Satellite Communication
4	NFHS-4	National Family Health Survey-4
5	Sabla	Rajiv Gandhi Scheme for Empowerment of Adolescent Girls
6	KSY	Kishori Shakti Yojana (KSY)
7	IFA	Iron Folic Acid tablet
8	NIPI	National Iron Plus Initiative
9	SNP	Supplementary Nutrition Programme
10	NHE	Nutrition and Health Education
11	ARSH and FW	Adolescent Reproductive and Sexual Health and Family Welfare
12	OOS AG	Out of School Adolescent girls
13	SG AG	School Adolescent girls
14	NGOs	Non-Governmental Organisations
15	BMI	Body Mass Index
16	ICMR	Indian Council of Medical Research
17	ANM	Auxiliary Nurse Midwife
18	FHW	Female Health Worker
19	LT	Lab Technician
20	UNICEF	United Nations Children's Fund
21	NI	Nutrition International

Acknowledgment

In this article, the author recognises the sincere efforts put by Ms. Ankur Vaidya, Sabla Consultant, who took the initiative to implement the programme with zeal and enthusiasm and assisted in structuring this article. Above all, she earnestly acknowledges the contributions by ICDS functionaries at all levels, most importantly, the Anganwadi workers who took time out to attend the sessions of SATCOM and implemented all the programme with utmost dedication. This article is just the beginning of the focused work which ICDS has started to improve the health and nutrition outcomes of adolescent girls in the State.

References

1. Black, R.E., Victora, C.G., Walker, S.P., Bhutta, Z.A., Christian, P., de Onis, M., Ezzati, M., Grantham-McGregor, S., Katz, J., Martorell, R., Uauy, R., and Maternal and Child Nutrition Study Group (2013) 'Maternal and child undernutrition and overweight in low-income and middle-income countries', The Lancet 382, 9890, pp 427-51. doi: 10.1016/S0140-6736(13)60937-X.
2. European Commission (2013) commission staff working document. Addressing Undernutrition in Emergencies.
3. Key J.D., Key L.L. Jr. (1994) Calcium needs of adolescents. Current Opinion in Pediatrics 6 pp.379-82
4. Lancet (2013) Maternal and Child Nutrition [online] http://www.thelancet.com/series/maternal-and-child-nutritions.
5. Nandi, S. and Schneider, H. (2014)'Addressing the social determinants of health: a case study from the Mitanin (community healthworker) programme in India', Health Policy and Planning, Vol.29, pp.71-81[online] Available at Downloaded from http://heapol.oxfordjournals.org (Accessed on 22nd February, 2016)
6. NFHS-4 (2015-16) Ministry of Health and Family Welfare, New Delhi.[online] http://rchiips.org/NFHS/pdf/NFHS4/India.pdf and http://rchiips.org/NFHS/pdf/NFHS4/GJ_FactSheet.pdf
7. Norhasmah, S1., Zalilah, M.S., Mohd Nasir, M.T, Kandiah, M. & Asnarulkhadi, A.S. (2010) 'A Qualitative Study on Coping Strategies among Women from Food Insecurity Households in Selangor and Negeri Sembilan', Mal J Nutr, Vol. 16, No.1, pp 39-54 Available from http://nutriweb.org.my/publications/mjn0016/Norhasmah(edSP)39-54.pdf (Accessed on 6th January, 2016).
8. Patton, G.C., Coffey, C., Cappa, C., Currie, D., Riley, L., Gore, F., Degenhardt, L., Richardson, D., Astone, N., Sangowawa, A.O., Mokdad, A. and Ferguson, J. (2012) 'Health of the world's adolescents: a synthesis of internationally comparable data', The Lancet 379, 9826, pp 1665-75. doi: 10.1016/S0140-6736(12)60203-7.
9. Rees J.M., Christine MT. (1989) Nutritional influences on physical growth and behaviour in adolescence. In: Adams G. (Ed.). Biology of adolescent behaviour and development. California: Sage Publications,
10. Sawyer, S.M., Afifi, R.A., Bearinger, L.H., Blakemore, S.J., Dick, B., Ezeh, A.C. and Patton, G.C. (2012) Adolescence: a foundation for future health', The Lancet 379, 9826, pp 1630-40. doi: 10.1016/S0140-6736(12)60072-5.
11. WHO (2009) System Thinking for Health system strengthening [online] http://apps.who.int/iris/bitstream/10665/44204/1/9789241563895_eng.pdf

□

18

Improving Child Health and Development in Mewat: Role and limitations of Community-based Mechanism

—*Pradeep K. Mehta*

Abstract

Infant mortality rates (IMR) and Maternal Mortality rates (MMR) reflects the status of public health and socio-economic development of a region. Mewat, one of the districts in Haryana, has very high IMR (117) and MMR (480), which points to an alarming health situation (Manav S., 2015). The introduction of integrated development child scheme (ICDS) was one of the major initiatives to improve the health care outcomes for both mother and child. The ICDS aims to provide not only food and preschool education but also primary healthcare to children under six years of age and their mothers. However, several studies (Michael Lokshin et al., 2015; Jyotiranjan Sahoo et al., 2016; and Thomas Nidhi et al., 2015) found that the ICDS programme was not particularly effective largely because of implementation problems. To counter this, there are several initiatives that target to strengthen the community-based mechanism for increased effectiveness of ICDS to improve child health and development (REF). On this backdrop, this paper examines the role of participation mechanisms by rural people in improving service delivery under the ICDS. The study presents a case study of Mewat region where a community-based organisation (CBO) has increased awareness about their rights and entitlements and redressal mechanisms so that they can demand better implementation of ICDS. The results highlight that is increasing access to information about rights and entitlements and providing the community with tools to demand accountability from service providers does play a role in improving implementation of ICDS that results in better and improved access to child health and development facilities. However, the process of change from increased awareness to demand of services by the citizens and action by the government officials is slow. Initially, only a few people raise their voices against the service delivery mechanism after knowing about their rights and entitlements. This is due to two factors, i.e., lack of complete understanding of improved benefits of better child care facilities and lack of collective action. Towards this, it is vital to improve awareness of the benefits of better child health care facilities and improve leadership skills among citizens. The moderated platforms can be organised where citizens, local officials and policy makers can interact and discuss the issues about the implementation of the program. There is also a requirement to influence the supply side through the provision of regular training to Anganwadi *workers (AWWs) on budget utilisation and services provided under ICDS which can improve their responsiveness to demands raised by the local community.*

Introduction

India lags behind several countries in terms of child and mother health care facilities. This is reflected in the higher rate of malnourishment among children in India; nearly half of the children (46%) are underweight, and one in every three malnourished children in the world lives in India (Chandran KPV, and P. Sandhya, 2010; and EPW, 2007). Early childhood care and development are critical for addressing the current situation in India, which must address child health, child development/ education and child nutrition (*ibid*).

In order to address child health care and development, the Government of India has introduced Integrated Child Development Scheme (ICDS) that has three major components including child health, early child education and better nutrition for child and mother. The ICDS program explicitly targets the poorest segment of the society, promising that the government delivers critical social goods and services to all who are entitled, including those who reside in rural areas. Although ICDS guarantees a range of services for better child health care, many services fail to reach the targeted beneficiaries (Gupta and Deepa, 2009). While some blame the deplorable state of social service delivery on ineffectual public institutions, others attribute it to the absence of beneficiaries' demand for better public services due to lack of awareness (Jayanti and Chandrashekhar, 2009; Banerjee and Duflo, 2011; Cummins, 2007).

Given the gaps emerging on the ground, several initiatives have found a place in the country's rural development milieu. These initiatives are varied in nature. While some aim at improving the supply side through making public institutions more accountable and transparent, there are several which aim at improving the demand side. The demand side here encompasses the targeted beneficiaries. Talking about the rural context, these initiatives engage the rural communities in not only making them aware of their rights and entitlements but also facilitating their access to such benefits. Awareness is found to be an important input to improving people's access to entitlements and drive them to effect change. Generating awareness entails improving people's knowledge about their rights through imparting relevant information. Ben (2006) acknowledges that while the information in itself is not knowledge, it provides essential raw material which, in due, the course can lead to knowledge and action.

As mentioned above, there have been several initiatives by organisations which intend to engage rural communities in making them aware of their rights, entitlements and redressal mechanisms. There is a community-based organisation (CBO) that has launched a program aiming to foster transparent and accountable ICDS capable of delivering child health and development facilities to the entitled villagers in Mewat. Encouraging villagers to proactively participate in monitoring the ICDS, the program intends to increase the demand from villagers for competent public institutions and channel it through legal recourse mechanisms. To achieve this objective, the organisation provides selected villagers (trainees) with year-long training where it informs them of their rights, entitlements, and grievance redressal methods so that the trainees can effectively monitor ICDS. Trainees are expected to share their newly acquired knowledge with fellow villagers through conducting follow-up meetings that organisation coordinates in the field as well as disseminating it to peers through personal networks. This is expected to put pressure on the government and local ICDS centre to function effectively, which further increases the access to better child health care facilities by the community.

In this backdrop, this paper attempts to examine the role of improved awareness of the community in the effective delivery of ICDS and its utilisation in Mewat. It attempts to unleash the differences emerging in the functioning of ICDS across villages which are experimental (where CBO created awareness about rights and entitlements and use of redressal mechanisms) and control. It envisages establishing whether awareness can be a precursor to effective functioning or not. The paper is divided into six sections. The first section provides an introduction to the paper. The second section provides details about the intervention by the community-based organisation (CBO). The third section provides detail about the methodology. Overview of health infrastructure and status of reproductive child health in Mewat is covered in section four. Role and limitations of Community based mechanism ineffective functioning and utilisation of ICDS are discussed in the fifth section, followed by conclusions and which are presented in the sixth section.

Components of the CBO Intervention

The CBO program has three broad components, and each component complements each other to increase the overall effectiveness of the program. With this three-prong program input, CBO intends to bring about transparent and accountable ICDS in the intervention villages.

The first, most salient component of the program is classroom (training) sessions conducted to a selected group of people from each one of the intervention villages. Typically six to seven trainees are selected from one village which includes both males and females. Mobilizing fellow villagers and monitoring local government offices, trainees are expected to become change agents in the villages. As such, CBO carefully selects them, based on the levels of motivation; community-mindedness; and time availability for participation. During the training sessions, CBO's field trainers teach trainees their legal and constitutional rights, their entitlements under ICDS and several grievance redressal methods.

The second component is the incentivisation of trainees to disseminate newly acquired knowledge and skills to their fellow villagers. CBO's trainers support trainees in conducting knowledge-sharing activities for their peers and other villagers in both formal and informal settings.

The third component is channelling the newly created demand through recourse mechanisms. CBO's trainers demonstrate trainees how to use grievance redressal methods when ICDS delivering services are dysfunctional. For example, trainers often assist trainees in writing complaint letters and filing the Right for Information applications to authorities. After successful utilisation of such methods, trainees are encouraged to mentor non-trained villagers so that they can also use these redressal methods.

Also, the program also created awareness about the benefits of child care and development facilities provided by ICDS such as timely vaccination, child nutrition, pre-school education etc. The role of the program, therefore, goes beyond mere dissemination of knowledge and creation of awareness and demand for effective implementation of ICDS; it is also about the utilisation of services and demonstration of channelling of demand by the community through legitimate redressal mechanisms. When villagers understand the benefits of the facilities by the ICDS and are aware of community-based mechanism for effective functioning of the local institution, it is expected that they proactively monitor public social service delivery through capitalizing on such mechanisms, and provision and access to better child health care facilities is expected to take roots in the villages.

Methodology

The present study has been conducted in 45 villages from Mewat district of Haryana. The village selection for the study was done using the stratified random sampling approach. A coherent distribution of villages was done across the five[33] blocks in the district. For facilitating village selection, a reconnaissance study was done to estimate the level of awareness among the respondent population. After that, 30 villages were selected that rated better on awareness regarding ICDS (experimental

33. Mewat district is composed of 5 blocks namely, Tauru, Nagina, Firozpur Jhirka, Nuh and Punhana. Nuh is the district headquarter.

villages). Correspondingly, 15 villages were selected based on having low or no awareness of ICDS (control villages). The awareness was also found to be higher in experimental villages due to the presence of wall paintings describing the provisions under the ICDS scheme and beneficiary entitlements. The control villages selected for the study were ensured to be comparable based on the observed similarity in the socio-economic conditions (occupational pattern, and distribution of caste and religion). Geographical proximity was also taken into consideration. In both types of villages, a survey was conducted during July 2014, and another round of the survey was undertaken from June 2016. Table-1 shows the number of villages selected from each block for the study. The instruments included a dataset on 20 randomly selected households[34] per village, focus group discussions with villagers and Anganwadi *workers (*AWWs) and non-participant and participant observations of ICDS centres. The final sample for the first round of survey comprised of 900 households. In the second round of the survey, due to the attrition rate, responses from 804 households were compared.

Table-1: Village Wise Sample

Blocks	Experimental villages	Control villages
Nagina	5	2
Nuh	5	2
Punhana	5	2
F. Jhirka	8	5
Tauru	7	4
Total	30	15

Source: Primary Data

Status of Health infrastructure and Reproductive Child Health in Mewat

Good health is central to happiness and well-being. The healthy population are found to live longer and be more productive (WHO, 2014). Status of key indicators related to health infrastructure and situation is important to understand the overall health scenario in the region. Access to health care services is imperative to ensure health equity as well as increasing the quality of healthy life for everyone. The health infrastructure in Mewat is not well developed; there are only one general hospital, one gynaecologist and one paediatrician for 1.1 million population of Mewat (Population

34. Random sampling was used for selection: field surveyors randomly visited households in each village until they identified 20 eligible households for ICDS scheme.

Research Centre, 2014; Census 2011). The health care facilities at the village level are also grim; According to DLHS data for 2007-08, only 26.1 percent villages in Mewat had any government health facility (IDC, 2014). The average population served by Sub-health centre is around 10000, and merely 50% of the villages have ASHA workers. Due to the higher number of villages having ICDS (93.5%), the role of effective implementation of ICDS in ensuring better child health becomes very important and critical.

Table-2: Health Infrastructure in Mewat district

S. No.	Health infrastructure	Number
1.	Number of General Hospital	1
2.	Gynaecologist	1
3.	Paediatrician	1
4.	The average number of medical institutions (2011-12)	105
5.	No of Community Health Centre (CHC)	3
6.	No. of Primary Health Centre (PHC)	17
7.	Percentage of villages having any government health facilities	26.1
8.	Average population served by Sub Health Centre (SHC)	10395
9.	Average population served by PHC	64096
10.	Average population served by CHC	263275
11.	Percentage of villages having Accredited Social Health Activist (ASHA)	47.8
12.	Percentage of villages having AWWs	93.5

Source: Statistical Abstract (2014), Haryana, Census 2011, and IDC, 2014

Reproductive health is considered to be the most important aspect of assessing the health status of a society as it is considered to be an essential component of young people's ability to become well adjusted, responsible and productive members of the society (United Nations, 2003). Better reproductive health is also essential to bring down the infant mortality rate (IMR). The statistics for the district reveals that reproductive health care is found to be largely in a grim state (table 3). According to the recent DLHS survey, antenatal care[35] is received by less than half of the pregnant women (45.5%) in Mewat (table 3). The sorry state of affairs further gets heightened

35. Antenatal care refers to the regular medical and nursing care recommended for women during pregnancy. It is particularly important to ensure appropriate growth and development of the foetus and elimination of any health risks both, to the expectant mother and the baby (Nath, 2014).

with reduced access to institutional mechanisms of delivery; only 51.2% of women undergo an institutional delivery in Mewat, thereby magnifying the risk to the woman and the baby. Lack of access to institutional delivery mechanisms increases the risk of maternal and infant mortality. Health risks among neonates and infants further magnify with lack of access to vaccination and child health care facilities. Approximately only a quarter of the total children (27.3%) receive full vaccination in Mewat. The mortality rate among children under the age of five years is also very high in Mewat (858) as compared to state (Haryana) average of 307.1.

Table-3: Reproductive Child Health

	Mewat	Haryana
Fertility		
Births to women aged 15-19 year out of total births	5.0	2.7
Current use of Family Planning		
Any Method (in %)	23.5	50.1
Antenatal care		
Pregnant women who received any antenatal check-up (in %)	45.5	73.8
Delivery care		
Institutional delivery (in %)	51.2	80.3
Child Immunisation		
Received full vaccination (in %)	27.3	52.7
Under Five Mortality		
Under five year infant mortality (in numbers)	858.0	307.1
Under 5 year infant mortality (Females) (in numbers)	512.0	124.6
Under 5 year infant mortality (Males) (in numbers)	346.0	182.4

Source: DLHS, 2013 and Statistical Abstract 2014

Role and Limitations of Community based Mechanism in the Effective Functioning of ICDS

Given the poor child health indices and lack of infrastructure at the district level, the role of the local institution i.e., ICDS becomes very crucial to improve the child health care situation. Overtime, there has been increased importance of the involvement of the community in effective functioning and utilisation of child care facilities through ICDS. The AWW needs to be recruited either from the same village/ward or from nearby villages. Apart from central, state and district level monitoring committees, the villagers including *gram panchayat*, ASHA workers, and beneficiaries are also involved in monitoring the functioning of ICDS. Bottom up approach was promoted to check the coverage and quality of services provided to the intended beneficiaries. It is expected to improve the utilisation of child care facilities and consequently improve child health indices as it is driven by community needs, information and values.

But it is often argued that lack of information and awareness often results in weak community based monitoring and mechanism. The CBO program imbibed the importance of the facilities provided by the ICDS and increased awareness about the scheme and its entitlements. It is expected that this should lead to increased demand for the services and receipt of due entitlements that improves child health and development. The section outlines the community based monitoring and examines its effect on the functional status of the ICDS, and utilisation of ICDS services.

Community based Monitoring

In this section, we examine the measures undertaken by the villagers with the aim to improve the functioning of ICDS services. The results reveal that in the last three years, around 35% of the trainees and fellow villagers in the experimental villages (as against 9% in the control villages) have been involved in monitoring the functioning of ICDS (table 4). It is important to note that most of the monitoring are restricted to the provision of food than many other equally important aspects for child development such as quantity and quality of infrastructure.

Table-4: Monitoring of ICDS by Gram Panchayat and Community

		Experimental Villages	Control Villages
Monitoring of ICDS (Y/N)		35%	09%
Activities Monitored (Among the ones monitoring ICDS)	Meal provisions	98%	92%
	Regular opening	12%	6%
	Activities by AWWs	15%	10%
	Infrastructure available	35%	36%
	Infrastructure Quality	20%	15%

Source: Primary Data

In both group of villages (experimental and control), there are gaps in the implemenntation of ICDS. Around 85% and 81% of community members in experimental and control villages respectively have found problems in the proper implementation of ICDS (figure 1). However, a relatively large number of respondents (28%) in the experimental villages as against the 7% of community members in the control villages have raised issues regarding implementation of ICDS in their villages.

It is important to note that only a few community members (20% and 12% community members in experimental and control villages respectively) have used any redressal mechanism (right to information, visit to district office etc.) towards providing more or better facilities in the ICDS centers. Many villagers still believe that there is no use of filling any complaint. This is primarily because concerned functionary have hardly responded to their complaints. At the same time, few villagers are also found to be still ignorant about the mechanisms for filling any complaint to the government department. In-depth discussions with them reveal that villagers find it more convenient to put their grievance to government officials when the officials visit their villages than filling any formal complaints.

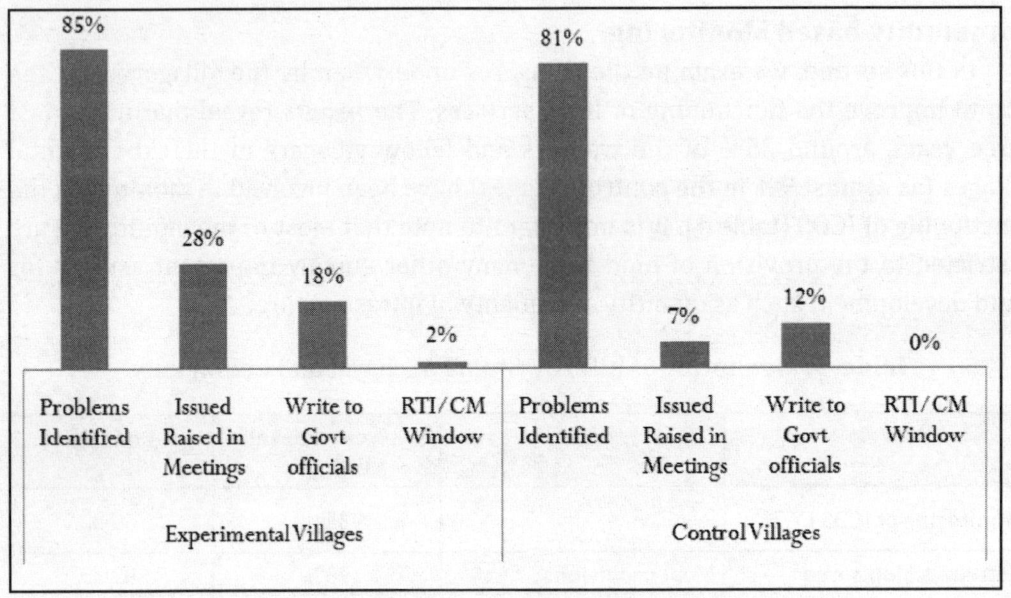

Fig. 1. Tools and mechanisms used by Gram Panchayat and Community

Source: Primary Data

Functioning of ICDS

In this section, we look at the availability of infrastructure and facilities at ICDS centers, provision of meals and display of services for more transparency. For effective and efficient functioning, ICDS centers require some basic infrastructure. There is a direct relationship between the availability of infrastructure in the centers and the quality of services provided to the beneficiary populace (Dhingra and Sharma, 2011). As is evident from table 5, there is an improvement over time in the condition of ICDS centers in both types of villages. It is evident that in the villages which are experimental, new arrangements have been made in the form of a separate building or alternative arrangements which include centers operating in *Chaupals*, government complexes, schools, *Panchayat* houses etc. Better condition of ICDS centers in the experimental villages could be attributed to community based monitoring. But when it comes to facilities in the ICDS centers, overtime there is not much improvement in the drinking water facilities and toilet facilities in ICDS centers in both experimental and control villages. Discussion with AWWs revealed that they have already put up the request for these facilities but there is not much response from the government. Lack of these essential facilities hampers AWWs in cooking food and ensuring children to stay in ICDS center for the stipulated time during the day.

Table-5: Infrastructure of ICDS center

	Maintained Building	Drinking water facilities	Toilet facilities
Experimental villages			
Baseline	82%	73%	60%
Endline	100%	80%	75%
Control Villages			
Baseline	73%	67%	60%
Endline	93%	73%	70%

Source: Primary Data

The overarching objective of the ICDS scheme is to provide nutrition to children in the age of 0 to 6 years and impart pre literacy skills such that children are adequately ready to enter into formal school. Pre literacy skills are imparted through cognitive activities using play as a medium. Teaching aids are provided to ICDS centre for improving the cognitive abilities of children. These teaching aids help make learning creative and improve retention ability in children. AWW is also supposed to provide medicine for treating common ailments of children and first aid in case of injuries and accidents. Pre-school kits, IEC materials, growth charts, medicine kits are some of the materials needs to be available in ICDS centres. Field observations yield that in the experimental villages, there has been an increase in the availability of materials (table 6). Contrarily, in case of control villages, the availability of materials is either the same or has marginally increased over the same period.

Table-6: Availability of material for Preschool activities

	Experimental Villages		Control Villages	
	Baseline	Endline	Baseline	Endline
Pre-school kits	43.0%	66.2%	48.1%	52.6%
IEC/training materials	38.2%	52.1%	33.4%	38.8%
Medicine kits	37.9%	45.4%	40.2%	40.2%
Growth Charts	48.0%	55.2%	37.5%	40.2%
Weighing machine	42.4%	45.8%	33.8%	35.9%

Source: Primary Data

Displaying the facilities provided by ICDS centers plays a crucial role in increasing the awareness level among the community regarding the benefits of the scheme. The ICDS centers are mandated to display the lists in the centre premises. The results from the survey reveals that not all ICDS centers have put up the lists of services in the ICDS center; 73% and 53% of ICDS centers in experimental and control villages respectively have displayed services list at the time of endline survey (table 7). In both experimental and control villages, the lists displayed at ICDS centers are in the form of charts which are rolled out when the AWWs open the center. There are no wall paintings detailing the services provided at the centre. In addition, around 53 % and 40% ICDS centers in both the experimental and control villages respectively have displayed the phone numbers of concerned officials.

Table-7: Display Facilities at ICDS center

	Services	Immunisation list	Phone number of officials
	Experimental villages		
Baseline	46%	83%	20%
Endline	73%	96%	53%
	Control Villages		
Baseline	40%	86%	26%
Endline	53%	86%	40%

Source: Primary Data

Another objective of the ICDS scheme is to improve the nutritional and health status of pregnant women, lactating mothers and children up to six years of age. In doing so, nutritive meals are provided at the center for all beneficiary segments. The meals provided are cooked hot within the center premises. According to the revised nutritional norms under the ICDS scheme, children below six years of age are entitled to get 500 calories and 12-15 grams of protein every day whereas pregnant women and nursing mothers are entitled to have 600 calories and 18-20 grams of protein per day. Data obtained from the field suggests that in experimental villages, there has been a considerable increase in the percentage of households receiving quality meals. Contrastingly, there is considerable decrease in the percentage of households receiving the same in control villages (table 8). With respect the o regularity of meals being provided to children, there appears to be a lot of scope for improvement. As is evident from the table, regularity of meal provision has witnessed a decline. AWWs mentioned that cooking of meals is dependent on the supply of sufficient ration from the government. They cannot purchase the ingredients for cooking meals. The frequency of ration supply to the schools needs to be worked at in collaboration with the local administration.

A glance at the human resources at the ICDS centers reveal that there ia s sufficient number of AWWs and Anganwadi helpers (AWHs) positions across both the experimental and control villages. But attendance of AWWs and AWHs is more sporadic in control villages as compared to experimental villages. This also could be attributed to the fact that visits by Child Development Project Officer (CDPO) is more often in the ICDS centers experimental villages as compared to ICDS centers in control villages, which is due to more active community based monitoring. Though there are more interactions between CDPOs and AWWs in experimental villages, there is still room for change in the implementation of ICDS in the rural villages of Mewat.

Table-8: Meal and its quality

	Proportion of households from where children are visiting ICDS regularly	Proportion of children getting meal regularly	Perception of quality of Meal being good
Experimental villages			
Baseline	51.6%	61.2%	47.9%
Endline	86.9%	59.6%	70.8%
Control Villages			
Baseline	58.4%	56.0%	63.9%
Endline	70.7%	53.3%	60.8%

Source: Primary Data

Awareness about ICDS facilities and Utilisation of ICDS services by eligible households

The AWWs is the most important functionary in implementing the ICDS. She plays a crucial role in promoting a child's growth and development thereby contributing to the impact ICDS centers can make. She visits homes, provides trainings, and immunisation to pregnant women, lactating mothers and children. To understand the extent of awareness regarding the roles and responsibilities of *anganwadi* workers, a questionnaire was administered on households having children between 0 to 6 years of age. The results reveal that the households in experimental villages have higher awareness regarding the presence of an *anganwadi* worker in their village (table 9). This is also witnessed to have improved over the past two years by nearly 38%. Contrastingly, the escalation in awareness levels is found to be only 14% ithe n case of villages which are control.

A further exploration into the data reveals that even though, the awareness regarding the presence of an *anganwadi* worker in the village has increased, much needs to be done regarding awareness of her roles and responsibilities. Though there has been an increase in the frequencies of her visiting home and conducting vaccination, not many people are aware of her role of training or information on health and conducting health camps. The picture is nearly same for both experimental and control villages.

Table-9: Awareness about Anganwadi Worker and her Roles

	Experimental Villages		Control Villages	
	Baseline	**Endline**	**Baseline**	**Endline**
Awareness about AWW	56.5%	94.8%	62.2%	76.3%
Aware that following activities undertaken by AWW				
Visit homes	66.9%	86.7%	52.2%	65.5%
Training/information on health	20.8%	33.4%	23.6%	33.6%
Conduct health camps/checkups	8.3%	10.2%	6.1%	10.3%
Vaccination	53.1%	81.8%	50.1%	64.5%
Provide meals	69.4%	92.2%	73.0%	83.8%

Source: Primary Data

In terms of utilisation of child care services, there has been n increase in the number of households sending their children to ICDS in both the experimental and control group and the proportionate change is higher in the experimental group citing the perceptible impact of increased awareness of the people (table 10). Still around 15% of the households are not utilizing the services. Interviews with the households not sending their child to ICDS highlights two prominent reasons i.e., (i) perception that there is no use of sending children to any educational institute and (ii) irregularity the n opening of the ICDS center. Higher incidence of vaccination by the children in the experimental villages signifies the importance of community based monitoring in improving child health. If we look at other facilities availed by the eligible households, it is found that there is a perceptible change in the proportion of people receiving the benefits in the experimental villages but still there is room for improvement.

Table-10: Utilisation of ICDS services

Among the eligible households	Experimental Villages		Control Villages	
	Baseline	Endline	Baseline	Endline
Proportion of households sending children to ICDS	51.6%	86.9%	58.4%	70.7%
Proportion of households got their child immunised	50.0%	69.8%	46.1%	51.3%
Antenatal care to pregnant women	22.6%	40.0%	24.3%	27.9%
Received advice during pregnancy	52.1%	71.0%	55.0%	59.0%
Received supplementary food/ tablets	32.0%	50.7%	35.2%	39.1%

Source: Primary Data

In a nutshell, the results reveal that higher awareness levels among the respondent population and relatively more use of grievance redressal mechanisms in experimental villages result in acknowledgment of the presence of *anganwadi* workers in the respective villages. However, there is a need to build the awareness of inhabitants regarding the specific roles and responsibilities of these workers such that they can ensure that they discharge their duties more effectively. It is apparent that higher awareness among a population group can make a positive impact on the strengthening the infrastructural set ups as well as improve the accountability stake of public officials.

Major Conclusions

The paper attempts to understand the role and limitations of community based mechanism in the functioning of ICDS. The reconnaissance study has been conducted in 45 villages (30 experimental villages and 15 control villages). The instruments included a dataset of 20 randomly selected households per village, focus group discussions and non-participant and participant observations of ICDS. A quasi-experimental double difference method was adopted to examine the influence of differing information levels on the functioning of the ICDS scheme and utilisation of child health and development facilities.

The results reveal that increasing access to information about rights and entitlements and providing the community with tools to demand accountability from service providers does play a role in improving the governance of ICDS. Prior to the intervention by a CBO, citizen in the selected region were found to be generally ignorant of their actual rights and entitlements under the ICDS scheme. Once their knowledge was improved, some of them rise collectively for demanding their rights either through direct interaction with the local service providers or through using redressal mechanisms. It is also found that some of the direct trainees become the member of the committees such as *panchayati raj* institutions. This also helped in the better functioning of ICDS centres in the experimental villages as these members ensured to closely monitor the functioning of ICDS centers in their village and take uthe p matter with the officials as and when required. Despite this, the intervention has some limitations as well. The process of transformation through awareness is slow. Among the people who were informed about their rights and entitlements by the CBO, only few of them have actually raised their voices against the government service delivery mechanism. This is primarily because many of the trainees do not have e complete understanding of improved benefits of better child care facilities through ICDS. It is also found that trainees filled complaints only once and did not followed up with the government officials further. Towards this, it is vital to improve leadership skills among some citizens that influence the regularity with which they interact with local officials and demand for good governance. It is also equally important to motivate people through exposure visits to the district officials and create opportunities for the common citizens to interact with local and district officials. The moderated platforms can be organised where citizens, local officials and policy makers can interact and discuss the issues pertaining the implementation of the program. Ambiguity in implementation roles of different entities and lack of knowledge of all services with the local implementers further dents the process. There is also a requirement to influence the supply side through the provision of regular training to AWWs on budget utilisation and services provided under ICDS which can improve their responsiveness to demands raised by the local citizens.

References

1. Banerjee, Abhijit V., and Esther Duflo. 2011. Poor Economics: A Radical Rethinking of the Way to Fight Global Poverty. London: Random House.
2. Ben, U.N. 2006. Public Relations Communications and Conflict Resolution in Nigeria: the Niger Delta Question Conflict Management and Peace Building in Africa. 1(1): 51-66.
3. Cummins, Stephan. 2007. 'Community Participation in Service Delivery and Accountability'. UCLA School of Public Affairs. http://www.spa.ucla.edu/up/webfiles/publications/community_participation_and_service_delivery.doc. Last accessed in December, 2016.
4. Census, 2011. Census of India. Retrieved in June 2017 from www.census2011.co.in
5. Chandran KPV, and P. Sandhya, 2010. Child Nutrition in Rural India: Some Policy Priorities and Strategies. MPRA Paper no. 27101. Retreived from https://mpra.ub.uni-muenchen.de/27101/1/Child_Nutrition_in_Rural_India_Some_Policy_Priorities_and_Strategies.pdf in May 2018
6. DLHS, 2013. District Fact Sheet. District level Household Survey. International Institute for Population Sciences (IIPS), Mumbai. Retrieved on June 2017. https://nrhm-mis.nic.in/SitePages/DLHS-4.aspx
7. Dhingra, R. and I. Sharma. 2011. "Assessment of Preschool Education Component of ICDS Scheme in Jammu District." Global Journal of Human Social Science 11(6).
8. EPW, 2007.Strategies for Children under Six. Economic and Political Weekly. Special article. Vol. 42, Issue 52. 29th December, 2007
9. Jyotiranjan Sahoo, Preetam B Mahajan, Sourabh Paul, Vikas Bhatia, Abhinash K Patra, and Dilip Kumar Hembram, 2016. Operational Assessment of ICDS Scheme at Grass Root Level in a Rural Area of Eastern India: Time to Introspect. Retrieved from https://www.ncbi.nlm.nih.gov/pubmed/28208890 in May 2018
10. Government of Haryana 2014. Statistical Abstract (Various Issues), Haryana
11. Gupta, Amit Sen, and Deepa. 2009. "How Inclusive is the Five Year Plan: A Review of Selected Sectors." UNDP.
12. http://www.undp.org/content/dam/india/docs/how_inclusive_is_the_eleventh_five_year_plan_a_sectoral_review.pdfLast accessed in December, 2016.
13. Institute for Development and Communication, (IDC), 2014. Health Disparities in Mewat: Strategies for Removal. Department of Planning, Government of Haryana.
14. Jayanti, S. Ravi, and S. Chandrasekhar. 2009. "Transforming Public System Governance: A Way Forward." New Governance and Development–Challenges of Addressing Poverty and Inequality. Ed. H.S. Shylendra. Delhi: Academic Foundation.
15. Manav S., 2015. Mortality indicators shoa w dismal state of healthcare. Retrieved from http://www.tribuneindia.com/news/haryana/governance/mortality-indicators-show-dismal-state-of-healthcare-nhm/116504.html in May 2018
16. Michael Lokshin; Monica Das Gupta; Michele Gragnolati and Oleksiy Ivaschenko, 2005. "Improving Child Nutrition? The Integrated Child Development Services in India"(PDF). Development and Change. 36 (4): 613-640.

17. Nath, G.B. 2014. 'Importance of Antenatal care'. Retrieved from http://parentssquare.com/pregnancy/importance-of-antenatal-care/ in May 2017
18. Population Research Centre, 2014. A Report on Quality Monitoring of Mewat District. Programme Implementation Plan 2013-14. Retrieved from https://nrhm-mis.nic.in/Part%20B%20Demographic%20and%20Vital%20Indicators/PIP%20Monitoring%20of%20various%20districts%20during%202013-14/Districts%20PIP%20Report%202013-14/Haryana/Mewat%20-%20PIP%20Report.docx on May 2018
19. Thomas Nidhi, Paramita Sengupta and Anoop I Benjamin, 2015. An Assessment of the Integrated Child Development Services Programme in an Urban Area of Ludhiana, Punjab. IOSR Journal of Dental and Medical Sciences14(2):58-61 · March 2015
20. United Nations 2003. 'World Youth Report 2003': The Global Situation of Young People. Department of Economic and Social Affairs. United Nations
21. WHO 2014. 'Health and Development'. World Health Organisation. Retrieved from http://www.who.int/hdp/en/ on June, 2017.

□

19

Maternal Health Scenario In Gujarat

—Kranti Vora and Shahin Saiyed

Abstract

Gujarat has made tremendous economic progress in recent decades. To match progress on health indicators with the economic indicators, the Government of Gujarat has initiated several interventions to improve access to care for maternal health services in the state for the past couple of decades. This article examines trends in maternal health indicators, health infrastructure including human resources, innovative program implementation, programmatic successes and failures. It also evaluates new initiatives and different strategies implemented by Government of Gujarat for improving maternal healthcare utilisation and indicators of the state. It is based on a review of literature and analysis of secondary data from different government surveys. Innovations and persuasive efforts of the government have improved the situation. The progress has been some what hampered by human resources related Issues for the efficient implementation of the effective strategies.

Introduction

Gujarat is one of the prosperous and urbanised Indian states with one of the fastest growing economies in India. It is also, one of the most industrialised states with per capita income 1.4 times higher than that of the national average (State-wise: Population, GSDP 2009-10). About 17% of the population in Gujarat is below the official poverty line, which is better than national average of 22% Gujarat has made a rapid and commendable progress on the economic front while there is a huge scope of improvement in social indicators such as education, health and gender equality (Hirway and Mahadevia, 2004). As per last Census data (2011), child sex ratio, which is a reflection of how females are values as compared to male in a society, is lower than national average (Census of India, 2011) and according to SRS 2011-13, the percentage of maternal mortality ratio (MMR) of Gujarat is significantly decreased. (Sample Registration System [SRS], 2011-13). However, compared to the percentage of institutional delivery of Gujarat, which is close to 90% as per NFHS, 4 data (International Institute of Population Science [IIPS], 2015-16), this decline is not equivalent. This may be because of limited access to Emergency Obstetric Care (EmOC), inefficient referral system, inadequate quality of care and low coverage of postnatal care (IIPS, 2007-08).

Purpose

For Gujarat to progress further on maternal health indicators, it is important to examine the current situation and contextual factors affecting maternal healthcare utilisation and indicators. The purpose of this chapter is 1) to analyse the present scenario in Gujarat regarding maternal health situation, 2) Understand health system and social factors affecting maternal health indicators and 3) to study new programs/ initiatives implemented in the last decade.

Materials and Methods

The chapter documents the maternal health situation of Gujarat from various perspectives including trends in maternal health indicators, health infrastructure including human resources, innovative program implementation, programmatic successes and failures. It is based on a review of the literature (including published and unpublished reports of government and non-governmental agencies, doctorals these etc.), analysis of secondary data from the health management information systems (HMIS) at the state and district levels and demographic health survey data. Secondary data for maternal health indicators are taken from the National Family Health Survey 4 (2015-16), District Level Household Survey 3 (DLHS), and Health Management Information System (HMIS) (National Health Systems Resource Centre Gujarat, [NHSRC] 2015-16). Information regarding health infrastructure and human resources was collected from Rural Health Statistics (RHS) Bulletin 2015-16 (Rural Health Statistics in India [RHS], 2015-16). Data and information are also obtained from official website of the health and family welfare department of the Gujarat Government and other similar internet sources. Despite the use of multiple data sources, there are gaps and discrepancies in the information on maternal health care services utilisation, provision and maternal health indicators. For example, the private sector has a vital role to provide maternal health care services but routine data collection for these services is not conducted. Hence, it is difficult to assess utilisation of the current maternal health services, type of quality of care, and analyze determinants of improvement of the maternal health situation in Gujarat.

Current Scenario

Gujarat accounts for 6% of the surface area of India and 5% of the population of India resides in the state. Gujarat has a population of about 60 million and has 43% of the population living in urban areas (higher compared to the Indian average of 27%) (Census of India, 2011). It is among the better performing Indian states in terms of demographic indicators with a better life expectancy at birth and lower birth/death rates than the national average. The indicators such as life expectancy and Infant Mortality Rate (IMR) for Gujarat indicates improvement over time with a 9th rank among 17 major states. The life expectancy increased from 57 years in 1981 to 68.2 years during 2009-13.

Table-1: Comparison of demographic and mortality indicators of Gujarat and India

Indicator	Gujarat	India
Population (In crore) (2011)	6	121
Decadal Growth (%) (2011)	19	18
Population density per sq km (2011)	308	382
Birth rate (2015)	20	21
Death Rate (2015)	6.1	6.5
Total Fertility Rate (2015)	2.2	2.3
Mean Age (years) of effective marriage (2015)	22	22
Literacy rate: (2015)		
Total	79	74
Male	87	82
Female	71	65
Sex ratio (no. of females per 1,000 males) SRS (2013-15)	854	900
Life expectancy at birth—females (2010-14)	69	68
Infant Mortality Rate (2015)	33	37
Under 5 Mortality Rate 2015	39	43
Maternal mortality ratio (2011-13)	112	167

Source: Registrar General of India. Sample Registration System Statistical Report 2015

As seen in table-1, men are more literate compare to women in Gujarat, which indicates the need of education in women. Maternal Mortality Ratio has reduced significantly from 202 in 1999-2001 to 112 per 1,00,000 live births in 2011-13. Currently, Gujarat is 5th in ranking concerning MMR among major states. Similarly, the IMR has also reduced from 54 infant deaths per 1000 live births in 2005 to 35 in 2014 but Gujarat ranks 12th among major states. Among the other vital indicators such as Neonatal Mortality rate (NNR) and Under-5 Mortality Rate (U5MR), among major states, Gujarat ranked 9 and 10 respectively during 2016 and ranked 14th for birth rate and 8th for death rate respectively (SRS, 2016). Maternal mortality, child mortality and social status of women raise important concerns regarding health systems related and social factors affecting the maternal health indicators.

Table-2: Trends in maternal health care utilisation

Indicator	DLHS-3 (2007-08)	NFHS 4 (2015-16)	HMIS (2015-16)
Coverage of antenatal services			
Tetanus toxoid injection (2 or more)*	61	87	75
Completed 3 antenatal care visits	55	71	80.4
Consumption of iron/folic acid tablets	29	37	95.7
Full ANC	20	31	NA
Place of delivery			
Institutional deliveries	57	89	98.4
Domiciliary deliveries	42	11	1.6
Institutional deliveries			
Public	36	33	40.6
NGO/trust	2	NA	NA
Private	62	67	59.4
Type of delivery			
Vaginal delivery	92	82	88.8
Caesarean section	8	18	11.2
Deliveries conducted by health personnel (Delivery by Doctor, ANM/Nurse/LHV)	62	87	NA
Mothers received postnatal care within 2 days of delivery	56	NA	87.9
Any delivery complication	47	NA	NA
Any post-delivery complication	26	NA	NA

NA=Not available # Full ANC for DLHS 3 is at least 3 ANC, 1 TT and 100 IFA, for NFHS 4 is at least 4 ANC, at least 1 TT and consumption of at least 100 IFA.

Source: IIPS, 2015-16 NFHS 4, IIPS. 2007-08, DLHS 3, RHS, 2015-16.

Table-2 shows the trends in utilisation of maternal health indicators for three demographic surveys DLHS 3 (2007-08), NFHS 4 (2015-16) and HMIS (2015-16), which are the latest data available to understand trends in maternal health care utilisation in Gujarat. The coverage of full ANC is 20% in DLHS 3, which increased to 31% in NFHS 4. The potential reasons for low full ANC may be low IFA consumption (37%), as tetanus toxoid and at least 3 ANC visits are reported more than 70%. Institutional deliveries have increased from 57% to 89% between the two surveys but the percentage of Caesarean section has more than doubled from 8% to 18%. There seems to be a significant difference in maternal health indicators between two surveys but one needs to be cautious in interpretation as both surveys used different sampling strategies. Especially if one examines the utilisation of institutional deliveries, which shows more than a 30-point percentage difference in less than 10 years, which seems unrealistic. Numbers in NFHS-4 and state HMIS data is much closer, yet in some of the indicators, there are huge discrepancies. For example, a demographic survey (NFHS-4) reports less than 40% consumption of IFA tablets while HMIS reports more than 95%. Lack of reliable data sources is one of the major issues dogging Indian states especially to accurately establish the progress made in the improvement of maternal health services utilisation leading to better maternal and child health in India.

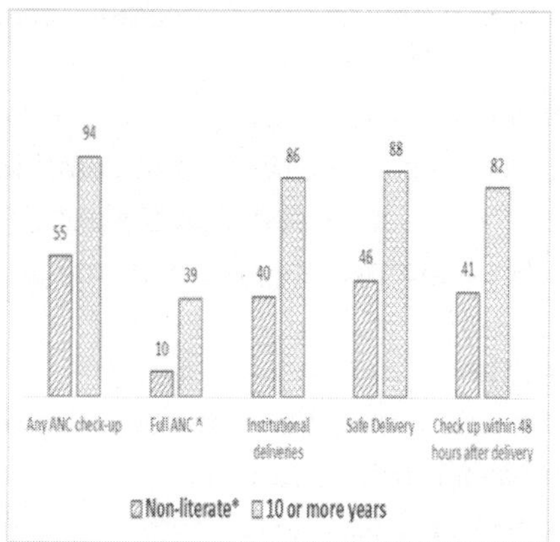

Fig. 1: Access to maternal health according to mother's education CES

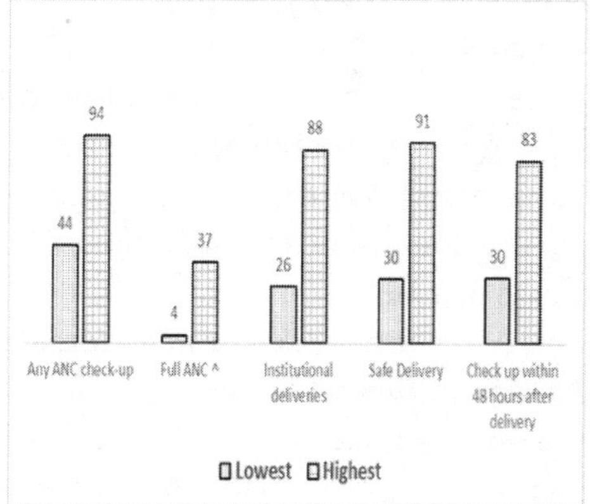

Fig. 2: Access to maternal health according to wealth index CES

Source: Own construction based on Coverage Evaluation Survey (CES) India 2009 Raw data.

The educational and economic status of women influences the use of maternal care. Figure 1 and 2 illustrate that illiterate mothers and mothers from the lowest wealth quintile are using basic maternal healthcare much less than their literate or wealthier counterparts and are far less likely to see a doctor. As per Figure 1, only

10% of illiterate mothers had full ANC compared to 39% of mothers with 12 or more year of education and 40% of mothers had institutional deliveries compared to 86% of mothers with 12 or more years of education; similar differences are observed in any ANC checkup, safe delivery and checkup within 48 hours after delivery. As per Figure 2, only 4% lowest wealth quintile mothers had full ANC compared to 37% of wealthier counterparts and 26% lowest wealth quintile mothers had institutional deliveries compared to 88% wealthier mothers; any ANC checkup, safe delivery and checkup within 48 hours after delivery show vast disparities based on wealth status of mother.

There is strong evidence that skilled attendance at birth and especially institutional deliveries are critical strategies for reducing maternal mortality. Improved access to maternal health services such as an antenatal checkup, institutional delivery/delivery by trained, EmOC skilled personnel and postnatal checkup reduces maternal morbidity and mortality. Though Gujarat has high proportions of institutional delivery, reduction of MMR is not equivalent because of the limited availability of EmOC within the public health system. There are 37 obstetricians available in all Community Health Centers (CHCs) of Gujarat, which reflect limited access to C-section. As Gujarat is unique in having a significant presence of the private sector at the sub-district level, it plays a very important role in the provision of maternal health care especially intra-natal care and EmOC

As seen in Table-2, a significant proportion of institutional deliveries take place in the private sector in Gujarat. Also the majority of childbirth-related complications as treated in the private sector due to limited access to a specialist in the public health system. It is important to understand the role of the private sector in the maternal healthcare delivery in Gujarat.

Role of the private sector in maternal healthcare delivery in Gujarat:

As seen in *Table*-3, about half of the maternal health care delivery takes place in the private sector including antenatal and intra-natal care in Gujarat. As part of the national trend, institutional deliveries in Gujarat also increased from 46% in DLHS-1(1998-99) to 56% in DLHS-3 (2007-08). While over a decade for NFHS survey, the institutional delivery increased from 53% (NHFS 3) to 89% (NFHS 4). In contrast to the national trend of the majority of institutional deliveries (58%) happening in the public sector, about 64% of institutional deliveries happened in the private sector in Gujarat. Even the trend of institutional deliveries in Gujarat from DLHS 2 to DLHS 3 shows a significant increase in the proportion of private sector deliveries (16%) (IIPS, DLHS 3, 2007-08; IIPS, DLHS 2, 2002-04). As De Costa et al noted, improvement in institutional deliveries in Gujarat is driven primarily by the private sector for more than 15 years now (De Costa et al., 2014).

Table-3: Role of the private sector in maternal healthcare delivery

Indicator	DLHS-3 (%)
ANC at a private facility	49
Received iron/folic acid tablets	46
The proportion of all deliveries	36
Type of delivery at the Private facility	
Vaginal delivery	83
Caesarean section	17
Any delivery complication	50
Any post-delivery complication	23

Source: Own construction based on IIPS, DLHS 3, raw data Gujarat, 2007-.08

It is noteworthy that in the private sector about 27% of all the deliveries are C-section that is a much higher proportion then that overall C-section rate of Gujarat (18%). This is consistent with the trend seen worldwide in the health systems where the thrust of institutional deliveries is in the private sector (Pomeroy et al., 2014). The supply-induced demand for C-section has important health system and maternal health indicator implications. A higher proportion of C-section increases the cost of maternal health care and leads to inequity in the access to the same.

The percentage of institutional delivery in the private sector is high in Gujarat because of a shortage of skilled healthcare providers in the public health sector and the presence of the private sector at the sub-district level. Hence the, quality of care in the private sector is also an important issue that warrants immediate attention. There are disparities in the size and composition of the private sector ranging from alternative medicine graduates conducting deliveries in less than 10-bedded hospitals in the remote rural areas to internationally trained specialists staffing more than 100-bedded corporate hospitals equipped with state-of-art facilities in the urban areas. This also makes it difficult to assess the quality of care and level of geographic and financial access (Vora & Mavalankar, 2014). Limited access to health care in the public sector along with low health literacy leads to higher out of pocket expense for the poor and marginalised population. Households with high health care needs (SCs/STs, and the poor) are in a more disadvantaged position in terms of spending on health care (Dwivedi & Pradhan, 2017).

Health Infrastructure Issues Including Human Resources

Maternal healthcare provision in Gujarat is three-tiered, ANM, staff nurse and medical officers provide antenatal care, basic delivery care including Basic EmOC and postnatal care at the Sub Centre (SC) and Primary Health Center (PHC). C-section facilities are available at some community health centres (CHC), all first referral units (FRU) and sub-district and district hospitals. Tertiary care is available at district hospitals and teaching hospitals.

Table-4: Status of facilities available at Public health facilities in Gujarat

Indicators	2011 (%)	2015 (%)
Facilities available at Sub Centers		
Total Subcenter	7274	8063
Sub Centers in Govt. Buildings	72	64
Number of Sub Centers with ANM Quarter	88	65
Number of Sub Centers with ANM living in Sub Center Quarter	88	65
Regular Water Supply	100	100
Electric Supply	100	100
All-Weather Motor-able Approach Road	100	100
Facilities at Primary Health Centers		
No of PHCs	1123	1247
PHCs functioning in Govt. Buildings	100	85
With Labor Room	100	90
With Operation Theatre	100	93
With at least 4 beds	100	90
Regular Water Supply	100	100
Electric Supply	100	100
All-Weather Motor-able Approach Road	100	100
With Telephone	100	93
With Computer	96	93
Referral Transport	83	93
Registered RKS	100	92
No. of PHCs Functioning as per IPHS norms	3	29
Facilities available at Community Health Centers		
CHCs	305	320
CHCs functioning in Govt. Buildings	98	91
With computer/ Statistical Asst. for MIS/ Accountant	100	99
With functional Laboratory	92	99

With functional O.T.	92	95
With functional Labor Room	95	95
With functioning Stabilisation Units for New Born	48	42
With New Born Care Corner	2	45
With at least 30 beds	95	99
With functional X-ray machine	83	79
With quarters for specialist Doctors	89	20
With specialist Doctors living in quarters	19	9
With referral transport available	92	99
With registered RKS	100	93
Functioning as per IPHS norms	44	31
Having a regular supply of Allopathic drugs for common ailments	100	99
Having a regular supply of AYUSH drugs for common ailments	100	95

Source: RHS, 2015-16; RHS, 2011.

As seen in Table-4, the number of public facilities have increased from 2011 to 2015, and functional laboratory, O.T. and labour room at CHCs are better than before. Availability of quarters for specialist doctors at CHCs has declined from 89% to 20% and only of 9% specialist doctors living in quarters. Physical infrastructure for health has improved and almost all of the health facilities have basic amenities such as 24*7 water supply and electricity. The majority (>90%) had labour room and operational theatre for providing delivery care. Almost all (>98%) the facilities had all-weather roads approachable throughout the year (RHS, 2015-16). In nutshell, physical infrastructure for healthcare in Gujarat is adequate and this is a result of investment by the government and focus of the majority of national-level programs on the development of infrastructure. The same can also be said for the logistics and supplies, with more than 95% of sub-centers and about 85% of PHCs havinag regular stock of essential supplies (IIP. DLHS 3, 2007-08).

On the other hand, human resource issues have remained the same over the past decade. Comparison of RHS data over a period of 10 years from 2005 to 2015 shows that the shortage of human resources in the health system has remained unchanged for over a decade (RHS, 2015-16). The maximum shortfall has been in the availability of specialists in the public health system, including obstetricians and pediatricians, who are available only in 11% of required positions consistently. Least shortfall has been in positions of general doctors at PHCs, which is 16%. This could be because the number of positions for doctors has increased from one to two including AYUSH doctors under NRHM/NHM. While vacant position against the sanctioned position of

ANM at SC and PHCs has increased from 2005 to 2015 which is 11% to 26%, which again could be due to increase in the number of sub-centres and lack of recruitment/ availability.

Table-5: Percentage of a shortfall of Human Resources at Public Health Sectors

	% of shortfall	
	2005	**2015**
The health worker (Female/ANM) at sub-centres & PHC	22	28
Doctors at Primary Health Centers	21	16
Total specialists at CHCs	92	89
Radiographers at CHCs	58	52
Pharmacists at PHCs & CHCs	40	18
Laboratory Technicians at PHCs & CHCs	35	31
Nursing Staff at PHCs & CHCs	51	24

Source: RHS, 2015-16; RHS, 2005.

One of the reasons for the shortage of medical graduates including specialists is less number of medical graduates joining the government service areas, migration of medical graduates out of the country and problems with the recruitment process. For example, during the year 2005-06 less than 10% of medical graduates joined government services. Furthermore, in order to meet the vacancies, recruitments are made on the ad-hoc/contractual basis (Central Bureau of Health Intelligence [CBHI], 2007). Poor posting and transfer practices have been documented as a cause of reluctance of medical graduates to join public services, low morale of in-service providers and crowding in urban areas with vacancies in the rural [Purohit & Martineau, 2016]. There have been concerns over the lack of formal mechanism or system for workforce planning on the continuous basis (Purohit & Martineau, 2016). One of the central issues of human resource planning is the challenge of getting skilled professionals to join public health systems and to stay and work in rural and remote areas.

Since most of the doctors come from urban middle-class backgrounds, they all experience constraints in opting for rural services. The first constraint is the economic loss-since rural stay would mean lesser opportunities for private practice and greater expenditure on maintaining the family's standard of living and expectations. The second constraint is professional isolation leading to erosion of skills directly correlated to the limitation of resources and lack of opportunity for further academic development and the last one is Social isolation-separation from families and cultural gaps between providers and the people they serve. Poor access and communication and inadequate residential facilities also act as barriers to rural retention of skilled health workers (NRHM, 2007-2012).

In summary, physical infrastructure and logistics supplies are adequate in the public health system of Gujarat but there are shortages of skilled staff and non-availability of posted healthcare providers. This might be because of deficient human resources policies.

Gujarat government has undertaken various initiatives to ensure universal access to maternal health care including public-private partnerships in rural and difficult areas for poor mothers especially from marginalised populations such as tribal.

Initiatives for improving maternal healthcare utilisation and indicators:

To improve maternal-child health situation and access to quality health care services, the Government of Gujarat has implemented innovative programs and schemes in the last decade. There are many publications highlighting the successes and failures of large schemes such as '*Chiranjeevi Yojana*' in the last few years. The literature indicates that CY was successful in improving geographic and financial access to skilled delivery care for poor and tribal women (Vora & Mavalankar, 2014; Yasobant et al., 2016). It also indicates that there is a need for including evaluation of innovative schemes when piloting and scaling up to know successes and issues with the innovations to improve them (De Costa et al., 2015). CY had a package of reimbursement for private providers to discourage supply-induced demand of C-section but studies show that this could have reduced access to indicated C-section, which in turn may lead to maternal and neonatal morbidity if not mortality (Altman et al., 2016; Bogg, Diwan, Vora, & De Costa, 2016). A lot has been published related to; CY hence; in the chapter newer initiatives are discussed.

Initiatives from Gujarat State:

1. **e-Mamta (Mother and Child Tracking System):** Gujarat State has initiated 'e-Mamta', a 'Mother and Child name-based information management system. 'e-Mamta', is innovative as it intends to harness the benefits of ICT to improve the effective and efficient delivery of healthcare services available. The program is designed to cover the entire state of Gujarat and specifically caters to rural and urban slum communities. The application developed in January 2010 is implemented all over Gujarat State. The government of India has appreciated and done National replication of the software as MCTS.
2. **108 Ambulance Services:** The Government of Gujarat (GoG) has introduced Free Emergency Response Services (ERS) on 29th August, 2007 in

partnership with GVK Emergency Management Research Institute. There are 585 ambulances serving over 6.03 crore people covering all 33 districts. The 108 Emergency Response Service is a comprehensive emergency service that serves not only medical emergencies but also police and fire emergencies. It has made remarkable progress in the 9 years of its operations. An emergency patient is now accessing modern emergency transport to a health facility with pre-hospital care.

3. **Obstetric ICUs:** To accelerate a reduction in MMR, Obstetric ICUs across all medical college hospitals of Gujarat were established. As of 2016-17, Government has approved the establishment of 14 Obstetric ICUs across the state. Currently, about five ICUs are functional and remaining is likely to be operationalised soon. These ICUs are dedicated Intensive Care Units nested within existing Obstetric department to cater to the pregnant mother developing serious complications. These mothers require intensive care as well as Obstetric Care. Obstetric ICUs have amalgamated these aspects of care into one unit. Obstetric ICUs have improved the access to tertiary care.
4. **Mamta Ghar:** This scheme facilitates access to the women in need of help to a continuum of care, including appropriate management of pregnancy, delivery, post-partum care and access to life-saving obstetric care when complications arise are crucial to Safe Motherhood. These are waiting for homes for high-risk mothers living in geographically difficult areas.
5. **Kasturba Poshan Sahay Yojana:** In Gujarat, pregnant women from BPL families benefit many schemes including Janani Suraksha Yojana. JSY however, does not address the issues regarding a woman's socioeconomic compulsions to work right up to the last stage of pregnancy and resuming work soon after childbirth. Hence, Kasturba Poshan Sahay Yojana was launched in February 2012 with the aims to provide partial compensation for the wage loss so that the woman is not under compulsion to work until the last stage of pregnancy and can take adequate rest before and after delivery (Kakkad et al., 2014).

Health Systems Improvement Strategies

The availability of the specialists and Medical Officers in the market poses a difficult challenge. To take care of this issue, Walk-in–Interviews are conducted for doctors to fill up Ad-hoc Posts. In addition, campus placements are also done. For the medical officers at the PHC, wherever possible, MBBS doctors have been recruited and for the remaining ones, AYUSH doctors have been placed to ensure quality services at PHCs. To provide specialised MCH and other services, the hiring of consultants for the CHCs and this task is delegated to the Regional Deputy Director and the district hospital authorities respectively who can also monitor their performance. Similarly, the powers to appoint ANMs and other paramedical are delegated to the concerned district authorities. Under NABH, both medical and paramedical staff are given training for their skill up gradation & deployed accordingly.

Gujarat has introduced program management units at the block, district and state levels to ensure sound monitoring of public health program. Each program management unit at the district level is staffed by a health management graduate and support staff. Data is collected from the village level by the ANMs and aggregated at the block, district, regional and state levels. Electronic reports are available to officers at each level to enable regular monitoring and planning.

Affordability of health care is a serious problem for the vast majority of the population, especially in tertiary care. Out of pocket expenditures arise even in public sector hospitals since lack of medicines means that patients have to buy them. This results in a very high financial burden on families in case of severe illness. A large fraction of the out of pocket expenditure arises from outpatient care and purchase of medicines, which are mostly not covered even by the existing insurance schemes. Until about the middle of 2008, public health facilities conducted free deliveries only for a woman's first two children. After that, the family had to pay for the delivery of the child. To encourage institutional deliveries, a Government Resolution was passed in 2008, instructing all public facilities to conduct all deliveries free of cost.

Conclusion

Gujarat has made significant progress on the economic front in past years, however social development indicators remain constant. Health indicators related to maternal health are improving at a slower pace due to the lack of skilled workforce to provide quality maternal healthcare. Large numbers of people incur heavy out of pocket expenditures on maternal health services. Large numbers of people to incur heavy out of pocket expenditures on maternal health services purchased from the private sector. Quality of health care services varies considerably in both the public and the private sector. In the past decade, Gujarat has implemented many innovative programs such as E-Mamta to improve the maternal health indicators which have shown promising results. 108 along with obstetric ICU are steps in the right direction to reduce maternal mortality by improving referral mechanism and availability of advanced obstetric care. Such innovations need to encourage and made integral to the system. Sustained political will and evidence-based implementation of strategies would help in to achieve the goals of safe motherhood.

References

1. Altman, R., Sidney, K., De Costa, A., Vora, K. & Salazar, M. (2016) Is Institutional Delivery Protective Against Neonatal Mortality Among Poor or Tribal Women? A Cohort Study From Gujarat, India. Matern Child Health J. DOI 10.1007/s10995-016-2202-y.
2. Bogg, L., Diwan, V., Vora, K. & De Costa, A. (2016) Impact of Alternative Maternal Demand-side Financial Support Programs in India on the Caesarean Section Rates: Indications of Supplier-Induced Demand. Matern Child Health J (2016) 20:11-15.
3. DOI: 10.1007/s10995-015-1810-2
4. Census of India, 2011. Retrieved from http://censusindia.gov.in/2011census/censusinfodashboard/stock/profiles/en/IND024_Gujarat.pdf Census, 2011
5. Census of India. 2011. Gujarat Population Census data. Retrieved from http://www.census2011.co.in/census/state/gujarat.html.
6. Central Bureau of Health Intelligence. 2007. Managing Human Resources for Health in India, A case study of Madhya Pradesh & Gujarat 2007. Website: www.cbhidghs.nic.in.
7. De Costa, A., Vora, K., Ryan, K., Raman, P., Santacatterina, M. & Mavalankar, D. (2014) The State-Led Large Scale Public Private Partnership 'Chiranjeevi Program' to Increase Access to Institutional Delivery among Poor Women in Gujarat, India: How Has It Done? What Can We Learn? PLOS One | www.plosone.org 1st May, 2014 | Volume 9 | Issue 5 | e95704. DOI: 10.1371/journal.pone.0095704.
8. De Costa, A., Vora, K., Schneider, E. & Mavalankar, D. (2015) Gujarat's Chiranjeevi Yojana–a difficult assessment in retrospect. Bull World Health Organ 2015; 93:436A–436B. doi: http://dx.doi.org/10.2471/BLT.14.137745
9. Dwivedi, R. & Pradhan, J. (2017). Does equity in healthcare spending exist among Indian states? Explaining regional variations from national sample survey data. International Journal for Equity in Health (2017) 16:15 DOI 10.1186/s12939-017-0517-y.
10. Hirway I. & Mahadevia D "Gujarat Human Development Report 2004". Mahatma Gandhi Labour Institute, Ahmedabad. Retrieved from http://www.in.undp.org/content/dam/india/docs/human_develop_report_gujarat_2004_report.pdf.
11. International Institute of Population Science. 2007-08. District Level Household and Facility Surveys (DLHS) 3, 2007-08. Fact sheet Gujarat. Retrieved from http://rchiips.org/pdf/rch3/state/Gujarat.pdf.
12. International Institute of Population Science. 2015-16. National Family Health Survey (NFHS) 4, 2015-16. State Factsheet, Gujarat. Retrieved from http://rchiips.org/NFHS/pdf/NFHS4/GJ_FactSheet.pdf.
13. International Institute of Population Science.2002-04. Reproductive and Child Health District Level Household Survey 2002-04 Gujarat Report. Retrieved from http://rchiips.org/pdf/state/Gujarat.pdf.
14. Kakkad, K., Patel, M., Patel, S. & Patel, S. (2014) Effect of 'Janani Shishu Suraksha Karyakram'–A Government Health Beneficiary scheme–on Admission rate and clinical outcome in NICU in a Tertiary care hospital. Natl J Community Med. 2014; 5(1): 118-

121. http://njcmindia.org/uploads/5-1_118-121.pdf
15. National Health Systems Resource Centre, Gujarat. 2015-16. Data Management & Analysis. HMIS Analysis 2015-16. Retrieved from: http://nhsrcindia.org/resource-detail/gujarat/MjQz.
16. NRHM in the Eleventh Five Year Plan (2007-2012), Strengthening Public Health Systems. Planning Commission Government of India. National Health Systems Resource Centre. Retrieved from nhsrcindia.org/index.php.
17. Pomeroy, A., Koblinsky, M. & Alva, S. 2014. Who gives birth in private facilities in Asia? A look at six countries. Health Policy and Planning 2014;29:i38–i47. DOI:10.1093/heapol/czt103.
18. Purohit, B. & Martineau, T. 2016 Issues and challenges in recruitment for government doctors in Gujarat, India. Human Resources for Health (2016) 14:43. DOI 10.1186/s12960-016-0140-9.
19. Registrar General of India. Sample Registration System Statistical Report 2015. Accessed from: http://www.censusindia.gov.in/vital_statistics/SRS_Reports_2015.html.
20. Rural Health Statistics in India 2011, Statistics Division, Ministry of Health and Family Welfare, Government of India. Retrieved from: https://data.gov.in/catalog/rural-health-statistics-india-2011.
21. Rural Health Statistics in India 2015-16, Statistics Division, Ministry of Health and Family Welfare, Government of India. Retrieved from: https://data.gov.in/catalog/rural-health-statistics-2016.
22. Sample Registration System. 2011-13. Registrar General of India. A special bulletin on Maternal Mortality in India 2011-13. Retrieved from http://www.censusindia.gov.in/vital_statistics/mmr_bulletin_2011-13.pdf.
23. State-wise: Population, GSDP, Per Capita Income and Growth Rate. 2009-10. Retrieved from http://pbplanning.gov.in/pdf/Statewise%20GSDP%20PCI%20and%20G.R.pdf.
24. Vora, K. & Mavalankar, D. (2014). Quality of Reproductive and Child Health Care in the Private Sector in India: Issues and Options. International Journal of Science and Research (IJSR). Volume 3 Issue 8, August 2014. DOI: https://www.ijsr.net/archive/v3i8/MDIwMTUyMTY=.pdf.
25. Yasobant, S., Vora K., Shewade, HD., Annerstedt, K.S., Isaakidis P., Mavalankar, D., Dholakia, N. & De Costa, A. (2016) Utilisation of the state-led public-private partnership program '*Chiranjeevi Yojana*' to promote facility births in Gujarat, India: a cross-sectional community-based study. BMC Health Services Research (2016) 16:266. https://doi.org/10.1186/s12913-016-1510-7.

□

20

Mothering and Child Development: Impact of Mothers' Well-being and Beliefs on Early Child Development

—Ms. Priscilla U. and Aneesh Kumar P.

Abstract

Mother has a crucial role in child development and parenting. Children are attached more to their mothers. But child rearing and parenting can be stressful for mothers. Studies have also found that mothers use higher levels of punishments and strict practices. The health and well-being of children are determined by their attachment and the well-being with their mother. The present study conducts a review from existing literature on maternal health and child rearing practices with an aim to understand maternal well-being, beliefs among mothers in India about child development and child rearing practices and how mothers' well-being and the belief's impact on early child development. The paper brings out the importance of understanding mothers' postpartum experiences, the belief's they hold regarding childrearing practices like breast feeding, illness and the use of corporal punishments, and their impact on physical and mental health. The existing health care policies and programs in India are also discussed highlighting the need for evidence based interventions and programs. The findings of the study call for the need for training, support and knowledge at family and community levels with support from medical and mental health professionals. Further it recommends for developing of parenting modules, providing help for mothers who experience problems and involvement of community members. This study has implications in understanding and developing positive and effective parenting modules including intervention and practices for Indian communities.

Introduction

Becoming a parent is an experience that not only makes one happy but it also makes one fear what's ahead and cause as potential decrease in the psychological well-being of a parent. Much research is limited to the maternal concerns about the infant and there are fewer studies done that concern the new mother and her adjustment to parenthood. The studies done are mostly in US and Canada (Harrison & Hicks, 1983); however, there is a need to study both the aspects in the light of the Indian traditions and ways of dealing with child-birth and maternity in India. There have been several changes in the way parenting is looked at and the way parenthood is viewed. In the 1900's children were considered to be valuable as they were able to economically contribute to the family's financial needs but that is slowly changing and the parents of today are less dependent on their children for economic support (McLanahan & Adams, 1987). The role of a caregiver plays a very significant role in providing a supportive environment for the development of the infant and the construct of self efficacy gives one a sense of one's ability to regulate one's life events (Bandura, 1982). This construct also is a pre-cursor to understand the bigger concept of 'parenting skills' (Cutrona & Troutman, 1986; Donovan, Leavitt & Walsh, 1990). The primary caretaker, usually the mother needs to respond effectively to the needs of the child which depends largely on how she perceives herself to be.

Motherhood is considered to be a profound and a unique experience for every woman. There are new responsibilities and tasks, and each individual copes differently to the significant life events, for instance child birth. Every woman who goes through the experience of motherhood goes through a set of life circumstances which makes her transition into parenthood a very meaningful one. Some of the aspects that influence these experiences could be family support, social support and work (Banik, 2015; Deb, Kumar, Bhattacharyya, & Sun, 2012). Studies on understanding the factors that determine how women respond to environmental demands of motherhood indicate that the beliefs and patterns that women develop before and after pregnancy matters. The women who experience certain complications during pregnancy, the period of childcare during the postpartum period and the characteristics of the infant plays a significant role in how the women react to their experience of motherhood (Hoffenaar, Balen & Hermanns, 2010). The study on maternal confidence among first time mothers during their child's infancy by Russell (2006), indicates that the relationship between the mother and the infant was often 'reciprocal in nature' wherein the mother was keen on responding appropriately and the infant often responds to the mother based on the mother's 'mood' and 'behaviour'. Hence the factors that are mentioned as significant in the process of mothering are supported by studies that were previously conducted. Other factors such as role conflicts, social support and appropriate care that needs to be given to the child shows that the attention is often directed towards how efficient the mother is, and this often leads to the mother experiencing a feeling of incompetence which will affect the infant-mother relationship (Donovan, Leavitt & Walsh, 1990). According to (Knaak, 2008) "The cultural context of mothering and the social-structuring of the postpartum environment" help us understand postpartum depression better. From the above statement, we understand that it is not only important for us to look at the experience of mothering as not only something unique but also look at the larger picture of the postpartum experience considering aspects such as the culture, the marital relationship, family structure, stressful life events etc.

Factors that Affect the Well-being of Mothers

An individual becomes a mother even before the child is brought into this world, but the transition to parenthood is often a process that involves physical, emotional and psychological change (George, 2005; Deb, Kumar, Bhattacharyya, & Sun, 2012). The mother is often anxious of the outcomes of the birthing experience as the control on childbirth is shifted from the mother to the doctors and the medical team involved (Allen, 2011). This anxiety in new mothers often causes them stress and this stress or perceived stress can lead to crisis. These stressors need to be identified and measures need to be taken to prevent them (Nancy, 2010). Researchers have found that once a woman becomes a mother, she experiences role strains and often the new mother experiences more stress in managing the maternal role than any other role that she plays; namely an employee, a wife, a daughter or a daughter-in-law (Miller, 2011). It is also found that the more a woman gets support from her spouse and supervisors, the chances of experiencing conflicts between balancing work life and family life is reduced (Erdwins, Buffardi Casper & O'Brien, 2001; Deb, Kumar, Bhattacharyya, & Sun, 2012). Most of the women of the 21st century are employed and the managing of both work and family seems like a huge task, the support that the mother receives from her employer has a very positive influence which helps reduce the strain that the woman experiences, it will help increase productivity and also her willingness to contribute to work (Thompson, Thomas, & Maier, 1992).

According to the study on maternal confidence among first time mothers during their child's infancy by Russell (2006), the relationship between the mother and the infant was often 'reciprocal in nature' wherein the mother was keen on responding appropriately and the infant often responds to the mother based on the mother's 'mood' and 'behaviour'. The study also focused on the aspect of infant temperament playing a significant role in the maternal experience of caring for her child including maternal depression, the interaction between the infant and the mother, cognitive and developmental effects on the infant and altered the maternal characteristics of the mother. The study also gives a lot of insight into the child-mother interaction as it plays a very significant role in the study that is currently conducted. Hence there arises a need to understand the level of competence from a cultural perspective which will be covered in the current study. The child related factors such as children born with disabilities strongly impact the maternal well-being and attachment (Thomas, Kumar, & Deb, 2014; Gireesan, Kumar, & Deb, 2013).

In the past decade, research has found that women suffer from maternal health problems not only during the postpartum period after the birth of the child but also during pregnancy mainly because of Intimate Partner Violence. Women in the South Asian countries especially suffer abuse by the in-laws as well as their partner in the marital relationship. The range of abuse begins with emotional, physical and moves on to economical abuse. There is a possibility for change in this situation only if there are efforts made to counter the culturally sanctioned beliefs that are part of the Indian culture and those will have to be addressed. Interventions that seek to promote gender equity needs to be initiated to sea e change in this situation in the future (Raj et al., 2010).

Policies for Maternal Care

One of the main reasons for the increase in maternal distress or postpartum depression has been identified as the negligence of maternal mental health in the primary health care system. There is internationally work done by the United Nations Fund for Population Activities and World Health Organisation which focuses on prevention of postpartum depression and maternal health problems. Depression in the early days of motherhood was considered to be linked to many risk factors such as marital discord, age of the mother and the gender of the infant etc. The care for child development module of Integrated Management of Childhood Illness was designed to test the maternal care for mother and also the child's developmental needs that can be provided by the primary health workers. The module was effective ta o certain extent in India, however, culturally sensitive psychological support is to be provided for the women along with the social support that is required for women during the postpartum period (Engle, 2009).

Policies are designed to enable all women and children to obtain the highest standard of health by sustaining effective health systems and also to provide an environment that promotes health. The important policy that is highly relevant to maternal care and health is the RMNCH (Reproductive, Maternal, Newborn and Child Health) policy. This policy was based oa n survey done in 2010 which found that an estimated 2,87,000 women died during pregnancy and childbirth. Hence the policy focused on evidence based intervention which not only focused infants but emphasised on care that needs to be provided along the continuum from the reproductive years, right through pregnancy up until the birth and attainment of childhood years of the children(Partnership for Maternal, Newborn & Child Health and WHO, 2014).

There are several policies under the RMNCH (Reproductive, Maternal, Newborn and Child Health) and the policies begin for adolescents who are of reproductive age right up to pregnancy, childbirth and infancy and childhood of their children. The guidelines for all of these policies are given by the WHO (World Health Organisation) (Partnership for Maternal, Newborn & Child Health and WHO, 2014). The aim of these policies is to provide essential, evidence based interventions to reduce reproductive, maternal, newborn and child mortality and to promote reproductive health. Some of the interventions are family planning, social support during child birth, detection and management of postpartum sepsis (serious infections after birth) and nutrition counselling. The community strategies such as home visits for women and children across the continuum of care and creation of women's groups for further assistance and help are provided for new mothers.

The policies are meant to establish appropriate management and organisational structures to deliver cross-cutting objectives through systematic governance process which includes, cross cutting objectives which are clearly defined, the need for joint working system is emphasised, barriers that affect effective collaboration are identified and the strategies to overcome them are also formulated and the implementation of the policy is considered to be a part of the policy making process.

Transition to Parenthood

The birth of a child is considered a life transforming experience not only for a mother who has given birth but also for fathers who experience the transition to parenthood. The family as a whole experiences physical, psychological and emotional change and this is the crucial time in the life of all of them including the newborn. The study conducted by Lynn George (2005), points that it is the time when women feel extremely vulnerable and their experience of fatigue and anxiety are considered common and often ignored whereas those are concerns that might require immediate attention or even rehospitalisation. The study also highlighted that women experienced a sense of abandonment and were over whelmed by the sudden increase in responsibility and this was often the result of a deficit in knowledge. The initial days can be quiet challenging and if the mothers are required to care for a temperamentally difficult child, the mother's sense of competence as a parent slowly fades away and there is an increase in fear and anxiety leading to postpartum depression (Cutrona & Troutman, 1986). Several other studies also point out the transition to motherhood which is described more as an adjustment to motherhood which determines how well she plays the role of a mother (Knaak, 2008).

The study done by Banik (2015) also points out that the ways of poor transition or "poor maternal functioning, which increased stress levels, caused unhealthy parent-child interactions and poor development of the child". Aspects such as low and high-socio-economic statuses, marital relationship satisfaction which are culturally more relevant were also studied and analysed (Deb, Kumar, Holden, & Rowe, 2017). There was emphasis given to the family support which helped understand the postpartum environment. The study done by Rodriques, Patel, Jaswal and De Souza (2003) gives a detailed description of the experiences of motherhood and the study was conducted in Goa, India. The paper was a rich source of information as it discovered aspects such as illnesses that were associated with child bearing and the lack of practical support and overworking which were identified as causes of illnesses during childbirth. The rituals performed after childbirth were considered to be good not only for the mother but also for the child, interestingly the rituals were considered to vary based on the gender of the child, there was a lack of emotional support that was reported by the women who were interviewed. These are very practical concerns that every mother might face in India and hence, the transition to motherhood is viewed differently by the new mothers based on the cultural and ethnic backgrounds that they come from.

Studies also found that the adaptation of the physical, emotional and social aspects of the transition to motherhood is sometimes makes the experience of motherhood to be rewarding for some and for some others the rewards might outweigh the costs (Hoffenaar, Balen & Hermanns, 2010). Each mother has a different experience when it comes to mothering and the experiences are predominantly subjective and the experience of transition depends largely on the external or environmental factors. The maternal confidence and the parental self-efficacy is affected if the mother assumes her transition was not the best or the ideal one. This leads to the mother feeling insecure and even leads to postpartum depression. The women who had experienced discomfort either during pregnancy or childbirth had an impact on the women who indicated low psychological well-being during the period of postpartum (Gausia, Ryder, Ali, Fisher, Moran & Koblinsky, 2012).

Cultural Aspects in the Process of Mothering in India

Childbirth is considered to be very auspicious and has a lot of traditions and cultural practices that are followed which are significant and are considered to be done for the protection and health of the infant and the new mother. There are several studies that are done on this aspect and one of the studies indicates that the new mothers receive a lot of help from their mothers, sisters, husbands and older child if any. The first time mothers enjoy the privileges of going to their mother's house during their postnatal period. There are also several reports that both the new mother and father are extremely nervous before the birth of the child and one of the main causes is the gender of the child and even today the gender of the infant plays a significant role. Study also points out that the gap between lack of motivation to complete work and the disturbed emotional state of mind during postpartum is often ignored off as fatigue and tiredness instead of it being a serious concern requiring psychiatric help.

It was also found that the postpartum rituals that were performed also varied based on the gender of the infant, when the infant born is a male a more expensive sweet was distributed in comparison to when a female infant was born (Rodrigues, Patel, Jaswal & De Souza, 2003).

There were also several rituals performed for the new mother which involved special oil massages which were considered to improve the strength and health for the new mother. They were also given a special diet which was meant to give them nourishment and help reduce the body pain and increase breast milk. While the period before and after childbirth involves a lot of financial requirement, economic difficulty was considered to be one of the pioneer reasons for distress among new mothers.

The need for not just support for new mothers but also child focused interventions is necessary to provide complete support and preventive measures to curb postpartum depression in the South Asian countries. Women also experience postnatal depression based on the gender of the infant, the women is often blamed if the infant born is a girl and the women in return go through extreme stress and get less access to reproductive healthcare. In the low income countries the maternal competence of the mother has a direct effect on the physical well-being of the infant. Emotionally the mother is not prepared to parent the child and hence because of this the quality of parenting by the mother, hence it does not contribute positively to the growth of the infant. There is a need to provide empowerment programs and the healthcare systems need to be strengthened in order to help the women providing sufficient community counselling which is aimed at preventing maternal depression (Patel, Rahman, Jacob & Hughes, 2004).

Prenatal exposure to various risk factors has long-term consequences on the infant and causes not only physical but also cognitive impairments. The direct consequences of prenatal stress or anxiety have been early delivery and the infant was seen to be born smaller than the ideal size. There were also impairments in the cognitive and social developments of the infants. It is found that maternal anxiety during the prenatal period of the mother results in the infants having negative affect from childhood to adulthood. It was also found that exposure to traumatic events during pregnancy resulted in the infants having cognitive challenges. However, it was found that the prenatal stress resulted in various behavioural outcomes but it was also found that it did not have the same impact on all the children (Talge et al., 2007).

Child Rearing Practices in India

In a study that was conducted in different parts of India, it was found that women from a lower socio-economic stratum of the society had to spend most part of their postpartum days outside their homes because they had the need to support their families financially. They mostly worked in fields, on construction sites, as sweepers and washer women. Statistics indicates that 93% of all lower status individuals nurturance from their mothers only from birth till the age of three years and the older children were considered to be capable of taking care of them and were forced to be self-reliant. However on the contrary the middle and upper status children received enough nurturance and are even encouraged to be physically dependent on their parents for all their needs. It was found that there is extreme diversity in the way children behave and this is a direct consequence of how they are brought up and this is also the vast complexity that exists in the child rearing practices in India (Seymour, 1976).

Conclusion

The new mothers often go through a lot of changes in order to take up and efficiently fulfil the role of a parent. The mother is often anxious of the new role that she has to play and often wants to be efficient and aims at having the perfect transition to parenthood. The mother also becomes distressed and worries if she is not playing the role of a perfect mother. The role of the infant is also considered significant as the temperament of the child directly affects the maternal confidence of the new mother. There is a need for the mother to be in a state of well-being and hence there are several policies for better maternal care which come under the RMNCH (Reproductive, Maternal, Newborn and Child Health). The policies and steps toward maternal care are effective and powerful tools that can be used to help new mothers to receive the aid that they require during their early years of transition to parenthood and also the policies are supposed to increase equality in receiving assistance from the government and the medical community.

In India, the transition to motherhood also has the aspect of culture which is considered to be a significant component. There is a lot of additional aid provided for the first-time mothers as they enjoy the privilege of going to their mother's homes after the birth of their child, they also have a lot of traditional rituals and practices that are practiced which help the mother cope with the transition and also contributes to the support system that the mother needs. The culture varies from place to place and the days are fast changing and women who become mothers or go through the transition into motherhood are seen to do it in isolation these days rather than follow traditional norms and cultural practices. The practices of child rearing are also contrastingly different in comparison to what is followed in the west. There is a contrasting way in which children are raised in India, there are families which raise their children with constant support and guidance and deny complete independence for any decision the child will make and the other extreme where the families are not able to provide the child complete attention as the family has a constant financial struggles which demands the child to be self-reliant since the very young age of three years.

Recommendations

There are several aspects of transition to parenthood that needs to be studied in the light of the Indian context and one such aspect is to understand the role of the husband during the period of postpartum and its implications can be studied in an elaborate manner, the role spirituality both before and after the birth of the child to further understand the role it plays in how the new mother views motherhood and see if it has any influence on the postpartum experience of the first time mothers. The current study has also looked at various aspects of motherhood and parenting but these trends seem to be changing rapidly and the transition into motherhood is perceived or viewed differently by the various generations that form the 'Indian Family'. There is a need to understand the parenting styles and child rearing practices that are observed in the recent years. With the increase in technology and the lack of quality time for families, there is still a wave of awakening towards the need to get back to basics. The only way to understand the trends better is by encouraging several studies to be conducted on the above mentioned aspects.

References

1. Allen, T., (2011). The Effects of Childbirth Expectations and experiences on Prevalence of Postpartum Mood and Anxiety Disorders in First-Time Mothers. Dissertation submission at Alliant International University California School of Professional Psychology, Fresno Campus.
2. Bandura, A. (1982). Self-efficacy mechanism in human agency. American Psychologist, 37, 122-147.
3. Banik, R. (2015). First-Time Mothers' Experiences of the Transition to Parenthood: The Role Of Socioeconomic Status On Prenatal Parenting Expectations and Postpartum Experiences. ProQuest LLC
4. Crist, N.G. (2010). Women's Perceptions of Postpartum Stress: A Narrative Analysis. ProQuest LLC.
5. Cutrona, E. C & Troutman, R.B. (Dec 1986). Social Support, Infant Temperament, and Parenting Self-Efficacy: A Mediational Model of Postpartum Depression. Wiley on behalf of the Society for Research in Child Development, 57, 1507-1518.
6. Deb, S., Kumar, A., Bhattacharyya, B., & Sun, J. (2012).Parents' perception about children's academic stress and child care related issues. Indian Journal of Health and Wellbeing, 3(3), 608-612.
7. Deb, S., Kumar, A., Holden, G.W., & Rowe, L.S. (2017). School corporal punishment, family tension, and students' internalizing problems: Evidence from India. School Psychology International, 38(1), 60-77.

8. Donovan, L.W., Leavitt, A.L., & Walsh, O.R. (1990). Maternal Self-Efficacy: Illusory Control and Its Effect on Susceptibility to Learned Helplessness. Wiley on behalf of the Society for Research in Child Development, 61, 1638-1647.
9. Engle, P.L. (2009). Maternal mental health: program and policy implications. The American Journal of Clinical Nutrition.
10. Erdwins, C.J., Buffardi, L.C., Casper, W.J., and O'Brien, A.S., (2001). The Relationship of Women's Role Strain to Social Support, Role Satisfaction, and Self-Efficacy. National Council on Family Relations
11. Gausia, K., Ryder, D., Ali, M., Fisher, C., Moran, A., & Koblinsky, M. (2012). Obstetric complications and psychological well-being: experiences of Bangladeshi women during pregnancy and childbirth. Journal of health, population, and nutrition, 30(2), 172.
12. George, L. (2005) Lack of Preparedness: Experiences of First-time mothers. MCN The American Journal of Maternal/Child Nursing.
13. Gireesan, A., Kumar, A., & Deb, S. (2013). Children with special needs: An exploration of child care from the perspective of their guardians and service providers. Indian Journal of Positive Psychology, 4(3), 472-477.
14. Harisson, M.J., & Hicks, S.A. (1983). Postpartum Concerns of Mothers and Their Sources of Help. Canadian Journal of Public Health/ Revue Canadienne de Sante Publique, 74, 325-328.
15. Hoffenaar, P.J., Balen, F.V.,& Hermanns, J. (2010). The Impact of Having a Baby on the Level and Content of Women's Well-Being. Social Indicators Research, 97, 279-295.
16. Knaak, J.S. (2008). The Process of Postpartum Adjustment. Published Heritage Branch. Library and Archives Canada.
17. McLanahan, S., & Adams. J. (1987). Parenthood and Psychological Well-Being. Annual Reviews, 13, 237-257.
18. Miller, A.R. (2011). The effects of motherhood timing on career path. Journal of Population Economics, 24, 1071-1100.
19. Partnership for Maternal, Newborn & Child Health and WHO. (2014) A Policy Guide for Implementing Essential Interventions for Reproductive, Maternal, Newborn and Child Health (RMNCH): A Multisectoral Policy Compendium for RMNCH. World Health Organisation. Geneva.
20. Patel, V., Rahman, A., Jacob, K.S., & Hughes, M. (2004). Effect of maternal mental health on infant growth in low income countries: new evidence from South Asia. London School of Hygiene and Tropical Medicine.
21. Raj, A., Sabarwal, S., Decker, M.R., Nair, S., Jethva, M., Krishnan, S., Donta, B., Saggurti, N., & Silverman, J.G. (2010). Abuse from In-Laws during Pregnancy and Post-Partum: Qualitative and Quantitative Findings from Low-income Mothers of Infants in Mumbai, India. Springer Science+Business Media, LLC 2010.
22. Rodrigues, M., Patel, V., Jaswal, S.,& De Souza, N. (2003). Listening to mothers: qualitative studies on motherhood and depression from Goa, India. Social Sciences and Medicine, 57, 1797-1806.

23. Russell, K. (2006). Maternal Confidence of First-time Mothers during their Child's Infancy. Dissertation, Georgia State University
24. Seymour, S. (1976). Caste/Class and Child Rearing in a Changing Indian Town. Wiley on behalf of the American Anthropological Asso2ciation, 3, 783-796.
25. Talge, N.M., Neal, C., Glover, V., and the early Translational Research and Prevention Science Network: Fetal and Neonatal Experience on Child and Adolescent Mental Health. (2007). Antenatal maternal stress and long-term effects on child neurodevelopment: how and why. Journal of Child Psychology and Psychiatry 48:3/4 pp245-261.
26. Thomas, S., Kumar, A., & Deb, S. (2014). Abuse of intellectually disabled children: Risks as Perceived by the Mothers. Social Science International, 30(2), 391.
27. Thompson, C.A., Thomas, C.C., & Maier, M. (1992). Work-family Conflict: Reassessing corporate policies and initiatives. In U. Sekaran & F.T.L. Leong (Eds). Womanpower: Managing in Times of Demographic Turbulance, Newbury Park, CA: Sage.

□

21

Remediation of Alphabetic-Alphasyllabary Biliterate Dyslexia: A Bridge from Despair to Hope

—*Saldanha, M.P.J. and Padakannaya, P.*

Abstract

India is a multiliterate and the second most populated nation in the world. Having a high rate of dyslexia, its vital to diagnose it early and remediate it at the earliest, lest they become a part of the vicious circle of academic failure and other socioeconomic consequences. As different writing systems exert varying cognitive demands on the reader, they show up in varying degrees of challenges faced in mastering efficient reading and spelling. It is not just the testing that needs to be done in indigenous languages, but also, the focus of remediation needs to be customised accordingly. The overall results confirm the view that phonological awareness training is a vital element in any dyslexia remediation protocol. The results support the view that the poor phonological awareness (PA) is the principal marker associated with Dyslexia.

Introduction

A rich diversity in linguistic, racial, cultural, and religious co-existence has been the nucleus of the existence of Indian heritage (Sharma, 2001). India takes pride in being one of the largest functionally multilingual nations in the world (Annamalai, 2001). Literacy skills in more than one language are very essential in the democratic, social, political and economic system of a country (Mohanty, 2008). Most schools in our country teach three languages to its pupils, as necessitated by the Three-Language Formula (TLF) which was recommended by The Report of the Education Commission (1964-1966) of Central Government India (Kothari, 1966). Therefore, to adhere to the TLF, following the approval of the parliament, it was executed into the National Policy on Education in 1968. Therefore, most schools in Karnataka teach Kannada, English, and Hindi (Saldanha, Siddaiah, Veerappa, Ramachandra, & Padakannaya, 2014).

With a population of around 1.34 billion in our country, nearly 39% is the children population, from which an estimated alarming rate of 7-20% of school going children have dyslexia(Child Protection and Child Rights, 2017; Tandon, 2016; Worldometers, 2017).

Dylexia currently referred to as Specific Learning Disorder, Diagnostic and Statistical Manual V Diagnostic code 315.00-With impairment in reading) is a common specific learning disability affecting nearly 80% of all those diagnosed to hava e learning disability (Karande, Sawant, Kulkarni, Kanchan & Sholapurwala, 2005; Medina, 2016). It is a genetic and neurocognitive disorder, and offers strong evidence to support the indispensable role of deficits in phonological skills, underlying the core difficulties in slow and inaccurate context-free single-word recognition and decoding skills (Shaywitz & Shaywitz, 2005; Thambirajah, 2010a; 2010b; Vellutino, Fletcher, Snowling, & Scanlon, 2004). Efficient phonological processing such as phonological awareness (PA) and rapid naming are indispensible for the mastery of literacy (Araújo, Inácio, Francisco, Faísca, Petersson, & Reis, 2011); Wagner, Torgesen, & Rashotte, 1999). Despite being independent sources the breakdown of reading dysfunction, they do have an additive say on efficient reading and spelling (Miller et al., 2006; Nicolson & Fawcett, 2005; Norton & Wolf, 2012; Verhagen, Aarnoutse, & Van Leeuwe, 2010; Vukovic & Siegel, 2006). Their main concern is the struggle to grasp how visual symbols in print are mapped onto speech sounds (and vice versa) and failure to master phonological recoding. They show weaker connections between visual-orthographic codes for words, thereby resulting in slow retrieval of words (Breznitz, 2002; Sunseth & Bowers, 2002). Their central problem in recognition of words in isolation, leading to poor accuracy of reading and spelling, eventually leads to impaired reading fluency (Thambirajah, 2010a; 2010b). A minimum of 5 cases have been reported in an average sized classroom Karande, Mehta, & Kulkarni, 2007; Mogasale, Patil, Patil, & Mogasale, 2012; Thomas, Bhanutej, & John, 2003).

Most schools in India teach two Indian languages and English. The English orthography is predominantly irregular and follows an alphabetic spelling system (Nag, 2007). It is linear in the visuospatial organisation (Padakannaya, Ramachandra, & Singh, 2008). It is challenging to the learner in comparison to other alphabetic languages, as the letter-sound mapping is less consistent with a lot of exceptions (Grigerenko, 2001; Landerl & Wimmer, 2008; Norton &Wolf, 2012; Seymour, Aro, & Erskine, 2003; Vellutino, Fletcher, Snowling, & Scanlon, 2004). A detailed phonemic discrimination is essential, and also several grapheme combinations are used for the same vowel sound and different consonant and vowel combination sounds to express different sounds. For example, the letter 'a', maps on to different phonemes in words like *cat, was, made* or *bar*. Likewise, the same letter or evea n sequence of letters can have different sounds when they occur in different positions (Goswami, 1997; Grigerenko, 2001). The phonological complexity at the syllable structure is very high, and there is more consistency when reading larger units such as rimes or syllables. There are a few words based on CV (Consonant Vowel) syllables (example: /Baby/). Most frequent syllable type is the CVC (Ex Dog, Cat). Most syllables have consonant clusters before (example: climb, sleep) or after (example: belt, song) the vowel. There is a lot of inconsistency when reading small units and less inconsistency when reading larger reading units, like rimes and syllables. Therefore, English children may be developing recoding strategies at more than one grain size. When the grain size is large, there will be more orthographic units to learn. There are around 3000 monosyllabic words in English at the rime level, and the reader is needed to learn around 400 phonological rimes and 600 different orthographic patterns. Relying on the mapping of the contained orthography of 26 letters onto the 44 phonemes alone will lead to sloppy recoding of English (Goswami, 2005; Treiman, Mullennix, Bijeljac-Babic, & Richmond-Welty, 1995; Ziegler & Goswami, 2005; 2006). The complexity is further made complex by the rich vowel system, of about 15 vowels, represented by just a few graphemes (Nag, 2007). Relying on grapheme—phoneme correspondences alones leads to erroneous recoding (Zeigler & Goswami, 2006).

All Indian scripts (except Urdu) have a common origin in '*Brahmi*', thereby sharing the similar salient features. Kannada, is one such language, is one of the oldest Dravidian languages of South India. It is distinctive from English in terms of transparency, grain size orthographic principle. It has a recorded history of over 2,300 years, unparalleled literature, spoken by over 60 million people and obtained a classical status granted by the Indian Central Government on the occasion of 52nd Kannada Rajyotsava and most number of Jnanapeeta awards (Express News Service, 2012). Sadly, not much spotlight is thrown on the dynamics of its reading processes (Karanth, Mathew, & Kurien, 2004). The script is an alphasyllabary (aka Abugidas) as they possess the characteristics of alphabets and also syllabaries (Sproat, 2006). The graphic complexes represent sounds at the syllabic level, and the sub syllabic decomposition shows the phonemes housed within, and these orthographic units of syllable—phoneme encodings are referred to as *akshara*. The scripts have symbols for syllabic vowels and consonants have an inherent 'a' sound, vowel diacritic marks (*matrās*) to represent consonant-vowel combinations, ligatures (secondary forms of consonants) to represent consonant blends, and diacritic to mute the housed vowel associated with the consonant symbol . All consonants and vowels have a primary symbol and a secondary form, and the writing of the graphosyllables is governed by specific rules. The secondary form of the vowel is more common than the primary form, until and unless the vowel is holding the beginning position or represents an independent morpheme (Nag, 2007; Nag, Treiman, & Snowling 2010; Padakannaya, Ramachandra, & Singh, 2008). The aforementioned linguistic features described are enough reason to conclude that the sound-print mapping differs greatly when compared to alphabetic and logographic orthographies. Despite the consistency favouring the rapid acquisition of the writing system, readers are faced with the challenge of mastering of over 510 orthographic units. The learner when faced with such complexities needs to invest a heavy processing cost (Gupta, 2004; Nag, 2007; Purushothama, 1994; Ramaa, 1993; Ramaa, Miles, & Lalithamma, 1993; Vaid & Gupta, 2002). A more detailed analysis of Kannada orthography can be found elsewhere Karanth, 2003, 2006; Nag, 2007; Nag & Snowling, 2012; Prakash & Joshi, 1989; 1995; Padakannaya & Ramachandra, 2011). Table-1 illustrates the major contrasts between Kannada and English writing system: mapping principles, graphic forms and level of transparency.

Table-1: Major contrast between Kannada and English language and writing systems

Contrasts	Kannada	English
	ºÉtÄÚ **/ºÉ/tÄÚ/**	Girl /[illegible]/[illegible][illegible]/l/
Grapheme mapping principle	Syllables	Morpheme
Graphic form and spatial layout	Non Linear	Linear
Level of Transparency	Shallow	Deep

Source: own construction

No writing system is indifferent to DD (Holopainen, Ahonen, & Lyytinen, 2001; Tressoldi, Stella, & Faggella, 2001). The intensity of deficits is greatly affected by the characteristics and phonological demands of the linguistic system, which modulates the specific demands on the phonological and orthographic processing skills (Grigerenko, 2001; Guardiola, 2001; Miles, 2000). English and Indian languages follow two distinct orthographies. English is an alphabetic system while Indian languages (Kannada, in the present study) are alphasyllabary systems. Vaid & Padakannaya (2004) pointed out that the cognitive processes underlying reading and the characteristic expression of dyslexia deficits vary across different writing systems.

Dyslexia and remediation: Every cloud has a silver lining

The challenge in mastering reading can have devastating effects in the form of low levels of general and academic self esteem, and also peer and teacher related areas of adjustment (Thambirajah, 2010a). Neuronal plasticity has given promising hopes researchers to successfully remediate struggling readers children, adolescents and adults with dyslexia across different age groups (Shaywitz & Shaywitz, 2005), thereby, proving biology is not final destiny (Leopold, 2013). Given what researchers know about the brain plasticity, has led researchers to successfully remediate children, adolescents and adults with DD benefit from behavioural intervention (Cramer et al., 2011; Draganski et al., 2004; Foorman & Moats, 2004; **Hudson, High, & Otaiba, 2007**; Nicolson, Fawcett, Moss, Nicolson, & Reason, 1999; Shastry, 2007; Shaywitz & Shaywitz, 2005). There are also not many studies that compare the compensated ones with normal typically developing readers. This article is focused on studying groups of children with dyslexia who are literate in Kannada and English: one group compensated and another without any type of remediation; and compare them with a CA matched control group *vis-à-vis* phonological awareness, reading rate, and rapid automatised naming. The comparison is unlike the conventional two groups, comparing readers with dyslexia with the typical readers or pre-post remediation. Such a study will also throw light on which of the languages respond more to remediation and also whether compensated ones can be differentiated from normal ones on any aspects of reading. The skills in Kannada (an alphasyllabary) and English (an alphabetic writing system) that are placed on either ends of the transparency continuum were compared. The study followed an ex post facto design with three groups of participants.

Participants

1. *Children with dyslexia remediated (CDR):* There were 49 students (37 boys and 12 girls, with a mean age of 14yrs and 2 months, SD=1.6), who were largely compensated at the time of testing. They were subjected to systematic and appropriate full time phonology-based pull out intervention as a part of their remedial programme, predominately in English and Kannada, and other core academic subjects with the frequency of sessions on an average of 5 days a week, and 3-5 hours per day, for a period of three academic years. In Kannada, the remediation protocol incorporated teaching *akshara* structure and *akshara* awareness explicitly (decomposition of *akshara* into its constituent parts and combining them to make syllabic *akshara*), sensitizing them to do fine visual and discriminations, and teaching visual and verbal associations between *aksharas* and corresponding sounds. There was a focus on fluency, emphasizing automation of the orthographic pattern recognition, by training to chunk word parts, as the sub-lexical pattern recognition facilitates more rapid recognition.

The remediation protocol for English incorporated training in phoneme awareness, alphabetic code, sound discrimination, grapheme-phoneme correspondence or phonics, blending phonemes into recognizable words, fluency (through emphasis on automatisation of the orthographic pattern recognition, by training to chunk word parts; necessary training was given at the sub-lexical, lexical, and connected text level through repeated guided oral reading or repeated reading), vocabulary and comprehension as well. .

Training was also focused on the vocabulary and comprehension level in both languages. It was integrated with fortifying the phonological skills (which focused on identifying rhyming words, manipulating syllables and phonemes in the form of synthesis and segmentation, sound elision from words, sound discrimination within words, sound substitution within words, and transposition of sounds within words).

2. *Children with dyslexia with no remediation (CDNR):* There were 46 students (36 boys and 10 girls; with a mean age of 12yrs and 9months, SD=1.3), in the group who never had exposure to any special education intervention or remediation prior to the testing.

   The children with DD (both CDR and CDNR) were officially diagnosed to be having developmental dyslexia by the certified clinical psychologists from government recognised institutions in Karnataka, India.

3. *Typically Developing children (TD):* There were 46 students (33 boys and 13 girls, with a mean age of 12yrs and 9 months, SD=1.02), who were age matched normally developing with normal academic achievement, language developments and intellectual ability.

The above three groups were compared on PA, RAN & Reading measures (Word/ Non-word reading and Reading rate).

Assessment tools

The testing of the CDR and CDNR children was preceded with an informal and a detailed noting of history that covered information pertaining to prenatal history, birth details, reaching milestones, medical history, sensory deficits, developmental difficulties, performance in academics, core curricular progress, emotional and behavioural problems were noted down either from their parents, teachers or case files. All details about the initial difficulties in language, math and writing, and the changes seen ever since were made. As a preliminary step to judge their current status, their handwritten note books were perused through, and an informal assessment of reading and writing using their text books was done.

Emotional/behavioural disorders were ruled out with Rutter's Proforma (A & B) (Rutter, 1967), Intellectual level of functioning was assessed with The Standard Progressive Matrices (Deshpande & Patwardhan, 2006; Raven, 1938; 1941), the level of Socio Economic Status was assessed with the Kuppuswamy's socioeconomic status scale: A Revision (Mishra & Singh, 2003) and The Socio-Economic Status Scale (Meenakshi, 2004).

Reading, PA and RAN subskills were assessed in both English and Kannada. Tests comprised of word reading lists to assess the accuracy and reading rate, non-word reading list to assess decoding accuracy and its reading rate, likewise, PA and RAN to assess phonological strengths. The tests were administered individually with sufficient practice trials prior to actual testing. A brief description is as follows

Reading Measures

Kannada

Word and Pseudo-word reading in Kannada (Saldanha et al., 2014): This tool was developed in the lines of Test of Word Reading Efficiency (TOWRE) (Torgesen, Wagner, & Rashotte, 1999), assessed Kannada word and pseudoword reading efficiency. There were 72 and 62 items in sight word efficiency (SWE) section and Pseudo-word efficiency (PDE) respectively. The total number of words and pseudo-words correctly read in 45 seconds and the total number of correctly read items (without time limit) were considered as one's scores. This test is one of the first quick and reliable test for assessment of decoding and sight-word reading skills in Kannada (Saldanha et al., 2014).

English

Test of Word Reading Efficiency (Torgesen et al., 1999): The test for English comprised Sight Word Reading Efficiency (SWE) and Phonological Decoding Efficiency (PDE) measures. It is a timed measure of single-word and pseudoword reading efficiency. The scoring is similar to the Word and Pseudo-word reading in Kannada (Saldanha et al., 2014).

Phonological Awareness Tests

Kannada

Phonological awareness (Saldanha & Padakannaya, 2010) Phoneme Reversal (PR): The participant had to orally repeat short non-words in the reverse order of phonemes (e.g., "I will say some made-up short words, one at a time. I want you to listen carefully and then tell me the real word you get when you reverse the order of the sounds in the made-up word. Say /elu/ (J®Ä).Now, tell me what word would you get if you say /elu/ (J®Ä) backwards?"). There were a total of 12 test items.

A time sampling test-retest reliability coefficients of the test for normal readers aged 8-17 years was 0.89 with a 2-week period between testing was reported for the subtests (Saldanha & Padakannaya, 2010). All the items assess PA, and were high on content validity. It was evident from the ratings of the experts that all items assess PA.

English

Comprehensive Test of Phonological Processing (Wagner, Torgesen, & Rashotte, 1999) assesses PA, phonological memory, and rapid naming ability. It can be administered to persons of age 7 through 24 years (persons in second grade through college). Wagner et al (1999) reported test-retest reliability coefficient for all the subtests ranging from 0.72 to 0.79 for ages 8-17 years.

Phoneme Reversal (PR): The participant was orally presented with phonemes and was required to tell the real word obtained when the presented order of the phonemes were reversed. (e.g., "I will say some made-up words in small parts, one part at a time. Please listen carefully, and tell me the real word you get when you reverse the order of the sounds in the made-up word. Say /tĭs/. Now tell me what word would you get if you say /tĭs/ backwards?"). The total number of items was 18. No of correct responses in each subtest constituted the score.

Rapid Automatised Naming

The Kannada version of the Rapid Automatised Naming (Siddaiah, Saldanha, Venkatesh, Ramachandra, & Padakannaya, 2016) to rapidly name color, object, digit and letter was adapted from Denckla & Rudel (1974). The corresponding names of colours in Kannada were [*haladi*] for yellow, [*nili*] for blue, [*kempu*] for red, [*kappu*] for black and [*hasiru*] for green. The time sampling test-retest reliability coefficient of the four subtests was 0.92 for colour. The total time in seconds to name the colours arranged in arrays was taken as the score.

Results

Phonological processing skills measure and characterize a struggling developmental dyslexic reader from typical readers, and performance oan n out-of-context measure of word reading and word reading efficiency index the progress of children's word reading ability. Table-2 presents the summary of the word, non-word reading and reading rate results by the three groups of readers in English and Kannada.

Table-2: Mean and standard deviation of reading word, non-words and reading rate of the three groups of readers in English and Kannada

	CDNR		CDR		TD	
	M	SD	M	SD	M	SD
English						
SWE (words read in 45 sec)	20.00	11.23	45.78	17.5	74.76	10.41
SWE (104)	36.54	20.32	77.9	22.16	101	3.78
PDE (non-words decoded in 45 secs)	9.48	5.65	24.14	11.62	46.35	10.27
PDE(63)	17.09	11.56	44.24	14.56	60.22	4.64
Kannada						
SWE (words read in 45 sec)	14.83	8.96	31.04	12.09	53.28	12.99
SWE(72)	28.57	18.71	60.43	11.87	70.46	2.31
PDE (Non-words Decoded in 45 sec)	11.09	5.96	22.47	7.69	38.72	10.63
PDE(62)	20.33	12.92	45.24	13.3	58.70	5.45

Source: own calculation based on collected data

Note: SWE—Sight Word Efficiency; PDE—Phonological Decoding Efficiency; CDNR =Children with Dyslexia with No Remediation; CDR=Children with Dyslexia Remediated; TD = Typically Developing. Maximum score in parenthesis beside the measure name

The group CDNR showed DD typical profile by obtaining the lowest scores on all the word and non-word reading and reading rate measures, with CDNR < CDR < TD trend. The performance was higher on word reading and its reading rate than on non-word reading counterpart. As expected, the TD group performed best in all the indices. The performance of the CDR group on all reading, non-word reading and reading rate measures was one standard deviation (mean ± 1SD) above the performance of the CDNR group reflecting the compensating effect of remediation. The performance on the word and non-word reading by the CDR group was twice that of the CDNR group. However, the performance of the CDR group was poor when compared to the performance of the TD group on all reading measures. Nevertheless, in terms of percentage, the overall performance of the CDR group was 70% and above on words and non-words read, and moreover, their accuracy and reading rate was better for words than non-words.

Table-3: Mean (percentage of accuracy is given in parenthesis) and standard deviation on Phoneme Reversal and of the RAN-Color tasks

	CDNR		CDR		TD	
	M	**SD**	**M**	**SD**	**M**	**SD**
English						
PR[a]	3.89(21.61)	2.58	11.18(62.11)	3.28	15.35(85.28)	2.27
Colour[b]	58.5	30.4	41.16	9.5	35.09	7.63
Kannada						
PR[a]	2.37(19.75)	3.14	9.22(76.83)	2.14	11.04(92)	0.99
Color[b]	116.83	70.8	77.92	45.18	53.96	16.24

Source: Own calculation

Note: [a] Measured in terms of mean PA items correctly performed (performance in percentage);

[b] Measured in seconds; PR-=Phoneme Reversal; CDNR =Children with Dyslexia with No Remediation; CDR=Children with Dyslexia Remediated; TD = Typically Developing.

Table-3 summarises the Phoneme Reversal and RAN –Color profiles of the three groups of readers in the two languages. The three groups differed on the level of performance on the PR tasks, with CDNR < CDR < TD trend. The CDNR showed typical profiles by obtaining the lowest percentage/ mean score; likewise, the TD has obtained the highest mean score. The performance of the CDR was more than 2SD higher than the performance of the CDNR on the PR measure, reflecting the ameliorating effects of the phonological remediation. As expected the CDNR have taken the longest mean time in seconds, and the TD have taken the shortest time in seconds to rapidly name the stimuli.

Table-4: Correlation between PA and RAN measures with reading measures across the groups

	Sight Word Reading			Non-word Reading		
	CDNR	**CDR**	**TD**	**CDNR**	**CDR**	**TD**
Kannada						
PR	**0.48****	**0.32***	**0.22**	**0.33***	**0.35***	**0.27**
RAN-Color	**–0.12**	**–0.31***	**–0.40****	**–0.90**	**–0.36***	**–0.47****
English						
PR	**0.31***	**0.55****	**0.26**	**0.34***	**0.40****	**0.48****
RAN-Color	**–0.40****	**–0.34***	**–0.41****	**–0.30***	**–0.26**	**–0.19**

Source: Saldanha & Siddaiah (2016)

Note: CDNR= Children with Dyslexia with no Remediation; CDR= Children with Dyslexia Remediated; TD=Typically Developing; PR=Phonological Reversal; RAN=Rapid Automatised Naming. $*p < 0.05$; $** p < 0.01$.

As mentioned in the introduction that phonological processing such as phonological awareness (PA) and rapid naming main and independent predictors and causes of breakdown underlying reading dysfunction, and have a collective effect on efficient reading and spelling (Miller et al., 2006; Nicolson & Fawcett, 2005; Norton & Wolf, 2012; Verhagen, Aarnoutse, & Van Leeuwe, 2010; Vukovic & Siegel, 2006). The two measures, viz. PR and RAN–Colour had significant correlations with word and non-word reading across the groups in both the languages (as shown in table 4). Further, in order to quantify and compare the shared and combined contributions of PA and RAN to sight word reading and non-word reading, a Regression Commonality Analysis (RCA) was applied to the scores. The RCA quantifies partitions unique and shared contribution of the different independent variables (PA and RAN) to the dependent variable (the word and non word reading measures) (Pedhazur, 1982). The SPSS script based on the R-code (Nimon, Lewis, Kane, & Haynes, 2008) was used for performing the statistical analysis. The results of the unique and shared contribution of PR and RAN color naming to the reading measures in the two languages by the three groups.

Table-5: The unique and common contributions of PR and RAN color naming to reading measures (%variance accounted for is given in the parenthesis)

	Sight Word Reading			**Nonword Reading**		
	CDNR	**CDR**	**TD**	**CDNR**	**CDR**	**TD**
Kannada						
Unique contributions						
PR	0.2321 (94.12)	0.0754 (43.83)	0.0431 (21.51)	0.1087 (93.12)	0.1014 (78.30)	0.067 (23.19)
RAN -Color	0.14 (5.88)	0.0678 (39.42)	0.1510 (75.34)	0.008 (6.87)	0.0021 (1.64)	0.2126 (73.58)
Common contributions						
PR & RAN – Color	0.000 (0.005)	0.0288 (16.74)	0.0063 (3.14)	0.0000 (0.005)	0.026 (20.05)	0.0093 (3.22)
Sum	0.2466	0.1720	0.2005	0.1168	0.1295	0.2889
English						
Unique contributions						
PR	0.0642 (29.12)	0.2505 (68.74)	0.0427 (20.32)	0.0915 (50.58)	0.1311 (66.21)	0.2068 (84.75)
RAN -Color	0.1256 (56.96)	0.0666 (18.28)	0.1440 (0.023)	0.0633 (34.99)	0.0404 (20.40)	0.0178 (7.30)

Common contributions						
PR & RAN – Color	0.0308 (13.97)	0.0473 (12.98)	0.0234 (10.95)	0.0260 (14.37)	0.0265 (13.38)	0.0194 (7.95)
Sum	0.2205	0.3645	0.2101	0.1809	0.1980	0.2440

Source: Saldanha & Siddaiah (2016)

Note: CDNR= Children with Dyslexia with no Remediation; CDR= Children with Dyslexia Remediated; TD=Typically Developing; PR=Phonological Reversal; RAN =Rapid Automatised Naming

Discussion and Conclusion

The results for Kannada revealed that the unique contribution by PA accounted for a greater proportion of variance. The variance of 94.12% and 93.12% to word and non-word reading of CDNR group respectively, and least to the TD group. It is interesting to note that the proportion othe f unique contribution of PA to reading decreased, as the level of reading expertise increased. The proportion othe f unique contribution of RAN colour to word and non-word reading, 75.34% and 73.58 % respectively, is highest for the TD group. Christo and Davis (2008) and Wolf (1997), report that PA plays a more prominent role in the early reading acquisition phase. As the reader graduates to the ceiling in their ability to decode, the rapid naming ability comes into play and gets stronger. The proportion of the unique contribution of RAN to word reading increased as the reading expertise increased.

The results for English showed that the unique contribution of PA to word and non word reading was greater than RAN except for the CDNR group. Further, the unique contribution of PA to non-word reading was directly proportional to the reading proficiency of the groups. Parallely, the unique contribution of RAN decreased as a function the f increase in the reading ability of the groups.

To conclude, the results suggest that remediation did prove to be effective to the CDR group as they performed much significantly better than the CDNR group on the word and non word reading measures. In fact, their performance on RAN was almost on par with the TD group. The naming speed was shorter in English by all groups and better PA performance in Kannada by almost groups (except CDNR). Despite intensive remediation at the phonemic level, children with dyslexia can never acquire complete mastery at the phonemic level due to the lack of consistency in grapheme-phoneme relations in a non-transparent orthography like English (Goswami, 2000).

In both the languages the CDNR group showed DD typical profile with the weakest PA and slowest naming speed. Remediation seemed to have helped the CDR group as the mean scores on reading and PA of the group are two standard deviation above the mean of the CDNR.

Further, the RCA analysis for Kannada showed that PA plays a major role during the early reading acquisition phase, but as reader scales to a higher level in decoding ability, the contribution of naming speed increases. In English, the relative contribution of PA is greater than the rapid naming. Therefore, during the early phases of learning reading, an intensive and consistent grounding in phonological awareness drills may fortify the mastery of the writing system. It could be in the form of phoneme or syllable identification, manipulation, blending, reversal, deletion, or spoonerisms. This can further strengthen the working memory, as it requires the mental segmentation of the phoneme, reversing their order and successively reassembling them. Poor ability to manipulate sub-lexical units in working memory is a pronounced phonological feature of DD (Démonet, Taylor, & Chaix, 2004).

By and large, this is applicable to other Indian scripts (except Urdu) that are alphasyllabaries and akin to Kannada phonology. However, In English, the combined contribution of PA and naming speed decreases as the reading proficiency increases. However, the results support the view that the poor PA is the principal marker associated with Dyslexia.

Acknowledgment

Special thanks to M.S. Thirumalai, Ph.D., Managing Editor, Language in India: Strength for Today and Bright Hope for Tomorrow

References

1. Annamalai, E. (2001). Managing multilingualism in India: Political and linguistic manifestations (Vol. 8). SAGE Publications Pvt. Limited.
2. Araújo, S., Inácio, F., Francisco, A., Faísca, L., Petersson, K.M., & Reis, A. (2011). Component processes subserving rapid automatised naming in dyslexic and non-dyslexic readers. Dyslexia, 17(3), 242-255.
3. Breznitz, Z. (2002). Asynchrony of visual orthographic and auditory phonological word recognition processes: An underlying factor in dyslexia. Reading and Writing: An Interdisciplinary Journal, 15(1-2), 15-42.
4. CHILD Protection & Child Rights.(2017). Child in India.
5. Retrieved from http://www.childlineindia.org.in/child-in-india.htm
6. Christo, C., & Davis, J. (2008). Rapid naming and phonological processing as predictors of reading and spelling. The California School Psychologist, 13(1), 7-18.
7. Cramer, S.C., Sur, M., Dobkin, B.H., O' Brien, C., Sanger, T.D., Trojanowski, J.Q., ...& Chen, W.G., S. (2011). Harnessing neuroplasticity for clinical applications. Brain: A Journal of Neurology, 134(6), 1591-1609.
8. Démonet, J.F., Taylor, M.J., & Chaix, Y. (2004). Developmental dyslexia. The Lancet, 363 (9419), 1451-1460.
9. Denckla, M.B., & Rudel, R. (1974). Rapid 'automatised' naming of pictured objects, colors, letters and numbers by normal children. Cortex, 10(2), 186-202.
10. Deshpande, C.G., & Patwardhan, V. (2006). Raven standard progressive matrices: Norms for Indian tribal areas. New Delhi: Manasayan.
11. Draganski, B., Gaser, C., Busch, V., Schuierer, G., Bogdahn, U., & May, A. (2004).

Neuroplasticity: Changes in grey matter induced by training. Nature, 427(6972), 311-312.

12. Express News Service. (1st November, 2012). Now, classical language status for Kannada. Retrieved from http://www.newindianexpress.com/states/karnataka/article9.ece
13. Foorman, B.R., & Moats, L.C. (2004). Conditions for sustaining research-based practices in early reading instruction. Remedial and Special Education, 25(1), 51-60.
14. Goswami, U. (1997). Rime-based coding in early reading development in English: Orthographic analogies and rime neighbourhoods. In C. Hulme & J.R. Malatesha (Eds.), Reading and spelling: Development and disorders (pp. 69-86). Mahwah, NJ: Erlbaum.
15. Goswami, U. (2000). Phonological representations, reading development and dyslexia: Towards a cross-linguistic theoretical framework. Dyslexia, 6, 133-151.
16. Goswami, U. (2005). Synthetic phonics and learning to read: A cross-language perspective. Educational Psychology in Practice, 21(4), 273-282.
17. Goswami, U. (2006). Neuroscience and education: from research to practice? Nature reviews neuroscience, 7(5), 406-413.
18. Grigerenko, E.L. (2001). Developmental dyslexia: An update on genes, brains, and environments. Journal of Child Psychology and Psychiatry, 42(1), 91-125.
19. Guardiola, J.G. (2001). The evolution of research on dyslexia. Annuario de Psicologia, 32(1), 3-30.
20. Gupta, A. (2004). Reading difficulties of Hindi-speaking children with developmental dyslexia. Reading and Writing: An Interdisciplinary Journal, 17, 79-99.
21. Holopainen, L., Ahonen, T., & Lyytinen, H. (2001). Predicting delay in reading achievement in a highly transparent language. Journal of Learning Disabilities, 34, 401-413.
22. Hudson, R.F., High, L., & Al Otaiba, S. (2007). Dyslexia and the brain: What does current research tell us? The Reading Teacher, 60(6), 506-515.
23. Karande, S., Mehta, V., & Kulkarni, M.(2007). Impact of an education program on parental knowledge of specific learning disability. Indian Journal of Medical Science, 61, 398-406.
24. Karande, S., Sawant, S., Kulkarni, M., Kanchan, S., & Sholapurwala, R. (2005). Cognition in specific learning disability. The Indian Journal of Pediatrics, 72(12), 1029-1033.
25. Karanth, P. (2003). Cross-linguistic study of acquired reading disorders. Dordrecht, The Netherlands: Kluwer Academic Publishers.
26. Karanth, P. (2006). The Kagunita of Kannada—Learning to read and write an Indian alphasyllabary. In R.M. Joshi & P. Aaron (Eds), Handbook of Orthography and Literacy, (pp. 389-404). Mahwah, NJ: Lawrence Erlbaum Associates.
27. Karanth, P., Mathew, A., & Kurien, P. (2004). Orthography and reading speed: Data from native readers of Kannada. Reading and Writing: An Interdisciplinary Journal, 17(1-2), 101-120.
28. Kothari, D.S. (1966). Report of the Education Commission, 1964-1966: Education and national development. New Delhi, India: Ministry of Education, Government of India.
29. Landerl, K., & Wimmer, H. (2008). Development of word reading fluency and spelling in a consistent orthography: An 8-year follow-up. Journal of Educational Psychology, 100, 150 –161.

30. Leopold, W. (13th February, 2013). Researchers discover a biological marker of dyslexia: Ability to consistently encode sound undergirds the reading process. Retrieved from http://www.northwestern.edu/newscenter//stories/2013/02/researchers-discover-a-biological-marker-of-dyslexia_mobile.html
31. Medina, J. (17th July, 2016). Specific Learning Disorder. Psychcentral. Retrieved from https://psychcentral.com/disorders/specific-learning-disorder/
32. Meenakshi (2004). Socio Economic Status Scale. Agra, India: Rakhi Prakashan.
33. Miles, E. (2000). Dyslexia may show a different face in different languages. Dyslexia, 6, 193-201.
34. Miller, C.J., Miller, S.R., Bloom, J.S., Jones, L., Lindstrom, W., Craggs, J.,... Hynd, G.W. (2006). Testing the double-deficit hypothesis in an adult sample. Annals of Dyslexia, 56(1), 83-102.
35. Mishra, D., & Singh, H.P.(2003). Kuppuswami's socioeconomic status scale: A Revision. Indian Journal of Pediatrics, 70, 273-274.
36. Mogasale, V.V., Patil, V.D., Patil, N.M., & Mogasale, V. (2012). Prevalence of specific learning disabilities among primary school children in a South Indian city. The Indian Journal of Pediatrics, 79(3), 342-347.
37. Mohanty, A. (2008). Multilingual Education in India. In N.H. Hornberger (Ed.), Encyclopedia of Language and Education (pp 1617-1626). USA: Springer.
38. Nag, S. (2007). Early reading in Kannada: the pace of acquisition of orthographic knowledge and phonemic awareness. Journal of Research in Reading, 30, 7-22.
39. Nag, S., & Snowling, M. (2012). Reading in an alphasyllabary: Implications for a language-universal theory of learning to read. Scientific Studies of Reading, 16, 404-423.
40. Nag, S., Treiman, R., & Snowling, M.J. (2010). Learning to spell in an alphasyllabary: The case of Kannada. Writing Systems Research, 2, 41-52.
41. Nicolson, R.I., & Fawcett, A.J. (2005).Developmental dyslexia, learning and the cerebellum. Journal of Neural Transmission Supplement, 69, 19-36.
42. Nicolson, R.I., Fawcett, A.J., Moss, H., Nicolson, M.K., & Reason, R. (1999). Early reading intervention can be effective and cost-effective. British Journal of Educational Psychology, 69, 47-62.
43. Nimon, K., Lewis, M., Kane, R., & Haynes, R.M. (2008). An R package to compute commonality coefficients in the multiple regression case: An introduction to the package and a practical example. Behavior Research Methods, 40(2), 457-466.
44. Norton, E.S. & Wolf, M. (2012). Rapid automatised naming (RAN) and reading fluency: Implications for understanding and treatment of reading disabilities. Annual Review of Psychology, 63, 427-452.
45. Padakannaya, P., & Ramachandra, N.B. (2011). Reading Akshara: Indian alphasyllabary. In P. McCardle, J.R. Lee, O. Tzeng, & B. Miller (Eds.), Dyslexia across languages: Orthography and the brain-gene-behaviour link. Maryland: Paul H. Brookes Publishing Co.
46. Padakannaya, P., Ramachandra, N.B., & Singh, N. (2008). Dyslexia, orthography and brain. Current Science, 95(10), 1381.
47. Pedhazur, E.G. (1982). Multiple regression in behavioural research: Explanation and prediction 2nd ed. New York: CBS College Publishing.

48. Prakash, P., Joshi, R.M. (1989). Language representation and reading in Kannada: A South Indian language. In Aaron, P.G., Joshi, R.M. (Eds.), Reading and writing disorders in different orthographic systems (pp. 223-230). Dordrecht, the Netherlands: Kluwer Academic Publishers.
49. Prakash, P., & Joshi, R.M. (1995). Orthography and reading in Kannada: A Dravidian language. In Taylor I., Olson D. (Eds.), Scripts and reading: Reading and learning to read the world's scripts (pp. 95-108). London, UK: Kluwer Academic Publishers.
50. Purushothama, G. (1994). A framework for testing Kannada reading on the basis of automaticity, rules of orthography and segmental processing. Manasagangotri, Mysore: Central Institute of Indian Languages.
51. Ramaa, S. (1993). Diagnosis and remediation of dyslexia: an empirical study in Kannada, an Indian language. Mysore: Vidyasagar Printing and Publishing House.
52. Ramaa, S., Miles, T.R., & Lalithamma, M.A. (1993). Dyslexia: Symbol processing difficulty in the Kannada language. Reading and Writing: An Interdisciplinary Journal, 5, 29-41.
53. Raven, J.C. (1938). Progressive matrices: A perceptual test of intelligence. London: H.K. Lewis.
54. Raven, J.C. (1941). Standardisation of progressive matrices, 1938. British Journal of Medical Psychology, 19, 137-150.
55. Rutter, M. (1967). Children's behaviour questionnaire for completion by teachers: preliminary findings. Journal of Child Psychology and Psychiatry, 8, 1-11.
56. Saldanha, M.P.J., & Padakannaya, P.(2010). Test of phonological processing. Mysore, KA: University of Mysore
57. Saldanha, M.P.J., & Siddaiah, A. (2016). Relative Contribution of Naming Speed and Phoneme Awareness To Reading Kannada and English in Dyslexic and Nondyslexic Biliterates. Language in India, 16(9), 117-131.
58. Saldanha, M., Siddaiah, A., Veerappa, A.M., Ramachandra, N.B., & Prakash, P. (2014). Catch them before they fall: a simple test of sight-word and pseudo-word reading in Kannada for a quick and early assessment. SAGE Open, 4(4), 1-8.
59. Seymour, P.H., Aro, M., & Erskine, J.M. (2003). Foundation literacy acquisition in European orthographies. British Journal of psychology, 94(2), 143-174.
60. Sharma, J.C. (8th December, 2001). Multilingualism in India. Language in India, Retrieved from http://www.languageinindia.com/dec2001/jcsharma2.html
61. Shastry, B.S. (2007). Developmental dyslexia: an update. Journal of Human Genetics, 52(2), 104-109.
62. Shaywitz, S.E., & Shaywitz, B.A. (2005). Dyslexia (Specific reading disability). Biological Psychiatry: A Journal of Psychiatrics Neuroscience and Therapeutics, 57(11), 1301-1309.
63. Siddaiah, A., Saldanha, M., Venkatesh, S.K., Ramachandra, N.B., & Padakannaya, P. (2016). Development of rapid automatised naming (RAN) in simultaneous Kannada-English biliterate children. Journal of psycholinguistic research, 45(1), 177-187.
64. Sproat, R. (2006). Brahmi-derived scripts, script layout, and segmental awareness. Written Language and Literacy, 9, 45-66.
65. Sunseth, K., & Bowers, P.G. (2002). Rapid naming and phonemic awareness: Contributions to reading, spelling, and orthographic knowledge. Scientific Studies of Reading, 6, 401-429.
66. Tandon, R. (16th May, 2016). PERSPECTIVE: India must do more for its talented dyslexic

students. Mail Online India.

67. Retrieved from http://www.dailymail.co.uk/indiahome/indianews/article-3593457/PERSPECTIVE-India-talented-dyslexic-students.html
68. Thambirajah, M.S. (2010a). Developmental dyslexia: An overview. Advances in Psychiatric Treatment, 16(4), 299-307.
69. Thambirajah, M.S. (2010b). Developmental Dyslexia: clinical aspects. Advances in Psychiatric Treatment, 16, 380-387.
70. Thomas, S., Bhanutej, K., & John, S. (2003). Dealing with Dyslexia. The Week, 21, 36-42. Retrieved on 28th June, 2011. Retrieved from http://www.actionresearch.net/living/rawalpdf/Ref.pdf
71. Torgesen, J.K., Wagner, R.K., & Rashotte, C.A. (1999). Examiner's Manual: Test of Word Reading Efficiency. Austin, TX: PRO-ED, Inc.
72. Treiman, R., Mullennix, J., Bijeljac-Babic, R., & Richmond-Welty, E.D.(1995). The special role of rimes in the description use and acquisition of English orthography. Journal of Experimental Psychology: General, 124, 107-136.
73. Tressoldi, P.E., Stella, G., & Faggella, M. (2001). The development of reading speed in Italians with dyslexia: A longitudinal study. Journal of Learning Disabilities, 34, 414-417.
74. Vaid, J., & Gupta, A. (2002). Exploring word recognition in a semi-alphabetic script: The case of Devanagari. Brain and Language, 81, 679-690.
75. Vaid, J., & Padakannaya, P.(2004). Introduction, Special issue on reading and writing in semi syllabic scripts. Reading and Writing: An interdisciplinary Journal, 17, 1-6.
76. Vellutino, F.R., Fletcher, J.M., Snowling, M.J., & Scanlon, D.M. (2004). Specific reading disability (dyslexia): what have we learned in the past four decades? Journal of child psychology and psychiatry, 45(1), 2-40.
77. Verhagen, W.G., Aarnoutse, C.A., & Van Leeuwe, J.F. (2010). Spelling and word recognition in Grades 1 and 2: Relations to phonological awareness and naming speed in Dutch children. Applied Psycholinguistics, 31(01), 59-80.
78. Vukovic, R.K., & Siegel, L.S. (2006). The Double-Deficit Hypothesis A Comprehensive Analysis of the Evidence. Journal of Learning disabilities, 39(1), 25-47.
79. Wagner, R.K., Torgesen, J.K., & Rashotte, C.A. (1999).CTOPP: Comprehensive Test of Phonological Processing. Examiner's manual. Austin, TX: PRO-ED.
80. Wolf, M. (1997). A provisional, integrative account of phonological and naming-speed deficits in dyslexia: Implications for diagnosis and intervention. In B. Blachman (Eds.), Foundations of reading acquisition and dyslexia: Implications for early intervention (pp. 67-92). Mahwah, NJ: Erlbaum.
81. Worldometers. (17th May, 2017). India Population. Retrieved from http://www.worldometers.info/world-population/india-population/
82. Ziegler, J.C., & Goswami, U. (2005). Reading acquisition, developmental dyslexia, and skilled reading across languages: A psycholinguistic grain size theory. Psychological Bulletin, 131(1), 3-29.
83. Ziegler, J.C., & Goswami, U. (2006). Becoming literate in different languages: Similar problems, different solutions. Developmental science, 9(5), 429-436.

□

22

Death Clustering among the Tribes of Central and Eastern Indian States

—Mukesh Ranjan, Laxmi Kant Dwivedi and Rahul Mishra

Abstract

Present study attempts to assess family level death clustering among mothers in the tribes of central and eastern Indian states of Jharkhand, Madhya Pradesh, Orissa and Chhattisgarh. Random effect logit model was applied to assess the family level death clustering using micro-data of National Family Health Survey-3 (2005-06), India. The raw data analysis show the s existence of clustering in all four states with maximum and minimum clustering exists among tribes of Chhattisgarh and Jharkhand respectively. The most important factor which increases the risk of infant deaths is the causal effect of any previous infant death in families on the risk of infant death on subsequent siblings (a scarring effect), after controlling for mother-level unobserved heterogeneity. Mother-level unobserved factors was found to be significant for the tribes of Jharkhand and Madhya Pradesh while in the states of Orissa and Chhattisgarh unobservable at mother level have limited power to explain death clustering. Results also shows that high-risk tribal families are more exposed to short birth intervals and are likely to reach higher parities in their attempts to achieve their desired family size.

Introduction

One of the targets under the Millennium Development Goal (MDG) is to reduce the infant mortality rate (IMR) by two-thirds between 1990 and 201 5.For India, it translates into a goal of reducing IMR from 88 infant deaths per thousand live births in 1990 to 29 infant deaths per thousand live births by201 5.The recent figure of IMR for India shows the val ofue of37 infant deaths per 1000 live births (Sample Registration System (SRS), 2015).Hence, it clearly reflects that India lagged far behind in achieving mortality related MDG goal. In India, the issue of high IMR exists with a lot of regional variations across the states. For example, among the bigger states, IMR varies from 12 infant deaths per 1000 live births in Kerala to 50 infant deaths per 1000 live births in Madhya Pradesh (SRS, 2015). Even post MDG era of Sustainable Development Goals set an ambitious target to reduce, neonatal mortality to at least as low as 12 per 1,000 live births and under-5 mortality to at least as low as 25 per 1,000 live births and also end preventable deaths of newborn and children under 5 years of age by 2030.

These goals could be achieved by adopting some different strategies like need to identify the most vulnerable high risk clusters of mothers which are frequently experiencing child deaths while progressing towards higher parity. In the present days, prevailing high mortality situation in the developing nation across the world including India is not only an issue of concern itself but it has strong linkages with intra-family clustering of deaths. Numerous literatures suggest that infant deaths were unevenly distributed among Indian families (Das Gupta 1990, 1997; Arulampalam and Bhalotra 2006, 2008; Pradhan and Arokiasamy 2006). In a study of rural Punjab, (one of the economically most prosperous state of India) it has been found that in the overall sample, 67 percent of women never experienced any child loss and only 13 percent of women experienced multiple child loss which accounted for nearly 62 percent of all child deaths (Das Gupta 1990).This disproportionate distribution of infant deaths is known as 'death clustering' in demographic literature. The obvious explanation of clustering is that, deaths are concentrated among poor and uneducated families and these families also share genetic or environmental risk factors that raises the risk of death (Arulampalam and Bhalotra, 2006). A recent study even highlighted that mortality hazard among tribes is higher than non-tribes in all the four central and eastern Indian states of Chhattisgarh, Jharkhand, Madhya Pradesh & Odisha (Ranjan, Dwivedi & Mishra, (2017a); Ranjan, Dwivedi & Mishra (2017b)). It has been found that on average, an Indian child had 25 percent lower likelihood of dying under age five as compared to an Adivasi or Tribal child (Das, Kapoor & Nikitin,, 2010).As per NFHS-3, (2005-06) estimates for the country, it is found that STs have lower infant mortality rate (62) than SCs (66) but higher than OBCs (57).

Present research was undertaken to investigate the clustering of infant deaths among tribal families of central and eastern states of India. These tribes varied in terms of their socio-economic and political development. The term 'Scheduled Tribes' refers to specific indigenous peoples whose status is acknowledged by the Constitution of India. The tribal population in India, according to the 2011 census, was 87 million and it constitutes around 8.2 percent of the total Indian population. Around 80 percent of them found in the central India and the rest was located in the north-eastern states. The maximum share in the tribal population is contributed by Madhya Pradesh (14.7 percent), followed by Odisha (9.2 percent), Jharkhand (8.3 percent) and Chhattisgarh (7.5 percent) to India's population in the central and eastern states. A majority of the tribal population living in these states are Particularly Vulnerable

Tribal Groups (PVTGs) (Ministry of Tribal affairs (MOTA), 2015). They are socially as well as economically very backward in the sense that they have little access to the resources for their development, low rate of literacy, relatively small population size, dwindling in numbers and some of the groups are at the verge of extinction.

Death Clustering: A Brief Description

Death clustering has been defined consistently in most of the studies in the following two ways: (i) counting the number women who have experienced more than one child loss and the extent of death clustered in them(Das Gupta, 1990; Guo, 1993; Curtis, Diamond & McDonald, 1993; Curtis & Steele, 199 6;Ranjan, Dwivedi & Mishra, 2017b) (ii).Whether the number of women with a different number of child deaths exceeds that which would be expected if the risks were constant for all women and their children (Ronsman, 1995; Zaba & David, 1996). Addressing this important issue of death clustering in the analysis of mortality needs to be addressed with caution as the observations are not independent since siblings living in the same family have similar exposure to the environment.

Hence, the present study is an attempt to quantify and highlight the issue of infant death clustering among the tribal families of four high infant mortality Indian states of Madhya Pradesh, Chhattisgarh, Odisha and Jharkhand. The study also try to understand the intra-family clustering of deaths due tthe o occurrence of previous siblings deaths in families and the contribution of unobserved factors (because of mother level unobserved factors like behavioural factors in child rearing, genetic factors etc.) in the concentration of deaths within the families of the tribes. The findings from the study would definitely help us in knowing the structure of family level death clustering and the interconnected survival prospects of siblings (scarring effect) as well as unobserved heterogeneity of mortality risk among mothers in these states.

Materials & Methods

In order to examine the family level infant death clustering, a bivariate analysis of a total number of children ever born to a family and infant deaths per family was carried out. Further, to establish and for capturing the linkages between survival prospects of siblings and mother specific unobserved heterogeneity, the random effect it log model was applied. This model has the advantage of simultaneously capturing unobserved heterogeneity and the causal positive or negative scarring mechanisms. Several previous studies have also employed this model to address the issue of death clustering (Sastry, 1997; Omariba, Rajulton, & Beaujot, 2008).

Data Source

The data used in the present study is taken from the third round of National Family health Survey which was conducted in the year 2005-06. It interviewed 124385 ever married women aged 15-49 at the time of the survey. It has a complete retrospective history of births together with a record of child deaths for each mother, for a period spanning more than 35 years (1968-2006). Thus, it would give a sufficient number of cases for analysis as well as it would provide the opportunity to construct (unbalanced) panel data for mothers. Further full retrospective birth history has been used for all the statistical analysis in the present study. Selecting tribal families from the birth history resulted in 2494 families had 9069 children born to them. So the, final sample for the analysis will be 9069 births.

The Empirical Model

The dependent variable i.e. infant death and the survival status of the preceding child (i.e. lagged variable) were both coded as binary variables—one if a child died before the age of 12 months and zero otherwise. By taking child specific and mother specific covariates along with preceding child (lagged variable), the random effect log it model was applied. Children who were younger than 12 months at the time of the survey were dropped from the sample because they had not had 12 months of exposure to mortality risk. Twins births were also dropped from the model so that siblings should be identified properly. In the present study, Infant death clustering is defined as two or more infant deaths in families. Children born to a mother has been considered as then same family hence mother is taken as a synonym for the family but a child may have different fathers.

Choice of Independent Variables

Child specific factors in the model: Birth order, Sex of the child, Survival status of the previous sibling.

Mother specific factors in the model: Her educational attainment and her partner's educational attainment, year of birth of a mother, mother's age at birth, mother age squared and religion.

Birth order has been categorised into 5 categories viz. '1', 3, 4, 5 and 6+ birth order. The educational attainment of the respondent's partner has been categorised into two categories viz. literate and illiterate. Respondent year of birth has been categorised into 3 categories those women who were born between 1956-1969, 1970-79 and after 1980. Information on household assets, immunisation, prenatal care, access to piped water, and relevant community level variables were not used because they are time inconsistent (Rosenzweig & Kenneth, 1986). The purpose of the mother-level random effects, which was included in the model, was to control for the time-invariant component of these omitted variables.

Statistical Model:

Random Effects Logit Model

Consider there are N children distributed in K different mother clusters. Each child has a vector of covariates, ***x*** and the parameters corresponding to the covariates are in vector β. The K mutually independent cluster variables $u_1, u_2, ..., u_k$, are not to be estimated, but rather the variation between clusters are to be quantified. Therefore, a normal distribution is assumed for the *u* values, and parameters characterizing this distribution can then be used to characterize the heterogeneity induced by the random effects.

The response variable 'infant survival status' (Y) is dichotomous in nature. A child is observed to die if Y = 1, and 0 otherwise.

Level 1: for a child with covariate *x*, corresponding to the *k*th cluster, the probability of observing an infant death, i.e. Y = 1 is:

$$P(Y = 1|u_k; x) = \exp(\eta(x, u_k))/(1+ \exp(\eta\ (x, u_k)).$$

Level 2: for that child, the second level equation is:

$$(\eta(x, u_k) = \beta x + \gamma Y_{nk-1} + u_{k,}$$

where $u_k \sim N(0, \sigma^2)$. The covariate vector *x* contains individual-level (Level 1) and cluster-level (Level 2) covariates. The model also includes the observed survival status of the previous siblings, Y_{nk-1}, the coefficient that picks up scarring. The estimated parameter γ should be interpreted as the 'average' effect of scarring over the time period considered. In models of this sort, the previous sibling's survival status Y_{ij-1} is necessarily correlated with mother level unobserved heterogeneity (random effect parameter) (Wiji Arulampalam and Sonia Bhalotra 2008).

Results

Sample Characteristics of the Study Population

The sample characteristics of the tribal population in selected states of central and eastern India is shown in Table-1 of total 12,534 families 20 percent (2494 families) were from Scheduled Tribes (STs). The distribution of sample shows that, over one-third of the tribal families' lived in Madhya Pradesh and nearly 20 percent were in Chhattisgarh.

Among 9069 children who were born to 2494 families and among these children, around1,632 children died at different ages in a period spanning more than 35 years from 1968 to 2006. Among these deaths, nearly two-third children were dead in their infancies. There are about 70 percent of families in the sample who never had an infant death, but 30 percent of families (712 families) had experience at least one infant death. Further, almost 8 percent of families (218 families) had experience at least two or more infant deaths which accounts for nearly 52 percent of the total infant deaths. Of total infant deaths, nearly 55 percent were males and 45 percent were females. Sixty percent of babies who died during infancy had younger sibling of age less than 24 months. With regard to religious composition portrays, a majority of families were from Hindus (90 percent). Further, parental educational attainment was also extremely poor among the tribal population. Nearly 80 percent of mothers and 55 percent of fathers had no formal schooling. Merely 10 percent of mothers and 30 percent of fathers were secondary and above educated.

Clustering of infant deaths across different caste groups in the central and eastern India

Clustering of infant deaths among families across different caste groups can be seen in Table-2.Although, it is clearly evident from the table that majority of infant deaths had come from the Other Backward Caste (OBCs) families but percentage contribution to infant death per family was highest among tribal families. It has been recorded over 40 percent among STs, followed by SCs (35 percent), OBCs (30 percent) and is noted lowest among other than SCs and STs and OBCs. Further, it has been observed that over half of infant death among SCs and STs were concentrated among those families, who had experience two or more infant deaths. The percentage of such families was 7 percent among SCs and 9 percent among STs. Therefore, maximum clustering of infant deaths was observed among tribal families and was least among Other than SCs, STs and OBCs. Overall the clustering of infant death in this region was 47 percent which clustered in just 6 percent families.

Clustering of infant deaths within tribal families is presented in Table-3. The sample has total 1,024 infant deaths among 2,494 tribal families. More than 95 percent of the children belonged to those families that contributed two or more children to the sample. Families with five or more children accounted for 17 percent of the families, but contributed over 50 percent of the total number of children in the sample. The mean number of children per tribal family was 3.6. It is clearly evident from the table that over half of deaths in the sample had come from 9 percent of those families who had experienced two or more deaths. It is worth mentioning that, only 3 percent of the families in the sample contributed three or more deaths; together these families accounted for approximately one-fourth of the total infant deaths. Largely, it can be concluded that the tribal women had high level of fertility, as half of the tribal families had three or more children. It makes mothers and their child at a greater risk of death.

The probability of infant death using raw data is shown in column 1 of Table-4. The raw data probabilities illustrates, that IMR was fairly high among tribal families.

It was highest in Madhya Pradesh (124) followed by Chhattisgarh, Odisha (111) and is recorded lowest in Jharkhand (103). The high mortality in all four states indicate the vulnerability of frequent infant deaths. There is not much differences in socio-economic and demographic indicators among families from different states. In column 2nd & 3rd, the raw probabilities of infant deaths for the index child was based on the condition of survival status of the previous sibling. Further, the difference between the two is calculated in column 4. It indicates the probability of the extent of death clustering within a family. Further it can be concluded that maximum probabilities of infant deaths clustering was existed in Chhattisgarh with 0.213. It is interesting to note that the probability of death for index child was highest among the families of Chhattisgarh followed by Madhya Pradesh, when there is a prior infant death in the family, but on contrary the probabilities of death is observed highest among the families of Madhya Pradesh instead of Chhattisgarh which have prior survived infant in the family. The probability of extent of death clustering was maximum in Chhattisgarh and minimum in Jharkhand which is early two and half times lower than Chhattisgarh, shown in column 4. Column 5 shows an alternate representation of data in terms of relative odds. The relative odds ratio of infant death based on previous sibling's death varies from 2.33 to 5.2 4. The relative risk shows the effect of previous infant death on the risk of death of the index child in a family. The relative odds ratio in Chhattisgarh was 5.24 which means that a new born in a tribal family would have five times more likely the risk of death during infancy, if one of his earlier sibling died as compared those families where none of the earlier siblings had died as an infant. The adjusted relative odds results based on the regression model is also quite close to what we have tried to capture from raw data and it is highly statistically significant ($p<0.01$) for all four states.

Overall, the data demonstrates a high degree of death clustering in tribes from Central and Eastern India. These are the observed tendencies in the data. Estimation of the statistical model allowed us to disentangle clustering effects into correlated risks amongst sibling and, conditional upon this, a causal effect of the death of one sibling on the risk of death of next sibling (Wiji Arulampalam and Sonia Bhalotra 2008).

Model based Clustering Analysis: Scarring

Column 1 of Table-5 records the probability of extent of death clustering persistence in the raw data that was first displayed in Table-4. Estimates of scarring from the model that ignored unobserved heterogeneity are in Panel, 1 and these were compared with estimates from the preferred model that allowed for it in Panel 2 of Table-5. The marginal effect associated with the estimated γ, the coefficient of the previous child's survival status, is computed as the difference between the sample averages of the probability of death predicted by the estimated model when

Y_{ij-1}=0 and when Y_{ij-1}=1. These were approximately equivalent to the first partial derivative of the conditional probability of infant death Y_{ij}=1 concerning Y_{ij-1}. The scarring effect observed from the above-explained model, is prominent among tribal families in all four states, after controlling exogenous factors at the individual and family level. The further result shows that the death during the infancy of a previous sibling in the family raises the probability of death for the index child during his infancy in every state of central and eastern region (Wiji Arulampalam and Sonia Bhalotra 2008).

It is evident from column 2 and 5 of Table-5 that irrespective of the inclusion of mother level heterogeneity in the model, it is observed that the marginal effect of scarring was statistically significant for all four states in both the panels. The maximum effect of scarring was observed in Chhattisgarh in both panels. There are nearly two hundred infant deaths per thousand live births that were clustered due to scarring in Chhattisgarh in Panel 1. After allowing unobserved heterogeneity at mother/family level, it may be derived that the effect of scarring related to clustering of infant deaths in the family was prominent in all states. The scarring associated clustered infant deaths in the family ranges from 73 infant deaths per thousand live births in Jharkhand ($p<0.01$) to a maximum of 182 infant deaths in Chhattisgarh ($p<0.01$).

Without taking into account the survival status of the previous sibling, the estimate for infant death would be underestimated. The underestimation of mortality varied between 9 percent (Jharkhand) and 25 percent (Chhattisgarh, as shown in column 4 of Table-5. A similar pattern can be observed in column 7, but underestimation in infant deaths was low. It implies that unobserved or hidden factors may be responsible for the clustering of infant deaths in the family to a certain extent. Without including the unobserved heterogeneity term in the model, the scarring factor explained 95 percent of the raw clustering in case of Chhattisgarh, as shown in column 3. Thus, scarring is putting maximum impact in Chhattisgarh, and it was a leading cause for explaining the clustering of infant deaths. The figure for Odisha was least where scarring explains only 82 percent of the raw probability of death clustering.

Column 5 and Column 6 of Panel 2 in Table-5, shows the marginal effect of scarring based on a model that has taken into account unobserved factors and its percentage contribution in raw clustering estimated in column 1.

The extent to which scarring effect explaining the raw data clustering varied between 75 percent in Odisha to 89 percent in Madhya Pradesh. We notice that, in column 3, the contribution of scarring explaining raw clustering of mortality in these two states was 82 percent and 90 percent respectively. The maximum reduction in the effect of scarring explaining the raw data under the presence of unobserved factors was observed for Chhattisgarh. The reduction was nearly 10 percent from 96 percent in column 3 to 86 percent in column 6. In each of the other three states, the reduction was occurred at a slower rate in comparison to Chhattisgarh. Thus a model that fails to allow for unobserved heterogeneity overestimated the level of scarring in every state. In other words, it would be wrong to neglect the familial and other components (unobserved factors) while estimating infant mortality.

Unobserved heterogeneity

Columns 8 and 9 of Table-5present the estimated variance of the unobserved heterogeneity term along with the intra class correlation coefficient. It shows that after adjusting for the scarring effect, along with mother and child level specific explanatory variables in the model, there was heterogeneity in the risk of mother experiencing the infant deaths (either due to genetic or some other unobservable factors) in Jharkhand and Madhya Pradesh as estimated variance was worked out to be significant at 1 percent as shown in column 8 of Table-5. It also shows that in these two states, mother level characteristics cannot be neglected while explaining the clustering of infant deaths. The percentage of error variance, attributable due to unobserved heterogeneity is shown in Column 9. It was lowest for Jharkhand as well as Madhya Pradesh and was highest for Chhattisgarh. The variance at mother level was statistically insignificant in Chhattisgarh and Odisha. Hence, in these two state, scarring performs a vital role in defining the clustering of infant deaths among tribal families of these two states. Demographers interpreted mother level effects as a measure of the importance of genetic traits (Sastry, 1997) or maternal ability (Das Gupta 1990, 1997). It explains that the inclusion of mother-specific factors in the model was not sufficient enough to explain mother level variation in these two states. It may be due to community level factors that are acting as a troubling parameter.

Discussion

This study assessed the clustering of infant death at a family level among tribal population of four selected states of India. Findings show that the STs has the highest number of families with at least two infant deaths (9%) and additionally, over half of the total infant deaths occurred only in those families who had experienced prior infant death. These results are supported by the finding of *Das Gupta* (1990), in rural Punjab, showing that families who had already experienced the loss of other children are at higher risk of losing further children. This relationship applied to the chance of survival of a child at all stages of childhood following the neonatal period. A sibling shares a large number of highly relevant demographic characteristics of a mother, such as age; breastfeeding patterns; and fecundity, which strongly correlates with the length of the birth interval. Zaba and David (1996) depicted the causal relationship between high-parity women and high-risk mothers. The present study also provided strong empirical evidence on this causal relationship, close to eighty percent of the infant deaths were attributed due to mothers of grand multiparity (≥4), identified them as 'high-risk' women. The sample selection effect (i.e., selection of families with higher than average incidence of prior child loss) and maternal depletion are the important factors in risk polarisation among high-parity mothers (Miller, Trussell, Pebley & Vaufhan, 1992).

Further, the study also observed the scarring effect under two different models. Scarring effect had played an important role in shaping intra-family death clustering in all the four selected states. It is possible to eliminate the risk of death of a first born child through public health intervention then the experience gained by mother in rearing this child would automatically reduce the risk of infant death for the younger child. After removing the scarring effect, the reduction in infant mortality was more in panel one than in panel 2. It shows that after inclusion of unobserved heterogeneity in the model, the level of infant mortality remains almost same for all the states. Arulampalam and Bhalotra (2006), in their research, also claimed that deaths might cluster due to both the unobserved heterogeneity and scarring effects. In light of the study, present states should carefully consider targeted interventions and appropriate policies to identify and improve the condition of tribal families with multiple infant deaths.

References

1. Arulampalam, W. and S. Bhalotra (2006). "Sibling death clustering in India: state dependence versus unobserved heterogeneity." Journal of the Royal Statistical Society: Series A. (Statistics in Society) 169(4): 829-848.
2. Arulampalam, W. and S. Bhalotra (2008). "The linked survival prospects of siblings: Evidence for the Indian states." Population Studies 62(2): 171-190.
3. Curtis, S.L., Diamond, I., & McDonald, J.W. (1993). Birth interval and family effects on postneonatal mortality in Brazil. Demography, 30(1), 33-43.
4. Curtis, S.L. and F. Steele (1996). "Variations in familial neonatal mortality risks in four countries." Journal of Biosocial Science 28(2): 141-159.
5. Das Gupta, M. (1990). "Death clustering, mothers' education and the determinants of child mortality in rural Punjab, India." Population Studies 44(3): 489-505.
6. Das Gupta, M. (1997). "Socio-economic status and clustering of child deaths in rural Punjab." Population Studies 51(2): 191-202.
7. Das M.B., Kapoor S., and Nikitin D. (2010). A closer look at child mortality among Adivasis in India. Policy Research Working Paper WPS5231. Human Development Department, The World Bank South Asia Region. Retrieved on 23rd March, 2015

from http://documents.worldbank.org/curated/en/955711468044086021/pdf/WPS5231.pdf.

8. Guo, G. (1993). "Use of sibling data to estimate family mortality effects in Guatemala." Demography 30(1): 15-32
9. Miller, J.E., J. Trussell, A.R. Pebley, and B. Vaughan. 1992. Birth spacing and child mortality in Bangladesh and the Philippines. Demography 29:305-318.
10. Ministry of Tribal Affairs (MOTA). (2013). Statistical Profile of Scheduled Tribes in India. (pp. 3-9). New Delhi: Statistics Division, Ministry of Tribal Affairs (MOTA). Retrieved on 2nd February, 2017 from http://tribal.nic.in/WriteReadData/userfiles/file/Statistics/StatisticalProfileofSTs2013.pdf
11. Omariba, D.W.R., Rajulton, F., & Beaujot, R. (2008). Correlated mortality of siblings in Kenya: The role of state dependence. Demographic Research, 18(11), 311-336.
12. Pradhan, J., & Arokiasamy, P. (2006). High infant and child mortality rates in Orissa: an assessment of major reasons. Population, Space and Place, 12(3), 187-200.
13. Ranjan, M., Dwivedi, L.K., & Mishra, R. (2017a). Infant mortality differentials among the tribal and non-tribal populations of Central and Eastern India. International Journal of Population Studies, 2(2).
14. Ranjan, M., Dwivedi, L.K., & Mishra, R. (2017b). Caste Differentials in Death Clustering In Central And Eastern Indian States. Journal of Biosocial Science, 1-21.
15. Registrar General of India (2015). Sample Registration System (SRS).India: Office of The Registrar General and Census Commissioner, Ministry of Home Affairs. Retrieved on 7 march, 2017 fromhttp://www.censusindia.gov.in/vital_statistics/SRS_Reports_2015.html
16. Ronsmans, C. (1995). "Patterns of clustering of child mortality in a rural area of Senegal." Population Studies 49(3): 443-461.
17. Rosenzweig, Mark R. and Kenneth I. Wolpin.(1986)."Evaluating the effects of optimally distributed public programs: Child health and family planning interventions", The American Economic Review 76(3): 470-482.
18. Sastry, N. (1997). "Family-level clustering of childhood mortality risk in Northeast Brazil." Population Studies 51(3): 245-261.
19. Wiji A. and Sonia B. (2008). "Persistence in Infant Mortality: Evidence for the Indian States", 1-43. https://warwick.ac.uk/fac/soc/economics/staff/swarulampalam/publications/popstud02jan08.pdf.
20. Zaba, B. and P.H. David (1996). "Fertility and the distribution of child mortality risk among women: an illustrative analysis." Population Studies 50(2): 263-278.

Table-1: The sample characteristics of tribal population in selected states, India, 1970-2006.

Background Characteristics	Jharkhand	Odisha	Chhattisgarh	MP	N
Caste					
Schedule Caste	11.4	29.7	18.1	40.8	2020
Schedule Tribe	17.8	22.3	26.0	34.0	2494
Other Backward Class	20.5	16.7	24.7	38.1	4920

Other	13.7	38.6	10.1	37.5	3100
Characteristics of Schedule Tribes in Selected States:	**Jharkhand**	**Odisha**	**Chhattisgarh**	**MP**	**N**
No. of Families	464	617	696	717	2,494
Total Births	1,655	2,028	2,456	2,930	9,069
Total Deaths among total births	15.4	20.0	24.3	40.4	1,632
Under 5 Deaths	15.7	20.0	24.0	40.3	1,493
Infant Deaths	15.9	19.3	24.7	40.1	1,024
Families with at least					
One Infant Death	17.5	20.7	23.1	38.7	712
Two Infant Deaths	15.1	16.4	24.5	44.0	218
Children born in families with at least					
One Infant Death	16.9	21.6	27.1	34.5	1024
Two Infant Death	14.3	18.7	29.4	37.5	530
Sex of child					
Male	16.4	19.8	27.2	36.5	570
Female	15.2	18.7	21.6	44.5	454
Religion					
Hindu	10.3	23.6	28.4	37.7	2,226
Muslim	66.4	22.1	11.5	0.0	89
Others	94.1	5.4	0.6	0.0	179
Mother's education					
Illiterate	17.1	22.9	24.7	35.3	1,969
Primary	13.6	20.4	29.8	36.3	235
Secondary	25.1	20.5	32.3	22.0	274
Higher and above	47.3	3.7	29.4	19.5	16
Father's education					
Illiterate	16.4	23.8	22.9	36.9	1321
Primary	8.8	23.5	31.2	36.5	466
Secondary	26.9	18.6	27.7	26.7	626
Higher and above	27.3	15.7	36.8	20.3	76

Note: Sample characteristics are based on the complete retrospective birth history of the women between 1970-2006, based on 3rd round of NFHS (2005-2006) All 'n' values are unweighted; *Abbr.,* JH—Jharkhand, OR—Odisha, CG—Chhattisgarh, MP—Madhya Pradesh.

Source: Author's construction

Table-2: Distribution of infant deaths among families of various caste groups in the central and eastern India, India 1970-2006.

	Families with infant deaths					Number of infant deaths				
Infant deaths	SC*	ST**	OBC	Others	Total	SC*	ST**	OBC	Others	Total
0	1,535	1,782	3,856	2,644	9817	0	0	0	0	0
1	345	494	786	364	1,989	345	494	786	364	1989
2	92	152	206	65	515	184	304	412	130	1030
3	31	44	51	20	146	93	132	153	60	438
4	12	17	14	3	46	48	68	56	12	184
5	3	4	4	2	13	15	20	20	10	65
6	0	1	2	1	4	0	6	12	6	24
7	2	0	1	1	4	14	0	7	7	28
Total	**2,020**	**2,494**	**4,920**	**3,100**	**12,534**	**699**	**1024**	**1446**	**589**	**3758**
	Families with at least 2 infant death	Families with at least 2 infant death	Families with at least 2 infant death	Families with at least 2 infant death	Families with at least 2 infant death	At least 2 infant death	At least 2 infant death	At least 2 infant death	At least 2 infant death	At least 2 infant death
Extent of infant death clustering	6.9	8.7	5.6	3.0	5.8	50.64	51.75	45.64	38.2	47.07

Source: Author's construction; **Abbreviation**: SC—Scheduled Caste; ST—Scheduled Tribes; OBC—Other backward castes; Others: Other than SC/ST and OBC.

Table-3: Distribution of infant deaths among Tribal families of central and eastern India, 1970-2006.

Children per family	No. of infant deaths per tribal family							Families	Total children	Percent Children
	0	1	2	3	4	5	6			
1	335	30	0	0	0	0	0	365	365	4.0
2	403	58	7	0	0	0	0	468	936	10.3
3	417	72	12	2	0	0	0	503	1509	16.6
4	285	95	24	5	0	0	0	409	1636	18.0
5	176	94	31	7	3	0	0	311	1555	17.1
6	97	68	33	8	0	0	0	206	1236	13.6
7	47	36	16	6	6	2	0	113	791	8.7

8	11	20	14	6	4	0	0	55	440	4.9
9	7	16	9	7	4	0	0	43	387	4.3
10	4	4	4	3	0	2	1	18	180	2.0
11	0	1	1	0	0	0	0	2	22	0.2
12	0	0	1	0	0	0	0	1	12	0.1
Families	1,782	494	152	44	17	4	1	2,494	9,069	100
% Families	71	20	6	2	1	0	0			
Percent of children:	60.8	24.6	9.6	3.2	1.4	0.4	0.1	100.0		
Percent of infant death:	0.0	48.2	29.7	12.9	6.6	2.0	0.6	100.0		

Source: Author's construction

Table-4: Raw data based probabilities of infant deaths among the Scheduled tribe in the central and eastern Indian states, 1970-2006.

State	Probability of death	Probability of death given the previous sibling's infant death	Probability of death given the previous sibling's survival	Death Clustering	Relative Odds Ratio	Relative Odds Ratio [*p*-value]
	[1]	[2]	[3]	[4]= [2]-[3]	[5]*	[6]**
Jharkhand:	**0.103**	**0.157**	**0.075**	**0.083**	**2.33**	**2.27 [0.002]**
Odisha:	**0.111**	**0.179**	**0.08**	**0.099**	**2.5**	**2.22 [0.004]**
Chhattisgarh:	**0.111**	**0.283**	**0.07**	**0.213**	**5.24**	**4.90 [0.000]**
Madhya Pradesh:	**0.124**	**0.249**	**0.092**	**0.157**	**3.28**	**3.33 [0.000]**

Source: Author's construction

Note: *The relative odds ratio is calculated as the ratio of Column [2]/(1-column [2]) to Column [3]/ (1-Column [3]).

This is the exponential of the estimated scarring coefficient in a simple logit model that includes an intercept and the survival status of the previous sibling.

**Column [6] reports the equivalent numbers from the estimated model which control for the effects of other covariates and unobserved mother—specific effects. These are exponentials of the estimated scarring coefficients γ. The *p*-values refer to those associated with the estimated γ.

Table-5: Effect of scarring on the clustering of infant mortality within the tribal families in central and eastern Indian states, India, 1970-2006. Results are based on the random effect of logit regression[1].

Panel 1: Model without unobserved heterogeneity (Col. 1 to 4)					Panel 2: Model with unobserved heterogeneity (Col. 5 to 9)				
State	Raw data death clustering[2]	Estimated marginal effects[3]	Raw clustering explained by scarring (%)	Reduction in infant mortality if no scarring	Estimated marginal effects[3]	Raw clustering explained by scarring (%)	Reduction in infant mortality if no scarring	The estimated variance of the mother level	estimated intra-mother correlation coefficient[5]
	[1]	[2]	[3]=[2]/[1]	(%)[4] [4]	[5]	[6]=[5]/[1]	(%)[4] [7]	[p-value][8]	[9]
Jharkhand:	0.083	0.0739 [0.002]	89.15	9.37	0.0737 [0.002]	88.86	1.02	0.00 [0.000]	0.0000
Orissa:	0.099	0.0806 [0.003]	81.51	12.6	0.0746 [0.004]	75.39	1.2	0.11 [0.170]	0.0340
Chhattisgarh:	0.213	0.2036 [0.000]	95.6	25.12	0.1823 [0.000]	85.77	2.8	0.15 [0.570]	0.0460
Madhya Pradesh:	0.157	0.1407 [0.000]	89.64	15.28	0.1398 [0.000]	89.05	2.1	0.00 [0.000]	0.0000

Source: Author's construction

Note: 1. The equation is estimated with the initial condition of the process. It means start of the process same as sample start.

The marginal effect associated with scarring is significant at the 1 percent level in all states. The p-values calculated to test whether the variance attributable to unobserved mother-specific heterogeneity is zero are computed accounting for the fact that the parameter under the null hypothesis is on boundary.

2. This is column [4] of Table-4.
3. The marginal effect is computed as the difference between the sample averages of the probability of death predicted by the estimated model when Yij-1=0 and when Yij-1=1(excluding the first born). This is approximately equivalent to the partial derivative of the conditional probability of death of the index child with respect to the covariate, Yij-1.
4. This is calculated as the difference between the predicted probability of death from the estimated model and predicted probability of death from the model when $\gamma=0$ is imposed after estimation, and excluding first-born children.
5. This is equal to column [8] as a proportion of estimated total variance.

□

23

Children's Right to Safe Sanitation in Urban Gujarat: Evidence from the Margins

—*Keshab Das*

Abstract

Lack of access to basic services such as water and sanitation are long recognised as a denial of human rights. While unsafe and inadequate sanitation and water affect all human beings, children suffer critically with both long term and short term losses which could severely compromise their potential capabilities in living an equal and aspiring citizen of the world. Based on information collected through a massive field survey of urban slums in Gujarat, this paper engages with issues of children's access to sanitation and a hygienic living environment both in the private and public spheres. The findings of the field surveys underscore the need for sustained efforts by the state towards educating and informing slum dwellers regarding benefits of sanitation and hygienic living. Increased investment towards building drainage and sewerage facilities, provision of water and regular management of collection and disposal of solid and liquid waste is an essential prerequisite towards promoting a safe sanitation environment for children and adults alike. Provision of sanitation infrastructure, awareness regarding hygienic practices and a vigilant society would contribute immensely towards ensuring children's right to safe sanitation and healthy living, especially those who reside in the urban margins.

Keywords: Urban sanitation; Children's rights; Slums; Drainage and sewerage, Gujarat.

JEL Classification: R58, I38, I18, I12

Acknowledgments

Sincere thanks are due to A.K. Rakesh (former MD, Nirmal Gujarat Mission), Irfan Khan (TALEEM Foundation), Jay N. Padalia (AIILSG), Rudra N. Mishra and Gani Memon (both at GIDR) for substantive support in accomplishing the larger study and to Sanjay Prasad (DG, MGLI) for offering an opportunity to present an earlier version of this paper at the National Seminar on 'Making Child Rights A Reality'. Special thanks are due to Indira Hirway (Director, CFDA) for constructive comments on an earlier draft of this paper.

Introduction

Lack of access to basic services such as water and sanitation are long recognised as a denial of human rights. The main challenges to taking a rights-based approach to water, sanitation and hygiene related to the fact that such a right is not construed (construed as) an explicit right, but derived from the right to an adequate standard of health and well-being enshrined in the Universal Declaration of Human Rights. Not until the Convention on the Rights of the Child was adopted in 1986 (ratified by all but two countries in the world) was the human right to safe water and sanitation made explicit (Häusermann, 1999). The issue of access to sanitation and a hygienic living environment—both at the private and public spheres—has acquired significance across the globe, at least since the conclusion of the United Nations proclaimed International Drinking Water Supply and Sanitation Decade (IDWSSD) during 1981-1990. The subsequent active perusal of the goal of ensuring universal access to clean water and sanitation facilities as through the Millennium Development Goals (MDG) (Goal #7) and, now, Sustainable Development Goals (SDG) (Goal #6) accorded primacy to these most basic amenities for every citizen of the world. As SDG #6 emphasises, "Water scarcity, poor water quality and inadequate sanitation negatively impact food security, livelihood choices and educational opportunities for poor families across the world."[36]

While unsafe and inadequate sanitation and water affect all human beings, children suffer critically with both long term and short term losses which could severely compromise their potential capabilities in living an equal and aspiring citizen of the world. For children, while falling ill, forced absences from attending school, non-school learning opportunities or playing are the most common immediate consequences of poor sanitation and water provision, these could emerge as life-long ineligibility in participating in a competitive job market or any field of human excellence. In short, the right to water and safe sanitation, directly and indirectly, ensures right to a dignified living, better education and healthy life. Emphasising the human security aspect in children's right to water and safe sanitation, Pink (2012: 85) observes that "It is imperative to recognise the critical link between clean water and adequate sanitation in the protection of child health. In many instances, inadequate sanitation and open sewage systems severely contaminate water supplies, causing disease and death. The human security approach is a relevant framework for the analysis of child rights due to its emphasis on security threats to the individual."

36. http://www.un.org/sustainabledevelopment/water-and-sanitation/ (Accessed 21st September, 2017)

In the developing world, the gross inadequacy of both the provision of and actual use of sanitation facilities has engaged policy formulators, civil society organisations and academics as to how best to address the crisis. It is possible to observe that in most these nations, sanitation is accorded a low priority in terms of budgetary spend and planning for universal access. For instance, the recent *GLAAS: 2016-2017* survey of the 75 developing and poor countries, including India, across SDG regions find that "80% of countries surveyed reported inadequate funding to meet their national targets...". This funding gap will be magnified as countries integrate the SDGs more fully into their national plans and targets" (UN-Water, 2017: 45). A recent study by the OECD indicates that several African countries have been spending less than 0.5 percent of their respective GDPs on sanitation and hygiene related activities (Martin and Watts, 2013: 39). While some of the poorest the African nations have come together in expressing their deep concern over the matter and efforts are on to raise the limit (the share of respective GDPs), the Indian state's record continues to be pitiable. As estimated by the Centre for Budget and Governance Accountability (CGBA), in terms of government spending on the water and sanitation sector, "In Budget 2015-16, there has been a decrease in the overall spending capacity of the government (both Centre and States combined). In addition, the net increase in the spending capacity of the State Governments has been modest at best. According to a report by CGBA, this amounts to a *miniscule 0.33 percent of Gross Domestic Product (GDP)* for the year" (Bhaduri, 2015. *Emphasis ours*). This is notwithstanding the claims made under the Swachh Bharat Mission. It needs to be underscored that comprehensive and comparable official statistics on the amount spent on sanitation at a disaggregated level is not available. This has seriously impaired any meaningful analysis of public investment in the sector.

A relatively less known and discussed aspect in the national health policies relates to a number of diseases caused or induced by poor sanitation and unsafe water. As per the World Health Organisation, about one-tenth of the global burden of disease is associated with these inadequacies. A particularly disturbing aspect of neglect of sanitation and hygiene has been a high incidence of diarrhoeal deaths reported from several of these countries; most victims have been children below the age of five. "As many as 1.7 million people die every year from diarrhoeal diseases and, of these, 90 percent are children under the age of five, living predominantly in developing countries" (Essity and WSSCC, 2017: 13). That diarrhoeal deaths in India top the global chart remains a shameful reminder to the country's huge neglect of this sector in particular and public health in general. As per a study published in *Lancet Infectious Diseases*, in 2015, India accounted for over one fifth (21 percent , about 105000 children) of all deaths of children due to diarrhoea, the country close to this record was Nigeria.[37] A recent study in semi-urban Gwalior in Madhya Pradesh has established that the spread of sanitation facilities could be a major driver in preventing stunted growth in children (Augsburg and Rodríguez-Lesmes, 2018).

In India, despite, such large initiatives as the Central Rural Sanitation Programme (CRSP-1986), Total Sanitation Campaign (TSC-1999)/ Nirmal Bharat Abhiyan (NBA-2012), and School Sanitation and Hygiene Education (SSHE) access to safe sanitation has remained an illusion, mainly in the rural areas and urban slums. Nevertheless, several states had a large proportion of households without access to any form of a toilet (Table-1).

Table-1: Households not having Toilets of Any Type, Indian States

States/National	Households (%)
India	53.08
Jharkhand	77.97
Odisha	77.96
Bihar	76.94
Chhatisgarh	75.41
Madhya Pradesh	71.18
Rajasthan	65.03
Uttar Pradesh	64.35
Gujarat	42.65

Source: Tables on Houses, Household Amenities and Assets, Census of India 2011.

The Swachchh Bharat Mission (SBM) to make India open defecation free (ODF) by 2019 could potentially contribute to children's sanitation and hygiene. Especially, the focus on building around 2.6 lakh individual toilets and 2.5 lakh community toilets across 4401 towns and cities across the country will have an impact on environmental cleanliness and personal hygiene. Similarly, the 'Clean India: Clean Schools' initiative has the scope of ensuring all schools to have functional and hygienic water supply and sanitation facilities. These efforts would also have positive behavioural changes at home as well. The moot point, however, is that if several loopholes and unscrupulous practices, those overwhelm implementation have been addressed effectively so far. (Suggestion: The moot point, however, is that whether several loopholes and unscrupulous practices, which overwhelm implementation have been addressed effectively so far or not.) In the eagerness to declare a state or region, ODF, manipulation of data needs to be strictly guarded against.

37. Details available at http://health.economictimes.indiatimes.com/news/industry/42-per-cent-global-child-deaths-due-to-diarrhoea-in-india-nigeria/58969275

It is in this broad context that this paper analyses field survey data collected through probably the highest ever coverage of slums and squatters in urban Gujarat. Although the larger research study (Das *et al.*, 2010) had addressed several issues, this paper engages with such information relevant to the aspect of children's sanitation in Gujarat's urban margins.

Sanitation in Slums in Urban Gujarat: Creating Database through Primary Surveys

Urbanisation has become an inevitable and unalterable process of economic progress. Ensuring access to basic amenities by the population from marginalised sections, those who (that) mostly live in slums has been a daunting task for most urban local bodies (ULBs). The problem is especially acute in small and medium towns with weaker ULBs and children in slums bear the brunt of governance deficit. Gujarat has been a front-runner in terms of the pace of urbanisation during recent decades. As per the last two Censuses, from 37.4 percent in 2001, the share of urban population has risen to 42.6 percent in 2011. A considerable proportion (6.53 percent) of the urban population would continue to live in slums due to various reasons.

When the state government decided to implement 'Nirmal Gujarat' to make the state ODF by 2010, it had no reliable baseline data. The Nirmal Gujarat Mission aimed at providing access to toilets to the urban slum population in the state through individual or community toilets. It was, hence, considered important to possess prior information regarding other basic necessities like availability of water. It was imperative to ascertain the characteristics of slum households, especially; the type of dwelling, occupation, the status of the migration, ownership of the house and hygienic and sanitation practices which might influence the demand and use of individual/community toilets. A baseline survey was needed to have an idea about the potential demand for toilets.[38] The following part of the paper heavily but selectively draws upon findings of this large scale survey.

The study had generated a baseline database of slum households in 20 urban centres across Gujarat: three cities, six A Class towns and 11 B Class towns. Table-2 presents the number of slums (organised and unorganised) and their sample household size by sample Municipal Corporations and *Nagarpalikas*. It may be noted that the sample size of the households relates *only* to the slums. The number might increase/decrease following the houselisting exercise under this study.

38. As part of the large scale study commissioned by the Nirmal Gujarat Mission of the Government of Gujarat (through the City Managers Association Gujarat) and based on the methodology developed in Das (2009), various field surveys had been undertaken by three Ahmedabad-based organisations, namely, Gujarat Institute of Development Research (GIDR), All India Institute of Local Self Government (AIILSG) and TALEEM Research Foundation.

Table-2: List and Number of Slum Households of Selected Municipal Corporations and Nagarpalikas

Sr. No.	District	Name of MC & NP	Number of Slums			Estimated No. of Slum Households	10% Sample of Households
			Org	Unorg	Total		
Municipal Corporation							
1	Vadodara	Vadodara*	NA	NA	NA	39514 (10.03)	3951
2	Jamnagar	Jamnagar	NA	NA	58	25914 (20.64)	2591
3	Junagadh	Junagadh	NA	NA	24	14000 (20.55)	1400
	Total					79428 (20.17)	7943
A Class Municipality (Nagarpalika)							
1	Anand	Anand	4	9	13	1269 (0.03)	127
2	Banaskantha	Palanpur	0	21	21	7000 (24.12)	700
3	Panchmahals	Godhra	0	21	21	4920 (17.14)	492
4	Valsad	Vapi	6	19	25	1760 (4.45)	176
5	Bhavnagar	Botad	0	8	8	901 (3.57)	90
6	Kutch	Gandhidham	0	6	6	6704 (12.29)	670
Total			**10**	**84**	**94**	**22554 (10.21)**	**2255**
B Class Municipality (Nagarpalika)							
1	Ahmedabad	Viramgam	0	16	16	2111 (17.32)	211
2	Anand	Khambhat	13	4	17	1875 (9.49)	188
3	Dahod	Dahod	4	6	10	675 (3.09)	68
4	Navsari	Vijalpor	17	4	21	4050 (21.84)	405
5	Patan	Sidhhpur	4	1	5	2100 (16.28)	210
6	Sabarkantha	Modasa	17	2	19	1172 (8.42)	117
7	Amreli	Savarkundala	0	14	14	1312 (8.51)	131
8	Bhavnagar	Mahuva	2	4	6	675 (3.83)	68
9	Junagadh	Mangrol	5	5	10	2097 (17.83)	210
10	Kutch	Anjar	25	5	30	10000 (52.89)	1000
11	Surendranagar	Dhangadhra	7	0	7	3468 (22.73)	347
Total			**104**	**61**	**165**	**29535 (16.59)**	**2955**
Grand Total						**131517 (13.33)**	**13152**

Notes: MC—Municipal Corporation; NP—Nagarpalika
Org—Organised; Unorg—Unorganised
NA—Not available
* Data on Vadodara was not provided by the concerned municipal authorities.
Figures in parentheses are percentages to Total Urban Households of the respective MCs/NPs as per *Census 2011*

The surveys were designed to obtain, *among other things*, a realistic picture of the nature of problems encountered by region, knowledge and practices concerning sanitation and hygiene and such other issues like the availability of water, etc. The study covered a staggering 153375 households in 783 slums, through a comprehensive houselisting exercise and further went in for a detailed sample survey of 15387 households. Additionally, over 300 focus group discussions (FGDs) were carried out with exclusive men and women groups separately to appreciate the concerns and opinion of slum dwellers. Data collected through Slum Cards had helped create a complete information base on basic aspects of all slums in the 20 urban centres.

Water and Sanitation in Slum Households: Status and Access

The major sources of potable water across the 20 urban areas could be identified as public sources as (such as) household taps, standposts and tubewells or handpumps. These accounted for around 80 to 90 percent of households suggesting very little dependence on private or open unprotected sources. The preponderance of these public sources also implied that for the water requirement for washing clothes/ utensils, bathing and toilets these were the same sources depended upon.

There was a wide variation in the proportion of households having any form of toilets. With 66 percent households with toilets, Vadodara was ahead of the remaining two sample corporations, namely, Junagadh (60 percent) and Jamnagar (40 percent). In all A-Class towns, less than half the sample households had some form of toilet. While Vapi had the maximum coverage of 49 percent , Palanpur had just about 38 percent . Among B Class towns, Mangrol had the highest coverage of toilets (70.5 percent), followed by Vijalpore (62.2 percent) and Anjar (53.5 percent). In the rest, the same was below 50 percent . In Mahuva and Dhrangadhra, nearly 80 percent of all sample slum households did not have toilets. What is important to note is that in several of these urban slums septic tanks with flush often occupied a low share. While some of the lowest covered areas were in Junagadh (22.0 percent), Anand (17.4 percent), Botad (4.7 percent), Dhrangadhra (4.2 percent), Mangrol (3.7 percent) and Godhra (3.0 percent), not a single sample household in Vapi and Modasa had a toilet with septic tank and flush. Moreover, given that the average quantity of water use varied between about 4 and 11 litres in different areas, in 11 out of the 20 urban areas surveyed there was no provision whatsoever of water inside the toilet, neither tap nor any storage for water. There were also several instances of toilets not in usable condition or were being used for storage and such other purposes.

Even in most slum households it was reported that all members, including children, were using toilets it remained unclear if availability of water irregularly or in small quantity was a deterrent for children to use toilets at home.

Hygienic Practices Concerning Children

Sanitation awareness and hygienic practices at the household level are crucial to the morbidity and long-term health outcome of its members, especially children. These relate to filtering of drinking water, handling of food, handwashing and disposing of solid and liquid wastes. A specific aspect is about the place of defecation by children and managing the disposal of excreta that is considered a major cause of diarrhoeal diseases in India. The questionnaire had included separate sections dealing with issues in hygienic practices, approaches to waste disposal and knowledge about and to manage sanitation-related diseases.

Filtering of Water and Handwashing

As shown in Table-2 (Table-3), almost all sample households agreed that they covered their vessels used to store food and drinking water. However, when asked about the mode of drawing potable water, it was found that except in a few urban centres, households seldom used a doya 39 as a protection against contamination. While all the sample slum households in Viramgam reported using a doya, the same figure for Vapi slums was 86 percent . Godhra, Botad and Vijalpore also reported above 65 percent of the sample households using a doya to draw water. In a number of urban centres including the two corporations of Vadodara and Jamnagar, the proportion was less than 50 percent . In fact, in Palanpur, Gandhidham, Siddhpur, Modasa, Sabarkundla, Mahuva, Anjar and Dhrangadhra only one-fourth of all sample households reported to be using a doya for drawing water. In Dhrangadhra, the figure was the lowest at 2 percent .

Use of filter devices while collecting water for drinking/cooking purpose is crucial to avoid water borne diseases due to contamination. However, as the survey revealed in most of the urban centres, households often used a piece of cloth to filter water. As reported in Table-3, use of filter devices was found to be very low in all urban centres, except Junagadh, Khambat and Mangrol, where above 30 percent of sample households said they used some filter devices to collect water. Nearly one-fifth of households in Anand, Godhra, Dahod and Vijalpore also did not use any water filter devices. The practice of the majority of slum dwellers filtering drinking water using proper devices would have potential health implications for children.

39. A tumbler-like vessel connected to a handle used exclusively for drawing water from a pot.

Table-3: Storage of Food/Water, Mode of Drawing Water from the Vessel and Filtering of Water

Urban Local Bodies	Covering of vessel for storing food/water	Mode of drawing water from the vessel		Filtering water			Number of households
		Doya	Other	Using cloth	Filter device	None	
Municipal Corporation							
Vadodara	5388 (99.7)	2364 (43.8)	3038 (56.2)	4866 (90.1)	51 (0.9)	485 (9.0)	5402 (100.0)
Jamnagar	1976 (99.8)	840 (42.4)	1139 (57.6)	1752 (88.5)	36 (1.8)	191 (9.7)	1979 (100.0)
Junagadh	1170 (100.0)	598 (51.1)	572 (48.9)	778 (66.5)	369 (31.5)	23 (2.0)	1170 (100.0)
A Class Nagarpalika							
Anand	219 (100.0)	78 (35.6)	141 (64.4)	163 (74.4)	15 (6.9)	41 (18.7)	219 (100.0)
Palanpur	531 (99.6)	114 (21.4)	419 (78.6)	356 (66.8)	118 (22.1)	59 (11.1)	533 (100.0)
Godhra	477 (99.6)	322 (67.2)	157 (32.8)	381 (79.5)	10 (2.1)	88 (18.4)	479 (100.0)
Vapi	947 (97.4)	841 (86.5)	131 (13.5)	946 (97.3)	13 (1.3)	13 (1.3)	972 (100.0)
Botad	332 (100.0)	241 (72.6)	91 (27.4)	328 (98.8)	1 (0.3)	3 (0.9)	332 (100.0)
Gandhidham	1114 (99.5)	222 (19.8)	898 (80.2)	1014 (90.5)	3 (0.3)	103 (9.2)	1120 (100.0)
B Class Nagarpalika							
Viramgam	172 (100.0)	172 (100.0)	0 (0.0)	164 (95.4)	4 (2.3)	4 (2.3)	172 (100.0)
Khambhat	164 (99.4)	65 (39.4)	100 (60.6)	63 (38.2)	64 (38.8)	38 (23.0)	165 (100.0)
Dahod	222 (96.9)	119 (52.0)	110 (48.0)	177 (77.3)	8 (3.5)	44 (19.2)	229 (100.0)
Vijalpore	214 (100.0)	142 (66.4)	72 (33.6)	165 (77.1)	9 (4.2)	40 (18.7)	214 (100.0)
Siddhpur	414 (100.0)	80 (19.3)	334 (80.7)	285 (68.8)	87 (21.0)	42 (10.1)	414 (100.0)

Modasa	268 (100.0)	47 (17.5)	221 (82.5)	211 (78.7)	30 (11.2)	27 (10.1)	268 (100.0)
Savarkundla	120 (99.2)	31 (25.6)	90 (74.4)	109 (90.1)	5 (4.1)	7 (5.8)	121 (100.0)
Mahuva	267 (99.3)	66 (24.5)	203 (75.5)	229 (85.1)	8 (3.0)	32 (11.9)	269 (100.0)
Mangrol	190 (100.0)	107 (56.3)	83 (43.7)	124 (65.3)	57 (30.0)	9 (4.7)	190 (100.0)
Anjar	767 (98.3)	92 (11.8)	688 (88.2)	733 (94.0)	35 (4.5)	12 (1.5)	780 (100.0)
Dhrangadhra	354 (98.6)	86 (24.0)	273 (76.0)	336 (93.6)	3 (0.8)	20 (5.6)	359 (100.0)

Source: Field Survey.

Similarly, handwashing has been identified as an important hygienic practice that could prevent contamination and, in fact, reduce the incidence of certain ailments. An idea about handwashing practices as prevalent in the sample urban centres may be had from Table-4. While Botad reported the highest proportion (over two-thirds) of slum households, who did not wash their hands before taking food, in Sabarkundla and Mahuva it was over one-third. Interestingly, these three towns also were the ones where the practice of covering food/water vessels was also found very low. A related question on if handwashing preceded feeding children were also asked to those households with kids below the age of five years of age. Whereas the practice was reported to be mostly prevalent in the three municipal corporations, among A Class and B Class towns, there were at least two, namely, Botad and Dhrangadhra where this practice was not much followed. These results indicate the absence of efforts at creating awareness regarding basic hygienic practices concerning handling potable water and food and handwashing. As regards the place of bathing, which was often a stone or concrete base enclosed with sacks near their houses, above 60 percent of slum households in the three corporations had access to the bathroom attached to the house. In more than 50 percent of households in Anand, Viramgam, Khambat and Anjar members reported using bathing platforms. Except for Botad, the proportion of slum households without bathroom varied from 30 percent in Vadodara to 75 percent in Anand.

Table-4: Handwashing before Eating and Feeding Children

Urban Local Bodies	Handwashing before eating			Handwashing before feeding children (< 5 years)				Number of households
	Always	At times	Never	Always	At times	Never	Households with children*	
Municipal Corporation								
Vadodara	4303 (79.7)	1037 (19.2)	62 (1.1)	3658 (76.9)	787 (16.6)	309 (6.5)	4754	5402 (100.0)
Jamnagar	1616 (81.7)	323 (16.3)	40 (2.0)	1407 (78.9)	238 (13.3)	138 (7.7)	1783	1979 (100.0)
Junagadh	1068 (91.3)	94 (8.0)	8 (0.7)	317 (86.6)	41 (11.2)	8 (2.2)	366	1170 (100.0)
A Class Nagarpalika								
Anand	208 (95.0)	7 (3.2)	4 (1.8)	167 (76.3)	51 (23.3)	1 (0.4)	219	219 (100.0)
Palanpur	444 (83.3)	82 (15.4)	7 (1.3)	150 (71.4)	55 (26.2)	5 (2.4)	210	533 (100.0)
Godhra	419 (87.5)	45 (9.4)	15 (3.1)	383 (92.1)	53 (12.7)	35 (8.4)	471	479 (100.0)
Vapi	921 (94.8)	49 (5.0)	2 (0.2)	756 (77.8)	214 (22.0)	2 (0.2)	972	972 (100.0)
Botad	117 (35.2)	211 (63.6)	4 (1.2)	82 (24.7)	250 (75.3)	0 (0.0)	332	332 (100.0)
Gandhidham	897 (80.1)	204 (18.2)	19 (1.7)	855 (77.6)	217 (19.7)	30 (2.7)	1102	1120 (100.0)
B Class Nagarpalika								
Viramgam	155 (90.1)	17 (9.9)	0 (0.0)	128 (74.4)	19 (11.0)	25 (14.5)	172	172 (100.0)
Khambhat	165 (100.0)	0 (0.0)	0 (0.0)	162 (98.2)	3 (1.8)	0 (0.0)	165	165 (100.0)
Dahod	198 (86.5)	25 (10.9)	6 (2.6)	183 (82.1)	27 (12.1)	13 (5.8)	223	229 (100.0)
Vijalpore	205 (95.8)	9 (4.2)	0 (0.0)	141 (65.9)	73 (34.1)	0 (0.0)	214	214 (100.0)
Siddhpur	375 (90.6)	37 (8.9)	2 (0.5)	126 (85.1)	20 (13.5)	2 (1.4)	148	414 (100.0)

Modasa	237 (88.4)	30 (11.2)	1 (0.4)	96 (79.3)	20 (16.5)	5 (4.1)	121	268 (100.0)
Savarkundla	75 (62.0)	43 (35.5)	3 (2.5)	73 (65.2)	26 (23.2)	13 (11.6)	112	121 (100.0)
Mahuva	163 (60.6)	93 (34.6)	13 (4.8)	154 (60.9)	54 (21.3)	45 (17.8)	253	269 (100.0)
Mangrol	173 (91.1)	17 (8.9)	0 (0.0)	63 (88.7)	8 (11.3)	0 (0.0)	71	190 (100.0)
Anjar	713 (91.4)	67 (8.6)	0 (0.0)	680 (87.1)	100 (12.8)	0 (0.0)	780	780 (100.0)
Dhrangadhra	312 (86.9)	43 (12.0)	4 (1.1)	178 (49.6)	44 (12.3)	137 (38.2)	359	359 (100.0)

Note: * Relevant for households with children.

Disposal of Solid and Liquid Waste and Awareness about Diarrhoea

Safe disposal of solid and liquid waste generated in households is crucial for maintaining a healthy living environment which impacts the health and well-being of children in particular. Table-5 shows the abysmal condition of garbage collection in all three types of ULBs. Except for Palanpur, where 51 percent (highest among all urban centres studied) of all slum households reportedly had been using box/plot provided by the concerned ULB for disposing of the solid waste, in the remaining urban centres common dumping yard (or, *ukarda*) was the major site of disposal of solid waste. In Vadodara and Dahod, only about one-third of the sample households used box/plot for disposing of solid waste. Poor use of box/plot provided by ULBs by slum households could be attributed to a variety of reasons, prominent among them being the inadequate facilities provided by the ULBs and households deliberately not using them.

The matter of disposal of liquid waste (mainly waste water) also was not done responsibly. Majority of the households simply threw liquid wastes on to the street or allowed it to flow into pits within the homestead. Among all the urban centres, in Vapi and Dahod, over 60 percent of households threw the liquid waste in drains nearby. Throwing waste water into drains might not be safe if the drains were not covered or water overflowed. In any case, the unhygienic disposal of solid and waste would continue to remain a major cause of various ailments in children who have no other alternative to play and move around. Children were certainly coming in direct contact with waste strewn all over.

Table-5: Disposal of Household Waste

Urban Local Bodies	Solid Waste				Liquid Waste				Total number of house-holds
	Box/pot within house site	Common dumping ground (*Ukarda*)	Box/plot by ULB	Others	Flows to pit within house site	Pour into the drain	Throw on the street	Others	
Municipal Corporation									
Vadodara	695 (12.9)	2477 (45.9)	1963 (36.3)	267 (4.9)	435 (8.1)	2127 (39.4)	2779 (51.4)	61 (1.1)	5402 (100.0)
Jamnagar	221 (11.2)	1120 (56.6)	533 (26.9)	105 (5.3)	131 (6.6)	974 (49.2)	850 (43.0)	24 (1.2)	1979 (100.0)
Junagadh	50 (4.3)	798 (68.2)	194 (16.6)	128 (10.9)	89 (7.6)	358 (30.6)	493 (42.1)	230 (19.7)	1170 (100.0)
A Class Nagarpalika									
Anand	20 (9.1)	186 (84.9)	13 (5.9)	0 (0.0)	89 (40.6)	25 (11.4)	105 (48.0)	0 (0.0)	219 (100.0)
Palanpur	20 (3.8)	408 (76.5)	64 (12.0)	41 (7.7)	37 (6.9)	63 (11.8)	346 (64.9)	87 (16.3)	533 (100.0)
Godhra	34 (7.1)	159 (33.2)	245 (51.1)	41 (8.6)	44 (9.2)	232 (48.4)	161 (33.6)	42 (8.8)	479 (100.0)
Vapi	59 (6.1)	656 (67.5)	257 (26.4)	0 (0.0)	185 (19.0)	635 (65.3)	152 (15.6)	0 (0.0)	972 (100.0)
Botad	22 (6.6)	307 (92.5)	3 (0.9)	0 (0.0)	3 (0.9)	12 (3.6)	317 (95.5)	0 (0.0)	332 (100.0)
Gandhidham	88 (7.9)	598 (53.4)	205 (18.3)	229 (20.4)	100 (8.9)	204 (18.2)	758 (67.7)	58 (5.2)	1120 (100.0)
B Class Nagarpalika									
Viramgam	34 (19.8)	103 (59.9)	35 (20.4)	0 (0.0)	60 (34.9)	75 (43.6)	35 (20.4)	2 (1.2)	172 (100.0)
Khambhat	0 (0.0)	159 (96.4)	6 (3.6)	0 (0.0)	1 (0.6)	55 (33.3)	109 (66.1)	0 (0.0)	165 (100.0)
Dahod	24 (10.5)	123 (53.7)	77 (33.6)	5 (2.2)	28 (12.2)	140 (61.1)	57 (24.9)	4 (1.7)	229 (100.0)
Vijalpore	91 (42.5)	79 (36.9)	42 (19.6)	2 (0.9)	51 (23.8)	22 (10.3)	131 (61.2)	10 (4.7)	214 (100.0)
Siddhpur	32 (7.7)	245 (59.2)	111 (26.8)	26 (6.3)	23 (5.6)	169 (40.8)	174 (42.0)	48 (11.6)	414 (100.0)

Modasa	25 (9.3)	204 (76.1)	33 (12.3)	6 (2.2)	16 (6.0)	40 (14.9)	193 (72.0)	19 (7.1)	268 (100.0)
Savarkundla	5 (4.1)	104 (86.0)	10 (8.3)	2 (1.7)	12 (9.9)	4 (3.3)	103 (85.1)	2 (1.7)	121 (100.0)
Mahuva	11 (4.1)	239 (88.8)	19 (7.1)	0 (0.0)	4 (1.5)	2 (0.7)	249 (92.6)	14 (5.2)	269 (100.0)
Mangrol	5 (2.6)	154 (81.1)	28 (14.7)	3 (1.6)	27 (14.2)	6 (3.2)	125 (65.8)	32 (16.8)	190 (100.0)
Anjar	188 (24.1)	522 (66.9)	70 (9.0)	0 (0.0)	74 (9.5)	457 (58.6)	249 (31.9)	0 (0.0)	780 (100.0)
Dhrangadhra	8 (2.2)	294 (81.9)	34 (9.5)	23 (6.4)	3 (0.8)	178 (49.6)	178 (49.6)	0 (0.0)	359 (100.0)

Source: Field Survey.

Although a majority of the sample households were aware of the fact that human excreta exposed on the ground could cause diseases, in Viramgam and Dahod more than above two-fifths of households surveyed had no idea if diseases could (or could not) be caused due to excreta left exposed. When asked to name particular diseases that human excreta could cause, most households across the urban areas identified only diarrhoea, additionally, in Junagadh, Palanpur, Siddhpur and Mangrol, most of the sample households reported that human excreta could cause nausea/vomiting. In order to find out awareness about symptoms of the most commonly occurring ailment of diarrhoea among children below age five, majority of households across all the 20 urban centres reported frequent watery stools as the major one followed by vomiting as well. This suggested that children suffering from diarrhoea would receive attention to be treated.

Hygienic Practices Following Defecation

Handwashing after defecation with soap and water, as distinct from washing with water only, has been considered a major step in keeping off faecal contamination. Excepting in Anand, Khambat, Vijalpore, Junagadh, Godhra, Botad and Dhrangadhra were more than 70 percent households reported using soap and water, in the remaining towns (except for Vapi), this proportion varied between 19 percent in Sabarkundla and 69 percent in Mangrol. In Vapi, 60 percent of sample households used clay to wash hands after defecation, which is an unhygienic practice. In Mahuva and Sabarkundla, 77 percent of households used only water for cleaning hands after defecation; in other sample towns, this proportion varied from 8 percent for Vijalpore to 53 percent in Modasa. It is possible to infer that a large part of slum households across the 20 urban centres (except for Anand, Khambat and Vijalpore) followed the unhygienic method of cleaning their hands after defecation making them vulnerable to various health hazards. That this is also reflective of children's handwashing practices causes concern.

Hygienic practices following defecation by children below the age of five are summarised in Table-6. In Botad only 27 percent of sample households reported cleaning their children after defecation, indicating poor awareness regarding health implications of such neglect for children. When asked whether the attendant to child washed her/his hands after cleaning the child, the responses were not encouraging. In 12 urban centres, the proportions of households who reported that the attendants wash their hands always after cleaning the child varied from 16 percent in Godhra to 49 percent in Anand. It suggests that the majority of slum households in eight out of the 20 urban centres did not clean their own hands after cleaning the child, which could cause diseases to both the adults and children in those households.

Table-6: Hygienic Practices Following Defecation by Children

Urban Local Bodies	Washing the child after defecation			Washing hand after cleaning the child			Number of households
	Always	At times	Never	Always	At times	Never	
Municipal Corporation							
Vadodara	1406(91.3)	130 (8.4)	4 (0.3)	460 (29.9)	1070 (69.5)	10 (0.6)	1540 (100.0)
Jamnagar	634 (91.2)	57 (8.2)	4 (0.6)	202 (29.1)	477 (68.6)	16 (2.3)	695 (100.0)
Junagadh	358 (97.8)	8 (2.2)	0 (0.0)	352 (96.2)	14 (3.8)	0 (0.0)	366 (100.0)
A Class Nagarpalika							
Anand	65 (53.2)	0 (0.0)	57 (46.7)	60 (49.2)	3 (2.5)	59 (48.4)	122 (100.0)
Palanpur	199 (94.8)	11 (5.2)	0 (0.0)	179 (85.2)	29 (13.8)	2 (1.0)	210 (100.0)
Godhra	198 (92.5)	16 (7.5)	0 (0.0)	36 (16.8)	177 (82.7)	1 (0.5)	214 (100.0)
Vapi	201(100.0)	0 (0.0)	0 (0.0)	173 (86.1)	9 (4.5)	19 (9.5)	201 (100.0)
Botad	82 (27.5)	10 (3.4)	206 (69.1)	77 (25.8)	15 (5.0)	206(69.1)	298 (100.0)
Gandhidham	492 (98.8)	6 (1.2)	0 (0.0)	155 (31.1)	343 (68.9)	0 (0.0)	498 (100.0)
B Class Nagarpalika							
Viramgam	150 (87.2)	22 (12.8)	0 (0.0)	131 (76.1)	40 (23.3)	1 (0.6)	172 (100.0)
Khambhat	60 (100.0)	0 (0.0)	0 (0.0)	60 (100.0)	0 (0.0)	0 (0.0)	60 (100.0)

Dahod	86 (81.1)	20 (18.9)	0 (0.0)	28 (26.4)	78 (73.6)	0 (0.0)	106 (100.0)
Vijalpur	53 (100.0)	0 (0.0)	0 (0.0)	51 (96.2)	0 (0.0)	2 (3.8)	53 (100.0)
Siddhpur	138 (93.9)	9 (6.1)	0 (0.0)	133 (89.9)	14 (9.5)	0 (0.0)	148 (100.0)
Modasa	109 (90.1)	12 (9.9)	0 (0.0)	109 (90.1)	12 (9.9)	0 (0.0)	121 (100.0)
Savarkundla	55 (96.5)	2 (3.5)	0 (0.0)	19 (33.3)	37 (64.9)	1 (1.8)	57 (100.0)
Mahuva	110 (84.0)	21 (16.0)	0 (0.0)	36 (27.5)	79 (60.3)	16 (12.2)	131 (100.0)
Mangrol	70 (98.6)	1 (1.4)	0 (0.0)	67 (94.4)	4 (5.6)	0 (0.0)	71 (100.0)
Anjar	238 (95.6)	10 (4.0)	1 (0.4)	229 (91.7)	15 (6.0)	5 (2.0)	249 (100.0)
Dhrangadhra	113 (95.8)	4 (3.4)	1 (0.8)	111 (94.1)	7 (6.0)	0 (0.0)	118 (100.0)

Source: Field Survey.

As can be seen from Table-7, most children below the age of five across the urban centres defecated either in the courtyard or outside the house in the open, except Anjar, where 76 percent of all children defecated in toilets. In Anand, Botad, Khambat, Sabarkundla and Mahuva less than 5 percent of sample households having children reported that their children used toilets, the lowest being in Botad. In the remaining urban centres, use of toilets by children varied from 8 percent in Vapi to 38 percent in Vijalpur. To an extent, this practice prevented children's excreta left in the open to potentially cause diseases.

While the majority of sample households reported removing children's excreta immediately (covering with sand/mud, or not) the variation could be observed across the urban centres. In Botad, only 1 percent of households reportedly removed children's excreta covering with sand and mud, followed by Anjar at 7 percent . In Viramgam, Vijalpore and Anjar over 50 percent of all slum households chose to throw the excreta after some time but covering with sand/mud. Public garbage dumps (*ukardas*) seemed to be the most preferred site for disposal of children's excreta across the 20 urban centres. It varied from cent percent in Khambat to 30 percent in Dhrangadhra. Use of toilets for disposal of children's excreta ranged between zero percent in Khambat and 41 percent in Mangrol. This highlights that disposal of children's excreta was not hygienically handled by the slum households across the urban centres, which could pose health hazards in children in the slums. Moreover, in all these above towns health care systems needed attention as a considerable proportion of slum population in certain towns were still dependent upon home remedies and local shops for treating diarrhoea.

Table-7: Site of Defecation by Children and Disposal of Excreta

Urban Local Bodies	Site of defecation				Time of removal					Site of disposal				Number of House-holds
	Toilet	Inside the house	Courtyard	Outside house	Immediately with sand/mud	Immediately without covering	After Sometime with sand/mud	After sometime without covering	Other	On street	Public garbage dump	In toilet	Other	
Municipal Corporation														
Vadodara	521 (33.8)	122 (7.9)	555 (36.0)	342 (22.2)	801 (52.0)	412 (26.8)	177 (11.5)	55 (3.6)	95 (6.2)	104 (6.8)	805 (52.3)	586 (38.1)	45 (2.9)	1540 (100.0)
Jamnagar	149 (21.4)	79 (11.4)	254 (36.5)	213 (30.6)	384 (55.3)	170 (24.5)	79 (11.4)	21 (3.0)	41 (5.9)	36 (5.2)	413 (59.4)	188 (27.1)	58 (8.3)	695 (100.0)
Junagadh	106 (29.0)	25 (6.8)	154 (42.1)	81 (22.1)	253 (69.1)	42 (11.5)	22 (6.0)	11 (3.0)	38 (10.4)	18 (4.9)	183 (50.0)	105 (28.7)	60 (16.4)	366 (100.0)
A Class Nagarpalika														
Anand	6 (4.9)	3 (2.5)	15 (12.3)	98 (80.3)	53 (43.4)	64 (52.5)	0 (0.0)	5 (4.1)	0 (0.0)	14 (11.5)	106 (86.9)	2 (1.6)	0 (0.0)	122 (100.0)
Palanpur	31 (14.8)	6 (2.9)	82 (39.0)	91 (43.3)	136 (64.8)	29 (13.8)	26 (12.4)	10 (4.8)	9 (4.3)	17 (8.1)	131 (62.4)	34 (16.2)	28 (13.3)	210 (100.0)
Godhra	71 (33.2)	32 (15.0)	65 (30.4)	46 (21.5)	116 (54.2)	52 (24.3)	25 (11.7)	11 (5.1)	10 (4.7)	27 (12.6)	81 (37.9)	85 (39.7)	21 (9.8)	214 (100.0)
Vapi	76 (37.6)	1 (0.5)	125 (61.9)	0 (0.0)	137 (67.8)	45 (22.3)	17 (8.4)	0 (0.0)	3 (1.5)	30 (14.9)	116 (57.4)	56 (27.7)	0 (0.0)	202 (100.0)
Botad	2 (0.7)	9 (3.0)	20 (6.7)	267 (89.6)	4 (1.3)	257 (86.2)	11 (3.7)	26 (8.7)	0 (0.0)	0 (0.0)	298 (100.0)	0 (0.0)	0 (0.0)	298 (100.0)
Gandhidham	142 (28.5)	11 (2.2)	171 (34.3)	174 (34.9)	354 (71.1)	61 (12.2)	22 (4.4)	7 (1.4)	54 (10.8)	74 (14.9)	240 (48.2)	139 (27.9)	45 (9.0)	498 (100.0)
B Class Nagarpalika														
Viramgam	36 (20.9)	1 (0.6)	114 (66.3)	21 (12.2)	22 (12.8)	39 (22.7)	92 (53.5)	6 (3.5)	13 (7.6)	91 (52.9)	61 (35.6)	20 (11.6)	0 (0.0)	172 (100.0)
Khambhat	1 (1.7)	0 (0.0)	2 (3.3)	57 (95.0)	60 (100.0)	0 (0.0)	0 (0.0)	0 (0.0)	0 (0.0)	0 (0.0)	60 (100.0)	0 (0.0)	0 (0.0)	60 (100.0)
Dahod	18 (17.0)	18 (17.0)	30 (28.3)	40 (37.7)	59 (55.7)	24 (22.6)	17 (16.0)	5 (4.7)	1 (0.9)	11 (10.4)	63 (59.4)	20 (18.9)	12 (11.3)	106 (100.0)
Vijalpur	20 (37.7)	0 (0.0)	13 (24.5)	20 (37.7)	16 (30.2)	3 (5.7)	29 (54.7)	4 (7.5)	1 (1.9)	14 (26.4)	38 (71.7)	1 (1.9)	0 (0.0)	53 (100.0)
Siddhpur	19 (12.8)	1 (0.7)	38 (25.7)	90 (60.8)	98 (66.2)	24 (16.2)	24 (16.2)	2 (1.4)	0 (0.0)	7 (4.7)	97 (65.5)	21 (14.2)	23 (15.5)	148 (100.0)
Modasa	17 (14.0)	1 (0.8)	34 (28.1)	69 (57.0)	84 (69.4)	14 (11.6)	14 (11.6)	6 (5.0)	3 (2.5)	11 (9.1)	80 (66.1)	18 (14.9)	12 (9.9)	121 (100.0)

Savarkundla	2 (3.5)	2 (3.5)	49 (86.0)	4 (7.0)	38 (66.7)	8 (14.0)	11 (19.3)	0 (0.0)	0 (0.0)	2 (3.5)	47 (82.5)	3 (5.3)	5 (8.8)	57 (100.0)
Mahuva	3 (2.3)	9 (6.9)	110 (84.0)	9 (6.9)	72 (55.0)	28 (21.4)	30 (22.9)	0 (0.0)	1 (0.8)	11 (8.4)	103 (78.6)	5 (3.8)	12 (9.2)	131 (100.0)
Mangrol	26 (36.6)	5 (7.0)	36 (50.7)	4 (5.6)	39 (54.9)	11 (15.5)	1 (1.4)	5 (7.0)	15 (21.1)	4 (5.6)	33 (46.5)	29 (40.8)	5 (7.0)	71 (100.0)
Anjar	190 (76.3)	8 (3.2)	51 (20.5)	0 (0.0)	18 (7.2)	61 (24.5)	143 (57.4)	27 (10.8)	0 (0.0)	8 (3.2)	187 (75.1)	54 (21.7)	0 (0.0)	249 (100.0)
Dhrangadhra	14 (11.9)	20 (16.9)	18 (15.3)	66 (56.0)	45 (38.1)	8 (6.8)	25 (21.2)	14 (11.9)	26 (22.0)	79 (66.9)	35 (29.7)	4 (3.4)	0 (0.0)	118 (100.0)

Source: Field Survey.

Through the survey findings, it is possible to surmise that a good number of slum households were aware of the health benefits of having an individual toilet in the house. The major reasons cited for opting to have a toilet at home was that it was more hygienic and also was convenient. As the earlier discussions in this paper have already shown, in many the aspects, like waste disposal, handwashing practices following defecation and drawing drinking water poor hygienic practices were being followed in the slums households quite widely, indicating children's right to health and hygienic environment had been grossly compromised.

Concluding Observations

The challenges of sanitation, particularly, in case of children belonging to economically weaker households, need to be contextualised through recognising the larger structural infirmities of poverty and unbridled urbanisation. It needs to be underscored that greater coverage of slum households by comprehensive sanitation facilities–not just toilet structures-has the potential of delivering higher quality health and productivity outcomes. A widely recognised reason for the poor sanitation practices in slum households has been a lack of *formal* access to the space of living. Community sanitation initiatives might offer a workable alternative, albeit the question of maintenance assumes huge significance. Even as this study has not enquired closely into the dynamics of children's behaviour and approach towards sanitation as across locality, income, education and gender categories, it certainly points to the fact that despite poverty and the crisis of unhygienic living conditions children, though in small numbers, have been willing to use an improved sanitation facility. A deeper enquiry is called for to appreciate the nuanced dynamics of sanitation for children in disadvantaged socio-economic and spatial contexts.

While sanitation and hygiene have remained one of the most neglected issues in India, the challenge of moving towards children's right to safe sanitation and hygiene (especially, those living in poverty) is enmeshed in a maze of larger issues such as:

Geography and legality of homesteads (space and ownership)

Discrimination based on caste, community and gender

Denial of (hence, inaction) existence of open defecation and manual scavenging

Supply inadequacy (depleting groundwater)

Contaminated water and sources

Poor attention to solid and liquid waste disposal

Lack of awareness and facilities to address water-borne and faecal ailments.

The findings of the field surveys underscore the need for sustained efforts by the state towards educating and informing slum dwellers regarding benefits of sanitation and hygienic living. Increased investment towards building drainage and sewerage facilities, provision of water and regular management of collection and disposal of solid and liquid waste is an essential prerequisite towards promoting a safe sanitation environment for children and adults alike. Hence, toilets *per se* would not bring about the desired health outcome to the local society, and, that would hardly help in ensuring the right to safe sanitation by children, especially from the urban margins.

References

1. Augsburg, Britta and Paul Andrés Rodríguez-Lesmes (2018), 'Sanitation and Child Health in India', World Development, 107, pp. 22-39.
2. Bhaduri, Amita (2015), 'Unpacking the Water and Sanitation Budget', India Water Portal. Available at http://www.indiawaterportal.org/articles/unpacking-water-and-sanitation-budget (Accessed on 24th September, 2017).
3. Das, Keshab (2009), Approach Paper for the Urban Sanitation Study in Gujarat. Submitted to the Nirmal Gujarat Mission, Government of Gujarat, Gandhinagar through the Gujarat Institute of Development Research, Ahmedabad. (Mimeo, Unpublished).
4. Das, Keshab, Rudra Narayan Mishra and Gani Memon (2010), Consolidated Report (Part I-Houselisting : Part II-Household Sample Survey): Baseline and Sample Study of All Slum Households in Twenty Urban Centres. Submitted to the Nirmal Gujarat Mission, Government of Gujarat, Gandhinagar through the Gujarat Institute of Development Research, Ahmedabad. (Mimeo, Unpublished).
5. Essity and Water Supply and Sanitation Collaborative Council (WSSCC) (2017), Joining Forces for Progress: Hygiene Matters Report 2016/17. Available at https://www.essity.com/Documents/en/Publications/Hygiene-Matters/Essity-HygieneMatters-2016-2018_lowres.pdf?epslanguage=sv (Accessed on 24th September, 2017).
6. Häusermann, Julia (1999), 'A Human Rights Approach to Development: Some Practical Implications for Water Aid's Work', The First WaterAid Lecture, City University, London, September 10. Available at http://www.righttowater.info/wp-content/uploads/wateraid_lecture.pdf (Accessed on 24th September, 2017).

7. Martin, Matthew and Richard Watts (2013), 'Putting Progress at Risk?: MDG Spending in Developing Countries', Government Spending Watch Report, Development Finance International and Oxfam International. Available at https://www.oxfam.org/sites/www.oxfam.org/files/file_attachments/putting-progress-at-risk-mdgs-160513-summ-en_0.pdf (Accessed on 24th September, 2017).
8. Pink, Ross (2012), 'Child Rights, Right to Water and Sanitation, and Human Security', Health and Human Rights, 14 (1), pp. 78-87.
9. UN—Water (2017), Financing Universal Water, Sanitation and Hygiene under the Sustainable Development Goals: UN—Water Global Analysis and Assessment of Sanitation and Drinking-Water (GLAAS) 2017 Report, World Health Organisation, Geneva. Available at http://www.publicfinanceforwash.com/sites/default/files/uploads/GLAAS%202017%20Report%20for%20Web_final.pdf (Accessed on 23rd September, 2017).

□□□